D1806857

Similes in the Bible (A Compendium)

Religions and Discourse

Edited by James M. M. Francis

Volume 63

PETER LANG

Oxford • Bern • Berlin • Bruxelles • New York • Wien

John E. Ziolkowski

Similes in the Bible (A Compendium)

PETER LANG

Oxford • Bern • Berlin • Bruxelles • New York • Wien

Bibliographic information published by Die Deutsche Nationalbibliothek.
Die Deutsche Nationalbibliothek lists this publication in the Deutsche National-
bibliografie; detailed bibliographic data is available on the Internet at
http://dnb.d-nb.de.

A catalogue record for this book is available from the British Library.

Library of Congress Cataloging-in-Publication Data

Names: Ziolkowski, John E., author.
Title: Similes in the Bible (a compendium) / John E. Ziolkowski.
Description: Oxford ; New York : Peter Lang, 2022. | Series: Religions and
    discourse, 1422-8998 ; vol. 63 | Includes bibliographical references.
Identifiers: LCCN 2021040935 (print) | LCCN 2021040936 (ebook) | ISBN
    9781800796737 (hardback) | ISBN 9781800795617 (ebook) | ISBN
    9781800795624 (epub)
Subjects: LCSH: Bible—Language, style. | Simile.
Classification: LCC BS537 .Z56 2022 (print) | LCC BS537 (ebook) | DDC
    220.6/6—dc23/eng/20211117
LC record available at https://lccn.loc.gov/2021040935
LC ebook record available at https://lccn.loc.gov/2021040936

Cover design by Peter Lang Ltd.

ISSN 1422-8998
ISBN 978-1-80079-673-7 (print)
ISBN 978-1-80079-561-7 (ePDF)
ISBN 978-1-80079-562-4 (ePub)

© Peter Lang AG 2022

Published by Peter Lang Ltd, International Academic Publishers,
52 St Giles, Oxford, OX1 3LU, United Kingdom
oxford@peterlang.com, www.peterlang.com

John E. Ziolkowski has asserted his right under the Copyright, Designs and Patents
Act, 1988, to be identified as Author of this Work.

All rights reserved.
All parts of this publication are protected by copyright.
Any utilisation outside the strict limits of the copyright law, without
the permission of the publisher, is forbidden and liable to prosecution.
This applies in particular to reproductions, translations, microfilming,
and storage and processing in electronic retrieval systems.

This publication has been peer reviewed.

* * *

For Alexandra

* * *

Contents

Acknowledgements

I would like to thank members of the Production Team at Peter Lang for their generous assistance to me at many points along the way: Lucy Melville, Ashita Shah and Jaishree Thiyagarajan. Professors Diane Bergant and Paul Duff were also very helpful.

Preface

Several years ago, my work concentrated on analyzing the similes in Plato's Dialogues, which involved distinguishing similes from metaphors, starting with Aristotle's discussion (*Rhetoric* Book 3.4.1–4 [1406b–1407]). Next some colleagues and I published a compendium of similes in the *Iliad* and *Odyssey*. (See Bibliography.) The purpose of the current study is to list all the similes in the Bible in three different versions (Greek, Latin, and English), noting especially the variation in the use of introductory words (*protheses*). There are over one thousand examples (not counting the predicate and genitive versions), a significant collection. The Introduction discusses the parts and types of similes as well as other similar figures of speech (e.g., analogies, comparisons, and metaphors); examples are provided of prothetic (*prothesis* expressed: he runs like a panther) and non-prothetic types (*prothesis* implied: he is [like] a lion in savagery).

The Conclusion points out various aspects of Biblical usage, some differing from those in classical Greek authors (Homer and Plato). The importance of similes in explaining abstractions accounts for their popularity in philosophers and religious writers, who compose similes to add clarity to their discussion. Examples are given of visualizing size (small as dust), love (kisses better than wine), and the senses (sweeter than honey). Similes are also an effective way of clarifying religious concepts (kingdom of heaven like a mustard seed or "the lord is my shepherd"). By comparing their presentation in different languages one can appreciate the variety of ways the same thoughts are expressed. (See examples below.) The eight Appendices provide abbreviated lists of the similes in the Old and New Testaments as well as examples of predicate and genitive similes, doublets (repeated similes with a slight change, e.g., Genesis 49.9, "he couched as a lion, and as an old lion," an unusual feature of the Old Testament), and factual comparisons (Daniel 7.3, "And *four great beasts came up from the sea*

... 4 The *first was* like *a lion*"). A chart provides an easy way to compare, for example, the use of the same prothetic words (*as*, ὡς and *sicut*) in different authors.

Here are two examples of similes in three languages (English, Greek, and Latin):

Proverbs 7.2 Keep my commandments, and live; and *my law* as *the apple of thine eye*.

7.2 φύλαξον ἐμὰς ἐντολάς, καὶ βιώσεις, τοὺς δὲ ἐμοὺς λόγους ὥσπερ κόρας ὀμμάτων·

7.2 Fili, serva mandata mea, et vives; et *legem meam* quasi *pupillam oculi tui:*

[my law (keep) ≈ the apple of your eye]

N.b. the variation: English has imperative "live" and the vehicle "apple"; whereas the Greek and Latin have future tense verbs (*vives* and βιώσεις) plus different words for the vehicle (*pupillam* and κόρας = *pupil and* "daughters")

Psalm 144.4 *Man* is like to *vanity*: *his days* are as *a shadow that passeth away.*

143.4 ἄνθρωπος ματαιότητι ὡμοιώθη, αἱ ἡμέραι αὐτοῦ ὡσεὶ σκιὰ παράγουσι.

143.4 *Homo vanitati* similis factus est; *dies ejus* sicut *umbra* praetereunt.

N.b. Greek has a verb for "is like," the Latin an adjective; in the second clause the verb is placed with *shadow* in English instead of with *days*.

* * *

1 Introduction

The **King James Bible** (KJB) has been read and cited widely since its completion in 1611 CE. The translation was done by forty-seven scholars, who used the Hebrew and Aramaic for the Old Testament (39 books) and the Greek for the New Testament (27 books). In this "treasure house of English prose"[1] similes have played an important role, since they employ such a rich field of references and emphasis. Consider these examples:

And I will make thy seed to multiply <u>as *the stars of heaven.*</u>
(Gen. 26.4)

Understand therefore this day, that the Lord thy God ... <u>*as a consuming fire*</u> he shall destroy them. (Deut. 9.3)

Hast thou not poured me out <u>as *milk*</u>, and curdled m*e* <u>like</u> <u>*cheese*</u>? (Job 10.10)

"*The kingdom of heaven* <u>is like to</u> <u>*a grain of mustard seed, which a man took and sowed in his field.*</u>" (Matt. 13.31)

For yourselves know perfectly that *the day of the Lord* **so** *cometh* <u>*as a thief in the night.*</u> (1 Thes. 5.2)

Such vivid comparisons help to clarify difficult concepts and add variety to the narrative.

Although collections of similes from various books of the Bible are available in print, currently there is no source that provides a complete compilation of Biblical similes (over one thousand in the Old Testament alone; see Appendix III). My work takes up this task with an additional feature: not only is the English provided but the Greek and Latin translations are also included. This is especially useful since it allows the reader to compare versions. Thus one finds that sometimes the simile is not included in other languages. Ideally one should also consult the Hebrew

---

1   C. S. Lewis, "The Literary Impact of the Authorised Version" (delivered March 20, 1950), reprinted in *Selected Literary Essays*, edited by Walter Hooper (1969), p. 142.

version (online texts are available), but this would have lengthened this study considerably. The Greek version is provided from the online text at <http://www.ellopos.net/ elpenor/physis/septuagint-genesis/default.asp>; and the Latin version from the online text at <http://www.drbo.org/lvb/chapter/ 28014.htm>. **Appendices I** (Old Testament) and **II** (New Testament) list all the similes in summary form; **Appendix III** locates them schematically in each book; and the two **Charts** present them in an abbreviated format. Thus there are various helpful ways to consult and compare the Biblical similes.

1 Parts of Similes

In copying the chosen passages, I have identified the three basic parts of similes: the *tenor (italicized),* the prothesis (underlined) and the *vehicle (underlined and italicized)*, with the occasional *apothesis* marked in **bold.** Here is an example:

Psalm 42.1 As [prothesis] *the hart* [vehicle] panteth after the water brooks, **so** [apothesis] panteth *my soul* [tenor] after thee, O God.

41.2 ON TPOΠON *ἐπιποθεῖ ἡ ἔλαφος ἐπὶ τὰς πηγὰς τῶν ὑδάτων,* **οὕτως** *ἐπιποθεῖ ἡ ψυχή μου πρός σέ, ὁ Θεός.*

41.1 Quemadmodum desiderat *cervus* ad fontes aquarum, **ita** desiderat *anima mea* ad te, Deus.

[my soul ≈ a hart desiring fountains of water]

Frequently the prothesis is contained in the verb or an adjective, as in the following Greek and Latin examples:

Verbal prothesis:

Matthew 25.1 Then shall *the kingdom of heaven* be likened unto *ten virgins.*

1 Τότε ὁμοιωθήσεται *ἡ βασιλεία τῶν οὐρανῶν* δέκα παρθένοις.

The prothesis is contained in the verb.

Adjectival prothesis:

Judges 14.18 *What* [tenor] is *sweeter* than [prothesis] *honey* [vehicle] and *what* is *stronger* than *a lion*?

18 τί *γλυκύτερον μέλιτος,* καὶ τί *ἰσχυρότερον λέοντος;*

18 Quid *dulcius melle*, et quid *fortius leone*?
The prothesis here is contained in the Greek and Latin adjectives.

2 Types of Similes

Similes are figurative comparisons that could be removed from the text with little logical effect and are usually not part of a series. There are two main types that may be distinguished by the presence or absence of an introductory "prothetic" word (e.g., "like" or "than"):

Prothetic (*prothesis* expressed): He runs <u>like</u> a panther.

or, He is fatter <u>than</u> a pig.

Non-prothetic (*prothesis* implied):

*a/1 Predicate nominative: He is [like] <u>a lion</u> in savagery.
    or Appositive: He, [like] <u>a lion</u> in savagery, attacked.

*a/2 Predicate accusative: They considered him [like] <u>a snake</u>.

*b/1 Comparative adjective: My love is <u>sweeter-than</u> honey.

*b/2 Comparative verb: What <u>is like</u> (e.g., ὁμοιωθήσεται) honey?

*c/ Genitive: He put on a <u>helmet of salvation</u> (= salvation [like] <u>a</u> <u>helmet</u>)

NB: it is not the genitive that is similetic, but rather the noun on which it depends. [See **Appendix V**.]

*d/ Verbal: They <u>trumpeted</u> (= sounded [like] a trumpet) their victory. [See **Appendix VII-3**]
    Similetic verbs, as in Daniel 13.5: ἐγὼ <u>ἐποίμανόν σε.</u>
    5 I tended-thee-[<u>as</u>]-a shepherd (≈ I <u>shepherded</u> thee).

3 Other Figures of Speech

The Bible contains various figures of speech that are like similes:

a **Analogy** – a factual comparison or concrete example closely tied to a specific passage, typically for the purpose of explanation or clarification. See *Job* 14.7–10: "hope of a tree, if it be cut down, that it will sprout again" … "but man dieth."

b **Comparison** – a discussion of the similarity between things. See Section 5 below and **Appendix VI**: Factual Comparisons.

c **Metaphor** – a figure of speech in which a word or phrase is applied to an object or action to which it is not literally applicable. See Section 4 below and **Appendix VII-2**: Examples of Metaphors.

d **Parable** – a short story designed to teach a moral or religious lesson. In the parables, Jesus teaches abstract spiritual concepts (how people react to the gospel, God's mercy, etc.) in the form of relatable stories, through which we gain a deeper understanding of God's truth. See Section 8 below.

Another group of figures occurs more rarely: allegories, aphorisms, fables, and riddles:

e **Allegory** – a story in which ideas are symbolized as people; some would call the parables of Jesus allegories. In these stories, the characters and events represent a truth about the Kingdom of God or the Christian life. For example, in the Parable of the Sower (Matthew 13:3–9) the seed and different types of soil illustrate the Word of God and various responses to it (as Jesus explains in verses 18–23). The story of the Prodigal Son also makes use of allegory. In this story (Luke 15:11–32), the titular son represents the average person: sinful and prone to selfishness. The wealthy father represents God, and the son's harsh life of hedonism and, later, poverty represents the hollowness of the ungodly lifestyle. When the son returns home in genuine sorrow, we have an illustration of repentance. In the father's mercy and willingness to receive his son back, we see God's joy when we turn from sin and seek His forgiveness.

f **Aphorism** – a concise saying or instructive maxim that contains a general truth, sometimes part of a simile (see Eccl. 10.1 below).

Also called an "apophthem" (from Greek *apophthegma*): a "terse, pointed saying." e.g., "Go to the ant, you sluggard; consider its ways and be wise!" (Proverbs 6:6) Or "Physician, heal Thyself" (Luke 4:23). A similetic aphorism (Eccl.10.1): "[just as] Dead flies cause the ointment of the apothecary to send forth a stinking savour: **so** [*apothesis*] doth a little folly him that is in reputation for wisdom and honour."

g **Fable** – a short story in which animals or objects speak a story, to teach a moral or religious lesson.

h **Riddle** – a question or statement intentionally phrased so as to require ingenuity in ascertaining its answer or meaning. Samson's riddle appears in the biblical narrative where Samson wagered a riddle to thirty Philistine guests, in these words: "Out of the eater came forth meat, and out of the strong came forth sweetness" (Judges 14.14). Also see Proverbs 30:18–19.

4 Similes and Metaphors

As a **simile** is an explicit figurative comparison ("But [God] made *his own people to go forth* like *sheep*," Ps. 78.52), a **metaphor** is an implied comparison ("Ye have plowed wickedness, ye have reaped iniquity; ye have eaten the fruit of lies," Hosea 10.13) based on a shift in meaning of the verb or other word (i.e., "plowed" is not meant literally). **The two figures may be distinguished by the fact that simile is a grammatical construction (where both tenor and vehicle are expressed with or without a prothesis), whereas metaphor is a play on the double meaning of a word.**

We should also note two types of metaphor, one like the example above ("Ye have **plowed wickedness**") and another ("The Lord **is my shepherd**" from Psalm 23), where **the metaphorical word is part of a simile** (with an implied "like": "The Lord is [like] my shepherd"). In the second example the metaphorical word ("shepherd") becomes the vehicle. Many "non-prothetic" or "predicate" similes (traditionally identified as metaphors) are included in this collection and placed in a separate **Appendix IV**.

Appendix V presents another type of grammatical construction not normally considered similetic: phrases like "he put ... an *helmet of salvation* upon his head" (Isaiah 59.17), here placed next to an explicit simile ("he put on *righteousness as a breast-plate*"). These expressions usually include an abstract word (salvation) visualized by a particular word (helmet). See 2 – *c/ above. Occasionally such constructions in the Greek or Latin are translated as normal similes in English: Lord, ... <u>*with favour*</u> wilt thou compass him <u>*as with a shield*</u> (for <u>*ut scuto bonae voluntatis tuae*</u> at Psalms 5.12).

We frequently add English words (especially verbs or protheses) that are understood in the Greek text:

For example, the Song of Solomon:

1.13 <u>ἀπόδεσμος τῆς στακτῆς</u> ἀδελφιδός μου ἐμοί, ἀνὰ μέσον τῶν μαστῶν μου αὐλισθήσεται.

13 *My kinsman* [<u>is</u>] to me [like] <u>a bundle of myrrh</u>; he shall lie between my breasts.

The justification for calling such constructions "similes" is that they are figurative comparisons with explicit *tenors* and *vehicles*, even though there is no expressed *prothesis*.

(a) Sometimes a second version of the English includes a *prothesis* (e.g. Deut. 4.24 is without a prothesis but the same phrase in Deut. 9.3 has one):

Deut. 4.24 For the Lord thy God is <u>a consuming fire</u>, even a jealous God.

Deut. 9.3 <u>As a consuming fire</u> he shall destroy them.

(b) Occasionally the prothesis that is missing in the English version is expressed in the Greek or Latin text, as at Exodus 14.22 (where the Latin translation adds a prothesis):

"*the waters* <u>were</u> <u>*a wall*</u> unto them on their right hand and on their left." 22 erat enim *aqua* <u>quasi</u> <u>*murus*</u> a dextra eorum et laeva.

Or *vice versa*: At Proverbs 25.25 the English has a prothesis (<u>As cold waters to a thirsty soul</u>, **so** is good news from a far country), whereas it is missing in the Latin version (<u>Aqua frigida animae sitienti</u>, et nuntius bonus de terra longinqua).

Other examples of this feature may be found at Job 8.14, Job 41.19, 1 Samuel 17.43 = I Kings, II Kings.21.14, and Jeremiah 9.11.

(c) Often a phrase with a **prothesis** (**like** *the great mountains)* is followed by a phrase without one (are a *great deep)*:

>Ps 36.6 Thy *righteousness* is <u>like</u> *the great mountains*; thy *judgments* are a *great deep*.
>
>35.7 ἡ δικαιοσύνη σου <u>ὡς</u> <u>ὄρη Θεοῦ</u>, τὰ κρίματά σου <u>ὡσεὶ</u> <u>ἄβυσσος πολλή</u>·
>
>35.7 *Justitia tua* <u>sicut</u> <u>montes Dei</u>; *judicia tua <u>abyssus multa</u>.*

(d) A non-prothetic simile (Deut. 4.24 For *the Lord thy God* is *a consuming fire)* may be followed by the same phrase with a prothesis in English (Deut. 9.3: **as** a consuming fire):

>24 ὅτι *Κύριος ὁ Θεός σου* <u>πῦρ καταναλίσκον</u> ἐστί, Θεὸς ζηλωτής. [the Lord ≈ a consuming fire] Moses quoting the Lord
>
>**24** quia *Dominus Deus tuus* <u>i̲gnis consumens</u> est.

These examples show that a prothesis (e.g., "like") is not a crucial part of a simile since it is expressed in some translations and omitted in others with no change in meaning.

5 Factual Comparisons

When the comparison is not figurative it is simply a factual statement rather than a simile:

>Thou through thy commandments hast made me <u>wiser than</u> mine enemies (Psalms 119.98). See **Appendix VI** for more examples.

6 Similes in the King James Bible

Sometimes the King James Bible has a simile where the online Greek or Latin text does not: e.g., at Job 3.24 the Latin version has a simile that is not in the Greek:

>Job 3.24 my roarings are poured out <u>like the waters</u>.
>
>24 δακρύω δὲ ἐγὼ συνεχόμενος φόβῳ·

24 et tamquam inundantes aquae, sic rugitus meus.
Occasionally the English differs considerably from the Greek and Latin:

Ps. 90.9 we spend our years <u>as a tale that is told</u>.

89.9 τὰ ἔτη ἡμῶν <u>ὡσεὶ ἀράχνη</u> ἐμελέτων.

89.9 Anni nostri <u>sicut aranea</u> meditabuntur;

[our years ≈ a tale/spider]

In some books of the Bible the chapter numbering of the Greek or Latin text differs from that of the King James version: e.g. Psalms [King James] 31.12 (2) = [Greek] 30.13.

7   Similes as (a) Words, (b) Phrases, or (c) Clauses

(a) He [behemoth] moveth *his tail* <u>like</u> <u>*a cedar*</u>. (Job 40.17)
(b) But the wicked shall perish; and *the enemies of the Lord* shall be <u>as</u> <u>*the fat of lambs*</u>. (Ps. 37.20)
(c) *I will wipe Jerusalem <u>as a man wipeth a dish</u>*, wiping it, and turning it upside down. (II Kings [= Kings IV] 21.13)

8   Parables

Parables are often introduced by similes:

Matthew 13.31 Another *parable* he presented to them, saying, "The *kingdom of the heavens* is <u>like</u> a *<u>mustard seed</u>*."

In the explanation of a parable the figurative element (the vehicle) often becomes the subject rather than the predicate:

Matthew 13.38 *<u>The field</u>* is *the world*; *<u>the good seed</u>* <u>are</u> *the children of the* kingdom; but the *<u>weeds</u>* are *the children of the wicked one*.

9 Doublet Similes

Frequently in the Old Testament a simile is repeated with a slight change (e.g., a lion + a young lion), making *doublet* similes. These are listed in **Appendix VIII.** The New Testament does not have this stylistic feature.

10 Divine Comparisons and Transformations

In Homer's *Iliad* and *Odyssey* divine comparisons and transformations occur so frequently that they form special categories. These types are not found in the Bible:

(A) Achilles is "like a god" or "god-like" (see *Compendium of Similes in Homer,* App. VIII);

(B) Athena departed "like a sea-bird" (see *Compendium of Similes in Homer,* App. IX).[2]

In this Introduction we have distinguished various types of similes and other similar figures. In the Conclusion (Chapter 5) we discuss the Biblical usage of similes as well as summarize the content of the eight Appendices.

---

2   See Ziolkowski (with Robert Farber and Denis Sullivan), *Compendium of Similes in Homer* (2016): <https://scholarspace.library.gwu.edu/files/rx913p90h>

For the various types of non-prothetic similes sometimes marked by asterisked figures (*a/1, *b/1 etc.) see the Introduction

Section 2.

An arrow (>) Indicates which of the Greek or Latin versions is closer to the English (if there is a notable difference).

Genesis (50 Chapters)[1]

Γένεσις

Gen. 13.16 And I will make *thy seed* <u>*as the dust of the earth*</u>.

    16 ποιήσω *τὸ σπέρμα σου* <u>ὡς</u> <u>*τὴν ἄμμον τῆς γῆς*</u>·

    16 Faciamque semen tuum <u>sicut</u> <u>*pulverem terrae:*</u>

    [thy seed ≈ dust]   The Lord to Abram

Gen. 22.17 I will multiply *thy seed* <u>as</u> <u>*the stars of the heaven*</u>, and <u>as</u> <u>*the sand which is upon the sea shore*</u>.

    17 πληθυνῶ *τὸ σπέρμα σου*, <u>ὡς</u> <u>*τοὺς ἀστέρας τοῦ οὐρανοῦ*</u> καὶ <u>ὡς</u> <u>*τὴν ἄμμον τὴν παρὰ τὸ χεῖλος τῆς θαλάσσης*</u>,

    17 multiplicabo semen tuum <u>sicut</u> <u>*stellas caeli*</u>, et <u>velut</u> <u>*arenam*</u> quae est in littore maris.

                         The Angel of the Lord to Abraham

    [thy seed ≈ stars; ≈ sand]

Gen. 25.25 And *the first* came out red, all over <u>*like an hairy garment*</u>.

    > 25 ἐξῆλθε δὲ ὁ πρωτότοκος πυρράκης, ὅλος <u>ὡσεὶ</u> <u>*δορὰ*</u> δασύς·

    25 Qui prior egressus est, rufus erat, et totus <u>in morem</u> pellis hispidus: Narrator

    [first twin (Esau) of Rebekah and Isaac ≈ an hairy garment]

---

1   See Appendix III for the number of similes in each Book.

Gen. 26.4 And I will make thy seed to multiply <u>as</u> *the stars of heaven.*

    4 καὶ πληθυνῶ τὸ σπέρμα σου <u>ὡς</u> <u>τοὺς ἀστέρας τοῦ οὐρανοῦ.</u>

    4 Et multiplicabo semen tuum <u>*sicut stellas caeli:*</u>

       [thy seed ≈ the stars of heaven]   The Lord to Isaac

Gen. 27.27 See, *the smell of my son* is <u>as</u> *the smell of a field* which the Lord hath blessed.

    27 ἰδοὺ ὀσμὴ τοῦ υἱοῦ μου <u>ὡς</u> <u>ὀσμὴ ἀγροῦ πλήρους, ὃν εὐλόγησε Κύριος</u>.   Isaac to his son Jacob

    27 Ecce odor filii mei <u>sicut</u> <u>*odor agri pleni*</u>, cui benedixit Dominus.

    [the smell of my son (Jacob) ≈ the smell of a blessed field]

Gen. 49.4 <u>Unstable as water</u>, thou shalt not excel.

    4 ἐξύβρισας <u>ὡς</u> <u>ὕδωρ</u>, μὴ ἐκζέσῃς·

    4 Effusus es <u>*sicut aqua*</u>, non crescas:

    [thou (Reuben) unstable ≈ water]

    Jacob to his son Reuben

Gen. 49.9 *Judah* is *a lion's whelp*: from the prey, my son, thou art gone up: he stooped down, he couched <u>as</u> *a lion*, and <u>as</u> *an old lion;*

    9 <u>σκύμνος λέοντος</u> Ἰούδα· ἐκ βλαστοῦ, υἱέ μου, ἀνέβης· ἀναπεσὼν ἐκοιμήθης <u>ὡς λέων</u> καὶ <u>ὡς σκύμνος</u>·

*a/1   9 <u>Catulus leonis</u> Juda: ad praedam, fili mi, ascendisti: requiescens accubuisti <u>ut leo</u>, et <u>quasi leaena</u>: Jacob to his sons

    [Judah ≈ a lion's whelp; thou (my son) ≈ a lion, an old lion]

Gen. 49.12 *His eyes* shall be red <u>with wine</u>, and his teeth white <u>with milk</u>.

    12 χαροποιοὶ οἱ ὀφθαλμοὶ αὐτοῦ <u>ἀπὸ οἴνου</u>, καὶ λευκοὶ οἱ ὀδόντες αὐτοῦ <u>ἢ γάλα</u>.

*/b1   12 <u>Pulchriores</u> sunt *oculi ejus <u>vino</u>*, et *dentes* ejus <u>*lacte*</u> candidiores.

    [his (Judah's) eyes (red) ≈ wine); his teeth (white) ≈ milk]   Jacob to his sons

Here the English translates the Greek, where 'with = from' and corresponds to 'like' or 'as'; 'white with milk' = 'white as / like milk'.

Gen. 49.27 *Benjamin shall ravin* <u>as</u> *a wolf: in the morning he shall devour the prey, and at night he shall divide the spoil.*

*a/1   27 Βενιαμὶν <u>λύκος ἅρπαξ</u>· τὸ πρωϊνὸν ἔδεται ἔτι καὶ εἰς τὸ ἑσπέρας δίδωσι τροφήν. (Benjamin, <u>*as a ravening wolf,*</u> *shall eat still in the morning, and at evening he gives food.*)

27 Benjamin <u>lupus rapax</u>, mane comedet praedam, et vespere dividet spolia. (Benjamin <u>*a ravenous wolf,*</u> in the morning shall eat the prey, and in the evening shall divide the spoil.)

[Benjamin ≈ a wolf]   Jacob to his sons

***

Exodus (40 Chapters)

Ἔξοδος

Exodus 4.6 And he put his hand into his bosom: and when he took it out, behold, <u>*his hand was leprous as snow.*</u>

6. καὶ ἐγενήθη ἡ χείρ αὐτοῦ <u>ὡσεὶ χιών.</u>

6 Quam cum misisset in sinum, protulit leprosam <u>*instar nivis.*</u>

[his hand ≈ snow]   Narrator

Exodus 15.10 *they* sank <u>as *lead*</u> in the mighty waters.

10 ἔδυσαν <u>ὡσεὶ μόλιβος</u> ἐν ὕδατι σφοδρῷ.

10 submersi sunt <u>*quasi plumbum*</u> in aquis vehementibus.

[they (Pharoah's army) ≈ lead]   Moses singing

Exodus 16.14 behold, upon the face of the wilderness there lay *a small round thing,* <u>as small as *the hoar frost*</u> on the ground.

14 καὶ ἰδοὺ ἐπὶ πρόσωπον τῆς ἐρήμου λεπτὸν <u>ὡσεὶ κόριον λευκόν,</u> <u>ὡσεὶ πάγος</u> ἐπὶ τῆς γῆς.

14 apparuit in solitudine minutum, et <u>*quasi pilo tusum in similitudinem pruinae*</u> super terram.

[a small round thing ≈ hoar frost]   Narrator

Exodus 16.31 And the house of Israel called the name thereof Manna; and it was <u>like *coriander seed*,</u> white: and the *taste* of it *was* <u>like *wafers made with honey.*</u> Narrator

31 καὶ ἐπωνόμασαν οἱ υἱοὶ ᾿Ισραὴλ τὸ ὄνομα αὐτοῦ, μάν· ἦν δὲ <u>ὡσεὶ σπέρμα κορίου λευκόν,</u> τὸ δὲ γεῦμα αὐτοῦ <u>ὡς ἐγκρὶς ἐν μέλιτι.</u>

31 Appellavitque domus Israel nomen ejus Man: quod erat <u>quasi *semen coriandri*</u> album, gustusque ejus <u>quasi *similae cum melle.*</u>

[it/Manna ≈ a white coriander seed; its taste ≈ wafers made with honey]
Exodus 19.18 and the *smoke* thereof ascended <u>as</u> *<u>the smoke of a furnace.</u>*

18 καὶ ἀνέβαινεν ὁ καπνὸς <u>ὡσεὶ</u> <u>*καπνὸς καμίνου*</u>,·

18 et ascenderet fumus ex eo <u>quasi</u> *<u>de fornace.</u>*

[smoke (the Lord's fire on Sinai) ≈ smoke of a furnace]   Narrator
Exodus 24.17 And *the sight of the glory of the Lord* was <u>like</u> *<u>devouring fire</u>*
<u>on the top of the mount</u> in the eyes of the children of Israel.   Narrator

17 τὸ δὲ εἶδος τῆς δόξης Κυρίου <u>ὡσεὶ</u> <u>πῦρ φλέγον ἐπὶ τῆς κορυφῆς τοῦ ὄρους</u>
ἐναντίον τῶν υἱῶν Ἰσραήλ.

17 Erat autem species gloriae Domini <u>quasi</u> ignis ardens super verticem
montis in conspectu filiorum Israel.

[the sight of the glory of the Lord ≈ devouring fire on Mt Sinai]
Exodus 33.11 And the Lord spake unto Moses face to face, <u>as</u> *<u>a man</u>*
<u>speaketh unto his friend.</u>

11 καὶ <u>ἐλάλησε</u> Κύριος πρὸς Μωυσῆν ἐνώπιος ἐνωπίῳ, <u>ὡς εἴ</u> <u>*τις λαλήσει*</u>
<u>*πρὸς τὸν ἑαυτοῦ φίλον.*</u>

11 Loquebatur autem Dominus ad Moysen facie ad faciem, <u>sicut</u> *solet*
<u>loqui homo ad amicum suum</u>.

[Lord spoke > Moses ≈ someone > a friend]   Narrator

***

Leviticus (27 Chapters)

Λευϊτικόν

***

Numbers (36 Chapters)

Ἀριθμοί

Numbers 11.7 And the manna was <u>as</u> *<u>coriander seed</u>*, and the colour thereof
<u>as</u> *<u>the colour of bdellium.</u>*

7 τὸ δὲ μάννα <u>ὡσεὶ</u> <u>*σπέρμα κορίου*</u> ἐστί, καὶ τὸ εἶδος αὐτοῦ <u>*εἶδος κρυστάλλου*</u>.

7 Erat autem man <u>quasi</u> *<u>semen</u>* coriandri, coloris *<u>bdellii</u>*.

[manna ≈ coriander seed; its color ≈ bdillium]

The children of Israel

Numbers 13.33 And there we saw the giants ... and we were in our own sight <u>as *grasshoppers.*</u>

34 καὶ ἐκεῖ ἑωράκαμεν τοὺς γίγαντας καὶ ἦμεν ἐνώπιον αὐτῶν <u>ὡσεὶ ἀκρίδες.</u>

34 Ibi vidimus monstra quaedam filiorum Enac de genere giganteo: quibus comparati, <u>quasi *locustae*</u> videbamur.

[we ≈ grasshoppers] The people to Moses

Numbers 23.24 Behold, the *people* shall rise up <u>as *a great lion*</u> and lift up himself <u>as *a young lion.*</u>

24 ἰδοὺ λαὸς <u>ὡς σκύμνος</u> ἀναστήσεται καὶ <u>ὡς λέων</u> γαυρωθήσεται· Balaam to Balak

24 Ecce populus ut *leaena* consurget, et <u>quasi *leo*</u> erigetur*:*

[the people ≈ a great lion; himself (Jacob) = a young lion]

***

Deuteronomy (34 Chapters)

Δευτερονόμιον

Deuteronomy 1.44 And *the Amorites,* which dwelt in that mountain, came out against you, and chased you, <u>as *bees do*</u>, and destroyed you in Seir, even unto Hormah.

44 καὶ ἐξῆλθεν ὁ Ἀμορραῖος ὁ κατοικῶν ἐν τῷ ὄρει ἐκείνῳ εἰς συνάντησιν ὑμῖν καὶ κατεδίωξαν ὑμᾶς, <u>ὡσεὶ ποιήσαισαν αἱ μέλισσαι,</u> καὶ ἐτίτρωσκον ὑμᾶς ἀπὸ Σηεὶρ ἕως Ερμᾶ.

44 Itaque egressus Amorrhaeus, qui habitabat in montibus, et obviam veniens, persecutus est vos, <u>*sicut solent apes*</u> persequi: et cecidit de Seir usque Horma.

[the Amorites ≈ bees] Narrator

Deut. 9.3 Understand therefore this day, that the Lord thy God ... <u>*as a consuming fire*</u> he shall destroy them.

3 καὶ γνώσῃ σήμερον, ὅτι Κύριος ὁ Θεός σου ... <u>πῦρ *a/1 καταναλίσκον</u> ἐστίν·

3 Scies ergo hodie quod *Dominus Deus tuus* ipse transibit ante te, <u>*ignis devorans atque consumens.*</u>

[the Lord thy God ≈ a consuming fire] Moses quoting the Lord

Deut. 32.2 My *doctrine* shall drop <u>as</u> *<u>the rain,</u>* my *speech* shall distil <u>as</u> *<u>the</u>* *<u>dew,</u>* <u>as</u> *<u>the small rain</u>* upon the tender herb, and <u>as</u> *<u>the showers</u>* upon the grass.   Moses

2 προσδοκάσθω <u>ὡς</u> <u>*ὑετὸς*</u> τὸ ἀπόφθεγμά μου, καὶ καταβήτω <u>ὡς</u> <u>*δρόσος*</u> τὰ ῥήματά μου, <u>ὡσεὶ</u> <u>*ὄμβρος*</u> ἐπ᾽ ἄγνωστιν καὶ <u>ὡσεὶ</u> <u>*νιφετὸς*</u> ἐπὶ χόρτον.
[NB 'snow' instead of 'showers'.]

2 Concrescat <u>ut</u> *<u>pluvia</u>* doctrina mea, fluat <u>ut</u> *<u>ros</u>* eloquium meum, <u>quasi</u> *<u>imber</u>* super herbam, et <u>quasi</u> *<u>stillae</u>* super gramina.
[my doctrine ≈ rain; my speech ≈ dew; ≈ small rain; ≈ showers]

***

Joshua (24 Chapters)

Ἰησοῦς Ναυῆ

Joshua 11.4 And *they* went out ... *much people, even* <u>as</u> *<u>the sand that is</u>* *<u>upon the sea shore</u>* in multitude.

4 καὶ ἐξῆλθον *αὐτοὶ καὶ οἱ βασιλεῖς αὐτῶν* μετ᾽ αὐτῶν, <u>*ὥσπερ ἡ ἄμμος τῆς*</u> <u>*θαλάσσης*</u> τῷ πλήθει.

4 Egressique sunt omnes cum turmis suis, populus multus nimis <u>sicut</u> *<u>arena quae est in littore maris.</u>*   *Narrator*
[they (the kings against Joshua) ≈ the sand of the sea]

***

Judges (21 Chapters)

Κριταί

Judges 6.5 For *they* came up with their cattle and their tents, and they came <u>as</u> *<u>grasshoppers</u>* for multitude.

5 *αὐτοὶ καὶ αἱ κτήσεις αὐτῶν* ἀνέβαινον *καὶ αἱ σκηναὶ αὐτῶν* παρεγίνοντο <u>καθὼς</u> <u>*ἀκρίς*</u> εἰς πλῆθος.

5 Ipsi enim et universi greges eorum veniebant cum tabernaculis suis, et <u>instar</u> *<u>locustarum</u>* universa complebant,
[they (the Midianites) ≈ grasshoppers]   *Narrator*

Judges 7.5 And the Lord said unto Gideon, *Every one* that lappeth of the water with his tongue, <u>as</u> *<u>a dog</u>* lappeth, him shalt thou set by himself.

5 καὶ εἶπε Κύριος πρὸς Γεδεών· πᾶς, ὃς ἂν λάψῃ τῇ γλώσσῃ αὐτοῦ ἀπὸ τοῦ ὕδατος <u>ὡς ἐὰν λάψῃ ὁ κύων</u>, στήσεις αὐτὸν κατὰ μόνας.

5 dixit Dominus ad Gedeon: *Qui lingua lambuerint aquas*, <u>sicut</u> solent <u>*canes*</u> lambere, separabis eos seorsum.

[whoever laps water with his tongue ≈ a dog]

The Lord to Gideon

Judges 7.12 And the Midianites … and *all* the children of the east lay along in the valley <u>like *grasshoppers*</u> for multitude; and *their camels* were without number, as *the sand by the sea side for multitude*.

12 καὶ Μαδιὰμ καὶ Ἀμαλὴκ καὶ *πάντες* οἱ υἱοὶ ἀνατολῶν βεβλημένοι ἐν τῇ κοιλάδι <u>ὡσεὶ ἀκρὶς</u> εἰς πλῆθος, καὶ ταῖς καμήλοις αὐτῶν οὐκ ἦν ἀριθμός, ἀλλ᾽ ἦσαν ὡς <u>ἡ ἄμμος ἡ ἐπὶ χείλους τῆς θαλάσσης εἰς πλῆθος</u>.

12 Madian autem et Amalec, et omnes orientales populi, fusi jacebant in valle, <u>ut</u> <u>*locustarum multitudo*</u>: *cameli* quoque innumerabiles erant, <u>sicut</u> *arena quae jacet in littore maris*.

[Midianites + Amalecites + all the easterners ≈ grasshoppers; their camels ≈ the sand by the sea side]   Narrator

Judges 14.18 *What* is <u>sweeter than</u> <u>*honey*</u>? and *what* is <u>stronger than</u> *a lion*? Men of the city to Samson

18 τί <u>γλυκύτερον μέλιτος</u>, καὶ τί <u>ἰσχυρότερον λέοντος</u>;

*b/1   18 Quid <u>dulcius</u> <u>*melle*</u>, et quid <u>fortius</u> *leone*?

[what is sweeter ≈ honey? what is stronger ≈ a lion?]

Judges 15.14 and the Spirit of the Lord came mightily upon him: and *the cords* that were upon his arms became <u>as *flax*</u> that was burnt with fire.

14 καὶ ἐγενήθη τὰ καλώδια τὰ ἐπὶ βραχίοσιν αὐτοῦ <u>ὡσεὶ στυππίον</u>, ὃ ἐξεκαύθη ἐν πυρί.

14 et sicut solent ad odorem ignis *lina* consumi, **ita** *vincula* quibus ligatus erat, dissipata sunt et soluta.

[the cords on his (Samson's) arms ≈ flax burnt with fire]   Narrator

Judges 16.9 and she [Delilah] said to him, the Philistines be upon thee, Sampson: and *he brake the withs,* as *a thread of tow is broken when it toucheth the fire.*

9 καὶ εἶπεν αὐτῷ· ἀλλόφυλοι ἐπὶ σέ, Σαμψών· καὶ διέσπασε τὰς νευράς, <u>ὡς εἴ τις ἀποσπάσοι στρέμμα στυπίου ἐν τῷ ὀσφρανθῆναι αὐτὸ πυρός·</u>

9 clamavitque ad eum: Philisthiim super te, Samson. *Qui rupit vincula, quomodo si rumpat quis filum de stuppae tortum putamine, cum odorem ignis acceperit*:
   [Samson broke cords ≈ a thread of tow broken in fire] Narrator

***

Ruth (4 Chapters)

Ῥούθ

***

1 Samuel = The First Book of the Kings (31 Chapters)

Βασιλειῶν Α´

***

2 Samuel = The Second Book of the Kings (24 Chapters)

Βασιλειῶν Β´

II Samuel 12.3 But the poor man had nothing, save *one little ewe lamb* … and was unto him as *a daughter.*
   3 καὶ τῷ πένητι οὐδὲν ἀλλ᾽ ἢ ἀμνὰς μία μικρά, … καὶ ἦν αὐτῷ ὡς θυγάτηρ·
   3 Pauper autem nihil habebat omnino, praeter ovem unam párvula … eratque illi sicut *filia*.   Narrator
   [lamb ≈ a daughter]
II Samuel 14.2 And Joab sent to Tekoah, and fetched thence a wise woman, and said unto her … put on now mourning apparel, and … be as *a woman that had a long time mounted for the dead*.
   2 καὶ ἀπέστειλεν Ἰωὰβ εἰς Θεκωέ, καὶ ἔλαβεν ἐκεῖθεν γυναῖκα σοφὴν καὶ εἴπε πρὸς αὐτήν· πένθησον δὴ καὶ ἔνδυσαι ἱμάτια πενθικὰ καὶ … ἔσῃ ὡς γυνὴ πενθοῦσα ἐπὶ τεθνηκότι τοῦτο ἡμέρας πολλὰς.
   2 misit Thecuam, et tulit inde mulierem sapientem : dixitque ad eam : Lugere te simula, et induere veste lugubri, et ne ungaris oleo, ut *sis* quasi *mulier jam plurimo tempore lugens mortuum.*   Joab
   [Tekoah/be ≈ a woman who has mourned a long time]

II Samuel 17.10 And he also that is valiant, whose *heart* is <u>as</u> <u>*the heart of a lion*</u>, shall utterly melt.

10 καί γε αὐτὸς υἱὸς δυνάμεως, οὗ ἡ καρδία <u>καθὼς</u> <u>ἡ καρδία</u> <u>τοῦ λέοντος</u>, τηκομένη τακήσεται.

10 Et fortissimus quisque, *cujus cor* est <u>quasi</u> <u>*leonis*</u>, pavore solvetur.   [the heart of a valiant man ≈ the heart of a lion]
Hushai to Absalom

II Samuel 21.19 and *the staff of whose spear* was <u>like</u> <u>*a weaver's beam*</u>.

19 καὶ τὸ ξύλον τοῦ δόρατος αὐτοῦ <u>ὡς</u> <u>ἀντίον ὑφαινόντων</u>.

19 Goliath Gethaeum, cujus *hastile* hastae erat <u>quasi</u> <u>*liciatorium*</u> texentium.   Narrator
[the staff of a spear (belonging to Goliath's brother) ≈ a weaver's beam]

II Samuel 22.34 He maketh *my feet* <u>*like hinds' feet.*</u>

   >   34 τιθεὶς τοὺς πόδας μου <u>ὡς</u> <u>ἐλάφων</u>

34 <u>Coaequans</u> pedes meos <u>cervis</u>
[my feet ≈ hind's feet]   David to the Lord in song

II Samuel 22.43 Then did I beat *them* <u>as small as</u> <u>*the dust of the earth*</u>, I did stamp *them* <u>as</u> <u>*the mire of the street.*</u>

43 καὶ ἐλέανα αὐτούς <u>ὡς</u> <u>χοῦν γῆς, ὡς</u> <u>πηλὸν ἐξόδων</u> ἐλέπτυνα αὐτούς.

43 Delebo *eos* <u>ut</u> <u>*pulverem terrae*</u>: quasi <u>lutum</u> platearum comminuam eos atque confringam.
David to the Lord in song
[them (who rose up against me) ≈ dust of the earth ≈ mud of the streets]

II Samuel 23.4 And *he* shall be <u>as</u> <u>*the light of the morning*</u> ... <u>as</u> the <u>*tender grass springing out of the earth by clear shinning after rain.*</u>

4 καὶ ἐν Θεῷ φωτὶ πρωΐας ἀνατείλαι ἥλιος, τὸ πρωῒ παρῆλθεν ἐκ φέγγους καὶ <u>ὡς</u> <u>ἐξ ὑετοῦ χλόης ἀπὸ γῆς</u>.

4 <u>Sicut</u> <u>*lux aurorae*</u>, oriente sole, mane absque nubibus rutilat, et <u>sicut</u> pluviis germinat <u>*herba*</u> de terra. [KJV closer to the Latin]   David singing
[a ruler ≈ morning light ≈ tender grass after rain]

***

I Kings = The Third Book of the Kings (22 Chapters)

Βασιλειῶν Γ΄

I Kings 20.27 And *the children of Israel* pitched before them like *two little flocks of kids*.

    27 ? Chapter 20 in Greek = Chapter. 21 in KJV; 20 is missing.

    27 Porro filii Israel recensiti sunt, et acceptis cibariis profecti ex adverso, castraque metati sunt contra eos, quasi *duo parvi grege*s *caprarum*: [the children of Israel ≈ two little flocks of kids]   Narrator

***

II Kings = The Fourth Book of the Kings (25 Chapters)

Βασιλειῶν Δ΄

II Kings 9.37 And *the carcase of Jezebel* shall be as *dung* upon the face of the field in the portion of Jezreel.

    37 καὶ ἔσται τὸ θνησιμαῖον Ἰεζάβελ ὡς κοπρία ἐπὶ προσώπου τοῦ ἀγροῦ ἐν τῇ μερίδι Ἰεζράελ.

    37 et erunt *carnes Jezabel* sicut *stercus* super faciem terrae in agro Jezrahel.   The Lord
    [carcase of Jezebel ≈ dung]

II Kings 21.13 and *I will wipe Jerusalem as a man wipeth a dish*, wiping it, and turning it upside down.

    13 καὶ ἀπαλείψω τὴν Ἰερουσαλήμ, καθὼς ἀπαλείφεται ὁ ἀλάβαστρος ἀπαλειφόμενος καὶ καταστρέφεται ἐπὶ πρόσωπον αὐτοῦ.

    13 et delebo Jerusalem, sicut *deleri solent tabulae*: et delens vertam.   The God of Israel
    [I (will wipe) > Jerusalem ≈ a man (wipes) a jar]

***

I Chronicles (29 Chapters)

Παραλειπομένων Α΄

I Chronicles 11.23 and in the Egyptian's hand was a *spear* like *a weaver's beam.*
    23 καὶ ἐν χειρὶ τοῦ Αἰγυπτίου δόρυ ὡς ἀντίον ὑφαινόντων,
    23 et habebat lanceam ut *liciatorium texentium.*
      [a spear ≈ a weaver's beam]   Narrator

***

II Chronicles (36 Chapters)

Παραλειπομένων Β΄

II Chronicles 4.5 *and the brim of it* [= the molten sea] like *the work of the brim of a cup,* with flowers of lilies;
    5 καὶ τὸ πάχος αὐτῆς [τὴν θάλασσαν χυτήν] παλαιστής, καὶ τὸ χεῖλος αὐτῆς ὡς χεῖλος ποτηρίου.
    5 et labium illius erat quasi *labium calicis*, vel *repandi lilii*:
      [brim/lip of sea ≈ the brim of a cup]   Narrator
    NB: '*the similitude* of oxen' (4.3).

***

Ezra (10 Chapters)

Ἔσδρας Α΄

***

Nehemiah (13 Chapters)

Ἔσδρας Β΄

***

Esther (10 Chapters)

Ἐσθήρ

***

Job (41 Chapters)

Ἰώβ

Job 3.21 Which (those in misery) long for *death*, but it cometh not; and dig for it <u>more than</u> for <u>*hid treasures.*</u>

    21 ἱμείρονται τοῦ θανάτου καὶ οὐ τυγχάνουσιν ἀνορύσσοντες <u>ὥσπερ</u> <u>θησαυρούς</u>,

    20 Qui expectant *mortem*, et non venit, <u>quasi</u> effodientes *thesaurum*;   Job

    [death ≈ hidden treasures]

Job 3.24 *my roarings* are poured out <u>like</u> the <u>*waters.*</u>

    24 δακρύω δὲ ἐγὼ συνεχόμενος φόβῳ· (simile **not in Greek**).

    24 et <u>tamquam</u> *inundantes aquae*, sic *rugitus meus.*

    [my roarings ≈ waters]   Job

Job 5.7 Yet *man is born unto trouble*, <u>as</u> *the sparks fly upward*.

    7 ἀλλὰ ἄνθρωπος γεννᾶται κόπῳ, <u>νεοσσοὶ δὲ γυπὸς τὰ ὑψηλὰ πέτονται</u>.

    7 *Homo nascitur ad laborem*, et *avis ad volatum*.

    [man > trouble ≈ sparks > fly upward]   Eliphaz

    NB a good example of a similetic aphorism without a pro-thesis in the Greek and Latin, expressed as a true simile in English. ('δὲ/et' conjunctions used for prothesis).

Job 5.25 Thou shalt know also that thy seed shall be great, and thine *off-spring* <u>as</u> <u>*the grass of the earth*</u>.

    25 τὰ δὲ τέκνα σου ἔσται <u>ὥσπερ</u> <u>τὸ παμβότανον τοῦ ἀγροῦ</u>.

    25 Scies quoque quoniam multiplex erit semen tuum, et *progenies tua* <u>quasi</u> <u>*herba terrae*</u>.

    [thine offspring ≈ the grass of the earth]   Eliphaz

Job 5.26 *Thou shalt come to thy grave in a full age*, <u>like as</u> a <u>*shock of corn cometh in in his season.*</u>

    26 ἐλεύσῃ δὲ ἐν τάφῳ <u>ὥσπερ σῖτος ὥριμος κατὰ καιρὸν θεριζόμενος</u> ἢ <u>ὥσπερ</u> <u>θιμωνία ἅλωνος καθ ᾿ ὥραν.συγκομισθεῖσα</u>. [**Greek adds a simile: or as a heap of the corn-flour collected in proper time.**]

    26 Ingredieris in abundantia sepulchrum, <u>sicut</u> *infertur acervus tritici* in tempore suo.   Eliphaz

    [thou at the grave ≈ shock of corn reaped (or ≈ heap of corn-flour)]

Job 6.3 For now it [*my grief*] would be <u>heavier than</u> *the sand of the sea.*

*b/1 3 καὶ [τὰς δὲ ὀδύνας μου] δὴ <u>*ἄμμου παραλίας*</u> <u>βαρυτέρα</u> ἔσται.

  3 Quasi *<u>arena</u>* maris *haec* <u>gravior</u> appareret;

  [my grief ≈ (heavier than) sand on the seashore]   Job

Job 6.7 The *things that my soul refused to touch* are <u>as</u> *<u>my sorrowful meat</u>.*

  7 βρόμον γὰρ ὁρῶ τὰ σῖτά μου <u>*ὥσπερ*</u> <u>*ὀσμὴν λέοντος·*</u>

  >   7 *Quae prius <u>nolebat</u> tangere anima mea*, nunc, prae angustia,
    <u>cibi</u> mei sunt.

    [what my soul refused to touch ≈ my sorrowful meat] Job

Job 6.15 *My brethren* have dealt deceitfully <u>as</u> *<u>a brook</u>*, and <u>as</u> *<u>the stream of</u>*
  <u>brooks</u> they pass away.

  15 οὐ προσεῖδόν με οἱ ἐγγύτατοί μου· <u>*ὥσπερ χειμάρρους ἐκλείπων*</u> ἢ <u>*ὥσπερ*</u>
  <u>*κῦμα*</u> παρῆλθόν με.

  15 Fratres mei praeterierunt me, <u>sicut</u> *<u>torrens qui raptim transit</u>* in
  convallibus.

    [my brethren ≈ a brook and a stream]   Job

Job 7.1 are not his [*a man's*] days also <u>like</u> the days *<u>of an hireling</u>*?

  1 ΠΟΤΕΡΟΝ οὐχὶ πειρατήριόν ἐστιν ὁ βίος ἀνθρώπου ἐπὶ τῆς γῆς καὶ
  <u>*ὥσπερ μισθίου αὐθημερινοῦ*</u> ἡ ζωὴ αὐτοῦ;

  1 Militia est. *vita hominis* super terram; et <u>sicut</u> *dies mercenarii, dies*
  ejus.   [man's life ≈ a hired day-laborer]   Job

Job 7.2 <u>As</u> *<u>a servant earnestly desireth the shadow,</u>* and <u>as</u> *<u>an hireling</u>*
  looketh for the reward of his work: **So** am I made to possess months
  of vanity.

  2 ἢ <u>*ὥσπερ θεράπων δεδοικὼς τὸν Κύριον αὐτοῦ*</u> καὶ τετευχὼς σκιᾶς; ἢ <u>*ὥσπερ*</u>
  <u>*μισθωτὸς ἀναμένων τὸν μισθὸν αὐτοῦ;*</u> 3 **οὕτως** κἀγὼ ...

  2 <u>Sicut</u> *<u>servus</u>* desiderat umbram, et <u>sicut</u> *<u>mercenarius</u>* praestolatur
  finem operis sui.   Job

    [I/any man ≈ a fearful servant or ≈ a hireling waiting for pay]

Job 7.6 *My days* are <u>swifter than</u> *<u>a weaver's shuttle</u>* and are spent
  without hope.

  *b/1 6 ὁ δὲ *βίος μου* ἐστιν <u>*ἐλαφρότερος λαλιᾶς*</u>, ἀπόλωλε δὲ ἐν κενῇ ἐλπίδι.

  6 *Dies mei* <u>velocius</u> transierunt <u>quam</u> a texente *tela* succiditur

    [my days ≈ (swifter than) a weaver's shuttle]   Job

Job 7.9 As _the cloud_ is consumed and vanisheth away: <u>so</u> _he that goeth_
   down to the grave shall come up no more.

>   9 καὶ οὐκέτι εἰμὶ <u>ὥσπερ νέφος</u> ἀποκαθαρθὲν ἀπ᾽ οὐρανοῦ. ἐὰν γὰρ ἄνθρωπος
>   καταβῇ εἰς ᾅδην, οὐκέτι μὴ ἀναβῇ.

>   9 <u>Sicut</u> consumitur <u>_nubes_</u>, et pertransit, **sic** _qui descenderit ad_ inferos,
>   non ascendet.

>   [he who dies ≈ a cloud vanishes]   Job

Job 7.20 why hast thou set _me_ <u>as</u> _a mark against thee_, so that I am a burden
   to myself?

>   20 διατί ἔθου <u>_με_</u> <u>_κατεντευκτήν_</u> σου;

>   20 Quare posuisti _me_ <u>_contrarium_</u> tibi?

>   [me ≈ a mark against thee]   Job

>   Not a simile in Greek or Latin; cf. 9.25 below, where the vehicle
>   is also abstract.

Job 8.2 How long shall _the words of thy mouth_ be <u>like</u> _a strong wind_?

>   2 μέχρι τίνος λαλήσεις ταῦτα, <u>_πνεῦμα πολυρρῆμον_</u> τοῦ στόματός σου;

*a/1   2 Usquequo loqueris talia, et <u>_spiritus multiplex_</u> sermones oris tui?

>   [your words ≈ a strong wind]   Bildad

>   **>>> NB a prothesis is added in English, not in Greek/Latin ori-
>   ginal. This lends strength to the argument that predicate
>   similes may be considered authentic similes.**

See also Job 8.9 below (where the Latin has a prothesis).

Job 9.25 Now _my days_ are <u>swifter than</u> _a post: they flee away._

*b/1   25 ὁ δὲ βίος μού ἐστιν <u>_ἐλαφρότερος_</u> <u>_δρομέως_</u>· ἀπέδρασαν καὶ οὐκ εἴδοσαν.

>   25 Dies mei <u>velociores</u> fuerunt <u>_cursore_</u>; fugerunt, et non viderunt
>   bonum.   [my days ≈ (swifter than) a post]   Job

Job 9.26 _They_ are passed away <u>as</u> _the swift ships_: <u>as</u> _the eagle_ that hasteth to
   the prey.

>   26 ἦ καί ἐστι <u>_ναυσὶν_</u> ἴχνος ὁδοῦ ἢ <u>_ἀετοῦ_</u> πετομένου ζητοῦντος βοράν;

>   26 Pertransierunt <u>quasi</u> <u>_naves_</u> poma portantes, <u>sicut</u> <u>_aquila_</u> volans
>   ad escam.

>   [my days ≈ swift ships ≈ an eagle]   Job

Job 10.10 Hast thou not poured me out <u>as</u> *milk*, and curdled me <u>like</u> *cheese*?

    10 ἢ οὐχ <u>ὥσπερ γάλα</u> με ἤμελξας, ἐτύρωσας δέ με <u>ἴσα</u> <u>τυρῷ</u>;

    10 Nonne <u>sicut</u> *lac* mulsisti me, et <u>sicut</u> *caseum* me coagulasti?

        [me ≈ milk or ≈ cheese]   Job

Job 10.16 *Thou* huntest *me as a fierce lion.*

    16 ἀγρεύομαι γὰρ <u>ὥσπερ λέων</u> εἰς σφαγήν,

    16 Et propter superbiam <u>quasi</u> *leaenam* capies *me*,

        [I ≈ a fierce lion]   Job

Job 11.8: It is <u>as high as</u> *heaven* … <u>deeper than</u> *hell*.

    8 ὑψηλὸς ὁ οὐρανός, καὶ τί ποιήσεις; <u>βαθύτερα</u> δὲ <u>τῶν ἐν ᾅδου</u> τί οἶδας;

    8 <u>Excelsior</u> *caelo* est, et quid facies? <u>profundior</u> *inferno*.

        [It ≈ (higher than) heaven … deeper than hell]   Zophar

Job 11.9 *The measure* thereof is *longer than the earth*, and <u>broader than</u> *the sea.*

    9 ἢ <u>μακρότερα</u> <u>μέτρου</u> γῆς ἢ <u>εὔρους</u> <u>θαλάσσης</u>;

    9 <u>Longior</u> *terra* mensura ejus et <u>latior</u> *mari*.

        [measure ≈ (longer than) the earth ≈ (broader than) the sea]   Zophar

Job 11.12 For vain man would be wise, though *man* be born like a wild *ass's colt*.

    12 βροτὸς δὲ γεννητὸς γυναικὸς <u>ἴσα</u> <u>ὄνῳ ἐρημίτῃ</u>.

    12 *Vir* vanus in superbiam erigitur, et <u>tamquam</u> *pullum onagri* se liberum natum putat.

        [man ≈ colt of a wild ass]   Zophar

Job 12.4 *I* am <u>as</u> *one mocked of his neighbour*, who calleth upon God.

    4 δίκαιος γὰρ ἀνὴρ καὶ ἄμεμπτος ἐγεννήθη εἰς χλεύασμα·(For a righteous and blameless man has become a subject for mockery.)

    4 *Qui deridetur ab amico suo*, <u>sicut</u> *ego*, invocabit Deum, et exaudiet eum; deridetur enim justi simplicitas.   Job

        [I ≈ one mocked by his neighbor]

Job 12.5 *He that is ready to slip with his feet* is <u>as</u> *a lamp despised* in the thought of him that is at ease.

    5 εἰς χρόνον γὰρ τακτὸν ἡτοίμαστο πεσεῖν ὑπὸ ἄλλων.

    5 *Lampas contempta* apud cogitationes divitum, parata ad tempus statutum.   Job

NB: The **Latin and Greek versions are quite different.**

[He … ≈ a despised lamp]

Job 12.25 They grope in the dark without light, and he maketh *them* to *stagger* like *a drunken man*.

25 ψηλαφήσαισαν σκότος καὶ μὴ φῶς, πλανηθείησαν δὲ <u>ὥσπερ ὁ μεθύων</u>.

25 Palpabunt quasi in tenebris, et non in luce, et *errare eos faciet* <u>quasi</u> *ebrios*.

[they (people of the earth) ≈ a drunken man]   Job

Job 13.12 *Your remembrances* are <u>like unto</u> *ashes, your bodies to bodies of clay.*

12 ἀποβήσεται δὲ ὑμῶν τὸ γαυρίαμα <u>ἴσα σποδῷ</u>, τὸ δὲ σῶμα <u>πήλινον</u>.

12 *Memoria vestra* <u>comparabitur</u> *cineri*, et redigentur in lutum cervices vestrae.   Job

[your remembrances ≈ ashes; your bodies ≈ clay)]

Job 13.28 And *he*, <u>as</u> *a rotten thing*, consumeth, <u>as</u> *a garment that is moth eaten*.

28 ὁ παλαιοῦται <u>ἴσα ἀσκῷ</u> ἢ <u>ὥσπερ ἱμάτιον σητόβρωτον</u>.

28 *qui* <u>quasi</u> *putredo* consumendus sum, et <u>quasi</u> *vestimentum quod comeditur a tinea*.

[he ≈ a rotten thing or ≈ a moth-eaten garment]   Job

Job 14.2 *He [man born of woman]* cometh forth <u>like</u> *a flower*, and is cut down; he fleeth also <u>as</u> *a shadow*, and continueth not.

2 ἢ <u>ὥσπερ ἄνθος ἀνθῆσαν</u> ἐξέπεσεν, ἀπέδρα δὲ <u>ὥσπερ σκιά</u> καὶ οὐ μὴ στῇ.

2 Qui <u>quasi</u> *flos* egreditur et conteritur, et fugit <u>velut</u> <u>umbra</u>, et numquam in eodem statu permanet.   Job

[he/a man ≈ flower that is cut down ≈ a shadow]

Job 14.6 Turn from him, that he may rest, till *he* shall accomplish, <u>as</u> an *hireling*, his day.

6 ἀπόστα ἀπ' αὐτοῦ, ἵνα … εὐδοκήσῃ τὸν βίον <u>ὥσπερ ὁ μισθωτός</u>.

6 Recede paululum ab eo, ut quiescat, donec optata veniat, <u>sicut</u> *mercenarii*, dies ejus.

[he/man ≈ a hireling]   Job

Job 14.11 <u>As</u> the *waters* fail from the sea, and <u>the flood</u> decayeth and drieth up: 12 **So** *man* lieth down, and riseth not.

11 χρόνῳ γὰρ σπανίζεται <u>θάλασσα</u>, ποταμὸς δὲ ἐρημωθεὶς ἐξηράνθη· 12 ἄνθρωπος δὲ κοιμηθεὶς οὐ μὴ ἀναστῇ.

11 <u>Quomodo</u> si recedant *aquae de mari*, et fluvius vacuefactus arescat: 12 **sic** *homo*, cum dormierit, non resurget.

    [man ≈ sea waters and floods dry up]   Job

Job 16.14 *He* [God] breaketh me with breach upon breach, he runneth upon me <u>like</u> *a giant*.

    14 κατέβαλόν με πτῶμα ἐπὶ πτώματι, ἔδραμον πρός με δυνάμενοι. (They overthrew me with fall upon fall: they ran upon me in [their] might.)

    15 Concidit [Deus] me vulnere super vulnus : irruit in me <u>quasi</u> *gigas*.   [God ≈ a giant]   Job

Job 16.21 O *that one might plead for man with God,* <u>as</u> *a man pleadeth for his neighbour*!

    21 εἴη δὲ ἔλεγχος ἀνδρὶ ἔναντι Κυρίου <u>καὶ</u> <u>υἱῷ ἀνθρώπου τῷ πλησίον</u> <u>αὐτοῦ</u>. [Job]

    22 atque utinam **sic** judicaretur vir cum Deo, <u>quomodo</u> judicatur filius hominis cum collega suo!

    [a man pleads for man with God ≈ a man pleads for his neighbor]   Job

Job 18.3 Wherefore are we counted <u>as</u> *beasts*?

    3 διατὶ δὲ <u>ὥσπερ</u> <u>τετράποδα</u> σεσιωπήκαμεν ἐναντίον σου;

    3 Quare reputati sumus <u>ut</u> *jumenta*

    [we ≈ beasts]   Bildad

Job 20.7 Yet *he* [the wicked] shall perish for ever <u>like</u> *his own dung*.

    7 ὅταν γὰρ δοκῇ ἤδη κατεστηρίχθαι, τότε εἰς τέλος ἀπολεῖται·

    7 <u>quasi</u> *sterquilinium* in fine perdetur.   Zophar

    [he/the wicked ≈ his own dung]

Job 20.8 *He* [the wicked] shall fly away <u>as</u> *a dream,* and shall not be found: yea, he shall be chased away <u>as</u> *a vision of the night*.

    8 <u>ὥσπερ</u> <u>ἐνύπνιον</u> ἐκπετασθὲν οὐ μὴ εὑρεθῇ, ἔπτη δὲ <u>ὥσπερ</u> <u>φάσμα</u> <u>νυκτερινόν</u>.

    8 <u>Velut</u> *somnium* avolans non invenietur: transiet <u>sicut</u> *visio nocturna*.   Zophar

    [he ≈ a dream that has fled away ≈ a vision of the night]

Job 21.18 *They* [the wicked] are <u>as</u> <u>*stubble before the wind*</u>, and <u>as</u> <u>*chaff*</u> that the storm carrieth away.

    2 ἔσονται δὲ <u>ὥσπερ</u> <u>ἄχυρα ὑπ' ἀνέμου</u> ἢ ὥσπερ <u>κονιορτός, ὃν ὑφείλετο</u> <u>λαῖλαψ</u>.

    18 Erunt <u>sicut</u> <u>*paleae ante faciem venti*</u>, et <u>sicut</u> <u>*favilla quam turbo*</u> <u>*dispergit*</u>.   Job

    [they ≈ stubble before the wind ≈ chaff carried away by a storm]

Job 22.24 Then shalt thou lay up *gold* <u>as</u> <u>*dust*</u>, and the *gold of Ophir* <u>as</u> the <u>*stones of the brooks*</u>.

    24 θήσῃ ἐπὶ χώματι ἐν πέτρᾳ καὶ <u>ὡς</u> <u>πέτρα χειμάρρου</u> Σωφίρ.

    24 Dabit <u>*pro terra*</u> silicem, et <u>*pro silice*</u> torrentes aureos.

    [gold ≈ dust; gold of Ophir ≈ stones of the brooks] Eliphaz

Job 24.5 Behold, <u>as</u> <u>*wild asses in the desert*</u>, go *they* forth to their work.

    5 ἀπέβησαν δὲ <u>ὥσπερ</u> <u>ὄνοι ἐν ἀγρῷ</u>.

    5 *Alii* <u>quasi</u> <u>*onagri in deserto*</u> egrediuntur ad opus suum:

    [They (the wicked) ≈ wild asses in the desert]   Job

Job 24.14 The *murderer* rising with the light killeth the poor and needy, and in the night is <u>as</u> <u>*a thief*</u>.

    14 καὶ νυκτὸς ἔσται <u>ὡς</u> <u>κλέπτης</u>. [ἀσεβεῖς – the ungodly]

    14 per noctem vero erit <u>quasi</u> *fur*.   *[homicida]*

    [the murderer in the night ≈ a thief]   Job

Job 24.17 For *the morning* is to them even <u>as</u> <u>*the shadow of death*</u>, if one know them, they are in the terrors of the <u>shadow of death</u>.

    17 ὅτι ὁμοθυμαδὸν αὐτοῖς τὸ πρωΐ <u>σκιὰ θανάτου</u>, ὅτι ἐπιγνώσεται τάραχος σκιᾶς θανάτου.

    17 Si subito apparuerit *aurora*, arbitrantur <u>*umbram mortis*</u> : et sic in tenebris quasi in luce ambulant.   Job

    [the morning ≈ the shadow of death; death ≈ a shadow]

Job 27.18 *He* buildeth his house <u>as</u> <u>*a moth*</u>, and <u>as</u> <u>*a booth that the keeper*</u> maketh.

    18 ἀπέβη δὲ οἱ οἶκος αὐτοῦ <u>ὥσπερ</u> <u>σῆτες</u> καὶ <u>ὥσπερ</u> <u>ἀράχνη</u>.

    18 Aedificavit <u>sicut</u> <u>*tinea*</u> domum suam, et <u>sicut</u> <u>*custos*</u> fecit umbraculum.

    [he ≈ a moth ≈ a booth/spider]   Job

Job 29.14 *My judgment* was <u>as</u> <u>*a robe and a diadem*</u>.

    14 δικαιοσύνην δὲ ἐνδεδύκειν, ἠμφιασάμην δὲ <u>*κρίμα ἴσα διπλοΐδι*</u>.

    14 Justitia indutus sum, et vestivi me, <u>sicut</u> <u>*vestimento et diademate*</u>, *judicio meo.*

    [my judgment ≈ a robe and a diadem]   Job

Job 29.18 Then I said, I shall die in my nest, and I shall multiply *my days* <u>as</u> <u>*the sand*</u>.

    18 εἶπα δέ· ἡ ἡλικία μου γηράσει <u>ὥσπερ</u> <u>*στέλεχος φοίνικος*</u>, πολὺν χρόνον βιώσω·

    18 In nidulo meo moriar, et <u>sicut</u> <u>*palma*</u> multiplicabo *dies.*

    [my days (growing old) ≈ the sand (palm)]   Job

Job 29.23 And they waited for *me* <u>as</u> for the <u>*rain*</u>; and they opened their mouth wide <u>as</u> for the <u>*latter rain*</u>.

    23 <u>ὥσπερ</u> <u>*γῆ διψῶσα προσδεχομένη τὸν ὑετόν*</u>, οὕτως οὗτοι τὴν ἐμὴν λαλιάν. [Job]

    (<u>As</u> <u>*the thirsty earth expecting the rain,*</u> *so they [waited for] my speech.*)

    23 *Expectabant me* <u>sicut</u> <u>*pluviam*</u>, et os suum *aperiebant* <u>quasi</u> ad <u>*imbrem serotinum*</u>.   Job

    [they waiting for my speech ≈ thirsty people expecting the rain]

Job 30.14 They [the youth] *came upon me* <u>*as a wide breaking in of waters*</u>.

    14 κέχρηται δέ μοι ὡς βούλεται, ἐν ὀδύναις πέφυρμαι.

    (And he has pleaded against me as he will: I am overwhelmed with pains.)

    14 <u>Quasi</u> *rupto muro*, et *aperta janua, irruerunt super me,* et ad meas miserias devoluti sunt.

    [they overwhelmed me ≈ a breaking-in of waters]   Job

Job 30.15 *They* [terrors] *pursue* my soul <u>as</u> <u>*the wind*</u>; and *my welfare passeth away* <u>as</u> <u>*a cloud*</u>.

    15 ἐπιστρέφονταί μου αἱ ὀδύναι, ᾤχετό μου ἡ ἐλπὶς <u>ὥσπερ</u> <u>*πνεῦμα*</u> καὶ <u>ὥσπερ</u> <u>*νέφος*</u> ἡ σωτηρία μου. [Job] (My pains return upon [me]; *my hope is gone* <u>like</u> *the* <u>*wind*</u>, and *my safety* <u>as</u> <u>*a cloud*</u>.)

    15 *abstulisti* <u>quasi</u> <u>*ventus*</u> desiderium meum, et <u>velut</u> <u>*nubes*</u> pertransiit *salus mea.*   Job

    [terrors pursue my soul ≈ wind; my welfare ≈ a cloud]

Job 30.18 By the great force of *my disease* is my garment changed: *it* bindeth me about <u>as</u> *<u>the collar of my coat</u>*.

18 ἐν πολλῇ ἰσχύϊ ἐπελάβετό μου τῆς στολῆς, <u>ὥσπερ</u> τὸ περιστόμιον τοῦ χιτῶνός μου περιέσχε με.

18 With great force [*my disease*] has taken hold of my garment: *it* has compassed me <u>as</u> *<u>the collar of my coat</u>*.

18 In multitudine eorum consumitur *vestimentum meum*, et <u>quasi *capito tunicae*</u> succinxerunt me.   Job
[my disease ≈ the collar of my coat]

Job 30.19 He hath cast me into the mire, and *I* am become <u>like</u> *<u>dust and ashes</u>*.

19 ἥγησαι δέ με <u>ἴσα</u> <u>*πηλῷ*</u>, <u>*ἐν γῇ καὶ σποδῷ*</u> μου ἡ μερίς· (And thou hast counted *me* <u>as</u> *<u>clay</u>*; *my portion* in *dust* and ashes.)

19 Comparatus sum <u>*luto*</u>, et <u>*assimilatus sum favillae*</u> et <u>*cineri*</u>.
[I ≈ dust and ashes (clay)]   Job

Job 31.36 Surely I would take it [my adversary's book] upon my shoulder, and bind *it* <u>as</u> *<u>a crown</u>* to me.

36 ἐπ᾽ ὤμοις ἂν περιθέμενος <u>*στέφανον*</u> ἀνεγίνωσκον.

36 ut in humero meo portem illum, et circumdem *illum* <u>quasi *coronam*</u> mihi?
[(my adversary's book) ≈ my crown]   Job

Job. 31.37 I would declare unto him the number of my steps; <u>as</u> *<u>a prince</u>* would *I* go near unto him.

37 καὶ εἰ μὴ ῥήξας αὐτὴν ἀπέδωκα, οὐθὲν λαβὼν παρὰ χρεωφειλέτου· (And if I did not read it and return it, having taken nothing from the debtor:)

>   37 Per singulos gradus meos pronuntiabo illum, et <u>quasi *principi*</u> offer*am* eum.   [I ≈ a prince]   Job

Job 32.19 Behold, *my belly* is <u>as</u> *<u>wine</u>* which hath no vent; it is ready to burst <u>like</u> *<u>new bottles</u>*.

32 ἡ δὲ γαστήρ μου <u>ὥσπερ</u> <u>*ἀσκὸς*</u> γλεύκους ζέων δεδεμένος ἢ <u>ὥσπερ</u> <u>*φυσητὴρ*</u> χαλκέως ἐρρηγώς.

19 En *venter* meus <u>quasi *mustum absque spiraculo*</u>, quod lagunculas novas disrumpit.   Job
[my belly ≈ wine or ≈ new bottles]

Job 34.7 *What man* is like *Job*, who drinketh up *scorning* like *water*?

    7 τίς ἀνὴρ ὥσπερ ᾿Ιώβ, πίνων μυκτηρισμὸν ὥσπερ ὕδωρ,

    7 Quis est *vir* ut est *Job*, qui bibit *subsannationem* quasi *aquam*?

        [a man like Job (a literal comparison) drinking *scorn* ≈
        water]   Elihu

Job 35.11 Who teacheth *us* more than the *beasts of the earth*, and maketh
us wiser than the *fowls of heaven*?

    11 ὁ διορίζων με ἀπὸ τετραπόδων γῆς, ἀπὸ δὲ πετεινῶν οὐρανοῦ; (who
    makes me to differ from the four-footed beasts of the earth, and
    from the birds of the sky?)

  >   11 qui docet *nos* super *jumenta terrae*, et super *volucres caeli* erudit
    nos?   Elihu

        [who? ≈ beasts of the earth; us (wiser than) ≈ the fowls of heaven]

Job 38.8 Or who shut up *the sea* with doors, *when it brake forth*, *as if* it had
issued out of the womb? 9 When I made *the cloud* *a/2 *the garment*
thereof, and *thick darkness a swaddling-band for it*.

    8 ἔφραξα δὲ θάλασσαν πύλαις, ὅτε ἐμαιοῦτο ἐκ κοιλίας μητρὸς αὐτῆς
    ἐκπορευομένη. ἐθέμην δὲ αὐτῇ νέφος ἀμφίασιν, ὁμίχλῃ δὲ αὐτὴν
    ἐσπαργάνωσα.

    8 Quis conclusit ostiis mare, quando *erumpebat* quasi *de vulva*
    procedens; cum ponerem *nubem* vestimentum ejus, et *caligine*
    illud quasi *pannis infantiae* obvolverem?

        [the sea broke out ≈ issued out to the womb; the cloud ≈ a gar-
        ment; thick darkness ≈ a swaddling-band]

    The Lord to Job

Job 38.14 *It* (the morning) is turned *as clay to the seal*; and *they* (the ends
of the earth) stand *as a garment*.

    14 ἢ σὺ λαβὼν γῆν πηλὸν ἔπλασας ζῷον καὶ λαλητὸν αὐτὸν ἔθου ἐπΙ γῆς;

    14 Restituetur ut *lutum* signaculum, et stabit sicut *vestimentum*.

    [It ≈ clay; they ≈ a garment]   The Lord to Job

Job 39.20 Canst thou make *him afraid* as *a grasshopper*?

    20 περιέθηκας δὲ αὐτῷ πανοπλίαν, δόξαν δὲ στηθέων αὐτοῦ τόλμῃ; (And
    hast thou clad him/a horse in perfect armour, and made his breast
    glorious with courage?)

> 20 Numquid suscitabis *eum* quasi *locustas*? gloria narium ejus
terror. [him/a horse afraid a grasshopper] The Lord to Job

Job 40.17 He [behemoth] moveth *his tail* like *a cedar*.

17 ἔστησεν οὐρὰν <u>ὡς</u> <u>κυπάρισσον.</u>

12 Stringit *caudam* suam quasi *cedrum*:   The Lord to Job
[a behemoth's tail ≈ a cedar]

Job 40.18 His *bones* are <u>as</u> strong *pieces of brass*; *his bones* are <u>like</u> bars
of *iron*.

*a/1   18 αἱ πλευραὶ αὐτοῦ <u>πλευραὶ χάλκειαι</u>, ἡ δὲ ῥάχις αὐτοῦ <u>σίδηρος χυτός.</u>
[behemoth]

13 *Ossa* ejus <u>velut</u> <u>*fistulae aeris*</u>, *cartilago* illius <u>quasi</u> <u>*laminae ferreae*</u>.   The
Lord to Job
[his bones ≈ pieces of brass ≈ bars of iron]

Job 41.15 His [the leviathan's] scales are his pride, *shut up together* <u>as</u> <u>*with*
a close seal</u>.

41: Greek and Latin chapters do not correspond.
There are other similes in the Latin text.
[leviathan's scales shut up ≈ a close seal]

Job 41.20 *Out of his nostrils* goeth smoke, <u>as</u> <u>*out of a seething pot*</u> or <u>*caldron*</u>.

12 ἐκ μυκτήρων αὐτοῦ ἐκπορεύεται καπνὸς <u>καμίνου καιομένης</u> πυρὶ
ἀνθράκων.

11 *De naribus ejus* procedit fumus, <u>sicut</u> <u>*ollae succensae*</u> atque
ferventis.   The Lord
[smoke from the leviathan's nostrils ≈ smoke out of a seething pot]

Job 41.24 His *heart* is <u>as firm as</u> a *stone*; yea, <u>as hard as</u> a *piece of the nether
millstone*.

16 ἡ καρδία αὐτοῦ πέπηγεν <u>ὡς λίθος</u>, ἔστηκε δὲ <u>ὥσπερ ἄκμων</u> ἀνήλατος.

15 *Cor* ejus indurabitur <u>tamquam</u> <u>*lapis*</u>, et stringetur <u>quasi</u> malleatoris
<u>*incus*</u>.   The Lord
[his heart (firm) ≈ a stone ≈ (hard) a piece of millstone]

Job 41.27 He esteemeth *iron* <u>as</u> <u>*straw*</u>, and *brass* <u>as</u> <u>*rotten wood*</u>.

19 ἥγηται μὲν γὰρ <u>σίδηρον ἄχυρα</u>, χαλκὸν δὲ <u>ὥσπερ ξύλον</u> σαθρόν.

18 reputabit enim <u>quasi</u> <u>*paleas ferrum*</u>, et <u>quasi</u> <u>*lignum putridum*</u>
aes. [iron ≈ straw; brass ≈ rotten wood]   The Lord

Job 41.29 *Darts* are counted <u>*as stubble*</u>.
    21 <u>ὡς καλάμη</u> ἐλογίσθησαν σφῦραι,
        20 <u>*Quasi stipulam*</u> aestimabit malleum   The Lord
        [darts ≈ stubble]
Job 41.31 He taketh the *deep* to boil <u>like</u> <u>*a pot*</u>: he maketh the sea <u>like</u> a *pot of ointment*.
    23 ἀναζεῖ τὴν ἄβυσσον <u>ὥσπερ χαλκεῖον</u>,
        22 Fervescere faciet <u>*quasi ollam*</u> profundum mare.   The Lord
        [the deep ≈ a pot/pot of ointment]
Job 41.33 Upon earth there is *not his* <u>*like*</u>, *who* is made without fear.
    25 οὐκ ἔστιν <u>οὐδὲν</u> ἐπὶ τῆς γῆς <u>ὅμοιον</u> <u>αὐτῷ.</u>
        24 *Non est* super terram *potestas* quae <u>comparetur</u> <u>*ei.*</u>
        [him ≈ nothing]

* * *

Psalms (150 Chapters)

Ψαλμοί

All speakers are David:

Ps. 1.3 And *he* [the blessed man] shall be <u>like</u> <u>*a tree planted by the rivers of water. that bringeth forth his fruit in his season.*</u>
    3 καὶ ἔσται [ΜΑΚΑΡΙΟΣ ἀνήρ] ὡς <u>τὸ ξύλον τὸ πεφυτευμένον παρὰ τὰς διεξόδους τῶν ὑδάτων.</u> ὃ τὸν καρπὸν αὐτοῦ δώσει ἐν καιρῷ αὐτοῦ,
    3 Et [Beatus vir] erit <u>tamquam</u> <u>*lignum quod plantatum est secus decursus aquarum,*</u> quod fructum suum dabit in tempore suo.
    [he (the blessed man) ≈ a tree planted by rivers]
Ps. 1.4 The ungodly … are <u>like</u> <u>*the chaff which the wind driveth away.*</u>
    4 οἱ ἀσεβεῖς … <u>ὡσεὶ χνοῦς,</u> ὃν ἐκρίπτει ὁ ἄνεμος ἀπὸ προσώπου τῆς γῆς.
    4 Non sic *impii*, non sic; sed <u>tamquam</u> <u>*pulvis*</u> quem projicit ventus a facie terrae.
    [the ungodly ≈ chaff scattered by wind]
Ps. 5.12 For thou, Lord, … *with favour wilt thou compass him*
    [the righteous] *as with a shield.*
*c/12 Κύριε, <u>ὡς ὅπλῳ εὐδοκίας</u> ἐστεφάνωσας ἡμᾶς.

*c/13 Domine, *ut scuto bonae voluntatis tuae* coronasti nos.

    [the Lord's favor ≈ a shield]

    *c/[In Greek and Latin a genitive simile: favor ≈ a shield]

Ps. 7.2 Lest he [*the enemy*] *tear* my soul <u>like</u> *a lion rending it in pieces.*

    2 μήποτε ἁρπάσῃ <u>ὡς</u> <u>λέων</u> τὴν ψυχήν μου, μὴ ὄντος λυτρουμένου μηδὲ σῴζοντος.

    2 nequando *rapiat* <u>ut</u> *leo* animam meam.

    [the enemy seizing my soul ≈ a lion]

Ps. 10.9 *He* [the wicked] lieth in wait secretly <u>as</u> *a lion in his den.*

    = 9.30 ἐνεδρεύει ἐν ἀποκρύφῳ <u>ὡς λέων ἐν τῇ μάνδρᾳ αὐτοῦ</u>,

    9.30 *insidiatur* in abscondito, <u>*quasi leo in spelunca sua.*</u>

    [He lying in wait ≈ a lion in his den]

Ps. 11.1 In the Lord put I my trust: how say ye to my soul, *Flee* <u>as</u> *a bird* to your mountain?

    = 10.1 ΕΠΙ τῷ Κυρίῳ πέποιθα· πῶς ἐρεῖτε τῇ ψυχῇ μου· <u>*μεταναστεύου ἐπὶ τὰ ὄρη ὡς στρουθίον;*</u>

    10.2 In Domino confido; quomodo dicitis animae meae: *Transmigra in montem* <u>sicut</u> *passer?*

    [you (my soul) fleeing to the mountains ≈ a bird/sparrow]

Ps. 12.6 The *words of the Lord* are pure words: <u>as</u> *silver tried in a furnace of earth,* purified seven times.

*a/1 = 11.6 τὰ λόγια Κυρίου λόγια ἁγνά, <u>*ἀργύριον πεπυρωμένον. δοκίμιον τῇ γῇ κεκαθαρισμένον ἑπταπλασίως.*</u>

    11.7 *Eloquia Domin*i, eloquia casta; <u>*argentum igne examinatum, probatum terrae, purgatum septuplum.*</u>

    [the words of the Lord ≈ silver hardened in fire]

    >>Only the English version includes a prothesis.

Ps. 17.8 Keep *me* <u>as</u> *the apple of the eye*, hide me under the shadow of thy wings.

    16.8 φύλαξόν *με* <u>ὡς</u> <u>κόρην ὀφθαλμοῦ</u>· ἐν σκέπῃ τῶν πτερύγων σου σκεπάσεις με.

    8 A resistentibus dexterae tuae custodi me, <u>ut</u> <u>*pupillam oculi.*</u> Sub <u>*umbra alarum tuarum*</u> protege me.

    [me ≈ the apple of the eye]

Ps. 17.12 <u>Like as</u> *a lion that is greedy of his prey*, and <u>as it were</u> *a young lion lurking in secret places*.

    = 16.12 ὑπέλαβόν με <u>ὡσεὶ</u> *λέων ἔτοιμος εἰς θήραν* καὶ <u>ὡσεὶ</u> *σκύμνος οἰκῶν ἐν ἀποκρύφοις*.

    12 Susceperunt me <u>sicut</u> *leo paratus ad praedam*, et <u>sicut</u> *catulus eonis habitans in abditis*.

    [they waited for me ≈ a lion greedy of its prey ≈ a young lion lurking]

Ps. 18.33 He [God] maketh *my feet* <u>like</u> *hinds' feet*.

    17.34 καταρτιζόμενος *τοὺς πόδας μου* <u>ὡσεὶ</u> *ἐλάφου* καὶ ἐπὶ τὰ ὑψηλὰ ἱστῶν με· (strengthening my feet <u>as</u> *hart's feet* and set me upon high places)

    17.34 qui [Deus] perfecit *pedes meos* <u>tamquam</u> *cervorum.*

    [my feet ≈ hinds' feet]

Ps. 19.5 Which is <u>as</u> *a bridegroom* coming out of his chamber, and rejoiceth <u>as</u> *a strong man* to run a race.

    18.6 ἐν τῷ ἡλίῳ ἔθετο τὸ σκήνωμα αὐτοῦ· καὶ αὐτὸς <u>ὡς</u> *νυμφίος* ἐκπορευόμενος ἐκ παστοῦ αὐτοῦ, ἀγαλλιάσεται <u>ὡς</u> *γίγας* δραμεῖν ὁδὸν αὐτοῦ. (In the sun He [God] has set his tabernacle; and He came forth *as a bridegroom* out of his chamber: he will exult <u>as a giant</u> to run his course.)

    18.6 In sole posuit tabernaculum suum; et *ipse* [Deus] <u>tamquam</u> *sponsus* procedens de thalamo suo. Exsultavit <u>ut</u> *gigas* ad currendam viam.

    [he/God ≈ a bridegroom ≈ a strong man/giant]

Ps. 19.10 <u>More</u> to be desired are they [judgments of the Lord] <u>than gold</u>, yea, <u>than</u> *much fine gold*: sweeter also than *honey and the honey-comb*.

    = 18.11 ἐπιθυμητὰ <u>ὑπὲρ</u> *χρυσίον* καὶ λίθον <u>τίμιον πολὺν</u> καὶ *γλυκύτερα* <u>ὑπὲρ</u> *μέλι καὶ κηρίον*.

    18.11 <u>Desiderabilia super</u> *aurum et lapidem* pretiosum multum; et <u>dulciora super</u> *mel et favum.*

    [(judgments of the Lord) more desirable ≈ gold ≈ (sweeter) honey and honey-comb]

Ps. 21.9 Thou shalt make *them* [those that hate thee] <u>as</u> *a fiery oven* in the time of thine anger.

    20.10 θήσεις *αὐτοὺς* <u>εἰς</u> *κλίβανον πυρὸς* εἰς καιρὸν τοῦ προσώπου σου·

20.10 Pones *eos* ut <u>*clibanum ignis*</u> in tempore vultus tui:
[them ≈ a fiery oven]

Ps. 22.13 They gaped upon me with their mouths, <u>as *a ravening and*</u> <u>*roaring lion.*</u>

21.14 ἤνοιξαν ἐπ᾽ ἐμὲ τὸ στόμα αὐτῶν <u>ὡς</u> <u>*λέων ἁρπάζων*</u> καὶ <u>ὠρυόμενος</u>.

21.14 Aperuerunt super me os suum, <u>sicut</u> l<u>*eo rapiens et rugiens*</u>.
[they ≈ a ravening and roaring ion]

Ps. 22.14 I am poured out <u>like *water*</u>, and all my bones are out of joint: my *heart* is <u>like *wax;*</u> it is melted in the midst of my bowels.

21.15 <u>ὡσεὶ</u> <u>*ὕδωρ*</u> ἐξεχύθην, καὶ διεσκορπίσθη πάντα τὰ ὀστᾶ μου, ἐγενήθη ἡ καρδία μου <u>ὡσεὶ</u> <u>*κηρὸς τηκόμενος*</u> ἐν μέσῳ τῆς κοιλίας μου·

21.15 <u>Sicut</u> <u>*aqua*</u> effusus *sum*; et dispersa sunt omnia ossa mea. Factum est cor meum <u>tamquam</u> <u>*cera*</u> liquescens in medio ventris mei.
[I (poured out) ≈ water; my heart ≈ melting wax]

Ps. 22.15 *My strength* is dried up <u>like *a potsherd;*</u> ... thou hast brought me into the <u>*dust of death*</u>.

21.16 ἐξηράνθη <u>ὡσεὶ</u> <u>*ὄστρακον*</u> ἡ ἰσχύς μου ... καὶ εἰς χοῦν θανάτου κατήγαγές με.

21.16 Aruit <u>tamquam</u> <u>*testa*</u> virtus mea, et ... in <u>*pulverem mortis*</u> deduxisti me.
[my strength (dried up) ≈ a potsherd; (death ≈ dust)]

Ps. 29.6 He maketh them also to skip <u>like *a calf*</u>; Lebanon and Sirion <u>like</u> <u>*a young unicorn.*</u>

28.6 καὶ λεπτυνεῖ αὐτὰς <u>ὡς</u> <u>*τὸν μόσχον*</u> τὸν Λίβανον, καὶ ὁ ἠγαπημένος. <u>ὡς</u> <u>*υἱὸς μονοκερώτων*</u>. (And he will beat them small, [even] Libanus itself, like a calf; and the beloved one is as a young unicorn.)

28.6 et comminuet eas <u>tamquam</u> <u>*vitulum*</u> Libani: et dilectus quemadmodum <u>*filius unicornium*</u>.
[they (cedars of Lebanon) ≈ a calf ≈ a young unicorm]

Ps. 31.12 I am forgotten <u>as *a dead man*</u> out of mind: *I* am <u>like *a broken*</u> <u>*vessel*</u>.

30.13 ἐπελήσθην <u>ὡσεὶ</u> <u>*νεκρὸς*</u> ἀπὸ καρδίας, ἐγενήθην <u>ὡσεὶ</u> <u>*σκεῦος*</u> <u>*ἀπολωλός*</u>.

30 13 Oblivioni datus sum, <u>tamquam</u> <u>*mortuus*</u> a corde. Factus sum <u>tamquam</u> <u>*vas perditum*</u>;
[I (forgotten) ≈ a dead man ≈ a broken vessel]

Ps. 32.9 Be *ye* not <u>as</u> the *horse or as the mule*, which have no understanding;

    31.9 μὴ γίνεσθε <u>ὡς</u> <u>*ἵππος καὶ ἡμίονος*</u>, οἷς οὐκ ἔστι σύνεσις,

    31.9 Nolite fieri <u>sicut</u> *equus et mulus,* quibus non est intellectus.

    [you ≈ (not) a horse or a mule]

Ps. 33.7 He *gathereth* the waters of the sea together <u>as</u> *an heap.*

    32.7 συνάγων <u>ὡσεὶ</u> <u>*ἀσκὸν*</u> ὕδατα θαλάσσης

    32.7 Congregans <u>sicut</u> *in utre* aquas maris;

    [the sea waters (gathered) ≈ a heap/bottle]

Ps. 35.14 *I* behaved myself <u>as</u> though *he* had been my *friend or brother*:;
I bowed down heavily, <u>as</u> *one that mourneth for his mother.*

    34.14 <u>ὡς</u> <u>*πλησίον*</u>, <u>ὡς</u> <u>*ἀδελφῷ*</u> ἡμετέρῳ οὕτως εὐηρέστουν· <u>ὡς</u> <u>*πενθῶν*</u>
    καὶ σκυθρωπάζων, οὕτως ἐταπεινούμην. (I humbled myself as one
    mourning and sad of countenance.)

    34.14 <u>Quasi</u> *proximum et quasi fratrem nostrum* **sic** *complacebam*; <u>quasi</u>
    lugens et contristatus **sic** *humiliabar.*

    [I behaved ≈ a friend or brother; and (bowed dowh) ≈ a mourner
    (for mother)]

Ps. 36.6 Thy *righteousness* is <u>like</u> *the great mountains*; thy *judgments* are a
great deep.

    35.7 ἡ δικαιοσύνη σου <u>ὡς</u> <u>*ὄρη Θεοῦ*</u>, τὰ κρίματά σου <u>ὡσεὶ</u> <u>*ἄβυσσος πολλή*</u>·

*a/   35.7 *Justitia tua* <u>sicut</u> *montes Dei*; *judicia tua* <u>abyssus multa</u>.

    [your righteousness ≈ great mountains; your judgments ≈ a
    great deep]

Ps. 37.2 For *they* shall soon be cut down <u>like</u> the *grass*, and wither <u>as</u> the
green herb.

    36.2 ὅτι <u>ὡσεὶ</u> <u>*χόρτος*</u> ταχὺ ἀποξηρανθήσονται καὶ <u>ὡσεὶ</u> <u>*λάχανα χλόης*</u> ταχὺ
    ἀποπεσοῦνται.

    36.2 quoniam <u>tamquam</u> *foenum* velociter arescent, et <u>quemadmodum</u>
    olera herbarum cito decident.

    [they (cut down) ≈ grass; (wither) ≈ green herb]

Ps. 37.6 And he shall bring forth t*hy righteousness* <u>as</u> *the light*, and thy
judgment <u>as</u> the *noonday.*

    36.6 καὶ ἐξοίσει <u>ὡς</u> <u>*φῶς*</u> τὴν δικαιοσύνην σου καὶ τὸ κρῖμά σου <u>ὡς</u> <u>*μεσημβρίαν*</u>.

    36.6 Et educet <u>quasi</u> *lumen* justitiam tuam, et *judicium tuum* <u>tamquam</u>
    meridiem.

    [thy righteousness ≈ light and thy judgment ≈ noonday]

Ps. 37.20 But the wicked shall perish; and *the enemies of the Lord* shall be
as *the fat of lambs*.

    36.20 ὅτι *οἱ ἁμαρτωλοὶ ἀπολοῦνται*, οἱ δὲ *ἐχθροὶ τοῦ Κυρίου* ἅμα τῷ
δοξασθῆναι αὐτοὺς καὶ ὑψωθῆναι ἐκλείποντες <u>ὡσεὶ <i>καπνὸς</i></u> ἐξέλιπον.
(and the enemies of the Lord at the moment of their being hon-
oured and exalted have utterly vanished <u>like *smoke*</u>)

    36.20 quia peccatores peribunt. *Inimici vero Domini* mox ut honorificati
fuerint et exaltati, deficientes <u>quemadmodum *fumus*</u> deficient.
[enemies of the Lord ≈ the fat of lambs / smoke]

Ps. 37.35 I have seen the wicked in great power, and spreading *himself* <u>like</u>
a *green bay tree*.

    36.35 εἶδον *τὸν ἀσεβῆ* ὑπερυψούμενον καὶ ἐπαιρόμενον <u>ὡς *τὰς κέδρους τοῦ
Λιβάνου*</u>· (like *the cedars of Libanus*)

    36.35 Vidi impium superexaltatum, et elevatum <u>sicut *cedros Libani*</u>;
[the wicked ≈ a green bay tree/cedars of Libanus]

Ps. 38.13 But *I,* <u>as</u> a *deaf man*, heard not; and I was <u>as</u> *a dumb man that*
openeth not his mouth.

    37.14 *ἐγὼ* δὲ <u>ὡσεὶ</u> <u>*κωφὸς*</u> οὐκ ἤκουον καὶ <u>ὡσεὶ</u> <u>*ἄλαλος*</u> οὐκ ἀνοίγων τὸ
στόμα αὐτοῦ·

    37.14 Ego autem, <u>tamquam *surdus*</u>, non audiebam; et <u>sicut *mutus*</u> non
aperiens os suum.
[I ≈ a deaf man ≈ a dumb man]

Ps 38.14 Thus *I* was <u>as *a man that heareth not*</u>.

Ps. 39.5 Behold, thou hast made *my days* <u>as an handbreadth</u>; and mine *age*
is <u>as *nothing before thee*</u>.

    38.5 γνώρισόν μοι, Κύριε, τὸ πέρας μου καὶ τὸν ἀριθμὸν τῶν ἡμερῶν μου,
τίς ἐστιν, ἵνα γνῶ τί ὑστερῶ ἐγώ.

    38.6 Ecce mensurabiles posuisti dies meos, et substantia mea <u>tamquam
nihilum ante te</u>.
[my days ≈ a handbreadth; my age ≈ nothing]

Ps. 42.1 <u>As *the hart panteth after the water brooks,*</u> **so** panteth *my soul after
thee*, O God.

    41.2 <u>ΟΝ ΤΡΟΠΟΝ</u> *ἐπιποθεῖ ἡ ἔλαφος ἐπὶ τὰς πηγὰς τῶν ὑδάτων,* **οὕτως**
ἐπιποθεῖ ἡ ψυχή μου πρός σέ, ὁ Θεός.

41.1 <u>Quemadmodum</u> desiderat cervus ad fontes aquarum, **ita** desiderat *anima mea* ad te, Deus.

[my soul ≈ a hart desiring brooks of water]

Ps. 44.11 Thou hast given *us* <u>like</u> <u>*sheep*</u> appointed for meat.

43.11x ἔδωκας ἡμᾶς <u>ὡς</u> <u>πρόβατα βρώσεως.</u>

43.12 Dedisti *nos* <u>tamquam</u> *<u>oves escarum</u>*;

[us ≈ sheep for meat]

Ps. 44.22 For thy sake *we* are counted <u>as</u> <u>*sheep for the slaughter.*</u>

43.23 ἐλογίσθημεν <u>ὡς</u> <u>πρόβατα σφαγῆς.</u>

43.22 aestimati sumus <u>sicut</u> *<u>oves occisionis.</u>*

[we ≈ sheep for slaughter]

Ps. 49.12 *He [a man being in honour]* <u>is like</u> <u>*the beasts that perish*</u>.

48.13 καὶ ἄνθρωπος ἐν τιμῇ ὢν οὐ συνῆκε, παρασυνεβλήθη τοῖς <u>κτήνεσι</u> <u>τοῖς ἀνοήτοις</u> καὶ ὡμοιώθη αὐτοῖς.

48.13 Et *homo, cum in honore esset*, non intellexit. Comparatus est *<u>jumentis insipientibus</u>*, et <u>similis factus est</u> illis.

[he ≈ beasts that perish] **cf. 49.20 (below).**

Ps. 49.14 <u>Like</u> *<u>sheep</u>* they are laid in the grave.

48.15 <u>ὡς</u> <u>πρόβατα</u> ἐν ᾅδῃ ἔθεντο, θάνατος ποιμανεῖ αὐτούς·

48.145 <u>Sicut</u> *<u>oves</u>* in inferno positi sunt:

[they (men held in honour) ≈ sheep]

Ps. 49.20 Man that is in honour, and understandeth not, <u>is like</u> the *<u>beasts</u> <u>that perish</u>*. **cf. 49.12.**

48.21 καὶ ἄνθρωπος ἐν τιμῇ ὢν οὐ συνῆκε, <u>παρασυνεβλήθη</u> ¨

*b/2   <u>τοῖς κτήνεσι τοῖς ἀνοήτοις</u> καὶ <u>ὡμοιώθη</u> <u>αὐτοῖς</u>.

21 Homo, cum in honore esset, non intellexit. Comparatus est jumentis insipientibus, et similis factus est illis.

[a man in honor but not understanding ≈ perishable beasts]

Ps. 51.7 Purge me with hyssop, and I shall be clean: wash me, and *I* shall be <u>whiter than</u> *<u>snow</u>*.

50.9 ραντιεῖς με ὑσσώπῳ, καὶ καθαρισθήσομαι, πλυνεῖς με, καὶ <u>ὑπὲρ χιόνα</u> <u>λευκανθήσομαι.</u>

50.9 Asperges me hyssopo, et mundabor; lavabis me, et <u>super</u> *<u>nivem</u>* dealbabor.

[I (whiter) ≈ snow]

Ps. 52.8 *I* am <u>like</u> *a green olive tree* in the house of God.

    51.10 ἐγὼ δὲ <u>ὡσεὶ</u> <u>ἐλαία κατάκαρπος</u> ἐν τῷ οἴκῳ τοῦ Θεοῦ·

    51.10 *Ego* autem, <u>sicut</u> *oliva fructifera in domo Dei*;

      [I ≈ green olive tree]

Ps. 55.6 And I said, Oh that I had *wings* <u>like</u> *a dove!* for then would I fly away, and be at rest.

    54.7 καὶ εἶπα· τίς δώσει μοι πτέρυγας <u>ὡσεὶ</u> <u>περιστερᾶς</u> καὶ πετασθήσομαι καὶ καταπαύσω;

    54.7 Et dixi: Quis dabit mihi *pennas* <u>sicut</u> *columbae*, et volabo, et requiescam?

      [me (wings) ≈ dove]

Ps. 55.21 The *words* of his mouth were <u>smoother than</u> *butter*, but war was in his heart: his *words* were <u>softer than</u> *oil* yet were they drawn swords.

    54.22 ἡπαλύνθησαν οἱ λόγοι αὐτοῦ <u>ὑπὲρ</u> <u>ἔλαιον</u>, καὶ αὐτοί εἰσι <u>βολίδες</u>.

    54.21 Molliti sunt *sermones* ejus <u>super</u> *oleum*; et ipsi sunt jacula.

      [words (smoother) ≈ butter; words (softer than) ≈ oil]

Ps. 58.4 Their [the wicked] *poison* is <u>like the</u> poison *of a serpent*; *they are* <u>like</u> *the* <u>*deaf adder*</u> that stoppeth her ear.

    57.5 ϑυμὸς αὐτοῖς <u>κατὰ τὴν ὁμοίωσιν</u> <u>τοῦ ὄφεως</u>, <u>ὡσεὶ</u> <u>ἀσπίδος κωφῆς</u> καὶ βυούσης τὰ ὦτα αὐτῆς,

    57.5 *Furor* illis <u>secundum similitudinem</u> *serpentis*, <u>sicut</u> *aspidis surdae et obturantis aures suas*,

      [their poison ≈ a serpent's; they ≈ a deaf adder]

Ps. 58.7 Let *them* [the wicked] melt away *as* <u>*waters which run continually*</u>; when he bendeth his bow to shoot his arrows, let *them* be <u>as</u> <u>*cut in pieces*</u>.

    57.8 ἐξουδενωϑήσονται <u>ὡσεὶ</u> <u>ὕδωρ διαπορευόμενον</u>· ἐκτενεῖ τὸ τόξον αὐτοῦ ἕως οὗ ἀσθενήσουσιν.

    57.8 Ad *nihilum* devenient <u>tamquam</u> <u>*aqua decurrens*</u>; intendit arcum suum donec infirmentur.

      [they (shall melt away) ≈ waters running continually; they ≈ cut in pieces]

Ps. 58.8 <u>As *a snail which melteth,*</u> let *every one of them* pass away: <u>like</u> the *untimely birth of a woman,* that they may not see the sun.

> 57.9 <u>ὡσεὶ *κηρὸς τακεὶς*</u> ἀνταναιρεθήσονται· ἔπεσε πῦρ ἐπ᾽ αὐτούς, καὶ οὐκ εἶδον τὸν ἥλιον.

> 57.9 <u>Sicut</u> *cera* quae fluit auferentur; supercecidit ignis, et non viderunt solem.

> [they (pass away) ≈ a melting snail/melted wax ≈ untimely birth of a woman]

Ps. 58.9 Before your pots can feel the thorns, he shall take *them* away <u>as</u> with a <u>*whirlwind*,</u> both living, and in his wrath.

> 57.10 πρὸ τοῦ συνιέναι τὰς ἀκάνθας αὐτῶν τὴν ῥάμνον, <u>ὡσεὶ *ζῶντας*, ὡσεὶ *ἐν ὀργῇ*</u> καταπίεται αὐτούς.

> 57.10 Priusquam intelligerent spinae vestrae rhamnum, <u>sicut *viventes* **sic**</u> in ira absorbet eos.

> [he (shall take them away) ≈ whirlwind]

Ps. 59.6 They [workers of iniquity, mine enemies] return at evening: *they* make a noise <u>like *a dog*,</u> and go round about the city.

> 58.7 ἐπιστρέψουσιν εἰς ἑσπέραν καὶ λιμώξουσιν <u>ὡς *κύων*</u> καὶ κυκλώσουσι πόλιν.

> 58.7 ≈ Convertentur ad vesperam, et famem *patientur* <u>ut *canes*</u>; et circuibunt civitatem.

> [they (shall make a noise) ≈ a dog] cf. 59.14.

Ps. 59.14 And at evening let them return; and *let them make a noise* <u>like *a dog*</u>, and go round about the city.

> 58.15 ἐπιστρέψουσιν εἰς ἑσπέραν, καὶ λιμώξουσιν <u>ὡς *κύων*</u> καὶ κυκλώσουσι πόλιν.

> 58.15 Convertentur ad vesperam, et famem *patientur* <u>ut *canes*</u>; et circuibunt civitatem.

> [they (shall make a noise/hunger) ≈ a dog]

Ps. 62.3 How long will ye imagine mischief against a man? ye shall be slain all of you: <u>as *a bowing wall* shall ye be, and as *a tottering fence*.</u>

> 61.4 ἕως πότε ἐπιτίθεσθε ἐπ᾽ ἄνθρωπον; φονεύετε πάντες <u>ὡς *τοίχῳ κεκλιμένῳ* καὶ *φραγμῷ ὠσμένῳ*.</u>

> 61.4 Quousque irruitis in hominem? interficitis universi vos, <u>tamquam *parieti inclinato*</u> et <u>*maceriae depulsa*e</u>?

> [you ≈ *a bowing wall and a broken fence*]

Ps. 64.3 Who [workers of iniquity] whet their *tongue* like *a sword,* and bend their bows to shoot their arrows, even bitter words.

> 63.4 οἵτινες ἠκόνησαν ὡς ῥομφαίαν τὰς γλώσσας αὐτῶν, ἐνέτειναν τόξον αὐτῶν πρᾶγμα πικρὸν.

> 63.4 Quia *exacuerunt* ut *gladium linguas suas;* intenderunt arcum rem amaram, 5 ut sagittent in occultis immaculatum.

> [(wicked people sharpen their) tongues ≈ a sword]

Ps. 68.2 As *smoke* is driven away, **so** *drive them away:* as *wax* melteth before the fire, *so let the wicked perish* at the presence of God.

> 67.3 ὡς ἐκλείπει καπνός, ἐκλιπέτωσαν· ὡς τήκεται κηρὸς ἀπὸ προσώπου πυρός, **οὕτως** ἀπολοῦνται οἱ ἁμαρτωλοὶ ἀπὸ προσώπου τοῦ Θεοῦ.

> 67.2 Sicut *deficit fumus,* deficiant; sicut *fluit cera a facie ignis,* **sic** *pereant peccatores a facie Dei.*

> [them (driven away) ≈ smoke; the wicked should perish ≈ wax melts]

Ps. 68.13 Though ye have lien among the pots, yet shall *ye* be as t*he wings of a dove covered with silver,* and her feathers with yellow gold.

> 67.14 ἐὰν κοιμηθῆτε ἀνὰ μέσον τῶν κλήρων (lots), πτέρυγες περιστερᾶς περιηργυρωμέναι, καὶ τὰ μετάφρενα αὐτῆς ἐν χλωρότητι χρυσίου.

> 67.14 Si dormiatis inter medios cleros (lots), pennae columbae deargentatae, et posteriora dorsi ejus in pallore auri.

> [ye ≈ wings of a dove]

> \>> **Not a simile in Greek/Latin (but note the alliteration in Greek).**

Ps. 68.14 When the Almighty scattered kings in it, *it* was *white as snow* in Salmon.

> 67.15 ἐν τῷ διαστέλλειν τὸν ἐπουράνιον βασιλεῖς ἐπ᾽ αὐτῆς, χιονωθήσονται ἐν Σελμών. [they shall be made snow-white]

> 67.15 Dum discernit caelestis reges super eam, *nive dealbabuntur* in Selmon.

> [it (Salmon) (white) ≈ snow; **a verbal simile in Greek (*d/)**]

Ps. 72.6 *He* (king Solomon) shall come down like *rain upon the mown grass:* as *showers that water the earth.*

> 71.6 καταβήσεται ὡς ὑετὸς ἐπὶ πόκον καὶ ὡσεὶ σταγὼν ἡ στάζουσα ἐπὶ τὴν γῆν.

71.6 Descendet <u>sicut</u> *<u>pluvia in vellus,</u>* et <u>sicut</u> *<u>stillicidia stillantia</u>* super terram.

[he/the king ≈ rain on grass ≈ showers watering the earth]

Ps. 73.20 <u>As</u> a *<u>dream when one</u> awaketh: so,* O Lord, when *thou* awakest, thou shalt despise their **image**.

72.20 <u>ὡσεὶ</u> <u>*ἐνύπνιον ἐξεγειρομένου*</u>, Κύριε, ἐν τῇ πόλει σου **τὴν εἰκόνα αὐτῶν** ἐξουδενώσεις.

72.20 <u>Velut</u> *<u>somnium surgentium</u>*, Domine, in civitate tua **imaginem** ipsorum ad nihilum rediges.

[Thou O Lord ≈ a dream of someone wakening up]

Ps. 73.22 So foolish was I, and ignorant: *I* was <u>as</u> *<u>a beast</u>* before thee.

72.20 κἀγὼ ἐξουδενωμένος καὶ οὐκ ἔγνων, <u>*κτηνώδης*</u> ἐγενόμην παρά σοι.

[beast-like]

72.22 et ego ad nihilum redactus sum, et nescivi; 23 <u>ut</u> *<u>jumentum</u> factus sum* apud te, et ego semper tecum.

[I ≈ a beast]

Ps 77.20 Thou leddest *thy people* <u>like</u> *<u>a flock</u>* by the hand of Moses and Aaron.

76.20 ὡδήγησας <u>*ὡς*</u> <u>*πρόβατα*</u> τὸν λαόν σου ἐν χειρὶ Μωϋσῆ καὶ ᾿Ααρών.

76.21 Deduxisti <u>sicut</u> *<u>oves</u> populum tuum*, in manu Moysi et Aaron.

[thy people ≈ a flock]

Ps. 78.13 He divided the sea, and caused them to pass through: *he made the waters to stand* <u>as</u> *<u>an heap.</u>*

77.13 διέρρηξε θάλασσαν καὶ διήγαγεν αὐτούς, παρέστησεν ὕδατα <u>*ὡσεὶ ἀσκόν.*</u>

77.13 Interrupit mare, et perduxit eos; et statuit *aquas* <u>quasi</u> *<u>in utre.</u>* [waters (standing) ≈ a heap]

Ps. 78.52 But [God] made *his own people to go forth* <u>like</u> *<u>sheep</u>*; and guided *them* in the wilderness <u>like</u> *<u>a flock</u>*.

77.52 καὶ ἀπῆρεν <u>*ὡς*</u> <u>*πρόβατα*</u> τὸν λαὸν αὐτοῦ καὶ ἀνήγαγεν αὐτοὺς <u>*ὡσεὶ ποίμνιον*</u> ἐν ἐρήμῳ

77.52 et abstulit <u>sicut</u> *<u>oves</u> populum suum*, et perduxit *eos* <u>tamquam</u> *<u>gregem</u>* in deserto;

[his people ≈ sheep ≈ a flock in the wilderness]

Ps. 78.69 And he built *his sanctuary* <u>like</u> <u>*high palaces*</u>, <u>like</u> <u>*the earth*</u> which he hath established for ever.

77.69 καὶ ᾠκοδόμησεν <u>ὡς</u> μονοκέρωτος [*as (the place) of a unicorn*] τὸ ἁγίασμα αὐτοῦ, ἐν τῇ γῇ ἐθεμελίωσεν αὐτὴν εἰς τὸν αἰῶνα. [*he founded it for ever on the earth*]

76.69 Et aedificavit <u>sicut</u> <u>*unicornium*</u> sanctificium suum, in terra quam fundavit in saecula.

[his sanctuary ≈ high palaces ≈ the earth] **NB: both Greek and Latin have a different reading for the vehicle.**

Ps. 79.3 *Their blood* have they shed [thy servants, thy saints] <u>like</u> <u>*water*</u>, round about Jerusalem: and there was none to bury them.

78.3 ἐξέχεαν *τὸ αἷμα αὐτῶν* <u>ὡσεὶ</u> <u>ὕδωρ</u> κύκλῳ Ἰερουσαλήμ, καὶ οὐκ ἦν ὁ θάπτων.

78.3 Effuderunt *sanguinem* eorum <u>tamquam</u> <u>*aquam*</u> in circuitu Jerusalem, et non erat qui sepeliret.

[their blood ≈ water]

Ps. 83.13 O my God, make *them* [thine enemies] <u>like</u> <u>*a wheel;*</u> as the <u>*stubble*</u> before the wind.

82.14 ὁ Θεός μου, θοῦ *αὐτοὺς* <u>ὡς</u> <u>τροχόν</u>, <u>ὡς</u> <u>καλάμην</u> κατὰ πρόσωπον ἀνέμου·

82.13 Deus meus, pone *illos* <u>ut</u> <u>*rotam*</u>, et <u>sicut</u> <u>*stipulam ante faciem venti*</u>.

[them ≈ a wheel ≈ stubble before the wind]

Ps. 83.14 <u>As</u> the <u>*fire*</u> burneth a wood, as <u>*the flame*</u> setteth the mountains on fire; 15 So persecute them with *thy tempest*.

82.15 <u>ὡσεὶ</u> <u>πῦρ</u>, ὃ διαφλέξει δρυμόν, <u>ὡσεὶ</u> <u>φλόξ</u>, ἣ κατακαύσει ὄρη, 16 οὕτως καταδιώξεις αὐτοὺς ἐν τῇ καταιγίδι σου, καὶ ἐν τῇ ὀργῇ σου συνταράξεις αὐτούς.

82.15 <u>Sicut</u> <u>*ignis*</u> qui comburit silvam, et <u>sicut</u> <u>*flamma*</u> comburens montes; 16 ita persequeris illos in *tempestate tua*, et in ira tua turbabis eos.

[thy tempest > enemies ≈ fire > wood ≈ a flame > mountains]

Ps. 84.10 For *a day in thy courts* is <u>better than</u> *a thousand.* I had <u>rather</u> *be a doorkeeper in the house of my God,* <u>than</u> *to dwell in the* tents of wickedness.

> 83.11 ὅτι <u>κρείσσων</u> ἡμέρα μία ἐν ταῖς αὐλαῖς σου <u>ὑπὲρ χιλιάδας</u>· ἐξελεξάμην <u>παραρριπτεῖσθαι ἐν τῷ οἴκῳ τοῦ Θεοῦ μου</u> μᾶλλον ἢ οἰκεῖν με ἐν σκηνώμασιν ἁμαρτωλῶν.

> *83.11 Quia* <u>melior</u> *est dies una in atriis tuis* <u>super</u> *millia;* <u>elegi</u> abjectus esse in domo Dei mei *magis quam habitare in tabernaculis peccatorum.*
> [a day in court (better) ≈ a thousand; to be a doorkeeper in the house of God ≈ (rather than) to dwell in the tents of wickedness]

Ps. 88.17 *They* [thy terrors, O Lord] came round about me daily <u>like</u> *water.*

> 87.18 ἐκύκλωσάν με <u>ὡσεὶ</u> <u>ὕδωρ</u> ὅλην τὴν ἡμέραν.

> 87.17 In me transierunt irae tuae, et *terrores tui* conturbaverunt me: 18 circumdederunt me <u>sicut</u> *aqua* tota die; circumdederunt me simul.
> [they (thy terrors, O Lord) ≈ water]

Ps. 89.46 How long, Lord? wilt thou hide thyself for ever? shall thy *wrath* burn <u>like</u> *fire*?

> 88.47 ἕως πότε, Κύριε, ἀποστρέφῃ εἰς τέλος, ἐκκαυθήσεται <u>ὡς</u> <u>πῦρ</u> ἡ ὀργή σου;

> 88.47 Usquequo, Domine, avertis in finem: exardescet <u>sicut</u> *ignis* ira tua?   [wrath ≈ fire]

Ps. 90.5 Thou [Lord] *carriest* them [children of men] *away* <u>as</u> <u>with</u> a *flood*; *they* are <u>as</u> a *sleep*: in the morning *they* are <u>like</u> *grass* which groweth up.

> 89.5 τὰ ἐξουδενώματα αὐτῶν ἔτη ἔσονται. τὸ πρωῒ <u>ὡσεὶ</u> <u>χλόη</u> παρέλθοι.
> 89.6 Mane <u>sicut</u> *herba* transeat.
> [the children are carried away ≈ a flood ≈ asleep; they ≈ grass]

Ps. 90.9 For all our days are passed away in thy wrath: we spend our *years* <u>as</u> *a tale* <u>that is told.</u>

> 89.9 ὅτι πᾶσαι αἱ ἡμέραι ἡμῶν ἐξέλιπον, καὶ ἐν τῇ ὀργῇ σου ἐξελίπομεν· τὰ ἔτη ἡμῶν <u>ὡσεὶ</u> <u>ἀράχνη</u> ἐμελέτων.

> 89.9 Quoniam omnes dies nostri defecerunt; et in ira tua defecimus. *Anni nostri* <u>sicut</u> *aranea* meditabuntur;
> [our years ≈ a tale/spider-!]

Ps. 92.7 When *the wicked* spring <u>as</u> *<u>the grass</u>*, and when all the workers of
iniquity do flourish; it is that they shall be destroyed for ever.

91.8 ἐν τῷ ἀνατεῖλαι *ἁμαρτωλοὺς* <u>ὡσεὶ</u> *<u>χόρτον</u>* καὶ διέκυψαν πάντες οἱ
ἐργαζόμενοι τὴν ἀνομίαν, ὅπως ἂν ἐξολοθρευθῶσιν εἰς τὸν αἰῶνα
τοῦ αἰῶνος.

91.8 Cum exorti fuerint *peccatores* <u>sicut</u> *<u>foenum</u>*, et apparuerint
omnes qui operantur iniquitatem, ut intereant in saeculum
saeculi;   [wicked ≈ grass]

Ps. 92.10 But *mine horn* shalt thou exalt <u>like</u> *<u>the horn of an unicorn</u>*;

91.11 καὶ ὑψωθήσεται <u>ὡς</u> *<u>μονοκέρωτος</u>* τὸ κέρας μου·

91.11 Et exaltabitur <u>sicut</u> *<u>unicornis</u>* cornu meum,
   [my horn ≈ a unicorn's horn]

Ps. 92.12 The *righteous* shall flourish <u>like</u> the *<u>palm-tree</u>*: *he shall grow* <u>like</u>
<u>a cedar in Lebanon</u>.

91.13 *δίκαιος* <u>ὡς</u> *<u>φοῖνιξ</u>* ἀνθήσει, <u>ὡσεὶ</u> *<u>ἡ κέδρος ἡ ἐν τῷ Λιβάνῳ</u>* πληθυνθήσεται.

91.123 *Justus* <u>ut</u> *<u>palma</u>* florebit; <u>sicut</u> *<u>cedrus Libani</u>* multiplicabitur.
   [the righteous ≈ a palm-tree ≈ the cedar in Lebanon]

Ps. 97.5 The *hills melted* <u>like</u> *<u>wax</u>* at the presence of the Lord.

96.5 τὰ ὄρη <u>ὡσεὶ</u> *<u>κηρὸς</u>* ἐτάκησαν ἀπὸ προσώπου Κυρίου,

96.5 *Montes* <u>sicut</u> *<u>cera</u>* fluxerunt a facie Domini;
   [hills ≈ wax]

Ps. 102.3 For *my days* are consumed <u>like</u> *<u>smoke</u>*, and *my bones* are burned
<u>as</u> *<u>an hearth</u>*.

101.4 ὅτι ἐξέλιπον <u>ὡσεὶ</u> *<u>καπνὸς</u>* αἱ ἡμέραι μου, καὶ τὰ ὀστᾶ μου <u>ὡσεὶ</u> *<u>φρύγιον</u>*
συνεφρύγησαν.

101.4 Quia defecerunt <u>sicut</u> *<u>fumus</u>* dies mei, et *ossa mea* <u>sicut</u> *<u>cremium</u>*
aruerunt.
   [my days (consumed) ≈ smoke; my bones ≈ (burned) an hearth]

Ps. 102.4 *My heart* is smitten, and withered <u>like</u> *<u>grass</u>*,

101.5 ἐπλήγην <u>ὡσεὶ</u> *<u>χόρτος</u>* καὶ ἐξηράνθη ἡ καρδία μου.

101.5 *Percussus sum* <u>ut</u> *<u>foenum</u>*, et aruit cor meum,
   [my heart ≈ grass]

Ps. 102.6 *I am* <u>*like a pelican*</u> of the wilderness; I am <u>like</u> *<u>an owl of the desert</u>*.

101.7 ὡμοιώθην *<u>πελεκᾶνι ἐρημικῷ</u>*, ἐγενήθην <u>ὡσεὶ</u> *<u>νυκτικόραξ ἐν οἰκοπέδῳ</u>*,

101.7 <u>Similis</u> factus sum *pellicano solitudinis*; factus sum <u>sicut</u> *nycticorax in domicilio.*

    [I ≈ a pelican in the wilderness ≈ an owl of the desert/in a house]

Ps. 102.7 I watch, and *am* <u>as</u> *a sparrow* alone upon the house top.

    101.8 ἠγρύπνησα καὶ ἐγενόμην <u>ὡς</u> <u>στρουθίον</u> μονάζον ἐπὶ δώματος.

    101.78 Vigilavi, et factus sum <u>sicut</u> *passer solitarius* in tecto.

    [I ≈ a sparrow]

Ps. 102.9 For I have eaten *ashes* <u>like</u> <u>*bread.*</u>

    101.10 ὅτι σποδὸν <u>ὡσεὶ</u> <u>ἄρτον</u> ἔφαγον.

    101.10 quia *cinerem* <u>tamquam</u> <u>*panem*</u> manducabam

    [ashes (eaten) ≈ bread]

Ps. 102.11 *My days* are <u>like</u> *a shadow* that declineth; and *I am withered* <u>like</u> *grass.*

    101.12 αἱ ἡμέραι μου <u>ὡσεὶ</u> <u>σκιὰ</u> ἐκλίθησαν, κἀγὼ <u>ὡσεὶ</u> <u>χόρτος</u> ἐξηράνθην.

    101.12 *Dies mei* <u>sicut</u> <u>*umbra*</u> declinaverunt, et *ego* <u>sicut</u> *foenum* arui.

    [my days (declined) ≈ a shadow; I (withered) ≈ grass]

Ps. 103.11 For <u>as</u> *the heaven is high above the earth,* **so great** is *his mercy* toward them that fear him.

    102.11 <u>*ὅτι κατὰ τὸ ὕψος τοῦ οὐρανοῦ ἀπὸ τῆς γῆς*</u> ἐκραταίωσε Κύριος τὸ ἔλεος αὐτοῦ ἐπὶ τοὺς φοβουμένους αὐτόν·

    102.11 Quoniam <u>secundum altitudinem caeli a terra</u>, corroboravit misericordiam suam super timentes se;

    [heaven (high) : earth ≈ the Lord's mercy (great) : them that fear Him]

Ps. 103.12 <u>As far as</u> the east is from the west, **so far** *hath he removed our transgressions from us.*

    102.12 <u>καθόσον</u> <u>ἀπέχουσιν ἀνατολαὶ ἀπὸ δυσμῶν</u>, ἐμάκρυνεν ἀφ᾽ ἡμῶν τὰς ἀνομίας ἡμῶν

    12 <u>quantum distat</u> <u>*ortus ab occidente*</u>, *longe fecit a nobis iniquitates* nostras.

    [the east : (far from) the west ≈ our transgressions : us]

Ps. 103.13 <u>Like as</u> *a father pitieth his children*, **so** *the Lord pitieth them that fear him.*

    102.13 <u>καθὼς</u> <u>*οἰκτείρει πατὴρ υἱούς*</u>, ᾤκτείρησε Κύριος τοὺς φοβουμένους αὐτόν.

102.13 <u>Quomodo</u> *miseretur pater filiorum*, misertus est Dominus timentibus se.

  [father : (pities) his children ≈ the Lord : them that fear him]

Ps. 103.15 As for man, *his days* are <u>as</u> <u>*grass*</u>; <u>as</u> <u>*a flower of the field*</u>, **so** *he flourisheth*.

  102.15 ἄνθρωπος, <u>ὡσεὶ</u> <u>χόρτος</u> αἱ ἡμέραι αὐτοῦ· <u>ὡσεὶ</u> <u>ἄνθος τοῦ ἀγροῦ</u>, **οὕτως** *ἐξανθήσει·*

  102.15 Homo, <u>sicut</u> *foenum* dies ejus; <u>tamquam</u> *flos agri*, **sic** *efflorebit*:
  [a man's days ≈ grass; he will flourish ≈ a flower of the field]

Ps. 104.2 Who coverest thyself with *light* <u>as</u> with a *garment*; who stretchest out the *heavens* <u>like</u> a *curtain* … 104.6 Thou coveredst it [the earth] *with the deep* <u>as</u> <u>*with a garment*</u>.

  103.2 ἀναβαλλόμενος *φῶς* <u>ὡς</u> <u>ἱμάτιον</u>, ἐκτείνων τὸν *οὐρανὸν* <u>ὡσεὶ</u> <u>δέρριν·</u>
  … 103.6 *ἄβυσσος* <u>ὡς</u> <u>ἱμάτιον</u> τὸ περιβόλαιον αὐτοῦ.

  103.2 amictus *lumine* <u>sicut</u> *vestimento*. Extendens *caelum* <u>sicut</u> *pellem*
  … 103.6 Abyssus <u>sicut</u> *vestimentum* amictus ejus.
  [(he covers himself with) light ≈ a garment; *heavens ≈ a curtain;*
  the deep ≈ a garment]

Ps. 109.18 As he clothed himself [a wicked man] with *cursing* <u>like as</u> <u>*with his garment,*</u> so let it come into his bowels <u>like</u> <u>*water*</u>, and <u>like</u> <u>*oil*</u> into his bones.

  108.18 καὶ ἐνεδύσατο *κατάραν* <u>ὡς</u> <u>ἱμάτιον</u>, καὶ εἰσῆλθεν <u>ὡσεὶ</u> <u>ὕδωρ</u> εἰς τὰ ἔγκατα αὐτοῦ καὶ <u>ὡσεὶ</u> <u>ἔλαιον</u> ἐν τοῖς ὀστέοις αὐτοῦ.

  108.18 Et induit *maledictionem* <u>sicut</u> *vestimentum*; et intravit <u>sicut</u> *aqua* in interiora ejus, et <u>sicut</u> *oleum* in ossibus ejus.
  ['he' (a wicked man) wears cursing ≈ a garment ≈ water in his
  bowels ≈ oil in his bones] **An awkward English version,
  with a double prothesis (*like* + *as*) and no distinction between the accusative (εἰς) and dative (ἐν) prepositional
  phras**es.

Ps. 109.23 *I* am gone <u>like</u> *the shadow* when it declineth: *I* am tossed up and down <u>as</u> the *locust*.

  108.23 <u>ὡσεὶ</u> <u>σκιὰ</u> ἐν τῷ ἐκκλῖναι αὐτὴν ἀντανηρέθην, ἐξετινάχθην <u>ὡσεὶ</u> <u>ἀκρίδες</u>.

108.23 Sicut *umbra* cum declinat ablatus sum, et excussus sum sicut *locustae.*

[I (gone) ≈ the shadow ≈ (tossed up and down) locust]

Ps. 114.4 The *mountains* skipped like *rams*, and the little *hills* like *lambs.*

113.4 τὰ ὄρη ἐσκίρτησαν ὡσεὶ κριοί καὶ οἱ βουνοὶ ὡς ἀρνία προβάτων.

113.4 *Montes* exsultaverunt ut *arietes*, et *colles* sicut *agni ovium.*

= >>> Repeated here:

Ps. 114.6 [5. What ailed thee?] Ye *mountains*, that ye skipped like *rams*, and ye little *hills*, like *lambs*?

5 [τί σοί ἐστι] 6 τὰ ὄρη, ὅτι ἐσκιρτήσατε ὡσεὶ κριοί, καὶ οἱ βουνοὶ ὡς ἀρνία προβάτων;

114.6 [5 Quid est tibi] *montes*, exsultastis sicut *arietes*? et *colles* sicut *agni ovium*?

[mountains (skipped) ≈ rams; hills ≈ lambs]

Ps. 118.12 T*hey* [all nations] compassed *me* about like *bees: they are quenched* as the *fire of thorns:* for in the name of the Lord I will destroy them.

117.12 ἐκύκλωσάν με ὡσεὶ μέλισσαι κηρίον καὶ ἐξεκαύθησαν ὡς πῦρ ἐν ἀκάνθαις, καὶ τῷ ὀνόματι Κυρίου ἠμυνάμην αὐτούς.

117.12 Circumdederunt me sicut *apes*, et exarserunt sicut *ignis* in spinis; et in nomine Domini, quia ultus sum in eos.

[they : me ≈ bees : (honeycomb); they : (flames) ≈ fire : thorns]

Ps. 119.70 *Their heart* is as fat as *grease*; but I delight in thy law.

118.70 ἐτυρώθη ὡς γάλα ἡ καρδία αὐτῶν, ἐγὼ δὲ τὸν νόμον σου ἐμελέτησα.

118.70 Coagulatum est sicut *lac cor eorum*; ego vero legem tuam meditatus sum.

[their heart ≈ grease / milk]

Ps. 119.72 The *law of thy mouth* is better unto me than *thousands of gold* and *silver*.

119.72 ἀγαθός μοι ὁ νόμος τοῦ στόματός σου ὑπὲρ χιλιάδας χρυσίου καὶ ἀργυρίου.

119.72 Bonum mihi *lex oris tui*, super *millia auri et argenti*.

[law of thy mouth ≈ [better than] thousands of gold and silver]

Ps. 119.83 For *I* am become <u>like</u> *a bottle in the smoke.*

118.83 ὅτι ἐγενήθην <u>ὡς</u> *<u>ἀσκὸς ἐν πάχνῃ</u>·*

118.83 Quia *factus sum* <u>sicut</u> *<u>uter in pruina.</u> [a bottle in the frost]*

[I ≈ a bottle in smoke / frost]

Ps. 119.103 *How sweet* are *thy words* unto my taste! yea, sweeter <u>than</u> *<u>honey</u>* to my mouth!

118.103 <u>ὡς</u> *γλυκέα τῷ λάρυγγί μου τὰ λόγιά σου*, <u>ὑπὲρ</u> <u>μέλι</u> τῷ στόματί μου.

118.103 Quam *dulcia* faucibus meis *eloquia tua*! <u>super</u> *<u>mel</u>* ori meo.

[your words (sweeter) ≈ honey]

Ps. 123.2 Behold, <u>as</u> *<u>the eyes of servants look unto the hand of their masters</u>*, and <u>as</u> *<u>the eyes of a maiden unto the hand of her mistress</u>*; **so** *our eyes wait upon the Lord our God,* until that he have mercy upon us.

122.2 ἰδοὺ <u>ὡς</u> <u>ὀφθαλμοὶ δούλων εἰς χεῖρας τῶν κυρίων αὐτῶν</u>, <u>ὡς ὀφθαλμοὶ</u> <u>παιδίσκης εἰς χεῖρας τῆς κυρίας αὐτῆς</u>, **οὕτως** οἱ ὀφθαλμοὶ ἡμῶν πρὸς Κύριον τὸν Θεὸν ἡμῶν, ἕως οὗ οἰκτειρῆσαι ἡμᾶς.

122.2 Ecce <u>sicut</u> *<u>oculi servorum</u>* in manibus dominorum suorum; <u>sicut</u> *<u>oculi ancillae</u>* in manibus dominae suae: **ita** *oculi nostri* ad Dominum Deum nostrum, donec misereatur nostri.

[servants' eyes > masters' hand ≈ maidservants' eyes > mistress' hand our eyes > the Lord]

Ps. 124.7 Our *soul* is escaped <u>as</u> *<u>a bird out of the snare of the fowlers</u>*: the snare is broken, and we are escaped.

123.7 ἡ ψυχὴ ἡμῶν <u>ὡς</u> <u>στρουθίον ἐρρύσθη ἐκ τῆς παγίδος τῶν θηρευόντων</u>· ἡ παγὶς συνετρίβη, καὶ ἡμεῖς ἐρρύσθημεν.

123.7 *Anima nostra* <u>sicut</u> *<u>passer</u>* erepta est de laqueo venantium; laqueus contritus est, et nos liberati sumus.

[our soul (escaped) ≈ a bird from the snare of fowlers]

Ps. 125.1 *They that trust in the Lord* shall be <u>as</u> *<u>mount Zion</u>*: which cannot be removed, but abideth forever.

124.1 *ΟΙ ΠΕΠΟΙΘΟΤΕΣ* ἐπὶ Κύριον <u>ὡς</u> <u>ὄρος Σιών</u>· οὐ σαλευθήσεται εἰς τὸν αἰῶνα ὁ κατοικῶν ῾Ιερουσαλήμ.

124.1 *Qui confidunt in Domino*, <u>sicut</u> *<u>mons Sion</u>*: non commovebitur in aeternum, qui habitat 2 in Jerusalem.

[they that trust in the Lord ≈ mount Zion]

Ps. 125.2 As t*he mountains are round about Jerusalem,* **so** the *Lord is round about his people* from henceforth even for ever.

    124.2 <u>ὄρη κύκλῳ αὐτῆς</u>, **καὶ** ὁ Κύριος κύκλῳ τοῦ λαοῦ αὐτοῦ ἀπὸ τοῦ νῦν καὶ ἕως τοῦ αἰῶνος.

    124.2 Montes in circuitu ejus; **et** Dominus in circuitu populi sui, ex hoc nunc et usque in saeculum.

    [the Lord around his people ≈ mountains around Jerusalem]

Ps. 127.4 As <u>*arrows are in the hand of a mighty man*</u>; **so** are *children of the youth.*

    126.4 <u>ὡσεὶ βέλη ἐν χειρὶ δυνατοῦ</u>, **οὕτως** οἱ υἱοὶ τῶν ἐκτετιναγμένων.

    126.4 <u>Sicut</u> <u>*sagittae in manu potentis*</u>, **ita** *filii excussorum.*

    (the children of them that have been shaken)

    [children of the youth ≈ arrows of a mighty man]

Ps. 128.3 Thy *wife* shall be as <u>*a fruitful vine by the sides of thine house*</u>: thy children <u>like</u> <u>*olive-plants*</u> round about thy table.

    127.3 ἡ γυνή σου <u>ὡς</u> <u>ἄμπελος εὐθηνοῦσα ἐν τοῖς κλίτεσι τῆς οἰκίας σου</u>· οἱ υἱοί σου <u>ὡς</u> <u>νεόφυτα ἐλαιῶν κύκλῳ τῆς τραπέζης σου</u>.

    127.3 *Uxor tua* <u>sicut</u> <u>*vitis abundans*</u>, in lateribus domus tuae; *filii tui* <u>sicut</u> <u>*novellae olivarum*</u> in circuitu mensae tuae.

    [your wife ≈ a fruitful vine; your children ≈ olive-plants]

Ps. 131.2 Surely *I have behaved* and quieted myself, as <u>*a child that is weaned*</u> of his mother: *my soul* is <u>even as</u> <u>*a weaned child.*</u>

    130.2 <u>ὡς</u> <u>τὸ ἀπογεγαλακτισμένον ἐπὶ τὴν μητέρα αὐτοῦ</u>, <u>ὡς</u> ἀνταποδώσεις ἐπὶ τὴν ψυχήν μου.

    (<u>according to</u> [the relation of] <u>*a weaned child to his mother*</u>, **so** *wilt thou recompense my soul.*)

    130.2 <u>sicut</u> <u>*ablactatus est super matre sua*</u>, **ita** *retributio in anima mea.*

    [I ≈ a weaned child; my soul ≈ a weaned child]

Ps. 133.2 [1-Behold, how good and how pleasant it is for brethren to dwell together in unity!] 2 *It is* <u>like</u> <u>*the precious ointment upon the head,*</u> that ran down upon the beard, ... 3 As t*he dew of Hermon, and as the dew that descended upon the mountains of Zion.*

    132.2 [1-ΙΔΟΥ δὴ τί καλὸν ἢ τί τερπνόν, ἀλλ᾽ ἢ τὸ κατοικεῖν ἀδελφοὺς ἐπὶ τὸ αὐτό;] <u>ὡς</u> <u>μύρον ἐπὶ κεφαλῆς</u> τὸ καταβαῖνον ἐπὶ πώγωνα, ... 3 <u>ὡς</u> <u>δρόσος Αερμὼν ἡ καταβαίνουσα ἐπὶ τὰ ὄρη Σιών</u>·

2 [Ecce quam bonum et quam jucundum, habitare fratres in unum!]
   2 Sicut *unguentum in capite*, quod descendit in barbam, …
   3 sicut *ros Hermon*, *qui descendit in montem Sion*.
   [for brothers to dwell together ≈ ointment on the head ≈ the
   dew of Hermon]

Ps. 140.3 *They have sharpened their tongues* like *a serpen*t; adders' poison is
under their lips. Selah.
   139.4 ἠκόνησαν γλῶσσαν αὐτῶν ὡσεὶ ὄφεως, ἰὸς ἀσπίδων ὑπὸ τὰ χείλη αὐτῶν.
   139.4 Acuerunt linguas suas sicut serpentis; venenum aspidum sub
   labiis eorum.
   [their tongues (sharp) ≈ (the tongue) of a serpent]

Ps. 141.2 Let my *prayer* be set forth before thee as *incense*; and the *lifting
up of my hands* as *the evening sacrifice*.
   140.2 κατευθυνθήτω ἡ προσευχή μου ὡς θυμίαμα ἐνώπιόν σου, ἔπαρσις
   τῶν χειρῶν μου θυσία ἑσπερινή.
   140.2 Dirigatur *oratio mea* sicut *incensum* in conspectu tuo; *elevatio
   manuum mearum sacrificium vespertinum*.
   [my prayer to you ≈ incense; my hands lifted up ≈ the evening
   sacrifice]

Ps. 141.7 *Our bones are scattered at the grave's mouth,* as when one cutteth
and cleaveth wood upon the earth.
   140.7 ὡσεὶ πάχος γῆς ἐρράγη ἐπὶ τῆς γῆς, διεσκορπίσθη τὰ ὀστᾶ αὐτῶν
   παρὰ τὸν ᾅδην. (As a lump of earth is crushed)
   140.7 Sicut *crassitudo terrae erupta est* super terram; *dissipata sunt ossa
   nostra secus infernum*.
   [our bones (scattered on the grave) ≈ one cuts wood on the earth]

Ps. 144.4 *Man* is like to *vanity*: his days are as *a shadow that passeth away.*
   143.4 ἄνθρωπος ματαιότητι ὡμοιώθη, αἱ ἡμέραι αὐτοῦ ὡσεὶ σκιὰ παράγουσι.
   143.4 *Homo vanitati* similis factus est; *dies ejus* sicut *umbra* praetereunt.
   [Man ≈ vanity; his days ≈ a shadow]

Ps. 144.12 [11 deliver me from the hand of strange children] 12 That *our
sons* may be as *plants grown up* in their youth: that our *daughters* may
be as *corner stones*, polished after the similitude of a *palace*.
   143.12 ὧν οἱ υἱοὶ ὡς νεόφυτα ἱδρυμένα ἐν τῇ νεότητι αὐτῶν, αἱ θυγατέρες
   αὐτῶν κεκαλλωπισμέναι, περικεκοσμημέναι ὡς ὁμοίωμα ναοῦ.

143.12 Quorum *filii* sicut <u>*novellae plantationes*</u> in juventute sua; *filiae* eorum compositae, circumornatae <u>*ut similitudo templi.*</u>

> [our sons ≈ plants; our daughters ≈ corner stones (simile: a palace)]

Ps. 147.16 [12 Praise the Lord, O Jerusalem] He giveth *snow* <u>like wool</u>: he scattereth the *hoarfrost* <u>like ashes.</u>

147.5 διδόντος *χιόνα* αὐτοῦ <u>ὡσεὶ</u> <u>*ἔριον*</u>, *ὀμίχλην* <u>ὡσεὶ</u> <u>*σποδὸν*</u> πάσσοντος·

147.5 Qui dat *nivem* sicut <u>*lanam*</u>, *nebulam* sicut <u>*cinerem*</u> spargit.

> [snow ≈ wool; hoarfrost (scattered) ≈ ashes]

Ps. 147.17 He casteth forth *his ice* <u>like</u> <u>*morsels.*</u>

147.6 βάλλοντος *κρύσταλλον* αὐτοῦ <u>ὡσεὶ</u> <u>*ψωμούς.*</u>

147.6 Mittit *crystallum suum* sicut <u>*buccellas*</u>:

> [his ice (thrown) ≈ morsels]

* * *

The Proverbs (31 Chapters)

Παροιμίαι

Prov. 1.27 When *your fear* comes <u>as</u> <u>*desolation*</u>, and *your destruction* cometh <u>as</u> <u>*a whirlwind*</u>.

27 καὶ ὡς ἂν ἀφίκηται **ὑμῖν** ἄφνω θόρυβος, ἡ δὲ *καταστροφὴ* <u>ὁμοίως</u> <u>*καταιγίδι*</u> παρῇ,

27 Cum irruerit repentina calamitas, et *interitus* <u>quasi</u> <u>*tempestas*</u> ingruerit;

> [your destruction ≈ a whirlwind]   **NB the first comparison has an abstract vehicle, whereas the second one has a figurative vehicle, and thus is a more traditional simile.**

Prov. 2.4 If thou seekest *her* [wisdom] <u>as *silver*</u>, and searchest for her <u>as *for* hid *treasures;*</u> [5 Then shalt thou understand the fear of the Lord and find the knowledge of God.]

2.4 καὶ ἐὰν ζητήσῃς αὐτὴν *[τὴν σοφίαν]* <u>ὡς</u> <u>*ἀργύριον*</u> καὶ <u>ὡς</u> <u>*θησαυροὺς*</u> ἐξερευνήσῃς αὐτήν.

2.4 si quaesieris *eam* <u>quasi *pecuniam*</u>, et sicut <u>*thesauros*</u> effoderis illam: 5 tunc intelliges timorem Domini, et scientiam Dei invenies.

> [wisdom ≈ silver ≈ hidden treasures]

Prov. 3.12 For *whom the Lord loveth* he correcteth; even <u>as</u> *<u>a father the son</u>* in whom he delighteth.

> 3.12 ὃν γὰρ ἀγαπᾷ Κύριος παιδεύει, μαστιγοῖ δὲ πάντα υἱὸν ὃν παραδέχεται.
>
> **[No simile in Greek]**

> 3.12 *quem enim diligit Dominus* corripit, et <u>quasi</u> *<u>pater in filio</u>* complacet sibi.
>
> [the Lord ≥ whom he loves ≈ a father ≥ his son]

Prov. 3.14 For *the merchandise of it [wisdom]* is <u>better than</u> *<u>the merchandise of silve</u>*r, and *the gain thereof* <u>than</u> *<u>fine gold</u>*

> 3.14 <u>κρεῖσσον</u> γὰρ *αὐτὴν* [σοφίαν] *ἐμπορεύεσθαι* <u>ἢ χρυσίου καὶ ἀργυρίου</u> <u>θησαυρούς</u>.

> 3.14 <u>Melior</u> est *acquisitio ejus* <u>*negotiatione argenti*</u>, et <u>*auri*</u> primi et purissimi *<u>fructus ejus</u>*.
>
> [wisdom (better than) ≈ merchandise of gold and silver]

Prov. 3.15 *She* is <u>more precious than</u> *<u>rubies:</u>* and all the things thou canst desire are not to be compared unto her [wisdom].

> 3.15 <u>τιμιωτέρα</u> δέ ἐστι <u>λίθων πολυτελῶν</u> ... πᾶν δὲ τίμιον οὐκ ἄξιον αὐτῆς ἐστι.

> 3.15 <u>Pretiosior</u> est *<u>cunctis opibus</u>*, et omnia quae desiderantur huic non valent comparari.
>
> [she (wisdom) ≈ (more precious) rubies]

Prov. 5.3 For the *lips of a strange woman* drop <u>as</u> *<u>an honeycomb</u>*, and *her mouth* is <u>smoother than</u> *<u>oil</u>*: 4 But *her end* is <u>bitter as</u> *<u>wormwood</u>*,sharp <u>as</u> *<u>a two-edged sword</u>*.

> 5.3 μὴ πρόσεχε **φαύλῃ γυναικί**· μέλι γὰρ ἀποστάζει ἀπὸ χειλέων γυναικὸς πόρνης, ἢ πρὸς καιρὸν λιπαίνει σὸν φάρυγγα, 4 ὕστερον μέντοι <u>πικρότερον χολῆς</u> εὑρήσεις καὶ <u>ἠκονημένον μᾶλλον</u> <u>μαχαίρας διστόμου</u>.

> 5.3 favus enim distillans labia meretricis, et <u>nitidius</u> *<u>oleo guttur ejus</u>*: [4] novissima autem illius *amara* <u>quasi</u> *<u>absinthium</u>*, et *acuta* <u>quasi</u> *<u>gladius biceps</u>*.
>
> [lips of a strange woman an honeycomb; her mouth(smoother than) oil; her end ≈ (bitter) wormwood ≈ (sharp) a two-edged sword]

Prov. 5.19 Let her [*the wife of thy youth*] be <u>as</u> the <u>*loving hind and pleasant*</u> <u>*roe;*</u> let her breasts satisfy thee at all times; and be thou ravished always with her love.

    5.19 [γυναικὸς τῆς ἐκ νεότητός σου] <u>ἔλαφος</u> φιλίας καὶ <u>πῶλος</u> σῶν χαρίτων ὁμιλείτω σοι·

    5.19 [mulier adolescentiae tuae] <u>*Cerva carissima*</u>, et gratissimus <u>*hinnulus*</u>: ubera ejus inebrient te in omni tempore, in amore ejus delectare jugiter.

    [the wife of your youth ≈ the loving hind and pleasant roe]

Prov. 6.5 Deliver *thyself* <u>as</u> <u>*a roe from the hand of the hunter*</u>, and <u>as</u> <u>*a bird*</u> from the hand of the fowler.

    6.5 ἵνα σώζῃ <u>ὥσπερ</u> <u>δορκὰς ἐκ βρόχων</u> καὶ <u>ὥσπερ</u> <u>ὄρνεον ἐκ παγίδος</u>.

    6.5 Eruere <u>quasi</u> <u>*damula*</u> de manu, et <u>quasi</u> <u>*avis*</u> de manu aucupis.

    [you (delivered) ≈ a roe (from a hunter) ≈ a bird (rescued from a fowler)]

Prov. 7.2 Keep my commandments, and live; and *my law* <u>as</u> <u>*the apple of*</u> <u>*thine eye*</u>.

    7.2 φύλαξον ἐμὰς ἐντολάς, καὶ βιώσεις, τοὺς δὲ ἐμοὺς λόγους <u>ὥσπερ</u> <u>κόρας</u> <u>ὀμμάτων</u>·

    2 Fili, serva mandata mea, et vives; et *legem meam* <u>quasi</u> <u>*pupillam*</u> <u>*oculi tui*</u>:

    [my law (keep) ≈ the apple of your eye]

Prov. 7.22 And *he goeth after her* straightway, <u>as</u> an <u>*ox goeth to the slaughter,*</u> or <u>as</u> *a fool to the correction of the stocks*.

    7.22 ὁ δὲ ἐπηκολούθησεν αὐτῇ κεπφωθείς, <u>ὥσπερ</u> δὲ <u>βοῦς ἐπὶ σφαγὴν ἄγεται</u> <u>καὶ ὥσπερ κύων ἐπὶ δεσμούς</u> 22 Statim *eam sequitur* <u>quasi</u> <u>*bos ductus*</u> <u>*ad victimam*</u>, et <u>quasi</u> <u>*agnus lasciviens*</u>; et <u>*ignorans quod ad vincula*</u> <u>*stultus trahatur.*</u>

    [he > her ≈ an ox > slaughter or ≈ a fool > the stocks]

Prov. 7.23 Till a dart strike through his liver; <u>as a bird hasteth to the snare.</u>

    23 ἢ <u>ὡς ἔλαφος τοξεύματι πεπληγὼς εἰς τὸ ἧπαρ</u>, σπεύδει δὲ <u>ὥσπερ ὄρνεον</u> <u>εἰς παγίδα</u>.

    23 donec transfigat <u>*sagitta jecur ejus*</u>; <u>velut si</u> <u>*avis festinet ad laqueum*</u>, et nescit quod de periculo animae illius agitur.

    [he > her ≈ a bird > a snare]

Prov. 8.11 For *wisdom* is <u>better than</u> <u>*rubies*</u>; and all the things that may be desired are not to be compared to it.

11 <u>κρείσσων</u> γὰρ σοφία <u>λίθων πολυτελῶν</u>, πᾶν δὲ τίμιον οὐκ ἄξιον αὐτῆς ἐστιν.

11 <u>melior</u> est enim *sapientia* <u>*cunctis pretiosissimis*</u>, et omne desiderabile ei non potest comparari.

[wisdom (better) ≈ rubies]

Prov. 8.19 My fruit is <u>better than</u> <u>*gold, yea,*</u> than *<u>fine gold</u>: and my revenue* <u>than</u> *<u>choice silver</u>.*

19 <u>βέλτιον</u> ἐμὲ <u>καρπίζεσθαι</u> <u>ὑπὲρ χρυσίον καὶ λίθον τίμιον</u>, τὰ δὲ ἐμὰ γεννήματα <u>κρείσσω ἀργυρίου ἐκλεκτοῦ</u>.

19 <u>Melior</u> est enim *fructus meus <u>auro et lapide pretioso</u>*, et *genimina* me(a) <u>*argento electo*</u>.

[my fruit (better) ≈ gold and fine gold; my revenue (better) ≈ choice silver]

Prov. 10.20 The *tongue of the just* is <u>*as choice silver*</u>; the heart of the wicked is little worth.

*a/ 20 <u>ἄργυρος πεπυρωμένος</u> γλῶσσα δικαίου, καρδία δὲ ἀσεβοῦς ἐκλείψει.

20 <u>*Argentum electum*</u> *lingua justi*; *cor autem impiorum <u>pro nihilo</u>*.

[tongue of the just ≈ choice silver]

Prov. 10.25 <u>As</u> *<u>the whirlwind</u>* passeth, **so** is *the wicked* no more: but *a/1 the righteous* is an *<u>everlasting foundation</u>.*

25 παραπορευομένης καταιγίδος ἀφανίζεται ἀσεβής, δίκαιος δὲ ἐκκλίνας σώζεται εἰς τὸν αἰῶνα. (When the storm passes by, the ungodly vanishes away; but the righteous turns aside and escapes forever.)

25 <u>Quasi</u> *tempestas transiens* non erit impius; *justus* autem <u>quasi</u> <u>*fundamentum sempiternum*</u>.

[wicked ≈ a whirlwind; righteous ≈ an everlasting foundation]

Prov. 10.26 <u>As</u> *<u>vinegar to the teeth,</u>* and as *<u>smoke to the eyes</u>*, **so** is the sluggard to them that send him.

26 <u>ὥσπερ ὄμφαξ ὀδοῦσι βλαβερὸν</u> καὶ <u>καπνὸς ὄμμασιν</u>, **οὕτως** παρανομία τοῖς χρωμένοις αὐτῇ.

26 <u>Sicut</u> <u>*acetum dentibus*</u>, et *<u>fumus oculis</u>*, **sic** *piger his qui miserunt* eum.

[the sluggard > them that send him ≈ vinegar > the teeth and smoke > eyes]

Prov. 11.22 As <u>*a jewel of gold in a swine's snout*</u>, **so** is *a fair woman which is without discretion*.

   22 <u>ὥσπερ ἐνώτιον ἐν ῥινὶ ὑός</u>, **οὕτως** γυναικὶ κακόφρονι κάλλος.

   22 <u>*Circulus aureus in naribus suis*</u>, *mulier pulchra et fatua*

      [a fair woman without discretion ≈ a jewel of gold in a swine's snout]

Prov. 12.4 *A virtuous woman* <u>is</u> <u>*a crown to her husband*</u>: but she that
*a/   maketh ashamed is as *rottenness in his bones*.

   γυνὴ ἀνδρεία <u>στέφανος τῷ ἀνδρὶ αὐτῆς</u>· ὥσπερ δὲ <u>ἐν ξύλῳ σκώληξ</u>, **οὕτως** ἄνδρα ἀπόλλυσι γυνὴ κακοποιός.

   4 *Mulier diligens* <u>*corona est viro suo*</u>; et <u>*putredo in ossibus ejus*</u>, *quae confusione res dignas gerit*.

      [a virtuous woman ≈ a crown to her husband; (a bad woman) : her husband ≈ rottenness (a worm : wood)])

Prov. 12.18 There is *that speaketh* <u>like</u> <u>*the piercings of a sword*</u>: but the tongue of the wise is health.

   18 εἰσὶν οἳ λέγοντες τιτρώσκουσι μαχαίρᾳ, γλῶσσαι δὲ σοφῶν ἰῶνται.

   18 Est qui *promittit*, et <u>quasi</u> *<u>gladio</u> pungitur* conscientiae, lingua autem sapientium sanitas est.

      [that speaks ≈ the piercings of a sword]

Prov. 15.19 The *way of the slothful man* is <u>as</u> an <u>*hedge of thorns*</u>.

   19 ὁδοὶ ἀεργῶν ἐστρωμέναι ἀκάνθαις.

   19 *Iter pigrorum* <u>quasi</u> <u>*sepes spinarum*</u>;

*a/[the way of the slothful man ≈ an hedge (consisting) of thorns]

Prov. 16.15 In the *light of the king's countenance* is *life*; and his favor is <u>as</u> a *cloud <u>of the latter rain</u>*.

   15 ἐν <u>φωτὶ ζωῆς</u> υἱὸς βασιλέως, οἱ δὲ προσδεκτοὶ αὐτῷ <u>ὥσπερ</u> <u>νέφος ὄψιμον</u>.

   15 In <u>*hilaritate*</u> vultus regis *vita*, et *clementia ejus* <u>quasi</u> <u>*imber serotinus*</u>.

      [a king's favor ≈ a cloud of rain]

Prov. 16.16 How much better is it to get *wisdom* <u>than</u> <u>*gold*</u>! and to get *understanding* <u>rather</u> to be chosen <u>than</u> <u>*silver*</u>!

   16 νοσσιαὶ σοφίας <u>αἱρετώτεραι χρυσίου</u>, νοσσιαί δὲ φρονήσεως <u>αἱρετώτεραι</u> <u>ὑπὲρ ἀργύριον</u>.

   16 Posside *sapientiam*, quia <u>*auro*</u> <u>melior</u> est, et acquire *prudentiam*, quia <u>pretiosior</u> est <u>*argento*</u>.

[wisdom (better than) ≈ gold; understanding (to be chosen) ≈ silver]

Prov. 17.1 <u>Better</u> is *a dry morsel*, and *quietness therewith,* <u>than</u> *<u>an house full of sacrifices with strife</u>.*

    1 <u>ΚΡΕΙΣΣΩΝ</u> ψωμὸς μεϑ᾽ ἡδονῆς ἐν εἰρήνη <u>ἢ</u> <u>οἶκος πλήρης πολλῶν ἀγαθῶν καὶ ἀδίκων θυμάτων μετὰ μάχης</u>.

    1 <u>Melior</u> est *buccella sicca cum gaudio*, <u>quam</u> *domus plena victimis cum jurgio*.

    [a dry morsel + quietness (better than) ≈ a house of strife]

Prov. 17.8 *A gift* is <u>as</u> *<u>a precious stone</u>* in the eyes of him that hath it: whithersoever it turneth, it prospereth.

    8 μισθὸς χαρίτων ἡ παιδεία τοῖς χρωμένοις, οὗ δ᾽ ἂν ἐπιστρέψῃ εὐοδωθήσεται. (*Instruction is to them that use it a gracious reward*;)

    8 *<u>Gemma gratissima</u> exspectatio praestolantis*; quocumque se vertit, prudenter intelligit.

    [a gift ≈ a precious stone]

Prov. 17.10 A *reproof entereth* <u>more</u> into a wise man <u>than</u> a*<u>n hundred stripes into a fool</u>.*

    10 συντρίβει ἀπειλὴ καρδίαν φρονίμου, ἄφρων δὲ μαστιγωθεὶς οὐκ αἰσθάνεται. [**no simile**]

    10 <u>Plus</u> proficit *correptio* apud prudentem, <u>quam</u> *centum plagae* apud stultum.

    [reproof > a wise man ≈ a hundred stripes > a fool]

Prov. 17.12 Let *a <u>bear robbed of her whelps meet a man,</u>* <u>rather than</u> *a fool in his folly.*

    12 ἐμπεσεῖται μέριμνα ἀνδρὶ νοήμονι, οἱ δὲ ἄφρονες διαλογιοῦνται κακά. [no simile in Greek]

    12 Expedit <u>magis</u> *<u>ursae occurrere raptis foetibus</u>*, <u>quam</u> *fatuo confidenti in stultitia sua*.

        [to meet a fool (rather than) ≈ to meet a bear robbed of her whelps]

Prov. 17.14 The *beginning of strife* is <u>as when</u> <u>*one letteth out water*</u>; therefore leave off contention before it be meddled with.

14 ἐξουσίαν δίδωσι λόγοις ἀρχὴ δικαιοσύνης, προηγεῖται δὲ τῆς ἐνδείας στάσις καὶ μάχη. (*The beginning of justice gives power to words; but sedition and strife precede poverty.*)

14 <u>*Qui dimittit aquam*</u> caput est *jurgiorum*, et antequam patiatur contumeliam judicium deserit.

[beginning of strife ≈ letting out water]·

Prov. 17.22 A *merry heart doeth good* <u>like</u> *a medicine*: but a broken spirit drieth the bones.

22 καρδία εὐφραινομένη εὐεκτεῖν ποιεῖ, ἀνδρὸς δὲ λυπηροῦ ξηραίνεται τὰ ὀστᾶ. [**no simile**]

22 Animus gaudens aetatem floridam facit; spiritus tristis exsiccat ossa. [**no simile**]

[a merry heart doing good ≈ a medicine]

Prov. 18.4 The *words of a man's mouth* are <u>*as deep waters*</u>, and the wellspring of wisdom <u>as</u> *a flowing brook.*

18.4 <u>ὕδωρ βαθὺ</u> λόγος ἐν καρδίᾳ ἀνδρός, ποταμὸς δὲ ἀναπηδύει καὶ πηγὴ ζωῆς.

4 Aqua profunda verba ex ore viri, et <u>*torrens redundans fons sapientiae.*</u>

[words of the mouth ≈ deep waters; wellspring of wisdom ≈ a flowing brook]

Prov. 18.8 The *words of a talebearer* are <u>as</u> <u>*wounds*</u> …

8 ὀκνηροὺς καταβάλλει φόβος, …

8 *Verba bilinguis* <u>quasi</u> <u>*simplicia,*</u>

[words of a talebearer ≈ wounds]

Prov. 18.11 The *rich man's wealth* <u>is</u> <u>*his strong city*</u>; and <u>as</u> an <u>*high*</u> *a/* <u>*wall*</u> in his own conceit.

11 ὕπαρξις πλουσίου ἀνδρὸς <u>πόλις ὀχυρά</u>, ἡ δὲ δόξα αὐτῆς μέγα ἐπισκιάζει.

11 *Substantia divitis* <u>*urbs roboris ejus*</u>, et <u>quasi</u> <u>*murus validus*</u> circumdans eum.

[wealth of a rich man ≈ his strong city ≈ a high wall]

Prov. 18.19 A *brother offended* <u>is harder to be won than</u> *a strong city*; and their *contentions* are <u>like</u> the *bars of a castle.*

19 ἀδελφὸς ὑπὸ ἀδελφοῦ βοηθούμενος <u>ὡς</u> <u>πόλις ὀχυρὰ καὶ ὑψηλή</u>, ἰσχύει δὲ <u>ὥσπερ</u> <u>τεθεμελιωμένον βασιλειον</u>.

19 *Frater qui adjuvatur a fratre* <u>quasi</u> <u>*civitas firma*</u>, et *judicia* <u>quasi</u>
<u>*vectes urbium.*</u>
[brother offended / helped by brother ≈ a strong city; their contentions ≈ the bars of a castle]

Prov. 19.12 The *king's wrath* is <u>as</u> <u>*the roaring of a lion*</u>; but his favor is <u>as</u> <u>*dew*</u>
<u>*upon the grass.*</u>

12 *βασιλέως ἀπειλὴ* <u>ὁμοία</u> <u>βρυγμῷ λέοντος</u>, <u>ὥσπερ</u> δὲ <u>δρόσος ἐπὶ χόρτῳ</u>,
οὕτως *τὸ ἱλαρὸν αὐτοῦ.*

12 <u>Sicut</u> <u>*fremitus leonis*</u>, **ita** et *regis ira*, et <u>sicut</u> <u>*ros super herbam*</u>, **ita** et
hilaritas ejus
[king's wrath ≈ roaring of a lion; his favor ≈ dew on grass]

Prov. 20.2 The *fear of a king* <u>is as</u> <u>*the roaring of a lion*</u>;
>>**Note the re-wording of 19.12.**

2 <u>οὐ διαφέρει</u> *ἀπειλὴ βασιλέως* <u>θυμοῦ λέοντος</u>,

2 <u>Sicut</u> <u>*rugitus leonis*</u>, **ita** et *terror regis*:
[fear of a king ≈ a lion's roaring]

Prov. 20.5 *Counsel in the heart* of *a man is* <u>like</u> <u>*deep water*</u>;

5 <u>ὕδωρ βαθὺ</u> *βουλὴ ἐν καρδίᾳ ἀνδρός,*

5 <u>Sicut</u> <u>*aqua profunda*</u>, **sic** *consilium in corde viri*;
[counsel in a man's heart ≈ deep water]

Prov. 21.1 The *king's heart* is in the hand of the Lord, <u>as</u> <u>*the rivers of*</u>
<u>*water*</u>: he turneth it whithersoever he will.

1 <u>ΩΣΠΕΡ</u> <u>ὁρμὴ ὕδατος</u>, **οὕτως** *καρδία βασιλέως ἐν χειρὶ Θεοῦ·* οὗ ἐὰν θέλων
νεύσῃ, ἐκεῖ ἔκλινεν αὐτήν.

1 <u>Sicut</u> <u>*divisiones aquarum*</u>, **ita** *cor regis in manu Domini;* quocumque
voluerit inclinabit illud
[the king's heart in the Lord's hand ≈ the rivers of water]

Prov. 21.9 It is <u>better</u> *to dwell in a corner of the housetop*, <u>than</u> <u>*with a*</u>
<u>*brawling woman in a wide house.*</u>

9 <u>κρεῖσσον</u> *οἰκεῖν ἐπὶ γωνίας ὑπαίθρου* <u>ἢ</u> <u>ἐν κεκονιαμένοις μετὰ ἀδικίας καὶ</u>
<u>ἐν οἴκῳ κοινῷ</u>. ([It is] better to dwell in a corner on the house-top,
than in plastered [rooms] with unrighteousness, and in an open
house.)

>   9 <u>Melius</u> est *sedere in angulo domatis*, <u>quam</u> <u>*cum muliere litigiosa*</u>,
et in domo communi.

[to dwell in a corner of the housetop (better than) ≈ to live with a brawling woman in a big house] cf. 21.19.

Prov. 21.19 It is <u>better</u> *to dwell in the wilderness*, <u>than</u> <u>*with a contentious and an angry woman*</u>.

> 19 <u>κρεῖσσον</u> *οἰκεῖν ἐν γῇ ἐρήμῳ* <u>ἢ</u> <u>*μετὰ γυναικὸς μαχίμου*</u> καὶ γλωσσώδους καὶ ὀργίλου.

> 19 <u>Melius</u> est *habitare in terra deserta*, <u>quam</u> *cum muliere rixosa* et iracunda.

> [*to dwell in the wilderness* (better than) ≈ with a contentious and angry woman]

Prov. 23.32 At the last *it* [*red wine*] biteth <u>like</u> *<u>a serpent</u>*, and stingeth <u>like</u> <u>*an adder*</u>.

> 32 ὁ δὲ ἔσχατον <u>ὥσπερ</u> <u>*ὑπὸ ὄφεως πεπληγὼς*</u> ἐκτείνεται, καὶ <u>ὥσπερ</u> <u>*ὑπὸ κεράστου*</u> διαχεῖται αὐτῷ ὁ ἰός. (But at last [such a one] *stretches himself out* <u>as</u> *<u>one smitten by a serpent</u>*, and *venom is diffused through him* <u>as</u> *<u>by a horned serpent</u>*.)

> 32 sed in novissimo [*vinum*] mordebit <u>ut</u> *<u>coluber</u>*, et <u>sicut</u> *<u>regulus</u> venena diffundet.*

> [wine ≈ a serpent ≈ an adder]

Prov. 23.34 Yea, *thou* shalt be <u>as</u> *<u>he that lieth down in the midst of the sea</u>*, or <u>as</u> *<u>he that lieth upon the top of a mast</u>*.

> 34 καὶ κατακείσῃ <u>ὥσπερ</u> <u>*ἐν καρδίᾳ θαλάσσης*</u> καὶ <u>ὥσπερ</u> <u>*κυβερνήτης ἐν πολλῷ κλύδωνι*</u>.

> 34 Et eris <u>sicut</u> *<u>dormiens in medio mari</u>,* et <u>quasi</u> *<u>sopitus gubernator</u>,* amisso clavo.

> [you ≈ he that lieth down in the midst of the sea or ≈ he that lieth upon the top of a mast]

Prov. 24.34 So shall *thy poverty* come <u>as</u> *<u>one that travelleth</u>*; and *thy want* <u>as</u> an *<u>armed man</u>*.

> 34 ἐὰν δὲ τοῦτο ποιῇς, ἥξει προπορευομένη ἡ πενία σου καὶ ἡ ἔνδειά σου <u>ὥσπερ</u> <u>*ἀγαθὸς δρομεύς*</u>.

> \> 34 et veniet tibi <u>quasi</u> *<u>cursor</u>* egestas, et *mendicitas* <u>quasi</u> *<u>vir armatus</u>*.

> [your poverty ≈ one traveling; your want ≈ an armed man]

Prov. 25.11 A *word fitly spoken* is <u>like</u> <u>*apples of gold in pictures of silver*</u>.

11 <u>*μῆλον χρυσοῦν*</u> ἐν ὁρμίσκῳ σαρδίου, <u>οὕτως</u> *εἰπεῖν λόγον*

11 <u>*Mala aurea in lectis argenteis*</u>, *qui loquitur verbum in tempore suo*.

    [a word fitly spoken ≈ apples of gold in pictures of silver]

Prov. 25.12 As <u>*an earring of gold*</u>, and <u>*an ornament of fine gold*</u>, **so** is *a wise reprover upon an obedient ear*.

12 *εἰς ἐνώτιον χρυσοῦν καὶ σάρδιον πολυτελὲς δέδεται, λόγος σοφὸς εἰς εὐήκοον οὖς.*

12 <u>*Inauris aurea et margaritum fulgens*</u> *qui arguit sapientem et aurem obedientem.*

    [a wise reprover on an obedient ear ≈ an earring of gold and a
    golden ornament] **In Greek and Latin versions** a **simile
    without a prothesis or apothesis.**

Prov. 25.13 A<u>s</u> <u>*the cold of snow in the time of harvest*</u>, **so** is *a faithful mes-senger* to them that send him.

13 <u>*ὥσπερ ἔξοδος χιόνος ἐν ἀμήτῳ κατὰ καῦμα ὠφελεῖ*</u>, **οὕτως** ἄγγελος πιστὸς τοὺς ἀποστείλαντας αὐτόν·

13 <u>Sicut</u> <u>*frigus nivis in die messis,*</u> **ita** *legatus fidelis* ei qui misit eum.

    [a faithful messenger ≈ cold snow during harvest]

Prov. 25.14 *Whoso boasteth himself of a false gift* is <u>like</u> <u>*clouds and wind
without rain*</u>.

14 <u>*ὥσπερ ἄνεμοι καὶ νέφη καὶ ὑετοὶ ἐπιφανέστατα*</u>, **οὕτως** ὁ καυχώμενος ἐπὶ δόσει ψευδεῖ.

14 <u>*Nubes, et ventus, et pluviae non sequentes*</u>, *vir gloriosus* et *promissa
non complens.*

    [he that boasts of a false gift ≈ winds + clouds without rain]

Prov. 25.19 *Confidence in an unfaithful man in time of trouble* is <u>like</u> <u>*a
broken tooth*</u>, and <u>*a foot out of joint*</u>.

19 ὁδὸς κακοῦ καὶ ποὺς παρανόμου ὀλεῖται ἐν ἡμέρᾳ κακῇ.

19 <u>*Dens putridus*</u>, et <u>*pes lassus,*</u> *qui sperat super infideli* in die angustiae.

    [confidence in an unfaithful man ≈ a broken tooth ≈ a foot out
    of joint]

Prov. 25.20 As <u>*he that taketh away a garment in cold weather*</u>, and <u>as</u> <u>*vinegar upon nitre*</u>, **so** is *he that singeth songs to an heavy heart.*

20 <u>ὥσπερ ὄξος ἕλκει ἀσύμφορον</u>, **οὕτως** *προσπεσὸν πάθος ἐν σώματι καρδίαν λυπεῖ.* 20α <u>ὥσπερ *σὴς ἐν ἱματίῳ καὶ σκώληξ ξύλῳ*</u>, **οὕτως** *λύπη ἀνδρὸς βλάπτει καρδίαν.* (<u>As</u> *vinegar is bad for a sore*, **so** *trouble befalling the body afflicts the heart.* <u>As</u> <u>*a moth in a garment, and a worm in wood*</u>, **so** the *grief of a man hurts the heart.*)

20 et <u>*amittit pallium in die frigoris.*</u> *Acetum in nitro, qui cantat carmina cordi pessimo.* <u>Sicut</u> <u>*tinea vestimento*</u>, et <u>*vermis ligno*</u>, **ita** *tristitia viri nocet cordi.*

  [a singer of sad songs ≈ he who takes away a garment in cold death ≈ vinegar on nitre]

Prov. 25.23 <u>*The north wind driveth away rain:*</u> **so** doth a*n angry countenance a backbiting tongue.*

23 <u>ἄνεμος Βορέας ἐξεγείρει νέφη</u>, *πρόσωπον δὲ ἀναιδὲς γλῶσσαν ἐρεθίζει.*

23 <u>*Ventus aquilo*</u> <u>dissipat</u> <u>*pluvias*</u>, et *facies tristis linguam detrahentem.*

  [an angry countenance > a back-biting tongue ≈ the north wind > rain]

Prov. 25.24 It is *better to dwell in the corner of the housetop*, <u>than</u> <u>*with a brawling woman and in a wide house.*</u> **Cf 21.9 and 21.19.**

Prov. 25.25 <u>As *cold waters to a thirsty soul*</u>, **so** is *good news from a far country.*

25 <u>ὥσπερ *ὕδωρ ψυχρὸν ψυχῇ διψώσῃ προσηνές*</u>, **οὕτως** *ἀγγελία ἀγαθὴ ἐκ γῆς μακρόθεν.*

25 <u>*Aqua frigida animae sitienti*</u>, et *nuntius bonus de terra longinqua.*

  [good news from far away ≈ cold water > a thirsty soul]

  NB: the Latin version lacks prothesis and apothesis.

Prov. 25.26 *A righteous man falling down before the wicked* is <u>as</u> <u>*a troubled fountain, and a corrupt spring.*</u>

26 <u>ὥσπερ *εἴ τις πηγὴ φράσσοι καὶ ὕδατος ἔξοδον λυμαίνοιτο*</u>, **οὕτως** *ἄκοσμον δίκαιον πεπτωκέναι ἐνώπιον ἀσεβοῦς.*

26 <u>*Fons turbatus pede et vena corrupta*</u>, *justus cadens coram impio.*

  [a righteous man > a wicked man ≈ a troubled fountain ≈ a corrupt spring]

  NB: the Latin version lacks prothesis and apothesis.

Prov. 25.28 *He that hath no rule over his own spirit* is like *a city that is broken* d*own, and without walls.*

28 ὥσπερ *πόλις τὰ τείχει καταβεβλημένη καὶ ἀτείχιστος,* **οὕτως** *ἀνὴρ ὅς οὐ μετὰ βουλῆς τι πράσσει.*

28 Sicut *urbs patens et absque murorum ambitu,* **ita** *vir qui non potest in loquendo cohibere spiritum suum.*

[a man with no rule over his own spirit ≈ an unfortified city]

Prov. 26.1 As *snow in summer,* and *as* *rain in harvest,* **so** *honour is not seemly for a fool.*

1 ΩΣΠΕΡ *δρόσος ἐν ἀμήτῳ καὶ ὥσπερ ὑετὸς ἐν θέρει,* **οὕτως** *οὐκ ἔστιν ἄφρονι τιμή.*

1 Quomodo *nix in aestate,* et *pluviae in messe,* **sic** *indecens est stulto gloria.*

[honor > (unseemly to) a fool ≈ snow (in summer) ≈ rain (in harvest)]

Prov. 26.2 As *the bird by wandering,* as *the swallow by flying,* **so** *the curse causeless* shall not come.

2 ὥσπερ *ὄρνεα πέταται καὶ στρουθοί,* **οὕτως** *ἀρὰ ματαία οὐκ ἐπελεύσεται οὐδενί.*

2 Sicut *avis ad alia transvolans* et *passer quolibet vadens,* **sic** *maledictum frustra prolatum* in quempiam superveniet.

[a causeless curse ≈ bird wandering ≈ sparrow flying]

Prov. 26.7 The *legs of the lame are not equal*: **so** is *a parable in the mouth of fools.*

7 ἀφελοῦ πορείαν σκελῶν καὶ παρανομίαν ἐκ στόματος ἀφρόνων.

7 Quomodo *pulchras frustra habet claudus tibias,* **sic** *indecens est in ore stultorum parabola.*

[A parable in the mouth of fools ≈ the unequal legs of the lame]

Prov. 26.8 As *he that bindeth a stone in a sling,* **so** is *he that giveth honour to a fool.*

8 ὃς ἀποδεσμεύει *λίθον ἐν σφενδόνῃ,* ὅμοιός ἐστι *τῷ διδόντι ἄφρονι δόξαν.*

8 Sicut *qui mittit lapidem in acervum Mercurii,* **ita** *qui tribuit insipienti honorem.*

[one who gives honor to a fool ≈ he that binds a stone in a sling]

Prov. 26.9 <u>As</u> a *thorn goeth up into the hand of a drunkard,* **so** is *a parable in the mouth of fools.* [cf. 26.7]

    9 <u>*ἄκανθαι φύονται ἐν χειρὶ μεθύσου*</u>, δουλεία δὲ ἐν χειρὶ τῶν ἀφρόνων.

    9 <u>Quomodo</u> si *spina nascatur in manu temulenti*, **sic** *parabola in ore stultorum.*

        [a parable in the mouth of fools ≈ a thorn in the hand of a drunkard]

Prov. 26.11 <u>As</u> *a dog returneth to his vomit* **so** *a fool returneth to his folly.*

    11 <u>ὥσπερ</u> <u>*κύων*</u> ὅταν ἐπέλθῃ <u>*ἐπὶ τὸν ἑαυτοῦ ἔμετον*</u> καὶ μισητὸς γένηται, **οὕτως** ἄφρων τῇ ἑαυτοῦ κακίᾳ ἀναστρέψας ἐπὶ τὴν ἑαυτοῦ ἁμαρτίαν.

    11 <u>Sicut</u> *canis* qui revertitur ad vomitum suum, **sic** *imprudens* qui iterat stultitiam suam.

        [a fool > his folly ≈ a dog > his own vomit]

Prov. 26.14 <u>As</u> the *door turneth upon his hinge,* **so** does *the slothful upon his bed.*

    14 <u>ὥσπερ</u> <u>*θύρα στρέφεται ἐπὶ τοῦ στρόφιγγος*</u>, **οὕτως** ὀκνηρὸς ἐπὶ τῆς κλίνης αὐτοῦ.

    14 <u>Sicut</u> *ostium vertitur in cardine suo*, **ita** *piger in lectulo suo.*

        [a sluggard > his bed ≈ a door (turning on) > its hinge]

Prov. 26.16: The *sluggard* is <u>wiser</u> in his own conceit <u>than</u> *seven men* that can render a reason.

    16 <u>σοφώτερος</u> ἑαυτῷ ὀκνηρὸς φαίνεται <u>τοῦ ἐν πλησμονῇ ἀποκομίζοντος ἀγγελίαν.</u>

    16 <u>Sapientior</u> *sibi piger videtur* septem viris loquentibus sententias.

        [a sluggard (wiser than) ≈ seven men]

Prov. 26.17 *He that passeth by, and meddleth with strife belonging not to him*, is <u>like</u> *one that taketh a dog by the ears.*

    17 <u>ὥσπερ</u> <u>*ὁ κρατῶν κέρκου κυνός*</u>, **οὕτως** ὁ προεστὼς ἀλλοτρίας κρίσεως.

    17 <u>Sicut</u> *qui apprehendit auribus canem*, **sic** *qui transit impatiens* et *commiscetur rixae alterius.*

        [he that makes himself champion of another's cause ≈ someone who takes a dog by the ears]

Prov. 26.18 *As a madman who casteth firebrands, arrows, and death,* 19 *so is the man that deceiveth his neighbor.*

18 [The Greek text is quite different.] cf. 17: ὥσπερ ὁ κρατῶν κέρκου κυνός, οὕτως ὁ προεστὼς ἀλλοτρίας κρίσεως.

(As he that lays hold of a dog's tail, so is he that makes himself the champion of another's cause.)

18 *Sicut noxius est qui mittit sagittas et lanceas in mortem.*

[one who deceives his neighbor ≈ a madman who throws firebrands, arrows and death]

Prov. 26.21 As *coals are to burning coals*, and *wood to fire*: **so** is *a contentious man to kindle strife.*

21 ἐσχάρα ἄνθραξι καὶ ξύλα πυρί, ἀνὴρ δὲ λοίδορος εἰς ταραχὴν μάχης.

21 *Sicut* carbones ad prunas, *et* ligna ad ignem, **sic** *homo iracundus suscitat rixas.*

[a contentious man > (kindle) strife ≈ coals > burning coals ≈ wood > fire]

Prov. 26.22 The *words of a talebearer* are as *wounds,* and they go down into the innermost parts of the belly.

22 λόγοι κερκώπων μαλακοί, οὗτοι δὲ τύπτουσιν εἰς ταμιεῖα σπλάγχνων.

22 *Verba susurronis* quasi *simplicia*, et ipsa perveniunt ad intima ventris.   [words ≈ wounds]

Prov. 26.23 *Burning lips and a wicked heart* are like *a potsherd covered with silver dross.*

23 ἀργύριον διδόμενον μετὰ δόλου, ὥσπερ ὄστρακον ἡγητέον.

23 Quomodo si *argento sordido ornare velis vas fictile*, **sic** *labia tumentia cum pessimo corde sociata.*

[burning lips and a wicked heart ≈ a potsherd covered with silver]

Prov. 27.3 A *stone is heavy, and the sand weighty*; but *a fool's wrath* is heavier than *them both.*

3 βαρὺ λίθος καὶ δυσβάστακτον ἄμμος, ὀργὴ δὲ ἄφρονος βαρυτέρα ἀμφοτέρων.

3 *Grave est saxum, et onerosa arena*, sed *ira stulti* utroque gravior.

[a fool's wrath (heavier than) ≈ a heavy stone ≈ weighty sand]

Prov. 27.5 *Open rebuke* is better than *secret love.*

5 κρείσσους ἔλεγχοι ἀποκεκαλυμμένοι κρυπτομένης φιλίας.

5 Melior est *manifesta correptio* quam *amor absconditus.*

[open rebuke ≈ secret love]

Prov. 27.8 As *a bird that wandereth from her nest*, **so** is *a man that wandereth from his place*.

8 ὥσπερ ὅταν ὄρνεον καταπετασθῇ ἐκ τῆς ἰδίας νοσσιᾶς, **οὕτως** ἄνθρωπος δουλοῦται ὅταν ἀποξενωθῇ ἐκ τῶν ἰδίων τόπων.

8 Sicut *avis transmigrans de nido suo*, **sic** vir qui derelinquit locum suum.

[a man who wanders from his own place ≈ a bird flying from its own nest]

Prov. 27.15 A *continual dropping in a very rainy day* and a *contentious woman* are alike.

15 σταγόνες ἐκβάλλουσιν ἄνθρωπον ἐν ἡμέρᾳ χειμερινῇ ἐκ τοῦ οἴκου αὐτοῦ, ὡσαύτως καὶ γυνὴ λοίδορος ἐκ τοῦ ἰδίου οἴκου.

15 *Tecta perstillantia in die frigoris* et *litigiosa mulier* comparantur.

[a contentious woman ≈ a continual dropping in a very rainy day]

Prov. 27.17 *Iron sharpeneth iron*; **so** *a man sharpeneth the countenance of his friend*.

17 σίδηρος σίδηρον ὀξύνει, ἀνὴρ δὲ παροξύνει πρόσωπον ἑταίρου.

17 *Ferrum ferro exacuitur,* et *homo exacuit faciem amici sui*.

(Prothesis is missing here.)

[a man > (sharpens) his friend's countenance ≈ iron > iron]

Prov. 27.19 As in water *face answereth to face*, **so** the *heart of man to man*.

19 ὥσπερ οὐκ ὅμοια πρόσωπα προσώποις, **οὕτως** οὐδὲ αἱ διάνοιαι τῶν ἀνθρώπων.

19 Quomodo *in aquis resplendent vultus prospicientium*, **sic** corda hominum manifesta sunt prudentibus.

[heart > heart ≈ face > face]

Prov. 27.20 *Hell and destruction are never full*; **so** the *eyes of man are never satisfied*.

20 ᾅδης καὶ ἀπώλεια οὐκ ἐμπίμπλανται, **ὡσαύτως καὶ** οἱ ὀφθαλμοὶ τῶν ἀνθρώπων ἄπληστοι.

20 *Infernus et perditio numquam implentur*: similiter et oculi hominum insatiabiles.

[eyes of men (insatiable) ≈ hell and destruction (not full)]

Prov. 27.21 As is t*he fining pot for silver*, and t*he furnace for gold*; **so** is *a man
to his praise.*

21 δοκίμιον ἀργυρῷ καὶ χρυσῷ πύρωσις, ἀνὴρ δὲ δοκιμάζεται διὰ στόματος
ἐγκωμιαζόντων αὐτόν.

21 Quomodo *probatur in conflatorio argentum et in fornace aurum*, **sic**
probatur homo ore laudantis.

[a man > praise ≈ a fining pot > silver ≈ a furnace > gold]

Prov. 28.1 The wicked flee when no man pursueth: but *the righteous* are
bold as *a lion.*

1 ΦΕΥΓΕΙ ἀσεβὴς μηδενὸς διώκοντος, δίκαιος δὲ ὥσπερ λέων πέποιθε.

1 Fugit impius, nemine persequente; *justus autem*, quasi *leo confidens*,
absque terrore erit.

[a righteous man (bold) ≈ a lion]

Prov. 28.3 *A poor man that oppresseth the poor is* like *a sweeping rain which
leaveth no food.*

3 ἀνδρεῖος ἐν ἀσεβείαις συκοφαντεῖ πτωχούς ὥσπερ ὑετὸς λάβρος καὶ
ἀνωφελής,

3 *Vir pauper calumnians pauperes* similis est *imbri vehementi in quo
paratur fames.*

[a poor man oppressing the poor ≈ rain (sweeping) which leaves
no food]

Prov. 28.15 As *a roaring lion*, and *a ranging bear*; **so** is *a wicked ruler* over
the poor people.

15 λέων πεινῶν καὶ λύκος διψῶν, ὃς τυραννεῖ, πτωχὸς ὤν, ἔθνους πενιχροῦ.

15 *Leo rugiens et ursus esuriens, princeps impius super populum pauperem.*

[a wicked ruler ≈ a roaring/hungry lion ≈ a ranging bear/
thirsty wolf]

Prov. 30.14 There is a generation, whose *teeth* are as *swords*, and *their jaw
teeth* as *knives*. …

14 ? [Greek text ends at Chapter 29.]

14 *generatio quae pro dentibus gladios habet*, et commandit *molaribus
suis, ut comedat inopes de terra*, …

[the teeth of one generation ≈ swords and knives]

Prov. 31.10 Who can find *a virtuous woman*? for *her price is* <u>far above</u> <u>*rubies*</u>.

10 Γυναῖκα ἀνδρείαν τίς εὑρήσει; <u>τιμιωτέρα</u> δέ ἐστι <u>λίθων πολυτελῶν</u> ἡ τοιαύτη.

10 Mulierem fortem quis inveniet? procul et de ultimis finibus pretium ejus.

[a virtuous woman (far above) ≈ rubies]

Prov. 31.14 *She is* <u>like</u> <u>*the merchants' ships;*</u> she bringeth her food from afar.

14 ἐγένετο <u>ὡσεὶ</u> <u>ναῦς</u> ἐμπορευομένη μακρόθεν, συνάγει δὲ αὐτῆς τὸν πλοῦτον. (*She is* <u>like</u> <u>*a ship trading from a distance:*</u> so she procures her livelihood.)

14 *Facta et* <u>quasi</u> <u>*navis institoris, de longe portans panem suum.*</u>

[she (a virtuous woman) ≈ merchants' ships trading from a distance]

***

Ecclesiastes (12 Chapters)

Ἐκκλησιαστής

Ῥήματα ἐκκλησιαστοῦ υἱοῦ Δαβὶδ βασιλέως Ἰσραὴλ ἐν Ἱερουσαλήμ. 1 The words of the Preacher, the son of David, king of Israel in Jerusalem.

Eccl. 7.1 *A good name* is <u>better than</u> <u>*precious ointment*</u>; and the day of death *than the day of one's birth.* [**a simile (figurative) followed by a comparison (literal)**] **Also comparisons in the next two sentences.**

1 *ΑΓΑΘΟΝ* ὄνομα <u>ὑπὲρ</u> <u>ἔλαιον ἀγαθὸν</u> καὶ ἡμέρα τοῦ θανάτου ὑπὲρ ἡμέραν γεννήσεως.

2 <u>Melius</u> est *nomen bonum* <u>quam</u> <u>*unguenta pretiosa*</u>, et dies mortis die nativitatis.

[a good name (better than) ≈ precious ointment]

Eccl. 7.6 For <u>as</u> <u>*the crackling of thorns under a pot,*</u> **so** is *the laughter of the fool*: this also is vanity.

6 <u>ὡς φωνὴ ἀκανθῶν ὑπὸ τὸ *bbbὸν λέβητα,*</u> **οὕτως** γέλως τῶν ἀφρόνων· καί γε τοῦτο ματαιότης.

7 quia <u>sicut</u> <u>*sonitus spinarum ardentium sub olla*</u>, **sic** *risus stulti*. Sed et hoc vanitas.

[the laughter of a fool ≈ the crackling of thorns under a pot]

Eccl. 7.26 And I find <u>more bitter than</u> *death the woman,* <u>whose</u> *heart is* <u>snares</u> and *nets,* and *her hands* <u>as</u> *bands.*

26 καὶ εὑρίσκω ἐγὼ αὐτὴν καὶ ἐρῶ <u>πικρότερον ὑπὲρ θάνατον,</u> σὺν τὴν γυναῖκα, ἥτις ἐστὶ θήρευμα καὶ <u>σαγῆναι καρδία αὐτῆς δεσμὸς</u> εἰς χεῖρας αὐτῆς·

*b/1   27 et inveni <u>amariorem</u> *morte* mulierem, quae <u>laqueus venatorum</u> est, et *sagena* cor ejus; *vincula* sunt *manus illius.*

[a woman (whose heart ≈ snares; whose hands ≈ bands) ≈ (more bitter than) death]

Eccl. 9.4 for *a living dog* is <u>better than</u> *a dead lion.*

4 ὁ κύων ὁ ζῶν, αὐτὸς <u>ἀγαθὸς ὑπὲρ τὸν λέοντα τὸν νεκρόν.</u>

*b/1   4 <u>melior</u> est *canis vivus* <u>leone mortuo.</u>

Rationale: 5 For the living know that they shall die: but the dead know not any thing.

[a living dog (better than) ≈ a dead lion]

– A factual comparison? (See listing in Appendix V.)

Eccl. 9.12 For man also knoweth not his time: <u>as</u> the *<u>fishes that are taken in</u>* *<u>an evil net,</u>* and <u>as</u> the *<u>birds that are caught in the snare</u>*; **so** are *the sons of men snared in an evil time,* when it falleth suddenly upon them.

12 ὅτι καί γε οὐκ ἔγνω ὁ ἄνθρωπος τὸν καιρὸν αὐτοῦ· <u>ὡς</u> οἱ <u>ἰχθύες οἱ</u> <u>θηρευόμενοι ἐν ἀμφιβλήστρῳ κακῷ</u> καὶ ὡς <u>ὄρνεα τὰ θηρευόμενα ἐν</u> <u>παγίδι,</u> <u>ὡς</u> αὐτὰ παγιδεύονται οἱ υἱοὶ τοῦ ἀνθρώπου εἰς καιρὸν πονηρόν, ὅταν ἐπιπέσῃ ἐπ᾽ αὐτοὺς ἄφνω.

12 Nescit homo finem suum; sed <u>sicut</u> *pisces* capiuntur hamo, et <u>sicut</u> <u>aves</u> laqueo comprehenduntur, **sic** *capiuntur homines* in tempore malo, cum eis extemplo supervenerit.

[sons of men (snared in an evil time) ≈ fishes taken in an evil net ≈ birds caught in a snare]

Eccl. 9.18 *Wisdom* is <u>better than</u> *<u>weapons of war</u>*: but one sinner destroyers much good.

18 ἀγαθὴ σοφία <u>ὑπὲρ</u> <u>σκεύη πολέμου,</u> καὶ ἁμαρτάνων εἰς ἀπολέσει ἀγαθωσύνην πολλήν.

18 <u>Melior</u> est *sapientia* <u>quam</u> *<u>arma bellica</u>*; et qui in uno peccaverit, multa bona perdet.

[wisdom ≈ (better than) weapons of war]

Eccl. 10.1 <u>*Dead flies cause the ointment of the apothecary to send forth a*</u> <u>*stinking savour*</u>: **so** doth *a little folly him that is in reputation for* *wisdom and honour.*

    1 <u>*ΜΥΙΑΙ ϑανατοῦσαι σαπριοῦσι σκευασίαν ἐλαίου ἡδύσματος·*</u> τίμιον ὀλίγον σοφίας <u>ὑπὲρ</u> δόξαν ἀφροσύνης μεγάλην,

    1 <u>*Muscae morientes perdunt suavitatem unguenti.*</u> <u>Pretiosior</u> est <u>*sapientia*</u> <u>*et gloria*</u>, *parva et ad tempus stultitia.*

> [**A simile in the form of an aphorism**: a little folly > (causes to stink) a reputation of wisdom and honor ≈ dead flies > an apothecary's ointment]
> – **Other similetic aphorisms follow (10.8–11).**

Eccl. 10.8 *He that diggeth a pit shall fall into it*; and <u>*whoso bracket an hedge,*</u> <u>*a serpent shall bite him.*</u>

    8 ὁ ὀρύσσων βόθρον εἰς αὐτὸν ἐμπεσεῖται, καὶ καθαιροῦντα φραγμόν, <u>δήξεται αὐτὸν ὄφις.</u>

    8 Qui fodit foveam incidet in eam, et qui dissipat sepem mordebit eum coluber.

> [digging a pit > falling in ≈ one bracketing a hedge > a serpent bite]

Eccl. 10.11 Surely <u>*the serpent will bite without enchantment*</u>: and *a babbler* *is no better.*

    11 ἐὰν δάκῃ ὄφις ἐν οὐ ψιθυρισμῷ, καὶ οὐκ ἔστι περισσεία τῷ ἐπᾴδοντι.

    11 Si mordeat serpens in silentio, nihil eo minus habet qui occulte detrahit.

> [a babbler ≈ a serpent biting]

Eccl. 12.11 *The words of the wise* are <u>as</u> <u>*goads*</u>, and <u>as</u> <u>*nails fastened*</u> *by the* *masters of assemblies, which are given from one shepherd.*

    11 *Λόγοι σοφῶν* <u>ὡς</u> <u>*τὰ βούκεντρα*</u> καὶ <u>ὡς</u> <u>ἥλοι</u> *πεφυτευμένοι*, οἳ παρὰ τῶν συνθεμάτων ἐδόθησαν ἐκ ποιμένος ἑνὸς

    11 *Verba sapientium* <u>sicut</u> <u>*stimuli*</u>, et <u>quasi</u> <u>*clavi in altum defixi,*</u> quae per magistrorum consilium data sunt a pastore uno.

> [words of wise ≈ goads ≈ nails fastened]

* * *

The Song of Solomon (8 Chapters)

ΑΣΜΑ ἀσμάτων, ὅ ἐστι τῷ Σαλωμών.
The Song of songs, which is Solomon's.

So-So. 1.2 Let him kiss me with the kisses of his mouth: for *thy love is* <u>better than *wine*</u>.

2 Φιλησάτω με ἀπὸ φιλημάτων στόματος αὐτοῦ, ὅτι ἀγαθοὶ *μαστοί σου* <u>ὑπὲρ *οἶνον*.</u> *(thy breasts)*

*b/1   1 Osculetur me osculo oris sui; quia <u>meliora</u> sunt *ubera tua vino*,   [your love/breasts (better than) ≈ wine]

So-So. 1.3 Because of the savour of thy good ointments *thy name* is <u>as *ointment poured forth*</u>, therefore do the virgins love thee.

3 καὶ *ὀσμὴ μύρων σου* ὑπὲρ πάντα τὰ ἀρώματα· μύρον ἐκκενωθὲν ὄνομά σου. διὰ τοῦτο νεάνιδες ἠγάπησάν σε.

*a/1   3 fragrantia unguentis optimis. *Oleum effusum nomen tuum*; ideo adolescentulae dilexerunt te.

[your name ≈ an ointment poured]

So-So. 1.4 We will remember *thy love* <u>more than *wine*</u>.

4 ἀγαπήσομεν *μαστούς σου* <u>ὑπὲρ *οἶνον.*</u>

3 memores *uberum tuorum* <u>super *vinum*</u>.

[your love/breasts (more than) ≈ wine]

So-So. 1.5 I am *black*, but *comely*, O ye daughters of Jerusalem, <u>as *the tents of Kedar*</u>, <u>as *the curtains of Solomon*</u>.

5 *μέλαινά* εἰμι ἐγὼ καὶ *καλή*, θυγατέρες Ἱερουσαλήμ, <u>ὡς *σκηνώματα Κηδάρ*</u>, <u>ὡς *δέρρεις Σαλωμών*</u>.

4 *Nigra sum, sed formosa*, filiae Jerusalem, <u>sicut *tabernacula Cedar*</u>, sicut *pelles Salomonis*.

[I/black & beautiful ≈ the tents of Kedar ≈ the curtains of Solomon]

So-So. 1.9 <u>I have compared</u> *thee*, O my love, <u>*to a company of horses in Pharaoh's chariots.*</u>

9 <u>*τῇ ἵππῳ μου*</u> ἐν ἄρμασι Φαραὼ <u>*ὡμοίωσά*</u> σε, ἡ πλησίον μου.

8 *Equitatui meo* in curribus Pharaonis <u>assimilavi</u> *te*, amica mea.

[you ≈ a company of Pharaoh's horses]

So-So. 1.14 *My beloved* is unto me <u>as</u> <u>*a cluster of camphor in the vineyards*</u> <u>*of Engedi.*</u>

14 βότρυς τῆς κύπρου ἀδελφιδός μου ἐμοί, ἐν ἀμπελῶσιν Ἐγγαδδί.

*a/1   13 <u>*Botrus cypri*</u> *dilectus meus* mihi in vineis Engaddi.

[my beloved/kinsman ≈ a cluster of camphor]

So-So. 2.2 <u>As</u> the <u>*lily among thorns,*</u> **so** is *my love among the daughters.*

3 <u>As</u> t<u>*he apple tree among the trees of the wood,*</u> **so** is my *beloved among the sons.*

2 <u>ὡς</u> <u>*κρίνον ἐν μέσῳ ἀκανθῶν*</u>, **οὕτως** ἡ *πλησίον μου ἀνὰ μέσον τῶν θυγατέρων.* 3 <u>ὡς</u> <u>*μῆλον ἐν τοῖς ξύλοις τοῦ δρυμοῦ*</u>, **οὕτως** *ἀδελφιδός μου ἀνὰ μέσον τῶν υἱῶν·*

2 SPONSUS. <u>Sicut</u> *lilium inte*r <u>*spinas*</u>, **sic** *amica mea inter filias.* 3 SPONSA. <u>Sicut</u> <u>*malus inter ligna silvarum*</u>, **sic** *dilectus meus inter filios.*

[my love among the daughters ≈ the lily among thorns; my beloved among the sons ≈ the apple tree among trees]

So-So. 2.9 *My beloved* is <u>like</u> <u>*a roe or a young hart.*</u>

9 <u>ὅμοιός</u> ἐστιν *ἀδελφιδός μου* <u>*τῇ δορκάδι ἢ νεβρῷ ἐλάφων ἐπὶ τὰ ὄρη Βαιθήλ.*</u>

9 <u>Similis</u> est *dilectus meus* <u>*capreae, hinnuloque cervorum.*</u>

[my beloved ≈ a roe ≈ a young hart]

So-So. 2.17 Until the day break, and the shadows flee away, turn, *my beloved*, and <u>be thou like</u> <u>*a roe or a young hart upon the mountains of*</u> <u>*Bether.*</u>

17 ἕως οὗ διαπνεύσῃ ἡ ἡμέρα καὶ κινηθῶσιν αἱ σκιαί. *b/2<u>ἀπόστρεψον,</u> <u>ὁμοιώθητι σύ, ἀδελφιδέ μου, τῷ δόρκωνι ἢ νεβρῷ ἐλάφων ἐπὶ ὄρη</u> <u>κοιλωμάτων.</u>

2.17 donec aspiret dies, et inclinentur umbrae. Revertere; <u>similis</u> esto, *dilecte mi,* <u>*capreae, hinnuloque cervorum super montes Bether.*</u>

[you ≈ a roe ≈ young hart]

So-So. 3.6 *Who is this* that cometh out of the wilderness <u>like</u> <u>*pillars of*</u> <u>*smoke*</u>, perfumed with myrrh and frankincense, with all powders of the merchant?

6 *Τίς αὕτη ἡ ἀναβαίνουσα ἀπὸ τῆς ἐρήμου* <u>ὡς</u> <u>*στελέχη καπνοῦ*</u> τεθυμιαμένη σμύρναν καὶ λίβανον ἀπὸ πάντων κονιορτῶν μυρεψοῦ;

6 Quae est *ista quae ascendit per desertum* <u>sicut</u> *<u>virgula fum</u>*i ex aromatibus myrrhae, et thuris, et universi pulveris pigmentarii?   [who? ≈ pillar(s) of smoke]

So-So. 4.1 Behold, thou art fair, my love; … thou hast *<u>doves' eyes</u>*; *thy hair* is <u>as</u> a *<u>flock of goats</u>*. 2 *Thy teeth* are <u>like a</u> *<u>flock of sheep that are even shorn</u>* which came up from the washing; … 3 *Thy lips* are <u>like</u> *<u>a thread of scarlet</u>*, and thy speech is comely: thy temples are <u>like</u> *<u>a piece of pomegranate</u>* within thy locks. 4 *Thy neck* is <u>like</u> t*<u>he tower of David</u>*, builded for an armoury: … 5 *Thy two breasts* are <u>like</u> *<u>two young roes, that are twins</u>*.

1 Ἰδοὺ εἶ καλή, ἡ πλησίον μου, ἰδοὺ εἶ καλή. ὀφθαλμοί σου <u>περιστεραὶ</u> ἐκτὸς τῆς σιωπήσεώς σου. τρίχωμά σου <u>ὡς ἀγέλαι τῶν αἰγῶν</u>, αἳ ἀπεκαλύφθησαν ἀπὸ τοῦ Γαλαάδ. 2 ὀδόντες σου <u>ὡς ἀγέλαι τῶν κεκαρμένων</u>, αἳ ἀνέβησαν ἀπὸ τοῦ λουτροῦ, … 3 <u>ὡς σπαρτίον τὸ κόκκινον χείλη σου</u>, καὶ ἡ λαλιά σου ὡραία, ὡς λέπυρον ῥοᾶς μῆλόν σου ἐκτὸς τῆς σιωπήσεώς σου. 4 <u>ὡς πύργος Δαυὶδ</u> τράχηλός σου, ὁ ᾠκοδομημένος εἰς θαλπιώθ·… 5 δύο μαστοί σου <u>ὡς δύο νεβροὶ δίδυμοι δορκάδος</u>.

1 SPONSUS. Quam pulchra es, amica mea! quam pulchra es! *Oculi* tui *<u>columbarum</u>*, … *Capilli tu*i <u>sicut</u> *<u>greges caprarum</u>* quae ascenderunt de monte Galaad. 2 *Dentes tui* <u>sicut</u> *<u>greges tonsarum</u>* quae ascenderunt de lavacro; … 3 <u>Sicut</u> *<u>vitta coccinea</u>* labia tua, et eloquium tuum dulce. <u>Sicut</u> *<u>fragmen mali punici</u>*, **ita** genae tuae, absque eo quod intrinsecus latet. 4 <u>Sicut</u> *<u>turris David</u>* collum tuum, quae aedificata est cum propugnaculis; … 5 *Duo ubera tua* <u>sicut</u> *<u>duo hinnuli, capreae gemelli</u>*, qui pascuntur in liliis.

[your eyes ≈ doves'; your hair ≈ flock of goats; your teeth ≈ a flock of shorn sheep; your lips ≈ a thread of scarlet; your temples ≈ a piece of pomegranate; your neck ≈ the tower of David; your two breasts ≈ two young roes that are twins]

So-So. 4.10 How fair is thy love, my sister, my spouse! how <u>much better</u> is *thy love* <u>than</u> *<u>wine!</u>* and *the smell of thine ointments* <u>than</u> *<u>all spices!</u>*

10 τί ἐκαλλιώθησαν μαστοί σου, ἀδελφή μου νύμφη; τί <u>ἐκαλλιώθησαν</u> μαστοί σου <u>ἀπὸ οἴνου</u>, καὶ ὀσμὴ ἱματίων σου <u>ὑπὲρ πάντα τὰ ἀρώματα</u>;

10 Quam pulchrae sunt mammae tuae, soror mea sponsa! *pulchriora* sunt *ubera tua <u>vino</u>, et odor unguentorum tuorum* <u>super</u> *<u>omnia aromata</u>.*

[your love/breasts (better than) ≈ wine; the smell of your ointments ≈ all spices]

So-So. 4.11 *Thy lips,* O my spouse, drop <u>as</u> *<u>the honeycomb</u>*; honey and milk are under thy tongue; and *the smell of thy garments* is <u>like</u> *<u>the smell of Lebanon</u>.*

11 κηρίον ἀποστάζουσι χείλη σου, νύμφη· μέλι καὶ γάλα ὑπὸ τὴν γλῶσσάν σου, καὶ *ὀσμὴ ἱματίων σου* <u>ὡς</u> *<u>ὀσμὴ Λιβάνου</u>.*

11 Favus distillans labia tua, sponsa; mel et lac sub lingua tua: et *odor vestimentorum tuorum* <u>sicut</u> *<u>odor thuris</u>*

[your lips ≈ the honeycomb; smell of your garments ≈ smell of Lebanon]

So-So. 5.11 His [my beloved's] *head* is <u>as</u> the *<u>most fine gold</u>, his locks* are bushy, and *black* <u>as</u> *<u>a raven</u>.* 12 *His eyes* are <u>as</u> *<u>the eyes of doves</u>* by the rivers of waters ... 13 *His cheeks* are <u>as</u> *<u>a bed of spices</u>,* <u>as</u> *<u>sweet flowers</u>: his lips* <u>like</u> *<u>lilies</u>,* dropping sweet smelling myrrh.

14 *His hands* are <u>as</u> *<u>gold rings</u>* set with the beryl: *his belly* is <u>as</u> *<u>bright ivory overlaid with sapphires</u>.* 15 His *legs* are <u>as</u> *<u>pillars of marble</u>,* set upon sockets of fine gold: *his countenance* is <u>as</u> *<u>Lebanon</u>,* excellent <u>as</u> the *<u>cedars</u>.*

11 κεφαλὴ αὐτοῦ *<u>χρυσίον καιφάζ</u>,* βόστρυχοι αὐτοῦ ἐλάται, <u>μέλανες ὡς</u> *<u>κόραξ</u>·* 12 ὀφθαλμοὶ αὐτοῦ <u>ὡς</u> *<u>περιστεραὶ</u>* ἐπὶ πληρώματα ὑδάτων λελουσμέναι ἐν γάλακτι, ... 13 *σιαγόνες αὐτοῦ* <u>ὡς</u> *<u>φιάλαι τοῦ ἀρώματος</u>* φύουσαι *<u>μυρεψικά</u>·* χείλη αὐτοῦ κρίνα στάζοντα σμύρναν πλήρη· 14 *χεῖρες αὐτοῦ* <u>τορευταὶ χρυσαῖ πεπληρωμέναι</u> Θαρσίς· κοιλία αὐτοῦ *<u>πυξίον ἐλεφάντινον</u>* ἐπὶ λίθου σαπφείρου· 15 κνῆμαι αὐτοῦ *<u>στῦλοι μαρμάρινοι</u>* τεθεμελιωμένοι ἐπὶ βάσεις χρυσᾶς· εἶδος αὐτοῦ <u>ὡς</u> *<u>Λίβανος</u>,* ἐκλεκτὸς <u>ὡς</u> *<u>κέδροι</u>·*

11 *Caput ejus* aurum optimum; *comae ejus* <u>sicut</u> *<u>elatae palmarum</u>, nigrae* <u>quasi</u> *<u>corvus</u>.* 12 *Oculi ejus* <u>sicut</u> *<u>columbae</u>* super rivulos aquarum, ... 13 *Genae illius* sicut *areolae aromatum,* consitae a pigmentariis. *Labia ejus <u>lilia</u>,* distillantia myrrham primam. 14 *Manus illius <u>tornatiles</u>,* aureae, plenae hyacinthis. *Venter ejus*

eburneus, distinctus sapphiris. 15 *Crura illius columnae marmoreae* quae fundatae sunt super bases aureas. *Species ejus* ut *Libani, electus* ut *cedri.*

> [my beloved's head ≈ fine gold; his locks (black) ≈ a raven; his eyes ≈ eyes of doves; his cheeks ≈ a bed of spices ≈ sweet flowers; his lips ≈ lilies; his hands ≈ gold rings; his belly ≈ bright ivory; his legs ≈ pillars of marble; his countenance ≈ Lebanon ≈ (excellent) cedars]

So-So. 6.4 *Thou* art beautiful, *O my love,* as *Tirzah,* comely as *Jerusalem, terrible* as an *army with banners.* 5 Turn away thine eyes from me, for they have overcome me: thy *hair* is as a *flock of goats* that appear from Gilead. 6 *Thy teeth* are as a *flock of sheep which go up from the washing,* … 7 As *a piece of pomegranate* are *thy temples* within thy locks.

4 Καλὴ εἶ, ἡ πλησίον μου, ὡς εὐδοκία, ὡραία ὡς ῾Ιερουσαλήμ, θάμβος ὡς τεταγμέναι. 5 ἀπόστρεψον ὀφθαλμούς σου ἀπεναντίον μου, ὅτι αὐτοὶ ἀνεπτέρωσάν με. τρίχωμά σου ὡς ἀγέλαι τῶν αἰγῶν, αἳ ἀνεφάνησαν ἀπὸ τοῦ Γαλαάδ. 6 ὀδόντες σου ὡς ἀγέλαι τῶν κεκαρμένων, αἳ ἀνέβησαν ἀπὸ τοῦ λουτροῦ, … 7 ὡς σπαρτίον τὸ κόκκινον χείλη σου καὶ ἡ λαλιά σου ὡραία, ὡς λέπυρον τῆς ῥοᾶς μῆλόν σου ἐκτὸς τῆς σιωπήσεώς σου.

3 Pulchra es, *amica mea*; suavis, et *decora* sicut *Jerusalem; terribilis* ut *castrorum acies ordinata.* 4 Averte oculos tuos a me, quia ipsi me avolare fecerunt. *Capilli tui* sicut *grex caprarum* quae apparuerunt de Galaad. 5 *Dentes* tui sicut *grex ovium* quae ascenderunt de lavacro: omnes gemellis foetibus, et sterilis non est in eis. 6 Sicut *cortex mali punici,* sic *genae tuae,* absque occultis tuis.

> [you my love (beautiful) ≈ Tirzah, (comely) ≈ Jerusalem, (terrible) ≈ armies with banners 5 your hair ≈ flock of goats 6 teeth ≈ a flock of sheep, your temples ≈ a piece of pomegranate]

So-So. 6.10 Who is *she* that looketh forth as the morning, *fair* as the moon, clear as the sun, and terrible as an army with banners?

10 τίς αὕτη ἡ ἐκκύπτουσα ὡσεὶ ὄρθρος, καλὴ ὡς σελήνη, ἐκλεκτὴ ὡς ὁ ἥλιος, θάμβος ὡς τεταγμέναι;

9 Quae est *ista* quae progreditur quasi *aurora consurgens, pulchra* ut *luna,* electa ut *sol,* terribilis ut *castrorum acies ordinata*?

[who? (looks forth) ≈ morning, (fair) ≈ moon, (clear) ≈ the sun, (terrible) ≈ an army with banners]

So-So. 6.12 Or ever I was aware, my soul made *me* like *the chariots of Amminabid*.

*a/2   12 οὐκ ἔγνω ἡ ψυχή μου· ἔθετό με ἅρματα Ἀμιναδάβ.

  11 Nescivi: anima mea conturbavit *me*, propter *quadrigas Aminadab*   [me ≈ chariots of Amminabid]

So-So. 7.1 How beautiful are thy feet with shoes, O prince's daughter!

joints of thy thighs are like *jewels*, the work of the hands of a cunning workman. 2 *Thy navel* is like *a round goblet*, which wanteth not liquor: *thy belly* is like *an heap of wheat set about with lilies*.

3 *Thy two breasts* are like *two young roes that are twins*. 4 *Thy neck* is as a *tower of ivory*; *thine eyes* like *the fish pools in Heshbon*, by the gate of Bathrabbim: *thy nose* is as *the tower of Lebanon* which looketh toward Damascus. 5 *Thine head* upon thee is like *Carmel*, and the *hair of thine head* like *purple*; the king is held in the galleries. …
7 *This thy stature* is like to *a palm tree*, and *thy breast* to *clusters of grapes*. 8 … now also *thy breasts* shall be as *clusters of the vine*, and *the smell of thy nose* like *apples*: 9 And *the roof of thy mouth* like t*he best wine for my beloved*, that goeth down sweetly causing the lips of those that are asleep to speak.

2 ὡραιώθησαν διαβήματά σου ἐν ὑποδήμασί σου, θύγατερ Ναδάβ· ῥυθμοὶ μηρῶν ὅμοιοι ὁρμίσκοις, ἔργον τεχνίτου·

3 ὀμφαλός σου κρατὴρ τορευτὸς μὴ ὑστερούμενος κρᾶμα· κοιλία σου θημωνία σίτου πεφραγμένη ἐν κρίνοις· 4 δύο μαστοί σου, ὡς δύο νεβροὶ δίδυμοι δορκάδος· 5 ὁ τράχηλός σου ὡς πύργος ἐλεφάντινος· οἱ ὀφθαλμοί σου ὡς λίμναι ἐν Ἐσεβών, ἐν πύλαις θυγατρὸς πολλῶν· μυκτήρ σου ὡς πύργος τοῦ Λιβάνου σκοπεύων πρόσωπον Δαμασκοῦ· 6 κεφαλή σου ἐπὶ σὲ ὡς Κάρμηλος, καὶ πλόκιον κεφαλῆς σου ὡς πορφύρα, βασιλεὺς δεδεμένος ἐν παραδρομαῖς. 7 … 8 τοῦτο μέγεθός σου, ὡμοιώθης τῷ φοίνικι καὶ οἱ μαστοί σου τοῖς βότρυσιν. … καὶ ἔσονται δὴ μαστοί σου ὡς βότρυες τῆς ἀμπέλου καὶ ὀσμὴ ῥινός σου ὡς μῆλα 10 καὶ ὁ λάρυγξ σου ὡς οἶνος ὁ ἀγαθός, πορευόμενος τῷ ἀδελφιδῷ μου εἰς εὐθύτητα, ἱκανούμενος χείλεσί μου καὶ ὀδοῦσιν.

1 Quam pulchri sunt gressus tui in calceamentis, filia principis! *Juncturae femorum tuorum* <u>sicut</u> *<u>monilia quae fabricata sunt manu</u>* artificis. 2 *Umbilicus tuus <u>crater tornatilis</u>*, numquam indigens poculis. *Venter tuus* <u>sicut</u> *<u>acervus tritici vallatus liliis</u>*. 3 *Duo ubera* tua <u>sicut</u> *<u>duo hinnuli, gemelli capreae</u>*. 4 *Collum tuum* <u>sicut</u> *<u>turris eburnea</u>*; *oculi tui* <u>sicut</u> quae sunt in porta filiae multitudinis. *Nasus tuus* <u>sicut</u> *<u>turris Liban</u>*i, quae respicit contra Damascum. 5 *Caput tuum* <u>ut</u> *<u>Carmelus</u>*; et *comae capitis tui* <u>sicut</u> *<u>purpura regis</u>* vincta canalibus. 6 ... 7 *Statura tua* assimilata est *<u>palmae</u>*, et *ubera tua <u>botris</u>*. 8 ... et erunt *ubera tua* <u>sicut</u> *<u>botri vineae</u>*, et *odor oris tui* <u>sicut</u> *<u>malorum</u>*. 9 *Guttur tuum* <u>sicut</u> *<u>vinum optimum</u>*, dignum dilecto meo ad potandum, labiisque et dentibus illius ad ruminandum. [joints of your thighs ≈ jewels, your nave ≈ a round goblet, your belly ≈ a heap of wheat, your two breasts ≈ two young twin roes, your neck ≈ a tower of ivory, your eyes ≈ fish pools in Heshbon, your nose ≈ the tower of Lebanon, your head ≈ Carmel, the hair on your head ≈ purple, your stature ≈ a palm tree, your breast ≈ clusters of grapes, your breasts ≈ clusters of the vine, the smell of your nose ≈ apples, the roof of your mouth ≈ the best wine]

So-So. 8.6 Set *me* <u>as</u> *<u>a seal upon thine heart,</u>* <u>as</u> *<u>a seal upon thine arm</u>*; for *love* <u>is strong as</u> *<u>death</u>*; *jealousy* is <u>cruel as</u> *<u>the grave</u>*, ...

6 θές με <u>ὡς</u> <u>*σφραγῖδα ἐπὶ τὴν καρδίαν σου*</u>, <u>ὡς</u> <u>*σφραγῖδα ἐπὶ τὸν βραχίονά σου*</u>· ὅτι <u>*κραταιὰ ὡς*</u> <u>*θάνατος ἀγάπη*</u>, <u>*σκληρὸς ὡς ᾅδης ζῆλος*</u>· περίπτερα αὐτῆς περίπτερα πυρός, φλόγες αὐτῆς·

6 Pone *me* <u>ut</u> *<u>signaculum super cor tuum,</u>* ut *<u>signaculum super</u>* *<u>brachium tuum,</u>* quia fortis est <u>ut</u> *<u>mors</u>* dilectio, *dura* <u>sicut</u> *<u>infernus</u>* aemulatio: [me ≈ a seal upon your heart ≈ a seal upon your arm; love (strong) ≈ death]

So-So. 8.10 *my breasts* <u>like</u> *<u>towers</u>*; then was I in his eyes <u>as one that found favor</u>.

10 ... καὶ *μαστοί μου* <u>ὡς</u> <u>*πύργοι*</u>· ἐγὼ ἤμην ἐν ὀφθαλμοῖς ὑτῶν <u>ὡς εὑρίσκουσα εἰρήνην</u>.

10 et *ubera mea* <u>sicut</u> *<u>turris</u>*, ex quo *facta sum* coram eo, <u>quasi</u> *<u>pacem reperiens</u>*.

[my breasts ≈ towers; I ≈ one that found favor]

[**The last is a comparison:** I ≈ one that found favor.]

So-So. 8.14 Make haste, my beloved, and be thou <u>like</u> to <u>*a roe or to a young hart up*</u>on the mountains of spices.

14 φύγε, ἀδελφιδέ μου, καὶ <u>ὁμοιώθητι</u> <u>*τῇ δορκάδι*</u> ἢ <u>*τῷ νεβρῷ*</u> τῶν ἐλάφων ἐπὶ ὄρη τῶν ἀρωμάτων.

14 Fuge, *dilecte mi*, et <u>assimilare</u> <u>*capreae, hinnuloque cervorum*</u> super montes aromatum.

[my beloved ≈ (be like) a roe or a young hart on mountains of spices]

* * *

Isaiah / Esaias (66 Chapters)

Isaiah 1.8 And the *daughter of Zion* is left <u>as</u> <u>*a cottage in a vineyard*</u>, <u>as</u> <u>*a lodge*</u> in a garden of cucumbers, <u>as</u> <u>*a besieged city.*</u>

8 ἐγκαταλειφθήσεται ἡ θυγάτηρ Σιὼν <u>ὡς</u> <u>*σκηνὴ ἐν ἀμπελῶνι*</u> καὶ <u>ὡς</u> <u>*ὀπωροφυλάκιον ἐν σικυηράτῳ*</u>, <u>ὡς</u> <u>*πόλις πολιορκουμένη·*</u>

8 Et *derelinquetur filia Sion* <u>ut</u> <u>*umbraculum in vinea*</u>, et <u>sicut</u> <u>*tugurium in cucumerario*</u>, et <u>sicut</u> <u>*civitas quae vastatur.*</u>

[daughter of Zion (deserted) ≈ a cottage in a vineyard ≈ a lodge in a garden of cucumbers ≈ a besieged city]

Isaiah 1.9 *We* should have been <u>as</u> <u>*Sodom*</u>, and *we* should have been <u>like unto</u> <u>*Gomorrah*</u>.

9 καὶ εἰ μὴ Κύριος σαβαὼθ ἐγκατέλιπεν ἡμῖν σπέρμα, <u>ὡς</u> <u>*Σόδομα*</u> ἂν ἐγενήθημεν καὶ <u>ὡς</u> <u>*Γόμορρα*</u> ἂν ὡμοιώθημεν.

9 Nisi Dominus exercituum reliquisset nobis semen, <u>quasi</u> <u>*Sodoma*</u> fuissemus, et <u>quasi</u> <u>*Gomorrha*</u> similes essemus.

[we ≈ Sodom and Gomorrah] (If the Lord had not left us a small remnant)

Isaiah 1.18 Come, now, and let us reason together, saith the Lord: though *your sins* be <u>as</u> <u>*scarlet*</u>, they shall be as *white* <u>as</u> <u>*snow*</u>; though they be <u>like</u> <u>*crimson*</u>, they shall be <u>as</u> <u>*wool*</u>.

18 καὶ δεῦτε διαλεχθῶμεν, λέγει Κύριος· καὶ ἐὰν ὦσιν αἱ ἁμαρτίαι ὑμῶν <u>ὡς</u> <u>*φοινικοῦν*</u>, <u>ὡς</u> <u>*χιόνα*</u> λευκανῶ, ἐὰν δὲ ὦσιν <u>ὡς</u> <u>*κόκκινον*</u>, <u>ὡς</u> <u>*ἔριον*</u> λευκανῶ.

18 Et venite, et arguite me, dicit Dominus. Si fuerint *peccata vestra* ut *coccinum*, quasi *nix dealbabuntur*; et si fuerint *rubra* quasi *vermiculus*, velut *lana alba* erunt

[your sins ≈ scarlet ≈ (white) as snow ≈ crimson ≈ (white) as wool]

Isaiah 1.30 For *ye [rulers of Sodom, people of Gemorrah (9)]* shall be as *an oak whose leaf fadeth,* and as *a garden that hath no water.* 31 And *the strong* shall be as *tow,* and *the maker of it* as a *spark,* and they shall both burn together, and none shall quench them.

30 ἔσονται [οἱ ἄνομοι καὶ οἱ ἁμαρτωλοὶ ἅμα] γὰρ ὡς τερέβινθος ἀποβεβληκυῖα τὰ φύλλα καὶ ὡς παράδεισος ὕδωρ μὴ ἔχων· 31 καὶ ἔσται ἡ ἰσχὺς αὐτῶν ὡς καλάμη στιππύου καὶ αἱ ἐργασίαι αὐτῶν ὡς σπινθῆρες πυρός, καὶ κατακαυθήσονται οἱ ἄνομοι καὶ οἱ ἁμαρτωλοὶ ἅμα, καὶ οὐκ ἔσται ὁ σβέσων.

30 cum *fueritis* velut *quercus defluentibus foliis,* et velut *hortus absque aqua.* 31 Et erit *fortitudo vestra* ut *favilla stuppae,* et *opus* vestrum quasi *scintilla,* et succendetur utrumque simul, et non erit qui extinguat.

[you (rulers of Sodom) ≈ an oak without leaves ≈ a garden without water] [the strong ≈ tow, its maker ≈ a spark]

Isaiah 3.18 In that day the Lord will take away the bravery of their tinkling ornaments about their feet, and their cauls, and t*heir round tires* like *the moon.* **Not a simile in the Latin or Greek text:** τοὺς μηνίσκους; *lunulas.*

[their round tires ≈ the moon]

Isaiah 5.24 Therefore as *the fire devoureth the stubble, and the flame consumeth the chaff,* **so** their *root* shall be as *rottenness,* and *their blossom* shall go up as *dust.*

24 διὰ τοῦτο ὃν τρόπον καυθήσεται καλάμη ὑπὸ ἄνθρακος πυρὸς καὶ συγκαυθήσεται ὑπὸ φλογὸς ἀνειμένης, ἡ ῥίζα αὐτῶν ὡς χνοῦς ἔσται καὶ τὸ ἄνθος αὐτῶν ὡς κονιορτὸς ἀναβήσεται·

24 Propter hoc, sicut *devorat stipulam lingua ignis,* et *calor flammae exurit,* **sic** *radix eorum* quasi *favilla* erit, et *germen eorum* ut *pulvis* ascendet.

[their root ≈ rottenness and their blossom ≈ dust ≈ fire > the stubble and the flame > the chaff]

Isaiah 5.28 Whose [the Lord's people against whom He is angry] arrows
are sharp, and all their bows bent, their *horses' hoofs* shall be counted
like *flint*: and t*heir wheels* like *a whirlwind*. 29 Their *roaring* shall be
like a *lion*, they shall roar like a young *lion* … 30 And in that day they
shall *roar* against them like *the roaring of the sea.*

28 ὧν τὰ βέλη ὀξέα ἐστὶ καὶ τὰ τόξα αὐτῶν ἐντεταμένα, οἱ πόδες τῶν ἵππων
αὐτῶν <u>ὡς</u> <u>*στερεὰ πέτρα*</u> ἐλογίσθησαν, *τροχοὶ τῶν ἁρμάτων αὐτῶν* <u>ὡς</u>
<u>*καταιγίς*</u>. 29 *ὁρμῶσιν* <u>ὡς</u> <u>*λέοντες*</u> καὶ παρέστηκαν <u>ὡς</u> <u>*σκύμνοι λέοντος*</u>.
… 30 καὶ *βοήσει* δι᾽ αὐτοὺς τῇ ἡμέρα ἐκείνη <u>ὡς</u> <u>*φωνὴ θαλάσσης*</u>
<u>*κυμαινούσης*</u>·

28 Sagittae ejus acutae, et omnes arcus ejus extenti. *Ungulae equorum*
ejus <u>ut</u> <u>*silex*</u>, et *rotae ejus* <u>quasi</u> <u>*impetus tempestatis*</u>. 29 *Rugitus ejus*
<u>ut</u> <u>*leonis*</u>; *rugiet* <u>ut</u> <u>*catuli leonum*</u>: … 30 Et *sonabit* super eum in
die illa <u>sicut</u> <u>*sonitus maris.*</u>

  [horses' hooves ≈ flint, chariot wheels ≈ a whirlwind, their roaring
    ≈ lion ≈ young lions … they (shall roar) ≈ the roaring of
    the sea]

Isaiah 6.13 As *a tail tree*, and as *an oak,* whose substance is in them, when
they cast their leaves: so *the holy seed* shall be the substance thereof.

13 καὶ ἔτι ἐπ᾽ αὐτῆς ἔστι τὸ ἐπιδέκατον, καὶ πάλιν ἔσται <u>*εἰς προνομὴν*</u> <u>ὡς</u>
<u>*τερέβινθος*</u> καὶ <u>ὡς</u> <u>*βάλανος*</u>, <u>*ὅταν ἐκπέσῃ ἐκ τῆς θήκης*</u> αὐτῆς.

13 Et adhuc in ea decimatio, et convertetur, et erit in ostensionem
<u>sicut</u> <u>*terebinthus*</u>, et <u>sicut</u> <u>*quercus quae expandit ramos suos*</u>; *semen
sanctum* erit id quod steterit in ea.   [the holy seed ≈ a tall tree
≈ an oak]

Isaiah 7.2 And it was told the house of David, saying, Syria is confederate
with Ephraim. And *his heart was moved*, and the heart of his people,
<u>as *the trees of the wood are moved with the wind*</u>.

2 καὶ ἀνηγγέλη εἰς τὸν οἶκον Δαυὶδ λέγων· συνεφώνησεν Ἀρὰμ πρὸς τὸν
Ἐφραίμ· καὶ *ἐξέστη ἡ ψυχὴ αὐτοῦ* καὶ ἡ ψυχὴ τοῦ λαοῦ αὐτοῦ, <u>ὃν
τρόπον *ἐν δρυμῷ ξύλον ὑπὸ πνεύματος σαλευθῇ*</u>.

2 Et *commotum est cor ejus*, et *cor populi ejus*, <u>sicut</u> moventur *ligna
silvarum a facie venti*.

  [his heart (moved) ≈ the trees (moved by the wind)]

Isaiah 9.18 For *wickedness* burneth <u>as</u> *<u>the fire:</u>* … and *they* shall mount up
<u>like</u> *<u>the lifting up of smoke</u>*. 19 … and t*he people* shall be <u>as</u> *<u>the fuel of</u>*
<u>the fire</u>.

    17 καὶ καυθήσεται <u>ὡς</u> <u>πῦρ</u> ἡ ἀνομία καὶ <u>ὡς</u> <u>ἄγρωσις ξηρὰ</u> βρωθήσεται
    ὑπὸ πυρός·(and shall be devoured by fire as dry grass) … 18 …
    καὶ ἔσται ὁ λαὸς <u>ὡς κατακεκαυμένος ὑπὸ πυρός·</u>

    18 *Succensa est* enim <u>quasi</u> <u>*ignis*</u> *impietas*: … et convolvetur superbia
    fumi. 19 … et erit *populus* <u>quasi</u> *<u>esca ignis.</u>*[wickedness (burns)
    ≈ fire; they (shall mount up) ≈ the lifting up of smoke; the people
    ≈ the fuel of the fire]

Isaiah 10.14 And my hand hath found <u>as</u> *<u>a nest</u>* *<u>the riches of the people</u>*: and
<u>as</u> *<u>one gathereth eggs that are left</u>*, have *I gathered all the earth*.

    14 καὶ σείσω πόλεις κατοικουμένας καὶ *τὴν οἰκουμένην ὅλην καταλήψομαι*
    τῇ χειρὶ <u>ὡς</u> <u>*νοσσιὰν*</u> καὶ <u>ὡς</u> <u>*καταλελειμμένα ᾠὰ*</u> ἀρῶ, καὶ οὐκ ἔστιν ὃς
    διαφεύξεταί με ἢ ἀντείπῃ μοι.

    14 Et invenit <u>quasi</u> <u>*nidum*</u> manus mea *fortitudinem populorum*; et
    <u>sicut</u> <u>*colliguntur ova*</u> quae derelicta sunt, **sic** *universam terram*
    ego *congregavi*.
    [the riches of the people ≈ a nest; I have gathered all the earth ≈
      one gathers eggs left behind]

Isaiah 10.15 Shall the axe boast itself against him that heweth therewith?
or *shall the saw magnify itself* against him that shaketh it? <u>as if</u> *the rod*
should shake itself against them that lift it up, or <u>as if</u> *<u>the staff should lift</u>*
<u>up itself</u>, <u>as if</u> i*t <u>were no wood.</u>*

    15 μὴ δοξασθήσεται ἀξίνη ἄνευ τοῦ κόπτοντος ἐν αὐτῇ; ἢ ὑψωθήσεται
    πρίων ἄνευ τοῦ ἕλκοντος αὐτόν; <u>ὡσαύτως *ἐάν τις ἄρῃ ῥάβδον ἢ ξύλον.*</u>

    15 Numquid gloriabitur securis contra eum qui secat in ea? aut
    exaltabitur serra contra eum a quo trahitur? <u>Quomodo si</u>
    elevetur virga contra elevantem se, et exaltetur baculus, qui utique
    lignum est.
    [an axe or a saw > the user ≈ a rod or staff > one (who lifts it)]

Isaiah 10.16 Therefore shall the Lord … under his glory *he shall kindle a burning* <u>like</u> <u>*the burning of a fire*</u>.

16 καὶ εἰς τὴν σὴν δόξαν πῦρ καιόμενον καυθήσεται.

10 Propter hoc mittet Dominator, Dominus exercituum, … et subtus *gloriam ejus succensa ardebit* <u>quasi</u> <u>*combustio ignis.*</u>[the Lord > a burning ≈ a fire]

Isaiah 10.17 And the *light of Israel* shall be <u>for</u> *<u>a fire</u>*, and h*is Holy One* <u>for</u> a *<u>flame</u>*: and it shall burn and devour his thorns and his briers in one day.

17 καὶ ἔσται τὸ φῶς τοῦ 'Ισραὴλ <u>εἰς</u> <u>πῦρ</u> καὶ ἁγιάσει αὐτὸν ἐν πυρὶ καιομένῳ καὶ φάγεται <u>ὡσεὶ</u> <u>χόρτον</u> τὴν ὕλην.

17 Et erit lumen Israel in igne, et Sanctus ejus in flamma;
[the light of Israel ≈ a fire; his Holy One ≈ a flame]

Isaiah 10.22 For though *thy people Israel* be <u>as</u> *<u>the sand of the sea</u>* …

22 καὶ ἐὰν γένηται ὁ λαὸς 'Ισραὴλ <u>ὡς</u> <u>ἡ ἄμμος τῆς θαλάσσης</u>,·

22 Si enim fuerit *populus tuus, Israel,* <u>quasi</u> *<u>arena maris</u>,* …
[the people of Israel ≈ the sand of the sea]

Isaiah 13.8 And they shall be afraid: pangs and sorrows shall shall take hold of them; *they shall be in pain* <u>as a woman that travaileth</u>: they shall be amazed one at another; *their faces* shall be <u>as</u> *<u>flames</u>*.

8 καὶ ταραχθήσονται οἱ πρέσβεις καὶ ὠδίνες αὐτοὺς ἕξουσιν, <u>ὡς</u> <u>γυναικὸς</u> <u>τικτούσης</u>· καὶ συμφοράσουσιν ἕτερος πρὸς τὸν ἕτερον καὶ ἐκστήσονται καὶ τὸ πρόσωπον αὐτῶν <u>ὡς</u> <u>φλὸξ</u> μεταβαλοῦσιν.

8 Torsiones et dolores tenebunt; <u>quasi</u> *<u>parturiens</u> dolebunt*: unusquisque ad proximum suum stupebit, *facies* <u>combustae</u> *vultus eorum*.
[elders (seized by pangs) ≈ woman in labor; their faces ≈ flames]

Isaiah 13.12 I will make a man <u>more precious than</u> fine *<u>gold</u>*; even a *man* than *<u>the golden wedge of Ophir</u>*.

12 καὶ ἔσονται οἱ καταλελειμμένοι <u>ἔντιμοι</u> <u>μᾶλλον ἢ</u> <u>τὸ χρυσίον τὸ ἄπυρον</u>, καὶ ὁ ἄνθρωπος <u>μᾶλλον ἔντιμος</u> ἔσται <u>ἢ</u> <u>ὁ λίθος ὁ ἐκ Σουφίρ</u>. (they that are left shall be more precious than gold tried in the fire)

12 <u>Pretiosior</u> erit *vir <u>auro</u>*, et *homo <u>mundo obrizo</u>*.
[a man (more precious) ≈ fine gold; a man (more precious) ≈ the golden wedge of Ophir]

Isaiah 13.14 And *it shall be* <u>as</u> *the chased roe*, and <u>as</u> *a sheep that no man taketh up*.

    14 καὶ ἔσονται οἱ καταλελειμμένοι <u>ὡς</u> <u>δορκάδιον φεῦγον καὶ ὡς πρόβατον</u> <u>πλανώμενον</u>, καὶ οὐκ ἔσται ὁ συνάγων, (And *they that are left* shall be <u>as</u> *a fleeing fawn, and as a stray sheep,* and there shall be none to gather [them].)

    14 Et erit <u>quasi</u> *damula fugiens*, et <u>quasi</u> *ovis*, et non erit qui congreget.

    [those left behind (Greek) ≈ a chased roe ≈ stray sheep]

Isaiah 14.19 But *thou art cast out* of thy grave <u>like</u> *an abominable branch*, and <u>as</u> *the raiment of those that are slain* ... <u>as</u> *a carcase trodden under feet*.

    19 σὺ δὲ ριφήσῃ ἐν τοῖς ὄρεσιν <u>ὡς</u> <u>νεκρὸς ἐβδελυγμένος</u> μετὰ πολλῶν τεθνηκότων ἐκκεκεντημένων μαχαίραις,

    19 tu autem *projectus es de sepulchro tuo*, <u>quasi</u> *stirps inutilis pollutus*, et obvolutus cum his qui interfecti sunt gladio, et descenderunt ad fundamenta laci, <u>quasi</u> *cadaver putridum*.

    [you (cast away) ≈ an abominable branch ≈ the raiment of the slain ≈ a carcase stepped on]

Isaiah 16.2 For it shall be, that, <u>as</u> *a wandering bird cast out of the nest*, **so** the *daughters of Moab* shall be at the fords of Arnon.

    2 ἔσῃ γὰρ <u>ὡς</u> πετεινοῦ ἀνιπταμένου <u>νεοσσὸς ἀφῃρημένος</u>, θύγατερ Μωάβ.

    1 Et erit: <u>sicut</u> *avis fugiens*, et *pulli de nido avolantes*, **sic** erunt *filiae Moab in transcensu Arnon*.

    [the daughters of Moab ≈ a wandering bird cast out of the nest]

Isaiah 16.11 Wherefore *my bowels* shall sound <u>like</u> *an harp for Moab*.

    11 διὰ τοῦτο ἡ κοιλία μου ἐπὶ Μωὰβ <u>ὡς</u> <u>κιθάρα</u> ἠχήσει, καὶ τὰ ἐντός μου <u>ὡσεὶ τεῖχος</u>, ὃ ἐνεκαίνισας.

    11 Super hoc *venter meus* ad Moab <u>quasi</u> *cithara* sonabit, et viscera mea ad murum cocti lateris.

    [my bowels (sound) ≈ a harp for Moab; (my inward parts ≈ a wall)]

Isaiah 17.5 And *it shall be* <u>as when</u> *the harvestman gathereth the corn* and *reapeth the ears with his arm;* and i*t shall be* <u>as</u> *he that gathereth ears in the valley of Rephaim.* 6 Yet *gleaning grapes shall be left in it,* <u>as the</u>

shaking of an olive tree, two or three berries in the top of the upper-most bought …

5 καὶ ἔσται ὃν τρόπον ἐάν <u>τις συναγάγῃ ἀμητὸν ἑστηκότα καὶ σπέρμα</u> <u>σταχύων ἐν τῷ βραχίονι αὐτοῦ ἀμήσῃ</u>, καὶ ἔσται ὃν τρόπον ἐάν <u>τις</u> <u>συναγάγῃ στάχυν ἐν φάραγγι στερεᾷ</u> 6 καὶ καταλειφθῇ ἐν αὐτῇ καλάμη, ἢ <u>ὡς ῥῶγες ἐλαίας δύο ἢ τρεῖς</u> ἐπ᾽ ἄκρου μετεώρου, ἢ τέσσαρες ἢ πέντε ἐπὶ τῶν κλάδων αὐτῶν καταλειφθῇ·

5 Et *erit* <u>sicut</u> *congregans in messe quod restiterit*, et brachium ejus spicas leget; et *erit* <u>sicut</u> *quaerens spicas in valle Raphaim.* 6 Et relinquetur in eo <u>sicut</u> *racemus* et <u>sicut</u> *excussio oleae duarum vel* *trium olivarum in summitate rami*, sive quatuor aut quinque in cacuminibus ejus fructus ejus, dicit Dominus Deus Israel.

[it shall be ≈ the harvestman gathers the corn and reaps the ears]
[gleaning grapes will be left ≈ the shaking of an olive tree]

Isaiah 17.9 In that day shall *his strong cities* be <u>as</u> *a forsaken bough*, and an *uppermost branch.*

9 τῇ ἡμέρᾳ ἐκείνῃ ἔσονται αἱ πόλεις σου *ἐγκαταλελειμμέναι*, <u>ὃν τρόπον</u> <u>κατέλιπον οἱ Ἀμορραῖοι καὶ οἱ Εὐαῖοι</u> ἀπὸ προσώπου τῶν υἱῶν Ἰσραήλ, καὶ ἔσονται ἔρημοι.

9 In die illa erunt *civitates fortitudinis ejus derelictae* <u>sicut aratra</u>, et segetes quae derelictae sunt a facie filiorum Israel; (In that day his strong cities shall be forsaken, as the ploughs, and the corn that were left before the face of the children of Israel)

[his strong cities ≈ a forsaken bough and an uppermost branch]

Isaiah 17.12 Woe to the multitude of many people, which make *a noise* <u>like</u> *the noise of the seas*, and to the rushing of nations, that make a *rushing* <u>like</u> *the rushing of mighty waters.* 13 *The nations shall rush* <u>like</u> <u>the rushing of many waters</u>: *but God shall rebuke them, and they shall flee far off, and shall be chased* <u>as the chaff of the mountains before the</u> <u>wind</u>, *and* <u>like a rolling thing before the whirlwind.</u>

12 Οὐαὶ πλῆθος ἐθνῶν πολλῶν· <u>ὡς θάλασσα κυμαίνουσα</u> **οὕτω** ταραχθήσεσθε, καὶ νῶτος ἐθνῶν πολλῶν <u>ὡς ὕδωρ</u> ἠχήσει. 13 <u>ὡς ὕδωρ πολὺ</u> ἔθνη πολλά, <u>ὡς ὕδατος πολλοῦ βία καταφερομένου·</u> καὶ ἀποσκορακιεῖ αὐτὸν καὶ πόρρω αὐτὸν διώξεται <u>ὡς χνοῦν ἀχύρου</u> λικμώντων ἀπέναντι ἀνέμου καὶ <u>ὡς κονιορτὸν τροχοῦ καταιγὶς φέρουσα.</u>

12 Vae multitudini populorum multorum, ut multitudo maris
sonantis; et tumultus turbarum, sicut *sonitus aquarum multarum.*
13 Sonabunt populi sicut *sonitus aquarum inundantium,* et
increpabit eum, et fugiet procul; et *rapietur* sicut *pulvis montium
a facie venti,* et sicut *turbo coram tempestate.*

[noise ≈ the noise of the seas; rushing ≈ the rushing of mighty
waters; *nations shall rush* ≈ *t*he rushing of many waters; *they
shall be chased* ≈ the chaff of the mountains before the wind
≈ a rolling thing before the whilrwind]

Isaiah 18.4 *I will consider* in my dwelling place like *a clear heat upon herbs,*
and like *a cloud of dew in the heat of harvest.*

4 διότι οὕτως εἶπέ μοι Κύριος· ἀσφάλεια ἔσται ἐν τῇ ἐμῇ πόλει ὡς φῶς
καύματος μεσημβρίας, καὶ ὡς νεφέλη δρόσου ἡμέρας ἀμήτου ἔσται.

4 Quiescam et considerabo in loco meo, sicut *meridiana lux clara est,*
et sicut *nubes roris in die messis.*

[I ≈ a clear heat upon herbs ≈ a cloud of dew in the heat of harvest]

Isaiah 19.14 The Lord hath mingled a perverse spirit in the midst
thereof: and they have *caused Egypt to err* in every work thereof as *a
drunken man staggereth in his vomit.*

14 Κύριος γὰρ ἐκέρασεν αὐτοῖς πνεῦμα πλανήσεως, καὶ ἐπλάνησαν
Αἴγυπτον ἐν πᾶσι τοῖς ἔργοις αὐτῶν, ὡς πλανᾶται ὁ μεθύων καὶ ὁ
ἐμῶν ἅμα.

14 Dominus miscuit in medio ejus spiritum vertiginis; et *errare fecerunt
Aegyptum in omni opere suo,* sicut *errat ebrius et vomens.*

[Egypt errs ≈ a drunk staggering in his vomit]

Isaiah 19.16 In that day shall *Egypt* be like unto *women.*

16 Τῇ δὲ ἡμέρᾳ ἐκείνῃ ἔσονται οἱ Αἰγύπτιοι ὡς γυναῖκες.

16 In die illa erit *Aegyptus* quasi *mulieres*;

[Egyptians ≈ women (in fear)]

Isaiah 21.1 As *whirlwinds in the south pass through*: **so** *it cometh from the
desert*, from a terrible land. 2 *A grievous vision is declared unto me.*

1 ΩΣ καταιγὶς δι᾽ ἐρήμου διέλθοι ἐξ ἐρήμου ἐρχομένη ἐκ γῆς, φοβερὸν 2 τὸ
ὅραμα καὶ σκληρὸν ἀνηγγέλη μοι.

1 Sicut *turbines ab africo veniunt, de deserto venit, de terra horribili.* 2
Visio dura nuntiata est mihi.

[a fearful vision ≈ a whirlwind coming from the desert]

Isaiah 21.3 Therefore are my loins filled with pains: *pangs have taken hold upon me* <u>as</u> *the pangs of a woman that travaileth.*

3 διὰ τοῦτο ἐνεπλήσθη ἡ ὀσφύς μου ἐκλύσεως, καὶ ὠδῖνες ἔλαβόν με <u>ὡς</u> <u>τὴν τίκτουσαν.</u>

3 Propterea repleti sunt lumbi mei dolore; *angustia possedit me* <u>sicut</u> <u>*angustia parturientis.*</u>

[me (in pain) ≈ a woman in labor]

Isaiah 22.18 *He [the Lord] will surely violently turn and toss thee,* <u>like</u> <u>*a ball*</u> into a large country: there shalt thou die.

18 καὶ [Κύριος] ῥίψει σε εἰς χώραν μεγάλην καὶ ἀμέτρητον, καὶ ἐκεῖ ἀποθανῇ·

18 Coronas [Dominus] cornonabit te tribulatione; <u>quasi *pilam*</u> mittet te in terram latam et spatiosam; ibi morieris.

[the Lord will toss you ≈ a ball]

Isaiah 23.15 And it shall come to pass in that day, that Tyre shall be forgotten … after the end of seventy years shall *Tyre sing* <u>as</u> an *harlot.*

15 καὶ ἔσται ἐν τῇ ἡμέρᾳ ἐκείνῃ καταλειφθήσεται Τύρος … καὶ ἔσται μετὰ ἑβδομήκοντα ἔτη, ἔσται *Τύρος* <u>ὡς</u> <u>ᾆσμα πόρνης.</u>

15 Et erit in die illa: in oblivione eris, o Tyre! … post septuaginta autem annos erit *Tyro* <u>quasi</u> <u>*canticum meretricis*</u>:

[Tyre ≈ (shall sing) a harlot]

Isaiah 24.13 When thus it shall be in the midst of the land among the people, there shall be <u>as</u> *the shaking of an olive tree,* and <u>as</u> *the gleaning grapes when the vintage is done.*

13 ταῦτα πάντα ἔσται ἐν τῇ γῇ ἐν μέσῳ τῶν ἐθνῶν, <u>ὃν τρόπον</u> <u>ἐάν</u> τις <u>καλαμήσηται ἐλαίαν,</u> **οὕτως** καλαμήσονται αὐτούς, καὶ ἐὰν παύσηται ὁ τρύγητος.

13 Quia haec erunt in medio terrae in medio populorum, *quomodo si paucae olivae quae remanserunt excutiantur ex olea* et *racemi, cum fuerit finita vindemia.*

[(the desolate city) ≈ the shaking of an olive tree ≈ gleaning grapes after the vintage]

Isaiah 24.20 The <u>earth</u> shall reel to and fro <u>like</u> *a drunkard,* and shall be removed <u>like</u> *a cottage* …

20 20 ἔκλινεν ὡς *ὁ μεθύων καὶ κραιπαλῶν*, καὶ σεισθήσεται ὡς
ὀπωροφυλάκιον ἡ γῆ.

20 agitatione agitabitur *terra* sicut *ebrius*, et auferetur quasi
tabernaculum unius noctis;
[the earth (shall reel) ≈ a drunkard; the earth (shall be removed)
≈ a cottage]

Isaiah 24.22 And *they* [*earthly kings*] shall be gathered together as *pris-*
oners are gathered in the pit …

22 καὶ συνάξουσι καὶ ἀποκλείσουσιν εἰς ὀχύρωμα καὶ εἰς δεσμωτήριον.

22 et congregabuntur in congregatione unius fascis in lacum, et
claudentur ibi in carcere, et post multos dies visitabuntur.
[earthly kings (gathered together) ≈ prisoners]
No simile in the Greek and Latin.

Isaiah 26.17 Like as *a woman with child, that draweth near the time of her*
delivery, is in pain … **so** *have we been in thy sight, O Lord.*.

17 καὶ **ὡς** *ἡ ὠδίνουσα ἐγγίζει τοῦ τεκεῖν* καὶ ἐπὶ τῇ ὠδῖνι αὐτῆς ἐκέκραξεν,
οὕτως ἐγενήθημεν τῷ ἀγαπητῷ σου διὰ τὸν φόβον σου, Κύριε.

17 Sicut *quae concipit, cum appropinquaverit ad partum*, dolens clamat
in doloribus suis, **sic** *facti sumus a facie tua, Domine.*
[we (in your sight, O Lord) ≈ a woman about to give birth]

Isaiah 26.18 We have been with child … we have as it were brought forth
wind; we have not wrought any deliverance in the earth.

18 ἐν γαστρὶ ἐλάβομεν … πνεῦμα σωτηρίας σου ἐποιήσαμεν ἐπὶ
τῆς γῆς.

18 Concepimus, et quasi *parturivimus*, et *peperimus spiritum*. Salutes
non fecimus in terra;
[deliverance (of a child) ≈ wind]

Isaiah 28.2 Behold, *the Lord hath a mighty and strong one,* which as *a*
tempest of hail and a destroying storm as *a flood of mighty waters*
overflowing, shall cast down to earth with the hand as a great body of
water sweeping away the soil, *he* shall make rest for the land.

2 ἰδοὺ ἰσχυρὸν καὶ σκληρὸν ὁ θυμὸς Κυρίου *ὡς χάλαζα καταφερομένη οὐκ*
ἔχουσα σκέπην, βίᾳ καταφερομένη· ὡς ὕδατος πολὺ πλῆθος σῦρον χώραν
τῇ γῇ ποιήσει ἀνάπαυσιν ταῖς χερσί.

2 Ecce validus et fortis Dominus <u>sicut</u> *impetus grandinis*; *turbo confringens*, <u>sicut</u> *impetus aquarum multarum inundantium* et emissarum super terram spatiosam.

[the Lord's anger ≈ a tempest of hail ≈ a flood of mighty water]

Isaiah 29.4 And thou shalt be brought down, and shall speak out of the ground ... and *thy voice* shall be <u>as</u> *of one that hath a familiar spirit*

4 καὶ ταπεινωθήσονται εἰς τὴν γῆν οἱ λόγοι σου, καὶ εἰς τὴν γῆν οἱ λόγοι σου δύσονται· καὶ ἔσται <u>ὡς οἱ φωνοῦντες ἐκ τῆς γῆς</u> ἡ φωνή σου, καὶ πρὸς τὸ ἔδαφος ἡ φωνή σου ἀσθενήσει.

4 Humiliaberis, de terra loqueris, ... et erit <u>quasi</u> *pythonis de terra vox tua*, et de humo eloquium tuum mussitabit.

[your voice ≈ a familiar spirit/a python]

Isaiah 29.5 Moreover *the multitude of thy strangers* shall be <u>like</u> *small dust,* and the *multitude of the terrible ones* shall be <u>as</u> *chaff that passeth away*.

5 καὶ ἔσται <u>ὡς κονιορτὸς ἀπὸ τροχοῦ</u> ὁ πλοῦτος τῶν ἀσεβῶν καὶ <u>ὡς χνοῦς φερόμενος</u> τὸ πλῆθος τῶν καταδυναστευόντων σε, καὶ ἔσται <u>ὡς στιγμὴ παραχρῆμα.</u>

5 Et erit <u>sicut</u> *pulvis tenuis* multitudo ventilantium te, et <u>sicut</u> *favilla pertransiens multitudo eorum* qui contra te praevaluerunt;   [the strangers ≈ small dust ≈ chaff]

Isaiah 29.7 And *the multitude of all the nations that fight against Ariel* ... shall be <u>as</u> *a dream of a night vision.* 8 *It shall even be* <u>as</u> *when an hungry man dreameth* ... *or* <u>as</u> *when a thirsty man dreameth* ... **so** shall *the multitude of all the nations be,* that fight against mount Zion.

7 καὶ ἔσται <u>ὡς ὁ ἐνυπνιαζόμενος καθ' ὕπνους νυκτὸς</u> ὁ πλοῦτος ἁπάντων τῶν ἐθνῶν, ὅσοι ἐπεστράτευσαν ἐπὶ Ἀριήλ, καὶ πάντες οἱ στρατευσάμενοι ἐπὶ Ἰερουσαλὴμ καὶ πάντες οἱ συνηγμένοι ἐπ' αὐτὴν καὶ θλίβοντες αὐτήν. 8 καὶ ἔσονται <u>ὡς οἱ ἐν τῷ ὕπνῳ πίνοντες καὶ ἔσθοντες,</u> καὶ ἐξαναστάντων μάταιον αὐτῶν τὸ ἐνύπνιον, καὶ <u>ὃν τρόπον ἐνυπνιάζεται ὁ διψῶν ὡς πίνων καὶ ἐξαναστὰς ἔτι διψᾷ,</u> ἡ δὲ ψυχὴ αὐτοῦ εἰς κενὸν ἤλπισεν, **οὕτως** ἔσται ὁ πλοῦτος τῶν ἐθνῶν πάντων, ὅσοι ἐπεστράτευσαν ἐπὶ τὸ ὄρος Σιών.

7 Et erit sicut somnium visionis nocturnae *multitudo omnium gentium quae dimicaverunt còntra Ariel,* et omnes qui militaverunt,

et obsederunt, et praevaluerunt adversus eam. [8] Et sicut *somniat esuriens*, et comedit, cum autem fuerit expergefactus, vacua est anima ejus; et sicut somniat sitiens et bibit, et postquam fuerit expergefactus, lassus adhuc sitit, et anima ejus vacua est: **sic** erit *multitudo omnium gentium quae dimicaverunt contra montem Sion*.
[*the multitude of nations* ≈ *a dream* ≈ a hungry man who dreams ≈ a thirsty man dreams]

Isaiah 29.11 And *the vision of all* is become unto you <u>as</u> <u>*the words of a book that is sealed.*</u>

11 καὶ ἔσονται ὑμῖν τὰ <u>*ῥήματα πάντα ταῦτα*</u> <u>ὡς</u> <u>*οἱ λόγοι τοῦ βιβλίου τοῦ ἐσφραγισμένου τούτου.*</u>

11 Et erit vobis *visio omnium* <u>sicut</u> <u>*verba libri signati*</u>,
[the vision of all ≈ the words of a sealed book]

Isaiah 30.17 One thousand shall flee at the rebuke of one; at the rebuke of five shall ye flee: <u>till ye be left as a beacon upon the top of a mountain,</u> and <u>as an ensign on an hill.</u>

17 χίλιοι διὰ φωνὴν ἑνὸς φεύξονται, καὶ διὰ φωνὴν πέντε φεύξονται πολλοί, <u>ἕως ἂν καταλειφθῆτε ὡς ἱστὸς ἐπ᾽ ὄρους, καὶ ὡς σημαίαν φέρων ἐπὶ βουνοῦ.</u>

17 *Mille homines a facie terroris unius*; et a facie terroris quinque fugietis, donec relinquamini <u>quasi *malus navis in vertice montis*</u>, et <u>quasi *signum super collem*.</u> hill]/
[many fleeing ≈ a beacon on a mountain ≈ an ensign on a /

Isaiah 30.22 Ye shall defile also the covering of thy graven images of silver ... thou shalt cast *them* away <u>as</u> <u>*a menstruous cloth.*</u>

22 καὶ ἐξαρεῖς *τὰ εἴδωλα τὰ περιηργυρωμένα καὶ τὰ περικεχρυσωμένα*, λεπτὰ ποιήσεις καὶ λικμήσεις <u>ὡς *ὕδωρ ἀποκαθημένης*</u> καὶ <u>ὡς *κόπρον*</u> ὥσεις *αὐτά*.

22 Et contaminabis laminas sculptilium argenti tui, ... et disperges *ea* <u>sicut *immunditiam menstruatae*.</u>
[them (the covering of graven images) ≈ a menstruous cloth]

Isaiah 30.27 Behold, the name of the LORD cometh from far, burning with his anger ... *his tongue* <u>as</u> <u>*a devouring fire.*</u>

27 Ἰδοὺ τὸ ὄνομα Κυρίου ἔρχεται διὰ χρόνου πολλοῦ, καιόμενος ὁ θυμός, ... καὶ ἡ ὀργὴ τοῦ θυμοῦ <u>ὡς *πῦρ*</u> ἔδεται.

27 Ecce nomen Domini venit de longinquo, ardens furor ejus, ...
et *lingua ejus* quasi *ignis devorans*.
[the Lord's tongue ≈ a devouring fire]

Isaiah 30.28 And *his breath*, as *an overflowing stream*, shall reach to
*c/ the midst of the neck, to sift the nations with *the sieve of vanity*:

28 καὶ τὸ πνεῦμα αὐτοῦ ὡς ὕδωρ ἐν φάραγγι σῦρον ἥξει ἕως τοῦ τραχήλου
καὶ διαιρεθήσεται τοῦ ταράξαι ἔθνη ματαίᾳ.

28 Spiritus ejus velut torrens inundans *usque ad medium colli, ad
perdendas gentes in nihilum, et* frenum *erroris quod erat in
maxillis populorum.*
[his breath ≈ an overflowing stream; vanity ≈ a sieve]

Isaiah 30.29 *Ye shall have a song*, as *in the night when a holy solemnity is
kept*; and *gladness of heart*, as *when one goeth with a pipe to come into
the mountain of the LORD*.

29 μὴ διαπαντὸς δεῖ ὑμᾶς εὐφραίνεσθαι καὶ εἰσπορεύεσθαι εἰς τὰ ἅγιά μου
διαπαντὸς ὡσεὶ ἑορτάζοντας καὶ ὡσεὶ εὐφραινομένους εἰσελθεῖν μετὰ
αὐλοῦ εἰς τὸ ὄρος Κυρίου;

29 *Canticum erit vobis* sicut *nox sanctificatae solemnitatis*, et *laetitia
cordis* sicut *qui pergit cum tibia, ut intret in montem Domini*.
[a song ≈ when a holy solemnity is kept; gladness of heart ≈ when
one goes with a pipe to the mountain of the Lord]

Isaiah 30.33 The *breath of the Lord*, like *a stream of brimstone*, doth kindle
it [Tophet].

33 ὁ θυμὸς Κυρίου ὡς φάραγξ ὑπὸ θείου καιομένη.

33 Nutrimenta ejus, ignis et ligna multa; *flatus Domini* sicut *torrens
sulphuris* succendens eam.
[the Lord's breath ≈ a stream of brimstone]

Isaiah 31.4 For thus hath the Lord spoken unto me, Like as the *lion* and
the *young lion* roaring on his prey, when a multitude of shepherds is
called forth against him ... 5 As *birds flying*, **so** will the *Lord of hosts
defend Jerusalem*.

4 ὅτι οὕτως εἶπέ μοι Κύριος· ὃν τρόπον ἐὰν βοήσῃ ὁ λέων ἢ ὁ σκύμνος ἐπὶ
τῇ θύρᾳ, ἣ ἔλαβε, καὶ κεκράξῃ ἐπ᾽ αὐτῇ, ἕως ἂν ἐμπλησθῇ τὰ ὄρη
τῆς φωνῆς αὐτοῦ, ... 5 ὡς ὄρνεα πετόμενα, **οὕτως** ὑπερασπιεῖ Κύριος
σαβαὼθ ὑπὲρ Ἱερουσαλήμ.

4 Quia haec dicit Dominus ad me: Quomodo si _rugiat leo_ et _catulus leonis_
super praedam suam; et cum occurrerit ei multitudo pastorum,
a voce eorum non formidabit, ... 5 Sicut _aves volantes_, **sic** _proteget
Dominus exercituum Jerusalem._

> [the Lord shall defend Jerusalem ≈ a lion roaring or a lion's whelp
> over a prey ≈ birds flying]

Isaiah 32.2 And _a man shall be_ as _an hiding place from the wind_, and _a
covert from the tempest_; as _rivers of water in a dry place_, as _the shadow
of a great rock in a weary land._

> 2 καὶ ἔσται ὁ ἄνθρωπος κρύπτων τοὺς λόγους αὐτοῦ καὶ κρυβήσεται ὡς
> ἀφ᾽ ὕδατος φερομένου· καὶ φανήσεται ἐν Σιὼν ὡς ποταμὸς φερόμενος
> ἔνδοξος ἐν γῇ διψώσῃ.

> 2 Et erit _vir_ sicut _qui absconditur a vento_, et _celat se a tempestate_; sicut
> _rivi aquarum in siti_, et _umbra petrae prominentis in terra deserta._

> [a man ≈ a hiding place from the wind ≈ a covert from the tempest
> ≈ rivers of water in a dry land ≈ the shadow of a great rock]

Isaiah 32.14 The _forts and towers_ shall be for _dens_ for ever, a _joy of wild
asses_, _a pasture of flocks._

> 14 καὶ ἔσονται αἱ κῶμαι σπήλαια ἕως τοῦ αἰῶνος, εὐφροσύνη ὄνων ἀγρίων,
> βοσκήματα ποιμένων,

> 14 tenebrae et palpatio factae sunt super speluncas usque in aeternum;
> gaudium onagrorum, pascua gregum.

> [forts and towers ≈ dens + a joy of wild asses + a pasture of flocks]
> – In Greek and Latin versions the second part consists of predi-
> cate similes.

Isaiah 33.4 And _your spoil shall be gathered_ like _the gathering of the
caterpiller:_ as _the running to and fro of locusts_ shall he run upon them.

> 4 νῦν δὲ συναχθήσεται τὰ σκῦλα ὑμῶν μικροῦ καὶ μεγάλου· ὃν τρόπον ἐάν
> τις συναγάγῃ ἀκρίδας, **οὕτως** ἐμπαίξουσιν ὑμῖν.

> 4 Et _congregabuntur spolia vestra_ sicut _colligitur bruchus_, velut _cum
> fossae plenae fuerint de eo._

> [your spoil gathered ≈ the gathering of the caterpiller; [the Lord]
> the running to and fro of locusts]

Isaiah 33.9 *Sharon* is <u>like</u> *<u>a wilderness</u>.*

   9 <u>ἕλη ἐγένετο</u> ὁ Σάρων·

   9 et factus est *Saron* <u>sicut</u> *<u>desertum.</u>*

   [Sharon ≈ a wilderness]

Isaiah 33.11 Ye shall conceive chaff, ye shall bring forth stubble: *your breath* <u>as</u> *<u>fire</u>* shall devour you.

   11 νῦν ὄψεσθε, νῦν αἰσθηθήσεσθε· ματαία ἔσται ἡ ἰσχὺς τοῦ πνεύματος ὑμῶν, πῦρ κατέδεται ὑμᾶς.

   11 Concipietis ardorem, parietis stipulam; *spiritus vester* <u>ut</u> *<u>ignis</u>* vorabit vos.   [your breath ≈ fire]

Isaiah 33.12 And the *people* shall be <u>as</u> *<u>the burnings of lime:</u>* <u>as</u> *<u>thorns cut up</u>* shall they be burned in the fire.

   12 καὶ ἔσονται ἔθνη κατακεκαυμένα <u>ὡς ἄκανθα ἐν ἀγρῷ</u> ἐρριμμένη καὶ κατακεκαυμένη.

   12 Et erunt *populi* <u>quasi</u> *<u>de incendio cinis</u>*; *<u>spinae congregatae</u>* igni comburentur.

   [the people ≈ burnings of lime ≈ thorns cutup]

Isaiah 34.4 And all the host of heaven shall be dissolved, and *the heavens* shall *be rolled together* <u>as</u> *<u>a scroll</u>*: and *all their host shall fall down,* <u>as</u> the *<u>leaf falleth off from the vine,</u>* and as *<u>a falling fig from the fig tree</u>*.

   4 καὶ τακήσονται πᾶσαι αἱ δυνάμεις τῶν οὐρανῶν, καὶ ἑλιγήσεται ὁ οὐρανὸς <u>ὡς βιβλίον</u>, καὶ πάντα τὰ ἄστρα πεσεῖται <u>ὡς φύλλα ἐξ ἀμπέλου</u> καὶ <u>ὡς πίπτει φύλλα ἀπὸ συκῆς</u>.

   4 Et tabescet omnis militia caelorum, et complicabuntur <u>sicut</u> *<u>liber caeli</u>* : et omnis militia eorum defluet, <u>sicut</u> defluit *<u>folium de vinea</u>* et de ficu.

   [the heavens (rolled up) ≈ a scroll; the host/stars falling ≈ a leaf from a vine ≈ a falling fig]

Isaiah 35.1 The wilderness and the solitary place shall be glad for them: and the *desert* shall rejoice, and *blossom* <u>as</u> *<u>the rose</u>.*

   1 ΕΥΦΡΑΝΘΗΤΙ, ἔρημος διψῶσα, ἀγαλλιάσθω ἔρημος καὶ ἀνθήτω <u>ὡς κρίνον</u>,

   1 Laetabitur deserta et invia, et exsultabit *solitudo*, et *florebit* <u>quasi lilium</u>.

   [the desert (rejoicing and blossoming) ≈ a rose]

Isaiah 35.6 Then* shall *the lame man leap* as an <u>*hart*</u>, and the tongue of the dumb sing; for in the wilderness shall waters break out, and streams in the desert. (*35.4 when 'your God will come with vengeance')

6 τότε ἀλεῖται <u>ὡς</u> <u>*ἔλαφος*</u> ὁ χωλός, τρανὴ δὲ ἔσται γλῶσσα μογιλάλων, ὅτι ἐρράγη ἐν τῇ ἐρήμῳ ὕδωρ καὶ φάραγξ ἐν γῇ διψώσῃ·

6 tunc saliet <u>sicut</u> <u>*cervus*</u> *claudus,* et aperta erit lingua mutorum: quia scissae sunt in deserto aquae, et torrentes in solitudine; [a lame man (leaping) ≈ an hart]

Isaiah 37.27 Therefore *their inhabitants* were of small power, they were dismayed and confounded: they were <u>as</u> <u>*the grass*</u> of the field, and <u>as *the green herb,*</u> as <u>*the grass on the housetops,*</u> and as <u>*corn blasted before it be grown up.*</u>

27 ἀνῆκα τὰς χεῖρας, καὶ ἐξηράνθησαν καὶ ἐγένοντο <u>ὡς *χόρτος ξηρὸς*</u> ἐπὶ δωμάτων καὶ <u>ὡς *ἄγρωστις.*</u>

27 *Habitatores* earum breviata manu contremuerunt, et confusi sunt. Facti sunt <u>sicut *foenum agri*</u>, et <u>*gramen pascuae*</u>, et <u>*herba tectorum*</u>, quae exaruit antequam maturesceret.

[they (defensed cities) ≈ (withered) grass of the field ≈ the green herb ≈ grass on the housetops ≈ corn blasted before it is grown]

Isaiah 38.12 *Mine age* is departed, and is removed from me <u>as *a shepherd's tent:*</u> *I* have cut off <u>like *a weaver*</u> my life: he will cut me off with pining sickness: from day even to night wilt thou make an end of me.

12 ἐξέλιπον ἐκ τῆς συγγενείας μου, κατέλιπον τὸ ἐπίλοιπον τῆς ζωῆς μου, ἐξῆλθε καὶ ἀπῆλθεν ἀπ' ἐμοῦ <u>ὥσπερ *ὁ καταλύων σκηνὴν πήξας,*</u> τὸ πνεῦμά μου παρ' ἐμοὶ ἐγένετο <u>ὡς *ἱστὸς ἐρίθου ἐγγιζούσης ἐκτεμεῖν.*</u>

12 *Generatio mea* ablata est, et convoluta est a me, <u>quasi *tabernaculum pastorum*</u>. Praecisa est <u>velut *a texente*</u> vita mea.

[mine age (departed) ≈ a shepherd's tent; I ≈ a weaver]

Isaiah 38.13 I reckoned till morning, that, <u>as *a lion,*</u> so will *he* break all my bones: from day even to night wilt thou make and end of me.

14 <u>Like *a crane or a swallow,*</u> **so** did *I* chatter: *I* did mourn <u>as *a dove:*</u> mine eyes fail with looking upward: O Lord, I am oppressed: undertake for me.

13 ἐν τῇ ἡμέρᾳ ἐκείνῃ *παρεδόθην* ἕως πρωΐ <u>ὡς *λέοντι·*</u> οὕτως συνέτριψε πάντα τὰ ὀστᾶ μου, ἀπὸ γὰρ τῆς ἡμέρα ἕως τῆς νυκτὸς παρεδόθην. 14 <u>ὡς</u>

χελιδών, **οὕτω** φωνήσω, καὶ <u>ὡς</u> <u>*περιστερά*</u>, **οὕτω** μελετήσω· ἐξέλιπον γάρ
μου οἱ ὀφθαλμοὶ τοῦ βλέπειν εἰς τὸ ὕψος τοῦ οὐρανοῦ πρὸς τὸν Κύριον,

13 Sperabam usque ad mane; <u>quasi</u> *<u>leo</u>* sic contriv*it* omnia ossa mea; de
mane usque ad vesperam finies me. [14] <u>Sicut</u> *<u>pullus hirundinis</u>*,
sic clamabo; meditabor <u>ut</u> *<u>columba</u>*. Attenuati sunt oculi mei,
suspicientes in excelsum. Domine, vim patior, responde pro me.

[he (the Lord) ≈ a lion; I ≈ a crane or a swallow ≈ a (mourning) dove]

Isaiah 40.11 *He* [the Lord] shall feed *his flock* <u>like</u> *<u>a shepherd</u>*. ...

11 <u>ὡς</u> *<u>ποιμὴν</u>* [Κύριος] *ποιμανεῖ τὸ ποίμνιον αὐτοῦ* ...

11 <u>Sicut</u> *<u>pastor gregem</u>* suum pascet, ...

[Lord > his flock ≈ a shepherd > (his flock)]

Isaiah 40.15 Behold, *the nations* are <u>as</u> *<u>a drop of a bucket</u>*, and are counted
<u>as</u> *<u>the small dust of the balance</u>*: behold, he taketh up *the isles* <u>as</u> *<u>a very</u>*
<u>little thing</u>.

15 εἰ *πάντα τὰ ἔθνη* <u>ὡς</u> *<u>σταγὼν ἀπὸ κάδου</u>* καὶ <u>ὡς</u> <u>*ῥοπὴ*</u> *<u>ζυγοῦ</u>* ἐλογίσθησαν
καὶ <u>ὡς</u> <u>*σίελος*</u> λογισθήσονται·

15 Ecce *gentes* <u>quasi</u> *<u>stilla situlae</u>*, et <u>quasi</u> *<u>momentum staterae</u>* reputatae
sunt; ecce *insulae* <u>quasi</u> *<u>pulvis exiguus</u>*.

[nations ≈ a drop of a bucket ≈ small dust of a balance; the isles
≈ a very little thing]

Isaiah 40.22 It is he [God] that sitteth upon the circle of the earth, and
the inhabitants thereof are <u>as</u> *<u>grasshoppers</u>*; that stretcheth out *the*
heavens <u>as</u> *<u>a curtain</u>*, and spreadeth *them* out <u>as</u> *<u>a tent</u>* to dwell in.

22 ὁ κατέχων τὸν γῦρον τῆς γῆς, καὶ οἱ *ἐνοικοῦντες* ἐν αὐτῇ <u>ὡς</u> <u>*ἀκρίδες*</u>, ὁ
στήσας <u>ὡς</u> <u>*καμάραν*</u> *τὸν οὐρανὸν* καὶ διατείνας <u>ὡς</u> <u>*σκηνὴν κατοικεῖν*</u>,

22 Qui sedet super gyrum terrae, et *habitatores* ejus sunt <u>quasi</u>
<u>locustae</u>; qui extendit <u>velut</u> *<u>nihilum</u>* caelos, et expandit *eos* <u>sicut</u>
<u>tabernaculum</u> ad inhabitandum;

[the inhabitants of the earth ≈ grasshoppers; heavens ≈ a curtain ≈ a tent]

Isaiah 40.24 and the whirlwind shall take *them* away <u>as</u> *<u>stubble</u>*.

24 καὶ *καταιγὶς* <u>ὡς</u> *<u>φρύγανα</u>* λήψεται αὐτούς.

24 et turbo <u>quasi</u> *<u>stipulam</u>* auferet *eos* [secretorum scrutatores ... judices
terrae]. [them (princes and judges) ≈ stubble]

Isaiah 40.31 But they that wait upon the Lord shall ... *mount up with wings* as *eagles*;

31 πτεροφυήσουιν ὡς ἀετοί,

31 *qui autem sperant in Domino* ... assument pennas sicut *aquilae,*[they (that wait upon the Lord) ≈ eagles]

Isaiah 41.2 He [the Lord] gave *them* [kings] as *the dust to his [the righteous man's] sword,* and as *driven stubble to his bow.*

2 ὡς φρύγανα ἐξωσμένα τὰ τόξα αὐτῶν·

2 dabit quasi *pulverem gladio ejus,* sicut *stipulam vento raptam arcui* ejus.
[them (kings) ≈ dust to the righteous man's sword ≈ driven stubble to his bow]

Isaiah 41.15 Behold ... thou shalt thresh the mountains, and beat them small, and shalt make *the hills* as *chaff.*

15 ἰδοὺ ... ἀλοήσεις ὄρη καὶ λεπτυνεῖς βουνοὺς καὶ ὡς χνοῦν θήσεις·

15 triturabis montes, et comminues, et *colles* quasi *pulverem* pones.   [hills ≈ chaff]

Isaiah 41.25 and he [one from the north] shall come upon *princes* as upon *morter,* and as the *potter treadeth clay.*

25 ἐρχέσθωσαν ἄρχοντες, καὶ ὡς πηλὸς κεραμέως καὶ ὡς κεραμεὺς καταπατῶν τὸν πηλόν, οὕτως καταπατηθήσεσθε.

25 et adducet *magistratus* quasi *lutum,* et velut *plastes conculans humum.*
[princes ≈ mortar ≈ potter's clay]

Isaiah 42.6 I the LORD ... will keep thee, and give *thee* for *a covenant* of the people, for *a light of the Gentiles.*

6 ἐγὼ Κύριος ὁ Θεὸς ... ἔδωκά σε εἰς διαθήκην γένους, εἰς φῶς ἐθνῶν.

6 Ego Dominus ... servavi te; et dedi *te* in *foedus populi, in lucem gentium.* [thee ≈ a covenant ≈ a light of the Gentiles]

Isaiah 42.13 The *LORD* shall go forth as *a mighty man, he* shall stir up jealousy like *a man of war.*

13 Κύριος ὁ Θεὸς τῶν δυνάμεων ἐξελεύσεται καὶ συντρίψει πόλεμον, ἐπεγερεῖ ζῆλον καὶ βοήσεται ἐπὶ τοὺς ἐχθροὺς αὐτοῦ μετὰ ἰσχύος.

13 *Dominus* sicut *fortis* egredietur, sicut *vir praeliator* suscitabit zelum.
[the Lord ≈ a mighty man ≈ a man of war]

Isaiah 42.14 I have long time holden my peace ... now I will cry <u>like *a travailing woman;*</u> I will destroy and devour at once.

    14 ἐσιώπησα, μὴ καὶ ἀεὶ σιωπήσομαι καὶ ἀνέξομαι; <u>ὡς ἡ τίκτουσα</u> ἐκαρτέρησα, ἐκστήσω καὶ ξηρανῶ ἅμα.

    14 Tacui semper, silui, patiens fui; <u>sicut *parturiens*</u> loqu*ar*; dissipabo, et absorbebo simul.

    [I (will cry) ≈ a travailing woman]

Isaiah 46.5 To whom *will ye <u>liken</u> me,* and make me equal, and *compare* me? 9 Remember ... I am God, and *there is none like me.*

    5 τίνι με ὡμοιώσατε; ... 9 καὶ μνήσθητε ... ὅτι ἐγώ εἰμι ὁ Θεός, καὶ οὐκ ἔστιν ἔτι <u>πλὴν ἐμοῦ.</u>'

    5 *Cui assimilastis me*, et adaequastis, et comparastis me, et fecistis *similem?* 9 Recordamini ... ego sum Deus, et non est ultra Deus nec est <u>similis *mei*.</u>   [no one ≈ me (God)]

Isaiah 47.14 Behold, they *shall be* as <u>*stubble;*</u> the fire shall burn them.

    14 ἰδοὺ πάντες <u>ὡς</u> <u>φρύγανα</u> ἐπὶ πυρὶ κατακαυθήσονται.

    14 Ecce facti sunt <u>quasi *stipula*</u>, ignis combussit eos.

    [they (astrologers, stargazers, prognosticators) ≈ stubble]

Isaiah 48.18 O that thou hadst hearkened to my commandments! then had *thy peace* been as <u>*a river,*</u> and *thy righteousness* as <u>*the waves of the sea:*</u> 19 *Thy seed* also had been as <u>*the sand,*</u> and *the offspring of thy bowels* like the <u>*gravel thereof.*</u>

    18 καὶ εἰ ἤκουσας τῶν ἐντολῶν μου, ἐγένετο ἂν <u>ὡσεὶ</u> <u>ποταμὸς</u> ἡ εἰρήνη σου καὶ ἡ δικαιοσύνη σου <u>ὡς κῦμα θαλάσσης·</u> 19 καὶ ἐγένετο ἂν <u>ὡς ἡ ἄμμος</u> τὸ σπέρμα σου καὶ τὰ ἔκγονα τῆς κοιλίας σου <u>ὡς ὁ χοῦς τῆς γῆς.</u>

    18 Utinam attendisses mandata mea: facta fuisset <u>sicut *flumen* pax tua</u>, et *justitia tua* <u>sicut *gurgites maris*</u>; 19 et fuisset <u>quasi *arena*</u> semen tuum, et *stirps uteri tui* <u>ut *lapilli ejus.*</u>

    [your peace ≈ a river; your righteousness ≈ waves of the see; your seed ≈ sand; your offspring ≈ gravel]

Isaiah 49.2 And he hath made *my mouth* like <u>*a sharp sword;*</u>

    2 καὶ ἔθηκε τὸ στόμα μου <u>ὡσεὶ</u> <u>μάχαιραν ὀξεῖαν</u>

    2 Et posuit *os meum* <u>quasi *gladium acutum,*</u> in umbra manus suae protexit me; et posuit *me* <u>sicut *sagittam electam,*</u> in pharetra sua abscondit me.

    [my mouth ≈ a sharp sword; me ≈ a polished shaft]

Isaiah 49.6 I (the Lord) will also give *thee* for *a light to the Gentiles,* that
thou mayest be my salvation unto the end of the earth.

    6 ἰδοὺ δέδωκά σε <u>εἰς διαθήκην γένους</u>, <u>εἰς φῶς ἐθνῶν</u> τοῦ εἶναί σε εἰς
σωτηρίαν ἕως ἐσχάτου τῆς γῆς.

    6 Et dixit: … ecce dedi *te* in *lucem gentium,* ut sis salus mea usque ad
extremum terrae.

    [you (Isaiah) ≈ a light to the Gentiles]

Isaiah 49.18 As I live, saith the Lord, thou shalt surely clothe thee *with
them all,* as *with an ornament*, and bind *them* on thee, *as a bride doeth.*

    18 ζῶ ἐγώ, λέγει Κύριος, ὅτι πάντας αὐτοὺς <u>ὡς κόσμον</u> ἐνδύσῃ καὶ περιθήσῃ
αὐτοὺς <u>ὡς κόσμον νύμφης</u>.

    18 Vivo ego, dicit Dominus, quia omnibus *his* <u>velut</u> <u>*ornamento*</u> vestieris,
et circumdabis tibi *eos* <u>quasi</u> *<u>sponsa</u>*.

    [thee (Zion) ≈ (clothed as) an ornament; ≈ a bride's attire]

Isaiah 51.6 *for the heavens shall vanish away* <u>like</u> *<u>smoke</u>*, and the *earth* shall
wax old <u>like</u> *<u>a garment.</u>*

    6 ὅτι ὁ οὐρανὸς <u>ὡς καπνὸς</u> ἐστερεώθη, ἡ δὲ γῆ <u>ὡς ἱμάτιον</u> παλαιωθήσεται

    6 quia *caeli* <u>sicut</u> *<u>fumus</u>* liquescent, et *terra* <u>sicut</u> *<u>vestimentum</u>* atteretur.

    [the heavens (shall vanish) ≈ smoke; the earth (grow old) ≈ a
garment]

Isaiah 51.8 For the moth shall eat *them* up <u>like</u> *<u>a garment,</u>* and the worm
shall eat *them* like *<u>wool</u>*: but my righteousness shall be for ever.

    8 <u>ὡς γὰρ ἱμάτιον βρωθήσεται ὑπὸ χρόνου</u> καὶ <u>ὡς ἔρια βρωθήσεται ὑπὸ σητός</u>·
ἡ δὲ δικαιοσύνη μου εἰς τὸν αἰῶνα ἔσται.

    8 <u>sicut</u> enim *<u>vestimentum</u>*, **sic** comedet *eos* vermis; et <u>sicut</u> *<u>lanam</u>*, **sic**
devorabit *eos* tinea:

    [they (men: shall be consumed by a moth) ≈ a garment ≈ wool
(by a worm)]

Isaiah 53.2 For *he* shall grow up before him <u>as</u> *<u>a tender plant,</u>* and <u>as</u> *<u>a root
out of a dry ground</u>*.

    2 ἀνηγγείλαμεν <u>ὡς παιδίον</u> ἐναντίον αὐτοῦ, <u>ὡς ῥίζα ἐν γῇ διψώσῃ</u>. οὐκ ἔστιν
εἶδος αὐτῷ οὐδὲ δόξα.

    2 Et ascendet <u>sicut</u> *<u>virgultum</u>* coram eo; et <u>sicut</u> *<u>radix de terra sitienti</u>*.

    [he (to whom the arm of the Lord is revealed) ≈ a tender plant
≈ a root out of dry ground]

Isaiah 53.6 All *we* like *sheep* have gone astray; we have turned every one to his own way; and the Lord hath laid on him the iniquity of us all.
7 He was oppressed, and he was afflicted, yet he opened not his mouth: he is brought as *a lamb to the slaughter,* and as *a sheep before her shearers* is dumb, **so** *he openeth not his mouth.*

6 πάντες ὡς πρόβατα ἐπλανήθημεν, ἄνθρωπος τῇ ὁδῷ αὐτοῦ ἐπλανήθη· καὶ Κύριος παρέδωκεν αὐτὸν ταῖς ἁμαρτίαις ἡμῶν. 7 καὶ αὐτὸς διὰ τὸ κεκακῶσθαι οὐκ ἀνοίγει τὸ στόμα αὐτοῦ· ὡς πρόβατον ἐπὶ σφαγὴν ἤχθη καὶ ὡς ἀμνὸς ἐναντίον τοῦ κείροντος αὐτὸν ἄφωνος, **οὕτως** οὐκ ἀνοίγει τὸ στόμα.

6 Omnes *nos* quasi *oves* erravimus, unusquisque in viam suam declinavit; et posuit Dominus in eo iniquitatem omnium nostrum. [7] Oblatus est quia ipse voluit, et non aperuit os suum; sicut *ovis* ad occisionem ducetur, et quasi *agnus* coram tondente se obmutescet, et non aperiet os suum.

[we ≈ sheep (gone astray); he (to whom the arm of the Lord is revealed) ≈ a lamb (to slaughter) ≈ a sheep before her shearers]

Isaiah 54.6 For the LORD hath called *thee* as a *woman forsaken* and grieved in spirit and a wife of youth, when thou wast refused, saith thy God.

6 οὐχ ὡς γυναῖκα καταλελειμμένην καὶ ὀλιγόψυχον κέκληκέ σε Κύριος, οὐδ᾽ ὡς γυναίκα ἐκ νεότητος μεμισημένην,

6 Quia et *mulierem derelictam et moerentem spiritu* vocavit *te* Dominus, et *uxorem ab adolescentia abjectam*, dixit Deus tuus. [you ≈ a forsaken woman ...]

Isaiah 54.9 For *this* is as *the waters of Noah* unto me: for as I have sworn ...

9 ἀπὸ τοῦ ὕδατος τοῦ ἐπὶ Νῶε τοῦτό μοί ἐστι·

9 Sicut *in diebus Noe istud* mihi est, cui juravi ne inducerem *aquas* Noe ultra super terram; **sic** juravi ut non irascar tibi, et non increpem te.

[this (a little wrath) ≈ the waters of Noah]

Isaiah 55.9 For <u>as</u> *the heavens are higher than the earth*, **so** are *my ways higher than your ways, and my thoughts than your thoughts.* 10 For <u>as</u> *the rain cometh down, and the snow from heaven,* ... 11 **So** *shall my word be that goeth forth* out of my mouth: ...

8 ἀλλ᾽ <u>ὡς</u> <u>ἀπέχει ὁ οὐρανὸς ἀπὸ τῆς γῆς</u>, **οὕτως** ἀπέχει ἡ ὁδός μου 9 ἀπὸ τῶν ὁδῶν ὑμῶν καὶ τὰ διανοήματα ὑμῶν ἀπὸ τῆς διανοίας μου. 10 <u>ὡς</u> γὰρ ἂν <u>καταβῇ ὁ ὑετὸς ἢ χιὼν ἐκ τοῦ οὐρανοῦ καὶ οὐ μὴ ἀποστραφῇ,</u> <u>ἕως ἂν μεθύσῃ τὴν γῆν,</u> καὶ ἐκτέκῃ καὶ ἐκβλαστήσῃ καὶ δῷ σπέρμα τῷ σπείραντι καὶ ἄρτον εἰς βρῶσιν, 11 οὕτως *ἔσται τὸ ῥῆμά μου,* ὃ ἐὰν ἐξέλθῃ ἐκ τοῦ στόματός μου, οὐ μὴ ἀποστραφῇ, ἕως ἂν τελεσθῇ ὅσα ἂν ἠθέλησα καὶ εὐοδώσω τὰς ὁδούς μου καὶ τὰ ἐντάλματά μου.

9 Quia <u>sicut</u> *exaltantur caeli a terra*, **sic** exaltatae sunt *viae meae a viis vestris*, et cogitationes meae a cogitationibus vestris. [10] Et <u>quomodo</u> *descendit imber et nix de caelo*, et illuc ultra non revertitur, sed inebriat terram, et infundit eam, et germinare eam facit, et dat semen serenti, et panem comedenti: 11 **sic** *erit verbum meum* quod egredietur de ore meo; non revertetur ad me vacuum, sed faciet quaecumque volui, et prosperabitur in his ad quae misi illud.

[my way > your ways ≈ the heaven (far from) > earth; my word (will not turn back) ≈ rain, snow (will not return to heaven)]

Isaiah 57.20 But *the wicked* are <u>like</u> *the troubled sea*, when it cannot rest, whose waters cast up mire and dirt.

20 <u>*οἱ δὲ ἄδικοι*</u> <u>*οὕτως*</u> <u>*κλυδωνισθήσονται*</u> καὶ ἀναπαύσασθαι οὐ δυνήσονται.

[***The simile is in the verb.**]

20 *Impii* autem <u>quasi</u> <u>*mare fervens*</u>, quod quiescere non potest, et redundant fluctus ejus in conculcationem et lutum.

[The wicked ≈ the troubled sea]

Isaiah 58.11 And the Lord shall guide thee continually, and satisfy thy soul in drought ... and thou shalt be like *a watered garden*, and <u>like</u> *a spring* of *water, whose waters fail not.*

11 καὶ ἔσται ὁ Θεός σου μετὰ σοῦ διαπαντός· καὶ ἐμπλησθήσῃ καθάπερ ἐπιθυμεῖ ἡ ψυχή σου, καὶ *τὰ ὀστᾶ σου* πιανθήσεται, καὶ ἔσῃ <u>ὡς</u> <u>*κῆπος*</u> <u>*μεθύων*</u> καὶ <u>ὡς</u> <u>*πηγὴ ἣν μὴ ἐξέλιπεν ὕδωρ*</u> καὶ τὰ ὀστᾶ σου <u>ὡς</u> <u>*βοτάνη*</u> <u>*ἀνατελεῖ*</u> καὶ πιανθήσεται καὶ κληρονομήσουσι γενεὰς γενεῶν.

11 Et requiem tibi dabit Dominus semper, et implebit splendoribus animam tuam, et ossa tua liberabit; et *eris* quasi <u>*hortus irriguus*</u>, et sicut f*ons aquarum cujus non deficient aquae.*

[thou ≈ well-watered garden ≈ a spring of water]

Isaiah 59.10 We grope *for the wall* <u>like the</u> *blind*, and *we grope* <u>as if we</u> <u>*had no eyes*</u>: we *stumble at noon-day* <u>as</u> *<u>in the night</u>: we are in desolate* places <u>as</u> <u>*dead men*</u>. 11 *We roar all* <u>like</u> <u>*bears*</u> and *mourn sore* <u>like</u> <u>*doves*</u>: we look for judgment, but there is none; for salvation, but it is far off from us.

10 ψηλαφήσουσιν <u>ὡς</u> <u>τυφλοί</u> τοῖχον καὶ <u>ὡς</u> <u>οὐχ ὑπαρχόντων ὀφθαλμῶν</u> ψηλαφήσουσι· καὶ πεσοῦνται ἐν μεσημβρίᾳ ὡς ἐν μεσονυκτίῳ, <u>ὡς</u> <u>ἀποθνήσκοντες</u> στενάξουσιν, 11 <u>ὡς ἄρκος καὶ ὡς περιστερὰ</u> ἅμα πορεύσονται· ἀνεμείναμεν κρίσιν, καὶ οὐκ ἔστι· σωτηρία μακρὰν ἀφέστηκεν ἀφ᾽ ἡμῶν.

10 *Palpavimus* sicut <u>*caeci*</u> parietem, et quasi <u>*absque oculis*</u> attrectavimus; *impegimus* meridie quasi <u>*in tenebris*</u>, *in caliginosis* quasi <u>*mortui*</u>.

[we ≈ blind men / with no eyes ≈ in the night (stumbling) ≈ dead men ≈ bears (roaring) and doves (mourning)]

Isaiah 59.17 For *he ... was clad with zeal* <u>as</u> *a cloak.*

17περιεβάλετο <u>ἱμάτιον ἐκδικήσεως</u> καὶ τὸ περιβόλαιον.

17 Indutus est *justitia* ut <u>*lorica*</u>, et *galea salutis* in capite ejus; indutus est vestimentis ultionis, et opertus est quasi <u>*pallio zeli.*</u>[zeal ≈ a cloak]

Isaiah 60.8 Who are *these* that fly <u>as</u> a <u>*cloud*</u>, and <u>as</u> the <u>*doves to their*</u> <u>*windows?*</u>

8 τίνες οἵδε <u>ὡς</u> <u>νεφέλαι</u> πέτανται καὶ <u>ὡσεὶ</u> <u>περιστεραὶ σὺν νεοσσοῖς</u>;

8 Qui sunt *isti* qui ut <u>*nubes*</u> volant, et quasi <u>*columbae*</u> ad fenestras suas?

[who are these? ≈ a cloud ≈ doves]

Isaiah 61.10 I will greatly rejoice in the Lord, ... <u>as</u> *a bridegroom decketh himself* with ornaments, and <u>*as a bride adorneth herself with jewels.*</u> 11 For <u>as t*he earth bringeth forth her bud, and as the garden causeth the*</u> <u>*things that are sown in it to spring forth;*</u> **so** the Lord God will cause *righteousness and praise to spring forth* before all nations.

10 Ἀγαλλιάσθω ἡ ψυχή μου ἐπὶ τῷ Κυρίῳ·... <u>ὡς νυμφίῳ</u> περιέθηκέ μοι μίτραν καὶ <u>ὡς</u> <u>νύμφην</u> κατεκόσμησέ με κόσμῳ. 11 καὶ <u>ὡς γῆ αὔξουσα τὸ</u>

ἄνθος αὐτῆς καὶ ὡς κῆπος τὰ σπέρματα αὐτοῦ, **οὕτως** ἀνατελεῖ Κύριος
δικαιοσύνην καὶ ἀγαλλίαμα ἐναντίον πάντων τῶν ἐθνῶν.

10 Gaudens gaudebo in Domino, ... quasi *sponsum* decoratum corona,
et quasi *sponsam ornatam monilibus suis*. [11] Sicut enim *terra
profert germen suum*, et sicut h*ortus semen suum germinat*, **sic**
*Dominus Deus germinabi*t *justitiam et laudem coram universis
gentibus*.

[I ≈ a bridegroom ≈ a bride; [the Lord > (causes to grow) righteousness ≈ the earth > flowers ≈ a garden > its seeds]

Isaiah 62.5 For *as a young man marrieth a virgin*, **so** *shall thy sons marry
thee: and* as *the bridegroom rejoiceth over the bride*, **so** shall thy God
rejoice over thee.

5 καὶ ὡς συνοικῶν νεανίσκος παρθένῳ, **οὕτω** κατοικήσουσιν οἱ υἱοί σου·
καὶ ἔσται ὃν τρόπον εὐφρανθήσεται νυμφίος ἐπὶ νύμφῃ, **οὕτως**
εὐφρανθήσεται Κύριος ἐπὶ σοί.

5 *Habitabit enim juvenis cum virgine*, et habitabunt in te filii tui; et
gaudebit sponsus super sponsam, et *gaudebit super te Deus tuus*.

[your sons will marry you ≈ a young man marries a virgin; the
Lord will rejoice over you ≈ a bridegroom over a bride]

Isaiah 63.13 [He = the Lord] that *led them through the deep*, *as an horse
in the wilderness*, that they should not stumble? 14 As *a beast goeth
down into the valley*, *the Spirit of the Lord caused him to rest*: **so** *didst
thou lead thy people*. to make thyself a glorious name.

13 ἤγαγεν αὐτοὺς διὰ τῆς ἀβύσσου ὡς ἵππον δι᾽ ἐρήμου, καὶ οὐκ ἐκοπίασαν.
14 καὶ ὡς κτήνη διὰ πεδίου, κατέβη πνεῦμα παρὰ Κυρίου καὶ ὡδήγησεν
αὐτούς· **οὕτως** ἤγαγες τὸν λαόν σου ποιῆσαι σεαυτῷ ὄνομα δόξης.

13 *qui eduxit eos per abyssos*, quasi *equum in deserto non* impingentem?
Quasi animal in campo descendens, *spiritus Domini* ductor ejus
fuit. **Sic** adduxisti populum tuum, ut faceres tibi nomen gloriae.

[he (the Lord) led them through the deep ≈ a horse in the wilderness ≈ a beast going into the valley]

Isaiah 64.2 As when *the melting fire burneth*, *the fire causeth the waters to
boil*, to make thy name known to thine adversaries, that the nations
may tremble at thy presence!

1 ΕΑΝ ἀνοίξῃς τὸν οὐρανόν, τρόμος λήψεται ἀπὸ σοῦ ὄρη, καὶ τακήσονται,
   2 <u>*ὡς κηρὸς ἀπὸ προσώπου πυρὸς τήκεται,*</u>

2 <u>Sicut</u> <u>*exustio ignis tabescerent,*</u> *aquae arderent igni,* ut notum fieret
   nomen tuum inimicis tuis, a facie tua gentes turbarentur.
   [nations will tremble ≈ fire burns / water boils]

Isaiah 64.6 But *we are all* <u>*as an unclean thing*</u>, and *all our righteousnesses*
are <u>*as filthy rags*</u>: and <u>*we all do fade as a leaf; and our iniquities, like the*</u>
<u>*wind, have taken us away.*</u>

   6 καὶ ἐγενήθημεν <u>ὡς ἀκάθαρτοι</u> πάντες ἡμεῖς, <u>ὡς ῥάκος ἀποκαθημένης</u> πᾶσα
   ἡ δικαιοσύνη ἡμῶν· καὶ <u>ἐξερρύημεν ὡς φύλλα</u> διὰ τὰς ἀνομίας ἡμῶν,
   οὕτως ἄνεμος οἴσει ἡμᾶς.

   6 Et facti sumus <u>ut</u> <u>*immundus*</u> omnes nos, et <u>quasi</u> <u>*pannus menstruatae*</u>
   universae justitiae nostrae; et cecidi*mus* <u>quasi</u> <u>*folium*</u> universi, et
   i*niquitates nostrae* <u>quasi</u> <u>*ventus*</u> abstulerunt nos.
   [we ≈ unclean; our righteousness ≈ filthy rags; we (fade) ≈ a leaf;
   our iniquities ≈ the wind]

Isaiah 65.8 Thus saith the Lord, <u>*As the new wine is found in the cluster*</u>, and
one saith, Destroy it not; for a blessing is in it: **so** *will I do for my ser-*
vants' sakes, that I may not destroy them all.

   8 Οὕτως λέγει Κύριος· <u>ὃν τρόπον</u> <u>*εὑρεθήσεται ὁ ῥὼξ ἐν τῷ βότρυϊ*</u> καὶ ἐροῦσι·
   μὴ λυμήνῃ αὐτόν, ὅτι εὐλογία ἐστὶν ἐν αὐτῷ, **οὕτως** ποιήσω ἕνεκεν τοῦ
   δουλεύοντός μοι, τούτου ἕνεκεν οὐ μὴ ἀπολέσω πάντας.

   8 Haec dicit Dominus: <u>Quomodo si</u> <u>*inveniatur granum in botro*</u>, et
   dicatur: Ne dissipes illud, quoniam benedictio est, **sic** *faciam*
   propter servos meos, ut non disperdam totum.
   [I will not destroy them all ≈ new wine found in the cluster]

Isaiah 65.22 for <u>as</u> <u>*the days of a tree are the days of my people,*</u>
   22 <u>κατὰ</u> γὰρ <u>*τὰς ἡμέρας τοῦ ξύλου τῆς ζωῆς*</u> ἔσονται αἱ ἡμέραι τοῦ λαοῦ μου·
   22 <u>*secundum enim dies ligni*</u> erunt *dies populi mei,* et opera manuum
   eorum inveterabint.
   [the days of my people ≈ of a tree]

Isaiah 65.25 The wolf and the lamb shall feed together, and the *lion* shall
eat straw <u>*like the bullock:*</u> and dust shall be the serpent's meal.
   25 τότε λύκοι καὶ ἄρνες βοσκηθήσονται ἅμα, καὶ λέων <u>ὡς βοῦς</u> φάγεται
   ἄχυρα, ὄφις δὲ γῆν <u>ὡς ἄρτον</u>·

25 *Lupus et agnus pascentur simul, leo et bos comedent paleas*, et *serpenti pulvis panis ejus*.

[lion (will eat straw) ≈ the bullock]

Isaiah 66.3 *He that killeth an ox is as if he slew a man; he that sacrificeth a lamb, as if he had cut off a dog's neck: he that offereth an oblation, as if he offered swine's blood; he that burnt incense, as if he blessed an idol.*

3 ὁ δὲ ἄνομος ὁ θύων μοι μόσχον ὡς ὁ ἀποκτένων κύνα, ὁ δὲ ἀναφέρων σεμίδαλιν ὡς αἷμα ὕειον, ὁ διδοὺς λίβανον εἰς μνημόσυνον ὡς βλάσφημος·

3 *Qui immolat bovem*, quasi *qui interficiat virum*; *qui mactat pecus*, quasi *qui excerebret canem*; *qui offert oblationem*, quasi *qui sanguinem suillum offerat*; *qui recordatur thuris*, quasi *qui benedicat idolo*.

[he who killed an ox ≈ someone who killed a man; he who sacrifices a lamb ≈ he who cut off a dog's neck; who offers an oblation ≈ he offers swine's blood; who burns incense ≈ he blessed an idol]

Isaiah 66.12 For thus saith the Lord, Behold, *I will extend peace to her like a river, and the glory of the Gentiles like a flowing stream.*

12 ὅτι τάδε λέγει Κύριος· ἰδοὺ ἐγὼ ἐκκλίνω εἰς αὐτοὺς ὡς ποταμὸς εἰρήνης καὶ ὡς χειμάρρους ἐπικλύζων δόξαν ἐθνῶν· 12 Ecce ego *declinabo super eam* quasi *fluvium pacis*, et quasi *torrentem inundantem gloriam gentium*, quam sugetis;   stream]/

[peace ≈ a river; the glory of the Gentiles ≈ a flowing /

Isaiah 66.14 And when ye see this, your heart shall rejoice, and *your bones shall flourish* like *an herb:* ... 15 For, behold, the Lord will come with fire, and *his chariots* like *a whirlwind,* to render his anger with fury, and his rebuke with flames of fire.

14 καὶ τὰ ὀστᾶ ὑμῶν ὡς βοτάνη ἀνατελεῖ·... 15 Ἰδοὺ γὰρ Κύριος ὡς πῦρ ἥξει καὶ ὡς καταιγὶς τὰ ἄρματα αὐτοῦ ἀποδοῦναι ἐν θυμῷ ἐκδίκησιν αὐτοῦ καὶ ἀποσκορακισμὸν αὐτοῦ ἐν φλογὶ πυρός.

14 Videbitis, et gaudebit cor vestrum; et *ossa vestra* quasi *herba* germinabunt; ... [15] Quia ecce Dominus in igne veniet, et quasi *turbo* quadrigae ejus, reddere in indignatione furorem suum et increpationem suam in flamma ignis;

[your bones ≈ an herb; the Lord's chariots ≈ a whirlwind]

* * *

Jeremiah (52 Chapters)

Ἰερεμίας

Jerem. 3.20 Surely *as a wife treacherously departeth from her husband,* **so** *have ye dealt treacherously with me,* O house of Israel, saith the Lord.

20 πλὴν <u>ὡς ἀθετεῖ γυνὴ εἰς τὸν συνόντα αὐτῇ,</u> **οὕτως** ἠθέτησεν εἰς ἐμὲ ὁ οἶκος Ἰσραήλ, λέγει Κύριος

20 Sed <u>quomodo si</u> *contemnat mulier amatorem suum,* **sic** *contempsit me domus Israel,* dicit Dominus.

[house of Israel (treacherous) > me (the Lord) ≈ a wife > her husband]

Jerem. 4.13 Behold, *he shall come up as clouds,* and *his chariots* shall be *as a whirlwind:* his horses are <u>swifter than</u> *eagles.*

13 ἰδοὺ <u>ὡς νεφέλη</u> ἀναβήσεται καὶ <u>ὡς καταιγὶς</u> τὰ ἅρματα αὐτοῦ, <u>κουφότεροι ἀετῶν</u> οἱ ἵπποι αὐτοῦ· οὐαὶ ἡμῖν, ὅτι ταλαιπωροῦμεν.

13 Ecce <u>quasi</u> *nubes* ascend*et:* et <u>quasi</u> *tempestas* currus ejus, <u>velociores aquilis</u> equi illius.

[He (the Lord) ≈ clouds; his chariots ≈ a whirlwind; his horses (swifter) ≈ eagles]

Jerem. 4.31 For I have heard *a voice as of a woman in travail,* and the anguish *as of her that bringeth forth her first child.*

31 ὅτι φωνὴν <u>ὡς ὠδινούσης</u> ἤκουσα, τοῦ στεναγμοῦ σου <u>ὡς πρωτοτοκούσης,</u> φωνὴ θυγατρὸς Σιών·

31 *Vocem* enim <u>quasi</u> *parturientis* audivi, *angustias* <u>ut</u> *puerperae:* vox filiae Sion intermorientis, expandentisque manus suas:

[a voice ≈ a voice of a woman giving birth; the anguish ≈ that of a woman giving birth for the first time]

Jerem. 5.8 *They* [Thy sons] were <u>as</u> *fed horses* in the morning: everyone neighed after his neighbour's wife.

8 <u>ἵπποι θηλυμανεῖς</u> ἐγενήθησαν [οἱ υἱοί σου], ἕκαστος ἐπὶ τὴν γυναῖκα τοῦ πλησίον αὐτοῦ ἐχρεμέτιζον.

8 *Equi amatores et emissarii facti sunt:* unusquisque ad uxorem proximi sui hinniebat.

[your sons ≈ fed/wanton horses]

Jerem. 5.16 Their *quiver* is <u>as</u> <u>*an open sepulchre*</u>.

   16 πάντες ἰσχυροὶ καὶ κατέδονται τὸν θερισμὸν ὑμῶν ([They are] all mighty men: 17 and they shall devour your harvest.]

   16 *Pharetra* ejus <u>quasi</u> <u>*sepulchrum patens*</u>, universi fortes.

    [their (= any nation invading Israel) quiver ≈ an open sepulchre]

Jerem. 5.27 <u>As</u> <u>*a cage is full of birds*</u>, **so** are *their houses full of deceit*

   27 <u>*ὡς παγὶς ἐφεσταμένη πλήρης πετεινῶν,*</u> **οὕτως** *οἱ οἶκοι αὐτῶν πλήρεις δόλου·*

   27 <u>Sicut</u> <u>*decipula plena avibus*</u>, **sic** *domus eorum plenae dolo.*

    [their (wicked men's) houses full of deceit ≈ a cage full of birds]

Jerem. 6.2 I have <u>likened</u> *the daughter of Zion* <u>to</u> <u>*a comely and delicate woman*</u>.

   2 καὶ ἀφαιρεθήσεται τὸ ὕψος σου, θύγατερ Σιών.

   2 <u>*Speciosae et delicatae*</u> <u>assimilavi</u> *filiam Sion.*

    [the daughter of Zion ≈ a comely and delicate woman]

Jerem. 6.7 <u>*As a fountain casteth out her waters*</u>, **so** *she [Jerusalem] casteth out her wickedness.*

   7 <u>*ὡς ψύχει λάκκος ὕδωρ,*</u> **οὕτω** *ψύχει κακία αὐτῆς·*

   7 Sicut <u>*frigidam fecit cisterna aquam suam*</u>, **sic** *frigidum fecit malitiam suam.*   water]/

    [Jerusalem > her wickedness ≈ a fountain (casts out) > its /

Jerem. 6.9 They shall throughly glean *the remnant of Israel* <u>as a vine</u>: turn back *thine* hand <u>as</u> <u>*a grapegatherer*</u> into the baskets.

   9 ὅτι τάδε λέγει Κύριος· καλαμᾶσθε, *καλαμᾶσθε <u>ὡς ἄμπελον</u>* τὰ κατάλοιπα τοῦ Ἰσραήλ, *ἐπιστρέψατε <u>ὡς ὁ τρυγῶν</u> ἐπὶ τὸν κάρταλλον αὐτοῦ.*

   9 Usque ad racemum colligent <u>quasi</u> in vinea *reliquias Israel.* Converte *manum tuam* <u>quasi</u> <u>*vindemiator*</u> ad cartallum.

    [the remnant of Israel ≈ a vine (to be gleaned thoroughly); you (Jerusalem) ≈ a grape-gatherer]

Jerem. 6.24 Anguish hath taken hold of us, and *pain,* <u>as</u> <u>*of a woman in travail*</u>.

   24 θλίψις κατέσχεν ἡμᾶς, ὠδῖνες <u>ὡς *τικτούσης*</u>.

   24 tribulatio apprehendit nos, *dolores* <u>ut</u> <u>*parturientem.*</u>

    [pain ≈ that of a woman in labor]

Jerem. 6.26 O daughter of my people … make thee *mourning*, <u>as for</u> *<u>an only son</u>*.

26 θύγατερ λαοῦ μου … πένθος <u>ἀγαπητοῦ</u> *ποίησαι* σεαυτῇ, κοπετὸν οἰκτρόν.

26 Filia populi mei … *luctum <u>unigeniti</u>* <u>fac</u> tibi, planctum amarum.

    [mourn ≈ an only son]

Jerem. 6.27 "I have set *<u>thee</u>* [for] *<u>a tower and a fortress</u>* among my people."

27 δοκιμαστὴν δέδωκά σε ἐν λαοῖς δεδοκιμασμένοις,

(I have caused thee to be tried among tried nations)

27 *<u>Probatorem</u>* dedi *te* in populo meo robustum.

    [you ≈ a tower and a fortress]

Jerem. 8.6 What have I done? *everyone turned to his course, <u>as the horse rusheth into the battle</u>. 7 Yea, <u>the stork in the heaven knoweth her appointed times: and the turtle and the crane and the swallow observe the time of their coming; but my people know not the judgment of the Lord</u>.*

6 τί ἐποίησα; διέλιπεν ὁ τρέχων ἀπὸ τοῦ δρόμου αὐτοῦ <u>ὡς ἵππος κάθιδρος ἐν χρεμετισμῷ αὐτοῦ</u>. 7 καὶ <u>ἡ ἀσίδα ἐν τῷ οὐρανῷ ἔγνω τὸν καιρὸν αὐτῆς, τρυγὼν καὶ χελιδών, ἀγροῦ στρουθία ἐφύλαξαν καιροὺς εἰσόδων ἑαυτῶν</u>, ὁ δὲ λαός μου οὗτος οὐκ ἔγνω τὰ κρίματα Κυρίου.

6 Quid feci? *Omnes conversi sunt ad cursum suum,* <u>quasi</u> *<u>equus impetu vadens ad praelium</u>. 7 <u>Milvus in caelo cognovit tempus suum: turtur, et hirundo, et ciconia custodierunt tempus adventus su</u>i: populus autem meus non cognovit judicium Domini.*

    [everyone (turned) ≈ a horse (rushes to battle); the people >
        NOT know the judgment of the Lord ≈ stork in heaven and
        turtle, crane and swallow > observe the time of their coming]

Jerem. 9.3 And they bend their *tongues* like *<u>their bow</u>* for lies.

3 καὶ ἐνέτειναν τὴν γλῶσσαν αὐτῶν <u>ὡς</u> <u>τόξον</u>,

3 Et extenderunt *linguam suam* <u>quasi</u> *<u>arcum</u>* mendacii et non veritatis.

    [tongue ≈ a bow]

Jerem. 9.8 Their *tongu*e is <u>as</u> *<u>an arrow shot out</u>.*

8 <u>βολὶς τιτρώσκουσα</u> ἡ γλῶσσα αὐτῶν

8 *<u>Sagitta vulnerans</u>* lingua eorum, dolum locuta est.

    [their tongue ≈ an arrow] **No prothesis in Greek and Latin texts**.

Jerem. 9.22 Even *the carcases of men* shall fall <u>as</u> <u>*dung*</u> upon the open field, and <u>as</u> the <u>*handful after the harvestman*</u>, and none shall gather them.

22 καὶ ἔσονται οἱ νεκροὶ τῶν ἀνθρώπων <u>εἰς</u> <u>*παράδειγμα*</u> ἐπὶ προσώπου τοῦ πεδίου τῆς γῆς ὑμῶν καὶ <u>ὡς</u> <u>*χόρτος ὀπίσω θερίζοντος*</u>, καὶ οὐκ ἔσται ὁ συνάγων.

22 Et cadet *morticinum hominis* <u>quasi</u> <u>*stercus*</u> super faciem regionis, et <u>quasi</u> *foenum post tergum metentis*, et non est qui colligat.

[men's carcasses ≈ dung ≈ handful]

Jerem. 10.5 *They* are upright <u>as</u> the <u>*palm tree*</u>.

5 θήσουσιν αὐτά, καὶ οὐ κινηθήσονται· (they will set them up and they will not move)

5 <u>in similitudinem</u> <u>*palmae*</u> *fabricata sunt*,

[they (the heathen) ≈ palm tree]

Jerem. 11.19 But <u>*I was like a lamb or an ox that is brought to the slaughter*</u>

19 ἐγὼ δὲ <u>*ὡς ἀρνίον ἄκακον*</u> ἀγόμενον τοῦ θύεσθαι οὐκ ἔγνων·

19 Et ego <u>quasi</u> <u>*agnus mansuetus*</u>, qui portatur ad victimam:

[I ≈ a lamb or ox brought to slaughter]

Jerem. 12.3 Pull them out <u>*like sheep for the slaughter.*</u>

3 ἅγνισον αὐτοὺς εἰς ἡμέραν σφαγῆς αὐτῶν.

(purify them for the day of their slaughter)

3 Congrega *eos* <u>quasi</u> <u>*gregem ad victimam*</u>,

[them (the wicked) ≈ sheep for slaughter]

Jerem. 12.8 *Mine heritage is unto* me <u>*as a lion in the forest.*</u>

8 ἐγενήθη ἡ κληρονομία μου ἐμοὶ <u>*ὡς λέων ἐν δρυμῷ*</u>·

8 Facta est mihi *haereditas mea* <u>quasi</u> <u>*leo in silva:*</u>

[my heritage ≈ a lion in the forest]

Jerem. 12.9 *Mine heritage* is unto me <u>*as a speckled bird.*</u>

9 μὴ <u>*σπήλαιον ὑαίνης*</u> ἡ κληρονομία μου ἐμοὶ ἢ <u>*σπήλαιον κύκλῳ αὐτῆς*</u>; (a hyena's cave or a cave round about her)

9 Numquid <u>*avis discolo*</u>r *haereditas mea* mihi? numquid avis tincta per totum?

[my heritage ≈ a speckled bird]

Jerem. 13.11 For <u>*as a girdle cleaveth to the loins of a man*</u>, **so** *have I caused to cleave unto me the whole house of Israel*, and the whole house of Judah.

11 ὅτι <u>*καθάπερ κολλᾶται τὸ περίζωμα περὶ τὴν ὀσφὺν τοῦ ἀνθρώπου*</u>, **οὕτως** *ἐκόλλησα πρὸς ἐμαυτὸν τὸν οἶκον τοῦ Ἰσραὴλ*

11 <u>Sicut</u> enim <u>*adhaeret lumbare ad lumbos viri,*</u> **sic** *agglutinavi mihi omnem domum Israel, et omnem domum Juda,* dicit Dominus,
[the house of Israel > me ≈ a girdle (around) > the loins of a man]

Jerem. 13.24 Therefore willI I scatter *them* <u>as</u> <u>*the stubble that passeth away by the wind of the wilderness.*</u>

24 καὶ *διέσπειρα αὐτοὺς* <u>*ὡς φρύγανα φερόμενα ἀπὸ ἀνέμου εἰς ἔρημον.*</u>

24 Et disseminabo *eos* <u>quasi</u> <u>*stipulam quae vento raptatur in deserto.*</u>
[them (scattered) ≈ stubble carried by the wind]

Jerem. 14.6 And the *wild asses* did stand in the high places, they *snuffed up the wind <u>like dragons.</u>*

6 *ὄνοι ἄγριοι ἔστησαν ἐπὶ νάπας· εἵλκυσαν ἄνεμον,*

6 Et *onagri* steterunt in rupibus, *traxerunt ventum* <u>quasi</u> <u>*dracones,*</u>
[wild asses (snuffed the wind) ≈ dragons]

Jerem. 14.9 Why shouldest *thou* [the hope of Israel] be <u>as</u> <u>*a man astonied,*</u> <u>as</u> <u>*a mighty man that cannot save?*</u>

9 μὴ *ἔσῃ* <u>*ὥσπερ ἄνθρωπος ὑπνῶν ἢ ὡς ἀνὴρ οὐ δυνάμενος σῴζειν;*</u>

9 Quare futurus *es* <u>velut</u> <u>*vir vagus,*</u> <u>ut</u> <u>*fortis qui non potest salvare?*</u> Tu autem in nobis es, Domine,
[you (hope of Israel) ≈ a man astounded ≈ a mighty man unable to save]

Jerem. 16.4 They shall die of grievous deaths; they shall not be lamented; neither shall they be buried; but *they* shall be <u>as</u> <u>*dung upon the face of the earth.*</u>

4 *ἐν θανάτῳ νοσερῷ ἀποθανοῦνται, οὐ κοπήσονται καὶ οὐ ταφήσονται· εἰς <u>παράδειγμα</u> ἐπὶ προσώπου τῆς γῆς ἔσονται καὶ τοῖς θηρίοις τῆς γῆς καὶ τοῖς πετεινοῖς τοῦ οὐρανοῦ·*

4 Mortibus aegrotationum morientur: non plangentur, et non sepelientur: in <u>*sterquilinium*</u> super faciem terrae *erunt.*
[they (people born here) ≈ dung on the face of the earth]

Jerem. 17.6 For *he* [5 *the man who trusts in man*] shall be <u>*like the heath in the desert.*</u>

6 καὶ *ἔσται* <u>*ὡς ἡ ἀγριομυρίκη ἡ ἐν τῇ ἐρήμῳ,*</u>

6 *Erit* enim <u>quasi</u> <u>*myricae in deserto,*</u> et non videbit cum venerit bonum:

[a trusting man ≈ a heath/myrica in the desert]

Jerem. 17.8 And *he* [the man who trusts in the Lord] *shall be <u>as a tree
    planted by the waters,</u>* etc

    8 καὶ ἔσται <u>ὡς ξύλον εὐθηνοῦν παρ' ὕδατα,</u>

    8 Et *erit* <u>quasi</u> <u>*lignum quod transplantatur super aquas,*</u> quod ad
    humorem mittit radices suas, et non timebit cum venerit aestus:

    [he (the man who trusts in the Lord) ≈ a thriving tree]

Jerem. 17.11 As t*<u>he partridge sitteth on eggs, and hatcheth them not;</u>* **so** *he
    that getteth riches, and not by right, shall leave them in the midst of his
    days, and at his end shall be a fool.*

    11 ἐφώνησε πέρδιξ, συνήγαγεν ἃ οὐκ ἔτεκε· ποιῶν πλοῦτον αὐτοῦ οὐ μετὰ
    <u>κρίσεως,</u>

    11 Perdix fovit quae non peperit: fecit divitias, et non in judicio: in
    dimidio dierum suorum derelinquet eas, et in novissimo suo erit
    insipiens.

    [a man gaining riches unjustly and losing them ≈ a partridge sit-
    ting on eggs but not hatching them]

Jerem. 18.6 O house of Israel, cannot *I* do with you *<u>as this potter</u>*? saith the
    Lord.Behold, *<u>as the clay is in the potter's hand,</u>* **so** *are ye in mine hand,
    O house of Israel..*

    6 εἰ <u>καθὼς ὁ κεραμεὺς οὗτος</u> οὐ δυνήσομαι τοῦ ποιῆσαι ὑμᾶς, οἶκος Ἰσραήλ;
    ἰδοὺ <u>ὡς ὁ πηλὸς τοῦ κεραμέως</u> ὑμεῖς ἐστε ἐν ταῖς χερσί μου.

    6 Numquid <u>sicut *figulus iste,*</u> non potero vobis facere, domus Israel?
    ait Dominus: ecce <u>sicut</u> <u>*lutum in manu figuli,*</u> **sic** *vos in manu
    mea,* domus Israel.

    [I/the Lord > you ≈ a potter > his clay]

Jerem. 18.17 *I will scatter them* <u>as</u> with *<u>an east wind</u> before the enemy;*

    17 <u>ὡς ἄνεμον καύσωνα</u> διασπερῶ αὐτοὺς κατὰ πρόσωπον ἐχθρῶν αὐτῶν,
    δείξω αὐτοῖς ἡμέραν ἀπωλείας αὐτῶν.

    17 Sicut <u>*ventus urens*</u> disperg*am* eos coram inimico.

    [I (will scatter my people) ≈ east wind (scatters the enemy)]

Jerem. 20.9 I will not make mention of him [the Lord] nor speak any
    more in his name. But *his word* was in my heart as *<u>a burning fire</u> shut
    <u>up in my bones.</u>*

    9 καὶ ἐγένετο <u>ὡς πῦρ καιόμενον φλέγον</u> ἐν τοῖς ὀστέοις μου.

9 [Non recordabor ejus, neque loquar ultra in nomine illius] et factus est in corde meo quasi *ignis exaestuans*, claususque in ossibus meis, et defeci, ferre non sustinens.

[the Lord's word in my heart ≈ a burning fire in my bones]

Jerem. 20.11 But the *LORD* is with me as a *mighty terrible one.*

11 ὁ δὲ Κύριος μετ᾽ ἐμοῦ καθὼς μαχητὴς ἰσχύων·

11 *Dominus* autem mecum est, quasi *bellator fortis.*

[the Lord with me ≈ a mighty fighter]

Jerem. 21.12 Execute judgment in the morning ... lest *my fury* go out like *fire*, and burn that none can quench it, because of the evil of your doings.

12 ἐξέλεσθε διηρπασμένον ἐκ χειρὸς ἀδικοῦντος αὐτόν, ὅπως μὴ ἀναφθῇ ὡς πῦρ ἡ ὀργή μου καὶ καυθήσεται, καὶ οὐκ ἔσται ὁ σβέσων.

21 Judicate mane judicium ... ne forte egrediatur ut *ignis indignatio mea*, et succendatur, et non sit qui extinguat, propter malitiam studiorum vestrorum.

[my fury ≈ fire]

Jerem. 23.9 Mine heart within me is broken because of the prophets; all my bones shake; *I am like a drunken man, and like a man whom wine hath overcome,* because of the Lord, and because of the words of his holiness.

9 Ἐν τοῖς προφήταις συνετρίβη ἡ καρδία μου, ἐν ἐμοὶ ἐσαλεύθη πάντα τὰ ὀστᾶ μου, ἐγενήθην ὡς ἀνὴρ συντετριμμένος καὶ ὡς ἄνθρωπος συνεχόμενος ἀπὸ οἴνου ἀπὸ προσώπου Κυρίου καὶ ἀπὸ προσώπου εὐπρεπείας δόξης αὐτοῦ.

9 Contritum est cor meum in medio mei, contremuerunt omnia ossa mea : *factus sum* quasi *vir ebrius,* et quasi *homo madidus a vino*, a facie Domini, et a facie verborum sanctorum ejus.

[I ≈ a drunken man ≈ a man overcome by wine]

Jerem. 23.12 Wherefore *their way* shall be unto them *as slippery way*s in the darkness.

12 διὰ τοῦτο γενέσθω ἡ ὁδὸς αὐτῶν αὐτοῖς εἰς ὀλίσθημα ἐν γνόφῳ,

12 Idcirco *via eorum* erit quasi *lubricum in tenebris*:

[their way (prophets and priests) ≈ slippery ways in darkness]

Jerem. 23.14 T*hey [prophets of Jerusalem] are all of them unto me as Sodom,*
and the inhabitants thereof *as Gomorrha.*

14 ἐγενήθησάν μοι πάντες ὡς Σόδομα καὶ οἱ κατοικοῦντες αὐτὴν ὥσπερ
Γόμορρα.

14 facti sunt [prophetae] mihi omnes ut *Sodoma,* et *habitatores* ejus
quasi *Gomorrha.*

[they (prophets of Jerusalem) ≈ Sodom; the inhabitants there
≈ Gomorrha]

Jerem. 23.29 Is not *my word* like as *a fire?* saith the Lord; and like *a hammer*
that breaketh the rock in pieces?

29 οὐκ ἰδοὺ οἱ λόγοι μου ὥσπερ πῦρ φλέγον, λέγει Κύριος, καὶ ὡς πέλυξ
κόπτων πέτραν;

29 Numquid non *verba mea* sunt quasi *ignis,* dicit Dominus, et quasi
malleus conterens petram?

[my word ≈ fire ≈ a hammer breaking a rock]

Jerem. 24.2 One basket had very good figs, even like the figs that are first
ripe: and the other basket had very naughty figs, which could not be
eaten, they were so bad. **A Comparison.**

The Lord showed Jeremiah two baskets of figs as an illustration
of the captives of Judah (the good figs) versus Zedekiah the
king of Judah and those that remain in the land and in Egypt
(the bad figs). Here we can see both literal comparisons (24.2)
and figurative similes.

Jerem. 24.5: Like *these good figs,* **so** will I acknowledge *them that are car-*
ried away captive of Judah;

24.5 ὡς τὰ σῦκα τὰ χρηστὰ ταῦτα, **οὕτως** ἐπιγνώσομαι τοὺς ἀποικισθέντας
Ἰούδα,

5 Sicut *ficus hae bonae,* **sic** cognoscam t*ransmigrationem Juda,* quam
emisi de loco isto in terram Chaldaeorum, i*n bonum.*

[Jews sent from Judah ≈ good figs]

Jerem. 24.8 And as *the evil figs, which cannot be eaten,* they are so evil;
surely thus saith the LORD, So will I give Zedekiah the king of
Judah, and his princes ... and them that dwell in the land of Egypt

8 καὶ ὡς τὰ σῦκα τὰ πονηρά, ἃ οὐ βρωθήσονται ἀπὸ πονηρίας αὐτῶν,
τάδε λέγει Κύριος, **οὕτως** παραδώσω τὸν Σεδεκίαν βασιλέα Ἰούδα

καὶ τοὺς μεγιστᾶνας αὐτοῦ καὶ τὸ κατάλοιπον Ἰερουσαλὴμ τοὺς
ὑπολελειμμένους ἐν τῇ γῇ ταύτῃ καὶ τοὺς κατοικοῦντας ἐν Αἰγύπτῳ.

8 Et sicut *ficus pessimae* quae comedi non possunt, eo quod sint
malae: haec dicit Dominus: **sic** dabo Sedeciam, regem Juda, et
principes ejus, et reliquos de Jerusalem, qui remanserunt in urbe
hac, et *qui habitant in terra Aegypti*.

[Zedikiah et al. + those who remain in this city etc. ≈ bad figs]

Jerem. 25.38 *He* hath forsaken his covert, as *the lion*.

= 32.24: ἐγκατέλιπεν ὥσπερ λέων κατάλειμμα αὐτοῦ,

25.38 Dereliqu*it* quasi *leo* umbraculum suum.

[He (the Lord) ≈ a lion]

NB the English and Latin of 25.38 correspond to the Greek text
of Chapter 32.24.

Jerem. 26.18 Thus saith the Lord of Hosts; *Zion* shall be plowed like *a
field*, and *Jerusalem* shall become *heaps*, and *the mountain of the house*
as the *high places of a forest*.

= 33.18 οὕτως εἶπε Κύριος· Σιὼν ὡς ἀγρὸς ἀροτριαθήσεται, καὶ Ἰερουσαλὴμ
εἰς ἄβατον ἔσται καὶ τὸ ὄρος τοῦ οἴκου εἰς ἄλσος δρυμοῦ.

26.18 *Sion* quasi *ager* arabitur, et *Jerusalem* in *acervum lapidum* erit,
et *mons domus* in *excelsa silvarum*.

[Zion ≈ a field for plowing ...]

Jerem. 29.17 Thus saith the Lord of hosts: Behold, I will send upon them
the sword, the famine, and the pestilence, and will make *them* [citi-
zens of Babylon] like *vile figs*, that cannot be eaten, they are so evil.

The equivalent Greek Chapter 36.17 is missing (all of 16–21).

17 ponam *eos* quasi *ficus malas*, quae comedi non possunt eo quod
pessimae sint:

[them [citizens of Babylon] ≈ vile figs]

Jerem. 30.6 Wherefore do I see *every man* with his hands on his loins, as
a woman in travail?

37.6 διότι ἑώρακα πάντα ἄνθρωπον καὶ αἱ χεῖρες αὐτοῦ ἐπὶ τῆς ὀσφύος
αὐτοῦ ... [**no simile**]

6 quare ergo vidi *omnis viri* manum super lumbum suum,
quasi *parturientis*,

[every man ≈ a woman in labor]

Jerem. 33.22 As *the host of heaven cannot be numbered, neither the sand of*
    the sea measured: **so** *will I multiply the seed of David my servant*, and
    the Levites that minister unto me.
    40.22 – Greek Chap. 40 ends at verse 13.
    22 Sicuti *enumerari non possunt stellae caeli, et metiri arena maris*, **sic**
        multiplicabo semen David servi mei, et Levitas ministros meos.
        [I will multiply David's seed ≈ the stars of heaven nor the sand
          of the sea can be measured]
    Note the long gap (Chapters 34–42) between similes.
    But there is a curious group of triplet expressions in this section:
    33.10–11 (without man without inhabitant without beast)
    36.10: (in the court at the entry in the ears)
    42.22 (by the sword by famine by pestilence)
    43.11 ('such as' – 3 times)
    44.13 (by the sword by famine by pestilence)
    44.20 (to the men, to the women, to all the people)
    44.23 (nor – nor – nor)
Jerem. 43.12 And I will kindle a fire in the houses of the gods of Egypt …
    And *he* [Nebuchadrezzar, the king of Babylon (43.10)] *shall array*
    *himself with the land of Egyp*t as *a shepherd putteth on his garment.*
    50.12 καὶ καύσει πῦρ ἐν οἰκίαις τῶν θεῶν αὐτῶν καὶ ἐμπυριεῖ αὐτὰς καὶ
        ἀποικιεῖ αὐτοὺς καὶ φθειριεῖ γῆν Αἰγύπτου, ὥσπερ φθειρίζει ποιμὴν
        τὸ ἱμάτιον αὐτοῦ, καὶ ἐξελεύσεται ἐν εἰρήνῃ, (And he shall kindle
        a fire in the houses of their gods, and shall burn them, and shall
        carry them away captives: and shall search the land of Egypt, <u>as</u>
        <u>a shepherd searches his garment</u>; and he shall go forth in peace.)
    43.12 et amicietur terra Aegypti <u>sicut</u> *amicitur pastor pallio suo.*
    [he > land of Egypt ≈ a shepherd > garment]
    KJB Jeremiah 44 = Greek 51; KJB 45 = Greek 51.31–35.
    KJB 46–52 does not correspond to the Greek. Thus there are no cor-
    responding Greek versions of the following similes.
Jerem. *46.8 Egypt riseth up* <u>like a flood</u>, and *his waters are moved* <u>like</u> *<u>the</u>*
    <u>rivers</u>.
    8 *Aegyptus <u>fluminis</u>* <u>instar</u> ascendit, et <u>velut</u> *<u>flumina</u>* movebuntur
        fluctus ejus.

[Egypt ≈ a flood; his waters ≈ the rivers]

Jerem. 46.20 *Egypt* is <u>like</u> *<u>a very fair heife</u>*r, but destruction cometh, it cometh out of the north. 21 Also *her hired men* are in the midst of her <u>like</u> *<u>fatted bullocks</u>*. ... 22 The *voice thereof shall go* <u>like</u> *<u>a serpent</u>*; for *they shall march with an army, and come against her with axes,* as <u>*hewers of wood*</u>. 23 ... *they* are <u>more than</u> *<u>the grasshoppers</u>*, and are innumerable.

20 *Vitula elegans atque formosa Aegyptus*, stimulator ab aquilone veniet ei. 21 *Mercenarii* quoque ejus, qui versabantur in medio ejus <u>quasi</u> *<u>vituli saginati</u>*, versi sunt, ... 22 *Vox ejus* <u>quasi</u> *<u>aeris</u>* sonabit: quoniam cum exercitu properabunt, et *cum securibus venient* ei <u>quasi</u> *<u>caedentes ligna</u>*. 23 ... *multiplicati* sunt <u>super</u> *<u>locustas</u>*, et non est eis numerus.

[Egypt ≈ a fair heifer; her hired men ≈ fatted bullocks; the voice ≈ a serpent; they ≈ hewers of wood; they ≈ grasshoppers]

Jerem. 48.6 Flee, save your lives, and *be* <u>like</u> *<u>the heath in the wilderness</u>*.

6 Fugite, salvate animas vestras, et *eritis* <u>quasi</u> *<u>myricae in deserto</u>*:

[you be ≈ the heath in the wilderness]

Jerem. 48.28 O *ye that dwell in Moab*, leave the cities, and dwell in the rock, and be <u>like</u> *<u>the dove that maketh her nest in the sides of the hole's mouth</u>*.

28 Relinquite civitates, et habitate in petra, *habitatores Moab*: et estote <u>quasi</u> *<u>columba nidificans in summo ore foraminis</u>*.

[dwellers in Moab ≈ the dove ...]

Jerem. 48.36 Therefore *mine heart* shall sound for Moab <u>like</u> *<u>pipes</u>*, and *mine heart* shall sound <u>like</u> *<u>pipes for the men of Kirheres</u>*.

36 Propterea *cor meum* ad Moab <u>quasi</u> *<u>tibiae</u>* resonabit, et *cor meum* ad viros muri fictilis <u>dabit</u> *<u>sonitum tibiarum</u>*:

[my heart (shall sound) ≈ pipes ≈ pipes for men of Kirheres]

Jerem. 48.38 for *I have broken Moab* <u>like</u> *<u>a vessel wherein is no pleasure</u>*, saith the LORD.

38 quoniam contrivi *Moab* <u>sicut</u> *<u>vas inutile</u>*, ait Dominus.

[Moab (broken) ≈ a vessel without pleasure]

Jerem. 49.16 though thou shouldest *make thy nest* <u>as high as</u> *<u>the eagle</u>*

16 cum *exaltaveris* <u>quasi</u> *<u>aquila</u> nidum tuum*,

[your nest (high) ≈ the eagle]

Jerem. 49.19 Behold, *he shall come up* like *a lion* ...
    19 Ecce <u>quasi</u> *leo* ascendet de superbia Jordanis ...
        [he ≈ a lion]
Jerem. 49.22 Behold, he shall come up and *fly* as *the eagle* ... *the heart of*
    the mighty men of Edom be <u>as</u> t<u>*he heart of a woman in her pangs*</u>.
    22 Ecce <u>quasi</u> *aquila* ascendet, et avolabit, et expandet alas suas super
        Bosran: et erit *cor fortium Idumaeae* in die illa <u>quasi</u> <u>*cor mulieris*</u>
        <u>*parturientis*</u>.
        [he (will fly) ≈the eagle; men's heart ≈ a woman's heart in
        her pangs]
Jerem. 50.37 A sword is upon their horses ... and *they* shall become
    <u>as</u> <u>*women*</u>.
    37 Gladius ad equos ejus, ... et *erunt* <u>quasi</u> <u>*mulieres*</u>:
        [they ≈ women]
Jerem. 50.42 *their voice* shall roar <u>like</u> *the sea*, and t*hey shall rid*e upon
    horses ... <u>like</u> <u>*a man to the battle.*</u>
    42 *vox eorum* <u>quasi</u> <u>*mare*</u> sonabit: et *super equos ascendent*, <u>sicut</u> <u>*vir*</u>
        <u>*paratus ad praelium*</u> contra te,
        [their voice (cruel people from the north) ≈ (shall roar) the sea;
        they shall ride horses ≈ a man to battle]
Jerem. 50.43 Anguish took hold of him [the king of Babylon], and *pangs*
    <u>as</u> <u>*of a woman in travail*</u>.
    43 angustia apprehendit eum, *dolor* <u>quasi</u> <u>*parturientem*</u>.
        [the king of Babylon ≈ a woman in labor]
Jerem. 50.44 Behold, *he* [the king of Babylon] *shall come up* like *a lion*.
    44 Ecce <u>quasi</u> *leo* ascendet,
        [he (shall come) ≈ a lion]
Jerem. 51.7 *Babylon* hath been <u>*a golden cup*</u> in the Lord's hand.
    7 <u>*Calix aureus*</u> Babylon in manu Domini.
Jerem. 51.14 Surely I will fill thee with *men* <u>as</u> with <u>*caterpillers;*</u> and they
    shall lift up a shout against thee.
    14 Quoniam replebo te *hominibus* <u>quasi</u> <u>*brucho*</u>, et super te celeuma
    cantabitur.
        [men ≈ caterpillers]

Jerem. 51.20 *Thou* are <u>*my battle-ax*</u> and weapons of war.

   20 <u>*Collidis*</u> *tu* mihi vasa belli.

Jerem. 51.30 The *mighty men of Babylon* … became <u>as</u> <u>*women*</u>.

   30 Cessaverunt *fortes Babylonis* a praelio, … et facti sunt <u>quasi</u>
     <u>*mulieres.*</u>

    [men of Babylon ≈ women]

Jerem. 51.33 The *daughter of Babylon* is <u>like</u> <u>*a threshingfloor*</u>, it is time to
thresh her.

   33 *Filia Babylonis* <u>quasi</u> <u>*area*</u>, tempus triturae ejus.

    [daughter of Babylon ≈ a threshingfloor]

Jerem. 51.34 Nebuchadnezzar the king of Babylon hath devoured me …
hath <u>made</u> *me* a<u>*n empty vessel,*</u> *he* hath swallowed me up <u>like</u> <u>*a*</u>
<u>*dragon*</u>.

     34 Comedit me, devoravit me *Nabuchodonosor rex*
      Babylonis: reddidit *me* <u>quasi</u> <u>*vas inane*</u>: absorbuit me
      <u>quasi</u> <u>*draco*</u>.

*a/2   [me ≈ an empty vessel; he ≈ a dragon]

Jerem. 51.38 *They* shall roar together <u>like</u> <u>*lions*</u>: *they* shall yell <u>as</u> <u>*lions'*</u>
<u>*whelps*</u>.

   38 Simul <u>ut</u> <u>*leones*</u> *rugient, excutient* comas <u>veluti</u> <u>*catuli leonum*</u>.

    [they ≈ lions / *lions' whelps*]

Jerem. 51.40 I will bring *them* down <u>like</u> <u>*lambs*</u> to the slaughter, <u>like</u> <u>*rams*</u>
with he goats.

   40 Deducam *eos* <u>quasi</u> <u>*agnos*</u> ad victimam, et <u>quasi</u> <u>*arietes*</u> cum haedis.

    [they ≈ lambs / rams]

Jerem. 51.55 Her [Babylon's] *waves* do roar <u>like</u> <u>*great waters*</u>.

   55 et sonabunt *fluctus eorum* <u>quasi</u> <u>*aquae multae.*</u>

    [Babylon's waves ≈ great waters]

* * *

Lamentations of Jeremiah (5 Chapters)

ΘΡΗΝΟΙ ΙΕΡΕΜΙΟΥ

Lam/Jerem. 1.1 How doth the city sit solitary, that was full of people! how
is she become <u>as a widow!</u> she that was great among the nations, and
princess among the provinces, how is she become tributary!

1 Πῶς ἐκάθισε μόνη ἡ πόλις ἡ πεπληθυμμένη λαῶν; ἐγενήθη <u>*ὡς χήρα*</u>
πεπληθυμμένη ἐν ἔθνεσιν.

1 Quomodo sedet sola civitas plena populo! Facta est
<u>quasi</u> *<u>vidua</u> domina gentium*; princeps provinciarum facta est sub
tributo.

[the city ≈ a widow]

Lam/Jerem. 1.6 *her princes are become* <u>like</u> *<u>harts, that find no pasture,</u>*
...

6 ἐγένοντο οἱ ἄρχοντες αὐτῆς <u>*ὡς κριοὶ οὐχ εὑρίσκοντες νομὴν*</u> καὶ ἐπορεύοντο
ἐν οὐκ ἰσχύϊ κατὰ πρόσωπον διώκοντος.

6 facti sunt *principes* ejus <u>velut</u> *<u>arietes non invenientes pascua</u>*,

[princes ≈ harts finding no pastures]

Lam/Jerem. 1.17 *Jerusalem is* <u>as</u> *<u>a menstruous woman</u>* among them.

17 ἐγενήθη Ἰερουσαλὴμ <u>εἰς</u> <u>*ἀποκαθημένην ἀναμέσον αὐτῶν.*</u>

17 facta est *Jerusalem* <u>quasi</u> *<u>polluta menstruis</u>* inter eos.

[Jerusalem ≈ menstruous woman]

Lam/Jerem. 2.3 [The Lord] he *burned against Jacob* <u>like</u> *a flaming fire* ...

4 He hath bent *his bow* <u>like</u> *an enemy*: he *stood with his right hand* <u>as</u>
<u>*an adversary*</u> ... he *pored out his fury* <u>like</u> *fire*. 5 The *Lord* was <u>as</u>
an *enemy* ... 6 And he hath violently taken away *his tabernacle* <u>as</u>
<u>if</u> it *were of a garden* ... 7 ... they have made *a noise in the house*
of the LORD <u>as</u> *in the day of a solemn feast.*

3 ἀνῆψεν ἐν Ἰακὼβ <u>*ὡς πῦρ φλόγα*</u> [Κύριος] ... 4 Ἐνέτεινε τόξον αὐτοῦ
<u>*ὡς ἐχθρός*</u>, ἐστερέωσε δεξιὰν αὐτοῦ <u>*ὡς ὑπεναντίος*</u> ... ἐξέχεεν <u>*ὡς πῦρ*</u>
τὸν θυμὸν αὐτοῦ. 5 Ἐγενήθη Κύριος <u>*ὡς ἐχθρός*</u> ... 6 Καὶ διεπέτασεν
<u>*ὡς ἄμπελον*</u> τὸ σκήνωμα αὐτοῦ, διέφθειρεν ἑορτὴν αὐτοῦ· ... 7 ...
φωνὴν ἔδωκαν ἐν οἴκῳ Κυρίου <u>*ὡς ἐν ἡμέρᾳ ἑορτῆς.*</u>

3 *succendit* in Jacob <u>quasi</u> *<u>ignem flammae devorantis</u>* in gyro ...

4 Tetendit *arcum suum* <u>quasi</u> *<u>inimicus</u>*, firmavit *dexteram suam* <u>quasi</u> *<u>hostis</u>* ... *effudit* <u>quasi</u> *<u>ignem indignationem suam</u>*. *5 Factus est Dominus* <u>velut</u> *<u>inimicus</u>* ... *6 Et dissipavit* <u>quasi</u> *<u>hortum tentorium suum; demolitus est tabernaculum suum. ... 7 ... Vocem dederu*n*t in domo Domini* <u>sicut</u> *<u>in die solemni</u>*.

    [he (burned) ≈ fire; he (bent his bow) ≈ an enemy; he (with his right hand) ≈ adversary; his fury ≈ fire; the Lord ≈ an enemy; his tabernacle ≈ a garden; (they made) noise ≈ on a feast day]

Lam/Jerem. 2.13 for *thy breach is great* <u>like</u> *<u>the sea</u>*.

    13 ὅτι ἐμεγαλύνθη *ποτήριον συντριβῆς σου·* (the cup of thy destruction is enlarged)

    13 magna est enim <u>velut</u> *<u>mare</u> contritio tua*:

      [your breach (large) ≈ the sea]

Lam/Jerem. 2.18 let *tears run down* <u>like</u> *<u>a river</u>* day and night: give thyself no rest; let not *<u>the apple of thine eye</u>* cease.

    18 καταγάγετε <u>ὡς χειμάρρους δάκρυα</u> ἡμέρας καὶ νυκτός· μὴ δῷς ἔκνηψιν σεαυτῇ, μὴ σιωπήσαιτο, θύγατερ, <u>ὁ ὀφθαλμός σου</u>.

    18 Deduc <u>quasi</u> *<u>torrentem</u> lacrimas* per diem et noctem; non des requiem tibi, neque taceat *<u>pupilla oculi tui</u>.*

      [tears ≈ a river]

Lam/Jerem. 3.10 *He* was unto me <u>as</u> *<u>a bear</u>* lying in wait, and <u>as</u> *<u>a lion</u>* in secret places.

    10 *<u>Ἄρκος ἐνεδρεύουσα</u>* αὐτός μοι, <u>λέων ἐν κρυφαίοις</u>·

    10 *<u>Ursus insidians</u> factus est* mihi, <u>leo</u> in absconditis.

      [he (the Lord) ≈ a bear ≈ a lion]

Lam/Jerem. 3.12 He hath bent his bow, and set *me* <u>as</u> *<u>a mark for the arrow</u>.*

    12 <u>ἐνέτεινε τόξον αὐτοῦ καὶ ἐστήλωσέ</u> *me* ὡς σκοπὸν εἰς βέλος.

    12 Tetendit arcum suum, et posuit *me* <u>quasi</u> *<u>signum ad sagittam</u>.*

      [me ≈ a mark for his arrow]

Lam/Jerem. 3.45 Thou hast made *us* <u>as</u> *<u>the offscouring and refuse</u>* in the midst of the people.

    45 καμμύσαι με καὶ ἀπωσθῆναι ἔθηκας ἡμᾶς ἐν μέσῳ τῶν λαῶν.

    45 *<u>Eradicationem et abjectionem</u>* posuisti *me* in medio populorum.

      [us ≈ offscouring and refuse]

Lam/Jerem. 3.52 Mine enemies chased *me* sore, <u>like</u> <u>*a bird*</u>, without cause.

52 Θηρεύοντες ἐθήρευσάν <u>*με ὡς στρουθίον*</u> πάντες οἱ ἐχθροί μου δωρεάν,

52 Venatione ceperunt *me* <u>quasi</u> <u>*avem*</u> inimici mei gratis

[me ≈ a bird]

Lam/Jerem. 4.2 The precious *sons of Zion*, <u>comparable to</u> <u>*fine gold*</u>, how are they esteemed <u>*as earthen pitchers*</u>?

2 Υἱοὶ Σιὼν οἱ τίμιοι, *οἱ ἐπηρμένοι ἐν χρυσίῳ*, πῶς ἐλογίσθησαν <u>*εἰς ἀγγεῖα*</u> <u>*ὀστράκινα*</u>

2 *Filii Sion inclyti,* et amicti auro primo: quomodo <u>reputati sunt in</u> <u>*vasa testea,*</u> opus manuum figuli!

[sons of Zion ≈ fine gold ≈ earthen pitchers]

Lam/Jerem. 4.3 *the daughter of my people* is become cruel, <u>like</u> <u>*the ostriches*</u> <u>*in the wilderness*</u>.

3 Καί γε δράκοντες ἐξέδυσαν μαστούς, ἐθήλασαν σκύμνοι αὐτῶν· θυγατέρες λαοῦ μου εἰς ἀνίατον <u>*ὡς στρουθίον ἐν ἐρήμῳ*</u>.

3 *filia populi me*i crudelis <u>quasi</u> <u>*struthio in deserto.*</u>

[daughter of my people (cruel) ≈ the ostrich(es) in the wilderness]

Lam/Jerem. 4.7 Her *Nazarites* were <u>*purer*</u> than <u>*snow*</u>, they were <u>*whiter*</u> than <u>*milk*</u>, they were <u>*more ruddy in body than rubies, their polishing*</u> <u>*was of sapphire; 8 Their visage is blacker than a coal … their skin …*</u> <u>*is withered, it is become like a stick.*</u> *9 They that be slain with the sword are* <u>better than</u> <u>*they that be slain with hunger*</u> …

7 Ἐκαθαριώθησαν Ναζιραῖοι αὐτῆς <u>ὑπὲρ χιόνα</u>, <u>ἔλαμψαν ὑπὲρ γάλα,</u> <u>ἐπυρώθησαν ὑπὲρ λίθους σαπφείρου</u> τὸ ἀπόσπασμα αὐτῶν. 8 <u>*Ἐσκότασεν ὑπὲρ ἀσβόλην*</u> τὸ εἶδος αὐτῶν, οὐκ ἐπεγνώσθησαν ἐν ταῖς ἐξόδοις· ἐπάγη δέρμα αὐτῶν ἐπὶ τὰ ὀστέα αὐτῶν, ἐξηράνθησαν, <u>ἐγενήθησαν ὥσπερ ξύλον</u> 9 <u>Καλοὶ</u> ἦσαν οἱ τραυματίαι ῥομφαίας ἢ <u>οἱ</u> <u>τραυματίαι λιμοῦ</u> …

7 <u>Candidiores</u> *Nazaraei* ejus <u>*nive*</u>, nitidiores <u>*lacte*</u>, <u>*rubicundiores ebore*</u> <u>*antiquo*</u>, <u>*sapphiro*</u> pulchriores. 8 *Denigrata est* <u>super</u> <u>*carbones*</u> facies eorum et non sunt cogniti in plateis; adhaesit cutis eorum ossibus: aruit, et *facta est* <u>quasi</u> <u>*lignum*</u>. 9 <u>Melius</u> fuit *occisis gladio* <u>quam</u> <u>*interfectis fame*</u>, …

[Nazarites (purer) ≈ snow ≈ (whiter) milk ≈ (polishing) sapphire; visage (blacker) ≈ coal; their skin ≈ a stick; slain with sword (better) ≈ slain with hunger]

Lam/Jerem. 4.14 *They* have wandered <u>as</u> <u>*blind men*</u> in the streets.

14 Ἐσαλεύθησαν ἐγρήγοροι αὐτῆς ἐν ταῖς ἐξόδοις.

14 Erraverunt *caeci* in plateis, polluti sunt in sanguine;
[(the sons of Zion) ≈ blind men]

Lam/Jerem. 4.19 Our *persecutors* are <u>swifter than</u> <u>*the eagles of the heaven*</u>.

19 Κοῦφοι ἐγένοντο οἱ διώκοντες ἡμᾶς <u>ὑπὲρ ἀετοὺς οὐρανοῦ,</u>

19 <u>Velociores</u> fuerunt *persecutores nostri* <u>*aquilis caeli.*</u>
[our persecutors (swifter) ≈ eagles of heaven]

Lam/Jerem. 5.10 *Our skin* was <u>*black*</u> <u>like</u> <u>*an oven*</u> because of the terrible famine.

10 τὸ δέρμα ἡμῶν, <u>ὡς κλίβανος</u> ἐπελιώθη συνεσπάσθησαν ἀπὸ προσώπου <u>καταιγίδων λιμοῦ.</u>

5.10 *Pellis nostra* <u>quasi</u> <u>*clibanus*</u> exusta est, a facie tempestatum famis.
[our skin (black) ≈ an oven]

* * *

Ezekiel /Jezekiel (48 Chapters)

Ezek. 1.4 And I looked, and, behold, a whirlwind came out of the north, a great cloud, and a fire infolding itself, and a brightness was about it, and out of the midst thereof <u>as</u> *the colour <u>of amber,</u>* out of the midst of the fire.

4 καὶ εἶδον καὶ ἰδοὺ πνεῦμα ἐξαῖρον ἤρχετο ἀπὸ βορρᾶ, καὶ νεφέλη μεγάλη ἐν αὐτῷ, καὶ φέγγος κύκλῳ αὐτοῦ καὶ πῦρ ἐξαστράπτον, καὶ ἐν τῷ μέσῳ αὐτοῦ <u>ὡς ὅρασις ἠλέκτρου ἐν μέσῳ τοῦ πυρὸς</u> καὶ φέγγος ἐν αὐτῷ.

4 Et vidi, et ecce ventus turbinis veniebat ab aquilone, et nubes magna, et ignis involvens, et *splendor* in circuitu ejus: et de medio ejus, <u>quasi</u> <u>*species electri*</u>, id est, de medio ignis:
[the color of the brightness of the whirlwind ≈ amber]

Ezek. 1.5 Also out of their midst thereof came *the likeness of four living creatures*. And this was their appearance. They had <u>*the likeness of a man*</u>.

5 καὶ ἐν τῷ μέσῳ ὡς <u>ὁμοίωμα τεσσάρων ζῴων,</u> καὶ αὕτη ἡ ὅρασις αὐτῶν· ὁμοίωμα <u>ἀνθρώπου</u> ἐπ' αὐτοῖς,

5 et in medio ejus *similitudo quatuor animalium.* Et hic aspectus eorum, *similitudo hominis* in eis.

  [appearance of 4 creatures ≈ likeness of a man]

Ezek. 1.7 And their feet were straight feet; and *the sole of their feet* was <u>like the *sole of a calf's foot*</u>: and *they sparkled* <u>like *the color of burnished brass*</u>.

  7 καὶ τὰ σκέλη αὐτῶν ὀρθά, καὶ πτερωτοὶ οἱ πόδες αὐτῶν, καὶ <u>*σπινθῆρες ὡς ἐξαστράπτων χαλκός,*</u> καὶ ἐλαφραὶ αἱ πτέρυγες αὐτῶν.

  7 Pedes eorum, pedes recti, et *planta pedis eorum* <u>quasi</u> *planta pedis vituli*: et *scintillae* <u>quasi</u> *aspectus aeris candentis*.

  [sole of their feet ≈ sole of a calf's foot; they (sparkled) ≈ the color of burnished brass]

Ezek. 1.8 And they had *the hands* of <u>*aman*</u> under their wings on their four sides.

  8 καὶ χεὶρ ἀνθρώπου ὑποκάτωθεν τῶν πτερύγων αὐτῶν ἐπὶ τὰ τέσσαρα μέρη αὐτῶν·

  8 Et *manus hominis* sub pennis eorum, in quatuor partibus : et facies et pennas per quatuor partes habebant.

  [their hands ≈ a man's hands]

Ezek. 1.10 And as for *the likeness of their faces, they four had <u>the face of a man, and the face of a lion</u>* on the right side; and they four had <u>the face of an ox</u> on the left side; and they four also had <u>the face of an eagle</u>.

  10 καὶ <u>*ὁμοίωσις τῶν προσώπων αὐτῶν· πρόσωπον ἀνθρώπου καὶ πρόσωπον λέοντος*</u> ἐκ δεξιῶν τοῖς τέσσαρσι καὶ πρόσωπον μόσχου ἐξ ἀριστερῶν τοῖς τέσσαρσι καὶ πρόσωπον ἀετοῦ τοῖς τέσσαρσι.

  10 *Similitudo autem vultus eorum,* <u>*facies hominis et facies leonis*</u> a dextris ipsorum quatuor, <u>*facies autem bovis*</u> a sinistris ipsorum quatuor, et <u>*facies aquilae*</u> desuper ipsorum quatuor.

  [they had faces ≈ a man, a lion, an ox, an eagle]

  This perhaps is best considered a <u>literal description</u> – but still figurative: they had faces [like that] of a lion etc.

Ezek. 1.13 And as for the likeness of the living creatures, their *appearance was* <u>like *burning coals of fire,*</u> and <u>like the *appearance of lamps.*</u>

  13 καὶ ἐν μέσῳ τῶν ζῴων <u>*ὅρασις ὡς ἀνθράκων πυρὸς καιομένων, ὡς ὄψις λαμπάδων συστρεφομένων ἀναμέσον τῶν ζῴων καὶ φέγγος τοῦ πυρός,*</u> καὶ ἐκ τοῦ πυρὸς ἐξεπορεύετο ἀστραπή.

13 Et *similitudo animalium, aspectus eorum* <u>quasi</u> <u>*carbonum ignis ardentium*</u>, et <u>quasi</u> <u>*aspectus lampadarum*</u>:

   [their appearance ≈ burning coals of fire ≈ lamps]

Ezek. 1.14 And *the living creatures ran and returned* <u>as</u> <u>*the appearance of a flash of lightning*</u>.

   13 καὶ φέγγος τοῦ πυρός, καὶ ἐκ τοῦ πυρὸς ἐξεπορεύετο ἀστραπή.

   14 Et *animalia ibant et revertebantur*, <u>in similitudinem</u> <u>*fulguris coruscantis*</u>.

   [their appearance ≈ a flash of lightning]

Ezek. 1.16 <u>*The appearance of their wheels and their work was*</u> <u>like unto</u> <u>*the colour of a beryl*</u>: and they four had one likeness: and <u>*their appearance and their work*</u> was <u>as it were</u> <u>*a wheel in at the middle of a wheel.*</u>

   16 καὶ <u>*τὸ εἶδος τῶν τροχῶν ὡς εἶδος θαρσείς*</u>, καὶ ὁμοίωμα ἐν τοῖς τέσσαρσι, <u>*καὶ τὸ ἔργον αὐτῶν ἦν καθὼς ἂν εἴη τροχὸς ἐν τροχῷ*</u>.

   16 Et *aspectus rotarum et opus earum* <u>quasi</u> <u>*visio maris*</u>: et una *similitudo* ipsarum quatuor: et *aspectus earum et opera* <u>quasi</u> sit <u>*rota in medio rotae*</u>.

   [wheels (color) ≈ beryl; their appearance ≈ a wheel in a wheel]

Ezek. 1.22 And t<u>*he likeness of the firmament upon the heads of the living creature was*</u> <u>as</u> <u>*the colour of the terrible crystal*</u>, stretched forth over their heads above.

   22 καὶ <u>*ὁμοίωμα ὑπὲρ κεφαλῆς αὐτοῖς τῶν ζῴων ὡσεὶ στερέωμα ὡς ὅρασις κρυστάλλου*</u> ἐκτεταμένον ἐπὶ τῶν πτερύγων αὐτῶν ἐπάνωθεν·

   22 Et *similitudo super capita* animalium firmamenti, <u>quasi</u> <u>*aspectus crystalli horribilis*</u>, et extenti super capita eorum desuper.

   [the likeness of the firmament over their heads ≈ the color of terrible crystal]

Ezek. 1.24 And when they went, I heard <u>*the noise of their wings,*</u> <u>like</u> <u>*the noise of great waters,*</u> <u>as</u> <u>*the voice of the Almighty,*</u> … <u>as</u> <u>the noise of an host.</u>

   24 καὶ ἤκουον <u>*τὴν φωνὴν τῶν πτερύγων αὐτῶν ἐν τῷ πορεύεσθαι αὐτὰ ὡς φωνὴν ὕδατος πολλοῦ*</u>·

   24 Et audiebam *sonum alarum*, <u>quasi</u> <u>*sonum aquarum multarum,*</u> <u>quasi</u> <u>*sonum sublimis Dei*</u>: cum ambularent, <u>quasi</u> *sonus* erat <u>*multitudinis*</u> <u>ut</u> <u>*sonus castrorum*</u>:

[the noise of their wings ≈ the noise of great waters ≈ the voice of the Almighty ≈ the noise of an host]

Ezek. 1.26 And above the firmament that was over their heads was *the likeness of a throne, as the appearance of a sapphire* stone : and *upon the likeness of the throne was the likeness as the appearance of a man above it.*

26 ὡς ὅρασις λίθου σαπφείρου ὁμοίωμα θρόνου ἐπ᾽ αὐτοῦ, καὶ ἐπὶ τοῦ ὁμοιώματος τοῦ θρόνου ὁμοίωμα ὡς εἶδος ἀνθρώπου ἄνωθεν.

26 Et super firmamentum, quod erat imminens capiti eorum, quasi *aspectus lapidis sapphiri similitudo throni*: et super similitudinem throni *similitudo* quasi *aspectus hominis desuper.*

[likeness ≈ a throne ≈ a sapphire stone ≈ the appearance of a man]

Ezek. 1.27 And I saw as the colour *of amber, as the appearance of fire* round about within it … and from the appearance of his loins even downward, I saw as it were the *appearance of fire, a*nd it had brightness round about.

27 καὶ εἶδον ὡς ὄψιν ἠλέκτρου ἀπὸ ὁράσεως ὀσφύος καὶ ἐπάνω, καὶ ἀπὸ ὁράσεως ὀσφύος καὶ ἕως κάτω εἶδον ὡς ὅρασιν πυρὸς καὶ τὸ φέγγος αὐτοῦ κύκλω.

27 Et vidi quasi *speciem electri,* velut *aspectus ignis,* intrinsecus ejus per circuitum: … vidi quasi *speciem ignis splendentis in circuitu,*

[color ≈ amber ≈ the appearance of fire]

Ezek. 1.28 As *the appearance of the bow that is in the cloud in the day of rain* **so** was *the appearance of the brightness round about.* This was the *appearance of the likeness of the glory of the LORD.*

28 ὡς ὅρασις τόξου, ὅταν ᾖ ἐν τῇ νεφέλῃ ἐν ἡμέραις ὑετοῦ, οὕτως ἡ στάσις τοῦ φέγγους κυκλόθεν. αὕτη ἡ ὅρασις ὁμοιώματος δόξης Κυρίου·

28 velut *aspectum arcus cum fuerit in nube in die pluviae.* **Hic** erat *aspectus splendoris per gyrum.*

[brightness around, the glory of the Lord ≈ a [rain?]bow in a rainy cloud]

Ezek. 3.3 Then did I eat it; and *it was in my mouth as hone*y for sweetness.

3 καὶ ἔφαγον αὐτήν, καὶ ἐγένετο ἐν τῷ στόματί μου ὡς μέλι γλυκάζον.

3 Et comedi *illud,* et factum est in ore meo sicut *mel dulce.*

[volumen istud]

[the taste of a roll (sweet) ≈ honey]

Ezek. 3.9 As <u>*an adamant*</u> harder than <u>*flint*</u> have I made *thy forehead*.

9 καὶ (8 – καὶ τὸ νῖκός σου κατισχύσω κατέναντι τοῦ νίκους αὐτῶν) ἔσται διαπαντὸς <u>κραταιότερον πέτρας</u>.

9 ut <u>*adamantem*</u> et ut <u>*silicem*</u> dedi *faciem tuam*:

[your forehead (harder) ≈ flint]

Ezek. 7.16 But *they that escape of them* … shall be on the mountains <u>*like doves of the valley*</u>.

18 καὶ ἀνασωθήσονται *οἱ ἀνασῳζόμενοι ἐξ αὐτῶν* καὶ ἔσονται ἐπὶ τῶν ὀρέων· πάντας ἀποκτενῶ.

18 Et salvabuntur *qui fugerint ex eis*: et erunt in montibus quasi <u>*columbae convallium omnes trepidi*</u>, unusquisque in iniquitate sua.

[Those who escape ≈ doves of the valley]

Ezek. 7.17 And *all knees* shall be <u>*weak as water.*</u>

17 πᾶσαι *χεῖρες* ἐκλυθήσονται, καὶ πάντες *μηροὶ* μολυνθήσονται ὑγρασίᾳ.

17 Omnes *manus* dissolventur, et *omnia genua* <u>*fluent aquis*</u>.

[knees (weak) ≈ water]

Ezek. 8.2 Then I beheld, and lo a *likeness* <u>as</u> <u>*the appearance of fire*</u> … as the <u>*appearance of brightness*</u>, as <u>*the colour of amber*</u>. 3 And he put forth <u>*the form of an hand*</u>, and took me by a lock of mine head.

2 καὶ εἶδον καὶ ἰδοὺ <u>ὁμοίωμα ἀνδρός</u>, ἀπὸ τῆς ὀσφύος αὐτοῦ καὶ ἕως κάτω πῦρ, καὶ <u>ἀπὸ τῆς ὀσφύος αὐτοῦ ὑπεράνω αὐτοῦ ὡς ὅρασις ἠλέκτρου</u>. 3 καὶ <u>ἐξέτεινεν ὁμοίωμα χειρὸς</u> καὶ ἀνέλαβέ με τῆς κορυφῆς μου.

2 et vidi: et ecce *similitudo* quasi *aspectus ignis*: … quasi <u>*aspectus splendoris*</u>, ut <u>*visio electri*</u>. 3 Et emissa <u>*similitudo manus*</u> apprehendit me in cincinno capitis mei.

[a likeness ≈ appearance of fire / of brightness ≈ the color of amber; form ≈ a hand]

Ezek. 10.1 Then I looked, and, behold, in the firmament that was above the head of the cherubim there appeared over them <u>as it were</u> <u>*a sapphire stone,*</u> <u>as</u> the appearance of <u>*the likeness of a throne*</u>.

1 ΚΑΙ εἶδον καὶ ἰδοὺ ἐπάνω τοῦ στερεώματος τοῦ ὑπὲρ κεφαλῆς τῶν Χερουβὶμ <u>ὡς λίθος σαπφείρου ὁμοίωμα θρόνου ἐπ' αὐτῶν</u>.

1 Et vidi: et ecce in firmamento quod erat super caput cherubim, <u>quasi</u> <u>*lapis sapphirus*</u>, <u>quasi</u> <u>*species similitudinis solii*</u>, apparuit super ea.

[there appeared over them ≈ a sapphire stone ≈ a throne]

Ezek. 10.8 And there appeared in the cherubim *the form of a man's hand* under their wings.

> 8 καὶ εἶδον τὰ Χερουβὶμ <u>ὁμοίωμα χειρῶν ἀνθρώπων ὑποκάτωθεν τῶν πτερύγων αὐτῶν.</u>

> 8 Et apparuit in cherubim *similitudo <u>manus hominis subtus pennas</u>* eorum.

> [the form/likeness ≈ a man's hand]

Ezek. 10.9 and *<u>the appearance of the wheels</u>* was as *<u>the colour of a beryl stone.</u>*

> 9 καὶ <u>ἡ ὄψις τῶν τροχῶν ὡς ὄψις λίθου ἄνθρακος.</u>

> 9 *species autem rotarum* erat <u>quasi</u> *<u>visio lapidis chrysolith</u>*i:

> [the appearance of the wheels ≈ a beryl stone]

Ezek. 10.10 And *<u>as for their appearances, they four had one likeness,</u> as if <u>a wheel had been in the midst of a wheel.</u>*

> 10 καὶ <u>ἡ ὄψις αὐτῶν ὁμοίωμα ἓν τοῖς τέσσαρσιν, ὃν τρόπον ὅταν ᾖ τροχὸς ἐν μέσῳ τροχοῦ.</u>

> 10 et *aspectus earum* <u>similitudo una quatuor, quasi</u> sit *<u>rota in medio rotae.</u>*

> [one likeness ≈ a wheel in the middle of a wheel]

Ezek. 10.21 Every one had four faces apiece … and *the likeness <u>of the hands of a man</u>* was under their wings. 22 And *the likeness of their faces* <u>was the same faces which I saw by the river of Chebar.</u>

> 21 τέσσαρα πρόσωπα τῷ ἑνί, καὶ ὀκτὼ πτέρυγες τῷ ἑνί, καὶ ὁμοίωμα χειρῶν ἀνθρώπου ὑποκάτωθεν τῶν πτερύγων αὐτῶν. 22 καὶ ὁμοίωσις τῶν προσώπων αὐτῶν, ταῦτα τὰ πρόσωπά <u>ἐστιν</u> <u>ἃ εἶδον ὑποκάτω τῆς δόξης τοῦ Θεοῦ Ἰσραὴλ ἐπὶ τοῦ ποταμοῦ τοῦ Χοβάρ.</u>

> 21 Quatuor vultus uni, et quatuor alae uni: et *similitudo manus* hominis sub alis eorum. 22 Et *similitudo vultuum eorum, <u>ipsi vultus quos videram juxta fluvium Chobar.</u>*

> [the hands ≈ hands of a man; the likeness of their faces ≈ the same faces which I saw by the river Chebar]

Ezek. 13.4 O Israel, thy *<u>prophets are</u> <u>like</u> <u>the foxes in the deserts.</u>*

> 4 <u>ὡς ἀλώπεκες ἐν ταῖς ἐρήμοις, οἱ προφῆταί σου Ἰσραήλ.</u>

> 4 Quasi *<u>vulpes in desertis</u>* prophetae tui, Israel, erant.

> [your prophets ≈ foxes in the deserts]

Ezek. 16.7 I have caused *thee to multiply* <u>as</u> *the bud of the field.*

7 <u>*καθὼς ἡ ἀνατολὴ τοῦ ἀγροῦ*</u> δέδωκά σε·

7 Multiplicatam <u>quasi</u> *germen agri* dedi *te:*

[you ≈ the bud of the field]

Ezek. 16.30 How weak is thine heart, saith the Lord God [to Jerusalem], seeing *thou doest all these thing*s, <u>the work of</u> *an imperious whorish woman:* ... 31 hast not been <u>as</u> *an harlot,* in that thou scornest hire: 32 But <u>as</u> *a wife that committed adultery,* which taketh strangers instead of her husband! ... 35 Wherefore, *O harlot,* hear the word of the Lord.

30 τί διαθῶ τὴν θυγατέρα σου, λέγει Κύριος, ἐν τῷ ποιῆσαί σε πάντα ταῦτα, <u>*ἔργα γυναικὸς πόρνης*</u>; ... 31 καὶ ἐγένου <u>*ὡς πόρνη*</u> συνάγουσα μισθώματα. ... 35 Διὰ τοῦτο, <u>*πόρνη*</u>, ἄκουε λόγον Κυρίου·

30 In quo mundabo cor tuum, ait Dominus Deus, cum facias omnia *haec opera mulieris meretricis et procacis*? 31 nec facta es <u>quasi</u> *meretrix fastidio augens pretium* ... 35 Propterea, *meretrix*, audi verbum Domini.

[thou/Israel ≈ a harlot]

Ezek. 16.44 Behold, every one that useth **proverbs** shall use **this proverb** against thee, saying, <u>As</u> is *the mother*, **so** is *her daughter.*

44 ταῦτά ἐστι πάντα, ὅσα εἶπαν κατὰ σοῦ ἐν **παραβολῇ** λέγοντες· <u>*καθὼς ἡ μήτηρ, 45 καὶ ἡ θυγάτηρ*</u>·

44 Ecce omnis qui dicit vulgo **proverbium**, in te assumet illud, dicens: <u>Sicut</u> *mater*, **ita** et *filia ejus.*

[her daughter ≈ the mother]

Ezek. 19.2 What <u>is</u> *thy mother? A lioness* ...

2 τί ἡ μήτηρ σου; <u>*σκύμνος*</u>·

2 Quare *mater tua* <u>*leaena*</u> inter leones cubavit? **19.9)**

[your mother ≈ a lioness] **(similetic story continues to /**

Ezek. 19.10 Thy *mother* is <u>like</u> *a vine in thy blood,* planted by the waters:

10 <u>*ἡ μήτηρ σου ὡς ἄμπελος καὶ ὡς ἄνθος ἐν ῥόᾳ ἐν ὕδατι πεφυτευμένη*</u>,

10 *Mater tua* <u>quasi</u> *vinea in sanguine tuo* super aquam plantata est: [your mother ≈ a vine in your blood]

Ezek. 20.32 *We* will be <u>as</u> *the heathen*, <u>as</u> t*he families of the countries*, to
serve wood and stone.

   32 ἐσόμεθα <u>ὡς</u> <u>τὰ ἔθνη καὶ ὡς αἱ φυλαὶ τῆς γῆς</u>

   32 Erimus <u>sicut</u> <u>*gentes*</u> et <u>sicut</u> <u>*cognationes terrae*</u>,

      [we ≈ the heathen]

Ezek. 21.32 *Thou* shalt <u>be for</u> *fuel to the fire*;

   32 ἐν πυρὶ ἔσῃ <u>κατάβρωμα</u>,

   32 <u>*Igni*</u> eris <u>*cibus*</u>;

      [You ≈ fuel for the fire]

Ezek. 22.20 <u>As</u> *they gather silver, and brass etc. into the midst of the furnace*
… **so** *will I gather you in mine anger and in my fury,* and I will leave
you there, and melt you.

   20 <u>καθὼς</u> <u>εἰσδέχεται ἄργυρος καὶ χαλκὸς καὶ σίδηρος καὶ κασσίτερος καὶ</u>
      <u>μόλιβος εἰς μέσον καμίνου τοῦ ἐκφυσῆσαι εἰς αὐτὸ πῦρ τοῦ χωνευθῆναι</u>,
      οὕτως εἰσδέξομαι ἐν ὀργῇ μου καὶ συνάξω καὶ χωνεύσω ὑμᾶς

   20 <u>*congregatione argenti, et aeris, et stanni, et ferri, et plumbi, in medio*</u>
      <u>*fornacis, ut succendam in ea ignem ad conflandum.*</u> **Sic** *congregabo*
      in furore meo, et in ira mea, et requiescam, et conflabo vos.

      [I will gather you in my anger ≈ they gather silver etc. into a
      furnace]

Ezek. 22.22 <u>*As silver is melted into the midst of the furnace,*</u> **so** *shall ye be*
melted in the midst thereof.

   22 <u>ὃν τρόπον χωνεύεται ἀργύριον ἐν μέσῳ καμίνου</u>, **οὕτως** χωνευθύσεσθε
      ἐν μέσῳ αὐτῆς· καὶ ἐπιγνώσεσθε διότι ἐγὼ Κύριος ἐξέχεα τὸν θυμόν
      μου ἐφ᾽ ὑμᾶς.

   22 Ut <u>*conflatur argentum in medio fornacis,*</u> **sic** *eritis in medio ejus:*[you
      melted in their midst ≈ silver melted in a furnace]

Ezek. 22.27 *Her princes in the midst thereof are* <u>*like wolves ravening the prey.*</u>

   27 οἱ ἄρχοντες αὐτῆς ἐν μέσῳ αὐτῆς <u>ὡς λύκοι ἁρπάζοντες ἁρπάγματα τοῦ</u>
      <u>ἐκχέαι αἷμα</u>, ὅπως πλεονεξίᾳ πλεονεκτῶσι.

   27 *Principes ejus in medio illius,* <u>quasi</u> <u>*lupi rapientes praedam*</u> ad
      effundendum sanguinem,

      [her princes ≈ wolves]

Ezek. 23.45 And *the righteous men*, they shall judge them after the manner of *adulteresses*, and after the manner of *women that shed blood*.

45 καὶ ἄνδρες δίκαιοι αὐτοὶ καὶ ἐκδικήσουσιν αὐτὰς ἐκδικήσει *μοιχαλίδος* καὶ ἐκδικήσει αἵματος, ὅτι *μοιχαλίδες* εἰσί, καὶ αἷμα ἐν χερσὶν αὐτῶν.

45 Viri ergo justi sunt : hi judicabunt eas judicio *adulterarum*, et judicio *effundentium sanguinem*, quia *adulterae* sunt.

[(righteous men shall judge) them ≈ adulteresses ≈ murderesses]

Ezek. 26.14 And *I will make thee* like *the top of a rock*: thou shalt be a *place to spread nets upon*;

14 καὶ *δώσω σε εἰς λεωπετρίαν, ψυγμὸς σαγηνῶν ἔσῃ*, οὐ μὴ οἰκοδομηθῇς ἔτι.

14 Et *dabo te* in *limpidissimam petram*, siccatio sagenarum eris, nec aedificaberis ultra, quia ego locutus sum, ait Dominus Deus.

[I will make you ≈ top of a rock]

Ezek. 32.2 Son of man, take up a lamentation for Pharaoh king of Egypt, and say unto him, *Thou* art like *a young lion of the nations*, and *thou* art as *a whale in the seas*:

2 υἱὲ ἀνθρώπου λαβὲ θρῆνον ἐπὶ Φαραὼ βασιλέα Αἰγύπτου καὶ ἐρεῖς αὐτῷ· *λέοντι ἐθνῶν ὡμοιώθης καὶ σὺ ὡς δράκων ὁ ἐν τῇ θαλάσσῃ.*

2 Fili hominis, assume lamentum super Pharaonem regem Aegypti, et dices ad eum: *Leoni gentium* assimilatus es, et *draconi qui est in mari*,

[you/Pharoah ≈ a young lion ≈ a whale]

Ezek. 38.9 *Thou* [Gog] shalt ascend and come like *a storm*, *thou* shalt be like *a cloud* to cover the land.

9 καὶ *ἀναβήσῃ ὡς ὑετὸς καὶ ἥξεις ὡς νεφέλη κατακαλύψαι γῆν* καὶ ἔσῃ σὺ καὶ πάντες οἱ περὶ σὲ καὶ ἔθνη πολλὰ μετὰ σοῦ.

9 Ascendens autem quasi *tempestas* venies, et quasi *nubes*, ut operias terram.

[you ≈ storm ≈ a cloud]

Ezek. 40.3 And he brought me thither, and, behold, there was a man, whose *appearance was like the appearance of brass.*

3 καὶ εἰσήγαγέ με ἐκεῖ, καὶ ἰδοὺ ἀνήρ, καὶ *ἡ ὅρασις αὐτοῦ ἦν ὡσεὶ ὅρασις χαλκοῦ στίλβοντος.*

3 et ecce vir cujus erat *species* quasi *species aeris.*

[a man ≈ brass]

Ezek. 43.2 And, behold, the glory of the God of Israel came from the way
of the east: and *his voice* was <u>like</u> <u>*the noise of many waters.*</u>
  2 καὶ φωνὴ τῆς παρεμβολῆς <u>ὡς φωνὴ διπλασιαζόντων πολλῶν,</u> καὶ ἡ γῆ
    ἐξέλαμπεν <u>ὡς φέγγος ἀπὸ τῆς δόξης κυκλόθεν.</u>
  2 Et ecce gloria Dei Israel ingrediebatur per viam orientalem: et
    vox erat ei <u>quasi</u> <u>*vox aquarum multarum,*</u> et terra splendebat a
    majestate ejus.
    [his voice ≈ the noise of many waters]

***

Daniel (12 Chapters)

Δανιήλ

Daniel 2.35 Then was the *iron, the clay* … broken to pieces together, and
  became <u>like</u> <u>*the chaff of the summer threshing floors.*</u>
    35 τότε ἐλεπτύνθησαν εἰς ἅπαξ τὸ ὄστρακον, ὁ σίδηρος, ὁ χαλκός, ὁ ἄργυρος,
    ὁ χρυσός, καὶ ἐγένετο <u>ὡσεὶ</u> <u>κονιορτὸς ἀπὸ ἅλωνος θερινῆς·</u>
    35 Tunc contrita sunt pariter *ferrum, testa, aes, argentum, et aurum,* et
    redacta <u>quasi</u> <u>*in favillam aestivae areae,*</u>
    [iron, clay etc. ≈ the chaff of summer threshing floors]
    (Daniel's interpretation of King Nebuchadnezzar's dream)
Daniel 2.40 And *the fourth kingdom* shall be <u>strong as</u> <u>*iron*</u> etc.
    40 καὶ βασιλεία τετάρτη, ἥτις ἔσται ἰσχυρὰ <u>ὡς</u> <u>σίδηρος·</u>
    40 Et *regnum quartum* erit <u>velut</u> <u>*ferrum*</u> .
    [the fourth kingdom ≈ (strong) iron]
Daniel 2.42 And <u>as</u> <u>*the toes of the feet were part of iron, and part of clay,*</u> **so**
  the kingdom shall be partly strong, and partly broken.
    42 καὶ <u>οἱ δάκτυλοι τῶν ποδῶν μέρος μέν τι σιδηροῦν μέρος δέ τι ὀστράκινον,</u>
    μέρος τι τῆς βασιλείας ἔσται ἰσχυρὸν καὶ ἀπ᾽ αὐτῆς ἔσται συντριβόμενον.
    42 Et <u>*digitos pedum ex parte ferreos, et ex parte fictiles*</u> : ex parte *regnum*
    erit solidum, et ex parte contritum.
    [kingdom part strong and broken ≈ toes part iron and part
      clay]   [Daniel's allegorical interpretation continues]

Daniel 4.33 and he [Nebuchadnezzar] was driven from men, and *did eat grass <u>as oxen</u>. ...* till *his hairs were grown* <u>like eagles'</u> <u>feathers</u> and *his nails* <u>like</u> <u>*birds' claws.*</u>

30 αὐτῇ τῇ ὥρᾳ ὁ λόγος συνετελέσϑη ἐπὶ Ναβουχοδονόσορ, καὶ ἀπὸ τῶν ἀνϑρώπων ἐξεδιώχϑη καὶ χόρτον <u>ὡς</u> <u>βοῦς</u> ἤσϑιε, καὶ ... ἕως οὗ αἱ τρίχες αὐτοῦ <u>ὡς</u> <u>λεόντων</u> ἐμεγαλύνϑησαν καὶ οἱ ὄνυχες αὐτοῦ <u>ὡς</u> <u>ὀρνέων.</u>

30 Eadem hora sermo completus est super Nabuchodonosor, et ex hominibus abjectus est, et foenum <u>ut</u> <u>bos</u> comedit, ... donec capilli ejus <u>in similitudinem</u> <u>aquilarum</u> crescerent, et ungues ejus <u>quasi</u> <u>avium.</u>

[he (ate grass) ≈ oxen; his hair ≈ eagles's feathers; his nails ≈ birds' claws] **NB > the Greek and Latin similes are in different verses in this chapter.**

Daniel 7.4 The *first* [of the four great beasts] was <u>like *a lion*</u>, and had eagle's wings ... 5 And behold *another beas*t, a second, <u>like</u> to a *<u>bear</u>* ... 6 After this I beheld, and lo *another,* <u>like</u> *a leopard* ...

4 τὸ πρῶτον <u>ὡσεὶ</u> <u>λέαινα</u>, καὶ πτερὰ αὐτῇ <u>ὡσεὶ</u> <u>ἀετοῦ</u>· ...

5 καὶ ἰδοὺ ϑηρίον δεύτερον <u>ὅμοιον</u> <u>ἄρκῳ</u>, ... 6 καὶ ἰδοὺ ϑηρίον ἕτερον <u>ὡσεὶ</u> <u>πάρδαλις.</u>

4 Prima <u>quasi</u> *<u>leaena</u>*, et alas habebat *<u>aquilae</u>* ... 5 Et ecce *bestia* alia <u>similis</u> <u>urso</u> ... 6 et ecce *alia* <u>quasi</u> *<u>pardus</u>*, et *alas* habebat <u>quasi</u> <u>*avis.*</u>

[first beast ≈ a lion, second ≈ a bear, third ≈ a leopard]

Daniel 7.8 In this horn were *eyes* <u>like</u> *<u>the eyes of a man</u>.*

8 καὶ ἰδοὺ ὀφϑαλμοὶ <u>ὡσεὶ</u> <u>ὀφϑαλμοὶ ἀνϑρώπου</u> ἐν τῷ κέρατι τούτῳ.

8 et ecce oculi, quasi oculi hominis erant in cornu isto.

[eyes ≈ eyes of a man]

Daniel 7.9 and the Ancient of days did sit, *whose garment was white* <u>as snow</u>, and *the hair of his head* <u>like</u> the *<u>pure wool</u>*: *his throne* was <u>like</u> the *<u>fiery flame</u>*, and *his wheels* <u>as</u> <u>*burning fire.*</u>

9 καὶ παλαιὸς ἡμερῶν ἐκάθητο, καὶ τὸ ἔνδυμα αὐτοῦ λευκὸν <u>ὡσεὶ</u> <u>χιών</u>, καὶ ἡ ϑρὶξ τῆς κεφαλῆς αὐτοῦ <u>ὡσεὶ</u> <u>ἔριον καϑαρόν</u>, ὁ ϑρόνος αὐτοῦ <u>φλὸξ πυρός</u>, οἱ τροχοὶ αὐτοῦ <u>πῦρ φλέγον</u>·

9 Aspiciebam donec throni positi sunt, et antiquus dierum sedit. *Vestimentum ejus candidum* quasi *nix, et capilli capitis ejus* quasi *lana munda: thronus ejus flammae ignis: rotae ejus ignis accensus.* [garment white ≈ snow, hair ≈ pure wool, throne ≈ fiery flame, wheels ≈ burning fire]

Daniel 10.5 Daniel's vision of "a certain man clothed in linen":

6 *His body also* was like *the beryl,* and *his face* as *the appearance of lightning, and his eyes* as *lamps of fire, and his arms and his feet* like *in colour to polished brass, and the voice of his words* like *the voice of a multitude.*

6 καὶ *τὸ σῶμα αὐτοῦ* ὡσεὶ *θαρσίς, καὶ τὸ πρόσωπον αὐτοῦ* ὡσεὶ *ὅρασις ἀστραπῆς, καὶ οἱ ὀφθαλμοὶ αὐτοῦ* ὡσεὶ *λαμπάδες πυρός, καὶ οἱ βραχίονες αὐτοῦ καὶ τὰ σκέλη* ὡς *ὅρασις χαλκοῦ στίλβοντος καὶ ἡ φωνὴ τῶν λόγων αὐτοῦ* ὡς *φωνὴ ὄχλου.*

6 et *corpus ejus* quasi *chrysolithus,* et *facies ejus* velut *species fulguris,* et *oculi ejus* ut *lampas ardens:* et *brachia ejus,* et quae deorsum sunt usque ad pedes, quasi *species aeris candentis:* et *vox sermonum ejus* ut *vox multitudinis.*

[his body ≈ beryl, face ≈ lightning, eyes ≈ lamps of fire, arms and legs ≈ polished brass, his voice ≈ the voice of a multitude]

Daniel 12.3 And *they that be wise shall shine* as *the brightness of the firmament;* and *they that turn many to righteousness* as *the stars for ever and ever.*

3 καὶ οἱ συνιέντες ἐκλάμψουσιν ὡς ἡ λαμπρότης τοῦ στερεώματος καὶ ἀπὸ τῶν δικαίων τῶν πολλῶν ὡς οἱ ἀστέρες εἰς τοὺς αἰῶνας καὶ ἔτι.

3 *Qui autem docti fuerint, fulgebunt* quasi *splendor firmamenti:* et *qui ad justitiam erudiunt multos,* quasi *stellae in perpetuas aeternitates.*

[the wise (shall shine) ≈ the brightness of the firmament; *they that turn many to righteousness* ≈ the stars]

Note: Three additional chapters (13, 14, 15), not found in the Hebrew and Aramaic text of Daniel, are also not included in the King James Bible.

* * *

Hosea (14 Chapters)

Ὡσηέ Α

Hosea 1.10 Yet *the number of the children of Israel* shall be as *the sand of the sea,* which cannot be measured nor numbered.

> 2.1 ΚΑΙ ἦν *ὁ ἀριθμὸς τῶν υἱῶν Ἰσραὴλ ὡς ἡ ἄμμος τῆς θαλάσσης,* ἣ οὐκ ἐκμετρηθήσεται οὐδὲ ἐξαριθμηθήσεται.

> 1.10 Et erit *numerus filiorum Israel* quasi *arena maris,* quae sine mensura est, et non numerabitur.

> [number of Israelis ≈ the sand of the sea]

Hosea 2.3 and set *her* [your mother] like *a dry land,* and slay her with thirst.

> 3 καὶ θήσω αὐτὴν ἔρημον καὶ τάξω *αὐτὴν ὡς γῆν ἄνυδρον* καὶ ἀποκτενῶ αὐτὴν ἐν δίψει.

> 3 et ponam *eam* quasi *solitudinem,* et statuam *eam* velut *terram inviam,* et interficiam eam siti.

> [her ≈ dry land]

Hosea 4.16 For *Israel slideth back as a back-sliding heifer:* now the *Lord will feed them as a lamb in a large place.*

> 16 διότι *ὡς δάμαλις παροιστρῶσα παροίστρησεν Ἰσραήλ·* νῦν νεμήσει αὐτοὺς Κύριος *ὡς ἀμνὸν ἐν εὐρυχώρῳ.*

> 16 Quoniam sicut *vacca lasciviens* declinavit *Israel;* nunc pascet *eos* Dominus, quasi *agnum in latitudine.*

> [Israel ≈ a back-sliding heifer ≈ a lamb in a large place]

Hosea 5.10 The *princes of Judah* were like *them that remove the bound:* therefore I will pour out *my wrath upon them* like *water.*

> 10 ἐγένοντο οἱ ἄρχοντες *Ἰούδα ὡς μετατιθέντες ὅρια,* ἐπ᾽ *αὐτοὺς ἐκχεῶ ὡς ὕδωρ τὸ ὅρμημά μου.*

> 10 Facti sunt *principes Juda* quasi *assumentes terminum;* super eos effundam quasi *aquam* iram meam.

> [princes of Judah ≈ they that remove the bound (boundary?); my wrath ≈ water]

Hosea 5.14 For *I* will be unto Ephraim as *a lion,* and as *a young lion* to the house of Judah.

> 14 διότι ἐγώ *εἰμι ὡς πανθὴρ τῷ Ἐφραίμ* καὶ *ὡς λέων τῷ οἴκῳ Ἰούδα·*

14 Quoniam *ego* quasi *leaena* Ephraim, et quasi *catulus leonis* domui Juda.

[I ≈ a lion / a young lion]

Hosea 6.3 and *he* [the Lord] shall come unto us as *the rain*, as *the latter and former rain* unto the earth.

3 διώξωμεν τοῦ γνῶναι τὸν Κύριον, ὡς ὄρθρον ἕτοιμον εὑρήσομεν αὐτόν, καὶ ἥξει ὡς ὑετὸς ἡμῖν πρώϊμος καὶ ὄψιμος γῇ.

3 sequemurque ut cognoscamus *Dominum*: quasi *diluculum* praeparatus est egressus ejus, et veniet quasi *imber* nobis *temporaneus et serotinus* terrae.

[the Lord ≈ the rain, the latter and former rain]

Hosea 6.4 O Judah, what shall I do unto thee? for *your goodness is* as *a morning cloud*, and as *the early dew* it goeth away.

4 τί σοι ποιήσω Ἰούδα; τὸ δὲ ἔλεος ὑμῶν ὡς νεφέλη πρωϊνὴ καὶ ὡς δρόσος ὀρθρινὴ πορευομένη.

4 quid faciam tibi, Juda? *misericordia vestra* quasi *nubes matutina*, et quasi *ros mane pertransiens*.

[your goodness ≈ a morning cloud ≈ early dew]

Hosea 6.7 But *they* [Gilead?] like *men* have transgressed the covenant:

7 αὐτοὶ δέ εἰσιν ὡς ἄνθρωπος παραβαίνων διαθήκην·

7 *Ipsi* autem sicut *Adam* transgressi sunt pactum: ibi praevaricati sunt in me.

[people (of Gilead?) ≈ men]

Hosea 6.9 And as *troops of robbers* wait for a man, **so** *the company of priests* murder in the way by consent: for they commit lewdness.

9 καὶ ἡ ἰσχύς σου ἀνδρὸς πειρατοῦ· ἔκρυψαν ἱερεῖς ὁδόν, ἐφόνευσαν Σίκιμα, ὅτι ἀνομίαν ἐποίησαν.

9 Et quasi *fauces virorum latronum*, particeps sacerdotum, in via interficientium pergentes de Sichem: quia scelus operati sunt.

[company of priests ≈ troops of robbers]

Hosea 7.4 They are all *adulterers,* as *an oven heated by the baker, who ceaseth from raising after he hath kneaded the dough, until it be leavened.*

4 πάντες μοιχεύοντες, ὡς κλίβανος καιόμενος εἰς πέψιν κατακαύματος ἀπὸ τῆς φλογός, ἀπὸ φυράσεως στέατος ἕως τοῦ ζυμωθῆναι αὐτό.

4 Omnes *adulterantes*, <u>quasi</u> <u>*clibanus succensus a coquente;*</u> quievit paululum civitas a commistione fermenti, donec fermentaretur totum.

[they (Samarians) ≈ an oven glowing with flame]

Hosea 7.6 For they have made ready their *heart* like <u>*an oven*</u>, whiles they lie in wait: their baker sleepeth all the night; in the morning *it burneth* as <u>*a flaming fire*</u>.

6 διότι <u>*ἀνεκαύθησαν ὡς κλίβανος αἱ καρδίαι αὐτῶν*</u>, ἐν τῷ καταράσσειν αὐτούς, ὅλην τὴν νύκτα ὅπου Ἐφραὶμ ἐνεπλήσθη, πρωΐ ἐγενήθη, <u>*ἀνεκαύθη ὡς πυρὸς φέγγος*</u>.

6 Quia applicuerunt <u>quasi</u> <u>*clibanum*</u> *cor suum*, cum insidiaretur eis; tota nocte dormivit coquens eos: mane *ipse succensus* <u>quasi</u> <u>*ignis flammae*</u>.

[their heart ≈ an oven ≈ a flaming fire]

Hosea 7.7 *They* are all *hot* <u>as</u> <u>*an oven,*</u> and have devoured their judges.

7 <u>*πάντες ἐθερμάνθησαν ὡς κλίβανος*</u> καὶ κατέφαγον τοὺς κριτὰς αὐτῶν·

7 *Omnes calefacti* sunt <u>quasi</u> <u>*clibanus*</u>, et devoraverunt judices suos.   [They all (hot) ≈ an oven]

Hosea 7.11 *Ephraim* also is <u>like</u> <u>*a silly dove, without heart.*</u>

11 καὶ ἦν <u>*Ἐφραὶμ ὡς περιστερὰ ἄνους οὐχ ἔχουσα καρδίαν*</u>·

11 Et factus est *Ephraim* <u>quasi</u> <u>*columba seducta non habens co*</u>r.

[Ephraim ≈ a silly dove without heart]

Hosea 7.12 *I will bring them down* <u>as</u> <u>*the fowls of the heaven*</u>. I will chastise them *as their congregation hath heard.*

12 καθὼς ἂν πορεύωνται, ἐπιβαλῶ ἐπ᾽ αὐτοὺς τὸ δίκτυόν μου· <u>*καθὼς τὰ πετεινὰ τοῦ οὐρανοῦ κατάξω αὐτούς*</u>, παιδεύσω αὐτοὺς ἐν τῇ ἀκοῇ τῆς θλίψεως αὐτῶν.

12 <u>quasi</u> <u>*volucrem cael*</u>i detraham *eos*; caedam eos secundum auditionem coetus eorum.

[them ? ≈ fowls of the heaven] **NB factual clause beginning with the second 'as'.**

Hosea 7.16 *They* are <u>like</u> <u>*a deceitful bow*</u>.

16 ἀπεστράφησαν εἰς οὐδέν, <u>*ἐγένοντο ὡς τόξον ἐντεταμένον*</u>

16 *facti* sunt <u>quasi</u> <u>*arcus dolosus*</u>:

[they (Samarians) ≈ a deceitful bow]

Hosea 8.1 Set the trumpet to thy mouth. *He* shall come <u>as *an eagle against the house of the Lord,*</u> because they have transgressed my covenant, and trespassed against my law.

   1 ΕΙΣ κόλπον αὐτῶν <u>ὡς γῆ</u>, <u>ὡς ἀετὸς ἐπὶ οἶκον Κυρίου</u>, ἀνθ᾽ ὧν παρέβησαν τὴν διαθήκην μου καὶ κατὰ τοῦ νόμου μου ἠσέβησαν.

   1 In gutture tuo sit tuba <u>quasi</u> <u>*aquila*</u> super domum Domini, pro eo quod transgressi sunt foedus meum, et legem meam praevaricati sunt.   [he ≈ an eagle]

Hosea 8.8 Israel is swallowed up: now shall *they* be among the nations <u>as a *vessel wherein is no pleasure.*</u>

   8 κατεπόθη ᾿Ισραήλ, νῦν ἐγένετο ἐν τοῖς ἔθνεσιν <u>ὡς σκεῦος ἄχρηστον</u>,

   8 Devoratus est *Israel*; nunc factus est in nationibus quasi <u>*vas immundum.*</u>

   [Israel ≈ a worthless vessel]

Hosea 9.4 *Their sacrifices* shall be unto them <u>as *the bread of mourners:*</u> all that eat thereof shall be polluted.

   4 αἱ θυσίαι αὐτῶν <u>ὡς ἄρτος πένθους αὐτοῖς,</u> πάντες οἱ ἐσθίοντες αὐτὰ μιανθήσονται.

   4 *Sacrificia eorum* quasi *panis lugentium*; omnes qui comedent eum, contaminabuntur.

   [their sacrifices ≈ the bread of mourning]

Hosea 9.10 I found *Israel* <u>like *grapes in the wilderness;*</u> I saw <u>*your fathers as the firstripe in the fig tree*</u> at her first time.

   10 <u>Ὡς σταφυλὴν ἐν ἐρήμῳ εὗρον τὸν ᾿Ισραήλ</u> καὶ <u>ὡς σκοπὸν ἐν συκῇ πρώϊμον πατέρας αὐτῶν εἶδον·</u>

   10 Quasi <u>*uvas in deserto*</u> inveni *Israel*, quasi <u>*prima poma ficulneae*</u> in <u>*cacumine ejus*</u> vidi *patres eorum*:

     [Israel ≈ grapes in the wilderness; your/their fathers ≈ first ripe in a fig tree]

Hosea 9.11 As for *Ephraim, their glory* shall fly away <u>like *a bird*</u>, from the birth, and from the womb, and from the conception.

   11 Εφραὶμ <u>ὡς ὄρνεον</u> ἐξεπετάσθη, αἱ δόξαι αὐτῶν ἐκ τόκων καὶ ὠδίνων καὶ συλλήψεων·

   11 *Ephraim* quasi <u>*avis*</u> avolavit; gloria eorum a partu, et ab utero, et a conceptu.

   [Ephraim / glory ≈ a bird]

Hosea 10.4 thus *judgment springeth up* <u>as</u> <u>*hemlock in the furrows of the field.*</u>

4 ἀνατελεῖ <u>ὡς</u> *ἄγρωστις* <u>κρίμα ἐπὶ χέρσον ἀγροῦ.</u>

4 et germinabit <u>quasi</u> <u>*amaritudo* judicium</u> super sulcos agri.

[judgment ≈ hemlock]

Hosea 10.7 As for Samaria, *her king* is cut off <u>as</u> <u>*the foam upon the water.*</u>

7 <u>ἀπέρριψε Σαμάρεια βασιλέα αὐτῆς ὡς φρύγανον ἐπὶ προσώπου ὕδατος.</u>

7 Transire fecit Samaria *regem suum* <u>quasi</u> <u>*spumam super faciem aquae.*</u>

[Samaria's king (cast off) ≈ the foam on the water]

Hosea 10.11 And *Ephraim* is <u>as</u> <u>*an heifer that is taught,*</u> and loveth to tread out the corn.

11 <u>*Εφραὶμ δάμαλις δεδιδαγμένη ἀγαπᾶν νεῖκος,*</u>

11 *Ephraim* <u>*vitula docta diligere trituram,*</u>

[Ephraim ≈ an heifer taught to tread corn/love threshing]

Hosea 11.10 They shall walk after the Lord: *he shall roar* <u>like</u> <u>*a lion:*</u> when he shall roar, then *the children* shall tremble from the west. 11 *They* shall tremble <u>as</u> <u>*a bird out of Egypt,*</u> and <u>as</u> <u>*a dove out of the land of Assyria:*</u> and I will place them in their houses, saith the Lord.

10 ὀπίσω Κυρίου πορεύσομαι· <u>ὡς λέων ἐρεύξεται,</u> ὅτι αὐτὸς ὠρύσεται, καὶ ἐκστήσονται τέκνα ὑδάτων. 11 <u>ἐκστήσονται ὡς ὄρνεον ἐξ Αἰγύπτου</u> <u>καὶ ὡς περιστερὰ ἐκ γῆς Ἀσσυρίων·</u> καὶ ἀποκαταστήσω αὐτούς εἰς τοὺς οἴκους αὐτῶν, λέγει Κύριος.

10 Post *Dominum* ambulabunt; <u>quasi</u> <u>*leo*</u> rugiet, quia ipse rugiet, et formidabunt filii maris. 11 Et avolabunt <u>quasi</u> <u>*avis ex Aegypto*</u>, et <u>quasi</u> <u>*columba de terra Assyriorum*</u>: et collocabo eos in domibus suis, dicit Dominus.

[the Lord (shall roar) ≈ a lion; they (shall tremble) ≈ a bird ≈ a dove]

Hosea 13.3 Therefore *they shall be* <u>as</u> <u>*the morning cloud*</u>, and <u>as</u> <u>*the early dew*</u> that passeth away, <u>as</u> <u>*the chaff that is driven with the whirlwind*</u> out of the floor, and <u>as</u> <u>*the smoke out of the chimney*</u>.

3 διὰ τοῦτο ἔσονται <u>ὡς νεφέλη πρωϊνὴ</u> καὶ <u>ὡς δρόσος ὀρθρινὴ</u> πορευομένη, <u>ὥσπερ χνοῦς ἀποφυσώμενος ἀφ᾽ ἅλωνος</u> καὶ <u>ὡς ἀτμὶς ἀπὸ δακρύων.</u>

3 Idcirco erunt <u>quasi</u> <u>*nubes matutina*</u>, et sicut <u>*ros matutinus*</u> praeteriens; sicut <u>*pulvis turbine raptus ex area*</u>, et sicut <u>*fumus de fumario*</u>.

[they (Israelites-?) ≈ morning cloud ≈ early dew ≈ chaff ≈ smoke]

Hosea 13.7 Therefore I [the Lord] will be unto them <u>as *a lion*</u>: <u>as *a leopard*</u> by the way will I observe them. 8 I will meet them <u>as *a bear that is bereaved*</u> of her whelps ... and there will I devour them <u>like *a lion*</u>.

7 καὶ *ἔσομαι* αὐτοῖς <u>ὡς</u> <u>*πανθὴρ*</u> καὶ <u>ὡς</u> <u>*πάρδαλις*</u> κατὰ τὴν ὁδὸν Ἀσσυρίων· 8 ἀπαντήσομαι αὐτοῖς <u>ὡς</u> <u>*ἄρκος ἀπορουμένη*</u> καὶ ... καὶ καταφάγονται αὐτοὺς ἐκεῖ σκύμνοι δρυμοῦ, <u>*θηρία ἀγροῦ*</u> διασπάσει αὐτούς.

7 Et *ego* ero eis <u>quasi</u> <u>*leaena*</u>, sicut *pardus* in via Assyriorum. 8Occurram eis <u>quasi</u> <u>*ursa raptis catulis*</u>, ... et consumam eos ibi <u>quasi</u> <u>*leo*</u>: bestia agri scindet eos.

[I/the Lord ≈ a lion ≈ a leopard ≈ a bear ≈ lion]

Hosea 14.5 *I* will be <u>as *the dew*</u> unto Israel: *he* [Ashur] shall grow <u>as the *lily*</u>, and cast forth his roots <u>as *Lebanon*</u>.

6 *ἔσομαι* <u>ὡς</u> <u>*δρόσος*</u> τῷ Ἰσραήλ, ἀνθήσει <u>ὡς</u> <u>*κρίνον*</u> καὶ βαλεῖ τὰς ῥίζας αὐτοῦ <u>ὡς</u> <u>*ὁ Λίβανος*</u>·

6 *Ero* <u>quasi</u> <u>*ros*</u>; *Israel* germinabit <u>sicut</u> <u>*lilium*</u>, et erumpet radix ejus <u>ut</u> <u>*Libani*</u>.

[I/the Lord ≈ dew; he/Ashur ≈ the lily ≈ Lebanon]

Hosea 14.6 His branches shall spread, and *his beauty* shall be <u>as the *olive tree*</u>, and *his smell* <u>as *Lebanon*</u>.

7 πορεύσονται οἱ κλάδοι αὐτοῦ, καὶ ἔσται <u>ὡς</u> <u>*ἐλαία κατάκαρπος*</u>, καὶ ἡ ὀσφρασία αὐτοῦ <u>ὡς</u> <u>*Λιβάνου*</u>·

7 Ibunt rami ejus, et erit <u>quasi</u> <u>*oliva gloria*</u> ejus, et *odor ejus* <u>ut</u> <u>*Libani*</u>.

[Ashur's beauty ≈ olive tree; his smell ≈ Lebanon]

Hosea 14.7 *they* shall revive <u>as *the corn*</u>, and grow <u>as t*he vine*</u>: the *scent* thereof shall be <u>as *the wine of Lebanon*</u>. 8 *Ephraim* shall say ... I am <u>like a *green fir tree*</u>.

8 ζήσονται καὶ *μεθυσθήσονται* <u>*σίτῳ*</u>· καὶ ἐξανθήσει <u>ὡς</u> <u>*ἄμπελος*</u> μνημόσυνον αὐτοῦ, <u>ὡς</u> <u>*οἶνος Λιβάνου*</u>. 9 τῷ Ἐφραίμ, ... ἐγὼ <u>ὡς</u> <u>*ἄρκευθος πυκάζουσα*</u>, ἐξ ἐμοῦ ὁ καρπός σου εὕρηται.

8 germinabunt <u>quasi</u> <u>*vinea*</u>; *memoriale ejus* <u>sicut</u> <u>*vinum Libani*</u>. 9*Ephraim*, quid mihi ultra idola? Ego ... <u>ut</u> <u>*abietem virentem*</u>; ex me fructus tuus inventus est.

[they ≈ corn ≈ the vine; the scent ≈ wine of Lebanon; Ephraim ≈ a green fir tree]

* * *

Joel (3 Chapters)

Ἰωήλ Δ´

Joel 1.8 Lament like *a virgin girded with sackcloth for the husband of her youth.*

    8 θρήνησον πρός με *ὑπὲρ νύμφην περιεζωσμένην σάκκον ἐπὶ τὸν ἄνδρα αὐτῆς τὸν παρθενικόν.*

    8 Plange quasi *virgo accincta sacco super virum pubertatis suae.*

    [you (lament for) > me ≈ a virgin > her husband]

Joel 2.3 the *land is as the garden of Eden before them,* and behind them a desolate wilderness.

    3 *ὡς παράδεισος τρυφῆς ἡ γῆ πρὸ προσώπου αὐτοῦ, καὶ τὰ ὄπισθεν αὐτοῦ* πεδίον ἀφανισμοῦ.

    3 Quasi *hortus voluptatis terra coram eo,* et post eum solitudo deserti.

    [the land before them ≈ the garden of Eden]

Joel 2.4 *The appearance of them* is as *the appearance of horses;* and as *horsemen, so shall they run.*

    4 *ὡς ὅρασις ἵππων ἡ ὄψις αὐτῶν, καὶ ὡς ἱππεῖς οὕτως* καταδιώξονται·

    4 Quasi *aspectus equorum,* aspectus eorum; et quasi *equites,* sic *current.*

    [their appearance ≈ horses; they run ≈ horsemen]

Joel 2.5 Like *the noise of chariots on the tops of mountains shall they leap,* like *the noise of a flame of fire that devoureth the stubble,* as *a strong people set in battle array.*

    5 *ὡς φωνὴ ἁρμάτων ἐπὶ τὰς κορυφὰς τῶν ὀρέων ἐξαλοῦνται καὶ ὡς φωνὴ φλογὸς πυρὸς κατεσθιούσης καλάμην καὶ ὡς λαὸς πολὺς καὶ ἰσχυρὸς παρατασσόμενος εἰς πόλεμον.*

    5 Sicut *sonitus quadrigarum super capita montium* exilient, sicut *sonitus flammae ignis devorantis stipulam,* velut *populus fortis praeparatus ad praelium.*

    [they (shall leap) ≈ the noise of chariots ≈ the noise of a flame of fire ≈ strong people preparing for battle]

Joel 2.7 *They shall run* like *mighty men; they shall climb the wall* like *men of war.*

    7 *ὡς μαχηταὶ δραμοῦνται καὶ ὡς ἄνδρες πολεμισταὶ ἀναβήσονται ἐπὶ τὰ τείχη.*

    7 Sicut *fortes* current; quasi *viri bellatores* ascendent murum.

[they (shall run) ≈ mighty men; (shall climb the wall) ≈ men of war]

Joel 2.9 They shall enter in at the windows <u>like</u> *a thief.*

    9 διὰ θυρίδων εἰσελεύσονται <u>ὡς κλέπται.</u>

    9 per fenestras intrab*unt* <u>quasi</u> *fur.*   [they ≈ thief]

* * *

Amos (9 Chapters)

Ἀμὼς Βʹ

Amos 2.9 Yet destroyed I the Amorite before them, *whose height was* <u>like</u> the *height of the cedars,* and *he was strong* as *the oaks.*

    9 ἐγὼ δὲ ἐξῆρα τὸν Ἀμορραῖον ἐκ προσώπου αὐτῶν, οὗ ἦν, <u>καθὼς ὕψος</u> <u>κέδρου</u> τὸ ὕψος αὐτοῦ, καὶ ἰσχυρὸς ἦν <u>ὡς δρῦς,</u>

    9 Ego autem exterminavi Amorrhaeum a facie eorum, cujus *altitudo,* *cedrorum altitudo* ejus, et *fortis ipse* <u>quasi</u> *quercus;*

       [his height ≈ a cedar; he (strong) ≈ an oak]

Amos 2.13 Behold, I *am pressed under you,* as <u>*a cart is pressed that is full of*</u> <u>*sheaves.*</u>

    13 διὰ τοῦτο ἰδοὺ *ἐγὼ κυλίω ὑποκάτω ὑμῶν,* <u>ὃν τρόπον</u> <u>κυλίεται ἡ ἄμαξα</u> <u>ἡ γέμουσα καλάμης·</u>

    13 Ecce *ego stridebo subter vos,* <u>sicut</u> <u>*strident plaustrum onustum foeno.*</u>   [I (am pressed) ≈ a cart full of sheaves]

Amos 3.12 Thus saith the Lord; <u>As</u> <u>*the shepherd taketh out of the mouth of*</u> the <u>*lion two legs, or a piece of an ear,*</u> **so** *shall the children of Israel be taken out that dwell in Samaria.*

    12 τάδε λέγει Κύριος· <u>ὃν τρόπον ὅταν ἐκσπάσῃ ὁ ποιμὴν ἐκ στόματος τοῦ</u> <u>λέοντος δύο σκέλη ἢ λοβὸν ὠτίου,</u> **οὕτως** ἐκσπασθήσονται οἱ υἱοὶ Ἰσραὴλ οἱ κατοικοῦντες ἐν Σαμαρείᾳ

    12 Haec dicit Dominus: <u>Quomodo si</u> *eruat pastor de ore leonis duo* *crura, aut extremum auriculae,* **sic** *eruentur filii Israel, qui hab-itant in Samaria.*

       [the children of Israel in Samaria (taken out) ≈ two legs or an ear from the mouth of a lion by a shepherd]

Amos 4.11 *I have overthrown some of you,* **as God overthrew Sodom and Gomorrha,** *and ye were* <u>as</u> <u>*a firebrand plucked out of the burning*</u>:

11 κατέστρεψα ὑμᾶς, <u>*καθὼς κατέστρεψεν ὁ Θεὸς Σόδομα καὶ Γόμορρα*</u>, καὶ <u>*ἐγένεσθε ὡς δαλὸς ἐξεσπασμένος ἐκ πυρός·*</u> καὶ οὐδ᾽ ὡς ἐπεστρέψατε πρός με, λέγει Κύριος.

11 Subverti vos **sicut subvertit Deus Sodomam et Gomorrham,** et *facti estis* <u>quasi</u> <u>*torris raptus ab incendio*</u>:

NB – a literal comparison followed by *a figurative simile*:

[I > (overthrew) you ≈ God > Sodom and Gomorrha; you ≈ a firebrand plucked out of the fire]

Amos 5.19 <u>As if a</u> <u>*man did flee from a lion, and a bear met him*</u>; or <u>*went into the house, and leaned his hand on the wall, and a serpent bit him.*</u> 20 *Shall not the day of the LORD be darkne*ss, and not light?

19 <u>ὃν τρόπον</u> <u>*ἐὰν φύγῃ ἄνθρωπος ἐκ προσώπου τοῦ λέοντος καὶ ἐμπέσῃ αὐτῷ ἡ ἄρκος, καὶ εἰσπηδήσῃ εἰς τὸν οἶκον αὐτοῦ καὶ ἀπερείσηται τὰς χεῖρας αὐτοῦ ἐπὶ τὸν τοῖχον καὶ δάκῃ αὐτὸν ὄφις.*</u> 20 *οὐχὶ σκότος ἡ ἡμέρα τοῦ Κυρίου καὶ οὐ φῶς;*

19 Quomodo si f<u>*ugiat vir a facie leonis, et occurrat ei ursus; et ingrediatur domum, et innitatur manu sua super parietem, et mordeat eum coluber.*</u> 20 *Numquid non tenebrae dies Domini,* et non lux?

[the Lord's day shall be darkness and not light ≈ a man flees from a lion and met a bear OR went into his house and was bitten by a serpent]

Amos 5.24 But let *judgment run down as waters,* and *righteousness as a mighty stream.*

24 καὶ <u>*κυλισθήσεται ὡς ὕδωρ κρίμα*</u> καὶ <u>*δικαιοσύνη ὡς χειμάρρους ἄβατος.*</u>

24 Et revelabitur <u>quasi</u> *aqua judicium,* et *justitia* <u>quasi</u> *torrens fortis.*

[judgment (run down) ≈ water; righteousness ≈ a mighty stream]

Amos 9.9 For … I will *sift the house of Israel among all nations,* <u>like as</u> <u>*corn is sifted in a sieve,*</u> yet shall not the least grain fall upon the earth.

9 διότι ἰδοὺ ἐγὼ ἐντέλλομαι καὶ λικμήσω ἐν πᾶσι τοῖς ἔθνεσι τὸν οἶκον Ἰσραήλ, <u>ὃν τρόπον</u> <u>*λικμᾶται ἐν τῷ λικμῷ*</u> καὶ οὐ μὴ πέσῃ σύντριμμα ἐπὶ τὴν γῆν.

9 Ecce enim mandabo ego, et *concutiam in omnibus gentibus domum
Israel*, sicut *concutitur triticum in cribro*, et non cadet lapillus super
terram.
[(I will sift) the house of Israel ≈ corn sifted in a sieve]

* * *

Obadiah (1 Chapter)

Ὀβδιού Ε΄

Obad. 1.4 Though *thou exalt thyself* as *the eagle*, and though thou *set thy
nest among the stars, thence will I bring thee down*, saith the Lord.
　　4 ἐὰν *μετεωρισθῇς ὡς ἀετὸς* καὶ ἐὰν *ἀνὰ μέσον τῶν ἄστρων θῇς νοσσιάν σου*,
　　ἐκεῖθεν κατάξω σε, λέγε Κύριος.
　　4 *Si exaltatus fueris* ut *aquila*, et si inter sidera posueris nidum tuum,
　　inde detraham te, dicit Dominus.
　　[you ≈ an eagle]
Obadiah 1.18 And *the house of Jacob* shall be a *fire*, ... and *the house of Esau*
for *stubble* ...
　　18 καὶ ἔσται ὁ οἶκος Ἰακὼβ *πῦρ*, ... ὁ δὲ οἶκος Ἡσαῦ *εἰς καλάμην*,
　　18 Et erit *domus Jacob* ignis, ... et *domus Esau* stipula:
*a/1　[house of Jacob ≈ a fire; the house of Joseph ≈ a flame; the house
　　of Esau ≈ stubble]

***

Jonah (4 Chapters)

Ἰωνᾶς Ϛ΄

***

Micah (7 Chapters)

Μιχαίας Γ΄

Micah 1.4 And the mountains shall be molten under him, and *the valleys
shall be cleft*, as *wax before the fire,* and as the *waters that are poured
down a steep place.*

4 καὶ σαλευθήσεται τὰ ὄρη ὑποκάτωθεν αὐτοῦ, καὶ *αἱ κοιλάδες τακήσονται* *ὡς κηρὸς ἀπὸ προσώπου πυρὸς καὶ ὡς ὕδωρ καταφερόμενον ἐν καταβάσει.*

4 Et consumentur montes subtus eum, et *valles scindentur* sicut *cera a* *facie ignis*, et sicut *aquae quae decurrunt in praeceps*.

[valleys (cleft) ≈ wax before fire ≈ water rushing down]

Micah 1.6 Therefore *I will make Samaria* as *an heap of the field, and* as *plantings of a vineyard*.

6 καὶ *θήσομαι Σαμάρειαν εἰς ὀπωροφυλάκιον ἀγροῦ καὶ εἰς φυτείαν* *ἀμπελῶνος.*

6 Et ponam *Samariam* quasi *acervum lapidum in agro*, cum plantatur vinea.

[Samaria ≈ a heap of the field ≈ plantings of a vineyard]

Micah 1.8 Therefore I will wail and howl, I will go stripped and naked: *I* *will make a wailing* like *the dragons*, and *mourning* as *the owls*.

8 ἕνεκεν τούτου κόψεται καὶ θρηνήσει, πορεύσεται ἀνυπόδετος καὶ γυμνή, *ποιήσεται κοπετὸν ὡς δρακόντων καὶ πένθος ὡς θυγατέρων σειρήνων·*

8 Super hoc plangam, et ululabo; vadam spoliatus, et nudus; *faciam* *planctum* velut *draconum*, et *luctum* quasi *struthionum*:

[I (wailing) ≈ dragons ≈ (mourning) owls]

Micah 1.16 Make thee bald ... *enlarge thy baldness* as *the eagle*;

16 ξύρησαι καὶ κεῖραι ἐπὶ τὰ τέκνα τὰ τρυφερά σου, *ἐμπλάτυνον τὴν χηρείαν* *σου ὡς ἀετός.*

16 Decalvare, et tondere super filios deliciarum tuarum; dilata *calvitium* *tuum* sicut *aquila*.   [become bald ≈ an eagle]

Micah 2.12 I will put *them* together as *the sheep of Bozra,* as *the flock in the* *midst of their fold*.

12 θήσομαι τὴν ἀποστροφὴν αὐτοῦ· *ὡς πρόβατα ἐν θλίψει, ὡς ποίμνιον ἐν* *μέσῳ κοίτης αὐτῶν·*

12 pariter ponam *illum* quasi *gregem in ovili,* quasi *pecus in medio* *caularum*.

[Jacob and his people (returning) ≈ sheep of Bozra ≈ a flock in the midst of their fold]

Micah 5.8 And *the remnant of Jacob shall be among the Gentiles* in the midst of many people as *a lion among the beasts of the forest,* as *a* *young lion among the flocks of sheep* ...

7 καὶ ἔσται τὸ ὑπόλειμμα Ἰακὼβ ἐν τοῖς ἔθνεσιν ἐν μέσῳ λαῶν πολλῶν <u>ὡς</u> <u>λέων ἐν κτήνεσι ἐν τῷ δρυμῷ καὶ ὡς σκύμνος ἐν ποιμνίοις προβάτων</u>.

7 Et erunt *reliquiae Jacob* in gentibus, in medio populorum multorum, <u>quasi</u> <u>*leo in jumentis silvarum*</u>, et <u>quasi</u> <u>*catulus leonis in gregibus*</u> <u>*pecorum*</u>, qui cum transierit, et conculcaverit, et ceperit, non est qui eruat.

    [the remnant of Jacob among the Gentiles ≈ a lion among the beasts of the forest ≈ a young lion among flocks of sheep]

Micah 7.1 Woe is me! for I am <u>as</u> <u>*when they have gathered the summer*</u> *fruits*, as *the grape-gleanings in the vintage; there is no cluster to eat.*

1 ΟΙΜΟΙ, ὅτι ἐγενήθην <u>ὡς</u> <u>συνάγων καλάμην ἐν ἀμήτῳ, καὶ ὡς ἐπιφυλλίδα</u> <u>ἐν τρυγητῷ</u>, οὐχ ὑπάρχοντος βότρυος τοῦ φαγεῖν τὰ πρωτόγονα. οἴμοι, ψυχή,

1 Vae mihi, quia factus *sum* <u>sicut</u> <u>*qui colligit in autumno racemos*</u> <u>*vindemia*</u>! non est botrus ad comedendum.

    [I ≈ someone gathering summer fruits ≈ one gathering grape-gleanings in the vintage]

Micah 7.4 The *best of them* is <u>as</u> *a brier*: the *most upright* is <u>sharper than</u> <u>*a*</u> *thorn hedge.*

4 <u>ὡς</u> <u>σὴς ἐκτρώγων</u> καὶ βαδίζων ἐπὶ κανόνος ἐν ἡμέρᾳ σκοπιᾶς. οὐαὶ οὐαί, αἱ ἐκδικήσεις σου ἥκασι, νῦν ἔσονται κλαυθμοὶ αὐτῶν.

4 *Qui optimus in eis est*, <u>quasi</u> *paliurus*, et *qui rectus*, <u>quasi</u> *spina de sepe.*

    [the best of them ≈ a brier; most upright (sharper) ≈ a thorn hedge]

***

Nahum (3 Chapters)

Ναούμ Ζ΄

Nahum 1.6   *His fury* is poured out *like fire.*

6 ἀπὸ προσώπου ὀργῆς αὐτοῦ τίς ὑποστήσεται; καὶ τίς ἀντιστήσεται ἐν ὀργῇ θυμοῦ αὐτοῦ; ὁ θυμὸς αὐτοῦ τήκει ἀρχάς, καὶ αἱ πέτραι διεθρύβησαν ἀπ' αὐτοῦ. [**No simile**]

6 *Indignatio ejus* effusa est <u>ut</u> *ignis*, et petrae dissolutae sunt ab eo. [The Lord's fury ≈ fire]

Nahum 1.10 For while *they* be folded together <u>as</u> *<u>thorns</u>*, and while they are drunken <u>as</u> *<u>drunkards</u>*, they shall be devoured <u>as</u> *<u>stubble</u>* fully dry.

10 ὅτι ἕως θεμελίου αὐτοῦ χερσωθήσεται καὶ <u>ὡς</u> <u>*σμῖλαξ περιπλεκομένη*</u> <u>*βρωθήσεται καὶ ὡς καλάμη ξηρασίας μεστή*</u>.

10 quia <u>sicut</u> *<u>spinae</u>* se invicem complectuntur, **sic** convivium eorum pariter potantium; consumentur <u>quasi</u> *<u>stipula</u>* ariditate plena.

[the Lord's enemies ≈ thorns ≈ drunkards ≈ stubble]

* * *

Habakkuk (3 Chapters)

Ἀμβακούμ H

Habak. 1.8 Their *horses* also are <u>swifter than</u> the *<u>leopards</u>*, and are <u>more fierce than</u> the *<u>evening wolves</u>*: another horsemen shall spread themselves, and their horsemen shall come from far: *they shall fly* <u>as</u> *the eagle* that hasteth to eat. 9 They shall come all for violence: their *faces* shall sup up <u>as</u> the <u>ea*st wind*</u>, and they shall gather the captivity <u>as</u> the *<u>sand</u>*.

8 καὶ ἐξαλοῦνται <u>ὑπὲρ</u> <u>*παρδάλεις*</u> οἱ ἵπποι αὐτοῦ καὶ <u>*ὀξύτεροι*</u> ὑπὲρ <u>*τοὺς λύκους τῆς Ἀραβίας·*</u> καὶ ἐξιππάσονται οἱ ἱππεῖς αὐτοῦ καὶ ὁρμήσουσι μακρόθεν καὶ πετασθήσονται <u>*ὡς ἀετὸς πρόθυμος εἰς τὸ*</u> <u>*φαγεῖν.*</u> 9 συντέλεια εἰς ἀσεβεῖς ἥξει, ἀνθεστηκότας προσώποις αὐτῶν ἐξεναντίας καὶ <u>*συνάξει ὡς ἄμμον αἰχμαλωσίαν.*</u>

8 <u>Leviores</u> *<u>pardis</u>* equi ejus, et <u>velociores</u> *<u>lupis vespertinis</u>*: et diffundentur equites ejus: equites namque ejus de longe venient; *volabunt* <u>quasi</u> *<u>aquila festinans ad comedendum</u>*. [9] Omnes ad praedam venient, facies eorum ventus urens; et *congregabit* <u>quasi</u> *<u>arenam captivitatem</u>*.

[his horses (run more swiftly) ≈ leopards; fiercer than ≈ evening wolves; (shall fly) ≈ an eagle hurrying to eat; faces ≈ east wind; his captives (gathered) ≈ sand]

Habak. 1.14 And *makest men* <u>as</u> *<u>the fishes of the sea, and</u>* <u>as</u> *<u>the creeping things, that have no ruler over them</u>*?

14 καὶ ποιήσεις τοὺς ἀνθρώπους ὡς <u>*τοὺς ἰχθύας τῆς θαλάσσης*</u> καὶ <u>*ὡς τὰ*</u> <u>*ἑρπετὰ τὰ οὐκ ἔχοντα ἡγούμενον*</u>;

14 Et *facies homines* <u>quasi</u> *pisces mari*s, et <u>quasi</u> *reptile non habens principem.*

   [men ≈ fish of the sea ≈ creeping things with no ruler]

Habak. 3.4 And his (God's) *brightness* was <u>as</u> *the light*; he had horns coming out of his hand.

   4 καὶ φέγγος αὐτοῦ <u>ὡς</u> <u>φῶς</u> ἔσται, κέρατα ἐν χερσὶν αὐτοῦ,

   4 *Splendor ejus* <u>ut</u> *lux* erit, cornua in manibus ejus.

   [His brightness ≈ light]

Habak. 3.14 T*hey* [the villagers] came out <u>as</u> *a whirlwind* to scatter me.

   14 διανοίξουσι χαλινοὺς αὐτῶν <u>ὡς</u> <u>ἐσθίων πτωχὸς λάθρα</u>.

   ([they shall be] as a poor man devouring in secret)

14 venientibus <u>ut</u> *turbo* ad dispergendum me.

   [they (villagers) ≈ a whirlwind]

Habak. 3.19 The Lord God is my strength, and he will make *my feet* <u>like</u> *hinds' feet.*

   19 Κύριος ὁ Θεὸς δύναμίς μου καὶ τάξει τοὺς πόδας μου εἰς συντέλειαν·

   (he will perfectly strengthen my feet)

   19 Deus Dominus fortitudo mea, et ponet *pedes meos* <u>quasi</u> *cervorum*:

   [my feet ≈ hinds' feet]

* * *

Zephaniah (3 Chapters)

Σοφονίας Θ΄

***

Haggai (2 Chapters)

Ἀγγαῖος Ι΄

***

Zechariah (14 Chapters)

Ζαχαρίας ΙΑ΄

Zech. 4.1 And the angel that talked with me came again, and waked *me* <u>as</u> *a man that is waken out of his sleep.*

1 ΚΑΙ ἐπέστρεψεν ὁ ἄγγελος ὁ λαλῶν ἐν ἐμοὶ καὶ ἐξήγειρέ *με* <u>ὃν τρόπον</u> <u>ὅταν ἐξεγερθῇ ἄνθρωπος ἐξ ὕπνου αὐτοῦ.</u>

1 Et reversus est angelus qui loquebatur in me, et suscitavit *me* <u>quasi</u> <u>*virum qui suscitatur de somno suo.*</u>

[me ≈ a man that is waken out of his sleep]

Zech. 5.9 Behold, there came out *two women*, and the wind was in their wings; for they had *wings* <u>like *the wings of a stork*</u>.

9 αὗται εἶχον <u>πτέρυγας ὡς πτέρυγας</u> ἔποπος (online)

9 et ecce *duae mulieres* egredientes: et spiritus in alis earum, et habebant *alas* <u>quasi</u> <u>*alas milvi.*</u>   [wings ≈ wings of a stork]

Zech. 7.12 Yea, they made *their hearts* <u>as</u> <u>*an adamant stone*</u>, lest they should hear the law.

12 καὶ τὴν καρδίαν αὐτῶν ἔταξαν <u>ἀπειθῆ</u> τοῦ μὴ ἐσακούειν τοῦ νόμου μου καὶ τοὺς λόγους. ('disobedient' – no simile)

12 Et *cor suum* posuerunt <u>ut *adamantem*</u>, ne audirent legem.

[their hearts ≈ an adamant stone]

Zech. 9.3 And Tyrus did build herself a strong hold, and heaped up *silver* <u>as</u> *the dust,* and <u>*fine gold as the mire of the streets*</u>.

3 καὶ ᾠκοδόμησε Τύρος ὀχυρώματα ἑαυτῇ καὶ ἐθησαύρισεν <u>ἀργύριον ὡς</u> <u>χοῦν</u> καὶ συνήγαγε <u>χρυσίον ὡς πηλὸν ὁδῶν.</u>

3 Et aedificavit Tyrus munitionem suam, et coacervavit *argentum* <u>quasi</u> <u>*humum*</u>, et *aurum* <u>ut *lutum platearum.*</u>

[silver (heaped up) ≈ dust; gold ≈ mire of the streets]

Zech. 9.14 And the Lord shall be seen over them, and *his arrow* shall go forth <u>as t*he lightning*</u>; and the Lord God shall blow the trumpet.

14 καὶ Κύριος ἔσται ἐπ᾽ αὐτοὺς καὶ ἐξελεύσεται <u>ὡς ἀστραπὴ</u> βολίς, καὶ **Κύριος παντοκράτωρ ἐν σάλπιγγι σαλπιεῖ.**

14 Et Dominus Deus super eos videbitur, et exibit <u>ut *fulgur* jaculum</u> ejus: **et Dominus Deus in tuba canet.**

[the Lord's arrow ≈ lightening]

Zech. 10.2 They [*the diviners*] comfort in vain; therefore *they* went their way <u>as a *flock*</u>, they were troubled, because there was no shepherd.

2 διὰ τοῦτο ἐξηράνθησαν <u>ὡς πρόβατα</u> καὶ ἐκακώθησαν, διότι οὐκ ἦν ἴασις.

2 idcirco abducti sunt [*divini*] <u>quasi *grex*</u>: affligentur, quia non est eis pastor. [they (diviners) went away ≈ a flock]

Zech. 10.3 Mine anger was kindled against *the shepherds*, and I punished the *goats*: for the Lord of hosts hath visited <u>*his flock*</u> *the house of Judah*, and hath made *them* <u>as</u> <u>*his goodly horse*</u> in the battle.

3 ἐπὶ τοὺς *ποιμένας* παρωξύνθη ὁ θυμός μου, καὶ ἐπὶ τοὺς *ἀμνοὺς* ἐπισκέψομαι· καὶ ἐπισκέψεται Κύριος ὁ Θεὸς ὁ παντοκράτωρ τὸ *ποίμνιον αὐτοῦ* τὸν οἶκον ᾿Ιούδα καὶ τάξει *αὐτοὺς* <u>ὡς</u> <u>ἵππον εὐπρεπῆ αὐτοῦ</u> ἐν πολέμῳ.

3 Super *pastores* iratus est furor meus, et super *hircos* visitabo: quia visitavit Dominus exercituum <u>*gregem suum*</u>, *domum Juda*, et posuit *eos* <u>quasi</u> <u>*equum gloriae suae*</u> in bello.

[the house of Judah ≈ his flock ≈ his horse in battle]

Zech. 10.5 And *they* shall be <u>as</u> <u>*mighty men*</u> …

5 καὶ ἔσονται <u>ὡς</u> <u>*μαχηταὶ πατοῦντες*</u> πηλὸν ἐν ταῖς ὁδοῖς ἐν πολέμῳ.

10.5 Et erunt <u>quasi</u> <u>*fortes*</u> conculcantes lutum viarum in praelio,

Zech. 10.7 And *they of Ephraim shall be* <u>like</u> *a mighty man*, and *their heart shall rejoice* <u>as</u> <u>*through wine*</u>:

7 καὶ ἔσονται ὡς <u>μαχηταὶ</u> τοῦ ᾿Εφραίμ, καὶ χαρήσεται ἡ καρδία αὐτῶν <u>ὡς ἐν οἴνῳ·</u>

7 Et erunt <u>quasi</u> <u>*fortes*</u> Ephraim, et *laetabitur* cor eorum <u>quasi</u> <u>*a vino.*</u>

[they (warriors of Ephraim) *shall rejoice* ≈ through wine]

Zech. 12.6 In that day *I will make the governors of Judah* <u>like</u> <u>*an hearth of fire*</u> *among the wood, and* <u>like</u> <u>*a torch of fire in a sheaf.*</u>

6 ἐν τῇ ἡμέρᾳ ἐκείνῃ <u>θήσομαι</u> τοὺς <u>χιλιάρχους</u> ᾿Ιούδα <u>ὡς δαλόν πυρὸς ἐν ξύλοις καὶ ὡς λαμπάδα πυρὸς ἐν καλάμῃ,</u>

6 In die illa ponam duces Juda <u>sicut</u> <u>*caminum ignis in lignis*</u>, et sicut <u>*facem ignis in foeno*</u> :

[the governors of Judah ≈ an hearth of fire among wood ≈ a torch of fire in a sheaf]

* * *

Malachi (4 Chapters)

Μαλαχίας IB′

Malach. 4.1 For, behold, the *day cometh, that shall burn* <u>as</u> <u>*an oven*</u>, and *all the proud*, yea, and *all that do wickedly*, shall be <u>*stubble*</u>: and the day that cometh shall burn them up, saith the Lord of hosts.

1 ΔΙΟΤΙ ἰδοὺ *ἡμέρα* Κυρίου ἔρχεται *καιομένη* <u>ὡς</u> <u>*κλίβανος*</u> καὶ φλέξει αὐτούς, καὶ ἔσονται πάντες οἱ ἀλλογενεῖς καὶ *πάντες οἱ ποιοῦντες ἄνομα* <u>*καλάμη*</u>, καὶ ἀνάψει αὐτοὺς ἡ ἡμέρα ἡ ἐρχομένη, λέγει Κύριος παντοκράτωρ,

1 Ecce enim *dies veniet succensa* <u>quasi</u> <u>*caminus*</u>: et erunt omnes *superbi et omnes facientes impietatem* <u>*stipula*</u>: et inflammabit eos dies veniens, dicit Dominus exercituum.

[a burning day ≈ an oven; all the wicked ≈ stubble consumed by fire]

* * *

3 Similes in the New Testament

For the various types of non-prothetic similes sometimes marked by asterisked figures (*a/1, *b/1 etc.) see the Introduction.

Section 2.

An arrow (>) Indicates which of the Greek or Latin versions is closer to the English (if there is a notable difference).

Matthew (28 Chapters / 29 similes)

ΚΑΤΑ ΜΑΘΘΑΙΟΝ

Matt. 3.16 He [Jesus] saw *the Spirit of God* descending <u>like</u> <u>*a dove*</u> and lighting upon him.

    16 εἶδεν [τὸ] *πνεῦμα* [τοῦ] θεοῦ καταβαῖνον <u>ὡσεὶ</u> <u>περιστερὰν</u>.

    16 vidit Spiritum Dei descendentem <u>sicut</u> <u>*columbam,*</u>

    [the spirit of God (descending) ≈ a dove]

Matt. 6.25 Take no thought for your life, what ye shall eat, or what ye shall drink; nor yet for your body, what ye shall put on. Is not *the life* <u>more</u> <u>than</u> <u>*meat*</u>, and the *body* <u>than</u> <u>*raiment*</u>?

    25 μὴ μεριμνᾶτε τῇ ψυχῇ ὑμῶν τί φάγητε καὶ τί πίητε, μηδὲ τῷ σώματι ὑμῶν τί ἐνδύσησθε· οὐχὶ ἡ ψυχὴ <u>πλεῖόν</u> ἐστι <u>τῆς τροφῆς</u> καὶ τὸ σῶμα <u>τοῦ ἐνδύματος;</u>

    25 ne solliciti sitis animae vestrae quid manducetis, neque corpori vestro quid induamini. Nonne *anima* <u>plus est quam</u> <u>*esca*</u>, et *corpus* <u>plus quam</u> <u>*vestimentum*</u>?

    [life (more than) ≈ meat; body ≈ raiment]

Matt. 7.24 Therefore *whoever heareth these sayings of mine, and doeth them,* <u>I will liken him unto</u> <u>*a wise man, which built his house upon a rock.*</u>

    24 Πᾶς οὖν ὅστις ἀκούει μου τοὺς λόγους τούτους καὶ ποιεῖ αὐτούς, <u>ὁμοιώσω</u> <u>αὐτὸν ἀνδρὶ φρονίμῳ, ὅστις ᾠκοδόμησε τὴν οἰκίαν αὐτοῦ ἐπὶ τὴν πέτραν·</u>

24 *Omnis ergo qui audit verba mea haec, et facit ea,* <u>assimilabitur</u> <u>*viro*</u>
   <u>*sapienti, qui aedificavit domum suam supra petram,*</u>

*a/2   [who listens to me and follows ≈ a wise man who built his house
       upon a rock] cf. Luke 6.48

Matt. 7.26 *Everyone that heareth these sayings of mine, and doeth them*
   not, <u>shall be likened unto</u> <u>*a foolish man, which built his house upon*</u>
   <u>*the sand.*</u>

   26 καὶ πᾶς ὁ ἀκούων μου τοὺς λόγους τούτους καὶ μὴ ποιῶν αὐτοὺς
      <u>ὁμοιωθήσεται</u> <u>ἀνδρὶ μωρῷ, ὅστις ᾠκοδόμησεν αὐτοῦ τὴν οἰκίαν ἐπὶ</u>
      <u>τὴν ἄμμον.</u>

   26 *Et omnis qui audit verba mea haec, et non facit ea,* <u>similis erit</u> <u>*viro*</u>
      <u>stulto, qui aedificavit domum suam super arenam:</u>
      [everyone who hears my words without following them ≈ a fool
      who built his house on the sand]

Matt. 9.36 He [Jesus] was moved with compassion on them, because *they*
   [the multitudes] fainted, and were scattered abroad, <u>as *sheep having*</u>
   <u>*no shepherd.*</u>

   36 Ἰδὼν δὲ τοὺς ὄχλους ἐσπλαγχνίσθη περὶ αὐτῶν, ὅτι ἦσαν ἐκλελυμένοι
      καὶ ἐρριμμένοι <u>ὡς πρόβατα μὴ ἔχοντα ποιμένα.</u>

   36 *Videns autem turbas, misertus est eis: quia erant vexati, et jacentes*
      <u>sicut *oves non habentes pastorem.*</u>
      [they ≈ sheep having no shepherd]

Matt. 10.16 Behold I send you forth <u>as *sheep in the midst of wolves*</u>; be ye
   therefore *wise* <u>as *serpents*</u> and *harmless* <u>as *doves*</u>.

   16 Ἰδοὺ ἐγὼ ἀποστέλλω ὑμᾶς <u>ὡς</u> <u>πρόβατα ἐν μέσῳ λύκων</u>: γίνεσθε οὖν
      φρόνιμοι <u>ὡς</u> <u>οἱ ὄφεις</u> καὶ ἀκέραιοι <u>ὡς</u> <u>αἱ περιστεραί.</u>

   16 Ecce ego mitto *vos* <u>sicut</u> <u>*oves in medio luporum.*</u> Estote ergo *prudentes*
      <u>sicut</u> <u>*serpentes*</u>, et *simplices* <u>sicut</u> <u>*columbae.*</u>
      [you ≈ sheep among wolves; (be wise) ≈ serpents; (be harmless)
      ≈ doves]

Matt. 10.31 Fear ye not therefore, *ye are* <u>of more value than</u> <u>*many sparrows.*</u>
   31 μὴ οὖν φοβεῖσθε: <u>πολλῶν στρουθίων</u> <u>διαφέρετε</u> ὑμεῖς.
   31 Nolite ergo timere: <u>*multis passeribus*</u> meliores estis *vos.*
      [you (more valuable) ≈ many sparrows]

Matt. 11.16 But whereunto *shall I liken this generation?* It is <u>like unto</u> <u>*children sitting in the markets, and calling unto their fellows.*</u>

   16 Τίνι δὲ ὁμοιώσω <u>*τὴν γενεὰν ταύτην*</u>; <u>ὁμοία</u> ἐστὶν <u>*παιδίοις καθημένοις*</u> <u>*ἐν ταῖς ἀγοραῖς*</u> ἃ προσφωνοῦντα τοῖς ἑτέροις.

   16 Cui autem similem aestimabo *generationem istam?* <u>Similis</u> est *pueris* *sedentibus in foro: qui clamantes coaequalibus.*

     [this generation ≈ children]

Matt. 12.12 How much then is *a man* <u>better than</u> *a sheep?*

   12 πόσῳ οὖν <u>διαφέρει</u> ἄνθρωπος <u>προβάτου</u>;

   12 Quanto <u>magis melior</u> est *homo* <u>ove</u>?

     [man ≈ sheep]   **Simile or comparison.**

Matt. 13.24 "*The kingdom of heaven* <u>is likened unto</u> *a man which sowed* *good seed in his field.*"

   24 <u>Ὡμοιώθη</u> ἡ βασιλεία τῶν οὐρανῶν <u>*ἀνθρώπῳ σπείραντι καλὸν σπέρμα*</u> <u>*ἐν τῷ ἀγρῷ αὐτοῦ*</u>.

   24 <u>Simile factum est</u> *regnum caelorum* <u>*homini, qui seminavit bonum*</u> *semen in agro suo*:

     [kingdom of heaven ≈ a man sowing good seed]

Matt. 13.31 "*The kingdom of heaven* <u>is like to</u> *a grain of mustard seed, which* *a man took and sowed in his field.*"

   31 <u>Ὁμοία</u> ἐστὶν ἡ βασιλεία τῶν οὐρανῶν <u>*κόκκῳ σινάπεως*</u>, ὃν λαβὼν ἄνθρωπος ἔσπειρεν ἐν τῷ ἀγρῷ αὐτοῦ:

   31 <u>Similis est</u> *regnum caelorum* <u>*grano sinapis*</u>, quod accipiens homo seminavit in agro suo:

     [kingdom of heaven ≈ a mustard seed]

Matt. 13.33 "*The kingdom of heaven* <u>is like</u> *unto leaven, which a woman took* *and hid in three measure of meal, till the whole was leavened.*"

   33 <u>Ὁμοία</u> ἐστὶν ἡ βασιλεία τῶν οὐρανῶν <u>*ζύμῃ*</u>, ἣν λαβοῦσα γυνὴ ἐνέκρυψεν εἰς ἀλεύρου σάτα τρία ἕως οὗ ἐζυμώθη ὅλον.

   33 <u>Similis est</u> *regnum caelorum* <u>*fermento*</u>, quod acceptum mulier abscondit in farinae satis tribus, donec fermentatum est totum.

     [kingdom of heaven ≈ leaven hidden by a woman in meal]

Matt. 13.44 Again *the kingdom of leaven* is <u>like unto</u> <u>*treasure hid in a field*</u>
...

44 Πάλιν <u>ὁμοία</u> ἐστὶν ἡ βασιλεία τῶν οὐρανῶν <u>θησαυρῷ κεκρυμμένῳ ἐν</u>
<u>τῷ ἀγρῷ</u>,

44 <u>Simile</u> est *regnum caelorum* <u>*thesauro abscondito in agro*</u> :
   [the kingdom of heaven ≈ treasure hidden in a field]

Matt. 13.45 Again, the *kingdom of heaven* is <u>like unto</u> <u>*a merchant man,*</u>
<u>*seeking goodly pearls.*</u>

45 Πάλιν <u>ὁμοία</u> ἐστὶν ἡ βασιλεία τῶν οὐρανῶν <u>ἀνθρώπῳ ἐμπόρῳ ζητοῦντι</u>
<u>καλοὺς μαργαρίτας</u>:

45 Iterum <u>simile est</u> *regnum caelorum* <u>*homini negotiatori*</u>, <u>*quaerenti*</u>
<u>*bonas margaritas.*</u>
   [kingdom of heaven ≈ a merchant man seeking goodly pearls]

Matt. 13.47 Again, *the kingdom of heaven* is <u>like</u> unto <u>*a net, that was cast*</u>
<u>*into the sea and gathered of every kind.*</u>

47 Πάλιν <u>ὁμοία</u> ἐστὶν ἡ βασιλεία τῶν οὐρανῶν <u>σαγήνῃ βληθείσῃ εἰς τὴν</u>
<u>θάλασσαν</u> καὶ ἐκ παντὸς γένους συναγαγούσῃ:

47 Iterum <u>simile</u> est *regnum caelorum* <u>*sagenae missae in mare*</u>, et ex
omni genere piscium congreganti.
   [The kingdom of heaven ≈ a net cast into the sea]

Matt. 13.52 Therefore *every scribe* which is instructed unto the kingdom of
heaven is <u>like</u> unto a man that is an <u>*house-holder which bringeth forth*</u>
<u>*out of his treasure things new and old.*</u>

52 ὁ δὲ εἶπεν αὐτοῖς, Διὰ τοῦτο πᾶς γραμματεὺς μαθητευθεὶς τῇ βασιλείᾳ
τῶν οὐρανῶν <u>ὅμοιός</u> ἐστιν <u>ἀνθρώπῳ οἰκοδεσπότῃ ὅστις ἐκβάλλει ἐκ</u>
<u>τοῦ θησαυροῦ αὐτοῦ καινὰ καὶ παλαιά.</u>

52 Ait illis: Ideo *omnis scriba* doctus in regno caelorum, <u>similis</u>
<u>est</u> *homini patrifamilias*, qui profert de thesauro suo nova et vetera.
   [every scribe ... ≈ a house-holder who brings out of his
   treasure ...]

Matt. 17.20 And Jesus said unto them, "Because of your unbelief: for
verily I say unto you, if ye have *faith* <u>as</u> <u>*a grain of mustard seed* ...</u> "

20 ὁ δὲ λέγει αὐτοῖς, Διὰ τὴν ὀλιγοπιστίαν ὑμῶν: ἀμὴν γὰρ λέγω ὑμῖν, ἐὰν
ἔχητε *πίστιν* <u>ὡς</u> <u>κόκκον σινάπεως</u> ...

19 Amen quippe dico vobis, si habueritis *fidem* <u>sicut</u> <u>*granum sinapis*</u>,
   [faith ≈ a grain of mustard seed]

Matt. 18.3 "Except *ye* be converted, and become <u>as</u> *little children*, ye shall not enter into *the kingdom of heaven*."

3 ἀμὴν λέγω ὑμῖν, ἐὰν μὴ στραφῆτε καὶ γένησθε <u>ὡς</u> <u>*τὰ παιδία*</u>, οὐ μὴ εἰσέλθητε εἰς τὴν βασιλείαν τῶν οὐρανῶν.

3 Amen dico vobis, nisi conversi fueritis, et efficiamini <u>sicut</u> *parvuli*, non intrabitis in regnum caelorum.

[ye ≈ little children; heaven ≈ a kingdom]

Cf. Matt. 18.4: a comparison –

18.4 *Whosoever* therefore shall humble himself <u>as</u> *this little childe* …

4 ὅστις οὖν ταπεινώσει ἑαυτὸν <u>*ὡς*</u> <u>*τὸ παιδίον τοῦτο*</u>, οὗτός ἐστιν ὁ μείζων ἐν τῇ βασιλείᾳ τῶν οὐρανῶν.

4 Quicumque ergo humiliaverit *se* <u>sicut</u> *parvulus iste*, hic est major in regno caelorum.

[you ≈ little child]

Matt. 18.23 Therefore is *the kingdom of heaven* <u>likened unto</u> *a certain king*, which would take account of his servants.

23 Διὰ τοῦτο <u>ὡμοιώθη</u> ἡ βασιλεία τῶν οὐρανῶν <u>*ἀνθρώπῳ βασιλεῖ ὃς ἠθέλησεν*</u> <u>*συνᾶραι λόγον μετὰ τῶν δούλων αὐτοῦ*</u>. … 23 Ideo assimilatum est *regnum caelorum* <u>*homini regi*</u>, qui voluit rationem ponere cum servis suis.

[kingdom of the heaven ≈ a certain king]

Matt. 19.24 And again I say unto you, It is <u>easier for</u> *a camel to go through the eye of a needle,* <u>than for</u> *a rich man to enter the kingdom of God.*

24 πάλιν δὲ λέγω ὑμῖν, <u>εὐκοπώτερόν</u> ἐστιν <u>*κάμηλον*</u> διὰ τρυπήματος ῥαφίδος διελθεῖν ἢ πλούσιον εἰσελθεῖν εἰς τὴν βασιλείαν τοῦ θεοῦ.

24 Et iterum dico vobis: <u>Facilius est</u> *camelum per foramen acus transire,* <u>quam</u> *divitem intrare in regnum caelorum.*

[rich man entering the kingdom of God (easier than) ≈ a camel going through the eye of a needle]

Matt. 20.1 For the kingdom of heaven is <u>like</u> unto a man that is *an householder,* which went out early in the morning to hire laborers into his vineyard.

1 <u>Ὁμοία</u> γάρ <u>ἐστιν</u> ἡ βασιλεία τῶν οὐρανῶν <u>*ἀνθρώπῳ οἰκοδεσπότῃ ὅστις*</u> <u>*ἐξῆλθεν ἅμα πρωῒ μισθώσασθαι ἐργάτας εἰς τὸν ἀμπελῶνα αὐτοῦ.*</u>

1 Simile est *regnum caelorum homini patrifamilias, qui exiit* primo
mane conducere operarios in vineam suam.

[kingdom of God ≈ a householder out to hire workers]

A simile turning into a long parable (20.2–16).

Matt. 21.13 See Predicate Accusatives: my house ≈ a den of thieves

Matt. 22.2 The *kingdom of heaven is* like unto *a certain king*, which made
a marriage for his son.

2 Ὡμοιώθη ἡ βασιλεία τῶν οὐρανῶν ἀνθρώπῳ βασιλεῖ, ὅστις ἐποίησεν γάμους
τῷ υἱῷ αὐτοῦ.

2 Simile factum est *regnum caelorum homini regi, qui fecit nuptias
filio suo.*

[kingdom of heaven ≈ a king who made a marriage for his son]

(**continues to 22.14, which has a rather strange conclusion: after punishment of a guest who was not wearing a
wedding garment, the conclusion (22.14) is "For many are
called, but few are chosen":**14 πολλοὶ γάρ εἰσι κλητοί, ὀλίγοι
δὲ ἐκλεκτοί. 14 Multi enim sunt vocati, pauci vero electi.)

Matt. 22.30 "For in the resurrection *they* neither marry, nor are given in
marriage, but are as *the angels of God in heaven.*"

30 ἐν γὰρ τῇ ἀναστάσει οὔτε γαμοῦσιν οὔτε ἐκγαμίζονται, ἀλλ᾿ ὡς ἄγγελοι
Θεοῦ ἐν οὐρανῷ εἰσι.

30 In resurrectione enim neque nubent, neque nubentur : sed erunt
sicut *angeli Dei in caelo.*

[they (the seven brothers) ≈ the angels of God in heaven]

Jesus' answer to the Sadducees.

Matt. 23.27 Woe unto you, *scribes and Pharisees,* hypocrites! for ye are like
unto *whited sepulchres,* which indeed appear beautiful outward, but
are within full of dead men's bones, and of all uncleanness.

27 Οὐαὶ ὑμῖν, γραμματεῖς καὶ Φαρισαῖοι ὑποκριταί, ὅτι παρομοιάζετε τάφοις
κεκονιαμένοις, οἵτινες ἔξωθεν μὲν φαίνονται ὡραῖοι ἔσωθεν δὲ γέμουσιν
ὀστέων νεκρῶν καὶ πάσης ἀκαθαρσίας.

27 Vae vobis scribae et pharisaei hypocritae, quia similes estis *sepulchris
dealbatis,* quae a foris parent hominibus speciosa, intus vero pleni
sunt ossibus mortuorum, et omni spurcitia!

[you (scribes and Pharissees) ≈ whited sepulchres]

Matt. 24.27 For a<u>s *the lightning cometh out of the east, and shineth even unto the west;*</u> **so** shall also t*he coming of the son of man be.*

27 <u>ὥσπερ</u> γὰρ <u>*ἡ ἀστραπὴ*</u> ἐξέρχεται ἀπὸ ἀνατολῶν καὶ φαίνεται ἕως δυσμῶν, **οὕτως** ἔσται ἡ παρουσία τοῦ υἱοῦ τοῦ ἀνθρώπου. 27 <u>Sicut</u> enim *<u>fulgur exit ab oriente, et paret usque in occidentem</u>*: **ita** erit et *adventus Filii hominis.*

[the coming of the son of man ≈ lightning]

Matt. 25.1 Then shall *the kingdom of heaven* be <u>likened</u> unto *<u>ten virgins</u>*, which took their lamps, and what forth to to meet the bridegroom.

1 Τότε <u>ὁμοιωθήσεται</u> ἡ βασιλεία τῶν οὐρανῶν <u>*δέκα παρθένοις*</u>, αἵτινες λαβοῦσαι τὰς λαμπάδας ἑαυτῶν ἐξῆλθον εἰς ὑπάντησιν τοῦ νυμφίου.

1 Tunc <u>simile erit</u> *regnum caelorum <u>decem virginibus</u>*: quae accipientes lampades suas exierunt obviam sponso et sponsae.

[kingdom of the heavens ≈ ten virgins with their lamps]

Matt. 25.14 For *the kingdom of heaven* is <u>as</u> *<u>a man traveling into a far country</u>*, who called his own servants, and delivered unto them his goods.

14 [ἡ βασιλεία τῶν οὐρανῶν] <u>Ὥσπερ</u> γὰρ *<u>ἄνθρωπος ἀποδημῶν ἐκάλεσεν τοὺς ἰδίους</u>* δούλους καὶ παρέδωκεν αὐτοῖς τὰ ὑπάρχοντα αὐτοῦ.

14 <u>Sicut</u> enim *<u>homo peregre proficiscens,</u> vocavit servos suos,* et *tradidit illis bona sua.*

[the kingdom of the heavens ≈ a man going on a journey ...]

Matt. 25.32 And before him shall be gathered all nations: and he shall *separate them from one another*, <u>as</u> a shepherd divideth his sheep from the goats.

32 καὶ συναχθήσονται ἔμπροσθεν αὐτοῦ πάντα τὰ ἔθνη, καὶ ἀφορίσει αὐτοὺς ἀπ᾽ ἀλλήλων, <u>ὥσπερ *ὁ ποιμὴν ἀφορίζει τὰ πρόβατα ἀπὸ τῶν ἐρίφων.*</u>

32 et congregabuntur ante eum *omnes gentes,* et *separabit eos ab* invicem, <u>sicut *pastor segregat oves ab haedis*</u>:

[He will separate the nations ≈ a shepherd > his sheep]

Matt. 28.3 His *countenance* was <u>like</u> *<u>lightning,</u>* and his *raiment* white <u>as</u> <u>snow:</u> *4* And for fear of him the keepers did shake, and became <u>as</u> <u>dead men.</u>

3 ἦν δὲ ἡ εἰδέα αὐτοῦ <u>ὡς</u> <u>ἀστραπὴ</u> καὶ τὸ ἔνδυμα αὐτοῦ λευκὸν <u>ὡς</u> <u>χιών</u>. 4 ἀπὸ δὲ τοῦ φόβου αὐτοῦ ἐσείσθησαν οἱ τηροῦντες καὶ ἐγενήθησαν <u>ὡς</u> <u>νεκροί</u>.

3 erat autem *aspectus ejus* <u>sicut</u> *<u>fulgur</u>*: et *vestimentum ejus* <u>sicut</u> *<u>nix</u>*. 4 Prae timore autem ejus exterriti sunt custodes, et facti sunt <u>velut</u> <u>mortui.</u>

[His appearance ≈ lightning; his raiment (white) ≈ snow; his keepers ≈ dead men]

* * *

Mark (16 Chapters / 9 similes)

ΚΑΤΑ ΜΑΡΚΟΝ

Mark 1.10 And straightway coming up out of the water, he [Jesus] saw the heavens opened, and *the Spirit* <u>like</u> *<u>a dove</u>* descending upon him.

10 καὶ εὐθὺς ἀναβαίνων ἐκ τοῦ ὕδατος εἶδεν σχιζομένους τοὺς οὐρανοὺς καὶ τὸ πνεῦμα <u>ὡς</u> <u>περιστερὰν</u> καταβαῖνον εἰς αὐτόν: 10 Et statim ascendens de aqua, vidit caelos apertos, et *Spiritum* <u>tamquam</u> <u>columbam</u> descendentem, et manentem in ipso.

[the spirit = a dove]

Mark 4.26 And he said, "**So** is the kingdom of God, <u>as if</u> *<u>a man should cast</u>* *<u>seed</u> into <u>the ground.</u>*

26 Καὶ ἔλεγεν, **Οὕτως** ἐστὶν ἡ βασιλεία τοῦ θεοῦ <u>ὡς</u> <u>ἄνθρωπος βάλῃ τὸν</u> <u>σπόρον ἐπὶ τῆς γῆς</u>

26 Et dicebat: Sic est *regnum Dei*, <u>quemadmodum si</u> *<u>homo jacia</u>*t <u>sementem in terram.</u>

[the kingdom of God ≈ a man casting seed into the ground]

Mark 4.30 And he said, "Whereunto <u>shall we liken</u> the kingdom of God? or with what <u>comparison</u> shall we compare it? 31 It is <u>like</u> *<u>a grain of</u>* *<u>mustard seed,</u>* which, when it is sown in the earth, is less than all the seeds that be in the earth: …

30 Καὶ ἔλεγεν, Πῶς <u>ὁμοιώσωμεν</u> *τὴν βασιλείαν τοῦ θεοῦ, ἢ ἐν τίνι αὐτὴν* <u>παραβολῇ</u> θῶμεν; 31 <u>*ὡς κόκκῳ σινάπεως,*</u> ὃς ὅταν σπαρῇ ἐπὶ τῆς γῆς, μικρότερον ὂν πάντων τῶν σπερμάτων τῶν ἐπὶ τῆς γῆς.

30 Et dicebat: Cui <u>assimilabimus</u> regnum Dei? aut cui <u>parab-olae</u> comparabimus illud? 31 <u>Sicut</u> *granum sinapis,* quod cum seminatum fuerit in terra, minus est omnibus seminibus, quae sunt in terra.

33 And **with many such parables** spake he ... 34 But **without a parable spake he not unto them.**

[the kingdom of god = a grain of mustard seed]

Mark 6.34 And Jesus, when he came out, saw much people, one was moved with compassion toward them, because *they* were <u>as *sheep not having a shepherd*</u>, and he began to teach them many things.

34 καὶ ἐξελθὼν εἶδεν *πολὺν ὄχλον,* καὶ ἐσπλαγχνίσθη ἐπ' αὐτοὺς ὅτι ἦσαν <u>*ὡς πρόβατα μὴ ἔχοντα ποιμένα,*</u> καὶ ἤρξατο διδάσκειν αὐτοὺς πολλά.

34 Et exiens vidit *turbam multam* Jesus: et misertus est super *eos,* quia erant <u>sicut</u> <u>*oves non habentes pastorem*</u>, et coepit docere multa.

[the crowd = sheep without a shepherd]

Mark 8.24 And he [the blind man] looked up, and said, I see *men* <u>as</u> *<u>trees, walking</u>*.

24 καὶ ἀναβλέψας ἔλεγε· βλέπω τοὺς ἀνθρώπους <u>*ὡς δένδρα περιπατοῦντας.*</u>

24 Et aspiciens, ait : Video *homines* <u>velut</u> *<u>arbores ambulantes</u>*.

[men ≈ trees]

Mark 9.3 And his *raiment* became shining, *exceeding white* <u>as</u> *<u>snow; so</u>* <u>as</u> *<u>no fuller on earth can white them</u>*.

3 καὶ *τὰ ἱμάτια* αὐτοῦ ἐγένετο στίλβοντα λευκὰ λίαν <u>οἷα</u> *<u>γναφεὺς ἐπὶ τῆς γῆς οὐ δύναται οὕτως λευκᾶναι.</u>*

2 Et *vestimenta ejus* facta sunt *splendentia,* et *candida* <u>nimis velut</u> *<u>nix,</u>* qualia fullo non potest super terram candida facere.

[his raiment ≈ (white as) snow]

Mark 10.25 It is <u>easier</u> for a *<u>camel</u>* to go through the eye of a needle, *than for <u>a rich man to enter into the kingdom of God</u>.*

25 <u>εὐκοπώτερόν</u> ἐστιν *<u>κάμηλον διὰ [τῆς] τρυμαλιᾶς [τῆς] ῥαφίδος διελθεῖν</u>* <u>ἢ πλούσιον εἰς τὴν βασιλείαν τοῦ θεοῦ εἰσελθεῖν.</u>

25 <u>Facilius</u> est <u>*camelum per foramen acus transire*</u>, <u>quam</u> *divitem intrare in regnum Dei.*

[a wealthy man > kingdom of God NOT≈ a camel > the eye of a needle]

Mark 12.25 For when they shall rise from the dead, *they* neither marry, nor are given in marriage; but are <u>as</u> <u>*the angels which are in heaven*</u>.

25 ὅταν γὰρ ἐκ νεκρῶν ἀναστῶσιν, οὔτε γαμοῦσιν οὔτε γαμίζονται, ἀλλ' εἰσὶν <u>ὡς</u> <u>*ἄγγελοι οἱ ἐν τοῖς οὐρανοῖς*</u>.

25 Cum enim a mortuis resurrexerint, neque nubent, neque nubentur, sed *sunt* <u>sicut</u> <u>*angeli in caelis*</u>.

[they ≈ angels in heaven] Jesus' answer to the Sadducees.

Mark 13.34 For *the Son of man* is <u>as</u> <u>*a man taking a far journey*</u> ...

34 <u>ὡς</u> <u>*ἄνθρωπος ἀπόδημος*</u>, ἀφεὶς τὴν οἰκίαν αὐτοῦ, ...

34 <u>Sicut</u> <u>*homo qui peregre profectus reliquit domum suam*</u>,

[the Son of man ≈ a man taking a far journey]   Jesus

* * *

Luke (24 Chapters / 15 similes)

ΚΑΤΑ ΛΟΥΚΑΝ

Luke 3.22 And *the Holy Ghost* descended in a bodily shape <u>like</u> <u>*a dove*</u> upon him.

22 καὶ καταβῆναι τὸ *Πνεῦμα τὸ Ἅγιον* σωματικῷ εἴδει <u>ὡσεὶ</u> <u>*περιστερὰν*</u> ἐπ' αὐτόν.

22 et descendit *Spiritus Sanctus* corporali specie <u>sicut</u> <u>*columba*</u> in ipsum.

[the Holy Ghost ≈ a dove]

Luke 6.47 Whosoever cometh to me, and heareth my sayings, and doeth them, I will show you *whom he is like*: 48 *He* is <u>like</u> <u>*a man which built an house ... on a rock ...*</u>

47 πᾶς ὁ ἐρχόμενος πρός με καὶ ἀκούων μου τῶν λόγων καὶ ποιῶν αὐτούς, <u>ὑποδείξω ὑμῖν τίνι ἐστὶν ὅμοιος:</u> 48 <u>ὅμοιός ἐστιν *ἀνθρώπῳ οἰκοδομοῦντι οἰκίαν ὃς ἔσκαψεν καὶ ἐβάθυνεν καὶ ἔθηκεν θεμέλιον ἐπὶ τὴν πέτραν*.</u>

47 Omnis qui venit ad me, et audit sermones meos, et facit eos, ostendam vobis *cui similis sit*: 48 <u>Similis</u> est <u>*homini aedificanti domum*</u>, ... et posuit fundamentum <u>*super petram*</u>:

[he who hears my sayings and does them ≈ a man who built his
house on a rock]

Luke 6.49 But *he that heareth, and doeth not,* is <u>like</u> <u>*a man that without*</u>
<u>*a foundation built an house upon the earth*</u> ... and the ruin of that
house was great.

49 ὁ δὲ ἀκούσας καὶ μὴ ποιήσας <u>ὅμοιός</u> ἐστιν <u>ἀνθρώπῳ οἰκοδομήσαντι</u>
<u>οἰκίαν ἐπὶ τὴν γῆν χωρὶς θεμελίου</u>, ᾗ προσέρηξεν ὁ ποταμός, καὶ εὐθὺς
συνέπεσεν, καὶ ἐγένετο τὸ ῥῆγμα τῆς οἰκίας ἐκείνης μέγα.

49 *Qui autem audit, et non facit,* <u>similis</u> est <u>*homini aedificanti domum*</u>
<u>*suam super terram sine fundamento*</u>: ... et facta est ruina domus
illius magna.

[he who hears me and does not do them ≈ a man who builds his
house on the earth without a foundation]

Luke 7.31 And the Lord said, <u>Whereunto</u> then <u>shall I liken</u> *the men of this*
generation? and <u>to what</u> are they like? 32 They are like unto *children*
sitting in the marketplace, and calling one to another ...

31 <u>*Τίνι*</u> οὖν <u>ὁμοιώσω</u> τοὺς ἀνθρώπους τῆς γενεᾶς ταύτης, καὶ <u>τίνι</u> εἰσὶν <u>ὅμοιοι</u>;
32 <u>ὅμοιοί</u> εἰσιν <u>παιδίοις τοῖς ἐν ἀγορᾷ καθημένοις καὶ</u> <u>προσφωνοῦσιν</u>
<u>ἀλλήλοις</u>, ...

31 Ait autem Dominus: <u>*Cui*</u> ergo <u>similes</u> dicam *homines generationis*
hujus? et <u>*cui*</u> <u>similes</u> *sunt?* 32 <u>Similes</u> sunt *pueris sedentibus in foro,*
et loquentibus ad invicem, et dicentibus: Cantavimus vobis tibiis,
et non saltastis: lamentavimus, et non plorastis.

[the people of this generation ≈ children sitting in the market]

Luke 10.3 Go your ways: behold, I send *you* forth <u>as</u> <u>*lambs among wolves.*</u>

3 ὑπάγετε· ἰδοὺ ἀποστέλλω ὑμᾶς <u>ὡς</u> <u>ἄρνας ἐν μέσῳ λύκων</u>.

3 Ite: ecce ego mitto *vos* <u>sicut</u> <u>*agnos inter lupos.*</u>

[you ≈ lambs among wolves]

Luke 10.18 And he said unto them, I beheld *Satan* <u>as</u> <u>*lightning fall from*</u>
<u>*heaven*</u>. Jesus

18 εἶπεν δὲ αὐτοῖς, Ἐθεώρουν τὸν Σατανᾶν <u>ὡς</u> <u>ἀστραπὴν ἐκ τοῦ οὐρανοῦ</u>
<u>πεσόντα</u>.

18 Videbam *Satanam* <u>sicut</u> <u>*fulgor de caelo cadentem.*</u>

[Satan ≈ lightening falling from heaven]

Luke 12.36 And *ye yourselves* <u>like unto</u> *<u>men that wait for their lord</u>*, when
he will return from the wedding …

36 καὶ ὑμεῖς <u>ὅμοιοι</u> <u>*ἀνθρώποις προσδεχομένοις τὸν κύριον*</u> ἑαυτῶν, πότε
ἀναλύσει ἐκ τῶν γάμων.

36 et *vos* <u>similes</u> *<u>hominibus exspectantibus dominum suum</u>* quando
revertatur a nuptiis :

[you ≈ men who wait for their lord to return from the wedding]

Luke 13.18 Then said he, Unto what <u>is</u> *the kingdom of God* <u>like</u>? and
whereunto shall I resemble it?

18 Ελεγεν οὖν, *<u>Τίνι</u>* <u>ὁμοία</u> ἐστὶν ἡ βασιλεία τοῦ θεοῦ, καὶ τίνι <u>ὁμοιώσω</u> αὐτήν;

18 Dicebat ergo: *<u>Cui</u>* <u>simile</u> est *regnum Dei*, et *cui* <u>simile aestimabo</u> *illud*?

[the kingdom of God = what (simile)?]

Simile follows in 19–21.

Luke 13.19 *It* is <u>like</u> *<u>a grain of mustard seed,</u>* which a man took, and cast
into his garden; and it grew, and waxed a great tree; and the fowls of
the air lodged in the branches of it.

19 <u>ὁμοία</u> ἐστὶν *<u>κόκκῳ σινάπεως</u>*, ὃν λαβὼν ἄνθρωπος ἔβαλεν εἰς κῆπον
ἑαυτοῦ, καὶ ηὔξησεν καὶ ἐγένετο εἰς δένδρον, καὶ τὰ πετεινὰ τοῦ
οὐρανοῦ κατεσκήνωσεν ἐν τοῖς κλάδοις αὐτοῦ.

19 <u>Simile</u> est *<u>grano sinapis</u>*, quod acceptum homo misit in hortum
suum, et crevit, et factum est in arborem magnam: et volucres
caeli requieverunt in ramis ejus.

[it (the kingdom of God) ≈ a mustard seed etc.]

Luke 13.20 And again he said, Whereunto <u>shall I liken</u> *the kingdom of God*?

20 Καὶ πάλιν εἶπεν, *<u>Τίνι</u>* <u>ὁμοιώσω</u> τὴν βασιλείαν τοῦ θεοῦ;

20 Et iterum dixit: *<u>Cui</u>* <u>simile</u> aestimabo *regnum Dei*?

[the kingdom of God ≈ to what?]

Luke 13.21 *It* is <u>like</u> *<u>leaven</u>*, which a woman took and hid in three measures
of meal, till the whole was leavened.

21 <u>ὁμοία</u> ἐστὶν *<u>ζύμη</u>*, ἣν λαβοῦσα γυνὴ [ἐν]έκρυψεν εἰς ἀλεύρου σάτα τρία
ἕως οὗ ἐζυμώθη ὅλον.

21 <u>Simile</u> est *<u>fermento</u>*, quod acceptum mulier abscondit in farinae sata
tria, donec fermentaretur totum.

[it (the kingdom of God) ≈ leaven, which a woman took and hid
in three measures of meal]

>>> **NB several parables are not included here because they are not expressed as similes.**

Luke 13.34 How often would *I have gathered thy children together*, as a *hen doth gather her brood under her wings*, and ye would not!

> 34 ποσάκις ἠθέλησα ἐπισυνάξαι τὰ τέκνα σου ὃν τρόπον ὄρνις τὴν ἑαυτῆς νοσσιὰν ὑπὸ τὰς πτέρυγας, καὶ οὐκ ἠθελήσατε.

> 34 quoties *volui congregare filios tuos* quemadmodum *avis nidum* suum sub pennis, et noluisti?

> [I (Jesus) > your children ≈ a hen > her brood]

Luke 17.6 And the Lord said, If ye had *faith* as *a grain of mustard seed*, ye might say unto this sycamine tree, Be thou plucked up by the root, and be thou planted in the sea; and it should obey you.

> 6 εἶπεν δὲ ὁ κύριος, Εἰ ἔχετε πίστιν ὡς κόκκον σινάπεως, ἐλέγετε ἂν τῇ συκαμίνῳ [ταύτῃ], Ἐκριζώθητι καὶ φυτεύθητι ἐν τῇ θαλάσσῃ: καὶ ὑπήκουσεν ἂν ὑμῖν.

> 6 Dixit autem Dominus: Si habueritis *fidem* sicut *granum sinapis*, dicetis huic arbori moro: Eradicare, et transplantare in mare, et obediet vobis.

> [faith ≈ a grain of mustard seed]

Luke 18.25 For it is easier for *a camel to go through a needle's eye*, than for a *rich man to enter into the kingdom of God*.

> 25 εὐκοπώτερον γάρ ἐστι κάμηλον διὰ τρυμαλιᾶς ῥαφίδος εἰσελθεῖν ἢ πλούσιον εἰς τὴν βασιλείαν τοῦ Θεοῦ εἰσελθεῖν.

> 25 facilius est enim *camelum per foramen acus transire* quam *divitem intrare in regnum Dei*.

> [a rich man > kingdom of God ≈ (easier for) a camel > a needle's eye]

> Cf. Mark 10.25 [NB – Both similes are expressed as though the rich man were part of the vehicle (easier than).]

Luke 21.35 For as *a snare* shall it [the kingdom of God] *come* on all them that dwell on the face of the whole earth.

> 35 ὡς παγὶς γὰρ ἐπελεύσεται ἐπὶ πάντας τοὺς καθημένους ἐπὶ πρόσωπον πάσης τῆς γῆς.

35 tamquam _laqueus_ enim _superveniet_ in omnes qui sedent super faciem
omnis terrae.
[the kingdom of God coming ≈ a snare]

***

John (21 Chapters / 2 similes)

ΚΑΤΑ ΙΩΑΝΝΗΝ

John 1.32 And John bare record, saying, I saw the _Spirit_ descending from
heaven like _a dove_, and it abode upon him.

32 Καὶ ἐμαρτύρησεν Ιωάννης λέγων ὅτι Τεθέαμαι τὸ πνεῦμα καταβαῖνον
ὡς περιστερὰν ἐξ οὐρανοῦ, καὶ ἔμεινεν ἐπ' αὐτόν.

32 Et testimonium perhibuit Joannes, dicens: Quia vidi _Spiritum_
descendentem quasi _columbam de caelo_, et mansit super eum.
[the spirit descending from heaven ≈ a dove]

John 3.14 And as Moses lifted up the serpent in the wilderness, even **so**
must _the Son of man_ be lifted up.

14 καὶ **καθὼς** Μωϋσῆς ὕψωσεν τὸν ὄφιν ἐν τῇ ἐρήμῳ, **οὕτως** ὑψωθῆναι
δεῖ τὸν υἱὸν τοῦ ἀνθρώπου.

14 Et sicut _Moyses exaltavit serpentem in deserto_, **ita** exaltari oportet
Filium hominis:
[the Son of man (to be lifted up) ≈ the serpent in the desert]

* * *

Acts of the Apostles (28 Chapters)

ΠΡΑΞΕΙΣ ΤΩΝ ΑΠΟΣΤΟΛΩΝ

Acts 2.2 And suddenly there came _a sound from heaven_ as of _a rushing
mighty wind_, and it filled all the house where they were sitting. 3 And
there appeared unto them _cloven tongues_ like as _of fire._

2 καὶ ἐγένετο ἄφνω ἐκ τοῦ οὐρανοῦ ἦχος ὥσπερ φερομένης πνοῆς βιαίας …
3 καὶ ὤφθησαν αὐτοῖς διαμεριζόμεναι γλῶσσαι ὡσεὶ πυρός,

2 et factus est repente de caelo _sonus_, tamquam _advenientis spiritus
vehementis_, et replevit totam domum ubi erant sedentes. 3 Et
apparuerunt illis _dispertitae linguae_ tamquam _ignis_, seditque supra
singulos eorum

[sound ≈ rushing wind; tongues ≈ fire]

Acts 8.32 *He* was led as a *sheep* to the slaughter, and like *a lamb* dumb before his shearer, so *he* opened not his mouth.

    32 Ὡς <u>*πρόβατον*</u> ἐπὶ σφαγὴν ἤχθη, καὶ <u>ὡς *ἀμνὸς*</u> ἐναντίον τοῦ κείραντος αὐτὸν ἄφωνος, **οὕτως** οὐκ ἀνοίγει τὸ στόμα αὐτοῦ.

    32 Locus autem Scripturae, quem legebat, erat hic : <u>Tamquam *ovis*</u> ad occisionem <u>ductus est</u> : et <u>sicus *agnus*</u> coram tondente se, sine voce, **sic** *non aperuit os suum.*

    [he ≈ a sheep to slaughter ≈ a lamb]

Acts 9.18 And immediately there fell from his eyes <u>as it had been *scales*</u>:

    18 καὶ εὐθέως ἀπέπεσον ἀπὸ τῶν ὀφθαλμῶν αὐτοῦ <u>ὡσεὶ λεπίδες</u>,

    18 Et confestim ceciderunt ab oculis ejus, <u>tamquam *squamae*</u>, et visum recepit :

    [(things) ≈ scales in his eyes]

Acts 11.5 I was in the city of Joppa praying: and in a trance I saw a vision, A *certain vessel* descend, <u>as it had been *a great sheet, let down from heaven by four corners*</u>; and it came even to me.

    5 ἐγὼ ἤμην ἐν πόλει Ιόππῃ προσευχόμενος, καὶ εἶδον ἐν ἐκστάσει ὅραμα, καταβαῖνον σκεῦός τι <u>ὡς ὀθόνην μεγάλην τέσσαρσιν ἀρχαῖς καθιεμένην ἐκ τοῦ οὐρανοῦ,</u> καὶ ἦλθεν ἄχρις ἐμοῦ·

    5 Ego eram in civitate Joppe orans, et vidi in excessu mentis visionem, *descendens vas* <u>*quoddam*</u> <u>velut</u> <u>*linteum magnum*</u> quatuor initiis summitti de caelo, et venit usque ad me.

    [a vision: a vessel let down from heaven ≈ a great sheet] Peter

NB In the long narrative that follows (chapters 12–28) there is only one simile, in Paul's speech (17.22–31):

Acts 17.29 "We ought not to think that *the Godhead* is <u>like unto *gold, or silver, or stone, graven by art and man's device.*</u>"

    29 οὐκ ὀφείλομεν νομίζειν <u>*χρυσῷ ἢ ἀργύρῳ ἢ λίθῳ*</u>, χαράγματι τέχνης καὶ ἐνθυμήσεως ἀνθρώπου, τὸ θεῖον εἶναι <u>ὅμοιον</u>.

    29 Genus ergo cum simus Dei, non debemus aestimare <u>*auro*</u>, aut <u>*argento, aut lapidi*</u>, sculpturae artis, et cogitationis hominis, *divinum* <u>esse simile.</u>

    [the Godhead NOT ≈ gold, silver or stone]

***

Epistle of Paul to the Romans (16 Chapters)

ΠΡΟΣ ΡΩΜΑΙΟΥΣ

* * *

First Corinthians (16 Chapters)

(First Epistle of Paul)

ΠΡΟΣ ΚΟΡΙΝΘΙΟΥΣ Α΄

1st Cor. 13.1 THOUGH I speak with the tongues of men and of angels, and have not charity, *I* am become *as sounding brass, or a tinkling cymbal.*

13 Ἐὰν ταῖις γλώσσαις τῶν ἀνθρώπων λαλῶ καὶ τῶν ἀγγέλων, ἀγάπην δὲ μὴ ἔχω, *γέγονα χαλκὸς ἠχῶν ἢ κύμβαλον ἀλαλάζον.*

13 Si linguis hominum loquar, et angelorum, caritatem autem non habeam, *factus sum* velut *aes sonans, aut cymbalum tinniens.*

[I ≈ sounding brass / a tinkling cymbal]

* * *

Second Corinthians (13 Chapters)

(Second Epistle of Paul)

ΠΡΟΣ ΚΟΡΙΝΘΙΟΥΣ Β᾽

2nd Cor. 11.3 But I fear, lest by any means, *as the serpent beguiled Eve* through his subtilty, **so** *your minds should be corrupted from the simplicity that is in Christ.*

3 φοβοῦμαι δὲ μήπως, *ὡς ὁ ὄφις Εὔαν ἐξηπάτησεν* ἐν τῇ πανουργίᾳ αὐτοῦ, **οὕτω** φθαρῇ τὰ νοήματα ὑμῶν ἀπὸ τῆς ἁπλότητος τῆς εἰς τὸν Χριστόν.

3 Timeo autem ne sicut *serpens Hevam seduxit astutia sua,* **ita** *corrumpantur sensus vestri, et excidant a simplicitate, quae est in Christo.*

[your minds corrupted by Christ's simplicity ≈ Eve beguiled by the serpent]

* * *

Galatians (6 Chapters)

(Epistle of Paul)

ΠΡΟΣ ΓΑΛΑΤΑΣ

* * *

Ephesians (6 Chapters)

(Epistle of Paul)

ΠΡΟΣ ΕΦΕΣΙΟΥΣ

* * *

Philippians (4 Chapters)

(Epistle of Paul)

ΠΡΟΣ ΦΙΛΙΠΠΗΣΙΟΥΣ

Phil. 2.15 in the midst of a crooked and perverse nation, among whom *ye shine* <u>as</u> *<u>lights in the world.</u>*

22 ἐν μέσῳ γενεᾶς σκολιᾶς καὶ διεστραμμένης, ἐν οἷς φαίνεσθε <u>ὡς</u> <u>*φωστῆρες ἐν κόσμῳ*</u>,

15 inter quos *lucetis* <u>sicut</u> *<u>luminaria in mundo.</u>*

[you (Philippians) ≈ lights]

* * *

Colossians (4 Chapters)

(Epistle of Paul)

ΠΡΟΣ ΚΟΛΟΣΣΑΕΙΣ

* * *

First Thessalonians (5 Chapters)

(Epistle of Paul)

ΠΡΟΣ ΚΟΛΟΣΣΑΕΙΣ

1 Thes. 5.2 For yourselves know perfectly that *the day of the Lord so cometh as a thief in the night*.

2 αὐτοὶ γὰρ ἀκριβῶς οἴδατε ὅτι ἡ ἡμέρα Κυρίου ὡς κλέπτης ἐν νυκτὶ οὕτως ἔρχεται.

2 Ipsi enim diligenter scitis quia *dies Domini*, sicut *fur in nocte*, **ita** veniet :

[the day of the Lord ≈ a thief in the night]

1 Thes. 5.3 For when they shall say, Peace and safety; then *sudden destruction* cometh upon them, *as travail upon a woman with child*;

3 τότε αἰφνίδιος αὐτοῖς ἐφίσταται ὄλεθρος, ὥσπερ ἡ ὠδὶν τῇ ἐν γαστρὶ ἐχούσῃ,

3 tunc repentius eis superveniet *interitus*, sicut *dolor in utero habenti*,

[sudden destruction ≈ pain of childbirth]

* * *

Second Thessalonians (3 Chapters)

(Epistle of Paul)

ΠΡΟΣ ΘΕΣΣΑΛΟΝΙΚΕΙΣ Β′

* * *

First Timothy (6 Chapters)

(Epistle of Paul)

ΠΡΟΣ ΤΙΜΟΘΕΟΝ Α′

* * *

Second Timothy (4 Chapters)

(Epistle of Paul)

ΠΡΟΣ ΤΙΜΟΘΕΟΝ Β′

* * *

Titus (3 Chapters)

(Epistle of Paul)

ΠΡΟΣ ΤΙΤΟΝ

* * *

Philemon (1 Chapter)

(Epistle of Paul)

ΠΡΟΣ ΦΙΛΗΜΟΝΑ

* * *

Hebrews (11 Chapters)

(Epistle of Paul)

ΠΡΟΣ ΕΒΡΑΙΟΥΣ

Hebr. 4.12 For *the word of God is quick,* and powerful, and <u>*sharper than any two-edged sword*</u>, piercing even to the dividing as under of soul and spirit, and of the joints and marrow.

12 ζῶν γὰρ ὁ λόγος τοῦ Θεοῦ καὶ ἐνεργὴς καὶ <u>τομώτερος ὑπὲρ πᾶσαν</u> <u>μάχαιραν δίστομον</u> καὶ διϊκνούμενος ἄχρι μερισμοῦ ψυχῆς τε καὶ πνεύματος

12 Vivus est enim *sermo Dei,* et efficax et <u>penetrabilior</u> <u>*omni gladio*</u> <u>*ancipiti*</u>.

[the word of God (sharper) ≈ two-edged sword]

* * *

James (5 Chapters)

(General Epistle)

ΙΑΚΩΒΟΥ ΕΠΙΣΤΟΛΗ

James 1.11 For *the sun* is <u>no sooner risen</u> with a burning heat, but it *withereth the grass, and the flower thereof falleth, and the grace of the fashion of it perisheth*: **so** also *shall the rich man fade away in his ways.*

11 <u>ἀνέτειλε γὰρ ὁ ἥλιος σὺν τῷ καύσωνι καὶ ἐξήρανε τὸν χόρτον, καὶ τὸ ἄνθος αὐτοῦ ἐξέπεσε, καὶ ἡ εὐπρέπεια τοῦ προσώπου αὐτοῦ ἀπώλετο.</u> **οὕτω** καὶ ὁ πλούσιος ἐν ταῖς πορείαις αὐτοῦ μαρανθήσεται.

11 <u>*exortus est enim sol cum ardore, et arefecit foenum, et flos ejus decidit, et decor vultus ejus deperiit*</u> : **ita** *et dives in itineribus suis marcescet.*

[the rich man shall fade ≈ the sun withers the grass etc.]

James 1.23 For *if any be a hearer of the word, and not a doer, he is* <u>*like unto a man beholding his natural face in a glass*</u>: etc.

23 ὅτι εἴ τις ἀκροατὴς λόγου ἐστὶ καὶ οὐ ποιητής, οὗτος <u>ἔοικεν</u> <u>ἀνδρὶ κατανοοῦντι τὸ πρόσωπον τῆς γενέσεως αὐτοῦ ἐν ἐσόπτρῳ</u>·

23 Quia *si quis auditor est verbi, et non factor,* hic comparabitur *viro considerati vultum nativitatis suae in speculo.*

[a hearer of the word and not a doer ≈ a man beholding his face in a mirror]

James 5.3 *Your gold and silver* is cankered; and the rust of them shall be a witness against you, and shall *eat your flesh* <u>*as it were fire.*</u>

3 ὁ χρυσὸς ὑμῶν καὶ ὁ ἄργυρος κατίωται, καὶ ὁ ἰὸς αὐτῶν εἰς μαρτύριον ὑμῖν ἔσται καὶ φάγεται τὰς σάρκας ὑμῶν. <u>ὡς πῦρ</u> ἐθησαυρίσατε ἐν ἐσχάταις ἡμέραις.

3 *Aurum et argentum vestrum* aeruginavit : et aerugo eorum in testimonium vobis erit, et *manducabit carnes vestras* <u>sicut ignis.</u>

[the rust of your gold and silver (shall eat your flesh) ≈ fire]

* * *

First Peter (5 Chapters)

(1st Epistle)

ΠΕΤΡΟΥ ΕΠΙΣΤΟΛΗ ΠΡΩΤΗ

1 Peter 1.7 That the trial of *your faith,* <u>*being much more precious than of gold that perisheth, though it be tried with fire,*</u> might be found unto praise and honour and glory at the appearing of Jesus Christ.

7 ἵνα τὸ δοκίμιον ὑμῶν τῆς πίστεως <u>πολυτιμότερον χρυσίου τοῦ ἀπολλυμένου</u> <u>διὰ πυρὸς δὲ δοκιμαζομένου</u> εὑρεθῇ εἰς ἔπαινον καὶ τιμὴν καὶ δόξαν ἐν ἀποκαλύψει Ἰησοῦ Χριστοῦ …

7 ut probatio *vestrae fidei* <u>multo pretiosior</u> *auro* (quod per ignem probatur) inveniatur in laudem, et gloriam, et honorem in revelatione Jesu Christi :

[your faith (more precious) ≈ gold that perishes]

1 Peter 1.18 Ye know that ye were not redeemed with *corruptible things*, <u>as</u> <u>silver and gold</u> … 19 But with the *precious blood of Christ, <u>as of a lamb</u>* <u>*without blemish and without spot*</u>:

18 εἰδότες ὅτι *οὐ φθαρτοῖς, ἀργυρίῳ ἢ χρυσίῳ*, ἐλυτρώθητε ἐκ τῆς ματαίας ὑμῶν ἀναστροφῆς πατροπαραδότου, 19 ἀλλὰ <u>τιμίῳ αἵματι</u> <u>ὡς</u> <u>ἀμνοῦ</u> <u>ἀμώμου καὶ ἀσπίλου Χριστοῦ.</u>

18 Scientes quod *non corruptibilibus,* <u>auro vel argento,</u> redempti estis de vana vestra conversatione paternae traditionis : 19 sed *pretioso sanguine* <u>quasi *agni immaculati Christi,*</u> et incontaminati.

[the blood of Christ ≈ a perfect lamb]

+ a literal comparison: corruptible things ≈ silver and gold

1 Peter 1.24 For *all flesh* is *<u>as grass,</u>* and *all the glory of man <u>as the flower of</u>* <u>*grass.*</u> The grass withereth, and the flower thereof falleth away.

24 διότι *πᾶσα σὰρξ <u>ὡς χόρτος,</u>* καὶ *πᾶσα δόξα ἀνθρώπου <u>ὡς ἄνθος χόρτου·</u>* ἐξηράνθη ὁ χόρτος, καὶ τὸ ἄνθος αὐτοῦ ἐξέπεσε·

24 quia *omnis caro* <u>ut *foenum*</u> : et *omnis gloria ejus* <u>tamquam *flos foeni*</u> : exaruit foenum, et flos ejus decidit.

[flesh ≈ grass; the glory of man ≈ the flower of grass]

1 Peter 2.4 To whom coming, <u>as</u> unto *<u>a living stone</u>* … 5 *Ye* also, <u>as</u> lively <u>*stones*</u>, are built up a spiritual house.

4 πρὸς ὃν προσερχόμενοι, <u>λίθον ζῶντα,</u> … 5 καὶ αὐτοὶ <u>ὡς λίθοι ζῶντες</u> οἰκοδομεῖσθε οἶκος πνευματικός, ἱεράτευμα ἅγιον.

4 Ad quem accedentes lapidem vivum, … [5] et ipsi <u>tamquam *lapides*</u> *vivi* superaedificamini, domus spiritualis.

[(the Lord) ≈ a living stone; you ≈ lively stones]

1 Peter 2.16 As *free*, and not using your liberty for a cloke of maliciousness, but <u>as</u> the <u>*servants of God.*</u>

  16 ὡς ἐλεύθεροι, καὶ μὴ ὡς ἐπικάλυμμα ἔχοντες τῆς κακίας τὴν ἐλευθερίαν, ἀλλ' <u>ὡς δοῦλοι Θεοῦ.</u>

  16 quasi *liberi*, et non quasi velamen habentes malitiae libertatem, sed sicut <u>*servi De*i.</u>

  [(ye) free ≈ the servants of God]

1 Peter 5.8 Be sober, be vigilant; because *your adversary the devil, <u>as a roaring lion,</u>* walketh about, seeking whom he may devour.

  8 νήψατε, γρηγορήσατε· ὁ ἀντίδικος ὑμῶν διάβολος <u>ὡς λέων ὠρυόμενος</u> περιπατεῖ ζητῶν τίνα καταπίῃ.

  8 Sobrii estote, et vigilate : quia *adversarius vester diabolus* <u>tamquam</u> <u>*leo rugiens*</u> circuit, quaerens quem devoret.

  [the devil ≈ a roaring lion searching for a victim]

* * *

Second Peter (3 Chapters)

(2nd Epistle)

ΠΕΤΡΟΥ ΕΠΙΣΤΟΛΗ ΔΕΥΤΕΡΑ

2 Peter 3.10 But *the day of the Lord* will come <u>*as a thief in the night*</u>;

  10 ἥξει δὲ ἡ ἡμέρα Κυρίου <u>ὡς κλέπτης ἐν νυκτί,</u>

  10 Adveniet autem *dies Domin*i <u>ut *fur.*</u>

  [the day of the Lord (will come) ≈ a thief in the night]

* * *

First John (5 Chapters)

(1st Epistle)

ΙΩΑΝΝΟΥ ΕΠΙΣΤΟΛΗ ΠΡΩΤΗ

* * *

Second John (1 Chapter)

(2nd Epistle)

ΙΩΑΝΝΟΥ ΕΠΙΣΤΟΛΗ ΔΕΥΤΕΡΑ

* * *

Third John (1 Chapter)

(3rd Epistle)

ΙΩΑΝΝΟΥ ΕΠΙΣΤΟΛΗ ΤΡΙΤΗ

* * *

Jude (1 Chapter)

(General Epistle)

ΙΟΥΔΑ ΕΠΙΣΤΟΛΗ

Jude 10 But these speak evil of those things which they know not: but what t*hey know naturally*, as *brute beasts*, in those things they corrupt themselves.

10 οὗτοι δὲ ὅσα μὲν οὐκ οἴδασι βλασφημοῦσιν, *ὅσα δὲ φυσικῶς ὡς τὰ ἄλογα ζῷα ἐπίστανται*, ἐν τούτοις φθείρονται.

10 quaecumque autem naturaliter, tamquam *muta animalia*, norunt, in his corrumpuntur.

[those who speak what they know naturally ≈ brute beasts]

* * *

The Revelation of St. John the Divine (22 Chapters)

ΑΠΟΚΑΛΥΨΙΣ ΙΩΑΝΝΟΥ

Rev. John 1.10 I was in the Spirit on the Lord's day, and heard behind me a *great voice*, as *of a trumpet*,

10 ἐγενόμην ἐν πνεύματι ἐν τῇ κυριακῇ ἡμέρᾳ, καὶ ἤκουσα φωνὴν ὀπίσω μου μεγάλην *ὡς σάλπιγγος*

10 fui in spiritu in dominica die, et audivi post me *vocem magnam* tamquam *tubae*

[a voice ≈ sound of a trumpet]

Rev. 1.14 His head and his hairs were *white* like *wool*, as white as *snow*; and *his eyes* were *as a flame of fire.*

14 ἡ δὲ κεφαλὴ αὐτοῦ καὶ *αἱ τρίχες λευκαὶ ὡς ἔριον λευκόν, ὡς χιών*, καὶ οἱ ὀφθαλμοὶ αὐτοῦ *ὡς φλὸξ πυρός*

14 caput autem ejus, et *capilli erant candidi* tamquam *lana alba*, et tamquam *nix*, et *oculi ejus* tamquam *flamma ignis* :
[his hairs (white) ≈ wool ≈ snow; his eyes ≈ a flame of fire]

Rev. 1.15 And *his feet* like unto *fine brass*, as if *they burned in a furnace*; and *his voice* as *the sound of many waters.*

15 καὶ οἱ πόδες αὐτοῦ *ὅμοιοι χαλκολιβάνῳ, ὡς ἐν καμίνῳ πεπυρωμένοι*, καὶ ἡ φωνὴ αὐτοῦ *ὡς φωνὴ ὑδάτων πολλῶν*,

15 et *pedes ejus* similes *auricalco*, sicut *in camino ardenti*, et *vox* illius tamquam *vox aquarum multarum* :
[his feet ≈ fine brass ≈ burned in a furnace; his voice ≈ sound of many waters]

Rev. 1.16 And he had in his right hand seven stars: and out of his mouth went a sharp two-edged sword: and his *countenance* was as *the sun shineth in his strength.*

16 καὶ ἔχων ἐν τῇ δεξιᾷ χειρὶ αὐτοῦ ἀστέρας ἑπτά, καὶ ἐκ τοῦ στόματος αὐτοῦ ῥομφαία δίστομος ὀξεῖα ἐκπορευομένη, καὶ ἡ ὄψις αὐτοῦ *ὡς ὁ ἥλιος φαίνει ἐν τῇ δυνάμει αὐτοῦ.*

16 et habebat in dextera sua stellas septem : et de ore ejus gladius utraque parte acutus exibat : et *facies ejus* sicut *sol lucet in virtute* sua.   [his countenance ≈ the sun]

Rev. 1.17 And when I saw him, *I* fell at his feet as *dead.*

17 Καὶ ὅτε εἶδον αὐτόν, ἔπεσα πρὸς τοὺς πόδας αὐτοῦ *ὡς νεκρός.*

17 Et cum vidissem eum, *cecidi* ad pedes ejus tamquam *mortuus.*
[I (fell at his feet) ≈ a corpse]

Rev. 2.18 These things saith the Son of God, who hath his *eyes* like unto *a flame of fire*, and his *feet* are like *fine brass.*

18 τάδε λέγει ὁ υἱὸς τοῦ Θεοῦ, ὁ ἔχων τοὺς ὀφθαλμοὺς αὐτοῦ *ὡς φλόγα πυρός,* καὶ οἱ πόδες αὐτοῦ *ὅμοιοι χαλκολιβάνῳ·*

18 Haec dicit Filius Dei, qui habet *oculos* tamquam *flammam ignis*, et *pedes ejus* similes *auricalco*
[His eyes ≈ a flame of fire; His feet ≈ fine brass]

Rev. 3.3 If therefore thou shalt not watch, *I will come* on thee <u>as</u> <u>*a thief.*</u>

  3 ἐὰν οὖν μὴ γρηγορήσῃς, ἥξω ἐπὶ σὲ <u>ὡς κλέπτης,</u>

  3 Si ergo non vigilaveris, veni*am* ad te <u>tamquam *fur.*</u>

  [I ≈ a thief]

Rev. 4.1 and the *first voice* which I heard was <u>as it were</u> <u>*of a trumpet*</u> talking with me.

  1 καὶ ἰδοὺ θύρα ἀνεῳγμένη ἐν τῷ οὐρανῷ, καὶ ἡ φωνὴ ἡ πρώτη ἣν ἤκουσα <u>ὡς σάλπιγγος λαλούσης</u> μετ᾿ ἐμοῦ,

  1 et ecce ostium apertum in caelo, et *vox prima*, quam audivi <u>tamquam *tubae loquentis mecum,*</u>

  [the first voice I heard ≈ a trumpet talking with me]

Rev. 4.3 And *he that sat* was to look upon <u>like</u> <u>*a jasper and a sardine stone*</u>: and there was a *rainbow round about the throne*, in sight <u>like unto</u> <u>*an emerald.*</u>

  3 καὶ ἐπὶ τὸν θρόνον *καθήμενος*, <u>ὅμοιος</u> <u>ὁράσει λίθῳ ἰάσπιδι</u> καὶ σαρδίῳ· καὶ ἶρις κυκλόθεν τοῦ θρόνου, <u>ὁμοίως</u> <u>ὅρασις σμαραγδίνων.</u>

  3 Et *qui sedebat* <u>similis</u> erat <u>*aspectui lapidis jaspidis*</u>, et *sardinis* : et *iris erat in circuitu sedis* <u>similis</u> <u>*visioni smaragdinae.*</u>

  [he sitting ≈ a jasper and sardine stone; the rainbow around his throne ≈ an emerald]

Rev. 4.6 And before the throne there was *a sea of glass* <u>like unto</u> <u>*crystal*</u>: and in the midst of the throne, and round about the throne, were four beasts full of eyes before and behind.

  6 καὶ ἐνώπιον τοῦ θρόνου **ὡς** ϑάλασσα ὑαλίνη, <u>ὁμοία</u> <u>κρυστάλλῳ·</u> καὶ ἐν μέσῳ τοῦ θρόνου καὶ κύκλῳ τοῦ θρόνου τέσσαρα ζῷα γέμοντα ὀφθαλμῶν ἔμπροσθεν καὶ ὄπισθεν·

  6 Et in conspectu sedis **tamquam** *mare vitreum* <u>simile</u> <u>*crystallo*</u>

  [the sea of glass ≈ crystal]

Rev. 4.7 And *the first beast* was <u>like</u> <u>*a lion,*</u> and *the second beast* <u>like</u> <u>*a calf,*</u> and *the third beast* had a face <u>as</u> <u>*a man*</u>, and t*he fourth beast* was <u>like</u> <u>*a flying eagle.*</u>

  7 καὶ τὸ ζῷον τὸ πρῶτον <u>ὅμοιον</u> <u>λέοντι</u>, καὶ τὸ δεύτερον ζῷον <u>ὅμοιον</u> <u>μόσχῳ</u>, καὶ τὸ τρίτον ζῷον ἔχον τὸ πρόσωπον <u>ὡς</u> <u>ἀνθρώπου</u>, καὶ τὸ τέταρτον ζῷον <u>ὅμοιον</u> <u>ἀετῷ πετομένῳ.</u>

7 Et *animal primum* simile *leoni*, et s*ecundum animal* simile *vitulo*,
et *tertium animal* habens faciem quasi *hominis*, et *quartum animal*
simile aquilae volanti.
[first beast ≈ a lion; the second beast ≈ a calf; the third beast ≈
a man; the fourth beast ≈ a flying eagle]

Rev. 6.1 AND I saw when the Lamb opened one of the seals, and I heard,
as it were the noise of thunder, one of the four beasts saying, Come
and see.

1 Καὶ εἶδον ὅτε ἤνοιξε τὸ ἀρνίον μίαν ἐκ τῶν ἑπτὰ σφραγίδων· καὶ ἤκουσα
ἑνὸς ἐκ τῶν τεσσάρων ζῴων λέγοντος, ὡς φωνὴ βροντῆς· ἔρχου.

1 Et vidi quod aperuisset Agnus unum de septem sigillis, et audivi
unum de quatuor animalibus, dicens tamquam *vocem tonitrui*
: Veni, et vide.
[the voice of one of the four beasts ≈ the noise of thunder]

Rev. 6.12 And I beheld when he had opened the sixth seal, and, lo, there
was a great earthquake; and *the sun* became *black* as *sackcloth of hair,*
and *the moon* became as *blood;* 13 And the *stars of heaven fell* unto the
earth, even as *a fig tree casteth her untimely figs,* when she is shaken
of a mighty wind. 14 And *the heaven departed* as *a scroll when it is
rolled together*; and every mountain and island were moved out of
their places.

12 Καὶ εἶδον ὅτε ἤνοιξε τὴν σφραγῖδα τὴν ἕκτην, καὶ σεισμὸς μέγας ἐγένετο,
καὶ ὁ ἥλιος μέλας ἐγένετο ὡς σάκκος τρίχινος, καὶ ἡ σελήνη ὅλη ἐγένετο
ὡς αἷμα, 13 καὶ οἱ ἀστέρες τοῦ οὐρανοῦ ἔπεσαν εἰς τὴν γῆν, ὡς συκῆ
βάλλουσα τοὺς ὀλύνθους αὐτῆς, ὑπὸ ἀνέμου μεγάλου σειομένη, 14 καὶ
ὁ οὐρανὸς ἀπεχωρίσθη ὡς βιβλίον ἑλισσόμενον, καὶ πᾶν ὄρος καὶ νῆσος
ἐκ τῶν τόπων αὐτῶν ἐκινήθησαν·

12 Et vidi cum aperuisset sigillum sextum : et ecce terraemotus magnus
factus est, et *sol factus est niger* tamquam *saccus cilicinus* : et *luna
tota* facta est sicut *sanguis* : 13 et *stellae de caelo cecider*unt super
terram, sicut *ficus emittit grossos suos* cum a vento magno movetur
: 14 et *caelum recessit* sicut *liber involutus* : et omnis mons, et
insulae de locis suis motae sunt
[the sun (became black) ≈ sackcloth of hair; the moon ≈ blood;
the stars falling from heaven ≈ figs from a fig tree; heaven
(departing) ≈ a scroll rolled up]

Rev. 8.8 And the *second angel sounded*, and <u>as it were</u> <u>*a great mountain*</u>
<u>*burning with fire was cast into the sea*</u>: and the third part of the sea
became blood.

    8 Καὶ ὁ δεύτερος ἄγγελος ἐσάλπισε, καὶ <u>ὡς</u> <u>*ὄρος μέγα πυρὶ καιόμενον ἐβλήθη*</u>
    <u>*εἰς τὴν θάλασσαν,*</u> καὶ ἐγένετο τὸ τρίτον τῆς θαλάσσης αἷμα,

    8 Et *secundus angelus tuba cecinit* : et <u>tamquam</u> <u>*mons magnus igne*</u>
    <u>*ardens missus est in mare*</u>, et facta est tertia pars maris sanguis,

    [sound of second angel ≈ a great mountain burning with fire cast
    into the sea]

Rev. 8.10 And the third angel sounded, and there fell a great *star from*
heaven, <u>*burning*</u> as it were <u>*a lamp*</u>, and it fell upon the third part of
the rivers, and upon the fountains of waters.

    10 Καὶ ὁ τρίτος ἄγγελος ἐσάλπισε, καὶ ἔπεσεν ἐκ τοῦ οὐρανοῦ *ἀστὴρ μέγας*
    καιόμενος <u>*ὡς λαμπάς*</u>, καὶ ἔπεσεν ἐπὶ τὸ τρίτον τῶν ποταμῶν καὶ ἐπὶ
    τὰς πηγὰς τῶν ὑδάτων.

    10 Et tertius angelus tuba cecinit : et *cecidit de caelo stella magna,*
    ardens <u>tamquam</u> <u>*facula*</u>, et cecidit in tertiam partem fluminum,
    et in fontes aquarum.

    [a great star falling and burning ≈ a lamp]

Rev. 9.3 And there came out of the smoke locusts upon the earth: and
unto them was given power, <u>as</u> <u>*the scorpions of the earth have power*</u>.

    3 καὶ ἐκ τοῦ καπνοῦ ἐξῆλθον ἀκρίδες εἰς τὴν γῆν, καὶ ἐδόθη *αὐταῖς ἐξουσία*
    <u>*ὡς ἔχουσιν ἐξουσίαν οἱ σκορπίοι τῆς γῆς·*</u>

    3 et de fumo putei exierunt locustae in terram, et data est illis *potestas*,
    <u>sicut</u> <u>*habent potestatem scorpiones terrae.*</u>

    [power of locusts ≈ scorpions]

Rev. 9.5 and *their torment* was <u>as</u> <u>*the torment of a scorpion, when he*</u>
<u>*striketh a man.*</u>

    5 καὶ ὁ βασανισμὸς αὐτῶν <u>ὡς</u> <u>*βασανισμὸς σκορπίου*</u>, ὅταν παίσῃ ἄνθρωπον.

    5 et *cruciatus eorum,* <u>ut</u> <u>*cruciatus scorpii cum percutit hominem.*</u>

    [their (certain men's) torment ≈ a scorpion striking a man]

Rev. 9.7 And the shapes of the locusts were <u>like unto</u> <u>*horses prepared unto*</u>
<u>*battle;*</u> and *on their heads were* <u>as it were</u> <u>*crowns like gold*</u>, and *their*
faces were <u>as</u> <u>*the faces of men.*</u>

7 καὶ τὰ ὁμοιώματα τῶν ἀκρίδων ὅμοια ἵπποις ἡτοιμασμένοις εἰς πόλεμον,
καὶ ἐπὶ τὰς κεφαλὰς αὐτῶν ὡς στέφανοι ὅμοιοι χρυσίῳ, καὶ τὰ πρόσωπα
αὐτῶν ὡς πρόσωπα ἀνθρώπων,

7 Et *similitudines locustarum*, similes *equis paratis in praelium* : et
super *capita earum* tamquam *coronae similes auro* : et *facies earum*
tamquam *facies hominum.*

[locusts ≈ horses prepared for battle; on their heads ≈ golden
crowns; their faces ≈ men's faces]

Rev. 9.8 And they had *hair* as the hair of women, and their *teeth* were as
the teeth of lions.

8 καὶ εἶχον τρίχας ὡς τρίχας γυναικῶν, καὶ οἱ ὀδόντες αὐτῶν ὡς λεόντων ἦσαν,

8 Et habebant *capillos* sicut *capillos mulierum.* Et *dentes earum*, sicut
dentes leonum erant.

[their hair ≈ women's hair; their teeth ≈ lions' teeth]

Similes or comparisons? In a vision there's not much difference
between literal and figurative description.

Rev. 9.9 And they had *breastplates*, as it were *breastplates of iron*; and the
sound of their wings was as the sound of chariots of many horses running to battle.

9 καὶ εἶχον θώρακας ὡς θώρακας σιδηροῦς, καὶ ἡ φωνὴ τῶν πτερύγων αὐτῶν
ὡς φωνὴ ἁρμάτων ἵππων πολλῶν τρεχόντων εἰς πόλεμον.

9 et habebant *loricas* sicut *loricas ferreas*, et *vox alarum earum* sicut *vox
curruum equorum multorum currentium in bellum.*

[their breastplates ≈ iron; sound of their wings ≈ sound of chariots with many horses running to battle]

Rev. 9.10 And they had tails like unto *scorpions*, and there were stings in
their tails.

10 καὶ ἔχουσιν οὐρὰς ὁμοίας σκορπίοις καὶ κέντρα,

10 et habebant *caudas* similes *scorpionum*, et aculei erant in caudis
earum. [their tails ≈ scorpions with stings]

Rev. 9.17 And thus I saw the horses in the vision, and them that sat on
them, having breastplates of fire, and of jacinth, and brimstone: and
the *heads of the horses* were as the heads of lions; and out of their
mouths issued fire and smoke and brimstone.

17 καὶ οὕτως εἶδον τοὺς ἵππους ἐν τῇ ὁράσει καὶ τοὺς καθημένους ἐπ᾽ αὐτῶν, ἔχοντας θώρακας πυρίνους καὶ ὑακινθίνους καὶ θειώδεις· καὶ *αἱ κεφαλαὶ τῶν ἵππων* <u>ὡς</u> <u>*κεφαλαὶ λεόντων*</u>, καὶ ἐκ τῶν στομάτων αὐτῶν ἐκπορεύεται πῦρ καὶ καπνὸς καὶ θεῖον.

17 Et ita vidi equos in visione : et qui sedebant super eos, habebant loricas igneas, et hyacinthinas, et sulphureas, et *capita eorum* erant <u>tamquam</u> <u>*capita leonum*</u> : et de ore eorum procedit ignis, et fumus, et sulphur.

[the heads of horses ≈ heads of lions]

Rev. 9.19 For their power is in their mouth, and in their tails: for *their tails* were <u>like unto</u> <u>*serpents*</u>, and had heads, and with them they do hurt.

19 ἡ γὰρ ἐξουσία τῶν ἵππων ἐν τῷ στόματι αὐτῶν ἐστι καὶ ἐν ταῖς οὐραῖς αὐτῶν· *αἱ γὰρ οὐραὶ αὐτῶν* <u>ὅμοιαι</u> <u>*ὄφεσιν*</u>, ἔχουσαι κεφαλάς, καὶ ἐν αὐταῖς ἀδικοῦσι.

19 Potestas enim equorum in ore eorum est, et in caudis eorum, nam *caudae eorum* <u>similes *serpentibus*</u>, habentes capita : et in his nocent.

[their tails ≈ serpents]

Rev. 10.1 AND I saw another mighty angel come down from heaven, clothed with a cloud: and a rainbow was upon his head, and *his face* was <u>as it were</u> <u>*the sun*</u>, and *his feet* <u>as</u> <u>*pillars of fire.*</u>

1 Καὶ εἶδον ἄλλον ἄγγελον ἰσχυρὸν καταβαίνοντα ἐκ τοῦ οὐρανοῦ, περιβεβλημένον νεφέλην, καὶ ἡ ἶρις ἐπὶ τῆς κεφαλῆς αὐτοῦ, καὶ *τὸ πρόσωπον αὐτοῦ* <u>ὡς</u> <u>*ὁ ἥλιος*</u>, καὶ *οἱ πόδες αὐτοῦ* <u>ὡς</u> <u>*στῦλοι πυρός,*</u>

1 Et vidi alium angelum fortem descendentem de caelo amictum nube, et iris in capite ejus, et *facies ejus* erat <u>ut *sol*</u>, et *pedes ejus* <u>tamquam</u> <u>*columnae ignis.*</u>

[his face ≈ the sun; his feet ≈ pillars of fire]

Rev. 10.3 And *cried with a loud voice*, <u>as when</u> <u>*a lion roareth*</u>:

3 καὶ ἔκραξε φωνῇ μεγάλῃ <u>ὥσπερ *λέων μυκᾶται.*</u>

3 et *clamavit voce magna*, <u>quemadmodum</u> <u>*cum leo rugit.*</u>

[voice ≈ a lion's roar]

Rev. 10.9 And he said unto me, Take it, and eat it up; and it shall make thy belly bitter, but *it shall be in thy mouth sweet* <u>as</u> <u>*honey*</u>. 10 And I took the little book out of the angel's hand, and ate it up; and it was in

my mouth *sweet* as *honey*: and as soon as I had eaten it, my belly was
bitter.

9 καὶ λέγει μοι· λάβε καὶ κατάφαγε αὐτό, καὶ πικρανεῖ σου τὴν κοιλίαν,
ἀλλ᾿ ἐν τῷ στόματί σου ἔσται γλυκὺ *ὡς μέλι*. 10 καὶ ἔλαβον τὸ βιβλίον
ἐκ τῆς χειρὸς τοῦ ἀγγέλου καὶ κατέφαγον αὐτό, καὶ ἦν ἐν τῷ στόματί
μου *ὡς μέλι γλυκύ*· καὶ ὅτε ἔφαγον αὐτό, ἐπικράνθη ἡ κοιλία μου.

9 Et dixit mihi : Accipe librum, et devora illum : et faciet amaricari
ventrem tuum, sed *in ore tuo erit dulce* tamquam *mel*. 10 Et accepi
librum de manu angeli, et devoravi illum : et erat in ore meo
tamquam *mel dulce*, et cum devorassem eum, amaricatus est
venter meus :
[the taste of the book in my mouth ≈ honey-sweet]

Rev. 11.1 AND there was given me *a reed* like unto *a rod*:

1 Καὶ ἐδόθη μοι *κάλαμος* ὅμοιος *ῥάβδῳ*,

1 Et datus est mihi *calamus* similis *virgae.* [a reed ≈ a rod]

Rev. 13.2 And the *beast* which I saw was like unto *a leopard*, and *his feet*
were as *the feet of a bear*, and *his mouth* as *the mouth of a lion*:

2 καὶ τὸ θηρίον ὃ εἶδον ἦν *ὅμοιον παρδάλει*, καὶ οἱ πόδες αὐτοῦ *ὡς ἄρκου*,
καὶ τὸ στόμα αὐτοῦ *ὡς στόμα λέοντος*.

2 Et *bestia, quam vidi*, similis erat *pardo*, et *pedes ejus* sicut *pedes ursi*,
et *os ejus* sicut *os leonis*.
[the beast ≈ a leopard; his feet ≈ a bear's; his mouth ≈ a lion's]

Rev. 13.11 And I beheld another beast coming up out of the earth; and he
had *two horns* like *a lamb*, and *he spake* as *a dragon*.

11 Καὶ εἶδον ἄλλο θηρίον ἀναβαῖνον ἐκ τῆς γῆς, καὶ εἶχε *κέρατα δύο ὅμοια
ἀρνίῳ*, καὶ ἐλάλει *ὡς δράκων*.

11 Et vidi *aliam bestiam* ascendentem de terra, et habebat *cornua duo
similia Agni*, et *loquebatur* sicut *draco*.
[two horns of the beast ≈ a lambs; its speech ≈ a dragon's]

Rev. 14.2 And I heard a *voice from heaven*, as *the voice of many waters*, and
as *the voice of a great thunder*: and I heard the voice *of harpers harping
with their harps*:

2 καὶ ἤκουσα φωνὴν ἐκ τοῦ οὐρανοῦ *ὡς φωνὴν ὑδάτων πολλῶν καὶ ὡς φωνὴν
βροντῆς μεγάλης*· καὶ ἡ φωνὴ ἣν ἤκουσα, *ὡς κιθαρῳδῶν κιθαριζόντων
ἐν ταῖς κιθάραις αὐτῶν*.

2 Et audivi *vocem de caelo,* tamquam <u>*vocem aquarum multarum,*</u> et tamquam <u>*vocem tonitrui magni*</u> : et *vocem,* quam audivi, <u>sicut citharoedorum citharizantium in citharis suis.</u>

[the voice from heaven ≈ many waters ≈ great thunder ≈ harpers harping]

Rev. 15.2 And I saw <u>as it were</u> <u>*a sea of glass mingled with fire*</u>:

2 καὶ εἶδον <u>ὡς θάλασσαν ὑαλίνην μεμιγμένην πυρί,</u>

2 Et vidi tamquam <u>*mare vitreum mistum igne.*</u>

[I saw ≈ a sea of glass mingled with fire]

Rev. 18.21 And a mighty angel took up *a stone* <u>like</u> <u>*a great millstone,*</u> and cast it into the sea.

21 Καὶ ἦρεν εἷς ἄγγελος ἰσχυρὸς λίθον <u>ὡς μύλον μέγαν</u> καὶ ἔβαλεν εἰς τὴν θάλασσαν

2 Et sustulit unus angelus fortis *lapidem* <u>quasi</u> <u>*molarem magnum,*</u> et misit in mare.

[the angel's stone ≈ a great millstone]

Rev. 19.12 His *eyes* were <u>as</u> <u>*a flame of fire,*</u>

12 οἱ δὲ ὀφθαλμοὶ αὐτοῦ <u>ὡς φλὸξ πυρός,</u>

12 *Oculi autem ejus* <u>sicut</u> <u>*flamma ignis.*</u>

[his eyes ≈ a flame of fire]

Rev. 21.2 And I John saw *the holy city, new Jerusalem,* coming down from God out of heaven, <u>*prepared*</u> as <u>*a bride adorned for her husband.*</u>

2 καὶ τὴν πόλιν τὴν ἁγίαν Ἱερουσαλὴμ καινὴν εἶδον καταβαίνουσαν ἐκ τοῦ οὐρανοῦ ἀπὸ τοῦ Θεοῦ, <u>ἡτοιμασμένην ὡς νύμφην κεκοσμημένην τῷ ἀνδρὶ αὐτῆς.</u>

2 Et ego Joannes vidi *sanctam civitatem Jerusalem* novam descendentem de caelo a Deo, *paratam* <u>sicut</u> <u>*sponsam ornatam*</u> viro suo.

[new Jerusalem ≈ a bride adorned for her husband]

Rev. 21.11 Having the glory of God: and *her ligh*t was <u>like unto</u> <u>*a stone most precious,*</u> even <u>like</u> <u>*a jasper stone,*</u> clear as <u>*crystal*</u>;

11 ἔχουσαν τὴν δόξαν τοῦ Θεοῦ· ὁ φωστὴρ αὐτῆς <u>ὅμοιος λίθῳ τιμιωτάτῳ, ὡς λίθῳ ἰάσπιδι κρυσταλλίζοντι·</u>

11 habentem claritatem Dei : et *lumen ejus* <u>simile</u> <u>*lapidi pretioso tamquam lapidi jaspidis,*</u> sicut <u>*crystallum.*</u>

[her light ≈ a precious stone ≈ jasper crystal-clear]

Rev. 21.18 And the building of the wall of it was of jasper: and the city was
   pure gold, like unto clear glass.
   18 καὶ ἦν ἡ ἐνδόμησις τοῦ τείχους αὐτῆς ἴασπις, καὶ ἡ πόλις *χρυσίον*
      καθαρόν, ὅμοιον ὑάλῳ καθαρῷ.
   18 Et erat structura muri ejus ex lapide jaspide : ipsa vero civitas *aurum*
      mundum simile *vitro mundo*.
   [the city's pure gold ≈ clear glass]
Rev. 22.1 AND he shewed me a pure river of water of life, *clear as crystal*,
   proceeding out of the throne of God and of the Lamb.
   1 Καὶ ἔδειξέ μοι ποταμὸν ὕδατος ζωῆς *λαμπρὸν ὡς κρύσταλλον*,
      ἐκπορευόμενον ἐκ τοῦ θρόνου τοῦ Θεοῦ καὶ τοῦ ἀρνίου.
   1 Et ostendit mihi *fluvium* aquae vitae, *splendidum* tamquam *crystallum*,
      procedentem de sede Dei et Agni.
   [pure river of water ≈ crysal-clear]

* * *

4 Conclusion

A Biblical Usage of Similes

In this compendium we point out the *source of comparison* of similes (vehicles), the *form* (type of prothesis), and often the *purpose* (e.g., to illustrate bravery or size etc.), although it would not be easy to say why a simile is offered at one place rather than another (the *occasion*) and why in some authors and not in others.

Nothing works so well as a simile to clarify a difficult concept, which is why philosophers and religious writers find them useful. Thus they are often found in explaining abstractions. Other topics are given below.

1 Abstractions:

Visualization of **abstractions** like bravery, size and speed characterizes many similes (abstract *tenor* with a concrete *vehicle*). Thus they illustrate

> great numbers: grasshoppers, sand (Judges 6.5)
>
> bravery: lions (II Sam. 17.10)
>
> size: small as dust (II Sam. 22.43)
>
> number: offspring like grass (Job 5.25)
>
> heaviness: sand of the sea (Job 6.3)
>
> speed: swifter than a weaver's shuttle (Job 7.6).

Sometimes a double vehicle combines an **abstraction** with a figurative or visible word: e.g., the Lord is my <u>strength</u> and my <u>shield</u>. (Psalms 28.7); when your fear cometh as *desolation*, and your destruction cometh as a <u>whirlwind</u>. (Prov. 1.27). In the construction we have called "genitive"

similes, abstractions are combined with visible concepts: e.g., salvation as
a horn, a shield, a rock or tower:

He is my protector, and *the horn of my salvation.*
(II Samuel 22.3)
When *the waves of death* compassed me, (II Samuel 22.5)
Thou hast also given me *the shield* of thy *salvation.*
(II Samuel 22.36)
Exalted be the *God* of *the rock of my salvation.*
(II Samuel 22.47)
He is *the tower* of *salvation* for his king. (II Samuel 22.51)
Similarly, **death as a shadow, life as a tree, glory as a crown, the
body as a temple:**
Let darkness and *the shadow of death* stain it. (Job 3.5)
Yea, though I walk through *the valley of the shadow of death (Psalm 23.4)*
A *wholesome tongue* is *a tree of life. (Prov.15.4)*
The hoary head is a *crown of glory. (Prov. 16.31)*
For *he put on righteousness* as *a breast-plate*, and an
helmet of salvation upon his head. (Isaiah 59.17)
But he spake of *the temple of his body.* (John 2.21)

2 Love:

Let him kiss me with the kisses of his mouth: for *thy love is* <u>better than
wine</u>. (So-So. 1.2)
Behold, thou art fair, my love; ... thou hast *<u>doves' eyes</u>*;
(So-So.4.1 + many other passages)
Let her [*the wife of thy youth*] be <u>as</u> the *<u>loving hind and pleasant roe;</u>* let
her breasts satisfy thee at all times; and be thou ravished always with
her love. (Prov. 5.19)

3 The Five Senses (You Hear, Feel, See, Smell, and Taste):

Jerem. 4.31 For I have **heard** *a voice <u>as of a woman in travail,</u>*

Isaiah 59.10 We **grope** *for the wall* like the *blind*, and *we grope*
   as if we *had no eyes*:
Ezekiel 1.27 And I **saw** as the colour *of amber.*
So-So. *7. 8* … and *the* **smell** *of thy nose* like *apples*:
Judges 14.18 *What* is **sweeter** than *honey*?

4 Humans Compared with Animals:

Many similes in the Bible are based on comparisons with familiar **animals**: e.g., doves, grasshoppers, lambs, lions, serpents and sheep in **Appendix VIII-C.**

5 Cities as Tenors and Vehicles:

One **unusual type of comparison** found in the Old Testament is the use
   of **cities as vehicles**:
Thou art *beautiful, O my love, as Tirzah, comely as Jerusalem.*(So-So. 6.4)
Or ever I was aware, my soul made me *like the chariots of Amminabid.*
   (So-So. 6.12)
We should have been *as Sodom*, and we should have been *like unto*
   Gomorrah. (Isaiah 1.9)
They [prophets of Jerusalem] are all of them unto me *as Sodom*, and the
   inhabitants thereof *as Gomorrha.* (Jerem. 23.14)
Amos 4.11 *I have overthrown some of you, as God overthrew Sodom and*
   Gomorrha,
Isaiah 17.5 And *it shall be* as when *the harvestman gathereth the corn* and
   reapeth the ears with his arm; and *it shall be* as *he that gathereth ears*
   in the valley of Rephaim
Cities also appear as the *tenor*: Sharon is like a wilderness. (Isaiah 33.9);
   Judah is a lion's whelp (Gen. 49.9)

6 Doublets:

Another characteristic of the Old Testament is the use of two similes in
close succession (see **Appendix VIII-A**):
Deliver thyself *as a roe* from the hand of the hunter, and *as a bird* from the
hand of the fowler. (Prov. 6.5)
And it shall be *as the chased roe, and as a sheep* that no man taketh up.
(Isaiah 13.14)
I am *like a drunken ma*n, and *like a man whom wine hath overcome*, be-
cause of the Lord. (Jerem. 23.9)

7 Religious Concepts: Heaven and Divinity

One of the most important reasons for similes in the Bible is to clarify **religious concepts**. For example, "The *kingdom of heaven* is like a *mustard
seed planted in a field*" (Matthew 13:31) or "… like a *treasure hidden in a
field*" (Matthew 13:44).
   Divinity
The challenge that faces many authors in the Old Testament is the need
to portray God and **visualize divinity**. Hence:
   as a bridegroom (Exodus 24.17; Deut. 9.3; Ps. 19.5)
   Like ***as a father*** pitieth his children, so the Lord (Ps. 103.13)
   As the mountains are round about Jerusalem, so the Lord
      (Ps. 125.2)
   Behold, the name of the LORD cometh from far, burning with his
      anger … his tongue ***as a devouring fire.*** (Isaiah 30.27)
   The breath of the Lord, ***like a stream of brimstone***, doth kindle it.
      (Isaiah 30.33)
   For thus hath the Lord spoken unto me, ***Like as the lion* and the
      *young lion roaring on his prey***, (Isaiah 31.4)
   The Lord is *my shepherd*; I shall not want … (Psalm 23.1)
   The Lord is **my light** and my salvation. (Ps 27.1)
   Unto thee will I cry, O Lord *my rock*. (Psalm 28.1 +31.2 & 3)
   Our soul waiteth for the Lord; he is our help and ***our shield.***

(Ps 33.20; + Ps 84.11)

But now, O Lord, thou art *our father*, we are the clay, and thou *our potter*; and we all are the work of thy hand.(Isaiah 64.8)

There is also a special need to describe **the kingdom of heaven and the divinity of Jesus.** (See, for example, Matthew 13 on the kingdom of heaven.) This is done primarily by the use of predicate similes (that often sound like definitions, especially in the first person):

For *the Son of man is as a man taking a far journey.*
(Mark 13.34)

He answered and said unto them, "*He that soweth the good seed* is the Son of man." (Matt. 13.37)

Then spake Jesus again to them, saying, *I am the light of the world.*
(John 8.12)

Then said Jesus unto them again, Verily, verily, I say unto you, *I am the door of the sheep.* (John 10.7)

I am the true vine, and my Father is the husbandman.
(John 15.1)

I am the vine, ye are the branches. (John 15.5)

8 Style:

Sometimes the Biblical comparisons are earthy or somewhat coarse:

The wicked shall perish *like his own dung* (Job 20.7)

As a *dog returneth to his vomit so* a fool returneth to his folly.
(Proverbs 26.11)

Refresh my bowels in the Lord. (Philemon 1.20)

Dead flies cause the ointment of the apothecary to send forth a *stinking savour*: so doth a little folly him that is in reputation for wisdom and honour. (Ecclesiastes 10.1)

Wherefore *my bowels* shall sound like an harp for Moab.
(Isaiah 16.11)

The Lord hath mingled a perverse spirit in the midst thereof: and they have caused Egypt to err in every work thereof *as a drunken man staggereth in his vomit.* (Isaiah 19.14)

Ye shall defile also the covering of thy graven images of silver
… thou shalt cast *them* away *as a menstruous cloth.* (Isaiah 30.22) This
is particularly popular; cf. Jerem. 30.6; Jerem. 49.22; Jerem. 50.43;
Isaiah 13.8; Lam/Jerem. 1.17.

9 Special Characteristics:

a Occasionally the English Version Adds a Simile Not in the Greek or
Latin Text:

In that day the Lord will take away the bravery of their tinkling ornaments about their feet, and their cauls, and their round tires
like the moon. (Isaiah 3.18) **Not a simile in the Latin or Greek
text: τοὺς μηνίσκους;** *lunulas.*
And *they* [*earthly kings*] shall be gathered together as *prisoners* are
gathered in the pit (Isaiah 24.22).

b Or the English Differs Completely from the Greek and Latin:

Ps. 90.9 For all our days are passed away in thy wrath: we spend our
years as *a tale* that is told.
89.9 ὅτι πᾶσαι αἱ ἡμέραι ἡμῶν ἐξέλιπον, καὶ ἐν τῇ ὀργῇ σου ἐξελίπομεν·
τὰ ἔτη ἡμῶν ὡσεὶ ἀράχνη ἐμελέτων.
89.9 Quoniam omnes dies nostri defecerunt; et in ira tua defecimus.
Anni nostri sicut *aranea* meditabuntur;
[years ≈ a tale/spider-?]
No doubt the reasons for these anomalies vary with the individual
passages.

c The Greek or Latin Prototype May Be Simply a Parallel Clause Rather
Than a Simile with Prothesis:

Proverbs 25.25 As *cold waters to a thirsty soul,* **so** is *good news from a
far country.*

25 ὥσπερ ὕδωρ ψυχρὸν ψυχῇ διψώσῃ προσηνές, **οὕτως** ἀγγελία ἀγαθὴ ἐκ γῆς μακρόθεν.

25 *Aqua frigida animae sitienti*, et *nuntius bonus de terra longinqua*.
[good news from far away ≈ cold water > a thirsty soul]

d Prothetic Words:

Many prothetic words are used to introduce similes in Greek and Latin (English words are in quotations here): 'as' (with predicate nominative or predicate accusative), with single words, phrases or clauses: / ὡς / ὡσεὶ / instar / *quasi* / *sicut* / *velut* / 'like' / ἴσα / καθώς; 'as far as' / καθόσον / *quantum* / 'as if' / *in morem* ; be like / ὁμοιώθητι / *similis esto* / 'similar to' / ὁμοία-ος-ον (+ da-tive) / 'like as' / 'like to' / 'like unto' / κατὰ / 'more than' / μᾶλλον ἢ / 'of' = 'like that of' / 'similitude' / 'such as' / οἷα / 'in the manner as' / ὃν τρόπον + ἐάν or ὅταν / 'beyond' [= 'better / more than'] / ὑπέρ / *super* + accusative / 'than' ἢ / ὑπέρ / *super* / with (white with) / ἀπὸ / Comparative Adjective/Adverb +: κρεῖσσον … ἢ (better than).

Apotheses: Thus, so, 'so that' / (ὥσπερ / ὡσεὶ … οὕτως) / (ὡς … ὡς)(ὡς … οὕτως) – (ὡς … οὕτω) / (ὃν τρόπον ἐάν … οὕτως).

10 Why Are There Similes in the Bible?

Note Luke 13 where "the disciples came, and said unto him, Why speakest thou unto them in parables?" Christ's reply was that he spoke "to them in parables: because they seeing see not; and hearing they hear not, neither do they understand." Like parables, most similes seek to add understanding and clarification to the text.

11 Considerations in Enumerating Similes in the Bible:

1-Some similes could be categorized as literal comparisons (e.g., Matt. 3.16 He saw *the Spirit of God* descending like *a dove*). This would perhaps seem figurative to listeners but intended literally by Matthew. Consider also Matt. *12.12:* How much then is *a man* better than *a sheep*?

2-Should repeated similes be counted as separate similes? John 8.12 ("I am the light of the world"); also at 9.5; cf.12.46.

3-Should one count the parts of a parable as a single simile or separate similes? Consider Matthew 13.36 when the disciples asked Jesus to "[d]eclare unto us the parable [simile?] of the tares of this field." In the passage that follows Jesus uses several predicate similes [See **Appendix IV.**]. He answered and said unto them, "*He that soweth the good seed* is *the Son of man.*" (Matt. 13.37) "*The field* is *the world*; *the good seed* are *the children of the* kingdom; but the *tares* are *the children of the wicked one.*" (Matt. 13.38) "The enemy that sowed them is the devil: the harvest is the end of the world; and the reapers are the angels." (Matt. 13.39)

The numerical totals in this Compendium (especially in Appendix III) are provided to show the differences between authors in their use of similes. Similes are like goldfish in a huge pond. They are difficult to count because there are other similar fish in the pond and more goldfish in some areas than in others and they are completely absent from some places. Nevertheless, numbers are useful for comparative purposes.

12 Differences with Classical Greek Authors Plato and Homer:

Unlike Plato, the authors of the Bible felt no need for **literary embellishment** (quoting authors like Homer – although Jesus and others frequently refer to passages in the Old Testament), **humorous exaggeration** (like Meno saying "If I may jest, *you* [Socrates] seem to me to be in appearance and other respects most like a *flat torpedo sea-fish/sting ray* [*Meno* 80b]) or **clarification by telling what something is not** (e.g., "All these [five] parts of virtue are NOT like pieces of gold similar to one another and to the whole of which they are parts, but like the parts of the face … dissimilar to each other" [*Protagoras* 329d]).

Nowhere in the Bible do we find certain kinds of similes that reflect the textual discussion such as may be found in Plato's Dialogues.

To take three examples: (1) Meno accuses Socrates of being like a sting-ray that paralyzes people (*Meno* 80a-b). Socrates replies that the comparison is just only if it implies that Socrates becomes paralyzed as well with perplexity from which grows insight. (2) In another Dialogue (*Theaetetus* 151b-c) Socrates himself likens his activities to those of a midwife who helps others bring forth knowledge even though he cannot produce it himself. (3) Finally, in the *Apology* (30e) Socrates claims that God has given him as a kind of gadfly to the city of Athens since he goes around arousing people to philosophy. Thus ***Plato uses similes to develop ideas in his Dialogues in a way not found in the Bible.***

Nor are there any elaborate similes such as are characteristic of Homer's *Iliad* and *Odyssey*, where the description may continue for five or six verses:

But the armies rushed forward, / just like thick tribes of bees / that come from some hollow rock ever anew / and fly in clusters over the spring flowers, / some darting en masse here, others there; / even so did their many tribes march in line from ships and huts / in squads before the broad shore / to the assembly. (*Iliad* 1.86–93)

It is not uncommon, however, to find in the Old Testament a string of similes describing one thing:

e.g., So-So. 7.1 How beautiful are thy feet with shoes, O prince's daughter! the *joints of thy thighs* are like *jewels*, the work of the hands of a cunning workman. 2 *Thy navel* is like *a round goblet*, which wanteth not liquor: *thy belly* is like *an heap of wheat set about with lilies*.

Or Isaiah 1.18 Come, now, and let us reason together, saith the Lord: though *your sins* be as *scarlet*, they shall be as *white* as *snow*; though they be like *crimson*, they shall be as *wool*.

Cf. The Song of Solomon 7.1–8:

How beautiful are thy feet with shoes, O prince's daughter! the *joints of thy thighs* are *like jewels*, the work of the hands of a cunning workman. 2 Thy navel is *like a round goblet*, which wanteth not liquor: thy belly is *like an heap of wheat* set about with lilies …

In this respect the similes in the Bible are distinctive.

B Summary of the Eight Appendices

Appendix I – Bible Similes – Old Testament (Outline)
Summary of the similes in all the books of the Old and New Testaments.
Appendix II – Bible Similes – New Testament (Outline)
Appendix III – Location of Similes in Each Book of the Bible
Similes are noted by chapters within each Book with summaries of the numbers of similes in the Old and New Testament. In Exodus the list of chapters with similes in parentheses starts off like this:

1-2-3-4(**6**)-7-8-9-10(<u>7</u>)-11-12-13-14(<u>22</u>)-15(**10**)-16(**14,31x2**)-17-18-19. Totals are listed for both sections of the Bible by book: For example: in the book of **Revelation** (22 Chapters) there are 63 similes: 60 prothetic + 2 predicate + 1 genitive; in total for the Old Testament: 984 prothetic, 164 predicate and 65 genitive similes; in the New Testament: 145 prothetic, 52 predicate and 20 genitive similes.

There are twelve books with no prothetic similes in the New Testament and ten in the Old Testament.
Appendix IV – Predicate Similes (*a1/ and *a/2)
Predicate similes may be defined (see Introduction, #2) as figurative comparisons that lack a prothesis, which is implied, so that the relationship is nominative (e.g., 'Judah is [like] a lion's whelp,' [Genesis 49.9]), appositive or accusative ('they shall call Jerusalem <u>the throne of the Lord</u>,' [Jeremiah 3.17]). From the list of the passages in **Appendix IV** one may see that the greatest number of predicate similes are located in Psalms (30), Proverbs (19), Jeremiah (14) and Job (12); in the New Testament, John (13) and Matthew (9).
Appendix V – Genitive Similes
Again the Psalms provide most examples of Genitive similes in the Old Testament (14) as Ephesians (6) does in the New Testament. In the example, "he is a tower of strength," one should note that the similetic word is the nominative 'tower' and not the 'of' (genitive) word 'strength'. (See Introduction, p. 4.)

Appendix VI – Factual Comparisons

Many examples of factual comparisons from the Old and New Testaments are provided as examples of non-similes lacking a figurative element: e.g., Ecclesiastes 9.4 "for a *living dog* is <u>better than</u> a *dead lion.*"

Appendix VII – Words for Simile in Greek and Latin; Examples of Metaphor and Parable; Verbal Similes

VIIA – Greek and Latin Words for Simile, Parable

Thou shalt despise their image / τὴν εἰκόνα αὐτῶν / imaginem ipsorum. (Psalm 73.20)

VIIB – Examples of Metaphor

There are many metaphors in the English version of the Bible: e.g., "They that <u>plow iniquity</u>, and <u>sow wickedness</u>, reap the same." (Job 4.8)

VIIC – Verbal Similes (*d/)

Psalm 5.12 You have 'crowned' us.

Κύριε, ὡς ὅπλῳ εὐδοκίας <u>ἐστεφάνωσας</u> ἡμᾶς.

Psalm 23.1 The Lord 'is my shepherd' ...

22.1 ΚΥΡΙΟΣ <u>ποιμαίνει</u> με

Appendix VIII – Doublets and Recurring Vehicles

Repeated Similes in the Old Testament This Appendix collects the similes characteristic of the Old Testament (but absent from the New Testament) that appear in doublet form (A), for example, "he couched as a lion, and as an old lion" (Genesis 49.9). These are not usually treated as two similes unless the *prothesis* (<u>as</u>) is repeated. Most examples occur in Job, Psalms, Proverbs and Isaiah. A few cases of triplet expressions (e.g., "without man, without inhabitant, without beast" in Jeremiah 33.10–11) are also given (B), although these are not similes.

In section 'C' (pp. 674 ff.) a selection of "repeated simile-vehicles" is provided. For example, the word 'apple' occurs at least six times as a simile vehicle in the Old Testament; the word 'dove' appears in thirteen similes in the Old Testament and five times in the New Testament. 'Lamb' occurs as a vehicle six times in the Old Testament and four times in the New Testament. This is just a selection of eighteen such repetitions; a word-search in the text of the similes in the Old Testament and the New Testament would provide other repeated vehicles.

* * *

Bible Charts

The Old Testament: Summary of Similes

The following Chart summarizes the prothetic similes by *Tenor*, *Prothesis* and *Vehicle* (predicate and genitive similes not included).

Book Passage	Tenor	Prothesis	Vehicle	Speaker
Gen. 3.16	thy seed	as, ὡς, sicut	dust of the earth	The Lord
Gen. 22.17	thy seed	as, ὡς, sicut as, ὡς, velut	the stars of heaven and sand	The Angel of the Lord
Gen. 25.25	the first (twin)	like, ὡσεὶ, in morem	hairy garment	Narrator
Gen. 26.4	thy seed	as, ὡς, sicut	stars of heaven	The Lord
Gen. 27.27	smell of my son	as, ὡς, sicut	smell of a blessed field	Isaac
Gen. 49.4	thou (unstable)	as, ὡς, sicut	water	Jacob
Gen. 49.9	Judah he	– as, ὡς, quasi	lion's whelp a lion/an old lion	Jacob
Gen. 49.12	his eyes (red) his teeth (white)	with, ἀπό pulchriores, candidiores	wine milk	Jacob
Gen. 49.27	Benjamin	as, –, –	a wolf λύκος, lupus	Jacob
Exodus 4.6	his hand (leprous)	as, ὡσεὶ, instar	snow	Narrator
Exodus 15.10	they	as, ὡσεὶ, quasi	lead	Moses
Exodus 16.14	round thing (small)	as, ὡσεὶ, quasi	hoar frost	Narrator

Book Passage	Tenor	Prothesis	Vehicle	Speaker
Exodus 16.31	Manna (white) (taste)	like, ὡσεὶ, quasi like, ὡς, quasi	coriander seed honey wafers	Narrator
Exodus 19.18	smoke	as, ὡσεὶ, quasi	furnace smoke	Narrator
Exodus 24.17	glory of the Lord	as, ὡσεὶ, quasi	devouring fire	Narrator
Exodus 33.11	Lord spoke to Moses	as, ὡς, sicut	a friend	Narrator
Numbers 11.7	Manna (color)	as, ὡσεὶ, quasi as, –, quasi	coriander seed bdellium	children of Israel
Numbers 13.33	we	as, ὡσεὶ, quasi	grasshoppers	people to Moses
Numbers 23.24	the people himself (Jacob)	as, ὡς, ut as, ὡς, quasi	a great lion a young lion	Balaam to Blaak
Deuter. 1.44	you (Amorites)	as, ὡσεὶ, sicut	bees	Narrator
Deuter. 9.3	the Lord	as,–, –	consuming fire	Moses
Deuter. 32.2	my doctrine my speech	as, ὡς, ut as, ὡς, ut	rain dew small rain showers, νιφετός	Moses
Joshua 11.4	they (kings)	as, ὥσπερ, sicut	sand on shore	Narrator
Judges 6.5	they (Midianites)	as, καθὼς, instar	grasshoppers	Narrator
Judges 7.5	whoever laps water with tongue	as, ὡς, sicut	dog	the Lord
Judges 7.12	Midianites their camels	like, ὡσεὶ, ut as, ὡς, sicut	grasshoppers sand	Narrator
Judges 14.18	what (sweeter) what (stronger)	than, comp. adjs.	honey a lion	Men to Samson
Judges 15.14	cords on his arms	as, ὡσεὶ, sicut	flax	Narrator

Book Passage	Tenor	Prothesis	Vehicle	Speaker
Judges 16.9	Samson broke cords	as, ὡς, quomodo si	thread is broken	Narrator
II Samuel 12.3	a lamb	as, ὡς, sicut	a daughter	Narrator
II Samuel 14.2	Tekoah	as, ὡς, quasi	a mourning woman	Joab
II Samuel 17.10	heart of a valiant	as, καθὼς, quasi	heart of a lion	Hushai
II Samuel 21.19	staff of a spear	like, ὡς, quasi	a weaver's beam	Narrator
II Samuel 22.34	my feet	like, ὡς, –	hind's feet	David
II Samuel 22.43	them	as, ὡς, ut / as, ὡς, quasi	dust of earth mire of the street	David
II Samuel 23.4	he (a ruler)	as, –, sicut / as, ὡς, sicut	morning light tender grass	David
I Kings 20.27	children of Israel	like,?, quasi	two little flocks of kids	Narrator
II Kings 9.37	carcase of Jezebel	as, ὡς, sicut	dung	The Lord
II Kings 21.13	I will wipe Jerusalem	as, καθὼς, sick	a man wipes a dish	God of Israel
I Chronicles 11.23	a spear	like, ὡς, ut	a weaver's beam	Narrator
II Chronicles 4.5	brim of sea	like, ὡς, quasi	brim of a cup	Narrator
Job 3.21	death	more than, ὥσπερ, quasi	hidden treasures	Job
Job 3.24	my roarings	like, –, tamquam	waters	Job
Job 5.7	man > born to trouble	as, δὲ, et	sparks > fly upward	Eliphaz
Job 5.25	thine offspring	as, ὥσπερ, quasi	grass of the earth	Eliphaz

Book Passage	Tenor	Prothesis	Vehicle	Speaker
Job 5.26	thou at the grave	like, ὥσπερ, sicut	corn in season	Eliphaz
Job 6.3	my grief (heavier)	than, βαρυτέρα, quasi	sand of the sea	Job
Job 6.7	what my soul refused to touch	as, ὥσπερ, cibi mei	my sorrowful meat	Job
Job 6.15	my brethren	as, ὥσπερ, sicut	a brook a stream	Job
Job 7.1	man's life	like, ὥσπερ, sicut	a hired day-laborer	Job
Job 7.2	I	as, ὥσπερ, sicut	a fearful servant a hireling waiting for pay	Job
Job 7.6	my days (swifter)	than, comp. adj., comp. adverb	a weaver's shuttle	Job
Job 7.9	he who dies	as, ὥσπερ, sicut	a vanishing cloud	Job
Job 7.20	me	as, predicate accusatives	a mark against thee	Job
Job 8.2	your words	like, (no prothesis in Gr. & Lat.)	a strong wind	Bildad
Job 9.25	my days (swifter)	than, (comparative adjs. in Gr. & Lat.)	a post	Job
Job 9.26	my days	as, [different construct. in Gr.], quasi + situ	swift ships, an eagle	Job
Job 10.10	me	as, ὥσπερ, sicut like, ἴσα, sicut	milk cheese	Job
Job 10.16	me	as, ὥσπερ, quasi	a fierce lion	Job

Book Passage	Tenor	Prothesis	Vehicle	Speaker
Job 11.8	it (as high) (deeper)	as, –, excelsior than, comp. adjs.	heaven hell	Zophar
Job 11.9	measure (longer) (broader)	than, comp. adjs.	the earth the sea	Zophar
Job 11.12	man	like, ἴσα, tamquam	wild ass's colt	Zophar
Job 12.4	I	as, –, sicut	one mocked by his neighbor	Job
Job 12.5	He …	as, –, –	a lamp despised	Job
Job 12.25	they	like, ὥσπερ, quasi	a drunken man	Job
Job 13.12	your memories your bodies	like unto, ἴσα, comp. verb	ashes clay	Job
Job 13.28	He	like, ἴσα, quasi as, ὥσπερ, quasi	a rotten thing a moth-eaten garment	Job
Job 14.2	a man	like, ὥσπερ, quasi as, ὥσπερ, velut	a cut flower a shadow	Job
Job 14.6	he/man	as, ὥσπερ, sucut	an hireling	Job
Job 14.11	man (lies down)	as, –, quomodo	waters (fail) flood (dries up)	Job
Job 16.14	God	like, –, quasi	giant	Job
Job 16.21	man (pleads with God for man)	as, καὶ, quo modo	man (pleads for neighbor)	Job
Job 18.3	we	as, ὥσπερ, ut	beasts	Bildad
Job 20.7	he/the wicked	like, –, quasi	his own dung	Zophar
Job 20.8	he/the wicked	as, ὥσπερ, velut as, ὥσπερ, sick	a dream a night vision	Zophar

Book Passage	Tenor	Prothesis	Vehicle	Speaker
Job 21.18	they/the wicked	as, ὥσπερ, sicut as, ὥσπερ, sicut	stubble to wind chaff to storm	Job
Job 22.24	gold gold of Ophir	as, ὡς, pro as, –, pro	dust stones of brooks	Eliphaz
Job 24.5	they/the wicked	as, ὥσπερ, quasi	wild asses in desert	Job
Job 24.14	the murderer	as, ὡς, quasi	a thief	Job
Job 24.17	the morning death	as, –, accusative	the shadow of death; a shadow	Job
Job 27.18	he house	as, ὥσπερ, sicut	a moth / ἀράχνη a booth	Job
Job 29.14	my judgment	as, ἴσα, sicut	a robe a diadem	Job
Job 29.18	my days	as, ὥσπερ, sicut	the sand	Job
Job 29.23	me	as, ὥσπερ, sicut as, –, quasi	rain latter rain	Job
Job 30.14	they/the youth	as, –, quasi	a breaking-in of waters	Job
Job 30.15	terrors my welfare	as, ὥσπερ, quasi as, ὥσπερ, velut	the wind a cloud	Job
Job 30.18	my disease (binds me about)	as, ὥσπερ, quasi	the collar of my coat	Job
Job 30.19	I	like, ἴσα, assimi- lates sum	dust and ashes	Job
Job 31.36	my adversary's book	as, ἀνεγίνωσκον, quasi	a crown	Job
Job 31.37	I	as, –, quasi	a prince	Job
Job 32.19	my belly	as, ὥσπερ, quasi like, ὥσπερ, –	wine new bottles	Job

Book Passage	Tenor	Prothesis	Vehicle	Speaker
Job 34.7	what man scorning	like, ὥσπερ, ut like, ὥσπερ, quasi	Job water	Elihu
Job 35.11	who? (teaches us more) us (makes wiser)	than, ἀπὸ, super than, ἀπὸ, super	beasts of earth fowls of heaven	Elihu
Job 38.8	sea (broke out) the cloud thick darkness	as, –, quasi I made	[water] from womb the garment a swaddling-band	Lord to Job
Job 38.14	morning ends of earth	as, –, ut as, –, sick	clay to the seal a garment	Lord to Job
Job 39.20	him	as, –, quasi	a grasshopper	Lord to Job
Job 40.17	behemoth's tail	like, ὡς, quasi	a cedar	Lord to Job
Job 40.18	his bones (strong) his bones	as, –, vellum like, –, quasi	pieces of brass bars of iron	Lord to Job
Job 41.15	leviathan's scales (shut up together)	as with, –, –	a close seal	? The Lord
Job 41.20	smoke from nostrils	as, –, sick	out of a seething pot or caldron	the Lord
Job 41.24	his heart (as firm) (as hard)	as, ὡς, tamquam as, ὥσπερ, quasi	a stone piece of millstone	the Lord
Job 41.27	iron brass	as, –, quasi as, ὥσπερ, quasi	straw rotten wood	the Lord
Job 41.29	darts (counted)	as, ὡς, quasi	stubble	the Lord
Job 41.31	the deep (to boil) the sea	like, ὥσπερ, quasi like, –, –	a pot a pot of ointment	the Lord

Book Passage	Tenor	Prothesis	Vehicle	Speaker
Job 41.33	(him)	like, ὅμοιον, comparator	not (a thing)	the Lord
Psalms 1.3	(the blessed man)	like, ὡς, tamquam	a tree by a river	David
Psalms 1.4	the ungodly	like, ὡσεὶ, tamquam	chaff scattered by wind	"
Psalms 5.12	favor	as, ὡς, ut	a shield	"
Psalms 7.2	the enemy	as, ὡς, ut	a lion	"
Psalms 10.9	the wicked	as, ὡς, quasi	a lion in his den	"
Psalms 11.1	you (my soul)	as, ὡς, sicut	a bird	"
Psalms 12.6	words of the Lord	as, –, –	silver purified	"
Psalms 17.8	me	as, ὡς, ut	apple of the eye	"
Psalms 17.12	(they waited for me)	as, ὡσεὶ, sicut as, ὡσεὶ, sicut	a greedy lion a young lion	"
Psalms 18.33	my feet	like, ὡσεὶ, tamquam	hinds' feet	"
Psalms 19.5	he/God	as, ὡς, tamquam as, ὡς, ut	a bridegroom a strong man	"
Psalms 19.10	they [judgments of the Lord] (more) (sweeter)	than, ὑπὲρ, super than, –, – than, ὑπὲρ, super	gold fine gold honey and honey comb	"
Psalms 21.9	them (who hate you)	as, –, ut	a fiery oven	"
Psalms 22.13	they	as, ὡς, sicut	a ravening and roaring lion	"
Psalms 22.14	I my heart	like, ὡσεὶ, sicut like, ὡσεὶ, tamquam	water wax	"

Book Passage	Tenor	Prothesis	Vehicle	Speaker
Psalms 22.15	my strength dust	like, ὡσεὶ, tamquam; of	a potsherd death	"
Psalms 29.6	them (to skip) Lebanon & Sirion	like, ὡς, tamquam like, ὡς, quemadmodum	a calf a young unicorn	"
Psalms 31.12	I (forgotten) I	as, ὡσεὶ, tamquam like, ὡσεὶ, tamquam	a dead man a broken vessel	"
Psalms 32.9	you (not)	as, ὡς, sicut	the horse or mule	"
Psalms 33.7	sea waters	as, ὡσεὶ, secut	an heap	"
Psalms 35.14	he I	as though, ὡς, quasi; as, ὡς, quasi	friend or brother a mourner (for his mother)	"
Psalms 36.6	your righteousness your judgments	like, ὡς, sicut –, ὡσεὶ, –	great mountains a great deep	"
Psalms 37.2	they (cut down) (wither)	like, ὡσεὶ, tamquam; as, ὡσεὶ, quemadmodum	grass green herb	"
Psalms 37.6	thy righteousness thy judgment	as, ὡς, quasi as, ὡς, tamquam	the light the noonday	"
Psalms 37.20	enemies of the Lord	as, ὡσεὶ, quemadmodum	the fat of lambs {fumus}	"
Psalms 37.35	himself	like, ὡς, sicut	a green bay tree	"
Psalms 38.13	I	as, ὡσεὶ, tamquam; as, ὡσεὶ, sick	a deaf man a dumb man	"

Book Passage	Tenor	Prothesis	Vehicle	Speaker
Psalms 39.5	my days my age	as, –, – as, –, tamquam	an handbreadth nothing	"
Psalms 42.1	my soul > God	as, ON ΤΡΟΠΟΝ, quemadmodum	a hart > water brooks	"
Psalms 44.11	us	like, ὡς, tamquam	sheep for meat	"
Psalms 44.22	we	as, ὡς, sicut	sheep for slaughter	"
Psalms 49.12	he (a man of honor)	like, ὡμοιώθη, similis	beasts that perish	"
Psalms 49.14	they (honorable men)	like, ὡς, sicut	sheep	"
Psalms 49.20	an honorable man with no understanding	like, ὡμοιώθη, similis	perishable beasts	"
Psalms 51.7	I (whiter)	than, ὑπὲρ, super	snow	"
Psalms 52.8	I (am)	like, ὡσεὶ, sicut	a green olive tree	"
Psalms 55.6	I (wings)	like, ὡσεὶ, sicut	a dove	"
Psalms 55.21	words (smoother) (softer)	than, –, – than, ὑπὲρ, super	butter oil	"
Psalms 58.4	their poison they (are)	like, κατὰ, secundum simil. like, ὡσεὶ, sicut	a serpent's poison a deaf adder	"
Psalms 58.7	(the wicked) "	as, ὡσεὶ, tamquam as, –, –	con- tinuous waters cut in pieces	"
Psalms 58.8	they (pass away)	as, ὡσεὶ, sicut like, –, –	melted snail/ (wax) untimely birth	"

Book Passage	Tenor	Prothesis	Vehicle	Speaker
Psalms 58.9	he (shall take away)	as, ὡσεὶ, sicut	a whirlwind	"
Psalms 59.6	they (shall make noise)	like, ὡς, ut	a dog	"
Psalms 59.14	they (let them make noise/ suffer hunger)	like, ὡς, ut	a dog	"
Psalms 62.3	you	as, ὡς, tamquam	a bowing wall and a tottering fence	"
Psalms 64.3	tongue (of the wicked)	like, ὡς, ut	a sword	"
Psalms 68.2	them (drive away) the wicked (should perish)	as, ὡς, sicut as, ὡς, sicut	smoke wax (melts)	"
Psalms 68.13	you	as, –, –	wings of a dove	"
Psalms 68.14	it (white)	as, verbal sim., ditto in Latin	snow	"
Psalms 72.6	king Solomon	like, ὡς, sicut as, ὡσεὶ, sicut	rain showers	"
Psalms 73.20	Thou, O Lord	as, ὡσεὶ, velut	a dream	"
Psalms 73.22	I	as, (κτηνώδης), ut	a beast	"
Psalms 77.20	thy people	like, ὡς, sicut	a flock	"
Psalms 78.13	waters (standing)	as, ὡσεὶ, quasi	a heap	"
Psalms 78.52	God's people	like, ὡς, sicut like, ὡσεὶ, tamquam	sheep a flock	"
Psalms 78.69	his sanctuary	like, ὡς, sicut like, –, –	high palaces/ unicorn the earth	"

Book Passage	Tenor	Prothesis	Vehicle	Speaker
Psalms 79.3	their blood	like, ὡσεὶ, tamquam	water	"
Psalms 83.13	[thine enemies]	like, ὡς, ut as, ὡς, sicut	a wheel _stubble_ before the wind	"
Psalms 83.14	[God] > enemies with tempest	as, ὡσεὶ, sicut as, ὡσεὶ, sicut	fire > wood flame > mountains	"
Psalsms 84.10	a day in court (better) a doorkeeper in the house of God	than, ὑπὲρ, super than, ἤ, quam	a thousand to dwell in tents of wickedness	"
Psalms 88.17	[thy terrors]	like, ὡσεὶ, sicut	water	"
Psalms 89.46	thy wrath	like, ὡς, sicut	fire	"
Psalms 90.5	children (carried away by Lord)	as as like, ὡσεὶ, sicut	with a flood a sleep grass	"
Psalms 90.9	we spend our years	as, ὡσεὶ, sicut	a tale told a cobweb	"
Psalms 92.7	the wicked	as, ὡσεὶ, sicut	the grass	"
Psalms 92.10	my horn	like, ὡς, sicut	horn of unicorn	"
Psalms 92.12	the righteous he	like, ὡς, ut like, ὡσεὶ, sicut	the palm-tree cedar in Lebanon	"
Psalms 97.5	hills (melted away)	like, ὡσεὶ, sicut	wax	"
Psalms 102.3	days (consumed) my bones (burned)	like, ὡσεὶ, sicut as, ὡσεὶ, sicut	smoke an hearth	"
Psalms 102.4	my heart (withered)	like, ὡσεὶ, ut	grass	"

Book Passage	Tenor	Prothesis	Vehicle	Speaker
Psalms 102.6	I I	like, verb, similis like, ὡσεὶ, sicut	a pelican a desert owl	"
Psalms 102.7	I (watch)	as, ὡς, sicut	a sparrow	"
Psalms 102.9	ashes (eaten)	like, ὡσεὶ, tamquam	bread	"
Psalms 102.11	my days I	like, ὡσεὶ, sicut like, ὡσεὶ, sicut	a shadow grass	"
Psalms 103.11	heaven (high) > earth	as, ὅτι, quoniam	his mercy (so great) > them	"
Psalms 103.12	east > west	as far as, καθόσον ἀπέχουσιν quantum distant	our transgres- sions (so far) > us	"
Psalms 103.13	a father > his children	like as, καθὼς, quo modo	the Lord > them that fear him	"
Psalms 103.15	a man's days he (will flourish)	as, ὡσεὶ, sicut as, ὡσεὶ, sic	grass a flower of field	"
Psalms 104.2	light the heavens the deep	as, ὡς, sicut like, ὡσεὶ, sicut as, ὡς, sicut	a garment a curtain a garment	"
Psalms 109.18	cursing (clothed) cursing > bowels cursing > bones	like as, ὡς, sicut like, ὡσεὶ, sicut like, ὡσεὶ, sicut	his garment water oil	"
Psalms 109.23	I (gone) I (tossed)	like, ὡσεὶ, sicut as, ὡσεὶ, sicut	a shadow the locust	"
Psalms 114.4 = 114.6	mountains hills	like, ὡσεὶ, ut like, ὡς, sicut	rams lambs	"
Psalms 118.12	they (na- tions) > me they (quenched)	like, ὡσεὶ, sicut as, ὡς, sicut	bees fire of thorns	"

Book Passage	Tenor	Prothesis	Vehicle	Speaker
Psalms 119.70	their heart (fat)	as, ὡς, sicut	grease	"
Psalms 119.72	law of thy mouth (better)	than, ὑπὲρ, super	thousands of gold and silver	"
Psalms 119.83	I (become)	like, ὡς, sicut	a bottle in smoke	"
Psalms 119.103	your words (sweeter)	than, ὑπὲρ, super	honey	"
Psalms 123.2	servants' eyes > masters eyes of maiden > her mistress	as, ὡς, sicut as, ὡς, sicut	our eyes > the Lord	"
Psalms 124.7	our soul (escaped)	as, ὡς, sicut	a bird out of fowler's snare	"
Psalms 125.1	they that trust in the Lord	as, ὡς, sicut	mount Zion (abides forever)	"
Psalms 125.2	the Lord around his people	as, –, –	the moun-tains around Jerusalem	"
Psalms 127.4	the children of the youth	as, ὡσεὶ, sicut	arrows of a mighty man	"
Psalms 128.3	thy wife thy children	as, ὡς, sicut like, ὡς, sicut	a fruitful vine olive plants	"
Psalms 131.2	I my soul	as, ὡς, sicut as, ὡς, ita	a weaned child a weaned child	"
Psalms 133.2 133.3	for brethren to dwell together	like, ὡς, sicut as, ὡς, sicut	ointment on the head, the dew of Hermon, on Zion	"
Psalms 140.3	their tongues (sharpened)	like, ὡσεὶ, sicut	a serpent's	"
Psalms 141.2	my prayer my raised hands	as, ὡς, sicut as, –, –	incense the evening sacrifice	"

Book Passage	Tenor	Prothesis	Vehicle	Speaker
Psalms 141.7	our bones (scattered)	as, ὡσεὶ, sicut	wood cut and cleaved	"
Psalms 144.4	man	is like, ὡμοιώθη, similis factus as, ὡσεὶ, sicut	vanity a shadow passing away	"
Psalms 144.12	our sons our daughters	as, ὡς, sicut as, ὡς, ut similitude	grown up plants corner stones polished	"
Psalms 147.16	snow hoarfrost (scattered)	like, ὡσεὶ, sicut like, ὡσεὶ, sicut	wool ashes	"
Psalms 147.17	his ice (thrown)	like, ὡσεὶ, sicut	morsels	"
Proverbs 1.27	your fear destruction	as, ὡς, – as, ὁμοίως, quasi	desolation a whirlwind	Solomon son of David
Prov. 2.4	wisdom	as, ὡς, quasis as, ὡς, sicut	silver treasures hidden	Solomon to his son (Rehoboam)
Prov. 3.12	the Lord > whom he loves	as, – quasi	a father > his son	Solomon to his son
Prov. 3.14	wisdom (better)	than, ἤ, [abl.]	merchandise of gold and silver	Solomon to his son
Prov. 3.15	wisdom (more precious)	than, [gen.], [abl.]	rubies	Solomon to his son
Prov. 5.3 5.4	lips of a strange woman; her mouth (smoother) her end (bitter) (sharp)	as, –, – than, –, – as, comp., quasi as, μᾶλλον, quasi	a honeycomb oil wormwood a two-edged sword	Solomon to his son
Prov. 5.19	the wife of your youth	as, –, –	a loving hind and pleasant roe	Solomon

Book Passage	Tenor	Prothesis	Vehicle	Speaker
Prov. 6.5	you (delivered)	as, ὥσπερ, quasi as ὥσπερ, quasi	a roe a bird (rescued)	Solomon
Prov. 7.2	my law (keep)	as, ὥσπερ, quasi	apple of your eye	Solomon
Prov. 7.22	he > her	as, ὥσπερ, quasi as, ὥσπερ, quasi	an ox > slaughter a fool > stocks	Solomon
Prov. 7.23	he > her	as, ὡς, vellum si	a bird > a snare	Solomon
Prov. 8.11	wisdom (better)	than, gen., abl.	rubies	Solomon
Prov. 8.19	my fruit (better)	than, ὑπέρ, abl.	gold, fine gold choice silver	Solomon
Prov. 10. 20	tongue of the just	as, –, –	choice silver	Solomon
Prov. 10.25	the wicked the righteous	as, –, quasi –, –, quasi	a whirlwind everlasting foundation	Solomon
Prov. 10.26	the sluggard > senders	as, ὥσπερ, sicut as, –, –	vinegar > teeth smoke >eyes	Solomon
Prov. 11.22	a fair woman without discretion	as, ὥσπερ, –	a jewel of gold in a swine's mouth	Solomon
Prov. 12.4	a virtuous woman > her husband a bad woman	–, –, – as, ὥσπερ, –	a crown rottenness	Solomon
Prov. 12.18	who speaks	like, –, quasi	piercings of a sword	Solomon
Prov. 15.19	a slothful man	as, –, quasi	a hedge of thorns	Solomon
Prov. 16.15	a king's favor	as, ὥσπερ, quasi	a cloud of rain	Solomon
Prov. 16.16	wisdom (better) understanding	than, genit., ablat. than, ὑπὲρ, ablat.	gold silver	Solomon

Book Passage	Tenor	Prothesis	Vehicle	Speaker
Prov. 17.1	a dry morsel + quietness (better)	than, ἤ, quam	a house of strife	Solomon
Prov. 17.8	a gift	as, –, –	a precious stone	Solomon
Prov. 17.10	reproof > a wise man (more)	than, –, quam	100 stripes > a fool	Solomon
Prov. 17.12	to meet a fool	rather than, –, magis quam	to meet a bear robbed of her whelps	Solomon
Prov. 17.14	beginning of strife	as, –, –	letting out water	Solomon
Prov. 17.22	a merry heart doing good	like –, –	a medicine	Solomon
Prov. 18.4	words of mouth wellspring of wisdom	as, –, – as, –, –	deep waters a flowing brook	Solomon
Prov. 18.8	words of a talebearer	as, –, quasi	wounds	Solomon
Prov. 18.11	wealth of rich man	–, –, – as, –, quasi	his strong city a high wall	Solomon
Prov. 18.19	a brother offended their contentions	than, ὡς, quasi like, ὥσπερ, quasi	a strong city bars of a castle	Solomon
Prov. 19.12	king's wrath his favor	as, ὁμοία, sicut as, ὥσπερ, sicut	roaring of a lion dew on grass	Solomon
Prov. 20.2	fear of a king	as, οὐ διαφέρει sicut	roaring of a lion	Solomon
Prov. 20.5	counsel in a man's heart	like, –, sicut	deep waters	Solomon
Prov 21.1	king's hear in Lord's hand	as, ὥσπερ, sicut	rivers of water	Solomon

Book Passage	Tenor	Prothesis	Vehicle	Speaker
Prov. 21.9	to dwell in corner (better)	than, ἤ, quam	with a brawling woman	Solomon
Prov. 21.19	to dwell in wilderness (better)	than, ἤ, quam	with a contentious woman	Solomon
Prov. 23.32	red wine (bites) (stings)	like, ὥσπερ, ut like, ὥσπερ, sicut	a serpent an adder	Solomon
Prov. 23.34	you	as, ὥσπερ, sicut as, ὥσπερ, quasi	he who lies in the sea he who lies on the mast	Solomon
Prov. 24.34	your poverty your want	as, –, quasi as, ὥσπερ, quasi	one traveling an armed man	Solomon
Prov. 25.11	a word fitly spoken	like, –, –	apples of gold in pictures of silver	Solomon
Prov. 25.12	a wise reprover on an obedient ear	as, –, –	an earring of gold an ornament of fine gold	Solomon
Prov. 25.13	a faithful messenger	as, ὥσπερ, sicut	cold snow in time of harvest	Solomon
Prov. 25.14	who boasts of a false gift	like, ὥσπερ, –	winds + clouds without rain	Solomon
Prov. 25.19	confidence in an unfaithful man	like, –, –	a broken tooth a foot out of joint	Solomon
Prov. 25.20	a singer of sad songs	as, ὥσπερ, – as, ὥσπερ, sicut	he who takes away … vinegar on nitre	Solomon
Prov. 25.23	an angry countenance > a back-biting tongue	–, –, –	north wind > rain	Solomon

Book Passage	Tenor	Prothesis	Vehicle	Speaker
Prov. 25.24 cf. 21.9 + 21.19	to dwell in corner of house	better than	with a brawling woman	Solomon
Prov. 25.25	good news from afar	as, ὥσπερ, –	cold water to a thirsty soul	Solomon
Prov. 25.26	a righteous man > a wicked man	as, ὥσπερ, –	a troubled fountain a corrupt spring	Solomon
Prov. 25.28	a man with no rule over his spirit	like, ὥσπερ, sicut	a broken down city without walls	Solomon
Prov. 26.1	honor to a fool	as, ὥσπερ, quo modo	snow (in summer) rain (in harvest)	Solomon
Prov. 26.2	a causeless curse	as, ὥσπερ, sicut as, –, –	a bird wandering sparrow flying	Solomon
Prov. 26.7	a parable in the mouth of fools	–, –, quomodo	unequal legs of the lame	Solomon
Prov. 26.8	who honors a fool	as, ὅμοιός, sicut	who binds a stone in a sling	Solomon
Prov. 26.9	a parable in the mouth of fools	as, –, quomodo	a thorn in the hand of a drunkard	Solomon
Prov 26.11	a fool > his folly	as, ὥσπερ, sicut	a dog > his own vomit	Solomon
Prov. 26.14	a sluggard > his bed	as, ὥσπερ, sicut	a door (turning) > its hinge	Solomon
Prov. 26.16	a sluggard (wiser)	than, genit., ablat.	seven men	Solomon
Prov. 26.17	he who champions another's cause	like, ὥσπερ, sicut	one who takes a dog by the ears	Solomon

Book Passage	Tenor	Prothesis	Vehicle	Speaker
Prov. 26.18	one who deceives his neighbor	as, ὥσπερ, sicut	a madman …	Solomon
Prov. 26.21	a contentious man > kindling strife	as, –, sicut	coals > burning coals wood > fire	Solomon
Prov. 26.22	words of a talebearer	as, –, quasi	wounds	Solomon
Prov. 26.23	burning lips and a wicked heart	like, ὥσπερ, quomodo	a potsherd covered with silver	Solomon
Prov. 27.3	a fool's wrath (heavier)	than, genit., ablat.	a heavy stone weighty sand	Solomon
Prov. 27.5	open rebuke (better)	than, genit., quam	secret love	Solomon
Prov. 27.8	a man who wanders	as, ὥσπερ, sicut	a bird flying from her nest	Solomon
Prov. 27.15	a contentious woman (alike)	–, ὡσαύτως, comparantur	continuous rain	Solomon
Prov. 27.17	a man > his friend's face	–, –, –	iron > iron (sharpens)	Solomon
Prov. 27.19	heart > heart	as, ὥσπερ, quomodo	face > face	Solomon
Prov. 27.20	eyes of men (insatiable)	–, –, similiter	hell and destruction (never full)	Solomon
Prov. 27.21	a man to praise	as, –, quomodo	a fining pot > silver a furnace > gold	Solomon
Prov. 28.1	the righteous (bold)	as, ὥσπερ, quasi	a lion	Solomon
Prov. 28.3	a poor man oppressing the poor	like, ὥσπερ, similis	a sweeping rain leaving no food	Solomon

Book Passage	Tenor	Prothesis	Vehicle	Speaker
Prov. 28.15	a wicked ruler	as, –, –	a roaring lion a ranging bear	Solomon
Prov. 30.14	teeth jaw teeth	as, –, pro as	swords knives	Agur, son of Jakeh
Prov. 31.10	a virtuous woman (far)	above, compar.+ genitive, procul de	rubies	King Lemuel
Prov. 31.14	she (a virtuous woman)	like, ὡσεὶ, quasi	merchants' ships trading from afar	King Lemuel
Ecclesiastes 7.1	a good name (better)	than, ὑπὲρ, quam	precious ointment	The Preacher
Eccl. 7.6	laughter of a fool	as, ὡς, sicut	crackling of thorns under a pot	Son of David Solomon?
Eccl.7.26	woman (more bitter) whose heart her hands	than, ὑπὲρ, ablat. –, –, – as, –, –	death snares and nets bands	The Preacher
Eccl. 9.4	a living dog (better)	than, ὑπὲρ, ablat.	a dead lion	The Preacher
Eccl. 9.12	sons of men snared in an evil time	as, ὡς, sicut as, ὡς, sicut	fishes taken in an evil net birds caught in a snare	The Preacher
Eccl. 9.18	wisdom (better)	than, ὑπὲρ, quam	weapons of war	The Preacher
Eccl. 10.1	a little folly > good reputation	–, –, –	dead flies > an apothecary's ointment	The Preacher
Eccl. 10.8	digging a pit > falling in	–, –, –	bracketing a hedge > a ser- pent bite	The Preacher

Book Passage	Tenor	Prothesis	Vehicle	Speaker
Eccl. 10.11	a babbler (no better)	–, –, –	a serpent biting	The Preacher
Eccl. 12.11	words of the wise	as, ὡς, sicut as, ὡς, quasi	goads nails fastened	The Preacher
Sol's Song 1.2	your love (better)	than, ὑπὲρ, ablat.	wine	Solomon
Sol's Song 1.3	your name	as, –,–	ointment poured	Solomon
Sol's Song 1.4	your love (more)	than, ὑπὲρ, super	wine	Solomon
Sol's Song 1.5	I (black & beautiful)	as, ὡς, sicut as, ὡς, sicut	tents of Kedar curtains of Solomon	Solomon
Sol's Song 1.9	you	I have compared to, ὡμοίωσά, assimilavi	a company of Pharaoh's horses	Solomon
Sol' Song 1.14	my beloved	as, –, –	a cluster of camphor	Solomon
Sol's Song 2.2 2.3	my love among daughters my beloved among sons	as, ὡς, sicut as, ὡς, sicut	lily among thorns apple tree among trees	Solomon
Sol's Song 2.9	my beloved	like, ὅμοιός, similes	a roe a young hart	Solomon
Sol's Song 2.17	my beloved	be like, ὁμιώθητι, similis esto	a roe or young hart	Solomon
Sol's Song 3.6	who?	like, ὡς, sicut	pillars of smoke	Solomon

Book Passage	Tenor	Prothesis	Vehicle	Speaker
Sol's Song 4.1–5	thou hast your hair your teeth your lips your temples your neck your breasts	– as, ὡς, sicut like, ὡς, sicut like, ὡς, sicut like, ὡς, sicut like, ὡς, sicut ike, ὡς, sicut	doves' eyes flock of goats flock of sheep thread of scarlet pomegranate tower of David twin roes	Solomon
Sol's Song 4.10	your love (better) smell of your ointments	than, ἀπὸ, ablat. than, ὑπὲρ, super	wine all spices	Solomon
Sol's Song 4.11	your lips smell of your garments	as, –, – like, ὡς, sicut	the honeycomb the smell of Lebanon	Solomon
Sol's Song 5.11–15	my beloved's head his locks (black) his eyes his cheeks his lips his hands his belly his legs his countenance	11 as, –, sicut as, ὡς, quasi 12 as, ὡς, sicut 13 as, ὡς, sicut as, –, – like, –, – 14 as, –, – as, –, – 15 as, –, – as, ὡς, ut as, ὡς, ut	fine gold a raven dove's eyes a bed of spices/ sweet flowers lilies gold rings bright ivory pillars of marble Lebanon cedars	Solomon
Sol's Song 6.4–7	my love (beautiful) (comely) (terrible) 5 your hair 6 teeth 7 temples	4 as, ὡς, – as, ὡς, sicut as, ὡς, ut 5 as, ὡς, sicut 6 as, ὡς, sicut as, ὡς, sic	Tirzah Jerusalem an army 5 flock of goats 6 flock of sheep pomegranate	Solomon

Book Passage	Tenor	Prothesis	Vehicle	Speaker
Sol's Song 6.10	Who? (looks forth) (fair) (clear) (terrible)	as, ὡσεὶ, quasi as, ὡς, ut as, ὡς, ut as, ὡς, ut	morning the moon the sun an army	Solomon
Sol's Song 6.12	me	like, –, propter (?)	chariots of Amminabid	Solomon
Sol's Song 7.1–9	joints of thighs your navel your belly 3 your two breasts 4 your neck your eyes your nose 5 your head your hair 7 your stature your breast 8 your breasts your smell 9 roof of mouth	1 like, –, sicut 2 like, ὅμοιοι, – like, –, sicut 3 like, ὡς, sicut 4 as, –, sicut like, –, sicut as, –, sicut 5 like, ὡς, sicut like, ὡς, sicut 7 like, –, (dat.) (like) to, sicut 8 as, ὡμοιώθης like, ὡς, sicut 9 like, ὡς, sicut	jewels a round goblet a heap of wheat 3 young roes 4 tower of ivy fish pools tower of Lebanon 5 Carmel purple 7 a palm tree clusters of grapes 8 clusters of vine apples 9 the best wine	Solomon
Sol's Song 8.6	me love (strong) jealousy (cruel)	as, ὡς, ut as, ὡς, ut as, ὡς, ut – sicut	a seal on your heart a seal on your arm death the grave	Solomon
Sol's Song 8.10	my breasts I	like, ὡς, sicut as, ὡς, quasi	towers one that found favor	Solomon
Sol's Song 8.14	my beloved	like, ὁμοιώθητι, <u>assimilare</u>	a roe or young hart	Solomon

Book Passage	Tenor	Prothesis	Vehicle	Speaker
Isaiah 1.8	daughter of Zion	as, ὡς, ut as, ὡς, sicut as, ὡς, sicut	cottage (vineyard) lodge (garden) besieged city	Isaiah son of Amoz
Isaiah 1.9	we	as, ὡς, quasi like, ὡς, quasi	Sodom Gomorrah	Isaiah
Isaiah 1.18	your sins (white) they they	as, ὡς, ut as, ὡς, quasi like, ὡς, quasi as, ὡς, velut	scarlet snow crimson wool	Isaiah
Isaiah 1.30 1.31	you (rulers of Sodom) 31 the strong the maker	as, ὡς, velut as, ὡς, velut as, ὡς, ut as, ὡς, quasi	a leafless oak a water- less garden 31 tow a spark	Isaiah
Isaiah 3.18	round tires	like, –, –	the moon	Isaiah
Isaiah 5.24	root [as, ὡς, quasi] rottenness their blossom [as, ὡς, ut] dust	as, ὃν τρόπον, sicut	the fire > the stubble and the flame > the chaff	Isaiah
Isaiah 5.28–30	horses' hooves wheels 29 their roaring 30 they (shall roar)	like, ὡς, ut like, ὡς, quasi 29 like, ὡς, ut like, ὡς, quasi 30 like, ὡς, sicut	flint a whirlwind 29 a lion a young lion 30 roaring of the sea	Isaiah
Isaiah 6.13	the holy seed	as, ὡς, sicut as, ὡς, sicut	a tall tree an oak	Isaiah
Isaiah 7.2	his heart (moved)	as, ὃν τρόπον, sicut	trees (moved by wind)	Isaiah

Book Passage	Tenor	Prothesis	Vehicle	Speaker
Isaiah 9.18 9.19	wickedness (burns); they (shall mount); 19 people	as, ὡς, quasi like, ὡς, – 19 as, ὡς, quasi	the fire lifting of smoke 19 fuel of the fire	Isaiah
Isaiah 10.14	peoples' riches I gathered earth	as, ὡς, quasi as, ὡς, sicut	a nest one gathers eggs	Isaiah
Isaiah 10.15	an axe or saw > the user	as if, ὡσαύτως ἐάν, quo modo si as if	a rod or staff > one who uses it	Isaiah
Isaiah 10.16	the Lord > a burning	like, –, quasi	a fire > a burning	Isaiah
Isaiah 10.17	the light of Israel his Holy One	for, εἰς, in for, ὡσεὶ, in	a fire a flame	Isaiah
Isaiah 10.22	people of Israel	as, ὡς, quasi	sand of the sea	Isaiah
Israel 13.8	elders (in pain) their faces	as, ὡς, quasi as, ὡς, –	a woman in labor flames	Isaiah
Isaiah 13.12	a man (more precious); even a man	than, μᾶλλον ἤ, [ablative] than	fine gold the golden wedge of Ophit	Isaiah
Isaiah 13.14	(those left behind)	as, ὡς, quasi as, ὡς, quasi	the chased roe a stray sheep	Isaiah
Isaiah 14.19	you (cast away)	like, ὡς, quasi as, –, – as, –, quasi	abominable branch, raiment of the slain, a trodden carcase	Isaiah
Isaiah 16.2	the daughters of Moab	as, ὡς, sicut	a wandering bird cast out of nest	Isaiah
Isaiah 16.11	my bowels (sound)	like, ὡς, quasi	a harp for Moab	Isaiah

Book Passage	Tenor	Prothesis	Vehicle	Speaker
Isaiah 17.5 17.6	it shall be 6 gleaning grapes	as when, ὃν τρόπον ἐάν, sicut as, ὃν τρόπον ἐάν, sicut 6 as, ὡς, sicut	gathering corn and reaping; gathering ears in Rephaim; 6 shaking of an olive tree	Isaiah
Isaiah 17.9	his strong cities	as, ὃν τρόπον, sicut	a for- saken bough, an uppermost branch	Isaiah
Isaiah 17.12 17.13	noise rushing 13 rush they shall be chased	like, ὡς, ut like, ὡς, sicut 13 like, ὡς, sicut as, ὡς, sicut	noise of the seas rushing of mighty waters; 13 rushing of many waters; chaff of mountains 13 a rolling thing before a whirlwind	Isaiah
Isaiah 18.4	I	like, ὡς, sicut like, ὡς, sicut	a clear heat a cloud of dew	Isaiah
Isaiah 19.14	Egypt errs	as, ὡς, sicut	a drunk stag- gering in his vomit	Isaiah
Isaiah 19.16	Egypt	like, ὡς, quasi	women	Isaiah
Isaiah 21.1	a fearful vision	as, ὡς, sicut	whirlwinds	Isaiah
Isaiah 21.3	me (in pain)	as, ὡς, sicut	a woman in labor flames	Isaiah
Isaiah 22.18	you (tossed by the Lord)	like, –, quasi	a ball	Isaiah
Isaiah 23.15	Tyre (will sing)	as, ὡς, quasi	a harlot	Isaiah

Book Passage	Tenor	Prothesis	Vehicle	Speaker
Isaiah 24.13	(the desolate city)	as, ὃν τρόπονἐάν, *quomodo si,* *as, –, –*	the shaking of an olive tree, gleaning grapes after vintage	Isaiah
Isaiah 24.20	earth (shall reel) (shall be removed)	like, ὡς, sicut like, ὡς, quasi	a drunkard a cottage	Isaiah
Isaiah 24.22	earthly kings (gathered together)	as, –, – (no simile in Gr. & Latin)	prisoners	Isaiah
Isaiah 26.17	we (in your sight)	as, ὡς, sicut	a woman about to give birth	Isaiah
Isaiah 26.18	child-birth	as it were, –, quasi	wind	Isaiah
Isaiah 28.2	Lord's anger	as, ὡς, sicut as, –, – as, ὡς, sicut	a tempest of hail a flood a great body of water	Isaiah
Isaiah 29.4	your voice	as, ὡς, quasi	a familiar spirit	Isaiah
Isaiah 29.5	your many strangers	like, ὡς, sicut as, ὡς, sicut	small dust chaff	Isaiah
Isaiah 29.7–8	multitude of nations	as, ὡς, sicut 8 as, ὡς, sicut as, ὃν τρόπον, sicut	a dream 8 hungry/thirsty man's dream	Isaiah
Isaiah 29.11	the vision of all	as, ὡς, sicut	words of a sealed book	Isaiah
Isaiah 30.17	many fleeing	as, ὡς, quasi as, ὡς, quasi	a beacon/ensign on a mountain/ hill	Isaiah
Isaiah 30.22	covering of graven images	as, ὡς, sicut	a menstruous cloth	Isaiah

Book Passage	Tenor	Prothesis	Vehicle	Speaker
Isaiah 30.27	the Lord's tongue	as, ὡς, quasi	a devouring fire	Isaiah
Isaiah 30.28	his breath vanity	as, ὡς, velut of, –, genitive	overflowing stream a sieve	Isaiah
Isaiah 30.29	a song (you shall have) gladness of heart	as, ὡσεὶ, sicut as, ὡσεὶ, sicut	when a holy solemnity is kept, going with a pipe to Lord's mountain	Isaiah
Isaiah 30.33	the Lord's breath	like, ὡς, sicut	a stream of brimstone	Isaiah
Isaiah 31.4–5	the Lord (defending Jerusalem)	like, ὃν τρόπον ἐάν, quo modo si 5 as, ὡς, sicut	a lion roaring or a young lion 5 birds flying	Isaiah
Isaiah 32.2	a man (shall be)	as, –, sicut as, ὡς, sicut as, –, –	hiding place from wind / from a tempest / rivers / shadow of a rock	Isaiah
Isaiah 32.14	forts and towers	for, –, –	dens, a joy of wild asses, a pasture of flocks	Isaiah
Isaiah 33.4	your spoil (gathered) (the Lord)	like, ὃν τρόπον ἐάν, sicut as, –, velut	gathering of the caterpillar, running of locusts	Isaiah
Isaiah 33.9	Sharon	like, –, sicut	a wilderness	Isaiah
Isaiah 33.11	your breath	as, –, ut	fire	Isaiah
Isaiah 33.12	the people	as, ὡς, quasi as, –, –	burnings of lime cut up thorns	Isaiah
Isaiah 34.4	heavens (rolled up); hosts (fall)	as, ὡς, sicut as, ὡς, sicut as, ὡς, –	a scroll falling leaf falling fig	Isaiah

Book Passage	Tenor	Prothesis	Vehicle	Speaker
Isaiah 35.1	the desert (blossoming and rejoicing)	as, ὡς, quasi	the rose	Isaiah
Isaiah 35.6	a lame man (leaping)	as, ὡς, sicut	an hart	Isaiah
Isaiah 37.27	they (defending citizens)	as, ὡς, sicut as, –, – as, –, – as, ὡς, –	field grass green herb grass on housetop blasted corn	Isaiah
Isaiah 38.12	my age (departed) I > my life (cut off)	as, ὥσπερ, quasi like, ὡς, velut	a shepherd's tent a weaver >	Isaiah
Isaiah 38.13–14	He (the Lord) 14 I (chatter) I (mourn)	as, ὡς, quasi like, ὡς, sicut as, ὡς, sicut	a lion 14 a crane/ swallow a dove	Isaiah
Isaiah 40.11	He (the Lord) > his flock	like, ὡς, sicut	a shepherd > (his flock)	Isaiah
Isaiah 40.15	nations the isles	as, ὡς, quasi as, ὡς, quasi as, ὡς, quasi	a drop of a bucket small dust a very little thing	Isaiah
Isaiah 40.22	inhabitants heavens	as, ὡς, quasi as, ὡς, velut as, ὡς, sicut	grasshoppers a curtain a tent	Isaiah
Isaiah 40.24	them (princes and judges)	as, ὡς, quasi	stubble	Isaiah
Isaiah 40.31	they (that wait upon the Lord)	as, ὡς, sicut	eagles	Isaiah
Isaiah 41.2	them (kings)	as, ὡς, quasi as, –, sicut	dust to righteous stubble to his bow	Isaiah

Book Passage	Tenor	Prothesis	Vehicle	Speaker
Isaiah 41.15	the hills	as, ὡς, quasi	chaff	Isaiah
Isaiah 41.25	princes	as, ὡς, velut	morter, potter's clay	Isaiah
Isaiah 42.6	thee	for, εἰς, in for, εἰς, in	a covenant a light of Gentiles	Isaiah/the Lord
Isaiah 42.13	the Lord	as, –, sicut as, –, sicut	a mighty man a man of war	Isaiah
Isaiah 42.14	I (will cry)	like, ὡς, sicut	a travailing woman	Isaiah
Isaiah 46.5–9	no one	like, πλὴν, similis	me (God)	Isaiah
Isaiah 47.14	they (astrologers etc.)	as, ὡς, quasi	stubble	Isaiah
Isaiah 48.18–19	thy peace thy righteousness 19 thy seed thy offspring	as, ὡσεὶ, sicut as, ὡς, sicut as, ὡς, quasi like, ὡς, ut	a river waves of sea 19 the sand gravel	Isaiah/the Lord
Isaiah 49.2	my mouth	like, ὡσεὶ, sicut	a sharp sword	Isaiah
Isaiah 49.6	thee (Isaiah)	for, εἰς, in	a light to the Gentiles	Isaiah/the Lord
Isaiah 49.18	(Zion) clothed with them; bound	as, ὡς, velut as, ὡς, quasi	an ornament a bride's (attire)	Isaiah
Isaiah 51.6	heavens (vanish) earth (grow old)	like, ὡς, sicut like, ὡς, sicut	smoke a garment	Isaiah
Isaiah 51.8	they (eaten by a moth); them	like, ὡς, sicut like, ὡς, sicut	a garment wool	Isaiah
Isaiah 53.2	he (shall grow)	as, ὡς, sicut as, ὡς, sicut	a tender plant a root	Isaiah

Book Passage	Tenor	Prothesis	Vehicle	Speaker
Isaiah 53.6–7	we 7 he	like, ὡς, quasi 7 as, ὡς, sicut as, ὡς, sicut	sheep (astray) lamb to slaughter sheep to shearer	Isaiah
Isaiah 54.6	you	as, ὡς, –	a woman forsaken	Isaiah
Isaiah 54.9	this (little wrath)	as, –, sicut	waters of Noah	Isaiah/the Lord
Isaiah 55.9–10	my ways > your ways; 10 my word	as, ὡς, sicut as, ὡς, quo modo	heavens > earth 10 rain/snow > heaven	Isaiah/the Lord
Isaiah 57.20	the wicked	like, –, quasi	troubled sea	Isaiah
Isaiah 58.11	you	like, ὡς, quasi like, ὡς, sicut	well-watered garden; a spring	Isaiah
Isaiah 59.10–11	we (grope) (stumble) (desolate) 11 we (roar) we (mourn)	like, ὡς, sicut as, ὡς, quasi as, ὡς, quasi like, ὡς, quasi like, ὡς, –	the blind in the night dead men bears doves	Isaiah
Isaiah 59.17	(he clad with) zeal	as, –, ut	a cloak	Isaiah
Isaiah 60.8	who? (fly)	as, ὡς, ut as, ὡσεὶ, quasi	a cloud the doves	Isaiah
Isaiah 61.10–11	I (will rejoice in the Lord); 11 the Lord > righteousness	as, ὡς, quasi as, ὡς, quasi 11 as, ὡς, sicut	a bridegroom a bride 11 earth > flowers a garden > its seeds	Isaiah
Isaiah 62.5	your sons (marry) > you; God (rejoice over) > you	as, ὡς, – as, ὃν τρόπον, –	a young man > a virgin; bride-groom > the bride	Isaiah

Book Passage	Tenor	Prothesis	Vehicle	Speaker
Isaiah 63.13–14	the Lord led them 14 you led your people	as, ὡς, quasi 14 as, ὡς, quasi	a horse in wilderness; 14 a beast in the valley	Isaiah
Isaiah 64.2	nations will tremble	as, ὡς, sicut	fire burns, water boils	Isaiah
Isaiah 64.6	we our righteousness we fade our iniquities	as, ὡς, ut as, ὡς, quasi as, ὡς, quasi like, –, quasi	an unclean thing filthy rags a leaf the wind	Isaiah
Isaiah 65.8	I will not destroy all	as, ὃν τρόπον, quo modo	new wine found in the cluster	Isaiah/the Lord
Isaiah 65.22	the days of my people	as, κατὰ, secundum	days of a tree	Isaiah
Isaiah 65.25	the lion (will eat straw)	like, ὡς, –	the bullock	Isaiah
Isaiah 66.3	he who killed an ox; who sacrifices a lamb; who offers an oblation; who burnt incense	as, –, quasi as if, ὡς, quasi as if, ὡς, quasi as if, ὡς, quasi	someone who killed a man; who cut off a dog's neck; who offered swine's blood; who blessed an idol	Isaiah/the Lord
Isaiah 66.12	peace glory of Gentiles	like, ὡς, quasi like, ὡς, quasi	a river a flowing stream	Isaiah/the Lord
Isaiah 66.14–15	bones 15 chariots	like, ὡς, quasi like, ὡς, quasi	an herb 15 a whirlwind	Isaiah/the Lord
Jeremiah 3.20	Israel (treacherous) > me (the Lord)	as, ὡς, quo modo si	a wife (treacherous) > husband	Jeremiah

Book Passage	Tenor	Prothesis	Vehicle	Speaker
Jerem. 4.13	He (the Lord) his chariots his horses (swifter)	than, [genit.], [ablative]	clouds a whirlwind eagles	Jeremiah
Jerem. 4.31	a voice anguish	as, ὡς, quasi as, ὡς, ut	a woman in labor a woman giving birth for first time	Jeremiah
Jerem. 5.8	your sons	as, –, –	fed horses	Jeremiah
Jerem. 5.16	their quiver	as, –, quasi	an open sepulchre	Jeremiah
Jerem. 5.27	wicked men's houses (full of deceit)	as, ὡς, sicut	a cage full of birds	Jeremiah
Jerem. 6.2	Zion's daughter	likened to, –, assimilavi	a comely and delicate woman	Jeremiah
Jerem. 6.7	Jerusalem > her wickedness	as, ὡς, sicut	a fountain (casts out) > waters	Jeremiah
Jerem. 6.9	they > Israel [Jerusalem]	as, ὡς, quasi as, ὡς, quasi	[one] (gleans) > a wine; grape gatherer	Jeremiah/the Lord
Jerem. 6.24	anguish + pain > us	as, ὡς, ut	[pain] > a woman in labor	Jeremiah
Jerem. 6.26	mourn (for?)	as, –, –	for an only son	Jeremiah
Jerem. 6.27	you	for, –, –	a tower and a fortress	Jeremiah
Jerem. 8.6–7	everyone (turned) 7 people NOT know the Lord's judgment	as, ὡς, quasi –, –, –	a horse (rushes to battle); 7 stork in heaven, turtle, crane and swallow know the time of their coming	Jeremiah

Book Passage	Tenor	Prothesis	Vehicle	Speaker
Jerem. 9.3	(they bend) theirtongues	like, ὡς, quasi	a bow	Jeremiah
Jerem. 9.8	their tongue	as, –, –	an arrow	Jeremiah
Jerem. 9.22	carcases of men	as, εἰς, quasi as, ὡς, quasi	dung handful after harvestman	Jeremiah/the Lord
Jerem 10.5	they (heathen)	as, –, in similitudinem	palm tree	Jeremiah
Jerem. 11.19	I	like, ὡς, quasi	a labor ox brought to slaughter	Jeremiah
Jerem 12.3	them (the wicked)	like, –, quasi	sheep for slaughter	Jeremiah
Jerem. 12.8	my heritage	as, ὡς, quasi	a lion in the forest	Jeremiah
Jerem. 12.9	my heritage	as, –, –	a speckled bird	Jeremiah
Jerem. 13.11	the house of Israel > me	as, καθάπερ, sicut	a girdle (around) > the loins of a man	Jeremiah
Jerem. 13.24	I > (scatter) them	as, ὡς, quasi	wind > stubble	Jeremiah
Jerem. 14.6	wild asses (snuffed up the wind)	like, –, quasi	dragons	Jeremiah
Jerem. 14.9	thou (hope of Israel)	as, ὥσπερ, velut as, ὡς, ut	a man astounded a mighty man …	Jeremiah
Jerem. 16.4	they (people born here)	as, εἰς παράδειγμα, in	dung on face of earth	Jeremiah
Jerem. 17.6	a trusting man	like, ὡς, quasi	the heath in the desert	Jeremiah/the Lord
Jerem. 17.8	he (who trusts in the Lord)	as, ὡς, quasi	a tree planted by water	Jeremiah

Book Passage	Tenor	Prothesis	Vehicle	Speaker
Jerem. 17.11	a man gaining riches unjustly and losing them	as, –, –	a partridge sitting on eggs but not hatching them	Jeremiah
Jerem. 18.6	I/the Lord > you	as/as, καθὼς/ὡς, sicut/sicut	a potter > his clay	Jeremiah
Jerem. 18.17	I > (will scatter) my people	as, ὡς, sicut	east wind > the enemy	Jeremiah/theLord
Jerem. 20.9	the Lord's word in my heart	as, ὡς, quasi	a burning fire in my bones	Jeremiah
Jerem. 20.11	the Lord with me	as, καθὼς, quasi	a mighty fighter	Jeremiah
Jerem. 21.12	my fury	like, ὡς, ut	fire	Jeremiah/the Lord
Jerem 23.9	I	like, ὡς, quasi like, ὡς, quasi	a drunken man a man overcome by wine	Jeremiah
Jerem. 23.12	their way (prophets and priests)	as, εἰς, *quasi*	slippery ways in darkness	Jeremiah/the Lord
Jerem. 23.14	(prophets of Jerusalem) the inhabitants	as, ὡς, ut as, ὥσπερ, quasi	Sodom Gomorrha	Jeremiah/the Lord
Jerem. 23.29	my word (the Lord)	as, ὥσπερ, quasi like, ὡς, quasi	a fire a hammer	Jeremiah/the Lord
Jerem. 24.2	figs	like	ripe figs	[a comparison]
Jerem. 24.5	Jews captive of Judah	like, ὡς, sicut	good figs	Jeremiah/the Lord
Jerem. 24 8	Zedekiah et alii	as, ὡς, sicut	evil figs	Jeremiah/the Lord
Jerem. 25.38	He (the Lord)	as, ὥσπερ, quasi	the lion	Jeremiah

Book Passage	Tenor	Prothesis	Vehicle	Speaker
Jerem. 26.18	Zion (plowed)	like, ὡς, quasi	a field for plowing	Jeremiah/the Lord
Jerem. 29.17	them (citizens of Babylon)	like –, quasi	vile figs	Jeremiah/the Lord
Jerem. 30.6	every man	as, –, quasi	a woman in labor	Jeremiah/the Lord
Jerem. 33.22	the seed of David (unnumbered)	as, –, sicuti	stars of heaven and sand of sea	Jeremiah/the Lord
Jerem 43.12	king of Babylon > the land of Egypt	as, ὥσπερ, sicut	a shepherd > his garment	Jeremiah
Jerem. 46.8	Egypt (rises up) his waters (moved)	like, –, instar like, –, vellut	a flood the rivers	Jeremiah/the Lord
Jerem. 46.20–23	Egypt hired men 22 the voice they 23 they (more)	like like like as than	a fair heifer 21 fatted bullocks 22 a serpent hewers of wood 23 grasshoppers	Jeremiah/the Lord
Jerem 48.6	you	like, –, quasi	the heath in wild	Jeremiah/the Lord
Jerem. 48.28	dwellers in Moab	like, –, quasi	the dove …	Jeremiah/the Lord
Jerem. 48.36	my heart (shall sound)	like, – quasi like, –, –	pipes pipes for Kirheres	Jeremiah/the Lord
Jerem. 48.38	Moab (broken)	like, –, sicut	a vessel without pleasure	Jeremiah/the Lord
Jerem. 49.16	your nest (high)	as, –, quasi	the eagle	Jeremiah
Jerem. 49.19	he	like, –, quasi	a lion	Jeremiah

Book Passage	Tenor	Prothesis	Vehicle	Speaker
Jerem. 49.22	he (will fly) men of Edom (heart)	as, –, quasi as, –, quasi	the eagle heart of a birthing woman	Jeremiah
Jerem. 50.37	they	as, –, quasi	women	Jeremiah
Jerem. 50.42	their voice they shall ride	like, –, quasi like, –, sicut	the sea a man to battle	Jeremiah/the Lord
Jerem. 50.43	(king of Babylon)	as, –, quasi	a woman in labor	Jeremiah
Jerem 50.44	(king of Babylon)	like, –, quasi	a lion	Jeremiah/the Lord
Jerem 51.7	Babylon	–, –, –	a golden cup	"
Jerem. 51.14	men	as, –, quasi	caterpillars	Jeremiah/the Lord
Jerem 51.20	Thou	–, –, –,	my battle-ax	"
Jerem. 51.30	men of Babylon	as, –, quasi	women	Jeremiah/the Lord
Jerem. 51.33	daughter of Babylon	like, –, quasi	a threshingfloot	Jeremiah/the Lord
Jerem. 51.34	me he	–, –, quasi like, –, quasi	an empty vessel a dragon	Jeremiah/the Lord
Jerem. 51.38	they	like, –, ut as, –, voluti	lions lions' whelps	Jeremiah/the Lord
Jerem. 51.40	them	like, –, quasi like, –, quasi	lambs rams	Jeremiah/the Lord
Jerem. 51.55	Babylon's waves	like, –, quasi	great waters	Jeremiah
Lamentations of Jeremiah 1.1	the city	as, ὡς, quasi	a widow	Jeremiah
Lam/Jerem. 1.6	her princes	like, ὡς, velut	harts	Jeremiah
Lam/Jerem. 1.17	Jerusalem	as, εἰς, quasi	a menstruous woman	Jeremiah

Book Passage	Tenor	Prothesis	Vehicle	Speaker
Lam/Jerem. 2.3–7	the Lord (burned) 4 he (bent his bow) he (stood) his fury 5 the Lord 6 his tabernacle 7 they made a noise	like, ὡς, quasi 4 like, ὡς, quasi as, ὡς, quasi like, ὡς, quasi 5 as, ὡς, velut 6 as if, ὡς, quasi 7 as, ὡς, sicut	a flaming fire 4 an enemy an adversary fire 5 an enemy 6 a garden 7 day of solemn feast	Jeremiah
Lam/Jerem. 2.13	your breach (great)	like, –, velut	the sea	Jeremiah
Lam/Jerem. 2.18	tears (fun down)	like, ὡς, quasi	a river	Jeremiah
Lam/Jerem. 3.10	He (the Lord)	as, –, – as, –, –	a bear a lion	Jeremiah
Lam/Jerem. 3.12	me	as, ὡς, quasi	a mark for the arrow	Jeremiah
Lam/Jerem. 3.45	us	as, –, –	offscouring and refuse	Jeremiah
Lam/Jerem. 3.52	me	like, ὡς, quasi	a bird	Jeremiah
Lam/Jerem. 4.2	sons of Zion (comparable) (esteemed)	to, –, – as, εἰς, in	fine gold earthen pitchers	Jeremiah
Lam/Jerem. 4.3	daughter of my people (cruel)	like, ὡς, quasi	ostriches in the wilderness	Jeremiah

Book Passage	Tenor	Prothesis	Vehicle	Speaker
Lam/Jerem. 4.7–9	Nazarites (purer) (whiter) (more ruddy) 8 their visage (blacker), skin (withered) 9 slain with sword (better)	than, ὑπὲρ, (ablat.) than, ὑπὲρ, (ablat.) than, ὑπὲρ, (ablat.) 8 than, ὑπὲρ, super like, ὥσπερ, quasi 9 than, ἤ, quam	snow milk rubies 8 a coal a stick 9 slain with hunger	Jeremiah
Lam/Jerem 4.14	they (sons of Zion)	as, –, –	blind men	Jeremiah
Lam/Jerem. 4.19	our persecutors (swifter)	than, ὑπὲρ, (ablat.)	eagles of the heaven	Jeremiah
Lam/Jerem. 5.10	our skin (black)	like, ὡς, quasi	an oven	Jeremiah
Ezekiel 1.4	brightness of whirlwind	as, ὡς, quasi	colour of amber	Ezekiel
Ezek. 1.5	appearance of 4 creatures	had, ὡς, –	likeness of a man	Ezekiel
Ezek. 1.7	sole of their feet (sparkled)	like, –, quasi like, ὡς, quasi	sole of a calf's foot burnished brass	Ezekiel
Ezek. 1.8	hands under their wings	of, genitive, genitive	a man	Ezekiel
Ezek. 1.10	their faces	likeness, ὁμοίωσις, similitudo	of a man, a lion an ox, an eagle	Ezekiel
Ezek. 1.13	their appearance	like, ὡς, quasi like, ὡς, quasi	burning coals of fire appearance of lamps	Ezekiel

Book Passage	Tenor	Prothesis	Vehicle	Speaker
Ezek. 1.14	their appearance	as, –, in similtudinem	a flash of lightning	Ezekiel
Ezek. 1.16	wheels (color) their appearance	like unto, ὡς, quasi; as it were, καθὼς, quasi	beryl a wheel in a wheel	Ezekiel
Ezek. 1.22	likeness of the firmament	as, ὡσεὶ, quasi	color of terrible crystal	Ezekiel
Ezek. 1.24	noise of their winds	like, ὡς, quasi as, –, quasi as, –, quasi	noise of great waters; the voice of the Almighty; the noise of an host	Ezekiel
Ezek. 1.26	likeness	of as, ὡς, quasi as, ὡς, quasi	a throne a sapphire stone the appearance of a man	Ezekiel
Ezek. 1.27	color	as, –, quasi as, ὡς, velut as it were, ὡς, quasi	amber appearance of fire appearance of fire	Ezekiel
Ezek. 1.28	brightness, glory of the Lord	as, ὡς, velut	rainbow on a rainy day	Ezekiel
Ezek. 3.3	taste of a roll (sweet)	as, ὡς, sicut	honey	Ezekiel
Ezek. 3.9	your forehead (harder)	as (than), [comp.], ut (ut)	flint	Ezekiel
Ezek. 7.16	those who escape	like, –, quasi	doves of the valley	Ezekiel
Ezek. 7.17	knees (weak)	as, –, –	water	Ezekiel
Ezek. 8.2 8.3	a likeness 3 form	as, –, ὡς, quasi as / as, ὡς, quasi 3 of, [genit.], [gen.]	appearance of fire/brightness/ color of amber 3 hand	Ezekiel

Book Passage	Tenor	Prothesis	Vehicle	Speaker
Ezek. 10.1	there appeared	as it were, ὡς, quasi as, –, quasi	a sapphire stone likeness of a throne	Ezekiel
Ezek. 10.8	form	of, ὁμοίωμα, similitudo	a man's hand	Ezekiel
Ezek. 10.9	appearance of the wheels	as, ὡς, quasi	color of a beryl stone	Ezekiel
Ezek. 10.10	one likeness	as if, ὃν τρόπον, quasi	a wheel in a wheel	Ezekiel
Ezek. 10.21–22	the likeness 22 likeness of faces	of, –, – –, –, –	the hands of a man; 22 faces I saw by the river	Ezekiel
Ezek. 13.4	your prophets	like, ὡς, quasi	foxes in the desert	Ezekiel
Ezek. 16.7	you (to multiply)	as, καθὼς, quasi	bud of the field	Ezekiel/the Lord
Ezek. 16.31	thou, Israel	as, ὡς, quasi	a harlot	Ezekiel/the Lord
Ezek. 16.32	[thou, Israel]	as, ὡς, quasi	an adulterous wife	Ezekiel/the Lord
Ezek. 16.44	the daughter	as, καθὼς, sicut	the mother	Ezekiel/the Lord
Ezek. 19.2	your mother	–, –, –	a lionness	Ezekiel/the Lord
Ezek. 19.10	your mother	like, ὡς, quasi	a vine in your blood	Ezekiel/the Lord
Ezek. 20.32	we	as, ὡς, sicut	the heathen, the families of the countries	Ezekiel/the Lord
Ezek. 21.32	you	for, –, –	fuel for the fire	Ezekiel/the Lord
Ezek. 22.20	I will gather you in my anger	as, καθὼς, ut	they gather silver etc. in a furnace	Ezekiel/the Lord

Book Passage	Tenor	Prothesis	Vehicle	Speaker
Ezek. 22.22	you melted	as, ὃν τρόπον, ut	silver melted in a furnace	Ezekiel/the Lord
Ezek. 22.27	her princes	like, ὡς, quasi	ravening wolves	Ezekiel/the Lord
Ezek. 23.45	them	after the manner of, ἐκδικήσει, judicio	adulteresses; murderesses	Ezekiel/the Lord
Ezek. 26.14	you (I will make)	like, εἰς, in	top of a rock; a place to spread nets	Ezekiel/the Lord
Ezek. 32.2	you/Pharoah	like, ὡμοιώθης, assimilatus es as, ὡς, –	a young lion a whale	Ezekiel/the Lord
Ezek. 38.9	you [Gog]	like, ὡς, quasi like, –, quasi	a storm a cloud	Ezekiel/the Lord
Ezek. 40.3	a man	like, ὡσεὶ, quasi	brass	Ezekiel
Ezek. 43.2	his voice	like, ὡς, quasi	the noise of many waters	Ezekiel
Daniel 2.35	iron, clay, etc.	like, ὡσεὶ, quasi	chaff of summer	Daniel
Daniel 2.40	fourth kingdom (strong)	as, ὡς, velut	iron	Daniel
Daniel 2.42	kingdom (strong and broken)	as, –, –	toes part iron and part clay	Daniel
Daniel 4.33	he (ate grass) his hair his nails	like, ὡς, ut like, ὡς, in similitudinem like, ὡς, quasi	oxen eagles' feathers birds' claws	Daniel

Book Passage	Tenor	Prothesis	Vehicle	Speaker
Daniel 7.4–6	4 first beast 5 another beast 6 another beast	4 like, ὡσεὶ, quasi 5 like, ὡσεὶ, similis 6 like, ὡσεὶ, quasi	4 a lion 5 a bear 6 a leopard	Daniel
Daniel 7.8	eyes	like	a man's	Daniel
Daniel 7.9	garment (white) hair of head throne wheels	as, ὡσεὶ, quasi like, ὡσεὶ, quasi like, –, – as, –, –	snow pure wool fiery flame burning fire	Daniel
Daniel 10.6	his body his face his eyes his arms and feet his voice	like, ὡσεὶ, quasi the appearance of, ὡσεὶ, velut as, ὡσεὶ, ut like, ὡς, quasi like, ὡς, ut	the beryl lightning lamps of fire polished brass voice of a multitude	Daniel
Daniel 12.3	the wise (shall shine); those turning many to righteousness	as, ὡς, quasi as, ὡς, quasi	brightness of the firmament the stars	Daniel
Hosea 1.10	number of Israeli	as, ὡς, quasi	sand of the sea	Hosea
Hosea 2.3	her (your mother)	like, ὡς, velut	dry land	Hosea
Hosea 4.16	Israel them	as, ὡς, sicut as, ὡς, quasi	back- sliding door a lamb	Hosea
Hosea 5.10	princes of Judah my wrath	like, ὡς, quasi like, ὡς, quasi	them that remove the bound; water	Hosea
Hosea 5.14	I	as / as, ὡς / ὡς, quasi / quasi	a lion / young lion	Hosea

Book Passage	Tenor	Prothesis	Vehicle	Speaker
Hosea 6.3	he/the Lord	as /as, ὡς / ὡς, quasi / quasi	the rain / the latter and former rain	Hosea
Hosea 6.4	your goodness	as / as, ὡς / ὡς, quasi / quasi	a morning cloud the early dew	Hosea
Hosea 6.7	people (of Gilead)	like, ὡς, sicut	men	Hosea
Hosea 6.9	company of priests	as, –, quasi	troops of robbers	Hosea
Hosea 7.4	they (Samarians)	as, ὡς, quasi	an oven glowing	Hosea
Hosea 7.6	their heart	like, ὡς, quasi as, ὡς, quasi	an oven a flaming fire	Hosea
Hosea 7.7	they (hot)	as, ὡς, quasi	an oven	Hosea
Hosea 7.11	Ephraim	like, ὡς, quasi	a silly dove	Hosea
Hosea 7.12	them	as, καθὼς, quasi	fowls of heaven	Hosea
Hosea 7.16	they	like, ὡς, quasi	a deceitful bow	Hosea
Hosea 8.1	he	as, ὡς, quasi	an eagle	Hosea
Hosea 8.8	Israel	as, ὡς, quasi	a worthless vessel	Hosea
Hosea 9.4	sacrifices	as, ὡς, quasi	bread of mourning	Hosea
Hosea 9.10	Israel your fathers	like, ὡς, quasi as, ὡς, quasi	wild grapes first ripe figs	Hosea
Hosea 9.11	their glory	like, ὡς, quas	aa bird	Hosea
Hosea 10.4	judgment	as, ὡς, quasi	hemlock	Hosea
Hosea 10.7	Samaria's king (cast off)	as, ὡς, quasi	foam on water	Hosea
Hosea 10.11	Ephraim	as, –, –	a heifer taught	Hosea
Hosea 11.10–11	he (the Lord) 11 they (shall tremble)	like, ὡς, quasi as/as, ὡς/ὡς, quasi/quasi	a lion a bird / a dove	Hosea

Book Passage	Tenor	Prothesis	Vehicle	Speaker
Hosea 13.3	they (Israelites)	as, ὡς, quasi as, ὡς, sicut as, ὥσπερ, sicut as, ὡς, sicut	morning cloud early dew chaff smoke	Hosea
Hosea 13.7–8	I/the Lord (will be) 8 (will meet) (will devour)	as, ὡς, quasi as, ὡς, sicut 8 as, ὡς, quasi like, –, quasi	a lion a leopard a bear a lion	Hosea
Hosea 14.5	I/the Lord he/Ashur	as, ὡς, quasi as, ὡς, sicut as, ὡς, ut	the dew the lily Lebanon	Hosea
Hosea 14.6	Ashur's beauty his smell	as, ὡς, quasi as, ὡς, ut	the olive tree Lebanon	Hosea
Hosea 14.7–8	they (shall revive) (shall grow) the scent 8 Ephraim	as, –, quasi as, ὡς, sicut as, ὡς, sicut 8 like, ὡς, ut	the corn the vine wine of Lebanon green fir tree	Hosea
Joel 1.8	you (lament)	like, ὑπὲρ, quasi	a virgin	Joel
Joel 2.3	the land before them	as, ὡς, quasi	the garden of Eden	Joel
Joel 2.4	their appearance they shall run	as, ὡς, quasi as, ὡς, quasi	horses horsemen	Joel
Joel 2.5	they (shall leap)	like, ὡς, sicut like, ὡς, sicut as, ὡς, velut	noise of chariots noise of fire strong people set for battle	Joel
Joel 2.7	they (shall run) (shall climb the wall)	like, ὡς, sicut like, ὡς, quasi	mighty men men of war	Joel
Joel 2.9	they (shall enter)	like, ὡς, quasi	a thief	Joel
Amos 2.9	the Amorite's height, (strong)	like, καθὼς, – as, ὡς, quasi	height of cedars the oaks	Amos/the Lord

Book Passage	Tenor	Prothesis	Vehicle	Speaker
Amos 2.13	I (am pressed)	as, ὃν τρόπον, sicut	a cart full of sheaves	Amos/the Lord
Amos 3.12	the children of Israel (taken out)	as, ὃν τρόπον, quo modo si	2 legs or piece of ear (taken out of mouth of a lion)	Amos/the Lord
Amos 4.11	I (overthrew)>you you	as, καθὼς, sicut as, ὡς, quasi	God > Sodom & Gomorrha; a firebrand plucked out of the fire	Amos/the Lord
Amos 5.19	the Lord's day shall be darkness (and not light)	as if, ὃν τρόπον, quo modo si	a man fleeing from a lion met a bear Or went into his house and a serpent bit him [!]	Amos/the Lord
Amos 5.24	judgment (run down); justice	as, ὡς, quasi as, ὡς, quasi	water a mighty stream	Amos/the Lord
Amos 9.9	I (will sift) > the house of Israel	like as, ὃν τρόπον, sicut	corn sifted in a sieve	Amos/the Lord
Obadiah 1.4	you	as, ὡς, ut	eagle	Obadiah/the Lord
Obadiah 1.18	the house of Jacob the house of Esau	−, −, − for, εἰς, −	a fire stubble	Obadiah/the Lord
Micah 1.4	valleys (cleft)	as, ὡς, sicut as, ὡς, sicut	wax before fire waters from steep	Micah
Micah 1.6	Samaria	as, εἰς, quasi as, εἰς, −	heap of the field plantings of a vineyard	Micah/the Lord
Micah 1.8	I (wailing) (mourning)	like, ὡς, velut as, ὡς, quasi	dragons owls	Micah

Book Passage	Tenor	Prothesis	Vehicle	Speaker
Micah 1.16	become bald	as, ὡς, sicut	an eagle	Micah/the Lord
Micah 2.12	(Jacob and his people returning)	as, ὡς, quasi as, ὡς, quasi	the sheep of Bozra flock in the fold	Micah
Micah 5.8	remnant of Jacob among Gentiles	as, ὡς, quasi as, ὡς, quasi	a lion among beasts, a young lion among sheep	Micah
Micah 7.1	I	as when, ὡς, sicut as, ὡς, –	one gathering summer fruits, grape-gleanings	Micah
Micah 7.4	the best of them the most upright (sharper)	as, ὡς, quasi than, –, quasi	a brier a thorn hedge	Micah
Nahum 1.6	his fury	like, –, ut	fire	Nahum
Nahum 1.10	they [the Lord's enemies] (folded) (drunken) (devoured)	as, ὡς, sicut as, –, – as, ὡς, quasi	thorns drunkards stubble	Nahum
Habakkuk 1.8–9	his horses (swifter) (more fierce) (fly) 9 their faces (shall sup up) (gather captivity)	than, ὑπὲρ, [ablat.] than, ὑπὲρ, [ablat.] as, ὡς, quasi as, –, – as, ὡς, quasi	leopards evening wolves the eagle the east wind sand	Habakkuk
Habak. 1.14	men	as, ὡς, quasi as, ὡς, quasi	fish of the sea creeping things with no ruler	Habakkuk
Habak. 3.4	God's brightness	as, ὡς, ut	the light	Habakkuk
Habak. 3.14	they (villagers)	as, ὡς, ut	a whirlwind	Habakkuk
Habak. 3.19	my feet	like, –, quasi	hinds' feet	Habakkuk

Book Passage	Tenor	Prothesis	Vehicle	Speaker
Zechariah 4.1	me (awakened)	as, ὃν τρόπον, quasi	a man waken from sleep	Zechariah
Zecha. 5.9	wings	like, ὡς, quasi	wings of a stork	Zechariah
Zecha. 7.12	their hearts	as, –, ut	an adamant stone	Zechariah
Zecha. 9.3	silver fine gold	as, ὡς, quasi as, ὡς, ut	dust mire of the streets	Zechariah
Zecha. 9.14	the Lord's arrow	as, ὡς, ut	lightning	Zechariah
Zecha. 10.2	the diviners (went)	as, ὡς, quasi	a flock	Zechariah
Zecha. 10.3	the house of Judah	–, –, – as, ὡς, quasi	his flock his horse in battle	Zechariah
Zecha. 10.5	they	as, ὡς, quasi	mighty men	Zechariah
Zecha. 10.7	warriors of Ephraim; their heart (shall rejoice)	like, ὡς, quasi as, ὡς, quasi	a mighty man through wine	Zechariah
Zecha. 12.6	governors of Judah	like, ὡς, sicut like, ὡς, sicut	hearth of fire a torch of fire	Zechariah/ the Lord
Malachi 4.1	a day (burning) all the wicked	as, ὡς, quasi –, –, –	an oven stubble	Malachi

* * *

The New Testament Summary of Similes

The following Chart summarizes the similes by *Tenor, Prothesis* and *Vehicle*.

Book Passage	Tenor	Prothesis	Vehicle	Speaker
Matthew 3.16	spirit of God descending	like, ὡσεὶ, sicut	a dove	Matthew
Matt. 6.25	life (more) body	than, [gen.], quam than, [gen.], quam	meat raiment	Jesus
Matt. 7.24	him	liken unto, ὁμοιώσω, assimilabitur	a wise man who built house on a rock	Jesus
Matt. 7.26	everyone who hears and doth not	shall be likened to ὁμοιωθήσεται similis erit	a fool who built house on sand	Jesus
Matt. 9.36	they (multitude)	as, ὡς, sicut	sheep with no shepherd	Matthew
Matt. 10.16	you be (wise) (harmless)	as, ὡς, sicut as, ὡς, sicut as, ὡς, sicut	sheep among wolves serpents / doves	Jesus
Matt. 10.31	you (more valuable)	than, [gen.], [abl.]	many sparrows	Jesus
Matt. 11.16	this generation	like unto, ὁμοία, similes	children sitting in markets	Jesus
Matt. 12.12	a man (better)	than, [gen.], [abl.]	a sheep	Jesus
Matt. 13.24	kingdom of heaven	likened to, Ὡμοιώθη, simile	a man sowing good seed	Jesus

Book Passage	Tenor	Prothesis	Vehicle	Speaker
Matt. 13.31	kingdom of heaven	like to, Ὁμοία, similis	a grain of mustard seed	Jesus
Matt. 13.33	kingdom of heaven	like unto, Ὁμοία, similis	leaven	Jesus
Matt. 13.44	kingdom of heaven	like unto, ὁμοία, simile	treasure hid in a field	Jesus
Matt. 13.45	kingdom of heaven	like unto, ὁμοία, simile	a merchant man	Jesus
Matt. 13.47	kingdom of heaven	like unto, ὁμοία, simile	a net cast into the sea	Jesus
Matt. 13.52	every scribe …	like unto, ὅμοιός, similis	a house-holder …	Jesus
Matt. 17.20	faith	as, ὡς, sicut	a mustard seed	Jesus
Matt. 18.3	ye	as, ὡς, sicut	little children	Jesus
Matt. 18.23	kingdom of heaven	likened unto, ὡμοιώθη, assimilatum est	a certain king	Jesus
Matt. 19.24	a rich man into heaven (easier)	than, ἤ, quam	camel through the eye of a needle	Jesus
Matt. 20.1	kingdom of heaven	like unto, ὁμοία, simile	an householder	Jesus
Matt. 22.2	kingdom of heaven	like unto, Ὡμοιώθη, simile	a certain king …	Jesus
Matt. 22.30	the resurrected	as, ὡς, sicut	angels of God	Jesus
Matt. 23.27	scribes and hypocrites	like unto, παρομοιάζετε, similes	whited sepulchres	Jesus
Matt. 24.27	coming of the son of man	as, ὥσπερ, sicut	lightning from the east	Jesus

Book Passage	Tenor	Prothesis	Vehicle	Speaker
Matt. 25.1	the kingdom of heaven	likened unto, ὁμοιωθήσεται, simile est	ten virgins with lamps	Jesus
Matt. 25.14	kingdom of heaven	as, ὥσπερ, sicut	a man going on a journey	Jesus
Matt. 25.32	He > (separate) nations	as, ὥσπερ, sicut	a shepherd > his sheep	Jesus
Matt. 28.3–4	His countenance raiment (white) his keepers	like, ὡς, sicut as, ὡς, sicut as, ὡς, velut	lightning snow dead men	Matthew
Mark 1.10	the Spirit	like, ὡς, tamquam	a dove	Mark
Mark 4.26	the kingdom of God	as if, ὡς, quemadmodum si	a man sh. cast seed into ground	Jesus
Mark 4.30–31	the kingdom of God	like, ὡς, sicut	a grain of mustard seed	Jesus
Mark 6.34	the people	as, ὡς, sicut	sheep without a shepherd	Mark
Mark 8.24	men	as, ὡς, velut	trees	Jesus
Mark 9.3	his raiment (white)	as, οἷα, velut	snow, as no fuller could white	Mark
Mark 10.25	a wealthy man > kingdom of God	than, ἤ, quam	a camel > the eye of a needle (easier)	Jesus
Mark. 12.25	they (dead shall rise)	as, ὡς, sicut	angels in heaven	Jesus
Mark 13.34	the Son of man	as, ὡς, sicut	a man taking a far journey	Jesus
Luke 3.22	the Holy Ghost	like, ὡσεὶ, sicut	a dove	Luke
Luke 6.47–48	he who hears my sayings …	like, ὅμοιός, similis	a man who built his house on a rock	Jesus

Book Passage	Tenor	Prothesis	Vehicle	Speaker
Luke 6.49	he who hears and does not do …	like, ὅμοιός, similis	a man who builds without a foundation	Jesus
Luke 7.31–32	people of this generation	like, ὅμοιοί, similes	children sitting in the market	Jesus
Luke 10.3	you (Apostles)	as, ὡς, sicut	lambs among wolves	Jesus
Luke 10.18	Satan	as, ὡς, sicut	lightning from heaven	Jesus
Luke 12.36	you	like unto, ὅμοιοί, similes	men who wait for their lord	Jesus
Luke 13.18–19	the kingdom of God	like, ὁμοία, simile	a grain of mustard seed	Jesus
Luke 13.20–21	the kingdom of God	like, ὁμοία, simile	leaven hidden in meal	Jesus
Luke 13.34	I/Jesus > your children	as, ὃν τρόπον, quemadmodum	a hen > her brood	Jesus
Luke 17.6	faith	as, ὡς, sicut	a grain of mustard seed	Jesus
Luke 18.25	a rich man > kingdom of God	than, ἤ, quam	a camel > a needle's eye (easier)	Jesus
Luke 21.35	the coming kingdom of God	as, ὡς, tamquam	a snare	Jesus
John 1.32	the Spirit (descending)	like, ὡς, quasi	a dove	John
John 3.14	the Son of man (to be lifted up)	as, καθὼς, sicut	the serpent in the desert	Jesus
Acts 2.2–3	sound from heaven 3 cloven tongues	as, ὥσπερ, tamquam 3 like as, ὡσεὶ, tamquam	a mighty wind 3 fire	(Luke)

Book Passage	Tenor	Prothesis	Vehicle	Speaker
Acts 8.32	he	as, ὡς, tamquam like, ὡς, sicus	sheep to slaughter lamb to shearing	(Luke)
Acts 9.18	(things) fell from his eyes	as it had been, ὡσεὶ, tamquam	scales	(Luke)
Acts 11.5	a vision: a vessel from heaven	as it had been, ὡς, velut	a great sheet	Peter
Acts 17.29	Godhead (NOT)	like unto, ὅμοιον, simile	gold, silver or stone	Paul
1st Cor. 13.1	I	as, –, velut	sounding brass / a tinkling cymbal	Paul
2nd Cor. 11.3	your minds corrupted by > Christ's simplicity	as, ὡς, sicut	Eve beguiled by > serpent	Paul
Phil. 2.15	you (Philippians shine)	as, ὡς, sicut	lights in the world	Paul
1 Thess. 5.2	day of the Lord (comes)	as, ὡς, sicut	a thief in the night	Paul
1 Thess. 5.3	sudden destruction (comes)	as, ὥσπερ, sicut	pain of childbirth	Paul
Hebrews 4.12	the word of God (sharper)	than, ὑπὲρ, [ablat.]	a two-edged sword	Paul
James 1.11	the rich man shall fade	so, οὕτω, ita (no sooner)	the sun withers the grass, etc.	James
James 1.23	a hearer of the word and not a doer	like unto, ἔοικεν, comparabitur	a man be-holding his face in a mirror	James
James 5.3	rust of your gold and silver	as it were, ὡς, sicut	fire	James

Book Passage	Tenor	Prothesis	Vehicle	Speaker
1 Peter 1.7	your faith (more precious)	than, [genit.], [ablat.]	gold that perishes	Peter
1 Peter 1.18–19	(ye were re-deemed with) the previous blood of Christ	as of, ὡς, quasi	a perfect lamb	Peter
1 Peter 1.24	all flesh the glory of man	as, ὡς, ut as, ὡς, tamquam	grass the flower of grass	Peter
1 Peter 2.4–5	(the Lord) 5 you also	as, –, – as, ὡς, tamquam	a living stone 5 lively stones	Peter
1 Peter 2.16	ye (free)	as, ὡς, quasi	the servants of God	Peter
1 Peter 5.8	your adversary the devil	as, ὡς, tamquam	a roaring lion searching for a victim	Peter
2 Peter 3.10	the day of the Lord (will come)	as, ὡς, ut	a thief in the night	Peter
Jude 10	those who speak what they know naturally	as, ὡς, tamquam	brute beasts	Jude
Rev. 1.10	a great voice	as, ὡς, tamquam	(sound of) a trumpet	John the Apostle
Rev 1.14	his head/hairs (white) his eyes	like, ὡς, tamquam as, ὡς, tamquam as, ὡς, tamquam	wool snow a flame of fire	John the Apostle
Rev. 1.15	his feet his voice	like unto, ὅμοιοι, similes as if, ὡς, sicut as, ὡς, tamquam	fine brass burned in a furnace sound of water	John the Apostle
Rev. 1.16	His countenance	as, ὡς, sicut	the sun	John the Apostle

Book Passage	Tenor	Prothesis	Vehicle	Speaker
Rev. 1.17	I (fell at his feet)	as, ὡς, tamquam	dead (a corpse)	John the Apostle
Rev. 2.18	His eyes His feet	like unto, ὡς, tamquam; like, ὅμοιοι, similes	a flame of fire fine brass	the Son of God
Rev. 3.3	I	as, ὡς, tamquam	a thief	the Son of God
Rev. 4.1	first voice	as it were, ὡς, tamquam	a trumpet	John the Apostle
Rev. 4.3	he sitting a rainbow around	like, ὅμοιός, similis like unto, ὁμοίως, similes	a jasper and sardine stone; an emerald	John the Apostle
Rev. 4.6	a sea of glass	like unto, ὁμοία, simile	crystal	John the Apostle
Rev. 4.7	first beast second beast third beast (face) fourth beast	like, ὅμοιον, simile like, ὅμοιον, simile as, ὡς, quasi like, ὅμοιον, simile	a lion a calf a man a flying eagle	John the Apostle
Rev. 6.1	(the voice of) one of the four beasts	as it were, ὡς, tamquam	the noise of thunder	John the Apostle
Rev. 6.12–14	the sun (black) the moon 13 stars > heaven 14 heaven (departing)	as, ὡς, tamquam as, ὡς, sicut 13 as, ὡς, sicut 14 as, ὡς, sicut	sackcloth of hair blood 13 figs > tree 14 a scroll (rolled up)	John the Apostle
Rev. 8.8	sound of second angel	as it were, ὡς, tamquam	a burning mountain cast into the sea	John the Apostle
Rev. 8.10	a great star falling and burning	as it were, ὡς, tamquam	a lamp	John the Apostle
Rev. 9.3	power of locusts	as, ὡς, sicut	scorpions	John the Apostle

Book Passage	Tenor	Prothesis	Vehicle	Speaker
Rev. 9.5	their torment	as, ὡς, ut	torment of a scorpion > a man	John the Apostle
Rev. 9.7	shapes of locusts head-wear their faces	like, ὅμοια, similes as it were, ὡς, similes as, ὡς, tamquam	horses > battle golden crowns faces of men	John the Apostle
Rev. 9.8	their hair their teeth	as, ὡς, sicut as, ὡς, sicut	women's hair lions' teeth	John the Apostle
Rev. 9.9	their sound of their wings	as it were, ὡς, sicut as, ὡς, sicut	breastplates of iron, many-horse-chariots > battle	John the Apostle
Rev 9.10	their tails	like, ὁμοίας, similes	scorpions with stings	John the Apostle
Rev. 9.17	heads of horses	as, ὡς, tamquam	heads of lions	John the Apostle
Rev. 9.19	their tails	like unto, ὅμοιαι, similes	serpents	John the Apostle
Rev. 10.1	his face his feet	as it were, ὡς, ut as, ὡς, tamquam	the sun pillars of fire	John the Apostle
Rev. 10.3	his voice	as when, ὥσπερ, quemadmodum cum	a lion's roar	John the Apostle
Rev. 10.9–10	taste of book in my mouth (sweet)	as, ὡς, tamquam	honey	John the Apostle
Rev. 11.1	a reed	like, ὅμοιός, similis	a rod	John the Apostle
Rev. 13.2	the beast his feet his mouth	like unto, ὅμοιον, similis as, ὡς, sicut as, ὡς, sicut	a leopard feet of a bear a lion's mouth	John the Apostle

Book Passage	Tenor	Prothesis	Vehicle	Speaker
Rev. 13.11	two horns of the beast he spoke	like, ὅμοια, similia as, ὡς, sicut	a lamb a dragon	John the Apostle
Rev. 14.2	a voice from heaven	as, ὡς, tamquam as, ὡς, tamquam	voice of many waters, of great thunder, of harpers harping	John the Apostle
Rev. 15.2	I saw	as it were, ὡς, tamquam	a sea of glass mingled with fire	John the Apostle
Rev. 18.21	the angel's stone	like, ὡς, quasi	a great millstone	John the Apostle
Rev. 19.12	His eyes	as, ὡς, sicut	a flame of fire	John the Apostle
Rev. 21.2	new Jerusalem	as, ὡς, sicut	a bride adorned for her husband	John the Apostle
Rev. 21.11	her light (clear)	like unto, ὅμοιος, simile; even like, ὡς, tamquam; as, –, sicut	a precious stone a jasper stone crystal	John the Apostle
Rev. 21.18	the city	like unto, ὅμοιον, simile	clear glass	John the Apostle
Rev. 22.1	pure river of water of life (clear)	as, ὡς, tamquam	crystal	John the Apostle

Appendices

An Outline of Similes in the Old Testament

Genesis 13.16 [thy seed ≈ dust], 22.17 [thy seed ≈ stars; ≈ sand], 25.25 [first twin (Esau) of Rebekah and Isaac ≈ an hairy garment], 26.4 [thy seed ≈ the stars of heaven], 27.27 [the smell of my son (Jacob) ≈ the smell of a blessed field], 49.4 [thou (Reuben) unstable ≈ water], 49.9 [Judah ≈ a lion's whelp; thou (my son) ≈ a lion, an old lion], 49.12 [his (Judah's) eyes (red) ≈ wine; his teeth (white) ≈ milk], 49.27 [Benjamin ≈ a wolf].

Exodus 4.6 [his hand ≈ snow], 15.10 [they (Pharoah's army) ≈ lead], 16.14 [a small round thing ≈ hoar frost], 16.31 it/Manna ≈ a white coriander seed; [its taste ≈ wafers made with honey], 19.18 [smoke (the Lord's fire on Sinai) ≈ smoke of a furnace], 24.17 [the sight of the glory of the Lord ≈ devouring fire on Mt Sinai], 33.11 [Lord spoke > Moses ≈ someone > a friend].

Leviticus 0

Numbers 11.7 [manna ≈ coriander seed; its color ≈ bdillium], 13.33 [we ≈ grasshoppers], 23.24 [the people ≈ a great lion; himself (Jacob) = a young lion].

Deuteronomy 1.44 [the Amorites ≈ bees], 9.3 [the Lord thy God ≈ a consuming fire], 32.2 [my doctrine ≈ rain; my speech ≈ dew; ≈ small rain; ≈ showers].

Joshua 11.4 [they (the kings against Joshua) ≈ the sand of the sea].

Judges 6.5 [they (the Midianites) ≈ grasshoppers], 7.5 [whoever laps water with his tongue ≈ a dog], 7.12 [Midianites + Amalecites + all the easterners ≈ grasshoppers; their camels ≈ the sand by the sea side], 14.18 [what is sweeter ≈ honey? what is stronger ≈ a lion?], 15.14 [the cords on his (Samson's) arms ≈ flax burnt with fire], 16.9 [Samson broke cords ≈ a thread of tow broken in fire].

Ruth 0

1 Samuel = The First Book of the Kings 0

2 Samuel = The Second Book of the Kings 12.3 [lamb ≈ a daughter], 14.2 [Tekoah/be ≈ a woman who has mourned a long time], 17.10 [the heart of a valiant man ≈ the heart of a lion], 21.19 [the staff of a spear (belonging to Goliath's brother) ≈ a weaver's beam], 22.34 [my feet ≈ hind's feet], 22.43 [them (who rose up against me) ≈ dust of the earth ≈ mud of the streets], 23.4 [a ruler ≈ morning light ≈ tender grass after rain]

I Kings = The Third Book of the Kings 20.27 [the children of Israel ≈ two little flocks of kids].

II Kings = The Fourth Book of the Kings 9.37 [carcase of Jezebel ≈ dung], 21.13 [I (will wipe) > Jerusalem ≈ a man (wipes) a jar].

I Chronicles 11.23 [a spear ≈ a weaver's beam].

II Chronicles 4.5 [brim/lip of sea ≈ the brim of a cup].

Ezra 0

Nehemiah 0

Esther 0

Job 3.21 [death ≈ hidden treasures], 3.24 [my roarings ≈ waters], 5.7 [man > trouble ≈ sparks > fly upward], 5.25 [thine offspring ≈ the grass of the earth], 5.26 [thou at the grave ≈ shock of corn reaped (or ≈ heap of corn-flour)], 6.3 [my grief ≈ (heavier than) sand on the seashore], 6.7 [what my soul refused to touch ≈ my sorrowful meat], 6.15 [my brethren ≈ a brook and a stream], 7.1 [man's life ≈ a hired day-laborer], 7.2 [I/any man ≈ a fearful servant or ≈ a hireling waiting for pay], 7.6 [my days ≈ (swifter than) a weaver's shuttle], 7.9 [he who dies ≈ a cloud vanishes], 7.20 [me ≈ a mark against thee], 8.2 [your words ≈ a strong wind], 9.25 [my days ≈ (swifter than) a post], 9.26 [my days ≈ swift ships ≈ <u>an eagle</u>], 10.10 [me ≈ milk or ≈ cheese], 10.16 [I ≈ a <u>fierce lion</u>], 11.8 [It ≈ (higher than) heaven ... deeper than hell], 11.9 [measure ≈ (longer than) the earth ≈ (broader than) the sea], 11.12 [man ≈ <u>colt of a wild ass</u>], 12.4 [I ≈ one mocked by his neighbor], 12.5 [He ... ≈ a despised lamp], 12.25 [they (people of the earth) ≈ a drunken man], 13.12 [your remembrances ≈ ashes; (your bodies ≈ clay)], 13.28 [he ≈ a rotten thing or ≈ a moth-eaten garment], 14.2 [he/a man ≈ flower that is cut down ≈ a shadow], 14.6 [he/man ≈ a hireling], 14.11 [man ≈ sea waters and floods dry up], 16.14 [God ≈ a giant], 16.21

[a man pleads for man with God ≈ a man pleads for his neighbor],
18.3 [we ≈ <u>beasts</u>], 20.7 [he/the wicked ≈ his own dung], 20.8 [he ≈ a
dream that has fled away ≈ a vision of the night], 21.18 [they ≈ stubble
before the wind ≈ chaff carried away by a storm] 22.24 [gold ≈ dust;
gold of Ophir ≈ stones of the brooks], 24.5 [They (the wicked) ≈ <u>wild
asses</u> in the desert], 24.14 [the murderer in the night ≈ a thief], 24.17
[the morning ≈ the shadow of death; death ≈ a shadow], 27.18 [he ≈ a
moth ≈ a booth/<u>spider</u>], 29.14 [my judgment ≈ a robe and a diadem],
29.18 [my days (growing old) ≈ the sand (palm?)], 29.23 [they waiting
for my speech ≈ thirsty people expecting the rain], 30.14 [they over-
whelmed me ≈ a breaking-in of waters], 30.15 [terrors pursue my soul
≈ wind; my welfare ≈ a cloud], 30.18 [my disease ≈ the collar of my
coat], 30.19 [I ≈ dust and ashes (clay)], 31.36 [(my adversary's book)
≈ my crown], 31.37 [I ≈ a prince], 32.19 [my belly ≈ wine or ≈ new
bottles], 34.7 [a man like Job (a literal comparison) drinking scorn ≈
water], 35.11 [who? ≈ <u>beasts</u> of the earth; us (wiser than) ≈ the <u>fowls of
heaven</u>], 38.8 [the sea broke out ≈ issued out to the womb; the cloud
≈ a garment; thick darkness ≈ a swaddling-band], 38.14 [It ≈ clay;
they ≈ a garment], 39.20 [him/a horse afraid ≈ a <u>grasshopper</u>], 40.17
[a behemoth's tail ≈ a cedar] 40.18 [his bones ≈ pieces of brass ≈ bars
of iron], 41.15 [leviathan's scales shut up ≈ a close seal], 41.20 [smoke
from the leviathan's nostrils ≈ smoke out of a seething pot], 41.24 [his
heart (firm) ≈ a stone ≈ (hard) a piece of millstone], 41.27 [iron ≈
straw; brass ≈ rotten wood], 41.29 [darts ≈ stubble], 41.31 [the deep ≈
a pot/pot of ointment], 41.33 [him ≈ nothing]. 9 animals; 8 humans.
Psalms 1.3 [he (the blessed man) ≈ a tree planted by rivers], 1.4 [the ungodly ≈ chaff scattered by wind], 5.12 [the Lord's favor ≈ a shield],
7.2 [the enemy seizing my soul ≈ <u>a lion</u>], 10.9 [He lying in wait ≈ <u>a
lion</u> in his den], 11.1 [you (my soul) fleeing to the mountains ≈ <u>a bird</u>/
<u>sparrow</u>], 12.6 [the words of the Lord ≈ silver hardened in fire], 17.8
[me ≈ the apple of the eye], 17.12 [they waited for me ≈ <u>a lion</u> greedy
of its prey ≈ a young lion lurking], 18.33 [my feet ≈ <u>hinds'</u> feet], 19.5
[he/God ≈ a bridegroom ≈ a strong man/giant], 19.10 [(judgments of
the Lord) more desirable ≈ gold ≈ (sweeter) honey and honey-comb],
21.9 [them ≈ a fiery oven], 22.13 [they ≈ a ravening and <u>roaring lion</u>],

22.14 [I (poured out) ≈ water; my heart ≈ melting wax], 22.15 [my
strength (dried up) ≈ a potsherd; (death ≈ dust)], 29.6 [they (cedars
of Lebanon) ≈ <u>a calf</u> ≈ a young unicorn], 31.12 [I (forgotten) ≈ a dead
man ≈ a broken vessel], 32.9 [you ≈ (not) a <u>horse or a mule</u>], 33.7 [the
sea waters (gathered) ≈ a heap/bottle], 35.14 [I behaved ≈ a friend or
brother; and (bowed dowh) ≈ a mourner (for a mother)], 36.6 [your
righteousness ≈ great mountains; your judgments ≈ a great deep],
37.2 [they (cut down) ≈ grass; (wither) ≈ green herb], 37.6 [thy righteousness ≈ light and thy judgment ≈ noonday], 37.20 [enemies of the
Lord ≈ the fat of lambs / smoke], 37.35 [the wicked ≈ a green bay tree/
cedars of Libanus], 38.13 [I ≈ a deaf man ≈ a dumb man], 39.5 [my days
≈ a handbreadth; my age ≈ nothing], 42.1 [my soul ≈ <u>a hart</u> desiring
brooks of water], 44.11 [us ≈ <u>sheep</u> for meat], 44.22 [we ≈ <u>sheep</u> for
slaughter], 49.12 [he ≈ <u>beasts</u> that perish-cf. 49.20 (below)], 49.14
[they (men held in honour) ≈ <u>sheep</u>], 49.20 [a man in honor but not
understanding ≈ perishable <u>beasts</u>], 51.7 [I (whiter) ≈ snow], 52.8 [I
≈ green olive tree], 55.6 [me (wings) ≈ dove], 55.21 [words (smoother)
≈ butter; words (softer than) ≈ oil], 58.4 [their poison ≈ a serpent's;
they ≈ a deaf <u>adder</u>], 58.7 [they (shall melt away) ≈ waters running
continually; they ≈ cut in pieces], 58.8 [they (pass away) ≈ a melting
<u>snail</u>/melted wax ≈ untimely birth of a woman], 58.9 [he (shall take
them away) ≈ whirlwind], 59.6 [they (shall make a noise) ≈ a <u>dog</u>]
cf. 59.14 [they (shall make a noise/hunger) ≈ a <u>dog</u>], 62.3 [you ≈ a
bowing wall and a broken fence], 64.3 [(wicked people sharpen their)
tongues ≈ a sword], 68.2 [them (driven away) ≈ smoke; the wicked
should perish ≈ wax melts], 68.13 [ye ≈ wings of a <u>dove</u>], 68.14 [it
(Salmon) (white) ≈ snow; a verbal simile in Greek], 72.6 [he/the king
≈ rain on grass ≈ showers watering the earth], 73.20 [Thou O Lord
≈ a dream of someone wakening up], 73.22 [I ≈ a <u>beast</u>], 77.20 [thy
people ≈ a <u>flock</u>], 78.13 [waters (standing) ≈ a heap], 78.52 [his people
≈ <u>sheep</u> ≈ a flock in the wilderness], 78.69 [his sanctuary ≈ high palaces ≈ the earth], 79.3 [their blood ≈ water], 83.13 [them ≈ a wheel ≈
stubble before the wind], 83.14 [thy tempest > enemies ≈ fire > wood
≈ a flame > mountains], 84.10 [a day in court (better) ≈ a thousand;
to be a doorkeeper in the house of God ≈ (rather than) to dwell in

the tents of wickedness], 88.17 [they (thy terrors, O Lord) ≈ water], 89.46 [wrath ≈ fire], 90.5 [the children are carried away ≈ a flood ≈ asleep; they ≈ grass], 90.9 [our years ≈ a tale/spider-?], 92.7 [wicked ≈ grass], 92.10 [my horn ≈ a unicorn's horn], 92.12 [the righteous ≈ a palm-tree ≈ the cedar in Lebanon], 97.5 [hills ≈ wax], 102.3 [my days (consumed) ≈ smoke; my bones ≈ (burned) an hearth], 102.4 [my heart ≈ grass], 102.6 [I ≈ a <u>pelican</u> in the wilderness ≈ an <u>owl</u> of the desert/in a house], 102.7 [I ≈ a <u>sparrow</u>], 102.9 [ashes (eaten) ≈ bread], 102.11 [my days (declined) ≈ a shadow; I (withered) ≈ grass], 103.11 [heaven (high): earth ≈ the Lord's mercy (great): them that fear Him], 103.12 [the east: (far from) the west ≈ our transgressions: us], 103.13 [father: (pities) his children ≈ the Lord: them that fear him], 103.15 [a man's days ≈ grass; he will flourish ≈ a flower of the field],104.2 [(he covers himself with) light ≈ a garment; heavens ≈ a curtain; the deep ≈ a garment], 109.18 ['he' (a wicked man) wears cursing ≈ a garment ≈ water in his bowels ≈ oil in his bones], 109.23 [I (gone) ≈ the shadow ≈ (tossed up and down) locust], 114.4 [mountains (skipped) ≈ rams; hills ≈ <u>lambs</u>], 114.6 [mountains (skipped) ≈ rams; hills ≈ lambs] 118.12 [they: me ≈ bees: (honeycomb); they: (flames) ≈ fire: thorns], 119.103 [your words (sweeter) ≈ honey] 119.70 [their heart ≈ grease / milk], 119.72 [law of thy mouth ≈ [better than] thousands of gold and silver], 119.83 [I ≈ a bottle in smoke / frost], 119.103 [your words (sweeter): my taste ≈ honey: my mouth], 122.2 [servants' eyes > masters' hand ≈ maidservants' eyes > mistress' hand ≈ our eyes > the Lord], 124.7 [our soul (escaped) ≈ a bird from the snare of fowlers], 125.1 [they that trust in the Lord ≈ mount Zion], 125.2 [the Lord around his people ≈ mountains around Jerusalem], 127.4 [children of the youth ≈ arrows of a mighty man], 128.3 [your wife ≈ a fruitful vine; your children ≈ olive-plants], 131.2 [I ≈ a weaned child; my soul ≈ a weaned child], 133.2 [for brothers to dwell together ≈ ointment on the head ≈ the dew of Hermon], 140.3 [their tongues (sharp) ≈ (the tongue) of a <u>serpent</u>], 141.2 [my prayer to you ≈ incense; my hands lifted up ≈ the evening sacrifice], 141.7 [our bones (scattered on the grave) ≈ one cuts wood on the earth], 144.4 [Man ≈ vanity; his days ≈ a shadow], 144.12 [our sons ≈ plants; our daughters ≈ corner stones (simile: a palace)], 147.16 [snow ≈ wool; hoarfrost (scattered) ≈ ashes], 147.17 [his ice (thrown) ≈ morsels]. 30 animals; the Lord 9 times.

The Proverbs 1.27 [your destruction ≈ desolation + a whirlwind], 2.4 [wisdom ≈ silver + hidden treasures], 3.12 [the Lord ≥ whom he loves a father ≥ his son], 3.14 [wisdom (better than) ≈ merchandise of gold and silver], 3.15 [she (wisdom) ≈ (more precious) rubies], 5.3 [lips of a strange woman ≈ an honeycomb; her mouth (smoother than) ≈ oil; her end ≈ (bitter) wormwood ≈ (sharp) a two-edged sword], 5.19 [the wife of your youth ≈ the loving hind and pleasant roe], 6.5 [you (delivered) ≈ a roe (from a hunter) ≈ a bird (rescued from a fowler)], 7.2 [my law (keep) ≈ the apple of your eye], 7.22 [he > her ≈ an ox > slaughter or ≈ a fool > the stocks], 7.23 [he > her ≈ a bird > a snare], 8.11 [wisdom (better) ≈ rubies], 8.19 [my fruit (better) ≈ gold and fine gold; my revenue (better) ≈ choice silver], 10.20 [tongue of the just ≈ choice silver], 10.25 [wicked ≈ a whirlwind; righteous ≈ an everlasting foundation], 10.26 [the sluggard > them that send him ≈ vinegar > the teeth and smoke > eyes], 11.22 [a fair woman without discretion ≈ a jewel of gold in a swine's snout], 12.4 [a virtuous woman ≈ a crown to her husband; (a bad woman): her husband ≈ rottenness (a worm: wood)], 12.18 [tongue that speaks ≈ the piercings of a sword], 15.19 [the way of the slothful man ≈ an hedge (consisting) of thorns], 16.15 [a king's favor ≈ a cloud of rain], 16.16 [wisdom (better than) ≈ gold; understanding (to be chosen) ≈ silver], 17.1 [a dry morsel + quietness (better than) ≈ a house of strife], 17.8 [a gift ≈ a precious stone], 17.10 [reproof > a wise man ≈ a hundred stripes > a fool], 17.12 [to meet a fool (rather than) ≈ to meet a bear robbed of her whelps], 17.14 [beginning of strife ≈ letting out water], 17.22 [a merry heart doing good ≈ a medicine], 18.4 [words of the mouth ≈ deep waters; wellspring of wisdom ≈ a flowing brook], 18.8 [words of a talebearer ≈ wounds], 18.11 [wealth of a rich man ≈ his strong city ≈ a high wall], 18.19 [brother offended / helped by brother ≈ a strong city; their contentions ≈ the bars of a castle], 19.12 [king's wrath ≈ roaring of a lion; his favor ≈ dew on grass], 20.2 [fear of a king ≈ a lion's roaring], 20.5 [counsel in a man's heart ≈ deep water], 21.1 [the king's heart in the Lord's hand ≈ the rivers of water], 21.9 [to dwell in a corner of the housetop (better than) ≈ to live with a brawling woman in a big house], cf. 21.19: [to dwell in the wilderness (better than) ≈ with a contentious and angry woman], 23.32 [wine ≈ a serpent ≈ an adder], 23.34 [you ≈ he that lieth down in the midst of the sea or ≈ he that lieth upon the top of a mast], 24.34 [your poverty ≈ one traveling; your want ≈ an armed man], 25.11 [a word fitly spoken ≈ apples of gold in pictures of silver], 25.12 [a wise reprover on an obedient ear ≈ an earring of gold and a golden ornament], 25.13 [a faithful messenger ≈ cold snow during harvest], 25.14 [he that boasts of a false gift ≈ winds + clouds without rain], 25.19 [confidence in an unfaithful man ≈ a broken tooth ≈ a foot out of joint], 25.20 [a singer of sad songs ≈ he who takes away a garment in cold death ≈ vinegar on nitre], 25.23 [an angry countenance > a back-biting tongue ≈ the north wind > rain], 25.24 **Cf 21.9 and 21.19.** 25.25 [good news from far away ≈ cold water > a thirsty soul], 25.26 [a righteous man > a wicked man ≈ a troubled fountain ≈ a corrupt spring], 25.28 [a man with no rule over his own spirit ≈ an unfortified city], 26.1 [honor > (unseemly to) a fool ≈ snow (in summer) ≈ rain (in harvest)], 26.2 [a causeless curse ≈ bird wandering ≈ sparrow flying], 26.7 [A parable in the mouth of fools ≈ the unequal legs of the lame], 26.8 [one who gives honor to a fool ≈ he that binds a stone in a sling], 26.9 [a parable in the mouth of fools ≈ a thorn in the hand of a drunkard], 26.11 [a fool > his folly ≈ a dog > his own vomit], 26.14 [a sluggard > his bed ≈ a door (turning on) > its hinge], 26.16 [a sluggard (wiser than) ≈ seven men], 26.17 [he that makes himself champion of another's cause ≈ someone who takes a dog by the ears], 26.18 [one who deceives his neighbor ≈ a madman who throws firebrands, arrows and death], 26.21 [a contentious man > (kindle) strife ≈ coals > burning coals ≈ wood > fire], 26.22 [words of a talebearer ≈ wounds], 26.23 [burning lips and a wicked heart ≈ a potsherd covered with silver], 27.3 [a fool's wrath (heavier than) ≈ a heavy stone ≈ weighty sand], 27.5 [open rebuke ≈ secret love], 27.8 [a man who wanders from his own place ≈ a bird flying from its own nest], 27.15 [a contentious woman ≈ a continual dropping in a very rainy day], 27.17 [a man > (sharpens) his friend's countenance ≈ iron > iron], 27.19 [heart > heart ≈ face > face], 27.20 [eyes of men (insatiable)

≈ hell and destruction (not full)], 27.21 [a man > praise ≈ a fining pot > silver ≈ a furnace > gold], 28.1 [a righteous man (bold) ≈ a lion], 28.3 [a poor man oppressing the poor ≈ rain (sweeping) which leaves no food], 28.15 [a wicked ruler ≈ a roaring/hungry lion ≈ a ranging bear/thirsty wolf], 30.14 [the teeth of one generation ≈ swords and knives], 31.10 [a virtuous woman (far above) ≈ rubies], 31.14 [she (a virtuous woman) ≈ merchants' ships trading from a distance].

Ecclesiastes 7.1 [a good name (better than) ≈ precious ointment], 7.6 [the laughter of a fool ≈ the crackling of thorns under a pot], 7.26 [a woman (whose heart ≈ snares; whose hands ≈ bands) ≈ (more bitter than) death], 9.4 [a living dog (better than) ≈ a dead lion], 9.12 [sons of men (snared in an evil time) ≈ fishes taken in an evil net ≈ birds caught in a snare], 9.18 [wisdom ≈ (better than) weapons of war], 10.1 a little folly > (causes to stink) a reputation of wisdom and honor ≈ [dead flies > an apothecary's ointment], 10.8 [digging a pit > falling in ≈ one bracketing a hedge > a serpent bite], 10.11 [a babbler ≈ a serpent biting], 12.11 [words of wise ≈ goads ≈ nails fastened]. 6 with animals.

The Song of Solomon 1.2 [your love/breasts (better than) ≈ wine], 1.3 [your name ≈ an ointment poured], 1.4 [your love/breasts (more than) ≈ wine], 1.5 [I/black & beautiful ≈ the tents of Kedar ≈ the curtains of Solomon], 1.9 [you ≈ a company of Pharaoh's horses], 1.14 [my beloved/kinsman ≈ a cluster of camphor], 2.2 [my love among the daughters ≈ the lily among thorns; my beloved among the sons ≈ the apple tree among trees], 2.9 [my beloved ≈ a roe ≈ a young hart], 2.17 [you ≈ a roe ≈ young hart], 3.6 [who? ≈ pillar(s) of smoke], 4.1 [your eyes ≈ doves'; your hair ≈ flock of goats; your teeth ≈ a flock of shorn sheep; your lips ≈ a thread of scarlet; your temples ≈ a piece of pomegranate; your neck ≈ the tower of David; your two breasts ≈ two young roes that are twins], 4.10 [your love/breasts (better than) ≈ wine; the smell of your ointments ≈ all spices], 4.11 [your lips ≈ the honeycomb; smell of your garments ≈ smell of Lebanon], 5.11 [my beloved's head ≈ fine gold; his locks (black) ≈ raven; his eyes ≈ eyes of doves; his cheeks ≈ a bed of spices ≈ sweet flowers; his lips ≈ lilies; his hands ≈ gold rings; his belly ≈ bright ivory; his legs ≈ pillars of marble; his countenance ≈ Lebanon ≈ (excellent) cedars], 6.4 [you my love (beautiful)

≈ Tirzah, (comely) ≈ Jerusalem, (terrible) ≈ armies with banners 5 your hair ≈ flock of goats 6 [teeth ≈ a flock of sheep, your temples ≈ a piece of pomegranate], 6.10 [who? (looks forth) ≈ morning, (fair) ≈ moon, (clear) ≈ the sun, (terrible) ≈ an army with banners], 6.12 [me ≈ chariots of Amminabid], 7.1–9 [joints of your thighs ≈ jewels, your nave ≈ a round goblet, your belly ≈ a heap of wheat, your two breasts ≈ two young twin roes, your neck ≈ a tower of ivory, your eyes ≈ fish pools in Heshbon, your nose ≈ the tower of Lebanon, your head ≈ Carmel, the hair on your head ≈ purple, your stature ≈ a palm tree, your breast ≈ clusters of grapes, your breasts ≈ clusters of the vine, the smell of your nose ≈ apples, the roof of your mouth ≈ the best wine], 8.6 [me ≈ a seal upon your heart ≈ a seal upon your arm; love (strong) ≈ death], 8.10 [my breasts towers; I ≈ one that found favor], 8.14 [my beloved ≈ (be like) a roe or a young hart on mountains of spices]. Characterized by many similes in one passage.

Isaiah 1.8 [daughter of Zion (deserted) ≈ a cottage in a vineyard ≈ a lodge in a garden of cucumbers ≈ a besieged city], 1.9 [we ≈ Sodom and Gomorrah], 1.18 [your sins ≈ scarlet ≈ (white) as snow ≈ crimson ≈ (white) as wool], 1.30 [you (rulers of Sodom) ≈ an oak without leaves ≈ a garden without water] [the strong ≈ tow, its maker ≈ a spark], 3.18 [their round tires ≈ the moon], 5.24 [their root > rottenness and their blossom > dust ≈ fire > the stubble and the flame > the chaff], 5.28 [horses' hooves ≈ flint, chariot wheels ≈ a whirlwind, their roaring ≈ lion ≈ young lions … they (shall roar) ≈ the roaring of the sea], 6.13 [the holy seed ≈ a tall tree ≈ an oak], 7.2 [his heart (moved) ≈ the trees (moved by the wind)], 9.18 [wickedness (burns) ≈ fire; they (shall mount up) ≈ the lifting up of smoke; the people ≈ the fuel of the fire], 10.14 [the riches of the people ≈ a nest; I have gathered all the earth ≈ one gathers eggs left behind], 10.15 [an axe or a saw > the user ≈ a rod or staff > one (who lifts it)], 10.16 [the Lord > a burning ≈ a fire], 10.17 [the light of Israel ≈ a fire; his Holy One ≈ a flame], 10.22 [the people of Israel ≈ the sand of the sea], 13.8 [elders (seized by pangs) ≈ woman in labor; their faces ≈ flames], 13.12 [a man (more precious) ≈ fine gold; a man (more precious) ≈ the golden wedge of Ophir], 13.14 [those left behind (Greek) ≈ a chased roe ≈ stray sheep], 14.19 [you (cast away) ≈ an abominable branch ≈ the raiment of the slain ≈ a carcase stepped on], 16.2 [the daughters of Moab ≈ a wandering bird cast out of the nest], 16.11 [my bowels (sound) ≈ a harp for Moab; (my inward parts≈ a wall)], 17.5 [it shall be ≈ the harvestman gathers the corn and reaps the ears] [gleaning grapes will be left ≈ the shaking of an olive tree], 17.9 [his strong cities ≈ a forsaken bough and an uppermost branch], 17.12 [noise ≈ the noise of the seas; rushing ≈ the rushing of mighty waters; nations shall rush ≈ the rushing of many waters; they shall be chased ≈ the chaff of the mountains before the wind ≈ a rolling thing before the whilrwind], 18.4 [I ≈ a clear heat upon herbs ≈ a cloud of dew in the heat of harvest], 19.14 [Egypt errs ≈ a drunk staggering in his vomit], 19.16 [Egyptians ≈ women (in fear)], 21.1 [a fearful vision ≈ a whirlwind coming from the desert], 21.3 [me (in pain) ≈ a woman in labor], 22.18 [the Lord will toss you ≈ a ball], 23.15 [Tyre ≈ (shall sing) a harlot], 24.13 [(the desolate city) ≈ the shaking of an olive tree ≈ gleaning grapes after the vintage], 24.20 [the earth (shall reel) ≈ a drunkard; the earth (shall be removed) ≈ a cottage], 24.22 [earthly kings (gathered together) ≈ prisoners], 26.17 [we (in your sight, O Lord) ≈ a woman about to give birth], 26.18 [deliverance (of a child) ≈ wind], 28.2 [the Lord's anger ≈ a tempest of hail ≈ a flood of mighty water], 29.4 [your voice ≈ a familiar spirit], 29.5 [the strangers ≈ small dust ≈ chaff], 29.7 [*the multitude of nations ≈ a dream* ≈ a hungry man who dreams ≈ a thirsty man dreams], 29.11 [the vision of all ≈ the words of a sealed book], 30.17 [many fleeing ≈ a beacon on a mountain ≈ an ensign on a hill], 30.22 [them (the covering of graven images) ≈ a menstruous cloth], 30.27 [the Lord's tongue ≈ a devouring fire], 30.28 [his breath ≈ an overflowing stream; vanity ≈ a sieve], 30.29 [a song ≈ when a holy solemnity is kept; gladness of heart ≈ when one goes with a pipe to the mountain of the Lord], 30.33 [the Lord's breath ≈ a stream of brimstone], 31.4 [the Lord shall defend Jerusalem ≈ a lion roaring or a lion's whelp over a prey ≈ birds flying], 32.2 [a man ≈ a hiding place from the wind ≈ a covert from the tempest ≈ rivers of water in a dry land ≈ the shadow of a great rock], 32.14 [forts and towers ≈ dens + a joy of wild asses + a pasture of flocks], 33.4 [your spoil gathered ≈ the gathering of

the caterpiller; [the Lord] ≈ the running to and fro of locusts], 33.9
[Sharon ≈ a wilderness], 33.11 [your breath ≈ fire], 33.12 [the people
≈ burnings of lime ≈ thorns cutup], 34.4 [the heavens (rolled up) ≈
a scroll; the host/stars falling ≈ a leaf from a vine ≈ a falling fig], 35.1
[the desert (rejoicing and blossoming) ≈ a rose], 35.6 [a lame man
(leaping) ≈ an hart], 37.27 [they (defensed cities) ≈ (withered) grass
of the field ≈ the green herb ≈ grass on the housetops ≈ corn blasted
before it is grown], 38.12 [mine age (departed) ≈ a shepherd's tent;
I ≈ a weaver], 38.13 [he (the Lord) ≈ a lion; I ≈ a crane or a swallow ≈
(mourning) dove], 40.11 [Lord > his flock ≈ a shepherd > (his flock)],
40.15 [nations ≈ a drop of a bucket ≈ small dust of a balance; the isles
≈ very little thing], 40.22 [the inhabitants of the earth ≈ grasshoppers; heavens ≈ a curtain ≈ a tent], 40.24 [them (princes and judges)
≈ stubble], 40.31 [they (that wait upon the Lord) ≈ eagles], 41.2 [them
(kings) ≈ dust to the righteous man's sword ≈ driven stubble to his
bow], 41.15 [hills ≈ chaff], 41.25 [princes ≈ mortar ≈ potter's clay],
42.6 [thee ≈ a covenant ≈ a light of the Gentiles], 42.13 [the Lord
≈ a mighty man ≈ a man of war], 42.14 [I (will cry) ≈ a travailing
woman], 46.5 [no one ≈ me (God)], 47.14 [they (astrologers, star-
gazers, prognosticators) ≈ stubble], 48.18 [your peace ≈ a river; your
righteousness ≈ waves of the see; your seed ≈ sand; your offspring ≈
gravel], 49.2 [my mouth ≈ a sharp sword; me ≈ a polished shaft], 49.6
[you (Isaiah) ≈ a light to the Gentiles], 49.18 [thee (Zion) ≈ (clothed
as) an ornament; ≈ a bride's attire], 51.6 [the heavens (shall vanish)
≈ smoke; the earth (grow old) ≈ a garment], 51.8 [they (men: shall
be consumed by a moth) ≈ a garment ≈ wool (by a worm)], 53.2 [he
(to whom the arm of the Lord is revealed) ≈ a tender plant ≈ a root
out of dry ground], 53.6 [we ≈ sheep (gone astray); he (to whom the
arm of the Lord is revealed) ≈ a lamb (to slaughter) ≈ a sheep before
her shearers], 54.6 [you ≈ a forsaken woman ...]. 54.9 [this (a little
wrath) ≈ the waters of Noah], 55.9 [my way > your ways ≈ the heaven
(far from) > earth; my word (will not turn back) ≈ rain, snow (will not
return to heaven)], 57.20 [The wicked ≈ the troubled sea], 58.11 [thou
≈ well-watered garden ≈ a spring of water], 59.10 [we ≈ blind men /
with no eyes ≈ in the night (stumbling) ≈ dead men ≈ bears (roaring)

and doves (mourning)], 59.17 [zeal ≈ a cloak], 60.8 [who are these?
≈ a cloud ≈ doves], 61.10 [I ≈ a bridegroom ≈ a bride; [the Lord >
(causes to grow) righteousness ≈ the earth > flowers ≈ a garden > its
seeds], 62.5 [your sons will marry you ≈ a young man marries a virgin;
the Lord will rejoice over you ≈ a bridegroom over a bride], 63.13 [he
(the Lord) led them through the deep ≈ a horse in the wilderness ≈
a beast going into the valley], 64.2 [nations will tremble ≈ fire burns
/ water boils], 64.6 [we ≈ unclean; our righteousness ≈ filthy rags;
we (fade) ≈ a leaf; our iniquities ≈ the wind], 65.8 [I will not destroy
them all ≈ new wine found in the cluster], 65.22 [the days of my people
≈ of a tree], 65.25 [lion (will eat straw) ≈ the bullock], 66.3 [he who
killed an ox ≈ someone who killed a man; he who sacrifices a lamb ≈
he who cut off a dog's neck; who offers an oblation ≈ he offers swine's
blood; who burns incense ≈ he blessed an idol], 66.12 [peace ≈ a river;
the glory of the Gentiles ≈ a flowing stream], 66.14 [your bones ≈ an
herb; the Lord's chariots ≈ a whirlwind].

Jeremiah Jerem. 3.20 [house of Israel (treacherous) > me (the Lord) ≈ a
wife > her husband], 4.13 [He (the Lord) ≈ clouds; his chariots ≈ a
whirlwind; his horses (swifter) ≈ eagles], 4.31 [a voice ≈ a voice of a
woman giving birth; the anguish ≈ that of a woman giving birth for
the first time], 5.8 [your sons ≈ fed/wanton horses], 5.16 [their (= any
nation invading Israel) quiver ≈ an open sepulchre], 5.27 [their (wicked
men's) houses full of deceit ≈ a cage full of birds], 6.2 [the daughter of
Zion ≈ a comely and delicate woman], 6.7 [Jerusalem > her wickedness ≈ a fountain (casts out) > its water], 6.9 [the remnant of Israel ≈ a
vine (to be gleaned thoroughly); you (Jerusalem) ≈ a grape-gatherer],
6.24 [pain ≈ that of a woman in labor], 6.26 [mourn ≈ an only son],
6.27 [you ≈ a tower and a fortress], 8.6 [everyone (turned) ≈ a horse
(rushes to battle); the people > NOT know the judgment of the Lord
≈ stork in heaven and turtle, crane and swallow > observe the time of
their coming], 9.3 [tongue ≈ a bow], 9.8 [their tongue ≈ an arrow],
9.22 [men's carcasses ≈ dung ≈ handful], 10.5 [they (the heathen) ≈
palm tree], 11.19 [I ≈ a lamb or ox brought to slaughter], 12.3 [them
(the wicked) ≈ sheep for slaughter], 12.8 [my heritage ≈ a lion in the
forest], 12.9 [my heritage ≈ a speckled bird], 13.11 [the house of Israel

> me ≈ a girdle (around) > the loins of a man], 13.24 [them (scattered) ≈ stubble carried by the wind], 14.6 [wild asses (snuffed the wind) ≈ dragons], 14.9 [you (hope of Israel) ≈a man astounded ≈ a mighty man unable to save], 16.4 [they (people born here) ≈ dung on the face of the earth], 17.6 [a trusting man ≈ a heath/myrica in the desert], 17.8 [he (the man who trusts in the Lord) ≈ a thriving tree], 17.11 [a man gaining riches unjustly and losing them ≈ a partridge sitting on eggs but not hatching them], 18.6 [I/the Lord > you ≈ a potter > his clay], 18.17 [I (will scatter my people) ≈ east wind (scatters the enemy)], 20.9 [the Lord's word in my heart ≈ a burning fire in my bones], 20.11 [the Lord with me ≈ a mighty fighter], 21.12 [my fury ≈ fire], 23.9 [I ≈ a drunken man ≈ a man overcome by wine], 23.12 [their way (prophets and priests) ≈ slippery ways in darkness], 23.14 [they (prophets of Jerusalem) ≈ Sodom; the inhabitants there ≈ Gomorrha], 23.29 [my word ≈ fire ≈ a hammer breaking a rock], 24.5 [Jews sent from Judah ≈ good figs], 24.8 [Zedikiah et al. + those who remain in this city etc. ≈ bad figs], 25.38 [He (the Lord) ≈ a lion], 26.18 [Zion ≈ a field for plowing …], 29.17 [them [citizens of Babylon] ≈ vile figs], 30.6 [every man ≈ a woman in labor], 33.22 [I will multiply David's seed ≈ the stars of heaven nor the sand of the sea can be measured], 43.12 [he > land of Egypt ≈ a shepherd > garment], 46.8 [Egypt ≈ a flood; his waters ≈ the rivers], 46.20 [Egypt ≈ a fair heifer; her hired men ≈ fatted bullocks; the voice ≈ a serpent; they ≈ hewers of wood; they ≈ grasshoppers], 48.6 [you be ≈ the heath in the wilderness], 48.28 [dwellers in Moab ≈ the dove …], 48.36 [my heart (shall sound) ≈ pipes ≈ pipes for men of Kirheres], 48.38 [Moab (broken) ≈ a vessel without pleasure], 49.16 [your nest (high) ≈ the eagle], 49.19 [he ≈ a lion], 49.22 [he (will fly) ≈ the eagle; men's heart ≈ a woman's heart in her pangs], 50.37 [they ≈ women], 50.42 [their voice (cruel people from the north) ≈ (shall roar) the sea; they shall ride horses ≈ a man to battle], 50.43 [the king of Babylon ≈ a woman in labor], 50.44 [he (shall come) ≈ a lion], 51.7 [Babylon ≈ a golden cup], 51.14 [men ≈ caterpillers], 51.20 [you ≈ my battle-ax], 51.30 [men of Babylon ≈ women], 51.33 [daughter of Babylon ≈ a threshingfloor], 51.34 [me ≈

an empty vessel; he ≈ a dragon], 51.38 [they ≈ lions / lions' whelps], 51.40 [they ≈ lambs / rams], 51.55 [Babylon's waves ≈ great waters].

Lamentations of Jeremiah 1.1 [the city ≈ a widow], 1.6 [princes ≈ harts finding no pastures], 1.17 [Jerusalem ≈ menstruous woman], 2.3 [he (burned) ≈ fire; he (bent his bow) ≈ an enemy; he (with his right hand) ≈ adversary; his fury ≈ fire; the Lord ≈ an enemy; his tabernacle ≈ a garden; (they made) noise ≈ on a feast day], 2.13 [your breach (large) ≈ the sea], 2.18 [tears ≈ a river], 3.10 [he (the Lord) ≈ a bear ≈ a lion], 3.12 [me ≈ a mark for his arrow], 3.45 [us ≈ offscouring and refuse], 3.52 [me ≈ a bird], 4.2 [sons of Zion ≈ fine gold ≈ earthen pitchers], 4.3 [daughter of my people (cruel) ≈ the ostrich(es) in the wilderness], 4.7 [Nazarites (purer) ≈ snow ≈ (whiter) milk ≈ (polishing) sapphire; visage (blacker) ≈ coal; their skin ≈ a stick; slain with sword (better) ≈ slain with hunger], 4.14 [(the sons of Zion) ≈ blind men], 4.19 [our persecutors (swifter) ≈ eagles of heaven], 5.10 [our skin (black) ≈ an oven].

Ezekiel 1.4 [the color of the brightness of the whirlwind ≈ amber], 1.5 [appearance of 4 creatures ≈ likeness of a man], 1.7 [sole of their feet ≈ sole of a calf's foot; they (sparkled) ≈ the color of burnished brass], 1.8 [their hands ≈ a man's hands], 1.10 [they had faces ≈ a man, a lion, an ox, an eagle], 1.13 [their appearance ≈ burning coals of fire ≈ lamps], 1.14 [their appearance ≈ a flash of lightning], 1.16 [wheels (color) ≈ beryl; their appearance ≈ a wheel in a wheel], 1.22 [the likeness of the firmament over their heads ≈ the color of terrible crystal], 1.24 [the noise of their wings ≈ the noise of great waters ≈ the voice of the Almighty ≈ the noise of an host], 1.26 [likeness ≈ a throne ≈ a sapphire stone ≈ the appearance of a man], 1.27 [color ≈ amber ≈ the appearance of fire], 1.28 [brightness around, the glory of the Lord ≈ a [rain?]bow in a rainy cloud], 3.3 [the taste of a roll (sweet) ≈ honey], 3.9 [your forehead (harder) ≈ flint], 7.16 [Those who escape ≈ doves of the valley], 7.17 [knees (weak) ≈ water], 8.2 [a likeness ≈ appearance of fire / of brightness ≈ the color of amber; form ≈ a hand], 10.1 [there appeared over them ≈ a sapphire stone ≈ a throne], 10.8 [the form/ likeness ≈ a man's hand], 10.9 [the appearance of the wheels ≈ a beryl stone], 10.10 [one likeness ≈ a wheel in the middle of a wheel], 10.21

[the hands ≈ hands of a man; the likeness of their faces ≈ the same faces which I saw by the river Chebar], 13.4 [your prophets ≈ foxes in the deserts], 16.7 [you ≈ the bud of the field], 16.30 [thou/Israel ≈ a harlot], 16.44 [her daughter ≈ the mother], 19.2 [your mother ≈ a lioness], 19.10 [your mother ≈ a vine in your blood], 20.32 [we ≈ the heathen], 21.32 [You ≈ fuel for the fire], 22.20 [I will gather you in my anger ≈ they gather silver etc. into a furnace], 22.22 [you melted in their midst ≈ silver melted in a furnace], 22.27 [her princes ≈ wolves], 23.45 [(righteous men shall judge) them ≈ adulteresses ≈ murderesses], 26.14 [I will make you ≈ top of a rock], 32.2 [you/Pharoah ≈ a young lion ≈ a whale], 38.9 [you ≈ storm ≈ a cloud], 40.3 [a man ≈ brass], [his voice ≈ the noise of many waters], 43.2 [his voice ≈ the noise of many waters].

Daniel 2.35 [iron, clay etc. ≈ the chaff of summer threshing floors], 2.40 [the fourth kingdom ≈ (strong) iron], 2.42 [kingdom part strong and broken ≈ toes part iron and part clay], 4.33 [he (ate grass) ≈ oxen; his hair ≈ eagles's feathers; his nails ≈ birds' claws], 7.4 [first beast ≈ a lion, second ≈ a bear, third ≈ a leopard], 7.9 [garment white ≈ snow, hair ≈ pure wool, throne ≈ fiery flame, wheels ≈ burning fire], 10.5 [his body ≈ beryl, face ≈ lightning, eyes ≈ lamps of fire, arms and legs ≈ polished brass, his voice ≈ the voice of a multitude], 12.3 [the wise (shall shine) ≈ the brightness of the firmament; *they that turn many to righteousness* ≈ the stars].

Hosea 1.10 [number of Israelis ≈ the sand of the sea], 2.3 [her/your mother ≈ dry land], 4.16 [Israel ≈ a back-sliding heifer ≈ a lamb in a large place], 5.10 [princes of Judah ≈ they that remove the bound (boundary?); my wrath ≈ water], 5.14 [I ≈ a lion / a young lion], 6.3 [the Lord ≈ the rain, the latter and former rain], 6.4 [your goodness ≈ a morning cloud ≈ early dew], 6.7 [people (of Gilead?) ≈ men], 6.9 [company of priests ≈ troops of robbers], 7.4 [they (Samarians) ≈ an oven glowing with flame], 7.6 [their heart ≈ an oven ≈ a flaming fire], 7.7 [They all (hot) ≈ an oven], 7.11 [Ephraim ≈ a silly dove without heart], 7.12 [them (?) ≈ fowls of the heaven], 7.16 [they (Samarians) ≈ a deceitful bow], 8.1 [he ≈ an eagle], 8.8 [Israel ≈ a worthless vessel], 9.4 [their sacrifices ≈ the bread of mourning], 9.10 [Israel ≈ grapes in the wilderness; your/

their fathers ≈ first ripe in a fig tree], 9.11 [Ephraim / glory ≈ a bird],
10.4 [judgment ≈ hemlock], 10.7 [Samaria's king (cast off) ≈ the foam
on the water], 10.11 [Ephraim ≈ an heifer taught to tread corn/love
threshing], 11.10 [the Lord (shall roar) ≈ a lion; they (shall tremble)
≈ a bird ≈ a dove], 13.3 [they (Israelites-?) ≈ morning cloud ≈ early
dew ≈ chaff ≈ smoke], 13.7 [I/the Lord ≈ a lion ≈ a leopard ≈ a bear
≈ lion], 14.5 [I/the Lord ≈ dew; he/Ashur ≈ the lily ≈ Lebanon], 14.6
[Ashur's beauty ≈ olive tree; his smell ≈ Lebanon], 14.7 [they ≈ corn
≈ the vine; the scent ≈ wine of Lebanon; Ephraim ≈ a green fir tree],

Joel 1.8 [you (lament for) > me ≈ a virgin > her husband], 2.3 [the land
before them ≈ the garden of Eden], 2.4 [their appearance ≈ horses;
they run ≈ horsemen], 2.5 [they (shall leap) ≈ the noise of chariots ≈
the noise of a flame of fire ≈ strong people preparing for battle], 2.7
[they (shall run) ≈ mighty men; (shall climb the wall) ≈ men of war],
2.9 [they ≈ thief].

Amos 2.9 [his height ≈ a cedar; he (strong) ≈ an oak], 2.13 [I (am pressed)
≈ a cart full of sheaves], 3.12 [the children of Israel in Samaria (taken
out) ≈ two legs or an ear from the mouth of a lion by a shepherd],
4.11 [I > (overthrew) you ≈ God > Sodom and Gomorrha; you ≈ a
firebrand plucked out of the fire], 5.19 [the Lord's day shall be darkness
and not light ≈ a man flees from a lion and met a bear OR went into
his house and was bitten by a serpent], 5.24 [judgment (run down)
≈ water; righteousness ≈ a mighty stream], 9.9 [(I will sift) the house
of Israel ≈ corn sifted in a sieve].

Obadiah 1.4 [you ≈ an eagle], 1.18 [house of Jacob ≈ a fire; the house of
Joseph ≈ a flame; the house of Esau ≈ stubble].

Jonah 0

Micah 1.4 [valleys (cleft) ≈ wax before fire ≈ water rushing down], 1.6
[Samaria ≈ a heap of the field ≈ plantings of a vineyard], 1.8 [I (wailing)
≈ dragons ≈ (mourning) owls], 1.16 become bald ≈ an eagle] 2.12
[Jacob and his people (returning) ≈ sheep of Bozra ≈ a flock in the
midst of their fold], 5.8 [the remnant of Jacob among the Gentiles ≈
a lion among the beasts of the forest ≈ a young lion among flocks of
sheep], 7.1 [I ≈ someone gathering summer fruits ≈ one gathering

grape-gleanings in the vintage], 7.4 [the best of them ≈ a brier; most upright (sharper) ≈ a thorn hedge].

Nahum 1.6 [The Lord's fury ≈ fire], 1.10 [the Lord's enemies ≈ thorns ≈ drunkards ≈ stubble].

Habakkuk 1.8 [his horses (run more swiftly) ≈ leopards; fiercer than ≈ evening wolves; (shall fly) ≈ an eagle hurrying to eat; faces ≈ east wind; his captives (gathered) ≈ sand], 1.14 [men ≈ fish of the sea ≈ creeping things with no ruler], 3.4 [His brightness ≈ light], 3.14 [they (villagers) ≈ a whirlwind], 3.19 [my feet ≈ hinds' feet].

Zephaniah 0

Haggai 0

Zechariah 4.1 [me ≈ a man that is waken out of his sleep], 5.9 [wings ≈ wings of a stork], 7.12 [their hearts ≈ an adamant stone], 9.3 [silver (heaped up) ≈ dust; gold ≈ mire of the streets], 9.14 [the Lord's arrow ≈ lightening], 10.2 [they (diviners) went away ≈ a flock], 10.3 [the house of Judah ≈ his flock ≈ his horse in battle], 10.7 [they (warriors of Ephraim) shall rejoice ≈ through wine], 12.6 [the governors of Judah ≈ an hearth of fire among wood ≈ a torch of fire in a sheaf].

Malachi 4.1 [a burning day ≈ an oven; all the wicked ≈ stubble consumed by fire].

* * *

An Outline of Similes in the New Testament

Matthew 3.16 [the spirit of God (descending) ≈ a dove], 6.25 [life (more than) ≈ meat; body ≈ raiment], 7.24 *a/2 [who listens to me and follows ≈ a wise man who built his house upon a rock] cf. Luke 6.48. 7.26 [everyone who hears my words without following them ≈ a fool who built his house on the sand], 9.36 [they ≈ sheep having no shepherd], 10.16 [you ≈ sheep among wolves; (be wise) ≈ serpents; (be harmless) ≈ doves], 10.31 [you (more valuable) ≈ many sparrows], 11.16 [this generation ≈ children], 12.12 [man ≈/better than a sheep], 13.24 [3 in of heaven ≈ a man sowing good seed], 13.31 [kingdom of heaven ≈ a mustard seed], 13.33, [kingdom of heaven ≈ leaven hidden by a woman in meal], 13.44 [the kingdom of heaven ≈ treasure hidden in a field], 13.45 [kingdom of heaven ≈ a merchant man seeking goodly pearls], 13.47 [The kingdom of heaven ≈ a net cast into the sea], 13.52 [every scribe … ≈ a house-holder who brings out of his treasure …], 17.20 [≈ a grain of mustard seed], 18.3 [ye ≈ little children; heaven ≈ a kingdom], Cf. Matt. 18.4: a comparison – 18.4 *Whosoever* therefore shall humble himself **as** *this little childe* … [you ≈ little child], 18.23 [kingdom of the heaven ≈ a certain king], 19.24 [rich man entering the kingdom of God (easier than) ≈ a camel going through the eye of a needle], 20.1 [kingdom of God ≈ a householder out to hire workers], **A simile turning into a long parable (20.2–16)**. 21.13 See Predicate Accusatives: my house ≈ a den of thieves. 22.2 [kingdom of heaven ≈ a king who made a marriage for his son] (**continues to 22.14, which has an interesting conclusion: after punishment of a guest who wasn't wearing a wedding garment, the conclusion (22.14) is "For many are called, but few are chosen":** 14 πολλοὶ γάρ εἰσι κλητοί, ὀλίγοι δὲ ἐκλεκτοί. 14 Multi enim sunt vocati, pauci vero electi. 22.30 [they (the seven brothers) ≈ the angels of God in heaven], 23.27 [you (scribes and Pharissees) ≈ whited sepulchres], 24.27 [the coming of the son of man ≈ lightening], 25.1 [kingdom of the heavens ≈ ten virgins with their lamps], 25.14 [the kingdom of the heavens ≈ a man going on a journey ...], 25.32 [He will separate the nations ≈ a shepherd > his sheep], 28.3 [His appearance ≈ lightning; his raiment (white) ≈ snow; his keepers ≈ dead men].

Mark 1.10 [the spirit = a dove], 4.26 [the kingdom of God ≈ a man casting seed into the ground], 4.30 [the kingdom of god = a grain of mustard seed], 6.34 [the crowd = sheep without a shepherd], 8.24 [men ≈ trees walking], 9.3 [his raiment ≈ (white as) snow], 10.25 [a wealthy man > kingdom of God NOT≈ a camel > the eye of a needle], 12.25 [they ≈ angels in heaven] Jesus' answer to the Sadducees, 13.34 [the Son of man ≈ a man taking a far journey].

Luke 3.22 [the Holy Ghost ≈ a dove] Cf. the category in Homer for 'Divine Transformations'. 6.47 [he who hears my sayings and does them ≈ a man who built his house on a rock], 6.49 [he who hears me and does not do them ≈ a man who builds his house on the earth without a foundation], 7.31 [the people of this generation ≈ children sitting in the market], 10.3 [you ≈ lambs among wolves], 10.18 [Satan ≈ lightening falling from heaven], 12.36 [you ≈ men who wait for their lord to return from the wedding], 13.18 [the kingdom of God = what (simile)?] **Simile follows in 19–21.** 13.39 [it (the kingdom of God) ≈ a mustard seed etc.], 13.20 [the kingdom of God ≈ to what?], 13.21 [it (the kingdom of God) ≈ leaven, which a woman took and hid in three measures of meal] >>>NB several parables are not included here because they are not expressed as similes. 13.34 [I (Jesus) > your children ≈ a hen > her brood], 17.6 [faith ≈ a grain of mustard seed], 18.25 [a rich man > kingdom of God ≈ (easier for) a camel > a needle's eye] Cf. Mark 10.25 [NB – Both similes are expressed as though the rich man were part of the vehicle (easier than).], 21.35 [the kingdom of God coming ≈ a snare].

John 1.32 [the spirit descending from heaven ≈ a dove], 3.14 [the Son of man (to be lifted up) ≈ the serpent in the desert].

Acts of the Apostles 2.2 [sound ≈ rushing wind; tongues ≈ fire], 8.32 [he/ Jesus ≈ a sheep to slaughter ≈ a lamb], 9.18 [(things) ≈ scales in his eyes], 11.5 [a vision: a vessel let down from heaven ≈ a great sheet], 17.29 [the Godhead NOT ≈ gold, silver or stone].

Epistle of Paul to the Romans 0

First Epistle of Paul to the Corinthians 13.1 [I ≈ sounding brass / a tinkling cymbal].

Second Epistle of Paul to the Corinthians 11.3 [your minds corrupted by Christ's simplicity ≈ Eve beguiled by the serpent].

Epistle of Paul to the Galatians 0

Epistle of Paul to the Ephesians 0

Epistle of Paul to the Philippians 2.15 [you (Philippians) ≈ lights in the world].

Epistle of Paul to the Colossians 0

First Epistle of Paul to the Thessalonians 5.2 [the day of the Lord ≈ a thief in the night], 5.3 [sudden destruction ≈ pain of childbirth].

Second Epistle of Paul to the Thessalonians 0

First Epistle of Paul to Timothy 0

Second Epistle of Paul to Timothy 0

Epistle of Paul to Titus 0

Epistle of Paul to Philemon 0

Epistle of Paul to the Hebrews 4.12 [the word of God (sharper) ≈ any two-edged sword].

James General Epistle 1.11 [the rich man shall fade ≈ the sun withers the grass etc.], 1.23 [a hearer of the word and not a doer ≈ a man beholding his face in a mirror], 5.3 [the rust of your gold and silver (shall eat your flesh) ≈ fire].

First Epistle of Paul to Peter 1.7 [your faith (more precious) ≈ gold that perishes], 1.18 [the blood of Christ ≈ a perfect lamb], 1.24 [flesh ≈ grass; the glory of man ≈ the flower of grass], 2.4 [(the Lord) ≈ a living stone; you ≈ lively stones], 2.16 [(ye) free ≈ the servants of God], 5.8 [the devil ≈ a roaring lion searching for a victim].

Second Epistle of Paul to Peter 3.10 [the day of the Lord (will come) ≈ a thief in the night].

First Epistle to John 0

Second Epistle to John 0

Third Epistle to John 0

General Epistle to Jude 10 [those who speak what they know naturally ≈ brute beasts].

The Revelation of St. John the Divine 1.10 [a voice ≈ sound of a trumpet], 1.14 [his hairs (white) ≈ wool ≈ snow; his eyes ≈ a flame of fire], 1.15 [his feet ≈ fine brass ≈ burned in a furnace; his voice ≈ sound of many waters], 1.16 [his countenance ≈ the sun], 1.17 [I (fell at his feet) ≈ a corpse], 2.18 [His eyes ≈ a flame of fire; His feet ≈ fine brass], 3.3 [I ≈ a thief], [the first voice I heard ≈ a trumpet talking with me], 4.3 [he sitting ≈ a jasper and sardine stone; the rainbow around his throne ≈ an emerald], 4.6 [the sea of glass ≈ crystal], 4.7 [first beast ≈ a lion; the second beast ≈ a calf; the third beast ≈ a man; the fourth beast ≈ a flying eagle], 6.1 [the voice of one of the four beasts ≈ the noise of thunder], 6.12 [the sun (became black) ≈ sackcloth of hair; the moon ≈ blood; the stars falling from heaven ≈ figs from a fig tree; heaven (departing) ≈ a scroll rolled up], 8.8 [sound of second angel ≈ a great mountain burning with fire cast into the sea], 8.10 [a great star falling and burning ≈ a lamp], 9.3 [power of locusts ≈ scorpions], 9.5 [their (certain men's) torment ≈ a scorpion striking a man], 9.7 [locusts ≈ horses prepared for battle; on their heads ≈ golden crowns; their faces ≈ men's faces], 9.8 [their hair ≈ women's hair; their teeth ≈ lions' teeth] **Similes or comparisons? In a vision there's not much difference between literal and figurative description.** 9.9 [their breastplates ≈ iron; sound of their wings ≈ sound of chariots with many horses running to battle], 9.10 [their tails ≈ scorpions with stings], 9.17 [the heads of horses ≈ heads of lions], 9.19 [their tails ≈ serpents], 10.1 [his face ≈ the sun; his feet ≈ pillars of fire], 10.9 [the taste of the book in my mouth ≈ honey-sweet], 11.1 [a reed ≈ a rod], 13.2 [the beast ≈ a leopard; his feet ≈ a bear's; his mouth ≈ a lion's], 13.11 [two horns of the beast ≈ a lambs; its speech ≈ a dragon's], 14.2 [the voice from heaven ≈ many waters ≈ great thunder ≈ harpers harping], 15.2 [(what) I saw ≈ a sea of glass mingled with fire], 18.21 [the angel's stone ≈ a great millstone], 19.12 [his eyes ≈ a flame of fire], 21.2 [new Jerusalem ≈ a bride adorned for her husband], 21.11 [her light ≈ a precious stone ≈ jasper crystal-clear], 21.18 [the city's pure gold ≈ clear glass], 22.1 [pure river of water ≈ crysal-clear].

* * *

Location of Similes in Each Book of the Bible with Summaries

>**prothetic** (**bold** type) + <u>predicate</u> (*a/1–2) + genitive (*c/)

A– The Old Testament

Genesis (50 Chapters)
[17 similes: 12 prothetic + 5 <u>predicate</u>]

1-2-3-4-5-6-7-8-9-10-11-12-13(**16**)-14-15-16-17-18-19-20-21-22
(**17**x2)-23-24-25(**25**)-26(**4**)-27(**27**)-28-29-30-31-32-33-34-35-35-
37-38-39-<u>40(12)</u>-41-42-43-44-45-46-47-48-<u>49</u>(**4,9**x2,**12**x2,**27**,<u>9,17,21,</u>
<u>22</u>)-50.

    *a/1:40.12, 49.9, 49.17, 49.21, 49.22

* * *

Exodus (40 Chapters)

[10 similes: 8 prothetic + 2 <u>predicate</u>]

1-2-3-4(**6**)-7-8-9-10(<u>7</u>)-11-12-13-14(<u>22</u>)-15(**10**)-16(**14,31**x2)-17-18-19
(**18**)-20-21-22-23-24(**17**)-25-26-27-28-29-30-31-32-33(**11**)-34-35-36-37-38-
39-40.

    *a/1:10.7, 14.22

* * *

Leviticus (27 Chapters)

[No similes]

* * *

Numbers (36 Chapters)

[5 prothetic similes]

1-2-3-4-5-6-7-8-9-10-11(**7**x2)-12-13(**33**)-14-15-16-17-18-19-20-21-22-23(**24**x2)-24-25-26-27-28-29-30-31-32-33-34-35-36.

* * *

Deuteronomy (34 Chapters)

[8 similes: 6 prothetic + 2 predicate]

1(**44**)-2-3-4(24)-5-6-7-8-9(**3**)-10-11-12-13-14-15-16-17-18-19-20-21-22-23-24-25-26-27-28-29-30-31-32(**2**x4,4)-33-34.
    *a/1: 4.24, 32.4

* * *

Joshua (24 Chapters)

[1 prothetic simile]

1-2-3-4-5-6-7-8-9-10-11(**4**)-12-13-14-15-16-17-18-19-20-21-22-23-24.

* * *

Judges (21 Chapters)

[8 prothetic similes]

1-2-3-4-5-6(**5**)-7(**5,12**x2)-8-9-10-11-12-13-14(**18**x2)-15(**14**)-16(**9**)-17-18-19-20-21.

* * *

Ruth (4 Chapters)

[No similes]

* * *

I Samuel = The First Book of the Kings (31 Chapters)

[1 <u>predicate</u> simile]

1-2-3-4-5-6-7-8-9-10-11-12-13-1-4-15-16-17(<u>43</u>)-18-19-20-21-22-23-24-25-26-27-28-29-30-31.

    *a/1: 17.43

* * *

II Samuel = The Second Book of the Kings (24 Chapters)

[21 similes: 9 prothetic + 7 <u>predicate</u> + 6 genitive]

1-2-3-4-5-6-7-8-9-10-11-12(**3**)-13-14(**2**)-15-16-17(**10**)-18-19-20-21(**19**)-22(34,43x2)-23(4x2)-24.

    *a/1: <u>22.2</u> (2), <u>22.3</u> (2), <u>22.29</u>, <u>22.31</u>, <u>22.51</u>
    *c/: 22.3, 22.5 (2), 22.36, 22.47, 22.51

* * *

I Kings = The Third Book of the Kings (22 Chapters)

[1 prothetic simile]

1-2-3-4-5-6-7-8-9-10-11-12-13-14-15-16-17-18-19-20(**27**)-21-22.

* * *

II Kings = The Fourth Book of the Kings (25 Chapters)

[3 similes: 2 prothetic and 1 predicate]

1-2-3-4-5-6-7-8-9(**37**)-10-11-12-13-14-15-16-17-18-19-20-21(**13**)-22-23-24-25.

    *a/1: 21.14

* * *

I Chronicles (29 Chapters)

[1 prothetic simile]

1-2-3-4-5-6-7-8-9-10-11(**23**)-12-13-14-15-16-17-18-19-20-21-22-23-24-25-26-27-28-29.

* * *

II Chronicles (36 Chapters)

[1 prothetic simile]

1-2-3-4(**5**)-5-6-7-8-9-10-11-12-13-14-15-16-17-18-19-20-21-22-23-24-25-26-
27-28-29-30-31-32-33-34-35-36.

* * *

Ezra (10 Chapters)

[No similes]

* * *

Nehemiah (13 Chapters)

[No similes]

* * *

Esther (10 Chapters)

[No similes]

* * *

Job (41 Chapters)

[105 similes: 88 prothetic + 11 <u>predicate</u> + 6 genitive]

1-2-3(**21,24**)-4-5(**7,25,26**)-6(**3,7,<u>12x2</u>,15x2**)-7(**1,2x2,6,<u>7</u>,9,
<u>12x2</u>,20**)-8(**2,<u>9,14</u>**)-9(**25,26x2**)-10(**10x2,16**)-11(**8x2,9x2,12**)-12(**4,5,25**)-
13(**<u>4</u>,12x2,28x2**)-14(**2x2,6,11**)-15-16(**14,21**)-17-18(**3**)-19-20(**7,8x2**)-
21(**18x2**)-22(**24x2**)-23-24(**5,14,17**)-25-26-27(**18x2**)-28-29(**14x2,18,23x2**)-
30(**14,15x2,18,19x2**)-31(**<u>12</u>,36,37**)-32(**19x2**)-33-34(**7**)-35(**11x2**)-36-
37-38(**8,<u>9</u>x2,14x2**)-39(**20**)-40(**17,18x2**)-41(**15,20,24x2,27x2,29,3
1x2,33**).

    *a/1: **6.12x2,7.7,7.12x2,8.9,8.14,13.4,31.12,38.9x2**
    *c/: **3.5, 10.21-22,16.16, 24.17x2**

* * *

Psalms (150 Chapters)

[201 similes: 150 prothetic + 37 <u>predicate</u> + 14 genitive]

1(**3,4**)-2-3(**3**x2)-4-5(**12**)-6-7(**2**)-8-9-10(**9**)-11(**1**)-12(**6**)-13-14-
15-16-17(**8,12**x2)-18(2x4,**33**)-19(**5**x2,**10**x3)-20-21(**9**)-22(**6,13,14**x2,**15**x2)-
23(**1**)-24-25-26-27(**1**)-28(**1,7**)-29(**6**x2)-30-31(**2,3,12**x2)-32(**7,9**x2)-33(**7,20**)-
34-35(**14**x2)-36(**6,6**)-37(**2**x2,**6**x2,**20,35**)-38(**13**x2)-39(**5**x2)-40-41-42(**1**)-
43-44(**11,22**)-45(**1**)-46-47-48-49(**12,14,20**)-50-51(**7**)-52(**8**)-53-54-
55(**6,21**x2)-56-57(**4**x2)-58(**4**x2,**7**x2,**8**x2,**9**)-59(**6,14**)-60(**8**)-61(**3**x2)-
62(**2,3**x2)-63-64(**3**)-65-66-67-68(**2**x2,**13,14**)-69-70-71-72(**6**x2)-73(**20,
22**)-74-75-76-77(**20**)-78(**13,35,39**x2,**52**x2,**69**x2)-79(**3**)-80-81-82-83
(**13**x2,**14**x2)-84(**10**x2,**11**)-85-86-87-88(**17**)-89(**46**)-90(**5**x3,**9**)-91-92(**7,
10,12**x2,**15**)-93-94(**22**)-95-96-97(**5**)-98-99-100-101-102(**3**x2,**4,6**x2,**7,9,1
1**x2)-103(**11,12,13,15**x2)-104(2x2,**3,4,17**)-105-106-107-108(**9**)-109
(**18**x3,**23**x2)-110(**1**)-111-112-113-114(4x2=**114.6**x2)-115(**10=11**)-116-
117-118(**12**x2,**14**)-119(**70,72,83,103,105**x2)-120-121(**5**)-122-123(2x2)-
124(**7**)-125(**1,2**)-126-127(**4**)-128(3x2)-129-130-131(**2**)-132-133(**2,3**x2)-134-
135-136-137-138-139-140(**3**)-141(2x2,**7**)-142-143-144(**4**x2,**12**x2)-145-146-
147(**16**x2-**17**)-148-149-150.

Predicate (*a/ + *b/):
    3(3),18(2x4),22(6),23(1),27(1),28(1,7),31(2,3),32(7),
    33(20),36(6),45(1),57(4x2),60(8),61(3x2),62(2),78(35,39x2),
    84(11),92(15),94(22),104(3,4,17),108(9),110(1),115(10,11),
    118(14),119(105x2),121(5).
*c/: 4(6),13(3),18(2),18(35),22(15),23(4),36(9),45(6),60(3),
    95(1),104(3,7),110(2),116(13).

* * *

The Proverbs (31 Chapters)

[144 similes: 105 prothetic + 26 <u>predicate</u> + 13 genitive]

1(**27**x2)-2(**4**x2,**7**)-3(**12,14**x2,**15**)-4-5(**3**x2,**4**x2,**19**)-6(**5**x2,**23**x2)-7(**2,22**x
2,**23,27**x2)-8(**11,19**x3)-9-10(**20,25,25,26**x2)-11(**22**)-12(**4,4,18**)-13(**14**])-
14(**27**)-15(**4,19**)-16(**15,16**x2)-17(**1,6**x2,**8,10,12,14,22**)-18(**4**x2,**7**x2,**8,
10,11,11,19**x2)-19(**12**x2)-20(**2,5,27**)-21(**1,9,19**)-22(**14**)-23(**27**x2,**32**x2,

34x2)-24(34x2)-25(**11,12**x2,**13,14**,<u>18</u>x3,**19**x2,**20**x2,**23,24,25,26**x2,**28**)-26(**1**
x2,**2**x2,**7,8,9,11,14,16,17,18,21**x2,**22,23**)-27(**3,5,8,15,17,19,20**,
21x2)-28(**1,3,15**x2)-29-30(**14**x2)-31(**10,14**).

*a/1: 2.7, 3.18, 6.23x2, 7.27x2, 10.25, 12.4, 13.12, 13.14, `14.27, 15.4, 16.31,
17.6x2, 18.7x2, 18.10,18.11, 20.27, 22.14, 23.27x2, 25.18x3.

*c/: 3.18, 4.9, 4.17x2, 13.12, 13.14, 14.3, 14.27x2, 15.4, 16.31, 22.8, 22.15.

* * *

Ecclesiastes (12 Chapters)

[14 similes: 13 prothetic + 1 <u>predicate</u>]

1-2-3-4-5-6-7(**1,6,26**x2,<u>**26**</u>)-8-9(**4,12**x2,**18**)-10(**1,8,11**)-11-12(**11**x2).
*a/1: 7.26(27)

* * *

The Song of Solomon (8 Chapters)

[78 similes: 65 prothetic + 13 <u>predicate</u>]

1(**2,3,4,5**x2,**9**,<u>13</u>,**14**,<u>15</u>)-2(<u>1</u>x2,**2,3,9**,<u>14</u>,**17**)-3(**6**)-4(<u>1</u>,**1,2,3**x2,**4,5**,
10x2,**11**x2,<u>12</u>x3)-5(**11**x2,**12,13**x3,**14**x2,**15**x3)-6(**4**x3,**5,6,7,10**x4,
12)-7(**1,2**x2,**3,4**x3,**5**x2,**7**x2,**8**x2,**9**)-8(**6**x4,<u>**6**</u>,<u>**9**</u>x2,<u>10</u>,**10,14**x2).

*a/1: 1.13, 2.1x2, 2.14, 4.12x3, 8.6, 8.9x2, 8.10
*a/2: 1.15,4.1

* * *

Isaiah (66 Chapters)

[222 similes: 195 prothetic + 11 <u>predicate</u> + 16 genitive]

1(**8**x3,**9**x2,**18**x4,**30**x2,**31**x2)-2-3(**18**)-4-5(**24**x4,**28**x2,**29**x2,**30**)-6(**13**x2)-
7(**2**)-8-9(**18**x2,**19**)-10(**14**x2,**15**x2,**16,17**x2,**22**)-11([**4**])-12-13(**8**x2,**12**x2,
14x2)-14(**19**x3)-15-16(**2,11**)-17(**5**x2,**6,9**x2,**12**x2,**13**x3)-18(**4**x2)-19(**14**,
16)-20-21(**1,3**)-22(**18**)-23(**15**)-24(**13**x2,**20**x2,**22**)-25-26(**17,18**)-27-
28(**2**x3)-29(**4,5**x2,**7,8**x2,**11**)-30(**17**x2,**22,27,28,29**x2,**33**)-31(**4,5**)-
32(**2**x4,**14**x3)-33(**4**x2,**9,11,12**x2)-34(**4**x3)-35(**1,6**)-36-37(**27**x4)-
38(**12**x2,**13,14**x2)-39-40(**11,15**x3,**22**x3,**24,31**)-41(**2**x2,<u>15</u>,**15,2**

5x2,<u>29</u>)-42(6x2,13x2,14)-43-44-45-46(5)-47(14)-48(<u>4</u>x2,18x2,19x2)-
49(2,<u>2</u>,6,18x2)-50-51(6x2,8x2)-52-53(2x2,6,7x2)-54(6,9)-55(9,10x2)-
56-57(20)-58(11x2)-59(10x4,11x2,17)-60(8x2)-61(10x2,11x2)-62(5x2)-
63(13,14)-64(2,6x4,<u>8x4,10x2</u>)-65(8,22,25)-66(3x4,12x2,14,15).

   *a/1: 41.29,48.4x2,64.8x4,64.10x2

   *a/2: 41.15,49.2

   *c/: 11.4,28.5,30.20x2,30.28,51.22x2,59.17x2,61.3x4,
      61.10x2,63.9.

* * *

Jeremiah (52 Chapters)

[110 similes: 89 prothetic + 17 <u>predicate</u> + 4 genitive]

1 - 2 (<u>14</u>x2,<u>31</u>x2) - 3 (<u>17</u>,20) - 4 (13x3,31x2) - 5 (8,<u>13,</u>16,27) -
6(2,7,9x2,24,26,27,<u>28</u>)-7(<u>11</u>)-8(6,7[14])-9(3,8,<u>11</u>,22x2)-10(5)-11(<u>19</u>)-
12(3,8,9)-13(11,24)-14(6,9x2)-15-16(4)-17(6,8,11)-18(6x2,17)-19-
20(9,11)-21(12)-22-
23(9x2,12,14x2,29x2)-24(5,8,<u>9</u>)-25(38)-26(18x2)-27-28-29(17)-30(6)-
31-32-33(22x2)-34-35-36-37-38-39-40-41-42-43(12)-44-45-
46(8x2,20,21,22x2,23)-47(<u>6</u>)-48(6,28,36x2,38)-49(16,19,22x2)-
50(<u>6</u>,37,42x2,43,44)-51(<u>7</u>,14,<u>19,20</u>,30,33,34,<u>34</u>,38x2, 40x2,55).

   *a/1: 2.14x2, 2.31x2, 8.13, 5.13, 6.28, 7.11, 24.9
      47.6, 50.6, 51.7, 51.19-20

   *a/2: 3.17, 9.11, 51.34

   *c/: 1.11, 8d.14, 3.16, 25.15

* * *

Lamentations of Jeremiah ΘPHNOI IEPEMIOY (5 Chapters)

[32 Similes: 29 prothetic + 2 <u>predicate</u> + 1 genitive]

1(1,6,17)-2(3,4x3,5,6,7,13,18)-3(10x2,12,45,52,<u>63</u>)-4(2x2,3,7x3,
8x2,9,<u>10</u>,14,19)-5(10).

*a/1: 3.63, 4.10
*c/: 1.14

* * *

Ezekiel (48 Chapters)

[76 similes: 61 prothetic + 12 <u>predicate</u> + 3 genitive]

1(4,5,7x2,8,10x4-13x2,14,16x2,22,24x3,26x3,27x2,28)-2-3(3,9)-4-5-
6-7(16,17)-8(2x3,3)-9-10(1x2,8,9,10,21,22)-11(3x2)-12-13(4)-14)-15-
16(7,31,32,44)-17-18-19(2,10)-20(32x2)-21(32)-22(<u>18</u>x6,20,22,<u>24</u>,27)-
23(45x2)-24-25-26(14)-27-28-29-30-31(<u>3</u>)-32(2x2)-33-34-35-36-37-
38(9x2)-39-40(3)-41-42-43(2)-44-45-46-47-48.
    *a/1: 11.3x2, 16.30, 22.18x6, 22.24, 26.14, 31.3
    *c/: 5.16, 7.11, 14.3

* * *

Daniel (12 Chapters)

[21 prothetic similes]

1-2(35,40,42)-3-4(33x3)-5-6-7(4,5,6,8,9x4)-8-9-10(6x5)-11-12
(3x2).

* * *

Hosea (14 Chapters)

[56 similes: 50 prothetic + 5 <u>predicate</u> + 1 genitive]

1(10)-2(3)-3-4(16x2)-5(10x2,14x2)-6(3x2,4x2,7,9)-7(4,6x2,7,<u>8</u>,11,12,
16)-8(1,8,<u>9</u>)-9(4,<u>8</u>,10x2,11)-10(<u>1</u>,4,7,11)-11(10,11x2)-12(<u>7</u>)-13(3x4,
7x2,8x2)-14(5x3,6x2,7x3,8).
    *a/1: 7.8, 8.9, 9.8, 10.1, 12.7.
    *c/: 10.13

* * *

Joel (3 Chapters)

[12 similes: 10 prothetic + 2 <u>predicate</u>]

1(<u>6</u>x2,8)-2(3,4x2,5x3,7x2,9).

* * *

Amos (9 Chapters)

[10 prothetic similes]

1-2(9x2,13)-3(12)-4(11)-5(19x2,24x2)-6-7-8-9(9).

* * *

Obadiah (1 Chapter)

[4 similes: 2 prothetic and 2 <u>predicate</u>]

1(4,<u>18</u>x2,18).
      *a/1: 1.18x2

* * *

Jonah (4 Chapters)

[1 <u>predicate</u>]

    *a/1: 4(<u>6</u>).

* * *

Micah (7 Chapters)

[15 prothetic similes]

1(4x2,6x2,8x2,16)-2(12x2)-3-4-5(8x2)-6-7(1x2,4x2).

* * *

Nahum (3 Chapters)

[4 prothetic similes]

1(6,10x3).

* * *

Habakkuk (3 Chapters)

[10 prothetic similes]

1(8x3,9x2,14x2)-2-3(4,14,19).

* * *

Zephaniah (3 Chapters)

[2 <u>predicate</u> similes]

1-2-3.
    *a/1: 3.3x2.

* * *

Haggai (2 Chapters)

[No similes]

* * *

Zechariah (14 Chapters)

[17 similes: 13 prothetic + 3 <u>predicate</u> + 1 genitive]

1-2-3-4(**1**)-5(**9**)-6-7(**12**)-8-9(3x2,**14**)-10(**2,3,5,7**x2)-11(<u>3</u>)-12(<u>2,3</u>,**6**x2)-
13-14.
    *a/: 11.3,12.2,12.3
    *c/:12.2

* * *

Malachi (4 Chapters)

[2 similes: 1 prothetic + 1 <u>predicate</u>]

1-2-3-4(**1**,<u>1</u>).
    *a/: 4.1

* * *

Summary: Number of Similes Old Testament

Book	Prothetic Similes	Predicate	Genitive
Genesis	12	5	
Exodus	8	2	
Numbers	5		
Deuteronomy	6	2	
Joshua	1		
Judges	8		
I Samuel		1	
II Samuel	9	7	6
I Kings	1		
II Kings	2	1	
I Chronicles	1		
II Chronicles		1	
Job	88	11	6
Psalms	150	37	14
Proverbs	105	26	13
Ecclesiastes	13	1	
Solomon's Song	65	13	
Isaiah	195	11	16
Jeremiah	89	17	4
Lamentations	29	2	1
Ezekiel	61	12	3
Daniel	21		
Hosea	50	5	1
Joel	10	2	
Amos	10		
Obadiah	2	2	
Jonah	1		
Micah	15		
Nahum	4		
Habakkuk	10		
Zephaniah		2	
Zechariah	13	3	1
Malachi	1	1	
Totals:	984	164	65 (1213 Total Similes)

There are ten books with no prothetic similes:

Leviticus (27 Chapters), Ruth (4 Chapters), Ezra (10 Chapters), Nehemiah (13 Chapters), Esther (10 Chapters), Haggai (2 Chapters); Four of these have predicate or genitive similes: 1 Samuel (First Kings, 31 Chapters), II Chronicles (36 Chapters) Jonah (4 Chapters) and Zephaniah (3 Chapters). There are Five Groups of Similes in the Old Testament: The five <u>Poetical</u> books have the most similes (Job through Solomon's Song, 421 similes), followed by the five major <u>Prophets</u> (Isaiah through Daniel, 395 similes). The other three groups follow at a great distance with fewer similes (except for Hosea): the twelve minor <u>Prophets</u> (Hosea through Malachi, 115 similes), <u>Pentateuch</u> (5 books: Genesis through Deuteronomy, 31 similes) and <u>History</u> (12 books: Joshua through II Chronicles, 22 similes).

B– The New Testament

Matthew (28 Chapters)

[49 similes: 33 prothetic + 13 <u>predicate</u> + 3 genitive]

1-2-3(**16**)-4(<u>19</u>)-5(<u>13,14</u>)-6(<u>22,25</u>)-7(<u>15</u>,**24,26**)-8-9(**36**)-10(**16**x3,**31**)-11(**16**)-12(**12**)-13(**24,31,33,**<u>37</u>,<u>38</u>x3,<u>39</u>x3,**44,45,47,52**)-14-15-16-17(**20**)-18(**3,**<u>23</u>)-19(**24**)-20(**1**)-21(<u>13</u>)-22(**2,30**)-23(**27**)-24(**27**)-25(**1,14,32**)-26-27-28(**3**x2,**4**).

*a/1: 5.13, 5.14, 6.22, 7.15,13.37,13.38x3,13.39x3
*a/2: 4.19, 21.13 NB passim 'kingdom of [=] heaven'
*c/: 3.3, 4.17, 18.3

* * *

Mark (16 Chapters)

[10 prothetic similes]

1(**10**)-2-3-4(**26,31**)-5-6(**34**)-7-8(**24**)-9(**3x2**)-10(**25**)-11-12(**25**)-
13(**34**)-14-15-16.

* * *

Luke (24 Chapters)

[18 similes: 13 prothetic + 3 <u>predicate</u> + 2 genitive]

1-2-3(**22**)-4-5-6(**48,49**)-7(**32**)-8(<u>11</u>)-9(<u>58</u>)-10(**3,18**)-11(<u>34</u>)-12(**36**)-
13(**19,21,34**)-14-15-16-17(**6**)-18(**25**)-19-20-21(**35**)-22-23-24.
    *a/1: 8.11, 9.58, 11.34
    *c/: 1.69,1.79

* * *

John (21 Chapters)

[24 similes: 2 prothetic + 19 <u>predicate</u> + 3 genitive]

1(<u>4,23</u>,**32**)-2-3(**14**,<u>29</u>)-4(<u>34</u>)-5-6(<u>33,48,51</u>)-7-8-9(<u>5</u>)-10(<u>1-2-7-9-11-14</u>)-11-
12(<u>46</u>)-13-14-15(<u>1,5</u>)-16-17-18-19-20-21.
    *a/1: 1.4,1.23, 3.29, 4.34, 6.33, 6.35, 6.48, 6.51, 8.12,
        9.5, 10.1-2-7-9-11-14, 12.46, 15.1, 15.5
    *c/: 2.21, 6.35, 8.12

* * *

Acts of the Apostles (28 Chapters)

[11 similes: 7 prothetic + 4 <u>predicate</u>]

1-2(**2,3**,<u>35</u>)-3-4-5-6-7(<u>49x2</u>)-8(**32x2**)-9(<u>15</u>,**18**)-10-11(**5**)-12-13-14-
15-16-17(**29**)-18-19-20-21-22-23-24-25-26-27-28.
    *a/1: 7.49x2, 9.15
    *a/2: 2.35

* * *

Romans (16 Chapters)

[4 similes: 3 <u>predicate</u> + 1 genitive]

1-2(<u>19</u>)-3(<u>13</u>)-4-5-6-7-8-9-10-11(<u>17</u>)-12-13-14-15-16.
 *a/1: 2.19, 3.13, 11.17
 *c/: 9.33

* * *

First Corinthians (16 Chapters)

[3 similes: 2 prothetic + 1 <u>predicate</u>]

1-2-3-4-5-6(<u>19</u>)-7-8-9-10-11-12-13(**1x2**)-14-15-16.
 *a/1: 6.19

* * *

Second Corinthians (13 Chapters)

[1 prothetic simile]

1-2-3-4-5-6-7-8-9-10-11(**3**)-12-13.

* * *

Galatians (6 Chapters)

[2 <u>predicate</u> similes]

1-2-3(<u>24</u>)-4-5(<u>22</u>)-6.
 *a/1: 3.24, 5.22

* * *

Ephesians (6 Chapters)

[4] genitive similes]

1-2-3-4-5-6.
 *c/: 6.14, 6.16, 6.17x2

* * *

Philippians (4 Chapters)

[1 prothetic simile]

1-2$\left(\mathbf{15}\right)$-3-4.

* * *

Colossians (4 Chapters)

[1 <u>predicate</u> simile]

1-2$\left(\underline{17}\right)$-3-4.
   *a/1: 2.17

* * *

First Thessalonians (5 Chapters)

[3 similes: 2 prothetic + 1 genitive]

1-2-3-4-5$\left(\mathbf{2,3}\right)$.
   *c/: 2.5

* * *

Second Thessalonians (3 Chapters)

[No similes]

* * *

First Timothy (6 Chapters)

[2 <u>predicate</u> similes]

1-2-3$\left(\underline{15}\right)$-4-5-6$\left(\underline{10}\right)$.
   *a/1: 3.15,6.10

* * *

Second Timothy (4 Chapters)

[1 genitive simile]

1-2-3-4($\underline{8}$).
        *c/: 4.8

* * *

Titus (3 Chapters)

[No similes]

* * *

Philemon (1 Chapter)

[No similes]

* * *

Hebrews (13 Chapters)

[1 prothetic simile]

1-2-3-4(**12**)-5-6-7-8-9-10-11-12-13.

* * *

James (5 Chapters)

[6 similes: 3 prothetic + 2 <u>predicate</u> + 1 genitive]

1(**11,23**)-2-3($\underline{5,6}$)-4-5(**3**)
        *a/1: 3.5, 3.6
        *c/: 1.12

* * *

First Peter (5 Chapters)

[11 similes: 8 prothetic + 3 genitive]

1(7,19,24x2)-2(4,5,16)-3-4-5(8).
    *c/: 2.8x2, 2.16

* * *

Second Peter (3 Chapters)

[1 prothetic simile]

1-2-3(10).

* * *

First John (5 Chapters)

[No similes]

* * *

Second John (1 Chapter)

[No similes]

* * *

Third John (1 Chapter)

[No similes]

* * *

Jude (1 Chapter)

[1 prothetic simile]

1(10).

* * *

The Revelation of St. John (22 Chapters)

[63 similes: 60 prothetic + 2 **predicate** + 1 genitive]

1(**10,14**x3,**15**x3,**16,17,**<u>20x2</u>)-2(**18**x2)-3(**3**)-4(**1,3**x2,**6,7**x4)-5-
6(**1,12**x2,**13,14**)-7-8(**8,10**)-9(**3,5,7**x3,**8**x2,**9**x2,**10,17,19**)-10(**1**x2,
3,9=**10**)-11(**1**)-12-13(**2**x3,**11**x2)-14(**2**x2)-15(**2**)-16-17-18(**21**)-19
(**12**)-20-21(**2,11**x2,**18**)-22(**1**).

    *a/1: 1.20 (2)
    *c/: 2.7

Summary: Number of Similes (New Testament)

Book	Prothetic Similes	Predicate	Genitive
Matthew	33	13	3
Mark	10		
Luke	13	3	2
John	2	19	3
Acts/Apostles	7	4	
Romans		3	1
First Corinthians	2	1	
Second "	1		
Galatians		2	
Ephesians			4
Philippians	1		
Colossians		1	
First Thessalonians	2		1
First Timothy		2	
Second "			1
Hebrews	1		
James	3	2	1
First Peter	8		3
Second "	1		
Jude	1		
Revelation	<u>60</u>	<u>2</u>	<u>1</u>

Book	Prothetic Similes	Predicate	Genitive
Total:	145	52	20

There are twelve books without prothetic similes:
SecondThessalonians (3 Chapters), Titus (3 Chapters), Philemon (1 Chapter), First John (5 Chapters), Second John (1 Chapter), Third John (1 Chapter);
Six of these contain predicate or genitive similes:
Epistle of Paul to the Romans (16 Chapters), Galatians (6 Chapters), Ephesians (6 Chapters), Colossians (4 Chapters), First Timothy (6 Chapters), Second Timothy (4 Chapters).

* * *

Predicate Similes (*a1/ and *a/2) (Some predicate similes are also listed in the main collection if they occur in sentences with regular similes.)

The Old Testament

Gen. 40.12 The _three branches_ <u>are</u> _three days_. [three days ≈ three branches] Joseph's interpretation of the chief butler's dream is like a simile in that the symbolic dream of branches contains the vehicle. Cf. the interpretation of parables, where "the figurative element (the vehicle) often becomes the subject rather than the predicate." (See Introduction #8.).

Gen. 49.9 _Judah_ is _<u>a lion's whelp</u>_:
9 <u>σκύμνος λέοντος</u> Ἰούδα·
*a/1   9 <u>Catulus leonis</u> Juda
[Judah ≈ a lion's whelp]

Gen. 49.17 _Dan_ shall be _<u>a serpent by the way</u>_, an _<u>adder in the path</u>_, that _biteth the horse heels ..._
17 καὶ γενηθήτω Δὰν <u>ὄφις ἐφ᾿ ὁδοῦ ἐγκαθήμενος ἐπὶ τρίβου</u>, δάκνων πτέρναν ἵππου,
*a/1   17 Fiat Dan _<u>coluber in via</u>_, _<u>cerastes in semita</u>_, mordens ungulas equi.   Jacob to his sons
[Dan ≈ a serpent, an adder]

Gen. 49.21 Naphtali is _<u>a hind let loose:</u> he giveth goodly words._
*a/1   Νεφθαλεὶμ <u>στέλεχος ἀνειμένον</u>, ἐπιδιδοὺς ἐν τῷ γεννήματι κάλλος.
       (Nephthalim is a spreading stem, bestowing beauty on its fruit.)

Nephthali, _cervus emissus_, et dans eloquia pulchritudinis.
[Naphtali ≈ a hind let loose]   Jacob to his sons
*a/1   49.22 *Joseph is a fruitful bough, even a fruitful bough by a well;whose*
branches run over the wall.
    22 _υἱὸς ηὐξημένος_ ᾿Ιωσήφ, υἱὸς ηὐξημένος μου ζηλωτός, υἱός μου νεώτατος.
    (Joseph is _a son increased_; my dearly loved son is increased; my
    youngest son.)
    22 _Filius accrescens_ Joseph, filius accrescens et decorus aspectu: filiae
    discurrerunt super murum.
(Joseph is _a growing son_, a growing son and comely to behold.)   Jacob
    to his sons
[Joseph ≈ fruitful bough]

* * *

Exodus 10.7 How long shall this man be _a snare unto us_?
    *a/1   7 ἕως τίνος ἔσται τοῦτο _ἡμῖν σκῶλον_ [_stumbling block, hindrance_];
    7 Usquequo patiemur hoc scandalum [stumbling block]?
    [this man ≈ a snare to us] Pharaoh's servants
    Exodus 14.22 and _the waters_ were _a wall_ unto them on their right
    *a/1hand and on their left.
    22. καὶ τὸ ὕδωρ αὐτῆς _τεῖχος_ ἐκ δεξιῶν καὶ _τεῖχος_ ἐξ εὐωνύμων·
    22 erat enim aqua _quasi murus_ a dextra eorum et laeva.
    NB: The Latin adds a prothesis (quasi).
    22 [water ≈ a wall]   Narrator

* * *

Deut. 4.24 For _the Lord thy God_ is _a consuming fire_, even a jealous God.
    *a/1   24 ὅτι _Κύριος ὁ Θεός σου πῦρ καταναλίσκον_ ἐστί, Θεὸς ζηλωτής.
    24 quia _Dominus Deus tuus ignis consumens_ est, Deus aemulator.
    [the Lord ≈ a consuming fire] Moses quoting the Lord
    (NB: The simile is repeated at 9.3 with a prothesis in English: "as
    a consuming fire he shall destroy them.")
Deut. 32.4 He [the Lord] is the _Rock_, his work is perfect.
    4 Θεός, ἀληθινὰ τὰ ἔργα αὐτοῦ, καὶ πᾶσαι αἱ ὁδοὶ αὐτοῦ κρίσεις·
    4 Dei perfecta sunt opera, et omnes viae ejus judicia.

[the Lord ≈ the Rock] **No simile in Greek or Latin.**

* * *

1 Samuel 17.43 = I Kings

*a/1   And the Philistine said unto David, Am *I a dog*, that thou comest to me with staves?

43 καὶ εἶπεν ὁ ἀλλόφυλος πρὸς Δαυίδ· <u>ὡσεὶ κύων</u> ἐγώ εἰμι, ὅτι σὺ ἔρχῃ ἐπ᾽ ἐμὲ ἐν ῥάβδῳ καὶ λίθοις; καὶ εἶπε Δαυίδ· οὐχί, ἀλλ᾽ ἢ <u>χείρων κυνός</u>. (and David said, No but <u>worse than</u> *a dog*.)

>   43 Et dixit Philisthaeus ad David: Numquid ego <u>*canis*</u> sum, quod tu venis ad me cum baculo? A Philistine

[I ≈ a dog]

NB: The Greek adds a prothesis (ὡσεὶ).

* * *

II Samuel 22.2 And he said, The *Lord is <u>my rock</u>*, and <u>*my fortress*</u>, and my deliverer.

2 καὶ εἶπεν· Κύριε, <u>*πέτρα μου,*</u> καὶ <u>*ὀχύρωμά μου*</u> καὶ ἐξαιρούμενός με ἐμοί.

*a/1   2 et ait: Dominus <u>*petra mea,*</u> et <u>*robur meum*</u>, et salvator meus.

[Lord ≈ my rock and my fortress] David to the Lord in song

II Samuel 22.3 he is <u>*my shield*</u>, and <u>*the horn of my salvation*</u>, my

*c/   <u>*high tower,*</u> and my refuge, my saviour.

3 <u>*ὑπερασπιστής*</u> μου καὶ <u>*κέρας σωτηρίας μου,*</u> <u>*ἀντιλήπτωρ*</u> μου καὶ καταφυγή μου σωτηρίας μου.

*a/1   3 Deus fortis meus sperabo in eum: <u>*scutum*</u> meum, et <u>*cornu*</u> salutis meae: <u>*elevator*</u> meus, et refugium meum: salvator meus.

[he ≈ my shield ≈ the horn of my salvation ≈ my high tower] David to the Lord in song

II Samuel 22.29 For *thou* art <u>*my lamp*</u>, O Lord.

29 ὅτι <u>*σὺ ὁ λύχνος μου*</u>, Κύριε.

*a/1   29 Quia *tu <u>lucerna mea</u>*, Domine.

[thou/Lord ≈ my lamp]   David to the Lord in song

II Samuel 22.31 He is a <u>*buckler*</u> to all them that trust in him.

*a/1   31 <u>*ὑπερασπιστής*</u> ἐστι πᾶσι τοῖς πεποιθόσιν ἐπ᾽ αὐτόν.

31 <u>*scutum*</u> est omnium sperantium in se.

[the Lord ≈ a buckler (shield)]   David to the Lord in song

* * *

II Kings 21.14 and *they [the people of Jerusalem]* shall become <u>*a prey*</u> and <u>*a spoil*</u> to all their enemies.

　　14 καὶ <u>ἔσονται</u> εἰς <u>διαρπαγὴν καὶ εἰς προνομὴν</u> πᾶσι τοῖς ἐχθροῖς αὐτῶν

　　14 eruntque in vastitatem, et in rapinam cunctis adversariis suis.

　　　　[they ≈ a prey and a spoil]   The Lord

NB: A prothesis in Greek but no simile in Latin.

* * *

Job 6.12 Is *my strength* the <u>*strength of stones*</u>? or is *my flesh* of <u>*brass*</u>?

　　12 μὴ ἰσχὺς <u>λίθων</u> ἡ ἰσχύς μου; ἢ αἱ σάρκες μού εἰσι <u>χάλκεαι</u>;

　　*a/   12 Nec fortitudo <u>lapidum</u> *fortitudo mea, nec caro mea* aenea/

　　　　[my strength ≈ stones; my flesh ≈ brass] Job/*est.*

　　Job 7.7 O remember that *my life* is <u>*wind*</u>.

**a/1   7 μνήσθητι οὖν ὅτι <u>πνεῦμά</u> μου ἡ ζωὴ.

　　　7 Memento quia *ventus* est *vita mea.*

　　　　[my life ≈ wind]   Job

Job 7.12 Am *I* a <u>*sea, or a whale*</u>, that thou settest a watch over me?

**a/1   12 πότερον <u>θάλασσά εἰμι ἢ δράκων</u>, ὅτι κατέταξας ἐπ᾿ ἐμὲ φυλακήν;

　　　12 Numquid <u>*mare ego*</u> sum, aut <u>*cetus*</u>, quia circumdedisti me carcere?

　　　　[I ≈ a sea or a whale (serpent)?]   Job

Job 8.9 For we are but of yesterday, and know nothing, because *our days* upon earth are <u>*a shadow*</u>:

　　9 χθιζοὶ γὰρ ἐσμεν καὶ οὐκ οἴδαμεν, <u>σκιὰ</u> γάρ <u>ἐστιν</u> ἡμῶν ἐπὶ τῆς γῆς ὁ βίος.

　　9 (hesterni quippe sumus, et ignoramus, quoniam **sicut** <u>*umbra*</u> *dies nostri* sunt *super terram.*)

**a/1   [our days ≈ a shadow]   Bildad

Job 8.14 Whose hope shall be cut off, and whose *trust* shall be

**a/1   <u>*a spider's web*</u>.

　　14 ἀοίκητος γὰρ αὐτοῦ ἔσται ὁ οἶκος, <u>ἀράχνη</u> δὲ αὐτοῦ <u>ἀποβήσεται</u> ἡ σκηνή.

　　14 Non ei placebit vecordia sua, et <u>sicut</u> <u>*tela aranearum*</u> *fiducia ejus.*

　　　　[his trust ≈ a spider's web]   Bildad

Job 13.4 But ye are forgers of lies, *ye* are all <u>*physicians of no value*</u>.

4 ὑμεῖς δέ ἐστε ἰατροὶ ἄδικοι καὶ ἰαταὶ κακῶν πάντες.

*a/1 4 prius *vos* ostendens *fabricatores mendacii,* et *cultores perversorum dogmatum.*

[you all ≈ bad physicians]   Job

Job 17.14 Thou [*corruption*] art *my father: to the worm, Thou* art *my mother, and my sister.*

Job 20.14 Yet his meat in his bowels is turned, *it* is the *gall of asps* within him.

Job 29.15 *I* was *eyes to the blind*, and *feet* was *I* to the lame.

15 ὀφθαλμὸς ἤμην τυφλῶν, ποὺς δὲ χωλῶν.

15 Oculus fui caeco, et pes claudo.

[I ≈ eyes + feet]   Job

Job 31.12 For it [deception] is *a fire that consumeth to destruction.*

12 πῦρ γάρ ἐστι [θυμὸς γὰρ ὀργῆς] καιόμενον ἐπὶ πάντων τῶν μερῶν, οὗ δ᾽ ἂν ἐπέλθῃ ἐκ ριζῶν ἀπώλεσεν.

12 *Ignis* est [iniquitas maxima] usque ad perditionem devorans, et omnia eradicans genimina.

[deception ≈ a fire]   Job

Job 38.8 Or who shut up *the sea* with doors, *when it brake forth*, as if it had *issued out of the womb*? 9 When I made *the*
    a/2 cloud the garment thereof, and *thick darkness a swaddling-band for it.*

8 ἔφραξα δὲ θάλασσαν πύλαις, ὅτε ἐμαιοῦτο ἐκ κοιλίας μητρὸς αὐτῆς ἐκπορευομένη. ἐθέμην δὲ αὐτῇ νέφος ἀμφίασιν, ὁμίχλη δὲ αὐτὴν ἐσπαργάνωσα.

8 Quis conclusit ostiis mare, quando *erumpebat* quasi *de vulva* procedens; cum ponerem *nubem* vestimentum ejus, et *caligine* illud quasi *pannis infantiae* obvolverem? [the sea broke out ≈ issued out to the womb; the cloud ≈ a garment; thick darkness ≈ a swaddling-band] The Lord to Job

NB sometimes the English version leaves out the prothesis, expressed in the Greek or Latin:

Job 41.19 Out of his mouth go *burning lamps*, and sparks of fire leap out.

11 ἐκ στόματος αὐτοῦ ἐκπορεύονται ὡς λαμπάδες καιόμεναι καὶ διαρριπτοῦνται ὡς ἐσχάραι πυρός.

(This shows that the prothesis is often implicit in English.)

* * *

Psalm 3.3 But *thou*, O Lord, art <u>*a shield for me;*</u> my glory, and <u>*the lifter up*</u> of mine head.

> 4 <u>σὺ</u> δέ, Κύριε, <u>*ἀντιλήπτωρ*</u> [helper/protector] μου εἶ, δόξα μου καὶ <u>ὑψῶν</u> τὴν κεφαλήν μου

> 4 *Tu* autem Domine, <u>*susceptor meus*</u> es, gloria mea, et exaltans caput meum.

> *a/1   [thou (O Lord) ≈ a shield for me + lifter up]

Simile only in English.

18.2 The Lord is <u>*my rock*</u>, and my <u>*fortress*</u>, and my deliverer; my God, my strength, in whom I will trust; <u>*my buckler*</u>, and the <u>*horn of my salvation*</u> and my <u>*high tower*</u>.

> = 17.3 *Κύριος <u>στερέωμά μου</u> καὶ <u>καταφυγή μου</u> καὶ <u>ρύστης</u> μου.* ῾Ο Θεός μου βοηθός μου, ἐλπιῶ ἐπ᾽ αὐτόν, ὑπερασπιστής μου καὶ <u>κέρας σωτηρίας μου</u> καὶ ἀντιλήπτωρ μου.

> *a/1   17.3 Dominus firmamentum meum, et refugium meum, et liberator meus. Deus meus adjutor meus, et sperabo in
> *c/   eum; protector meus, et <u>*cornu salutis meae*</u>, et susceptor meus. [the Lord ≈ my rock, fortress, deliverer, strength, buckler, the horn of my salvation, my high tower]

> **– A combination of predicate similes and simple nouns, plus one genitive simile.**

Psalm 22.6 But *I* am a <u>*worm*</u>, and no man; a reproach of men, and despised of the people.

> 21.7 *ἐγὼ* δέ <u>εἰμι</u> <u>*σκώληξ*</u> καὶ οὐκ ἄνθρωπος, ὄνειδος ἀνθρώπων καὶ ἐξουθένημα λαοῦ.

> 21.7 Ego autem sum vermis, et non homo; opprobrium hominum, et abjectio plebis.

> *a/1   [I ≈ a worm]

Psalm 23.1 The *Lord* is <u>*my shepherd*</u>; I shall not want …

4 Yea, though I walk through <u>*the valley of the shadow of death*</u>, I will fear no evil … thy rod and thy staff they comfort me.

> *d/   22.1 ΚΥΡΙΟΣ <u>*ποιμαίνει*</u> με καὶ οὐδέν με ὑστερήσει … ἐὰν γὰρ καὶ πορευθῶ <u>ἐν μέσῳ σκιᾶς θανάτου</u>, οὐ φοβηθήσομαι κακά … ἡ ῥάβδος σου καὶ ἡ βακτηρία σου, αὐταί με παρεκάλεσαν.

22.1 Dominus regit me, et nihil mihi deert … 4 Nam, etsi ambulavero *in medio umbrae mortis*, non timebo mala, quoniam tu mecum es. Virga tua, et baculus tuus, ipsa me consolata sunt.

[Lord ≈ my shepherd; death ≈ a shadow]

NB: Here the Greek expresses the simile as a verb, while the English translates it as a predicate simile.

Psalm 27.1 The *Lord* is *my light* and my salvation.

    26.1 *ΚΥΡΙΟΣ φωτισμός μου* καὶ σωτήρ μου.

    26.1 *Dominus illuminatio mea* et salus mea.

    [the Lord ≈ my light]

Psalm 28.1 Unto thee will I cry, O Lord *my rock.*

    27.1 ΠΡΟΣ σέ, Κύριε, ἐκέκραξα, ὁ Θεός μου.

    27.1 Ad te, Domine, clamabo;   [Lord ≈ my rock]

    28.7 The Lord is my strength and *my shield.*

    27.8 Κύριος κραταίωμα τοῦ λαοῦ αὐτοῦ καὶ ὑπερασπιστὴς τῶν σωτηρίων τοῦ χριστοῦ αὐτοῦ ἐστι. (The Lord is the strength of his people, and the saving defender of his anointed.)

    27.8 Dominus fortitudo plebis suae, et protector salvationum christi sui est.

*a/1   [Lord ≈ my rock ≈ my shield]

Neither simile appears in Greek or Latin.

Psalm 31.2 Be *thou* my *strong rock,* for *an house of defense* to save me.

    30.3 γενοῦ μοι εἰς Θεὸν ὑπερασπιστὴν καὶ εἰς οἶκον καταφυγῆς

    30.3 *Esto* mihi i*n Deum protectorem*, et *in domum refugii*, ut salvum me facias.   [thou/Lord ≈ my rock]

Psalm 31.3 thou art *my rock and my fortress.*

    30.4 ὅτι <u>κραταίωμά μου καὶ καταφυγή μου</u> εἶ σύ.

    30.4 quoniam *fortitudo mea et refugium meum* es *tu*;

    [thou/Lord ≈ my rock and my fortress]

    30.3 γενοῦ μοι <u>εἰς Θεὸν ὑπερασπιστὴν</u> καὶ <u>εἰς οἶκον καταφυγῆς</u> τοῦ σῶσαί με. (Be thou to me for a protecting God, and for a house of refuge to save me.)

    30.3 Esto mihi in Deum protectorem, et in *domum refugii,* ut salvum me facias: 4 quoniam fortitudo mea et *refugium meum* es tu;

    [thou ≈ my strong rock and ≈ a house of defense ≈ my rock + fortress]

Psalm 32.7 *Thou* art *my hiding place.*

   31.7 σύ μου <u>εἶ</u> <u>καταφυγή ἀπὸ θλίψεως τῆς περιεχούσης με·</u>

   31.7 *Tu* es *refugium meum a tribulatione quae circumdedit me*;

   [thou/Lord ≈ hiding place]

Psalm 33.20 Our soul waiteth for the *Lord; he* <u>is</u> our help and *our shield.*

   32.20 ἡ ψυχὴ ἡμῶν ὑπομενεῖ τῷ Κυρίῳ, ὅτι *βοηθὸς καὶ ὑπερασπιστὴς*
   ἡμῶν ἐστιν·

   32.20 Anima nostra sustinet Dominum, quoniam *adjutor et protector*
   noster est.

   [the Lord ≈ our shield] **Not a simile in Greek or Latin.**

Psalm 36.6 Thy *righteousness* is <u>like</u> *the great mountains*; thy *judgments* are
a *great deep.*

   35.7 ἡ δικαιοσύνη σου <u>ὡς</u> <u>ὄρη Θεοῦ</u>, τὰ κρίματά σου <u>ὡσεὶ</u> <u>ἄβυσσος πολλή·</u>

   a/   35.7 Justitia tua <u>sicut</u> montes Dei; judicia tua abyssus multa.

   [your righteousness ≈ great mountains; your judgments ≈ a great deep]

Psalm 45.1 *My tongue* is *the pen of a ready writer.*

   44.2 ἡ γλῶσσά μου <u>κάλαμος γραμματέως ὀξυγράφου.</u>

   44.2 *Lingua mea calamus scribae velociter scribentis.*

   [my tongue ≈ pen of a ready writer]

Psalm 57.4 My soul is among lions: … among … the sons of men, whose
teeth are *spears and arrows*, and their *tongue* a *sharp sword.*

   56.5 υἱοὶ ἀνθρώπων, οἱ ὀδόντες αὐτῶν <u>ὅπλα καὶ βέλη</u>, καὶ ἡ γλῶσσα αὐτῶν
   <u>μάχαιρα ὀξεῖα.</u>

   56.5 Filii hominum *dentes* eorum *arma et sagittae*, et *lingua eorum*
   gladius acutus.

a/1 [men's teeth ≈ spears and arrows; their tongue ≈ *a sharp weapon]

Psalm 59.11 bring them down, O *Lord our shield.*

   58.12 <u>ὁ ὑπερασπιστής μου, Κύριε.</u>

   58.12 et depone eos, *protector meus, Domine.*

[Lord ≈ our shield]

   Psalm 60.8 Moab is my *washpot.*

   *a/   59.10 Μωὰβ <u>λέβης τῆς ἐλπίδος μου.</u>

   *c/   59.10 Moab olla *spei meae.*

   [Moab ≈ washpot/caldron of my hope]

   The English translation omits entirely the genitive phrase.

Psalm 61.3 For *thou* hast been *a shelter* for me, and *a strong tower* from the enemy.

60.4 ὅτι ἐγενήθης ἐλπίς μου, <u>*πύργος ἰσχύος*</u> ἀπὸ προσώπου ἐχθροῦ.

*c/   60.4 quia factus es spes mea, *turris fortitudinis* a facie inimici.

[you ≈ my shelter ≈ a strong tower]

Psalm 62.2 *He* only is <u>*my rock*</u> and my salvation; he is my defence.

61.3 καὶ γὰρ αὐτὸς Θεός μου καὶ σωτήρ μου, καὶ ἀντιλήπτωρ μου.

61.3 Nam et ipse Deus meus et salutaris meus.

[He ≈ my rock: **NB no figurative words in the Greek or Latin**] Cf. 62.6, 7 and 8.

Psalm 78.35 And they remembered that *God* <u>was</u> *their rock*.

77.35 καὶ ἐμνήσθησαν ὅτι <u>ὁ Θεὸς βοηθὸς αὐτῶν ἐστι.</u>

77.35 Et rememorati sunt quia <u>Deus adjutor est eorum,</u>

[Another 'God as a rock' translation]

Psalm 78.39 And he remembered that *they* <u>were but</u> *flesh*; *a wind that passeth away*, and cometh not again.

[the children of Ephraim, 78.9]

77.39 καὶ ἐμνήσθη ὅτι <u>*σάρξ*</u> εἰσι, <u>*πνεῦμα πορευόμενον*</u> καὶ οὐκ ἐπιστρέφον.

*a/1   77.39 Et recordatus est quia caro sunt, spiritus vadens et non rediens.

[they ≈ flesh ≈ a wind that disappears]

Psalm 84.11 For the *Lord God* is *a sun and shield.*

83.12 ὅτι ἔλεος καὶ ἀλήθειαν ἀγαπᾷ Κύριος ὁ Θεός, χάριν καὶ δόξαν δώσει·

83.12 Quia misericordiam et veritatem diligit Deus, gratiam et gloriam dabit Dominus.

[the Lord God ≈ a sun and shield]

Cf. 84.9 Behold, O God our shield.

Nothing corresponds in the Greek/Latin to 'sun and shield'.

Psalm 92.15 Again 'the Lord is my rock' + 94.22; 95.1.

104.3 who *maketh the clouds* his <u>chariot</u>:

103.3 ὁ <u>*τιθεὶς νέφη τὴν ἐπίβασιν αὐτοῦ*</u>,

103.3 qui ponis nubem ascensum tuum,

[clouds ≈ chariot]

104.4 who maketh his … *ministers a flaming fire.*

103.4 ὁ ποιῶν … <u>*τοὺς λειτουργοὺς αὐτοῦ πυρὸς φλόγα.*</u>

103.3 qui facis … *ministros tuos ignem urentem.*

[his ministers ≈ a flaming fire]

Psalm 104.17 As for the stork, the *fir trees* are *her house.*

103.17 τοῦ ἐρωδιοῦ ἡ οἰκία [the house of the heron]

103.17 herodii *domus*

[fir trees ≈ her house]

Psalm 108.9 *Moab* is *my washpot.*

107.10 Μωὰβ λέβης τῆς ἐλπίδος μου [caldron of my hope]

107.10 Moab *lebes* spei meae;

[Moab ≈ washpot / caldron of my hope]

Psalm 110.1 The Lord said unto my Lord, Sit thou at my right

a/2   hand, until I make thine *enemies thy footstoo*l.

109.1 ΕΙΠΕΝ ὁ Κύριος τῷ Κυρίῳ μου· κάθου ἐκ δεξιῶν μου, ἕως ἂν θῶ

τοὺς ἐχθρούς σου *ὑποπόδιον τῶν ποδῶν σου.*

109.1 Dixit Dominus Domino meo: Sede a dextris meis, donec ponam

inimicos tuos scabellum pedum tuorum.

[thine enemies ≈ a footstool]

Psalm 115.10–11 Trust in *the Lord: he is* their help and *their shield.*

113.17 βοηθὸς καὶ ὑπερασπιστὴς αὐτῶν ἐστιν. 18 … βοηθὸς καὶ

ὑπερασπιστὴς αὐτῶν ἐστιν.

113.17–18 adjutor eorum et protector eorum est.

[the Lord ≈ shield]

No similetic word in Greek or Latin.

Psalm 118.14 The *Lord* is my strength and *song,* and is become

my salvation.

117.14 ἰσχύς μου καὶ *ὕμνησίς* μου ὁ Κύριος καὶ ἐγένετό μοι εἰς σωτηρίαν.

117.14 *Fortitudo mea* et *laus mea* Dominus; et factus est mihi in salutem.

[The Lord ≈ my strength and *song* … salvation]

Psalm 119.105 Thy *word* is *a lamp unto my feet*, and *a light unto my path*.

118.105 *Λύχνος* τοῖς ποσί μου ὁ νόμος σου καὶ *φῶς* ταῖς τρίβοις μου.

118.105 *Lucerna* pedibus meis *verbum tuum*, et *lumen* semitis meis.

[your law ≈ a lamp to my feet ≈ a light to my path]

Psalm 121.5 The Lord is thy keeper: *the Lord* is *thy shade* upon thy

right-hand.

*a/   120.5 Κύριος φυλάξει σε, Κύριος *σκέπη σοι* ἐπὶ χεῖρα δεξιάν σου·

120.5 Dominus custodit te, Dominus *protectio tua* super manum dexteram tuam.

[the Lord ≈ thy shade]

* * *

Prov. 2.7 He [the Lord] layeth up sound wisdom for the righteous: *he* is *a buckler* to them that walk uprightly.

7 καὶ θησαυρίζει τοῖς κατορθοῦσι σωτηρίαν, ὑπερασπιεῖ τὴν πορείαν αὐτῶν.

7 Custodiet rectorum salutem, et proteget gradientes simpliciter.

[he/the Lord ≈ a buckler] **No simile in the Greek or Latin.**

Prov. 3.18 *She* [*wisdom*] **is** a <u>tree of life</u> to them that lay hold upon
*a/   her; and happy is every one that retaineth her.

3.18 <u>ξύλον ζωῆς</u> **ἐστι** πᾶσι τοῖς ἀντεχομένοις αὐτῆς,

3.18 *Lignum vitae* est his qui apprehenderint eam [sapientiam], et qui tenuerit eam beatus.

*c/   [wisdom ≈ a tree of life; life ≈ a tree] – **another good illustration**
of a similetic vehicle consisting of another simile.

Prov. 6.23 For *the commandment [of thy father]* is *a lamp;* and *the law [of thy mother] is light*; and reproofs of instruction are the way of life.

6.23 ὅτι <u>λύχνος</u> ἐντολὴ νόμου καὶ <u>φῶς</u>, ὁδὸς ζωῆς καὶ ἔλεγχος καὶ παιδεία.

6.23 Quia *mandatum* <u>lucerna</u> est, et *lex* <u>lux</u>, et via vitae increpatio disciplinae;

[commandment of thy father ≈ a lamp; the law of thy mother ≈ a light]

Prov. 7.27 *Her house* is *the way to hell*, going down *to the chambers of death*.

*a/   27 <u>ὁδοὶ ᾅδου</u> ὁ οἶκος αὐτῆς κατάγουσαι εἰς <u>τὰ ταμιεῖα τοῦ θανάτου</u>.

27 *Viae inferi* domus ejus, penetrantes in interiora mortis.

[her house ≈ the way to hell ≈ chambers of death]

Prov. 10.25 but *the righteous* is an *everlasting foundation*.
*a/   [See Greek and Latin versions in "I Similes in OT".]

Prov. 12.4 *A virtuous woman* is *a crown to her husband:* but
*a/   she that maketh ashamed is as *rottenness in his bones.*

γυνὴ ἀνδρεία <u>στέφανος τῷ ἀνδρὶ αὐτῆς</u>· ὥσπερ δὲ <u>ἐν ξύλῳ σκώληξ</u>, **οὕτως** ἄνδρα ἀπόλλυσι γυνὴ κακοποιός.

4 *Mulier diligens <u>corona est viro suo</u>*; et *<u>putredo in ossibus ejus</u>, quae confusione res dignas gerit.*

[a virtuous woman ≈ a crown to her husband; (a bad woman): her husband ≈ rottenness (a worm: wood)]

Prov. 13.12 Hope deferred taketh the heart sick: but when the

*a/   desire cometh, it <u>is</u> a *<u>tree of life</u>*.

12 <u>κρείσσων</u> ἐναρχόμενος βοηθῶν καρδίᾳ τοῦ ἐπαγγελλομένου καὶ εἰς ἐλπίδα ἄγοντος· <u>δένδρον γὰρ ζωῆς ἐπιθυμία ἀγαθή</u>.

(<u>Better</u> is he that begins to help heartily, *<u>than he</u>* that promises and leads [another] to hope: for *a good desire* is *<u>a tree of life</u>*.)

> 12 Spes quae differtur affligit animam; *lignum <u>vitae</u> desiderium veniens.*

*c/   [good desire ≈ a tree of life; tree ≈ life] **Again the vehicle consists of a genitive simile. The English follows the Latin text.***

Prov. 13.14 The *law* of the wise <u>is</u> a *<u>fountain</u>* of life, to depart from the *snares of death.* cf. 14.27.

14 *νόμος σοφοῦ <u>πηγὴ</u> ζωῆ.*

14 *Lex* sapientis *<u>fons</u>* vitae.

[law ≈ a fountain; life ≈ a fountain]

Prov. 14.27 The *fear of the Lord* <u>is</u> *<u>a fountain</u>* of life; to depart from the <u>snare</u>s of *death.*

27 πρόσταγμα Κυρίου <u>πηγὴ ζωῆς</u>, ποιεῖ δὲ ἐκκλίνειν ἐκ παγίδος θανάτου.

27 Timor Domini *<u>fons</u>* vitae, ut declinent a ruina mortis.

*a/   [fear of the Lord ≈ a fountain of life; life ≈ a fountain]

(snares of death = possessive genitive with personified 'death'; cf. 13.14)

Prov. 15.4 A *wholesome tongue* <u>is</u> *<u>a tree</u>* of life.

*a/   4 *ἴασις γλώσσης <u>δένδρον ζωῆς</u>,*

4 *Lingua placabilis <u>lignum</u> vitae*;

*c/   [wholesome tongue ≈ a tree of life; life ≈ a tree]

***Tree* is the vehicle of both a predicate simile and a genitive simile: wholesome tongue ≈ a tree; life ≈ a tree.**

Prov. 16.31 The hoary head is a *<u>crown of glory</u>* ...

31 <u>στέφανος</u> καυχήσεως γήρας,

*a/   31 *<u>Corona</u> dignitatis senectus, quae in viis justitiae reperietur.*

*c/   [hoary head ≈ a crown of glory; glory ≈ a crown]

Prov. 17.6 Children's *children* <u>are</u> *the crown of old men*; and the *glory of children* are their *fathers.*

6 <u>στέφανος</u> γερόντων τέχνα τέχνων, <u>καύχημα</u> δὲ τέχνων πατέρες αὐτῶν.

6 <u>Corona senum</u> *filii filiorum*, et gloria filiorum patres eorum.

*a/   [grandchildren ≈ the crown of old men; fathers ≈ the glory of children]

Prov. 18.7 A *fool's mouth* <u>is</u> *his destruction*, and *his lips* are *the snare* of his soul.

7 στόμα ἄφρονος συντριβὴ αὐτῷ, τὰ δὲ χείλη αὐτοῦ

*a/   <u>παγὶς</u> τῇ ψυχῇ αὐτοῦ.

7 Os stulti contritio ejus, et *labia* ipsius <u>ruina animae ejus</u>.

[(a fool's mouth ≈ his destruction); his lips ≈ snare of his soul]

Prov. 18.10 The *name of the Lord* is <u>a strong tower.</u>

a*/   10 ἐκ μεγαλωσύνης ἰσχύος ὄνομα Κυρίου ...

10 <u>Turris fortissima</u> nomen Domini;

[name of the Lord ≈ a strong tower]

Prov. 18.11 *The rich man's wealth* <u>is</u> *his strong city*; and <u>as</u> an

*a/   *high wall* in his own conceit.

11 ὕπαρξις πλουσίου ἀνδρὸς <u>πόλις ὀχυρά</u>, ἡ δὲ δόξα αὐτῆς μέγα ἐπισκιάζει.

11 *Substantia divitis* <u>urbs roboris ejus</u>, et <u>quasi</u> <u>murus validus</u> circumdans eum.

[wealth of a rich man ≈ his strong city ≈ a high wall]

Prov. 20.27 The *spirit of man* <u>is</u> *the candle of the Lord*, searching all the inward parts of the belly.

27 <u>φῶς Κυρίου</u> πνοὴ ἀνθρώπων, ὃς ἐρευνᾷ ταμιεῖα κοιλίας.

27 <u>Lucerna Domini</u> *spiraculum hominis*, quae investigat omnia secreta ventris.

*a/   [spirit of man ≈ the candle of the Lord]

Prov. 22.14 The *mouth of strange women* is <u>a deep pit</u>; he that is abhorred of the Lord shall fall therein.

14 <u>βόθρος βαθὺς</u> στόμα παρανόμου, ὁ δὲ μισηθεὶς ὑπὸ Κυρίου ἐμπεσεῖται εἰς αὐτόν.

(NB: 'the mouth of a transgressor')

>   14 <u>Fovea profunda</u> os alienae; cui iratus est Dominus, incidet in eam.

*a/   [mouth of a strange woman/transgressor ≈ a deep pit]
    Prov. 23.27 For *a whore* is *a deep ditch; and a strange woman is a*
        narrow pit.
    27 <u>πίθος γὰρ τετρημένος</u> <u>ἐστὶν</u> ἀλλότριος οἶκος, καὶ φρέαρ στενὸν ἀλλότριον·
        (For *a strange house* is *a vessel full of holes*; and a strange well is
        narrow.)
> 27 *<u>Fovea enim profunda</u>* est *meretrix,* et *<u>puteus angustus</u> aliena.*
*a/   [a whore/strange house ≈ a deep dish/vessel full of holes; a strange
    woman/well ≈ a narrow pit]
    Prov. 25.18 *A man that beareth false witness against his neighbor*
*a/   is *<u>a maul,</u>* and *<u>a sword, and a sharp arrow.</u>*
    18 <u>ῥόπαλον καὶ μάχαιρα καὶ τόξευμα ἀκιδωτόν,</u> **οὕτως** καὶ ἀνὴρ ὁ
        καταμαρτυρῶν τοῦ φίλου αὐτοῦ μαρτυρίαν ψευδῆ.
    18 *<u>Jaculum, et gladius, et sagitta acuta,</u> homo qui loquitur contra
        proximum suum falsum testimonium.*
    [a man who bears false witness ≈ a maul (club) + sword + arrow]

* * *

Eccl. 7.26 And I find <u>more bitter than</u> *death the woman,* <u>whose</u> *heart is*
    <u>snares</u> and *<u>nets,</u>* …
    26 καὶ εὑρίσκω ἐγὼ αὐτὴν καὶ ἐρῶ <u>πικρότερον ὑπὲρ θάνατον,</u> σὺν τὴν
        γυναῖκα, <u>ἥτις ἐστὶ θήρευμα</u> καὶ <u>σαγῆναι καρδία αὐτῆς</u>
    27et inveni <u>amariorem</u> *<u>morte</u> mulierem, quae <u>laqueus</u> venatorum est,*
        et *<u>sagena</u> cor* ejus;
    [heart ≈ snares and nets]

* * *

Song of So. 1.13 *A <u>bundle of</u> myrrh* is my well-beloved unto me; he shall lie
    all night betwixt my breasts.
    13 <u>ἀπόδεσμος τῆς στακτῆς</u> ἀδελφιδός μου ἐμοί, ἀνὰ μέσον τῶν μαστῶν μου
        αὐλισθήσεται.
    12 *<u>Fasciculus myrrhae</u> dilectus meus* mihi; *inter ubera mea commorabitur.*
    [my beloved ≈ a bundle of myrrh]
So-So. 1.15 Behold, thou art fair, my love; behold, thou art fair;
*a/2   *thou hast <u>doves' eyes.</u>*

15 ἰδοὺ εἶ καλή, ἡ πλησίον μου, ἰδοὺ εἶ καλή, *ὀφθαλμοί σου <u>περιστεραί.</u>*

14 Ecce tu pulchra es, amica mea! ecce tu pulchra es! *Oculi tu*i
<u>*columbarum.*</u>[your eyes ≈ doves']

So-So. 2.1 I <u>am</u> *the rose of Sharon*, and the <u>*lily of the valleys.*</u>

1 1 *ΕΓΩ <u>ἄνθος τοῦ πεδίου, κρίνον τῶν κοιλάδων.</u>*

1 *Ego <u>flos campi</u>*, et <u>*lilium convallium*</u>

[I ≈ rose of Sharon + the lily of the valleys]

So-So. 2.14 O <u>*my dove*</u>, that art in the clefts of the rock.

14 *σὺ <u>περιστερά μου</u>, ἐν σκέπῃ τῆς πέτρας, ἐχόμενα τοῦ προτειχίσματος·*

13 *amica mea* 14 <u>*columba mea,*</u> in foraminibus petrae,

*a/1   [you ≈ my dove]

So-So. 4.1 Behold, thou art fair, my love; behold, thou art fair;

*a/2   *thou hast <u>doves' eyes</u> within thy locks*:

1 Ἰδοὺ εἶ καλή, ἡ πλησίον μου, ἰδοὺ εἶ καλή. *ὀφθαλμοί σου <u>περιστεραί</u>* ἐκτὸς
τῆς σιωπήσεώς σου.

1 SPONSUS. Quam pulchra es, amica mea! quam pulchra es! *Oculi*
tui <u>*columbarum,*</u>

[eyes ≈ a dove's eyes]

So-So. 4.12 A <u>*garden enclosed*</u> is *my siste*r, *my spouse;*

*a/1   <u>a spring shut up</u>, <u>a fountain sealed</u>.

12 *<u>κῆπος κεκλεισμένος</u>, ἀδελφή μου νύμφη, κῆπος κεκλεισμένος, <u>πηγὴ
ἐσφραγισμένη.</u>*

12 *<u>Hortus conclusus</u>* soror mea, sponsa, <u>*hortus conclusus, fons signatus.*</u>

[my sister, my spouse ≈ an enclosed garden ≈ a spring shut up ≈ a
fountain sealed]

So-So. 8.6 *the coals thereof* <u>are</u> <u>*coals of fire,*</u> which hath a most vehe-
ment flame.

6 *περίπτερα αὐτῆς <u>περίπτερα πυρός, φλόγες</u> αὐτῆς·*

6 *lampades ejus <u>lampades ignis atque flammarum.</u>*

[her coals ≈ coals of fire]

So-So. 8.9 If she [our little sister] be *a <u>wall</u>*, we will build upon her

*a/1   a palace of silver; bulwarks; and if she be a *<u>door</u>*, we will enclose her
with boards of cedar. 10 *I* am a *<u>wall.</u>*

9 εἰ <u>*τεῖχός* <u>ἐστιν</u></u>, οἰκοδομήσωμεν ἐπ᾿ αὐτὴν ἐπάλξεις ἀργυρᾶς· καὶ εἰ <u>θύρα</u>
ἐστί, διαγράψωμεν ἐπ᾿ αὐτὴν σανίδα κεδρίνην. 10 ἐγὼ <u>τεῖχος.</u>

9 Si _murus_ est, aedificemus super eum propugnacula argentea; si _ostium_ est, compingamus illud tabulis cedrinis. 10 SPONSA. *Ego murus,* [she ≈ a wall ≈ a door; I ≈ a wall]

* * *

Isaiah 28.1 Woe to the crown of pride, to the drunkards of Ephraim, whose *glorious beauty* is *a fading flower* …

    1 ΟΥΑΙ τῷ στεφάνῳ τῆς ὕβρεως, οἱ μισθωτοὶ Ἐφραίμ· <u>τὸ ἄνθος τὸ ἐκπεσὸν</u> ἐκ τῆς δόξης ἐπὶ τῆς κορυφῆς τοῦ ὄρους τοῦ παχέος, οἱ μεθύοντες ἄνευ οἴνου.

    1 Vae coronae superbiae, ebriis Ephraim, et *flori decidenti*, gloriae exsultationis ejus, qui erant in vertice vallis pinguissimae, errantes a vino.

*a/1 [beauty ≈ a fading flower]

Isaiah 41.15 Behold, I will make *thee a new sharp threshing instrument* having teeth: thou shalt thresh the mountains, and beat them small, and shalt make *the hills* as *chaff*.

    15 ἰδοὺ ἐποίησά σε <u>ὡς τροχοὺς ἁμάξης ἀλοῶντας καινοὺς πριστηροειδεῖς</u>, καὶ ἀλοήσεις ὄρη καὶ λεπτυνεῖς βουνοὺς καὶ <u>ὡς χνοῦν</u> θήσεις·

    15 Ego posui *te* quasi *plaustrum triturans novum*, habens rostra serrantia; triturabis montes, et comminues, et *colles* quasi *pulverem* pones.

*a/2 [thee ≈ new sharp threshing instrument; hills ≈ chaff]

NB – From the English text one cannot tell whether the 'thee' is a dative case or direct object with the 'new sharp threshing instrument' as a simile. It becomes clear from the Greek and Latin.

Isaiah 41.29 Behold, they [people] are all vanity; their works are nothing: their *molten images* are *wind and confusion*.

    29 εἰσὶ γὰρ οἱ ποιοῦντες ὑμᾶς, καὶ μάτην οἱ πλανῶντες ὑμᾶς.

    29 Ecce omnes injusti et vana opera eorum; <u>ventus et inane simulacra eorum</u>.

*a/1 [people's molten images ≈ wind and confusion]

Isaiah 48.4 Because I knew that thou art obstinate, and *thy neck* is <u>an iron sinew,</u> and *thy brow* <u>brass</u>;

4 γινώσκω ὅτι σκληρὸς εἶ, καὶ <u>*νεῦρον σιδηροῦν*</u> ὁ τράχηλός σου, καὶ τὸ μέτωπόν σου <u>*χαλκοῦν*</u>.

4 Scivi enim quia durus es tu, et <u>*nervus ferreus*</u> cervix tua, et *frons* tua <u>*aerea*</u>.

*a/1   [your neck ≈ an iron sinew; your brow ≈ brass]

Isaiah 49.2 he hid me, and made *me a polished shaft*;

*a/2   in his quiver hath he hid me.

2 καὶ ὑπὸ τὴν σκέπην τῆς χειρὸς αὐτοῦ ἔκρυψέ με, ἔθηκέ *με* <u>*ὡς βέλος ἐκλεκτὸν*</u> καὶ ἐν τῇ φαρέτρᾳ αὐτοῦ ἔκρυψέ με.

2 in umbra manus suae protexit me; et posuit *me* <u>sicut</u> <u>*sagittam electam*</u>, in pharetra sua abscondit me.

Isaiah 64.8 But now, O Lord, *thou* art <u>*our father*</u>, <u>*we are the clay*</u>, and *thou* our <u>*potter*</u>; and *we all* are <u>*the work of thy hand*</u>.

8 καὶ νῦν, Κύριε, πατὴρ ἡμῶν σύ, <u>*ἡμεῖς δὲ πηλός*</u>, ἔργα τῶν χειρῶν σου πάντες.

8 Et nunc, Domine, <u>*pater noster*</u> es *tu*, *nos* vero <u>*lutum*</u>; et

*a/1   <u>*fictor noster*</u> *tu*, et <u>*opera manuum tuarum*</u> omnes nos.

(4x) [you ≈ our father; we ≈ clay; you ≈ our potter; we all ≈ the work of your hand]

Isaiah 64.10 Thy *holy cities* are <u>*a wilderness*</u>, Zon is <u>*a wilderness*</u>, Jerusalem a <u>*desolation*</u>.

(3x) 10 πόλις τοῦ ἁγίου σου ἐγενήθη <u>*ἔρημος*</u>, Σιὼν <u>*ὡς ἔρημος*</u> ἐγενήθη, Ιερουσαλὴμ <u>*εἰς κατάραν*</u>.

10 Civitas Sancti tui facta est deserta, Sion deserta facta est, Jerusalem desolata est.

[holy cities ≈ a wilderness; Zion ≈ a wilderness, Jerusalem ≈ a desolation]

* * *

Jeremiah 2.14 Is *Israel* <u>*a servant*</u>? <u>is</u> he <u>*a home-born slave*</u>?

*a/1   14 Μὴ <u>*δοῦλός*</u> <u>*ἐστιν*</u> Ἰσραὴλ ἢ <u>*οἰκογενής*</u> ἐστι; διατί εἰς (2) προνομὴν ἐγένετο;

14 Numquid <u>*servus*</u> <u>est</u> Israel, aut <u>*vernaculus*</u>?

[Israel ≈ a servant ≈ a slave]

Jeremiah 2.31 O generation, see ye the word of the Lord. Have *I* *a/1   been *a wilderness* unto Israel? *a land of darkness*?

     31 τάδε λέγει Κύριος· μὴ <u>*ἔρημος*</u> *ἐγενόμην* τῷ 'Ισραὴλ ἢ <u>*γῆ κεχερσωμένη*</u>;

     31 Numquid *solitudo* <u>factus sum</u> Israeli, aut *terra serotina*?

     [I/the Lord ≈ a wilderness, a land of darkness]

Jeremiah 3.17 At that time they shall call *Jerusalem* the <u>*throne of the Lord.*</u>

a/2   17 ἐν ταῖς ἡμέραις ἐκείναις καὶ ἐν τῷ καιρῷ ἐκείνῳ καλέσουσι <u>τὴν</u>
       <u>'Ιερουσαλὴμ Θρόνον Κυρίου,</u>

     17 In tempore illo vocabunt *Jerusalem* <u>*solium Domini:*</u>

     [Jerusalem ≈ the throne of the Lord]

     Jeremiah 5.13 And *the prophets* <u>shall become</u> <u>*wind*</u>, and the word is
       not in them.

     13 οἱ *προφῆται ἡμῶν* ἦσαν <u>εἰς</u> <u>*ἄνεμον*</u>, καὶ λόγος Κυρίου οὐχ ὑπῆρχεν ἐν
       αὐτοῖς·

     13 *Prophetae* fuerunt <u>in *ventum*</u> locuti, et responsum non fuit in eis.

*a/1   [our prophets ≈ wind]

Jeremiah 6.28 They (22: people from the north) are <u>*brass and iron*</u>.

*a/1   28 <u>*χαλκὸς καὶ σίδηρος*</u>, πάντες διεφθαρμένοι εἰσίν.

     28 *Omnes isti principes* declinantes, ambulantes fraudulenter, <u>*aes et*</u>
       <u>*ferrum*</u>: universi corrupta sunt.

     [(the people from the north) ≈ brass and iron]

Jeremiah 7.11 Is *this house,* which is called by my name, become <u>*a den of*</u>
     <u>*robbers*</u> in your eyes? Behold, I have seen it, saith the Lord.

     11 μὴ <u>*σπήλαιον ληστῶν*</u> ὁ οἶκός μου, οὗ ἐπικέκληται τὸ ὄνομά μου ἐπ' αὐτῷ
       ἐκεῖ, ἐνώπιον ὑμῶν; καὶ ἰδοὺ ἐγὼ ἑώρακα, λέγει Κύριος,

     11 Numquid ergo <u>*spelunca latronum*</u> facta est *domus ista*, in qua
       invocatum est nomen meum in oculis vestris?

*a/1   [my house ≈ a den of robbers]

Jeremiah 9.11 And I will make *Jerusalem* heaps, and <u>*a den of dragons*</u>.

*a/2   11 καὶ δώσω τὴν 'Ιερουσαλὴμ <u>εἰς</u> μετοικίαν καὶ εἰς <u>*κατοικητήριον*</u>
     <u>*δρακόντων*</u> .

11 Et dabo *Jerusalem* <u>in *acervos arenae*</u>, et *cubilia draconum*:

[Jerusalem ≈ a den of dragons] **No prothesis in English in contrast to
the Greek and Latin texts.**

Jeremiah 24.9 And I will deliver them to be removed ... to be **a reproach and a proverb, a taunt and a curse,** in all places whither I shall drive them etc..

9 καὶ δώσω αὐτοὺς **εἰς διασκορπισμὸν** εἰς πάσας τὰς βασιλείας τῆς γῆς, καὶ ἔσονται **εἰς ὀνειδισμὸν καὶ εἰς παραβολὴν καὶ εἰς μῖσος** καὶ **εἰς κατάραν ἐν παντὶ τόπῳ,** οὗ ἔξωσα αὐτοὺς ἐκεῖ.

9: Et dabo eos **in vexationem, afflictionemque** omnibus regnis terrae, **in opprobrium, et in parabolam, et in proverbium,** et in **maledictionem** in universis locis ad quae ejeci eos.

[them ≈ a reproach + a proverb + a taunt and a curse]

Cf. 25.11 And *this whole land* <u>shall be</u> <u>*a desolation, and an astonishment.*</u>

NB **After 25.13 the Greek text skips to 34 Prophesies against the Nations of Aelam and the correspondence ceases.**

Jeremiah 47.6 O *thou sword of the Lord*, how long will it be ere *thou* be quiet? put up thyself *into thy scabbard,* rest, and be still.

6 O *mucro Domin*i, usquequo non quiesces? Ingredere in *vaginam* tuam, refrigerare, et sile.

*a/1   [thou ≈ sword of the Lord (into your scabbard)]

Jeremiah 50.6 *My people* <u>hath been</u> l<u>*ost sheep*</u>: their shepherds have caused them to go astray.

6 *Grex perditus* factus est *populus meus*, pastores eorum seduxerunt eos,

*a/1   [my people ≈ lost sheep]

Jeremiah 51.7 *Babylon* hath <u>been</u> <u>*a golden cup*</u> in the LORD's hand, that made all the earth drunken: the nations have drunken of her wine; therefore the nations are mad.

7 *Calix aureus Babylon* in manu Domini, inebrians omnem terram: de vino ejus biberunt gentes, et ideo commotae sunt.

*a/1   [Babylon ≈ a golden cup]

Jeremiah 51.19 and *Israel* is *the rod of his [Jacob's] inheritance:* the Lord of hosts is his name. 20 *Thou* <u>art</u> *my battle axe and weapons of war*; for with thee will I break in pieces the nations.

19 et *Israel* <u>*sceptrum haereditatis ejus*</u>: Dominus exercituum nomen ejus. 21 Collidis *tu* mihi *vasa belli*: et ego collidam in te gentes, et disperdam in te regna.

*a/1   [Israel ≈ the rod of inheritance; thou ≈ my battle axe]

Jeremiah 51.34 Nebuchadnezzar the king of Babylon hath devoured me
    … hath <u>made</u> *me* a<u>*n empty vessel.*</u>

* * *

Lamentations of Jeremiah 3.63 *I* <u>am</u> *<u>their musick</u>*.
    63 ἐπίβλεψον ἐπὶ τοὺς ὀφθαλμοὺς αὐτῶν. (look upon their eyes)
    63 *ego* <u>sum</u> *<u>psalmus eorum</u>*.
*a/   [I ≈ their music/psalm]
    Lamentations of Jeremiah 4.10 The hands of the pitiful women have
sodden their own children: *they were <u>their meat</u>* in the destruction of the
daughter of my people.
    10 Χεῖρες γυναικῶν οἰκτριρμόνων ἥψησαν τὰ παιδία αὐτῶν, <u>ἐγενήθησαν</u>
        <u>εἰς βρῶσιν</u> αὐταῖς ἐν τῷ συνννντρίμματι τῆς θυγατρὸς τοῦ λαοῦ μου.
    10 Manus mulierum misericordium coxerunt filios suos; *facti sunt <u>cibus</u>*
        earum *<u>in contritione filiae populi</u>* mei.
    [they ≈ their meat]

* * *

Ezekiel 11.3 *This <u>city</u>* <u>is</u> *<u>the caldron</u>* and *we* <u>be</u> *<u>the flesh</u>*.
    3 – *αὕτη <u>ἐστὶν</u> ὁ <u>λέβης</u>, <u>νος</u> αὐτεμ <u>τὰ κρέα</u>.*
    3 *haec* est *<u>lebes</u>, <u>nos</u>* autem *<u>carnes</u>*.
*a/1   [this city ≈ cauldron; we ≈ the flesh]
    Cf. 11.7 ("they are the flesh")
Ezekiel 22.18 Son of man, the *house of Israel* is to me <u>become *<u>dross</u>*</u>: all they
    are *<u>brass</u>*, and *<u>tin</u>*, and *<u>iron</u>*, and *<u>lead</u>*, in the midst of the furnace; they
    are even *<u>the dross of silv</u>*er.
    18 υἱὲ ἀνθρώπου, ἰδοὺ γεγόνασί μοι ὁ οἶκος 'Ισραὴλ ἀναμεμειγμένοι πάντες
        χαλκῷ καὶ σιδήρῳ καὶ κασσιτέρῳ καὶ μολίβῳ, ἐν μέσῳ ἀργυρίου
        ἀναμεμειγμένος ἐστί.
    18 Fili hominis, versa est mihi domus Israel in *<u>scoriam</u>: omnes isti <u>aes,</u>*
        <u>et stannum, et ferrum, et plumbum in medio fornacis</u>: <u>scoria argenti</u>
        <u>facti sunt</u>.
*a/1   [house of Israel ≈ dross, brass, tin, iron, lead, the dross of silver]
Ezek. 22.24 Son of man, say unto her, *Thou* <u>art</u> *<u>the land that is not cleansed,</u>*
    <u>nor rained upon in the day of indignation.</u>

24 σὺ εἶ γῆ ἡ οὐ βρεχομένη, οὐδὲ ὑετὸς ἐγένετο ἐπὶ σὲ ἐν ἡμέρᾳ ὀργῆς·

24 *Tu es terra immunda*, et non compluta in die furoris.

[you ≈ the land that is not cleansed etc.]

Ezekiel 31.2 Whom art thou like in thy greatness? 31.3 Behold, *the Assyrian* was *a cedar in Libanon,* with fair branches, and with a shadowing shroud … and his top was among the thick boughs.
4 – 5 – 6 – 7 – 8

3 ἰδοὺ Ἀσσοὺρ κυπάρισσος ἐν τῷ Λιβάνῳ καὶ καλὸς ταῖς παραφυάσι καὶ ὑψηλὸς τῷ μεγέθει, εἰς μέσον νεφελῶν ἐγένετο ἡ ἀρχὴ αὐτοῦ.

3 Ecce *Assur* quasi *cedrus in Libano*, pulcher ramis, et frondibus nemorosus, excelsusque altitudine, et inter condensas frondes elevatum est cacumen ejus

Beginning of a long simile (4–8) / allegory (31.9–14).

*a/ [Assyrian ≈ a cedar in Libanon]

* * *

Hosea 7.8 *Ephraim* is *a cake not turned*.

8 Ἐφραὶμ ἐγένετο ἐγκρυφίας οὐ μεταστρεφόμενος.

8 *Ephraim* factus est *subcinericius panis, qui non reversatur.*

[Ephraim ≈ a cake not turned]

Hosea 8.9 For *they* are gone up to Assyria, *a wild ass* alone by himself.

[they ≈ a wild ass]

Hosea 9.8 The watchman of Ephraim was with my God: but *the prophet* is *a snare of a fowler* in all his ways.

8 σκοπὸς Ἐφραὶμ μετὰ Θεοῦ· προφήτης, παγὶς σκολιὰ ἐπὶ πάσας τὰς ὁδοὺς αὐτοῦ·

8 Speculator Ephraim cum Deo meo, propheta *laqueus ruinae factus* est super omnes vias ejus.

*a/1 [prophet ≈ a snare of a fowler]

Hosea 10.1 *Israel* is *an empty vine*, he bringeth forth fruit unto himself.

1 ΑΜΠΕΛΟΣ εὐκληματοῦσα Ἰσραήλ, ὁ καρπὸς εὐθηνῶν αὐτῆς·

1 *Vitis frondosa* Israel, fructus adaequatus est ei:

*a/1 [Israel ≈ an empty vine]

Hosea 12.7 He is *a merchant*, the balances of deceit are in his hand.

8 Χαναὰν ἐν χειρὶ αὐτοῦ ζυγὸς ἀδικίας, καταδυναστεύειν ἠγάπησε.

7 Chanaan, in manu ejus statera dolosa, calumniam dilexit.
[He / thy God ≈ a merchant]

* * *

Joel 1.6 For a nation is come up upon my land, strong, and without
number, whose *teeth* <u>are</u> *the teeth of a lion,* and he hath the *cheek teeth*
of a *great lion.*
   6 ὅτι ἔθνος ἀνέβη ἐπὶ τὴν γῆν μου ἰσχυρὸν καὶ ἀναρίθμητον, οἱ ὀδόντες
   αὐτοῦ, ὀδόντες λέοντος, καὶ αἱ μύλαι αὐτοῦ σκύμνου.
   6 Gens enim ascendit super terram meam, fortis et innumerabilis: dentes
      ejus *ut* <u>dentes leonis,</u> *et* molares ejus *ut* <u>catuli leonis.</u>
[its teeth ≈ a lion's teeth ≈ a great lion]

* * *

Obadiah 1.18 And *the house of Jacob* <u>shall be</u> a *fire,* and *the house of*
586 Joseph a *flame,* and *the house of Esau* <u>for</u> *stubble* ...
   18 καὶ ἔσται ὁ οἶκος 'Ιακὼβ <u>πῦρ</u>, ὁ δὲ οἶκος 'Ιωσὴφ <u>φλόξ</u>, ὁ δὲ οἶκος 'Ησαῦ
      <u>εἰς καλάμην,</u>
   18 Et erit *domus Jacob* <u>*ignis*</u>, et *domus Joseph* <u>*flamma*</u>, et *domus Esau*
      <u>*stipula*</u>:
*a/1 [house of Jacob ≈ a fire; the house of Joseph ≈ a flame; the house
       of Esau ≈ stubble]

* * *

Jonah 4.6   And the Lord God prepared *a gourd,* and made it to come
up over Jonah, <u>that</u> it <u>might be</u> *a shadow over his head,* to deliver him
from his grief.
   6 προσέταξε Κύριος ὁ Θεὸς <u>κολοκύνθῃ</u>, ... εἶναι <u>σκιὰν ὑπεράνω τῆς κεφαλῆς</u>
      <u>αὐτοῦ</u> τοῦ σκιάζειν αὐτῷ ἀπὸ τῶν κακῶν αὐτοῦ.
   6 Et praeparavit Dominus Deus *hederam*, ... <u>ut</u> esset <u>*umbra*</u> super
      caput ejus,
[a gourd ≈ a shadow]

* * *

Zephaniah 3.3 *Her princes within her* <u>are</u> <u>*roaring lions,*</u> *her judges* <u>are</u>
<u>*evening wolves*</u>; they gnaw not the bones till the morrow.

   3 οἱ ἄρχοντες αὐτῆς ἐν αὐτῇ ὡς λέοντες ὠρυόμενοι· οἱ κριταὶ αὐτῆς ὡς λύκοι
   <u>τῆς Ἀραβίας</u>, οὐχ ὑπελίποντο εἰς τὸ πρωΐ·

   3 *Principes ejus* in medio ejus <u>quasi</u> <u>*leones rugientes*</u>; *judices ejus* <u>*lupi*</u>
   <u>*vespere*</u>, non relinquebant in mane.

   [her (the filthy city's) princes ≈ roaring lions; her judges ≈ evening
   wolves]

* * *

Zechariah 11.3 There is a *voice of the howling of the shepherds*; for their
glory is spoiled: *a voice* <u>*of the roaring of young lions*</u>.

   3 φωνὴ θρηνούντων ποιμένων, ὅτι τεταλαιπώρηκεν ἡ μεγαλωσύνη αὐτῶν·
   <u>φωνὴ ὠρυομένων λεόντων.</u>

   3 Vox ululatus pastorum, quia vastata est magnificentia eorum: *vox*
   <u>*rugitus leonum.*</u>

*a/1   [voice of the shepherds ≈ the roaring of young lions]

12.2 Behold, I will make *Jerusalem* <u>*a cup of trembling*</u> *unto all the*
a/2   *people round about* ... 3 And in that day *I will make Jerusalem*
   <u>*a burdensome stone for all people.*</u>

   2 ἰδοὺ ἐγὼ τίθημι <u>τὴν Ἰερουσαλὴμ ὡς πρόθυρα σαλευόμενα</u> πᾶσι τοῖς λαοῖς
   κύκλῳ ... 3 καὶ ἔσται ἐν τῇ ἡμέρᾳ ἐκείνῃ θήσομαι τὴν Ιερουσαλὴμ
   <u>λίθον καταπατούμενον πᾶσι τοῖς ἔθνεσι.</u>

   2 Ecce ego ponam *Jerusalem* <u>*superliminare crapulae*</u> omnibus populis
   in circuitu ... 3 Et erit: in die illa ponam *Jerusalem* <u>*lapidem oneris*</u>
   <u>*cunctis populis.*</u>

*a/2   [Jerusalem ≈ a cup of trembling ≈ a burdensome stone for all
   people]

   Malachi 4.1 and *all that do wickedly* shall <u>be</u> <u>*stubble.*</u>

   1 καὶ πάντες οἱ ποιοῦντες ἄνομα <u>καλάμη</u>,

   1 et *erunt* ... *omnes facientes impietatem* <u>*stipula.*</u>

* * *

The New Testament

Matt. 4.19 Follow me, and I will make *you fishers of men*.

19 δεῦτε ὀπίσω μου καὶ ποιήσω ὑμᾶς <u>*ἁλιεῖς ἀνθρώπων*</u>.

19 Venite post me, et faciam *vos* fieri <u>*piscatores hominum.*</u>

*a/2   [you ≈ fishers of men] (Jesus)

Matt. 5.13 *Ye* are the <u>salt of the earth</u>: but if the salt have lost his savor, wherewith shall it be salted?

13 Ὑμεῖς ἐστε <u>*τὸ ἅλας τῆς γῆς·*</u> ἐὰν δὲ τὸ ἅλας μωρανθῇ, ἐν τίνι ἁλισθήσεται;

13 *Vos* estis <u>*sal terrae.*</u> Quod si sal evanuerit, in quo *a/1   salietur?

[you ≈ salt of the earth]

Matt. 5.14 Ye are the <u>light of the world</u>. A city that is set on an hill cannot be hid.

14 Ὑμεῖς ἐστε <u>*τὸ φῶς τοῦ κόσμου.*</u> οὐ δύναται πόλις κρυβῆναι ἐπάνω ὄρους κειμένη·

14 *Vos* estis <u>*lux mundi*</u>. Non potest civitas abscondi supra montem posita,

*a/1   [you ≈ light of the world]

Matt. 6.22 The <u>*light of the body*</u> is *the eye*: if therefore thine eye be single, thy whole body shall be full of light.

22 <u>*Ο λύχνος τοῦ σώματός*</u> ἐστιν ὁ ὀφθαλμός· ἐὰν οὖν ὁ ὀφθαλμός σου ἁπλοῦς ᾖ, ὅλον τὸ σῶμά σου φωτεινόν ἔσται·

22 <u>*Lucerna corporis tui*</u> est *oculus tuus*. Si oculus tuus fuerit simplex, totum corpus tuum lucidum erit.

*a/   [the eye ≈ the light of the body]

Matt. 7.15 Beware of *false prophets*, which come to you in sheep's clothing, but inwardly they <u>are</u> <u>*ravening wolves*</u>.

15 Προσέχετε δὲ ἀπὸ τῶν ψευδοπροφητῶν, οἵτινες ἔρχονται πρὸς ὑμᾶς ἐν ἐνδύμασι προβάτων, ἔσωθεν δέ <u>εἰσι λύκοι ἅρπαγες</u>.

15 Attendite a *falsis prophetis*, qui veniunt ad vos in vestimentis ovium, intrinsecus autem <u>sunt</u> <u>*lupi rapaces*</u>:

*a/1   [false prophets ≈ ravening wolves]

Matt. 13.37 He answered and said unto them, "<u>*He that soweth the good seed*</u> is *the Son of man*."

37 ὁ δὲ ἀποκριθεὶς εἶπεν, Ο σπείρων τὸ καλὸν σπέρμα ἐστὶν ὁ υἱὸς τοῦ ἀνθρώπου:

37 Qui respondens ait illis: *Qui seminat bonum semen*, est *Filius hominis.*

*a/1   [son of man ≈ the sower of the good seed]

Matt. 13.38 *The field* is *the world*; *the good seed* are *the children of the* kingdom; but the *tares* are *the children of the wicked one.*

38 ὁ δὲ ἀγρός ἐστιν ὁ κόσμος: τὸ δὲ καλὸν σπέρμα, οὗτοί εἰσιν οἱ υἱοὶ τῆς βασιλείας: τὰ δὲ ζιζάνιά εἰσιν οἱ υἱοὶ τοῦ πονηροῦ, [world ≈ the field; children of the kingdom ≈ the good seed; the children of the wicked one ≈ the tares]

Matt. 13.39 The *enemy that sowed them* is *the devil*: *the harvest* is *the end of the world;* and *the reapers* are *the angels.*

39 ὁ δὲ ἐχθρὸς ὁ σπείρας αὐτά ἐστιν ὁ διάβολος· ὁ δὲ θερισμὸς συντέλεια τοῦ αἰῶνός ἐστιν· οἱ δὲ θερισταὶ ἄγγελοί εἰσιν.

39 Inimicus autem, qui seminavit ea, est diabolus. Messis vero, consummatio saeculi est. Messores autem, angeli sunt.

[the devil ≈ the enemy that sowed the tares; the end of the world ≈ the harvest; the angels ≈ the reapers]

Matt. 21.13 It is written, *My house* shall be called the house of prayer; but ye have made it *a den of thieves*.

13 γέγραπται, ὁ οἶκός μου οἶκος προσευχῆς κληθήσεται· ὑμεῖς δὲ αὐτὸν ἐποιήσατε σπήλαιον λῃστῶν.

13 Scriptum est: *Domus mea* domus orationis vocabitur: vos autem fecistis illam *speluncam latronum*.

*a/2   [my house ≈ a den of thieves]

* * *

Mark

* * *

Luke 8.11 *The seed* is the *word of God.*

11 ἔστι δὲ αὕτη ἡ παραβολή· ὁ σπόρος ἐστὶν ὁ λόγος τοῦ Θεοῦ·

11 Est autem haec parabola: *Semen* est *verbum Domini.*

[the word of God ≈ a seed]

Luke 9.58 And Jesus said unto him [a certain man], _Foxes_ have holes, and _birds_ of the air have nests: but *the Son of man* hath not where to lay his head.

58 <u>*αἱ ἀλώπεκες*</u> φωλεοὺς ἔχουσι καὶ <u>*τὰ πετεινὰ*</u> τοῦ οὐρανοῦ κατασκηνώσεις, ὁ δὲ υἱὸς τοῦ ἀνθρώπου οὐκ ἔχει ποῦ τὴν κεφαλὴν κλίνῃ.

58 <u>*Vulpes*</u> foveas habent, et <u>*volucres*</u> caeli nidos: *Filius* autem *hominis* non habet ubi caput reclinet.

[the Son of man (not) ≈ foxes and birds] Jesus

Luke 11.34 The *light of the body* is *the eye.*

34 <u>*ὁ λύχνος τοῦ σώματός*</u> ἐστιν ὁ ὀφθαλμός·

34 <u>*Lucerna corporis tui*</u> est *oculus tuus.*

[the eye ≈ the light of the body]

* * *

John 1.4 In him was life; and the *life* <u>was</u> *the light of men.*

4 ἐν αὐτῷ ζωὴ ἦν, καὶ ἡ ζωὴ ἦν <u>τὸ φῶς τῶν ἀνθρώπων</u>:

4 In ipso vita erat, et *vita* <u>erat</u> <u>*lux hominum*</u>:

*a/1   [His life ≈ the light of men] St. John cf. 8.12; 9.5; 12.46.

John 1.23 *I* <u>am</u> *the voice of one crying in the wilderness.*

23 ἔφη· ἐγὼ <u>φωνὴ βοῶντος ἐν τῇ ἐρήμῳ</u>,

23 *Ego* <u>*vox clamantis in deserto*</u>

*a/1   [I (John the Baptist) ≈ the voice of one crying in the wilderness]

John 1.29 [28 I am not the Christ, but that I am sent before him.] 29 He that hath the bride is the bridegroom: but *the friend of the bridegroom* … this my joy therefore is fulfilled.

29 ὁ ἔχων τὴν νύμφην νυμφίος ἐστίν· <u>ὁ δὲ φίλος τοῦ νυμφίου</u>, ὁ ἑστηκὼς καὶ ἀκούων αὐτοῦ, χαρᾷ χαίρει διὰ τὴν φωνὴν τοῦ νυμφίου. αὕτη οὖν ἡ χαρὰ ἡ ἐμὴ πεπλήρωται.

29 Qui habet sponsam, sponsus est: <u>*amicus autem sponsi*</u>, qui stat, et audit eum, gaudio gaudet propter vocem sponsi. *Hoc ergo gaudium meum impletum est.*

[I (John the Baptist) ≈ the friend of the bridegroom]

John 4.34 Jesus saith unto them, <u>*My meat*</u> <u>is</u> *to do the will of him that sent me,* and to finish his work.

34 <u>ἐμὸν βρῶμά</u> ἐστιν ἵνα ποιῶ τὸ θέλημα τοῦ πέμψαντός με.

34 <u>*Meus cibus*</u> est *ut faciam voluntatem ejus qui misit me,*

[to do the will of him that sent me ≈ my meat] Jesus **Jesus speaking figuratively about his work (in reply to his disciples urging Him to eat)**

Cf. 4.37: One soweth, and another reapeth.

John 6.33 For <u>*the bread of God*</u> is *he which cometh down from heaven* …

35*I* am <u>*the bread of life.*</u>

33<u>ὁ γὰρ ἄρτος τοῦ Θεοῦ</u> ἐστιν ὁ <u>καταβαίνων ἐκ τοῦ οὐρανοῦ</u> καὶ ζωὴν διδοὺς τῷ κόσμῳ.

33 <u>*Panis enim Dei*</u> est, *qui de caelo descendit,* et dat vitam mundo.

[the one coming down from heaven ≈ the bread of god]

= John 6.48 I am that bread of life. Cf. 6.51 + 54.

John 8.12 Then spake Jesus again to them, saying, *I* am <u>*the light of the world*</u>: he that followers me shall not walk in darkness but shall have the light of life.

12 Πάλιν οὖν αὐτοῖς ὁ Ἰησοῦς ἐλάλησε λέγων· ἐγώ <u>εἰμι</u> <u>τὸ φῶς τοῦ κόσμου·</u> ὁ ἀκολουθῶν ἐμοὶ οὐ μὴ περιπατήσῃ ἐν τῇ σκοτίᾳ, ἀλλ᾽ ἕξει τὸ φῶς τῆς ζωῆς.

12 *Ego* <u>sum</u> <u>*lux mundi.*</u>

[I (Jesus) ≈ the light of the world] cf. 9.5.

John 10.1 Verily, verily, I say unto you, *He that entereth not by the door* into the sheepfold, but climbeth up some other way, *the same* is <u>*a thief*</u> and <u>*a robber.*</u>

1 Ἀμὴν ἀμὴν λέγω ὑμῖν, ὁ μὴ εἰσερχόμενος διὰ τῆς θύρας εἰς τὴν αὐλὴν τῶν προβάτων, ἀλλὰ ἀναβαίνων ἀλλαχόθεν, ἐκεῖνος <u>κλέπτης</u> ἐστὶ καὶ <u>λῃστής·</u>

1 Amen, amen dico vobis: *qui non intrat per ostium in ovile ovium,* sed ascendit aliunde, *ille <u>fur</u>* <u>est</u> et <u>*latro.*</u>

*a/1 [he that enters into a sheepfold not by the door ≈ a thief and robber]

2 But *he that entereth in by the door* is <u>*the shepherd of the sheep.*</u>

2 ὁ δὲ εἰσερχόμενος διὰ τῆς θύρας <u>ποιμήν</u> ἐστιν τῶν προβάτων.

2 *Qui autem intrat per ostium, <u>pasto</u>r est <u>ovium.</u>*

*a/1 2 [he who enters through the door ≈ the shepherd of the sheep]

John 10.7 Then said Jesus unto them again, Verily, verily, I say unto you,

I am *the door of the sheep*.

7 Εἶπεν οὖν πάλιν ὁ Ἰησοῦς, Ἀμὴν ἀμὴν λέγω ὑμῖν ὅτι γώ εἰμι *ἡ θύρα τῶν προβάτων*.

7 Amen, amen dico vobis, quia ego sum ostium ovium.

*a/1   [I (Jesus) ≈ the door of the sheep] cf. 10.9 (9 ἐγώ εἰμι ἡ θύρα).

NB – the predicate simile explains the parable.

*a/1   10.11 *I* am *the good shepherd*.

11 Ἐγώ εἰμι *ὁ ποιμὴν ὁ καλός*: ὁ ποιμὴν ὁ καλὸς τὴν ψυχὴν αὐτοῦ τίθησιν ὑπὲρ τῶν προβάτων:

11 *Ego* sum *pastor bonus*. Bonus pastor animam suam dat pro ovibus suis.
[I = the good shepherd] also 10.14.

John 12.46 *I* am come *a light into the world,* that whosoever believeth on me should not abide in darkness.

46 ἐγώ *φῶς* εἰς τὸν κόσμον *ἐλήλυθα*, ἵνα πᾶς ὁ πιστεύων εἰς ἐμὲ ἐν τῇ σκοτίᾳ μὴ μείνῃ.

46 *Ego lux in mundum* veni, ut omnis qui credit in me, in tenebris non maneat.

*a/1   [I ≈ a light into the world]

John 14.6 *I* am the *way*, the truth, and the life.6 λέγει αὐτῷ ὁ Ἰησοῦς· ἐγώ εἰμι *ἡ ὁδὸς* καὶ ἡ ἀλήθεια καὶ ἡ ζωή·

6 Dicit ei Jesus: *Ego* sum *via*, et veritas, et vita.
[I ≈ the way]

John 15.1 *I* am the true *vine*, and *my Father* is the *husbandman*.

1 Ἐγώ εἰμι *ἡ ἄμπελος ἡ ἀληθινή*, καὶ ὁ πατήρ μου
ὁ γεωργός ἐστι.

1 *Ego* sum *vitis vera*, et *Pater meus agricola* est.
[I ≈ true vine; my Father ≈ the husbandman]

John 15.5 *I* am the *vine*, ye are the *branches*.

5 ἐγώ εἰμι ἡ ἄμπελος, ὑμεῖς τὰ κλήματα.

5 *Ego* sum *vitis*, vos *palmites.*
[I ≈ the vine; you ≈ the branches]

                                                    * * *

Acts of Apostles
Acts 2.35   Until I make *thy foes* *thy footstool*.

35 ἕως ἂν θῶ τοὺς ἐχθρούς σου <u>ὑποπόδιον τῶν ποδῶν σου</u>.

35 donec <u>ponam</u> *inimicos tuos* <u>scabellum pedum tuorum</u>.

*a/2   [your foes ≈ your footstools]

Acts 7.49 *Heaven is my* <u>*throne*</u> *and earth is my* <u>*footstool*</u>.

49 Ο οὐρανός μοι <u>θρόνος</u>, ἡ δὲ γῆ <u>ὑποπόδιον τῶν ποδῶν μου</u>:

49 *Caelum* <u>*mihi sedes*</u> *est*: *terra* autem <u>*scabellum pedum meorum*</u>.

*a/1   [heaven ≈ my throne; earth ≈ my footstool]

Acts. 9.15 But the Lord said unto him, "Go thy way, for *he* is a <u>*chosen vessel*</u> unto me, to bear my name before the Gentiles."

15 εἶπεν δὲ πρὸς αὐτὸν ὁ κύριος, Πορεύου, ὅτι <u>σκεῦος ἐκλογῆς</u> ἐστίν μοι
οὗτος τοῦ βαστάσαι τὸ ὄνομά μου ἐνώπιον ἐθνῶν τε καὶ βασιλέων
υἱῶν τε Ἰσραήλ:

15 Dixit autem ad eum Dominus: Vade, quoniam <u>*vas electionis*</u> est
mihi *iste*, ut portet nomen meum coram gentibus, et regibus, et
filiis Israel.

*a/1   [he ≈ a chosen vessel] [Saul]

* * *

Epistle of Paul to the Romans

Romans 2.19 And [thou, O man] art confident that *thou thyself art a
guide of the blind,* <u>*a light of them which are in darkness.*</u>

19 πέποιθάς τε σεαυτὸν ὁδηγὸν εἶναι τυφλῶν, <u>φῶς τῶν ἐν σκότει</u>,

19 confidis teipsum esse *ducem caecorum*, <u>*lumen eorum qui in
tenebris sunt.*</u>

*a/1   [thou ≈ a light] 'Thou' = 'O Man' in 2.1.

Romans 3.13 *Their throat is* <u>*an open sepulchre*</u>; with *their tongues* they have
used deceit; the poison of asps is under their lips.

13 <u>τάφος ἀνεῳγμένος</u> ὁ λάρυγξ αὐτῶν, ταῖς γλώσσαις αὐτῶν ἐδολιοῦσαν, <u>ἰὸς
ἀσπίδων</u> ὑπὸ τὰ χείλη αὐτῶν·

13 <u>*Sepulchrum patens*</u> est *guttur eorum*, *linguis suis* dolose
agebant: <u>*venenum aspidum*</u> sub labiis eorum.

*a/1   [throat ≈ open sepulchre] **'Their'**= the Jews (3.1).

Romans 11.16–24 (parable of the tree)

17 And if some of the branches be broken off, and *thou*, <u>*being a wild olive tree*</u>, wert grafted in among them, and with them partakest of the root and fatness of the olive tree.

17 εἰ δέ τινες τῶν κλάδων ἐξεκλάσθησαν, <u>*σὺ δὲ ἀγριέλαιος ὢν*</u> ἐνεκεντρίσθης ἐν αὐτοῖς καὶ συγκοινωνὸς τῆς ῥίζης καὶ τῆς πιότητος τῆς ἐλαίας ἐγένου.

17 Quod si aliqui ex ramis fracti sunt, *tu* autem cum <u>*oleaster*</u> <u>esses.</u>

[you ≈ a wild olive tree]

* * *

First Epistle of Paul to the Corinthians

1 Corinth. 6.19 What? know ye not that *your body* <u>is</u> <u>*the temple of the Holy Ghost which is in you*</u>, which ye have of God, and ye are not your own?

19 ἢ οὐκ οἴδατε ὅτι *τὸ σῶμα ὑμῶν* <u>*ναὸς τοῦ ἐν ὑμῖν Ἁγίου Πνεύματός ἐστιν*</u>, οὗ ἔχετε ἀπὸ Θεοῦ, καὶ οὐκ ἐστὲ ἑαυτῶν;

19 An nescitis quoniam *membra vestra*, <u>*templum sunt Spiritus Sancti, qui in vobis est,*</u> quem habetis a Deo, et non estis vestri?

[your body ≈ the temple of the Holy Ghost]

* * *

Epistle of Paul to the Galatians

Galatians 3.24 Wherefore *the law* <u>was</u> <u>*our schoolmaster*</u> to bring us unto Christ, that we might be justified by faith.

24 ὥστε ὁ νόμος <u>*παιδαγωγὸς ἡμῶν γέγονεν*</u> εἰς Χριστόν, ἵνα ἐκ πίστεως δικαιωθῶμεν·

24 Itaque lex *paedagogus noster fuit* in Christo, ut ex fide justificemur.

*a/1   [the law ≈ our schoolmaster]

Galatians 5.22 But <u>*the fruit of the Spirit*</u> <u>is</u> *love, joy, peace, long suffering, gentleness, goodness, faith.*

22 <u>*ὁ δὲ καρπὸς τοῦ Πνεύματός ἐστιν*</u> ἀγάπη, χαρά, εἰρήνη, μακροθυμία, χρηστότης, ἀγαθωσύνη, πίστις,

22 *Fructus autem Spiritus* <u>est</u> *caritas, gaudium, pax, patientia, benignitas, bonitas, longanimitas, 23 mansuetudo, fides, modestia, continentia, castitas.*

[love, joy etc. ≈ the fruit of the Spirit: the Spirit > love ≈ (a tree) > fruit]

* * *

Epistle of Paul to the Colossians
> 2.16 Let no man therefore judge you in meat, or in drink etc.
> 17 *Which* are *a shadow of things to come*; but the body is of Christ.

> 16 Μὴ οὖν τις ὑμᾶς κρινέτω ἐν βρώσει ἢ ἐν πόσει ἢ ἐν μέρει ἑορτῆς ἢ νουμηνίας ἢ σαββάτων, 17 ἅ ἐστι σκιὰ τῶν μελλόντων, τὸ δὲ σῶμα Χριστοῦ.

> 16 Nemo ergo vos judicet in cibo, aut in potu, aut in parte diei festi, aut neomeniae, aut sabbatorum: 17 *quae* sunt *umbra* futurorum: corpus autem Christi.

*a/1   [meat, drink etc. ≈ a shadow of things to come]

* * *

First Epistle of Paul to Timothy
3.15 thou oughtest to behave thyself in *the house of God*, which is the church of the living God, *the pillar and ground of the truth*.

> 15 ἐὰν δὲ βραδύνω, ἵνα εἰδῇς πῶς δεῖ ἐν οἴκῳ Θεοῦ ἀναστρέφεσθαι, ἥτις ἐστὶν ἐκκλησία Θεοῦ ζῶντος, στῦλος καὶ ἑδραίωμα τῆς ἀληθείας.

> 15 si autem tardavero, ut scias quomodo oporteat te in *domo Dei* conversari, quae est ecclesia Dei vivi, *columna et firmamentum veritatis*.

*a/1   [the house of God ≈ the pillar and ground of truth]

1st Timothy 6.10 For *the love of money* is t*he root of all evil.*

> 10 *ῥίζα γὰρ πάντων τῶν κακῶν* ἐστιν ἡ φιλαργυρία,

> 10 *Radix enim omnium malorum* est *cupiditas*:

*a/1   [love of money ≈ the root of evil]

* * *

General Epistle to James
James 3.4 Behold also the *ships*, which though they be so great, and are driven of fierce winds, yet are they turned about with a very *small helm*, whithersoever the governor listen.
> 5 Even so *the tongue is a little member*, and boasteth great things … 6 And *the tongue* is *a fire*, a world of iniquity … it defileth the

whole body, and setteth on fire the course of nature; and it is set on fire or hell.

4 ἰδοὺ καὶ *τὰ πλοῖα*, τηλικαῦτα ὄντα καὶ ὑπὸ σκληρῶν ἀνέμων ἐλαυνόμενα, μετάγεται ὑπὸ ἐλαχίστου πηδαλίου ὅπου ἂν ἡ ὁρμὴ τοῦ εὐθύνοντος βούληται. 5 **οὕτω** καὶ ἡ γλῶσσα *μικρὸν μέλος* ἐστὶ καὶ μεγαλαυχεῖ. ἰδοὺ *ὀλίγον πῦρ* ἡλίκην ὕλην ἀνάπτει·

4 Ecce et *naves*, cum magnae sint, et a ventis validis minentur, circumferuntur a modico gubernaculo ubi impetus dirigentis voluerit. 5 **Ita et** *lingua modicum quidem membrum* est, et magna exaltat. Ecce *quantus ignis* quam magnam silvam incendit!

[the tongue ≈ a little member ≈ a fire]

***

The Revelation of St. John the Divine

Rev. 1.20 The *seven stars* are *the angels of the seven churches*: and the *seven candlesticks* which thou sawest are *the seven churches*.

20 οἱ ἑπτὰ ἀστέρες *ἄγγελοι τῶν ἑπτὰ ἐκκλησιῶν* εἰσι, καὶ αἱ λυχνίαι *αἱ ἑπτὰ ἑπτὰ ἐκκλησίαι* εἰσίν.

20 *septem stellae, angeli* sunt septem ecclesiarum: et *candelabra septem, septem ecclesiae* sunt.

[the angels of the seven churches ≈ seven stars; the seven churches ≈ seven candlesticks] Jesus to St. John

***

Summary

List of Predicate Similes

Old Testament

Genesis 40.12, 49.9, 49.17, 49.21, 49.22
Exodus 10.7, 14.22   Deuteronomy 4.24, 32.4
I Samuel 17.43   II Samuel 22.2, 22.3, 22.29, 22.31

II Kings 21.14

Job 6.12, 7.7, 7.12, 8.9, 8.14, 13.4, 17.14, 20.14, 29.15, 31.12, 38.8, 41.19

Psalms 3.3, 18.2, 17.3, 22.6, 23.1, 27.1, 28.1, 31.2, 31.3, 32.7, 33.20, 36.6, 45.1, 57.4, 59.11, 60.8, 61.3, 62.2, 78.35, 78.39, 84.11, 92.15, 104.4, 104.17, 108.9, 110.1, 115.10–11, 118.14, 119.105, 121.5

Proverbs 2.7, 3.18, 6.23, 7.27, 10.25, 12.4, 13.12, 13.14, 14.27, 15.4, 16.31, 17.6, 18.7, 18.10, 18.11, 20.27, 22.14, 23.27, 25.18

Ecclesiastes 7.26

Song Of Solomon 1.13, 1.15, 2.1, 2.14, 4.1, 4.12, 8.6, 8.9

Isaiah 28.1, 41.15, 41.29, 48.4, 49.2, 64.8, 64.10

Jeremiah 2.14, 2.31, 3.17, 5.13, 6.28, 7.11, 9.11, 24.9, 25.11, 47.6, 50.6, 51.7, 51.19, 51.34

Lamentations 3.63, 4.10	Ezekiel 11.3, 22.18, 22.24, 31.2
Hosea 7.8, 8.9, 9.8. 10.1, 12.7	Joel 1.6
Obadiah 1.18	Jonah 4.6
Zephaniah 3.3	Zechariah 11.3, 12.2
Malachi 4.1	

New Testament

Matthew 4.19, 5.13, 5.14, 6.22, 7.15, 13.37, 13.38, 13.39, 21.13

Luke 8.11, 9.58, 11.34

John 1.4, 1.23, 1.29, 4.34, 6.33, 8.12, 10.1, 10.7, 10.11, 12.46, 14.6, 15.1, 15.5

Acts 2.35, 7.49, 9.15	Epistle to Romans 2.19, 3.13, 11.16–24
1 Cointhians. 6.19	Galatians 3.24, 5.22
Colossians 2.16	1 Timothy 3.15, 6.10
James 3.4	Revelation 1.20

* * *

Genitive Similes

The justification for classifying some prepositional phrases with 'of' as similes may be found at **Isaiah** 59.17, where such phrases alternate with regular similes:

> Isaiah 59.17 For *he put on righteousness* as *a breast-plate*, and an *helmet of salvation* upon his head; and he put on the *garments of vengeance* for clothing, and was clad with *zeal* as *a cloak*.
>
> 'Salvation as a helmet' or 'vengeance as a garment' would express the similes in the more conventional way; in all four phrases there is a concrete vehicle with an abstract tenor.
>
> In Latin and Greek the genitive case expresses the tenor, hence the term "genitive simile".

* * *

The English phrases "stream of consciousness" (coined by William James) or "flood of mail" are familiar English examples. We are meant to visualize the abstract words as a stream or a flood, thus similes.

In most cases such phrases combine an abstract tenor with a concrete vehicle but occasionally both are concrete, as at John 2.21:

> But he spake of *the temple of his body*.
>
> ἐκεῖνος δὲ ἔλεγεν περὶ *τοῦ ναοῦ* *τοῦ σώματος* αὐτοῦ.
>
> Ille autem dicebat de *templo corporis sui*. [the body ≈ a temple]

Of course the Greek or Latin genitive case and English prepositional phrases with 'of' frequently express other relationships besides similetic: e.g., the sound of a trumpet ('coming from'), a rich man's wealth (possessive), fear of the Lord (objective) is the beginning of wisdom (partitive), a hedge of thorns or den of lions ('consisting of'). It is not always easy to define the relationship between the nouns. This Appendix contains a list of those genitive or 'of' expressions that seem most like similes.

Genitive Similes (*/c)

II Samuel 22.3 he is] my protector, and *the horn of my salvation*, my helper, and my sure refuge.

> 3 ὑπερασπιστής μου καὶ <u>κέρας σωτηρίας μου</u>, ἀντιλήπτωρ μου καὶ καταφυγή μου σωτηρίας μου.

> 3 Deus fortis meus sperabo in eum: scutum meum, et <u>*cornu* salutis</u> meae.

> [my salvation ≈ a horn]

II Samuel 22.5 When the <u>waves of death</u> compassed me, <u>the floods</u> *of ungodly men* made me afraid.

> 5 ὅτι περιέσχον με <u>συντριμμοὶ</u> θανάτου, <u>χείμαρροι</u> ἀνομίας ἐθάμβησάν με·

> 5 Quia circumdederunt me <u>contritiones mortis</u>: torrentes Belial terruerunt me.David to the Lord in song [death ≈ waves; (ungodly men ≈ floods)]

II Samuel 22.36 Thou hast also given me *the shield* of thy *salvation*.

> 36 καὶ ἔδωκάς μοι <u>ὑπερασπισμὸν σωτηρίας</u> μου.

*c/   36 Dedisti mihi <u>*clypeum salutis*</u> tuae.

[my/thy salvation ≈ a shield]   David to the Lord in song

NB 'my' salvation in Greek, 'your' in Latin.

II Samuel 22.47 and exalted be the *God* of *the rock of my salvation*.

[God ≈ the rock of my salvation; salvation ≈ a rock]

*c/   47 ὁ <u>*φύλαξ*</u> τῆς σωτηρίας μου.David to the Lord in song

47 exaltabitur Deus <u>*fortis*</u> salutis meae.

[salvation ≈ a rock]

NB: the simile is not in the Greek or Latin.

II Samuel 22.51 He is *the tower* of *salvation* for his king

51 μεγαλύνων τὰς σωτηρίας βασιλέως αὐτοῦ

*c/   51 magnificans salutes regis sui David to the Lord in song

[salvation ≈ a tower]

NB: the simile is not in the Greek or Latin.

* * *

Nehemiah 9.12 Moreover thou leddest them in the day by *a cloudy pillar*; and in the night by *a pillar of fire*.

This could be considered a genitive simile (pillar ≈ fire) as well as a descriptive genitive (a fiery pillar).

* * *

Job 3.5 Let darkness and <u>the shadow of death</u> stain it … let *the blackness of the day* terrify it.

5 ἐκλάβοι δὲ αὐτὴν <u>σκότος καὶ σκιὰ θανάτου</u>, ἐπέλθοι ἐπ᾽ αὐτὴν γνόφος. καταραθείη ἡ ἡμέρα

*c/ 5 Obscurent eum <u>tenebrae et umbra mortis</u>; occupet eum caligo, et involvatur amaritudine.

[death ≈ a shadow] Job

>>**This is one of those expressions that could be classified as a similetic genitive (death ≈ a shadow) or a possessive genitive (death's shadow).**

Job 10.21 I go whence I shall not return, even to the *land of darkness* *c/ and 'the <u>shadow</u> *of death*.' (repeated in 10.22)

21 με πορευθῆναι ὅθεν οὐκ ἀναστρέψω, εἰς γῆν σκοτεινὴν καὶ γνοφεράν.

21 vadam, et non revertar, ad *terram tenebrosam*, et opertam mortis caligine: (<u>umbra</u> mortis in 10.22) Job

[death ≈ a shadow]

Job 16.16: On my eyelids is <u>the shadow</u> *of death*.

16 ἐπὶ δὲ βλεφάροις μου <u>σκιά</u>;

16 palpebrae meae *caligaverunt*.

[death ≈ a shadow] Job

>> **Here the simile is only in the English version; cf. Job 24.17.**

Job 24.17 For *the morning* is to them even <u>as *the shadow of death:*</u> if *c/ one know them, they are in the terrors of the <u>*shadow of death*</u>.

17 ὅτι ὁμοθυμαδὸν αὐτοῖς τὸ πρωΐ <u>σκιὰ θανάτου</u>, ὅτι ἐπιγνώσεται τάραχος <u>σκιᾶς θανάτου</u>.

17 Si subito apparuerit aurora, arbitrantur <u>umbram mortis</u>: et sic in tenebris quasi in luce ambulant

[morning ≈ the shadow of death; death ≈ a shadow] Job

* * *

Psalm 4.6 Lord, lift thou up the <u>light</u> of *thy countenance* upon us.

　　6 Εσημειώθη ἐφ᾽ ἡμᾶς <u>τὸ φῶς</u> τοῦ προσώπου σου, Κύριε.

*c/　<u>The light</u> of *thy countenance*, O Lord, has been manifested to-
　　wards us.

　　7 Ἐσημειώθη ἐφ᾽ ἡμᾶς <u>τὸ φῶς τοῦ προσώπου σου,</u> Κύριε.

　　7 Signatum est super nos <u>*lumen vultus tui*</u>, Domine.

　　[your countenance ≈ a light]

　　Similetic or possessive genitive.

　　NB Greek and Latin versions have Genitive similes:

Psalm 5.12 For thou, Lord, ... *with favour wilt thou compass him* [the
　　righteous] <u>*as with a shield.*</u>

*c/　12 Κύριε, <u>ὡς ὅπλῳ εὐδοκίας</u> ἐστεφάνωσας ἡμᾶς.

*c/　13 Domine, <u>*ut scuto bonae voluntatis tuae*</u> coronasti nos.

　　[the Lord's favor ≈ a shield]

Psalm 13.3 Consider and hear me, O Lord my God: lighten mine eyes,

*/c　lest I sleep <u>*the sleep of death*</u>.

　　= 12.4 ἐπίβλεψον, εἰσάκουσόν μου, Κύριε ὁ Θεός μου· φώτισον τοὺς
　　ὀφθαλμούς μου, μήποτε <u>ὑπνώσω εἰς θάνατον.</u>

　　12.4 Respice, et exaudi me, Domine Deus meus. Illumina oculos meos,
　　ne *umquam* <u>obdormiam in morte</u>.

　　[death ≈ sleep]

　　Note – Psalm 17.8 Keep *me* <u>as</u> <u>*the apple of the eye,*</u> hide me under <u>*the*</u>
　　　<u>*shadow of thy wings.*</u>

　　[me ≈ an apple *of the eye:* **a possessive genitive followed by another**]

Psalm 18.2 The *Lord is* ... <u>*the horn of my salvation*</u>,

　　18.1 = 17.3 18.1 *Κύριος* ... ὑπερασπιστής μου καὶ
　　<u>κέρας σωτηρίας μου.</u>

　　17.3 Deus ... cornu salutis meae.

　　[salvation ≈ a horn]

Psalm 18.35 Thou hast also given me the <u>*shield of thy salvation*</u>.

　　17.36 καὶ ἔδωκάς μοι <u>ὑπερασπισμὸν σωτηρίας</u> (And thou hast made me
　　　secure in my salvation)

　　17.36 et dedisti mihi <u>*protectionem salutis tuae.*</u>

*c/　[thy salvation ≈ a shield: **no simile in Greek and Latin**]

Psalm 22.15 and thou hast brought me into the <u>*dust of death.*</u>

21.15 καὶ εἰς <u>*χοῦν θανάτου*</u> κατήγαγές με.

21.16 et <u>*in pulverem mortis*</u> deduxisti me.

[death ≈ dust]

Psalm 23.4 Yea, though I walk through the valley of <u>*the shadow of death*</u>, I will fear no evil.

22.4 ἐὰν γὰρ καὶ πορευθῶ ἐν μέσῳ <u>*σκιᾶς θανάτου*</u>, οὐ φοβηθήσομαι κακά,

22.4 Nam, etsi ambulavero in medio <u>*umbrae mortis,*</u> non timebo mala, quoniam tu mecum es.

[death ≈ a shadow]

Psalm 31.2, 3 (= 30.3) *γενοῦ μοι* ... <u>εἰς *οἶκον καταφυγῆς*</u> τοῦ σῶσαί με.

30.2 be *thou* to me ... <u>for *a house of refuge*</u> to save me.

Psalm 36.9 For with thee is <u>*the fountain of life*</u>.

*c/   35.10 ὅτι παρὰ σοὶ <u>*πηγὴ ζωῆς*</u>,

35.10 quoniam apud te est <u>*fons vitae.*</u>

[life ≈ a fountain]

**Cf. 36.11 'the foot of pride' and 'the hand of the wicked'
[possessive genitives] (pes superbiae, et manus peccatoris) +
36.12 'workers of iniquity' (objective genitive).**

Ps 45.6 the <u>*scepter of thy kingdom*</u> is a right sceptre.

44.7 ῥάβδος εὐθύτητος <u>ἡ *ῥάβδος τῆς βασιλείας σου*</u>.

44.7 virga directionis <u>virga regni tui.</u>

[thy kingdom ≈ a sceptre]

Ps 60.3 Thou hast made us to drink <u>*the wine of astonishment.*</u>

*c/   59.5 ἐπότισας ἡμᾶς <u>οἶνον *κατανύξεως.*</u>

59.5 Ostendisti populo tuo dura; potasti nos <u>vino *compunctionis.*</u>

[astonishment ≈ wine]

Ps 95.1 Let us make a joyful noise to <u>the rock of our salvation.</u>

94.1 ἀλαλάξωμεν τῷ Θεῷ τῷ Σωτῆρι ἡμῶν·

94.1 jubilemus Deo salutari nostro;

[our salvation ≈ a rock] **No simile in Greek or Latin.**

Ps 104.3 who walketh upon *the <u>wings of the wind</u>* ...

3 ὁ περιπατῶν ἐπὶ <u>*πτερύγων ἀνέμων*</u>·

3 qui ambulas super <u>*pennas ventorum*</u> ...

[wind ≈ wings]

Ps. 104.7 At <u>the voice of thy thunder</u> they hasted away.

103.7 ἀπὸ <u>φωνῆς βροντῆς σου</u> δειλιάσουσιν.

103.7 Ab increpatione tua fugient, a <u>*voce tonitrui tui*</u> formidabunt.

[your voice ≈ thunder]

Ps 110.2 The Lord shall send <u>the rod of thy strength</u> out of Zion.

109.2 <u>*ῥάβδον δυνάμεως*</u> ἐξαποστελεῖ σοι Κύριος ἐκ Σιών,

109.2 <u>*Virgam virtutis tuae*</u> emittet Dominus ex Sion

[thy strength ≈ a rod]

Ps 116.13 I will take <u>*the cup of salvation*</u> …

*c/   115.4 <u>*ποτήριον*</u> σωτηρίου λήψομαι.

115.4 <u>*Calicem*</u> salutaris accipiam,

[salvation ≈ a cup]

* * *

The Proverbs

Prov. 3.18 *She* [*wisdom*] is a <u>tree of life</u> to them that lay hold upon her.

18<u>ξύλον ζωῆς</u> ἐστι πᾶσι τοῖς ἀντεχομένοις αὐτῆς,

18 <u>*Lignum vitae*</u> est his qui apprehenderint eam

[life ≈ a tree]

*c/   [wisdom ≈ *a tree of life; life ≈ *a tree] – **a good illustration** of a
similetic vehicle consisting of another simile.

Prov. 4.9 She shall give to thine head an *ornament of grace*: a<u>*crown*</u> of
glory shall she deliver to thee.

9 ἵνα δῷ τῇ σῇ κεφαλῇ στέφανον χαρίτων, <u>στεφάνῳ δὲ τρυφῆς</u> ὑπερασπίσῃ σου.

9 Dabit capiti tuo *augmenta gratiarum*, et <u>*corona inclyta*</u> proteget te.

[glory ≈ a crown] ***No genitive in Latin.***

Prov. 4.17 For they eat <u>*the bread*</u> of *wickedness*, and drink the <u>*wine*</u> <u>of</u>
violence.

*c/   4.17 οἴδε γὰρ σιτοῦνται <u>σῖτα ἀσεβείας</u>, <u>οἴνῳ</u> δὲ παρανόμῳ μεθύσκονται.

4.17 Comedunt <u>*panem impietatis*</u>, et <u>*vinum iniquitatis*</u> bibunt.

[**Genitive similes:** wickedness ≈ bread; violence ≈ wine]

NB that the second phrase is NOT a genitive simile in Greek.

Cf. 'ornament of grace' (στέφανον χαρίτων, augmenta gratiarum) **and**
   'crown of glory' (στεφάνῳ δὲ τρυφῆς, corona inclyta) **in 4.9:**

**(Note that the second phrase is NOT a genitive simile in Greek –
but an adjective.)**

Prov. 13.12 for *a good desire* is a *tree of life*.
    12 <u>δένδρον γὰρ ζωῆς</u>
    12 27 *lignum* <u>*vitae.*</u>
    [life ≈ a tree]

Prov. 14.3 In the mouth of the foolish is *a rod of pride*:
    3 <u>*βακτηρία*</u> ὕβρεως,
    3 <u>*virga*</u> *superbiae*;
    [pride ≈ a rod]

Prov. 14.27 The *fear of the Lord* is *a fountain of life,* to depart from the *snare* of *death.*
    27 πρόσταγμα Κυρίου <u>πηγὴ ζωῆς</u>, ποιεῖ δὲ ἐκκλίνειν ἐκ <u>παγίδος θανάτου.</u>
    [fear of the Lord ≈ a fountain of life; life ≈ a fountain; death ≈ snares] **Perhaps the ambiguity lies in the tendency to personify death as a creature with a shadow and snares.**

Prov.15.4 A *wholesome tongue* is *a tree of life*,
    4 ἴασις γλώσσης <u>δένδρον ζωῆς</u>,
    4 Lingua placabilis lignum vitae;
    [*Tree* is the vehicle of both a predicate simile and a genitive simile: life ≈ a tree] Huston Smith, <u>The World's Religions</u>, p. 303, calls the 'tree of life' a simile.

Prov. 16.31 The hoary head is a *crown of glory* ...
    31 <u>στέφανος</u> καυχήσεως γήρας,
    31 31 <u>*Corona*</u> dignitatis *senectus*,
*c/   [a crown of glory; glory ≈ a crown]

Prov. 22.8 He that soweth iniquity shall reap vanity: and *the rod of his anger* shall fail.
    8 ὁ σπείρων φαῦλα θερίσει κακά, πληγὴν δὲ ἔργων αὐτοῦ συντελέσει.
    > 8 Qui seminat iniquitatem metet mala, et <u>*virga irae suae*</u> consummabitur. [anger ≈ a rod]
    The English follows the Latin here. The phrase could be a genitive simile (anger ≈ a rod) or a possessive genitive (anger's rod), but since the tenor is abstract I prefer the former. The metaphor of 'sowing' is in the first part.
    cf. 22.15: <u>*rod*</u> of *correction* [correction ≈ a rod]

* * *

Isaiah 11.4 He [the Lord] shall smite the earth with *the rod of his mouth* and with *the breath of his lips* shall he slay the wicked.

> 4 καὶ πατάξει γῆν <u>τῷ λόγῳ</u> <u>τοῦ στόματος αὐτοῦ</u> καὶ <u>ἐν πνεύματι διὰ χειλέων</u> ἀνελεῖ ἀσεβῆ· (and he shall smite the earth with the *word of his mouth*, and *with the breath of his lips* shall he destroy the ungodly one.)

> 4 et percutiet terram *virga oris sui*, et *spiritu labiorum suorum* interficiet impium.

*c/   [his mouth ≈ a rod ('breath of his lips' = possessive)]

Isaiah 28.5 In that day shall the Lord of hosts be for a *crown of glory*, and for a *diadem of beauty* unto the residue of his people.

> 5 τῇ ἡμέρᾳ ἐκείνῃ <u>ἔσται</u> Κύριος σαβαὼθ <u>ὁ στέφανος τῆς ἐλπίδος ὁ πλακεὶς τῆς δόξης</u> τῷ καταλειφθέντι μου λαῷ·

> 5 In die illa erit Dominus exercituum *corona gloriae*, et *sertum exsultationis* residuo populi sui;

*c/   [glory ≈ a crown; beauty ≈ a diadem]

Isaiah 30.20 And though the Lord give you the bread of adversity, and the water of affliction … thine eyes shall see thy teachers.

> 20 καὶ δώσει Κύριος ὑμῖν <u>ἄρτον θλίψεως</u> καὶ ὕδωρ στενόν,

> 20 Et dabit vobis Dominus *panem arctum, et aquam brevem*;

*c/   [adversity ≈ bread; affliction ≈ water]

NB one genitive expression in the Greek and none in Latin.

Isaiah 51.22 Behold, I have taken out of thine hand *the cup of trembling*, even the dregs of *the cup of my fury*; thou shalt no more drink it again.

> 22 ἰδοὺ εἴληφα ἐκ τῆς χειρός σου <u>τὸ ποτήριον τῆς πτώσεως</u>, τὸ <u>κόνδυ τοῦ θυμοῦ μου</u>, καὶ οὐ προσθήσῃ ἔτι πιεῖν αὐτό·

> 22 Ecce tuli de manu tua *calicem soporis*, fundum *calicis indignationis meae*; non adjicies ut bibas illum ultra.

*c/   [trembling ≈ a cup; fury ≈ a cup]

Isaiah 59.17 For *he put on righteousness* as *a breast-plate*, and an *helmet of salvation* upon his head; and he put on the *garments of vengeance* of clothing, and was clad with *zeal* as *a cloak*.

> 17 καὶ ἐνεδύσατο δικαιοσύνην <u>ὡς θώρακα</u> καὶ περιέθετο <u>περικεφαλαίαν σωτηρίου</u> ἐπὶ τῆς κεφαλῆς καὶ περιεβάλετο <u>ἱμάτιον ἐκδικήσεως</u> καὶ τὸ περιβόλαιον.

17 Indutus est *justitia* <u>ut</u> <u>*lorica*</u>, et <u>*galea*</u> *salutis* in capite ejus; indutus
est vestimentis ultionis, et opertus est <u>quasi</u> <u>*pallio zeli*</u>.

*c/ [righteousness ≈ a breast-plate; salvation ≈ a helmet; vengeance

*c/ ≈ a garment; zeal ≈ a cloak]

**NB – This series illustrates the closeness between genitive similes
and prothetic similes, since the phrases are interchangeable:** *right-
eousness* <u>as</u> <u>*a breast-plate*</u> ≈ the <u>*breast-plate*</u> of *righteousnes*s; *zeal* <u>as</u> <u>*a*</u>
<u>*cloak*</u> ≈ <u>*the cloa*</u>k of *zeal*.

Isaiah 61.3 To appoint unto them that mourn in Zion, to give unto them
beauty for ashes, *the oil of joy for* mourning, the *garment of praise* for
the *spirit of heaviness; that they might be called* trees of righteousness.

3 δοθῆναι τοῖς πενθοῦσι Σιὼν δόξαν ἀντὶ σποδοῦ, *ἄλειμμα εὐφροσύνης* τοῖς
πενθοῦσι, *καταστολὴν δόξης* ἀντὶ *πνεύματος ἀκηδίας*·

3 ut ponerem lugentibus Sion, et darem eis *coronam pro cinere*, *oleum*
gaudii pro luctu, *pallium laudis* pro *spiritu moeroris*; et vocabuntur
in ea *fortes justitiae*, plantatio Domini ad glorificandum.

*c/ [joy ≈ oil; praise ≈ garment; heaviness ≈ a spirit;
(4x) righteousness ≈ trees]

Isaiah 61.10 I will greatly rejoice in the Lord, ... for he hath clothed me
with t*he garments of salvation*, he hath covered me with the *robe of*
righteousness: <u>as</u> <u>*a bridegroom decketh himself*</u> with ornaments, and
<u>*as a bride adorneth herself with jewels.*</u> 11 For <u>as</u> t*he earth bringeth*
<u>*forth her bud, and as the garden causeth the things that are sown in it*</u>
<u>*to spring forth;*</u> **so** the Lord God will cause *righteousness and praise to*
spring forth before all nations.

10 Ἀγαλλιάσθω ἡ ψυχή μου ἐπὶ τῷ Κυρίῳ· ἐνέδυσε γάρ με *ἱμάτιον σωτηρίου*
καὶ *χιτῶνα εὐφροσύνης*, <u>ὡς</u> <u>*νυμφίῳ*</u> περιέθηκέ *μοι μίτραν* καὶ <u>ὡς</u> <u>*νύμφην*</u>
κατεκόσμησέ με κόσμῳ. 11 καὶ <u>ὡς</u> <u>*γῆ αὔξουσα τὸ ἄνθος αὐτῆς καὶ ὡς*</u>
<u>*κῆπος τὰ σπέρματα αὐτοῦ*</u>, **οὕτως** ἀνατελεῖ Κύριος δικαιοσύνην καὶ
ἀγαλλίαμα ἐναντίον πάντων τῶν ἐθνῶν.

10 Gaudens gaudebo in Domino, et exsultabit anima mea in Deo
meo, quia induit me *vestimentis salutis*, et i*ndumento justitiae*
circumdedit me, <u>quasi</u> <u>*sponsum*</u> decoratum corona, et <u>quasi</u>
<u>*sponsam ornatam monilibus suis.*</u> [11] <u>Sicut</u> enim <u>*terra profert*</u>

germen suum, et sicut h*ortus semen suum germinat*, **sic** *Dominus Deus germinabit justitiam et laudem coram universis gentibus.*
*c/   [salvation ≈ a garment; righteousness ≈ a robe; I ≈ a bridegroom ≈ a (2x) bride; [the Lord > (causes to grow) righteousness ≈ the earth > flowers ≈ a garden > its seeds]

Isaiah 63.9 The *angel of his presence* saved him.
9 οὐ πρέσβυς οὐδὲ ἄγγελος, ἀλλ᾽ αὐτὸς Κύριος ἔσωσεν αὐτούς.
9 *angelus faciei ejus* salvavit eos.
*c/   [his presence ≈ an angel]

* * *

Jeremiah 1.11 I see *a rod of* an almond tree.
11 τί σὺ ὁρᾷς Ἱερεμία; καὶ εἶπε· βακτηρίαν καρυΐνην.
11 *Virgam vigilantem* ego video.
[an almond tree ≈ a rod] **No simile in Greek or Latin.**

Jeremiah 4.4 Circumsize yourselves to the Lord, and take away the fore-skins of your heart, ye men of Judah …
4 περιτμήθητε τῷ Θεῷ ὑμῶν καὶ περιτέμνεσθε τὴν σκληροκαρδίαν ὑμῶν.
[your hardness of heart]
4.Circumcidimini Domino, et auferte *praeputia cordium* vestrorum,
[the heart ≈ foreskin]

Jeremiah 8.14 *water of gall* to drink.
14 Θεὸς ἀπέρριψεν ἡμᾶς καὶ ἐπότισεν ἡμᾶς ὕδωρ χολῆς.
14 et potum dedit nobis *aquam fellis.*
[gall ≈ water]

Jeremiah 13.16 shadow of death
16 σκιὰ θανάτου
16 ponet eam in *umbram mortis*, et in caliginem.
[death ≈ a shadow]

Jeremiah 25.15 For thus saith the Lord God of Israel unto me: Take *the wine cup* of *this fury* at my hand … and cause all the nations … to drink it.
15 [What happened to verses 14–33 of Chap. 25?]
25:14–19 = Heb. 49:34–39]

15 Sume *calicem vini furoris hujus* de manu mea, et propinabis de illo
cunctis gentibus, ad quas ego mittam te.
   *c/   [fury ≈ a cup of wine]

* * *

Lamentations of Jeremiah 1.14 The *yoke of my transgressions* is bound by
his hand.

   14 Ἐγρηγορήθη ἐπὶ τὰ ἀσεβήματά μου· ἐν χερσί μου συνεπλάκησαν,
   ἀνέβησαν ἐπὶ τὸν τράχηλόν μου·
   (He has watched over my sins, they are twined about my hands, they
   have come up on my neck.)
*c/   14 *jugum iniquitatum mearum*
   [my transgressions ≈ a yoke]
   Lamentations of Jeremiah 5.10 they are convulsed, because of [the
   appearance of] 'storms of famine'
   10 τὸ δέρμα ἡμῶν, ὡς κλίβανος ἐπελιώθη συνεσπάσθησαν ἀπὸ?-προσώπου
   καταιγίδων λιμοῦ.

* * *

Ezekiel 5.16 When I shall send upon them *the evil arrows of famine* ...
   16 καὶ ἐν τῷ ἀποστεῖλάι με βολίδας τοῦ λιμοῦ ἐπ᾽ αὐτοὺς
   16 quando misero *sagittas famis pessimas* in eos,
*c/   [famine ≈ arrows (of a bow)]
   [famine ≈ shafts (i.e., of a bow): possessive?]
Ezekiel 7.11 *Violence* is risen up into *a rod of wickedness*.
   10 εἰ καὶ ἡ ράβδος ἤνθηκεν, ἡ ὕβρις ἐξανέστηκε. 11 καί συντρίψει στήριγμα
   ἀνόμου καὶ οὐ μετὰ θορύβου οὐδὲ μετὰ σπουδῆς.
   11 *iniquitas* surrexit in *virga impietatis*:
*c/   [Violence ≈ a rod of wickedness (wickedness ≈ a rod)]
Ezekiel 14.3: These men [the elders of Israel] have ... put *the stumblingblock
of their iniquity* before their face.
   3 τὴν κόλασιν τῶν ἀδικιῶν αὐτῶν ἔθηκαν πρὸ προσώπου αὐτῶν.
   3 *scandalum iniquitatis suae* statuerunt contra faciem suam:
*c/   [their iniquity ≈ a stumblingblock]
   cf. 14.4 "the *stumbling block of his iniquity*"

***

Hosea 10.13 ye have eaten *the fruit of lies*.
   13 ἐφάγετε καρπὸν ψευδῆ [**false fruit**]
   13 comedistis *frugem mendacii*
   [lies ≈ fruit]

* * *

Zech. 12.2 Behold, I will make Jerusalem *a cup of trembling* unto all the people.
   2 ἰδοὺ ἐγὼ τίθημι τὴν Ἰερουσαλὴμ *ὡς πρόθυρα σαλευόμενα* πᾶσι τοῖς λαοῖς κύκλῳ.
   2 Ecce ego ponam Jerusalem *superliminare crapulae* omnibus populis in circuitu. [trembling ≈ a cup]

New Testament: – With 'of' (Genitive)

Matt. 3.3 For this is he that was spoken of by the prophet Esaias, saying,
   The *voice of one crying in the wilderness*, Prepare ye the way of the Lord.
   3 οὗτος γάρ ἐστιν ὁ ῥηθεὶς ὑπὸ Ἡσαΐου τοῦ προφήτου λέγοντος· *φωνὴ βοῶντος ἐν τῇ ἐρήμῳ*, ἑτοιμάσατε τὴν ὁδὸν Κυρίου.
   3 Hic est enim, qui dictus est per Isaiam prophetam dicentem:
   Vox clamantis in deserto: Parate viam Domini:
   [voice of one ≈ someone crying in the wilderness] = John the Baptist
   'of' = 'like that of'; thus 'of' may be considered the prothesis; but it is also a possessive genitive.
   Matt. 4.17 Repent, for the *kingdom of heaven* is at hand. (Jesus)
   17 μετανοεῖτε· ἤγγικε γὰρ *ἡ βασιλεία* τῶν οὐρανῶν.
   17 Poenitentiam agite: appropinquavit enim *regnum* caelorum.
*c/ [heaven ≈ a kingdom] **Also a possessive genitive (heaven's kingdom).** *Passim.* **e.g., 18.3.**

***

Mark

***

Luke 1.69 And [the Lord God of Israel] hath raised up an *horn of salvation* for us.

69 καὶ ἤγειρε *κέρας σωτηρίας* ἡμῖν …

*c/   69 Et erexit *cornu salutis* nobis in domo David pueri sui.

    [salvation ≈ a horn] **Or Salvation's horn.**

Luke 1.79 To give light to them that sit in darkness and in *the shadow of death*.

    79 ἐπιφᾶναι τοῖς ἐν σκότει καὶ *σκιᾷ θανάτου* καθημένοις,

    79 Illuminare his qui in tenebris et *in umbra mortis* sedent:

*c/   [death ≈ a shadow]

    Cf. 3.7 O generation of vipers

    NOT a genitive simile but rather a partitive-genitive (generation 'consisting' of vipers).

    7 γεννήματα ἐχιδνῶν / Genimina viperarum.

* * *

John 2.21 But he spake of *the temple of his body*.

    21 ἐκεῖνος δὲ ἔλεγεν περὶ *τοῦ ναοῦ τοῦ σώματος* αὐτοῦ.

    21 Ille autem dicebat de *templo* corporis sui.

*c/   [the body ≈ a temple]

John 6.35 And Jesus said unto them, *I* am *the bread of life*: he that cometh to me shall never hunger; and he that believeth on me shall never thirst.

    35 αὐτοῖς ὁ Ιησοῦς, *Εγώ* εἰμι *ὁ ἄρτος τῆς ζωῆς*: ὁ ἐρχόμενος πρός ἐμὲ οὐ μὴ πεινάσῃ, καὶ ὁ πιστεύων εἰς ἐμὲ οὐ μὴ διψήσει πώποτε.

    [I (Jesus) = the bread of life] Jesus cf. 6.48 and 51+54.

    Both a genitive simile (life = bread) and a partitive (bread = *the most important part* of life).

John 8.12 Then spake Jesus again unto them, saying, I am *the light of the world*: he that followeth me shall not walk in darkness,

*/c but shall have the *light of life*.

    12 Πάλιν οὖν αὐτοῖς ὁ Ιησοῦς ἐλάλησε λέγων· ἐγώ *εἰμι τὸ φῶς* τοῦ κόσμου· ὁ ἀκολουθῶν ἐμοὶ οὐ μὴ περιπατήσῃ ἐν τῇ σκοτίᾳ, ἀλλ᾽ ἕξει τὸ φῶς τῆς ζωῆς.

    12 Ego sum lux mundi: qui sequitur me, non ambulat in tenebris, sed habebit *lumen* vitae.

    [life ≈ a light]

***

Epistle of Paul to the Romans

Romans 9.33 *I* lay in Sion *a stumbling stone and rock of offense.*
    33 ἰδοὺ τίθημι ἐν Σιὼν *λίθον προσκόμματος καὶ πέτραν σκανδάλου,*
    33 Ecce *pono* in Sion *lapidem offensionis, et petram scandali:*
*c/   [offense ≈ a rock]

* * *

Epistle of Paul to the Ephesians

Ephesians 6 and 11: 'the whole armor of God'
    6.14 Stand therefore, having your loins girt about with truth, and
        having on *the breastplate of righteousness*;
        14 στῆτε οὖν περιζωσάμενοι τὴν ὀσφὺν ὑμῶν ἐν ἀληθείᾳ, καὶ ἐνδυσάμενοι
        τὸν θώρακα τῆς δικαιοσύνης,
        14 State ergo succincti lumbos vestros in veritate, et induti *loricam*
        justitiae,
        [righteousness ≈ a breastplate]
    6.15 And your feet shod with the preparation of *the gospel of peace.*
        15 καὶ ὑποδησάμενοι τοὺς πόδας ἐν ἑτοιμασίᾳ *τοῦ εὐαγγελίου* τῆς εἰρήνης,
        15 et calceati pedes in praeparatione *Evangelii pacis,*
        [peace ≈ gospel]
    6.16 Above all, taking *the shield of faith*, wherewith ye shall be able to
        quench all the fiery darts of the wicked.
        16 ἐπὶ πᾶσιν ἀναλαβόντες *τὸν θυρεὸν τῆς πίστεως,* ἐν ᾧ δυνήσεσθε πάντα
        τὰ βέλη τοῦ πονηροῦ τὰ πεπυρωμένα σβέσαι·
        16 in omnibus sumentes *scutum fidei,*
        [faith ≈ a shield]
    6. 17 And take *the helmet of salvation*, and the sword of the Spirit, which
        is the word of God:
        17 καὶ *τὴν περικεφαλαίαν τοῦ σωτηρίου* δέξασθε, καὶ *τὴν μάχαιραν τοῦ*
        Πνεύματος, ὅ ἐστι ῥῆμα Θεοῦ.
        17 et *galeam salutis* assumite, et *gladium spiritus.*
        [salvation ≈ a helmet; the Spirit ≈ a sword]
        NB – These could also be possessive (like God's word):

Salvation's helmet, the Spirit's sword.

* * *

First Epistle of Paul to the Thessalonians

2.5 For neither at any time used we flattering words, as ye know, nor a
cloak of covetousness: God is witness.

    5 οὔτε γάρ ποτε ἐν λόγῳ κολακείας ἐγενήθημεν, καθὼς οἴδατε, οὔτε ἐν
    προφάσει πλεονεξίας, Θεὸς μάρτυς,

    5 Neque enim aliquando fuimus in sermone adulationis, sicut
    scitis: neque *in occasione avaritiae*: Deus testis est:

*c/   [covetousness ≈ a cloak] **Simile only in English translation.**

* * *

James (5 Chapters)

(General Epistle)

1.12 Blessed is the man that endureth temptation: for when he is tried, he
shall receive *the crown of life*.
    [life ≈ a crown]

* * *

Second Epistle of Paul to Timothy

4.8 Henceforth there is laid up for me *a crown of righteousness,* which the
Lord, the righteous judge, shall give me at that day.

    8 λοιπὸν ἀπόκειταί μοι *ὁ* τῆς δικαιοσύνης *στέφανος,*

    8 In reliquo reposita est mihi *corona justitiae*, quam reddet mihi
    Dominus in illa die, justus judex.

*c/   [righteousness ≈ a crown]

* * *

First Epistle General of Peter

1 Peter 2.8 And *a stone of stumbling*, and *a rock of offense* …]
    2.8 *λίθος προσκόμματος* καὶ *πέτρα σκανδάλου.*

2.8 et *lapis offensionis, et petra scandali*
[stumbling ≈ a stone; offense ≈ a rock]
1 Peter 2.16 not using your liberty for *a cloke of maliciousness.*

    16 μὴ *ὡς ἐπικάλυμμα* ἔχοντες τῆς κακίας τὴν ἐλευθερίαν, ἀλλ᾽ ὡς δοῦλοι Θεοῦ.

    16 non quasi *velamen habentes malitiae* libertatem, sed sicut servi Dei.

*c/   [maliciousness ≈ a cloak]

* * *

The Revelation of St. John the Divine

Rev. 2.7 To him that overcometh will I give to eat of the *tree of life*, which is in the midst of the paradise of God.

    7 νικῶντι δώσω αὐτῷ φαγεῖν ἐκ *τοῦ ξύλου* τῆς ζωῆς, ὅ ἐστιν ἐν τῷ παραδείσῳ τοῦ Θεοῦ μου.

    7 Vincenti dabo edere de *ligno* vitae, quod est in paradiso Dei mei.

    [life ≈ a tree]

When the genitive is abstract, the expression seems more similetic than partitive. It is implied that righteousness is a kind of crown rather than that a crown belongs to an entity Righteousness. In other expressions the 'of' indicates partitive or possessive.

Ps. 17.8 Keep *me* as *the apple of the eye (i.e., the best part of the eye) under the shadow of thy wings. (possessive)*

Prov. 16.31 *στέφανος* καυχήσεως γῆρας,

    31 *Old age* is a *crown of honour.*   *[descriptive]*

[old age ≈ a crown of honour; honor ≈ a type of crown, /

Sometimes the KJV seems to be a translation of the Latin and sometimes of the Greek. Here the Greek is closer: Isaiah 28.5. cf. the Vulgate of Isaiah 30.20: Et dabit vobis Dominus panem arctum, et aquam brevem. Again the English is closer to the Greek. The Greek dates from 2nd century BC, the Latin from the 4th c. AD and the English translation (KJV) from 1608 AD.

* * *

Summary Genitive Similes

Old Testament

II Samuel 22.3, 22.5, 22.36, 22.47, 22.51

Nehemiah 9.12   Job 3.5, 10.21, 16.16, 24.17

Psalm 4.6, 5.12, 13.3, 17.8, 18.2, 18.35, 22.15, 23.4, 31.2–3, 35.9, 45.6,
    60,3, 95.1, 104.3, 104.7, 110.2, 116.13

Proverbs 3.18, 4.9, 4.17, 13.12, 14.3, 14.27, 15.4, 16.31, 16.31, 22.8

Isaiah, 11.4, 28.5, 30.20, 51.22, 59.17, 61.3, 61.10, 63.9

Jeremiah 1.11, 4.4, 8.14, 13.16, 25.15

Lamentations 1.14,5.10   Ezekiel 5.16, 7.11, 14.3

Hosea 10.13   Zecharia 12.2

New Testament

Matthew 3.3, 4.17   Luke 1.69, 1.79

John 2.21, 6.35, 8.12   Romans 9.33

Ephesians 6 + 11, 6.15, 6.16, 6.17

Thessalonians 2.5   James 1.12

2 Timothy 4.8 1   Peter 2.16

Revelation 2.7

Factual Comparisons
(Examples of literal transformations and comparisons that are more factual than figurative.)

A Old Testament

Genesis 19.26 But his wife looked back from behind him, and <u>became</u> a *pillar of salt.* Narrator 26 ἐγένετο στήλη ἁλός / versa est in statuam salis

* * *

Exodus 4.3 He cast it [a rod] on the ground and *it* <u>became</u> *a serpent.*
   3. καὶ ἔρριψεν αὐτὴν ἐπὶ τὴν γῆν, καὶ ἐγένετο ὄφις; also 4.4.
   (Cf. Gen. 19.26 above: ἐγένετο στήλη ἁλός) Narrator
Exodus 4.4 And he [Moses] put forth *his hand,* and caught it, and *it* <u>became</u> *a rod* in his hand. Narrator
Exodus 28.11 With the work of an engraver in stone, <u>like</u> *<u>the engravings of a signet</u>*, shalt thou engrave the two stones with the names of the children of Israel. The Lord to Moses
   See also 28.21.

* * *

Deuteronomy 2.10 *The Emims* dwelt therein in times past, a people great, and many, and *tall*, <u>as</u> *<u>the Anakims</u>*.

* * *

Judges 16.30 So *the dead which he [Samson] slew at his death* were <u>more</u> <u>than</u> *<u>they which he slew in his life</u>*.

* * *

II Samuel 13.15 *the hatred* wherewith he/Amnon hated her/his sister Tamar was <u>greater than</u> *<u>the love</u>* wherewith he had loved her.

* * *

Job 1.8 "Hast thou considered *my servant Job*, that there is *none* <u>like</u> <u>*him*</u> in the earth, a perfect and an upright man …?"

Job 34.26 He striketh *them* <u>as</u> *<u>wicked men</u>* in the open sight of others.
Elihu

Job 35.5 Behold the *<u>clouds</u>* which are <u>higher than</u> *thou*.
Elihu to Job

Job 40.7 Gird up thy loins now <u>like a man</u>. [NB = 40.2 in Latin 40.9 Hast thou an arm <u>like God</u>? /version.]

40.15 behemoth: he eateth grass <u>*as an ox*</u>.

Job 41.33 Upon earth there is not *his like,* who is made without fear.

25 οὐκ ἔστιν οὐδὲν ἐπὶ τῆς γῆς <u>ὅμοιον αὐτῷ</u> πεποιημένον

24 *<u>Non est super terram potestas quae comparetur</u>* ei, qui factus est ut nullum timere.[(the Lord) ≈ no equal]

* * *

Ps 8.5 For thou hast made *him* [man] a <u>little lower than</u> the *<u>angels</u>*.

Ps 68.15 the hill of God is as the hill of Bashan. Also at 69.31 (better than an ox or bullock).

Ps 80.10 The hills were covered with the shadow of it, and the *boughs* thereof were <u>like</u> the *goodly cedars*.

Ps 119.98 Thou through thy commandments hast made *me* <u>wiser than</u> <u>*mine enemies.*</u>

  118.ὑπὲρ τοὺς ἐχθρούς μου ἐσόφισάς με τὴν ἐντολήν σου,

  118.98 Super inimicos meos prudentem me fecisti mandato tuo.

Ps 119.99 I have <u>more understanding than all my teachers</u>.

  118.99 ὑπὲρ πάντας τοὺς διδάσκοντάς με συνῆκα.

  118.99 Super omnes docentes me intellexi,

Ps 119.100 <u>I understand more than the ancients</u>.

118.100 ὑπὲρ πρεσβυτέρους συνῆκα.

118.100 Super senes intellexi,

Ps 139.12 Yea, the darkness hideth not from thee: but *the night shineth* <u>as</u> *the day*.

138.12 ὅτι σκότος οὐ σκοτισθήσεται ἀπὸ σοῦ, καὶ **νὺξ ὡς ἡμέρα** φωτισθήσεται·

138.12 Quia tenebrae non obscurabuntur a te, et **nox sicut dies** illuminabitur;

* * *

Prov. 23.34 Yea, thou *shalt be* <u>as</u> *<u>he that lieth down in the midst of the sea</u>*, or <u>as</u> *<u>he that lieth upon the top of a mast</u>*.

34 καὶ *κατακείσῃ* <u>ὥσπερ</u> <u>*ἐν καρδίᾳ θαλάσσης*</u> καὶ <u>ὥσπερ</u> <u>*κυβερνήτης ἐν πολλῷ κλύδωνι.*</u> [a metaphor: καρδίᾳ θαλάσσης]

34 Et eris <u>sicut</u> <u>*dormiens in medio mari,*</u> et <u>quasi</u> <u>*sopitus gubernator,*</u> amisso clavo.

[you ≈ he who lies down in the middle of the sea ≈ he who lies upon the top of a mast] **Here a figurative-sounding comparison is expressed as though factual.**

* * *

Ecclesiastes 7.1 *A good name* is <u>better than</u> <u>*good oil*</u>; and the day of death *than the day of birth*. – **a figurative simile followed by a literal comparison; also comparisons in the next two sentences. But then (in 7.6) the comparison becomes figurative again.**

Ecclesiast 9.4 for *a living dog* is [above = better than] <u>*a dead lion*</u>.

4 ὁ κύων ὁ ζῶν, αὐτὸς <u>*ἀγαθὸς ὑπὲρ*</u> <u>*τὸν λέοντα τὸν νεκρόν.*</u>

* * *

Isaiah 30.26 Moreover t*he light of the moon* shall be <u>as</u> t*<u>he light of the sun</u>*, and the light of the sun shall be sevenfold <u>as</u> *<u>the light of seven day</u>*s.

26 καὶ ἔσται τὸ φῶς τῆς σελήνης <u>ὡς</u> <u>*τὸ φῶς τοῦ ἡλίου*</u> καὶ τὸ φῶς τοῦ ἡλίου ἔσται ἑπταπλάσιον ἐν τῇ ἡμέρᾳ,

26 et erit *lux lunae* <u>sicut</u> <u>*lux solis*</u>, et *lux solis* erit septempliciter <u>sicut</u> <u>*lux septem dierum,*</u>

[the light of the moon ≈ the light of the sun ≈ the light of seven days]

Jeremiah 32.42 For thus saith the Lord: <u>Like as</u> I <u>*have brought all this*</u> <u>*great evil upon this people*</u>, **so** *will I bring upon them all the good that I have promised them.*

39.42 ὅτι οὕτως εἶπε Κύριος· <u>καθὰ</u> ἐπήγαγον ἐπὶ τὸν λαὸν τοῦτον πάντα τὰ κακὰ τὰ μεγάλα ταῦτα, **οὕτως** ἐγὼ ἐπάξω ἐπ᾽ αὐτοὺς πάντα τὰ ἀγαθά, ἃ ἐλάλησα ἐπ᾽ αὐτούς.

32.42 <u>Sicut</u> adduxi super populum istum omne malum hoc grande, **sic** adducam super eos omne bonum quod ego loquor ad eos.

Also see 42.18: 'As mine anger and my fury hath been poured forth upon the inhabitants of Jerusalem, so shall my fury be poured forth upon you.'

* * *

Lamentations of Jeremiah 1.12 see if thereby any <u>sorrow like unto my sorrow.</u>

12 ἴδετε εἰ ἔστιν <u>ἄλγος κατὰ τὸ ἄλγος</u> μου,.

Lamentations of Jeremiah 1.20 abroad *the sword* bereaveth, at home there is <u>*as death*</u>.

2.5: The Lord is become <u>*as an enemy*</u>.

* * *

Ezekiel 23.44 Yet t*hey went in unto her*, <u>as</u> t<u>*hey go in unto a woman that playeth the harlot*</u>: **so** *went they in unto Aholah and unto Aholibah,* the lewd women.

cf. 26.19: When I shall make thee <u>*a desolate city, like the cities*</u> that are not inhabited.

Ezekiel 42.11 And *the way before them* was <u>like</u> <u>*the appearance of the chambers*</u> which were toward the north.

* * *

Daniel >> **The following are not similes but literal descriptions:**

7.3 And *four great beasts came up from the sea*, diverse one from another
4 The *first was* like *a lion*, and had eagle's wings ...
5 And, behold, *another beast* like *to a bear*, ... 6 ... and lo *another* like
a leopard, ... 7 After this ... *behold a fourth beast, dreadful and
terrible*, ... and it had ten horns ... 8 ... in this horn were *eyes* like
the eyes of man, and a mouth speaking great things.

3 καὶ τέσσαρα θηρία μεγάλα ἀνέβαινον ἐκ τῆς θαλάσσης διαφέροντα
ἀλλήλων. 4 τὸ πρῶτον ὡσεὶ λέαινα, καὶ πτερὰ αὐτῇ ὡσεὶ ἀετοῦ·
ἐθεώρουν ἕως οὗ ἐξετίλη τὰ πτερὰ αὐτῆς, καὶ ἐξήρθη ἀπὸ τῆς γῆς
καὶ ἐπὶ ποδῶν ἀνθρώπου ἐστάθη, καὶ καρδία ἀνθρώπου ἐδόθη αὐτῇ.
5 καὶ ἰδοὺ θηρίον δεύτερον ὅμοιον ἄρκῳ, καὶ εἰς μέρος ἓν ἐστάθη, καὶ
τρεῖς πλευραὶ ἐν τῷ στόματι αὐτῆς ἀναμέσον τῶν ὀδόντων αὐτῆς,
καὶ οὕτως ἔλεγον αὐτῇ· ἀνάστηθι, φάγε σάρκας πολλάς. 6 ὀπίσω
τούτου ἐθεώρουν καὶ ἰδοὺ θηρίον ἕτερον ὡσεὶ πάρδαλις, καὶ αὐτῇ
πτερὰ τέσσαρα πετεινοῦ ὑπεράνω αὐτῆς, καὶ τέσσαρες κεφαλαὶ τῷ
θηρίῳ, καὶ ἐξουσία ἐδόθη αὐτῇ. 7 ὀπίσω τούτου ἐθεώρουν καὶ ἰδοὺ
θηρίον τέταρτον φοβερὸν καὶ ἔκθαμβον καὶ ἰσχυρὸν περισσῶς, καὶ οἱ
ὀδόντες αὐτοῦ σιδηροῖ μεγάλοι, ἐσθίον καὶ λεπτῦνον καὶ τὰ ἐπίλοιπα
τοῖς ποσὶν αὐτοῦ συνεπάτει, καὶ αὐτὸ διάφορον περισσῶς παρὰ πάντα
τὰ θηρία τὰ ἔμπροσθεν αὐτοῦ, καὶ κέρατα δέκα αὐτῷ. ...

3.Et *quatuor bestiae grandes ascendebant de mari diversae inter se.* 4
Prima quasi *leaena*, et *alas habebat* aquilae: ... 5 Et *ecce bestia alia*
similis *urso* in parte stetit: ... 6 et ecce *alia* quasi *pardus*, et alas
habebat quasi *avis*, ... 7 Post haec aspiciebam in visione noctis, et
ecce *bestia quarta terribilis atque mirabilis*, ... et habebat cornua
decem. ... et ecce oculi, quasi *oculi hominis* erant in cornu isto,
et os loquens ingentia.

[4 beasts compared to animals]
Daniel 7.20 [the fourth beast] *whose look* was more stout than *his fellows.*

* * *

Hosea 9.9 They have deeply corrupted themselves, ***as in the days of Gibeah.***
Hosea 9.10 their abominations were according ***as*** they loved.

* * *

Zechariah 10.5 And *they* shall be <u>as</u> *<u>mighty men.</u>*

    5 καὶ <u>*ἔσονται ὡς μαχηταὶ*</u> πατοῦντες πηλὸν ἐν ταῖς ὁδοῖς

    5 Et erunt <u>quasi</u> *<u>fortes</u>* conculcantes lutum viarum in praelio

* * *

B Factual Comparisons in the New Testament

Matt. 12.12 How much then is *a man* <u>better than</u> *<u>a sheep</u>*?

    12 πόσῳ οὖν <u>διαφέρει</u> ἄνθρωπος <u>*προβάτου*</u>. ὥστε ἔξεστιν τοῖς σάββασιν

    καλῶς ποιεῖν. [man = a sheep]

    12 Quanto <u>magis melior</u> est *homo* <u>*ove*</u>?

    [a man ≈ a sheep]

* * *

Mark 1.22 [And they were astonished at his doctrine: for *he* taught them

    <u>as</u> *<u>one that had authority</u>*, and not <u>as</u> the *<u>scribes</u>*.]

    22 ἦν γὰρ διδάσκων αὐτοὺς <u>ὡς</u> ἐξουσίαν ἔχων καὶ οὐχ <u>ὡς</u> οἱ γραμματεῖς.

Mark 12.31 And the second [commandment] is <u>like</u>, namely this, Thou

    shalt love *thy neighbo*r <u>as</u> *<u>thyself</u>*. There is *none other commandment*

    <u>greater than</u> *<u>these</u>*.

    31 καὶ δευτέρα <u>ὁμοία</u>, αὕτη· ἀγαπήσεις τὸν πλησίον σου <u>ὡς ἑαυτόν</u>. <u>μείζων</u>

    <u>τούτων</u> ἄλλη ἐντολὴ οὐκ ἔστι.

    31 Secundum autem <u>simile</u> est illi: Diliges *proximum tuum* <u>tamquam</u>

    <u>teipsum</u>. <u>Majus</u> *<u>horum</u>* aliud *mandatum* non est.

    [thy neighbor ≈ thyself; no other commandment (greater than)

    ≈ these]

* * *

John 8.53 Art *thou* <u>greater than</u> *<u>our father Abraham</u>*, which is dead? 53 μὴ

    σὺ μείζων εἶ <u>*τοῦ πατρὸς*</u> ἡμῶν Ἀβραάμ, ὅστις ἀπέθανεν;

    [thou = our father] St. John

* * *

Romans 2.19 And art confident that *thou thyself art a guide of the blind, a light of them which are in darkness*

19 πέποιθάς τε <u>σεαυτὸν ὁδηγὸν εἶναι τυφλῶν</u>, <u>φῶς τῶν ἐν σκότει</u>,

1 (NB a comparison followed by a simile)

[you ≈ *a light]

Summary

Old Testament

Genesis 19.26   Exodus 4.3, 4.4, 28.11
Deuteronomy 2.10   Judges 16.30
II Samuel 13.15   Job 1.8, 34.26, 35.5, 40.7, 41.33
Psalms 8.5, 68.15, 80.10, 119.98–99–100, 139.12
Proverbs 23.34   Ecclesiastes 7.1, 9.4
Isaiah 30.26   Jeremiah 32.42
Lamentations 1.12, 1.20   Ezekiel 23.44, 42.11
Hosea 9.9–10   Zechariah 10.5

New Testament

Matthew 12.12   Mark 1.22, 12.31
John 8.53   Romans 2.19

* * *

Words for Simile; Some Metaphors; Verbal Similes

A Words for 'Simile' etc.
B Examples of Metaphors
C 'Verbal' Similes (similetic verbs)

* * *

A– Words for 'Simile' and 'Parable'

Old Testament

Psalm 73.20 <u>As a *dream when one* awaketh: so,* O Lord, when *thou* awakest,
thou shalt despise their **image**.

> 72.20 <u>ὡσεὶ ἐνύπνιον ἐξεγειρομένου</u>, Κύριε, ἐν τῇ πόλει σου **τὴν εἰκόνα
αὐτῶν** ἐξουδενώσεις.

> 72.20 <u>Velut *somnium surgentium*</u>, Domine, in civitate tua **imaginem**
ipsorum ad nihilum rediges.

> [Thou O Lord ≈ a dream of someone wakening up] NB use of **εἰκόνα**.

Ps 106.20 Thus they changed their glory into the **similitude** *of an ox that
eateth grass.*

> *105.20* καὶ ἠλλάξαντο τὴν δόξαν αὐτῶν ἐν **ὁμοιώματι** μόσχου ἐσθίοντος
χόρτον.

> 105.20 Et mutaverunt gloriam suam in **similitudinem** vituli comedentis
foenum.

> [their glory ≈ (a simile) a calf feeding on grass]

Ps 143.12 Quorum *filii* <u>sicut</u> <u>*novellae plantationes*</u> in juventute sua; *filiae* eorum compositae, circumornatae <u>*ut similitudo templi.*</u>

[our sons ≈ plants; our daughters ≈ corner stones (simile: a palace)]

Isaiah 40.18 To whom then will ye **liken** God? or **what likeness will ye compare** unto him?

18 τίνι **ὡμοιώσατε** Κύριον καὶ **τίνι ὁμοιώματι ὡμοιώσατε** αὐτόν;

18 Cui ergo **similem** fecisti Deum? aut **quam imaginem** ponetis ei?

[God ≈?]] [**cf. 40.25 below**]

Isaiah 40.25 To whom then **will ye liken me,** or **shall I be equal**: saith the Holy One.

25 νῦν οὖν τίνι με **ὡμοιώσατε** καὶ **ὑψωθήσομαι**; εἶπεν ὁ ἅγιος.

25 Et cui **assimilastis** me, et **adaequastis**, dicit Sanctus?

[the Holy One ≈?] [**cf. 40.18 above and 46.5 below.**]

Isaiah 46.5 **To whom will ye liken me, and make me equal, and compare me, that we may be like?** [**cf. 40.18 and 25 above**]

5 τίνι με **ὡμοιώσατε**; ἴδετε, τεχνάσασθε, οἱ πλανώμενοι.

5 Cui **assimilastis** me, et **adaequastis**, et **comparastis** me, et **fecistis similem?**

[I the Lord ≈ who?]

Isaiah 46.9 Remember the former things of old: **for I am God,** and there is none else; I am God, and there is **none like me.**

9 καὶ μνήσθητε τὰ πρότερα ἀπὸ τοῦ αἰῶνος, ὅτι ἐγώ **εἰμι ὁ Θεός,** καὶ **οὐκ ἔστιν ἔτι πλὴν ἐμοῦ.**

9 Recordamini prioris saeculi, quoniam **ego sum Deus,** et **non est ultra Deus nec est similis mei.**

[God ≈ none]

Hosea 12.10 I have also spoken by the prophets, and I have multiplied visions, and used **similitudes**, by the ministry of the prophets.

11 καὶ λαλήσω πρὸς προφήτας, καὶ ἐγὼ ὁράσεις ἐπλήθυνα καὶ ἐν χερσὶ προφητῶν **ὡμοιώθην.**

10 Et locutus sum super prophetas, et ego visionem multiplicavi, et in manu prophetarum **assimilatus sum.**

Hebrews

7.15 for that <u>after the similitude of Melchisedec</u> there ariseth another priest.

15 καὶ περισσότερον ἔτι κατάδηλόν ἐστιν, εἰ <u>κατὰ τὴν ὁμοιότητα</u> Μελχισεδὲκ ἀνίσταται ἱερεὺς ἕτερος.

15 Et amplius adhuc manifestum est: si <u>secundum similitudinem</u> Melchisedech exsurgat alius sacerdos.

Ezekiel 8.2 And I looked, and, behold, the **likeness of a man**: from his loins and downwards [there was] fire, and *from his loins upwards [there was] as the appearance of amber.* 3 And *he stretched forth the likeness of a hand*, and took me by the crown of my head;

2 καὶ εἶδον καὶ ἰδοὺ <u>ὁμοίωμα ἀνδρός</u>, ἀπὸ τῆς ὀσφύος αὐτοῦ καὶ ἕως κάτω πῦρ, καὶ <u>ἀπὸ τῆς ὀσφύος αὐτοῦ ὑπεράνω αὐτοῦ ὡς ὅρασις ἠλέκτρου.</u> 3 καὶ <u>ἐξέτεινεν ὁμοίωμα χειρὸς</u> καὶ ἀνέλαβέ με τῆς κορυφῆς μου.

Ezekiel 10.1 Then I looked, and, behold, over the firmament that was above the head of the cherubs [there was] *a **likeness** of a throne over them, as a sapphire stone.*

1ΚΑΙ εἶδον καὶ ἰδοὺ ἐπάνω τοῦ στερεώματος τοῦ ὑπὲρ κεφαλῆς τῶν Χερουβὶμ *ὡς λίθος σαπφείρου ὁμοίωμα θρόνου ἐπ᾽ αὐτῶν.*

1 Et vidi: et ecce in firmamento quod erat super caput cherubim, quasi lapis sapphirus, **quasi species similitudinis solii**, apparuit super ea.

Ezekiel 17. 2 Son of man, put forth a **riddle**, and *speak a **parable** unto the house of Israel.*

2 υἱὲ ἀνθρώπου, διήγησαι **διήγημα** καὶ εἰπὸν **παραβολὴν** πρὸς τὸν οἶκον τοῦ Ἰσραήλ.

2 *Fili hominis, propone* **aenigma**, *et narra* **parabolam** *ad domum Israel.*

Ezekiel 18.2 What mean ye, that ye use *this **proverb** concerning the land of Israel?* 3 ... this **proverb**.

2 υἱὲ ἀνθρώπου, τί ὑμῖν ἡ **παραβολὴ** αὕτη ἐν τοῖς υἱοῖς Ισραηλ λέγοντες· 3 ... λεγομένη ἡ **παραβολὴ αὕτη.**

2 Quid est quod inter vos **parabolam vertitis in proverbium istud** in terra Israel 3 ... **parabola haec in proverbium.**

Habakkuk 2.6 Shall not all these take up a **parable** against him? and a taunting **proverb** against him?

6 οὐχὶ ταῦτα πάντα κατ᾽ αὐτοῦ **παραβολὴν** λήψονται καὶ **πρόβλημα** εἰς διήγησιν αὐτοῦ;

6 Numquid non omnes isti super eum **parabolam** sument, et **loquelam aenigmatum** ejus.

* * *

New Testament

Matthew 13.3 He spoke many things to them in **parables** saying, Behold a sower went forth to sow.

  3 καὶ ἐλάλησεν αὐτοῖς πολλὰ ἐν **παραβολαῖς** λέγων, Ἰδοὺ ἐξῆλθεν ὁ σπείρων τοῦ σπείρειν.

  See also 13.13, 13.24, 13.31, 13.33, 13.36; Mark 13.28.

John 6 This **parable** Jesus spoke to them but they did not understand what things they were which he spake unto them.

  6 Ταύτην τὴν **παροιμίαν** εἶπεν αὐτοῖς ὁ Ἰησοῦς: ἐκεῖνοι δὲ οὐκ ἔγνωσαν τίνα ἦν ἃ ἐλάλει αὐτοῖς.

John 16.25 "These things I have spoken to you **in proverbs**; the time shall come when I will no longer speak **in proverbs** but I shall show you **plainly** about the father." Jesus

  25 Ταῦτα **ἐν παροιμίαις** λελάληκα ὑμῖν: ἔρχεται ὥρα ὅτε οὐκέτι **ἐν παροιμίαις** λαλήσω ὑμῖν ἀλλὰ **παρρησίᾳ** περὶ τοῦ πατρὸς ἀπαγγελῶ ὑμῖν.

  (figurative speech)

***

B– Examples of Metaphors

2 Samuel 22.11: he was seen upon *the wings of the wind*.

Job 3.11 Why did I not *give up the ghost*?

  NB the metaphor is not in Gr/Lat.: 11 διατί γὰρ ἐν κοιλίᾳ οὐκ ἐτελεύτησα / Quare non in vulva mortuus sum?

Job 4.8 They that *plow iniquity, and sow wickedness, reap the same*.

Psalms 23:1: The *Lord* is *my shepherd*; I shall not want

Proverbs 13:14: The *law* of the wise is a *fountain* of life.

Isaiah 24.7 The new wine *mourneth*, the vine *languisheth*.

Isaiah 64:8: But now, O Lord, ... *we are the clay*, and *thou* our *potter*; and *we all* are *the work of thy hand*.

John 6:35 John 8:12 John 14:6 John 15:5

Hosea 10.13 Ye have <u>plowed wickedness</u>, ye have <u>reaped iniquity;</u> ye have eaten <u>the fruit of lies.</u>

Habakkuk 2.11 For <u>the stone shall cry out</u> of the wall, and <u>the beam</u> out of the timber <u>shall answer it.</u>

Matthew 5:13: *Ye* are the <u>salt of the earth:</u> 5.14 Ye are the <u>light of the world.</u>

John 18.11 Then said Jesus unto Peter, Put up thy sword into the sheath: *the cup which my Father hath given me*, shall I not *drink* it?

Revelations 19:7: For *the marriage of the Lamb* is come, and his wife hath made herself ready.

Revelations 21:6: I am *Alpha and Omega,* the beginning and the end.

C – Verbal Similes

Psalm 5.12 You have 'crowned' us.

Κύριε, <u>ὡς ὅπλῳ εὐδοκίας</u> **ἐστεφάνωσας** ἡμᾶς.

Psalm 23.1 The *Lord* is *my shepherd*; I shall not want ...

*d/   22.1 ΚΥΡΙΟΣ *ποιμαίνει* με καὶ οὐδέν με ὑστερήσει

NB: Where Greek expresses the simile as a verb, the English translates it as a predicate simile.

Psalm Ps. 68.14 When the Almighty scattered kings in it, *it* was *white as snow* in Salmon.

67.15 ἐν τῷ διαστέλλειν τὸν ἐπουράνιον βασιλεῖς ἐπ᾽ αὐτῆς, *χιονωθήσονται* ἐν Σελμών [they shall be made snow-white]

67.15 Dum discernit caelestis reges super eam, *nive dealbabuntur* in Selmon.

[it (Salmon) white ≈ snow; **a verbal simile in Greek (*d/)**]

Daniel 2.3 And the king said unto them, I have **dreamed a dream** ...

3 καὶ εἶπεν αὐτοῖς ὁ βασιλεύς· <u>ἠνυπνιάσθην</u>,

3 Et dixit ad eos rex: <u>Vidi somnium</u>

Daniel 13.5: <u>ἐγὼ *ἐποίμανόν σε ἐν τῇ ἐρήμῳ,*</u>

    13.5 I tended thee <u>[as] a shepherd</u> (≈ I shepherded thee) in an unin-
        habited land.

    [I tended ≈ I shepherded, i.e., the occasional verbal simile]

Hosea 13.5: ἐγὼ *ἐποίμανόν σε ἐν τῇ ἐρήμῳ* (I *tended thee* [*as*] *a shepherd* in
    the wilderness).

    I Kings = 'The Third Book of the Kings' (online):

    1.39 And Zadoc the priest took an horn of oil out of the tabernacle,
        and anointed Solomon. And they <u>blew the trumpet</u>;

    39 ἔλαβε Σαδὼκ ὁ ἱερεὺς τὸ κέρας τοῦ ἐλαίου ἐκ τῆς σκηνῆς ἔχρισε τὸν
        Σαλωμὼν καὶ **ἐσάλπισε** τῇ κερατίνῃ =

    (3rd Kings) 1.39 Sumpsitque Sadoc sacerdos cornu olei de tabernaculo,
        et unxit Salomonem: et <u>cecinerunt buccina</u>.

***

There are also **similetic adjectives:** Ezekiel 11.19: I will take the <u>stony</u>
heart ('like' stone) out of thy flesh. Or Ezek. 13.11: a <u>stormy</u> wind shall
rend it. But not all such adjectives are similetic: <u>sunny</u> day + <u>starry</u> night
(= 'full of' not 'like').

* * *

Doublets and Recurring Vehicles

A Doublets
B Triplet Expressions in Jeremiah
C A Selection of Recurring Vehicles

* * *

A Doublet Similes in the Old Testament

(None in the New Testament)

Often a vehicle is repeated in a very similar form (e.g., as a lion + as an old lion in the first text below) – thus not really two different similes, but *doublets*. Yet since the *prothesis* (as) is repeated, technically they may be counted as two similes.

Gen. 49.9 he couched as *a lion*, and as *an old lion*

Gen. 49.17 *Dan* shall be *a serpent by the way*, an *adder in the path*

Gen. 49.22 Joseph is a fruitful bough, even a fruitful bough by a well;

Numbers 23.24 Behold, the *people* shall rise up as *a great lion* and lift up himself as *a young lion.*

Deut. 32.2 My *doctrine* shall drop as *the rain*, my *speech* shall distal as *the dew*, as *the small rain.*

II Samuel 22.43 Then did I beat *them* as small as *the dust of the earth*, I did stamp *them* as *the mire of the street.*

Job 6.15 *My brethren* have dealt deceitfully as *a brook*, and as *the stream of brooks* they pass away.

Job 7.2 As _a servant earnestly desireth the shadow,_ and as _an hireling_ looketh for the reward of his work:

Job 14.11 As the _waters_ fail from the sea, and the flood decayeth and drieth up:

Job 20.8 _He_ [the wicked] shall fly away as _a dream,_ and shall not be found: yea, he shall be chased away as _a vision of the night_.

Job 21.18 _They_ [the wicked] are as _stubble before the wind_, and as _chaff_ that the storm carrieth away.

Job 29.23 And they waited for _me_ as for the _rain_; and they opened their mouth wide as for the _latter rain_.

Job 30.19 He hath cast me into the mire, and _I_ am become like _dust and ashes_.

Job 41.24 His _heart_ is as firm as a _stone_; yea, as hard as a _piece of the nether millstone_.

Job 41. 31 He taketh the _deep_ to boil _like a pot_: he maketh the sea _like a pot of ointment_.

Psalms 17.12 Like as _a lion that is greedy of his prey_, and as it were _a young lion_

Psalms 19.10 More to be desired are they [judgments of the Lord] than gold, yea, than _much fine gold_: sweeter also than _honey and the honey-comb_.

Psalms 37.2 For _they_ shall soon be cut down like the _grass_, and wither as the _green herb_.

Ps. 59.6 They [workers of iniquity, mine enemies] return at evening: _they_ make a noise like _a dog_, and go round about the city.>>>

Ps. 59.14 And at evening let them return; and _let them make a noise_ like _a dog_, and go round about the city.

Ps. 72.6 _He_ (king Solomon) shall come down like _rain upon the mown grass_: as _showers that water the earth_.

Ps. 78.52 But [God] made _his own people to go forth_ like _sheep_; and guided _them_ in the wilderness like _a flock_.

Ps. 83.14 As the _fire_ burneth a wood, as _the flame_ setteth the mountains on fire;

Ps. 114.4 The _mountains_ skipped like _rams_, and the little _hills_ like _lambs_. + Ps. 114.6

Ps. 119.105 Thy *word* is <u>*a lamp unto my feet*</u>, and <u>*a light unto my path*</u>.
118.105 <u>Λύχνος</u> τοῖς ποσί μου ὁ νόμος σου καὶ <u>φῶς</u> ταῖς τρίβοις μου.
118.105 <u>Lucerna</u> pedibus meis *verbum tuum*, et <u>*lumen*</u> semitis meis.
[your law ≈ a lamp to my feet ≈ a light to my path]

Ps. 131.2 Surely *I have behaved* and quieted myself, <u>as</u> <u>*a child that is*</u> <u>*weaned*</u> of his mother: *my soul* is <u>even as</u> <u>*a weaned child.*</u>

Ps. *133*.3 <u>As t</u><u>*he dew of Hermon,*</u> and <u>*as the dew that descended upon the*</u> <u>*mountains of Zion.*</u>

Prov. 5.19 Let her [*the wife of thy youth*] be <u>as</u> the <u>*loving hind and*</u> <u>*pleasant roe;*</u>

Prov. 6.5 Deliver thyself *as a roe* from the hand of the hunter, and *as a bird* from the hand of the fowler.

Prov. 8.19 My fruit is <u>better than</u> *gold, yea,* <u>than</u> *fine gold:*

Prov. 23.32 At the last *it* [*red wine*] biteth <u>like</u> *a serpent*, and stingeth <u>like</u> *an adder.*

Prov, 25.12 <u>As</u> *an earring of gold*, and *an ornament of fine gold*, so is *a wise reprover upon an obedient ear.*

Prov. 25.26 *A righteous man falling down before the wicked* is <u>as</u> *a troubled fountain, and a corrupt spring*.

Prov. 26.2 <u>As</u> <u>*the bird by wandering,*</u> <u>as</u> <u>*the swallow by flying*</u>, **so** the *curse causeless* shall not come.

Prov. 83.14 <u>As</u> the *fire* burnt a wood, <u>as</u> *the flame* setteth the mountains on fire; 15 So persecute them with *thy storm.*

Song of Solomon 2.9 *My beloved* is <u>like</u> <u>*a roe or a young hart.*</u>

So-So 2.17 Until the day break, and the shadows flee away, turn, *my beloved,* and <u>be thou like</u> <u>*a roe or a young hart upon the moun-*</u><u>*tains of Bether.*</u>

So-So 4.1 *thy hair* is <u>as</u> a *flock of goats*, that appear from mount Galaad. 2 *Thy teeth* are <u>like</u> a *flock of sheep that are even shorn* which came up from the washing;

So-So. 6.5 thy *hair* is <u>as</u> a *flock of goats* that appear from Gilead. 6 *Thy teeth* are <u>as</u> a *flock of sheep which go up from the washing.*

So-So. 8.14 Make haste, my beloved, and be thou <u>like</u> to <u>*a roe or to a*</u> <u>*young hart up*</u>on the mountains of spices.

Isaiah 5.29 Their *roaring* shall be <u>like</u> a *lion*, they shall roar <u>like</u> a young *lions.*

Isaiah 6.13 As *<u>a tail tree</u>,* and <u>as *an oak*</u>

Isaiah 13.12 I will make a man <u>more precious than</u> fine *gold*; even a *man* <u>than</u> *<u>the golden wedge of Ophir.</u>*

Isaiah 13.14 And it shall be *as the chased roe, and as a sheep* that no man taketh up.

Isaiah 17.5 And *it shall be* <u>as when</u> *<u>the harvestman gathereth the corn</u>* and *<u>reapeth the ears with his arm;</u>* and i*t shall be* <u>as</u> *<u>he that gathereth ears in the valley of Rephaim.</u>*

Isaiah 17.9 In that day shall *his strong cities* be <u>as</u> *<u>a forsaken bough</u>*, and an *<u>uppermost branch.</u>*

Isaiah 17.12 Woe to the multitude of many people, which make *a noise* <u>like</u> *<u>the noise of the seas</u>*, and to the rushing of nations, that make a *rushing* <u>like</u> *<u>the rushing of mighty waters</u>*. 13 *The nations shall rush* <u>like *t*he rushing of many waters</u>*:*

Isaiah 31.4 For thus hath the Lord spoken unto me, <u>Like</u> a<u>s</u> the *lion* and the *<u>young lion</u>* roaring on his prey,

Isaiah 32.2 And *a man shall be* <u>as</u> *<u>an hiding place from the wind</u>*, and *<u>a covert from the tempest</u>*;

Isaiah 37.27 they were <u>as</u> *<u>the grass</u>* of the field, and <u>as</u> *<u>the green herb</u>*, <u>as</u> *<u>the grass on the housetops,</u>*

Isaiah 53.7 he is brought <u>as</u> *<u>a lamb to the slaughter,</u>* and <u>as</u> *<u>a sheep before her shearers</u>*

Isaiah 59.10 We grope *for the wall* <u>like the</u> *<u>blind</u>*, and *we grope* <u>as if we had no eyes</u>:

Isaiah 64.10 Thy *holy cities* are *<u>a wilderness</u>*, Zon is *<u>a wilderness.</u>*

Isaiah 66.12 For thus saith the Lord, Behold,*I will extend peace to her* <u>like</u> *<u>a river,</u> and the glory of the Gentiles* <u>like a flowing stream</u>.

Jerem. 4.31 For I have heard *a voice* *<u>as of a woman in travail,</u> and the anguish* *<u>as of her that bringeth forth her first child.</u> Cf. 6.24.*

Jerem. 23.9 *I am* like *<u>a drunken man, and</u> like a man whom wine hath overcome.*

Jerem. 23.14 *They [prophets of Jerusalem] are all of them unto me* <u>as</u> *<u>Sodom,</u> and the inhabitants thereof <u>as Gomorrha.</u>*

Jerem. 46.8 'like a flood, like rivers': Aegyptus <u>fluminis instar</u> ascendit, et <u>velut flumina</u> movebuntur fluctus ejus.

Jerem. 48.36 Therefore *mine heart* shall sound for Moab <u>like</u> <u>*pipes*</u>, and *mine heart* shall sound <u>like</u> <u>*pipes for the men of Kirheres.*</u>

Jerem. 51.38 t*hey* shall roar together <u>like</u> <u>*lions*</u>: *they* shall yell <u>as</u> <u>*lions'*</u> <u>*whelps.*</u>

Jerem. 51.40 I will bring *them* down <u>like</u> <u>*lambs*</u> to the slaughter, <u>like</u> <u>*rams*</u> with he goats.

Lam/Jerem. 2.3 [The Lord] he *burned against Jacob* like <u>*a flaming fire*</u> 4 … he pored out *his fury* <u>like</u> <u>*fire*</u>.

Lam/Jerem. 2.4 He hath bent *his bow* <u>like</u> <u>*an enemy*</u>: he *stood with his right hand* <u>as</u> <u>*an adversary*</u> .

Hosea 5.14 For *I* will be unto Ephraim <u>as</u> <u>*a lion,*</u> and <u>as</u> <u>*a young lion*</u> to the house of Judah.

Hosea 6.3 and *he* [the Lord] shall come unto us <u>as</u> <u>*the rain,*</u> <u>as</u> <u>*the latter and former rain*</u> unto the earth.

Hosea 7.6 For they have made ready their *heart* like <u>*an oven,*</u>

Hosea 7.7 *They* are all *hot* <u>as</u> <u>*an oven,*</u>

Hosea 11.11 *They* shall tremble <u>as</u> <u>*a bird out of Egypt*</u>, and <u>as</u> <u>*a dove out of the land of Assyria:*</u>

Hosea 13.7 Therefore I [the Lord] will be unto them <u>as</u> <u>*a lion*</u>: <u>as</u> <u>*a leopard*</u> by the way will I observe them; 8 and there will I devour them <u>like</u> <u>*a lion*</u>.

Ezekiel 1.27 And I saw <u>as</u> the colour <u>*of amber,*</u> <u>as</u> <u>*the appearance of fire*</u> round about within it … I saw <u>as it were</u> the <u>*appearance of fire,*</u>

Joel 1.6 For a nation is come up upon my land, strong, and without number, whose *teeth* <u>are</u> <u>*the teeth of a lion*</u>, and he hath the *cheek teeth* of a <u>*great lion.*</u>

Joel 2.7 *They* shall run <u>like</u> <u>*mighty men; they shall climb the wall*</u> <u>like</u> <u>*men of war.*</u>

Amos 2.9 Yet destroyed I the Amorite before them, *whose height was* <u>like</u> the <u>*height of the cedars,*</u> and *he was strong* <u>as</u> <u>*the oaks.*</u>

Amos 5.24 But let <u>*judgment run down as waters*</u>, and <u>*righteousness as a mighty stream*</u>.

Obadiah 1.18 And *the house of Jacob* <u>shall be</u> a *fire*, and *the house of Joseph* a <u>*flame*</u>,

Micah 2.12 I will put *them* together <u>as</u> *<u>the sheep of Bozra,</u>* <u>as</u> *<u>the flock in the midst of their fold.</u>*

Micah 5.8 And *the remnant of Jacob shall be among the Gentiles* in the midst of many people <u>as</u> *<u>a lion among the beasts of the forest,</u>* <u>as</u> *<u>a young lion among the flocks of sheep.</u>*

Micah 7.4 The *best of them* is <u>as</u> *<u>a brier</u>*: the *most upright* is <u>sharper</u> than *a thorn hedge*.

Zech. 12.6 In that day *I will make the governors of Judah* <u>like</u> *<u>an hearth of fire</u>* among the wood, and <u>like</u> *<u>a torch of fire in a sheaf.</u>*

Summary of Doublet Similes

Old Testament

Genesis 49.9, 49.17, 49.22	Numbers 23.24
Deuteronomy 32.2	II Samuel 22.43

Job 6.15, 7.2, 14.11, 20.8, 21.18, 29.23, 30.19, 41.24, 41.31

Psalms   17.12,   19.10,   37.2,   59.6,   59.14,   72.6,78.52,   83.14,   114.4   119.105, 131.2, 133.3

Proverbs 5.19, 8.19, 23.32, 25.12, 25.26, 26.2, 83.14

Song of Solomon 2.17, 6.5, 8.14

Isaiah   5.29,   6.13,   13.12,   13.14,   17.5,   17.9,   17.12,   31.4,   32.2,   37.27,   53.759.10, 64.10, 66.12

Jeremiah 4.31, 23.10, 23.14, 46.8, 48.36, 51.38, 51.40

Lamentations 2.3, 2.4	Hosea 5.14, 6.3, 7.6, 11.11,13.7
Ezekiel 1.27	Joel 2.7
Amos 2.9, 5.24	Obadiah 1.18
Micah 5.8, 7.4	Zechariah 12.6

B Triplet Expressions in Jeremiah

33.10–11 (without man without inhabitant without beast) absque homine, et absque habitatore, et absque pecore,

36.10: (in the court at the entry in the ears) in domo Domini, in gazophylacio Gamariae, filii Saphan scribae, in vestibulo superiori, in introitu portae novae domus Domni,

42.22 (by the sword by famine by pestilence) quia gladio, et fame, et peste moriemini

43.11 ('such as' – 3x) quos in mortem, in mortem, et quos in captivitatem, in captivitatem, et quos in gladium, in gladium

44.13 (by the sword by famine by pestilence) in gladio, et fame, et peste:

44.20 ('to the men, to the women, to all the people') Et dixit Jeremias ad omnem populum, adversum viros, et adversum mulieres, et adversum universam plebem,

44.23 ('nor – nor – nor')

C A Selection of Recurring Vehicles

apple(s)

Ps 17.8 Keep *me* as *the apple of the eye*

Prov. 7.2 Keep my commandments, and live; and *my law* as *the apple of thine eye.*

Prov. 25.11 A *word fitly spoken* is like *apples of gold in pictures of silver.*

So-So. 2.3 As t*he apple tree among the trees of the wood,*

So-So. 7. 8 ... and the smell of thy nose like *apples*:

Lam/Jerem. 2.18 let not *the apple of thine eye* cease.

dove(s)

Ps. 55.6 And I said, Oh that I had *wings* like *a dove!*

Ps. 68.13 yet shall *ye* be as t*he wings of a dove covered with silver*,

So-So. 1.15 behold, thou art fair;*thou hast* *doves' eyes.*

Song of S 2.14 *O my dove*, that art in the clefts of the rock

So-So. 4.1 Behold, *thou hast doves' eyes*

So-So. 5.12 *His eyes* are as *the eyes of doves*

Isaiah 38.14 *I* did mourn as *a dove:*

Isaiah 59.11 *We roar all* like *bears* and *mourn sore* like *doves*:

Isaiah 60.8 Who are *these* that fly as a *cloud*, and as the *doves?*

Jerem. 48.28 be like *the dove that maketh her nest in the sides*

Ezek. 7.16 But *they* … shall be *like doves of the valley*.

Hosea 7.11 *Ephraim* also is like *a silly dove, without heart.*

Hosea 11.11 *They* shall tremble … as *a dove out of Assyria:*

New Testament:

Matt. 3.16 He [Jesus] saw *the Spirit of God* descending like *a dove*.

Matt. 10.16 Behold I send you forth as *sheep in the midst of wolves*; be
   ye therefore *wise* as *serpents* and *harmless* as *doves*.

Mark 1.10 He [Jesus] saw the heavens opened, and *the Spirit* like *a
   dove* descending upon him.

Luke 3.22 And *the Holy Ghost* descended in a bodily shape like *a dove*
   upon him.

John 1.32 And John bare record, saying, I saw the *Spirit* descending
   from heaven like *a dove,*

fig(s)

Isaiah 34.4 *all their host shall fall down, …* as *a falling fig from the
   fig tree*.

Jerem. 24.2 One basket had very good figs, even like the figs that are
   first ripe

Jerem. 24.5: Like *these good figs*, **so** will I acknowledge *them*

Jerem. 24.8 And as *the evil figs, which cannot be eaten*, they are so evil;

Jerem. 29.17 Thus saith the Lord of hosts: Behold, I … will make *them*
   [citizens of Babylon] like *vile figs*,

Hosea 9.10 I found *Israel* like *grapes in the wilderness;* I saw *your fathers
   as the first ripe in the fig tree*

New Testament:

Rev. 6 13 And the *stars of heaven fell* unto the earth, even as *a fig tree
   casteth her untimely figs,*

fool(s)

Prov. 7.22 And *he goeth after her* straightway, as an *ox goeth to the slaughter*, or as *a fool* to the correction of the stocks.

Prov. 17.10 A *reproof entereth* more into a wise man than a*n hundred tripes into a fool*.

Prov. 17.12 Let *a bear robbed of her whelps meet a man*, rather than *a fool in his folly*.

Prov. 26.1 As *snow in summer*, and as *rain in harvest*, **so** *honour is not seemly for a fool*.

Prov. 26.7 The *legs of the lame are not equal*: **so** is *a parable in the mouth of fools*.

Prov. 26.8 As *he that bindeth a stone in a sling*, **so** is *he that giveth honour to a fool*.

Prov. 26.9 As a *thorn goeth up into the hand of a drunkard*, **so** is *a parable in the mouth of fools*.

Prov. 26.11 As *a dog returneth to his vomit* **so** *a fool returneth to his folly*.

Prov. 27.3 A *stone is heavy, and the sand weighty*; but *a fool's wrath* is heavier than *them both*.

Eccl. 7.6 For as *the crackling of thorns under a pot*, **so** is *the laughter of the fool*: this also is vanity.

.Jerem. 17.11 As t*he partridge sitteth on eggs, and hatcheth them not;* **so** *he that getteth riches, and not by right, … at his end shall be a fool*.

Ps. 73.22 So foolish was I, and ignorant: *I* was as *a beast* before thee.

New Testament:

Matt. 7.26 *Everyone that heareth these sayings of mine, and doeth them not*, shall be likened unto *a foolish man, which built his house upon the sand*.

grasshopper(s)

Numbers 13.33 And we were in our own sight as *grasshoppers.*

Judges 6.5 and they came as *grasshoppers* for multitude.

Judges 7.12 and *all* the children of the east lay along in the valley like *grasshoppers* for multitude;

Job 39.20 Canst thou make *him afraid* as *a grasshopper*?

Isaiah 40.22 and *the inhabitants* thereof are as *grasshoppers*;

Jeremiah 46.23 ... *they* are <u>more than</u> *<u>the grasshoppers</u>*, and are
    innumerable.
[Not found in New Testament]
heifer
    Jerem. 46.20 *Egypt* is <u>like</u> *<u>a very fair heife</u>*r.
    Hosea 4.16 For *<u>Israel slideth back as a back-sliding heifer.</u>*
    Hosea 10.11 And *Ephraim* is <u>as</u> *<u>an heifer that is taught,</u>*
    [Not in New Testament]
honey
    Ezek. 3.3 Then did I eat it; and *<u>it was in my mouth as hone</u>*y for sweetness.
    Exodus 16.31 And the house of Israel called the name thereof Manna;
        and ... the *taste* of it *was* <u>like</u> *<u>wafers made with honey</u>*.
    Judges 14.18 *What* is <u>sweeter than</u> *<u>honey</u>*?
    Ps. 19.10 <u>More</u> to be desired are they [judgments of the Lord] <u>than</u>
        gold, ... <u>sweeter also than</u> *<u>honey and the honey-comb</u>*.
    Ps. 119.103 *How sweet* are *thy words* unto my taste! yea, sweeter <u>than</u>
        <u>honey</u> to my mouth!
    Prov. 5.3 For the *lips of a strange woman* drop <u>as</u> *<u>an honeycomb</u>*,
    So-So. 4.11 *Thy lips,* O my spouse, drop <u>as</u> *<u>the honeycomb</u>*; honey and
        milk are under thy tongue.
    New Testament:
    Rev. 10.9 And he said unto me, Take it, and eat it up; and it shall make
        thy belly bitter, but *it shall be in thy mouth sweet* <u>as</u> *<u>honey</u>*. [+ 10.10]
lamb(s)
    Ps. 37.20 But the wicked shall perish; and *the enemies of the Lord* shall
        be <u>as</u> *<u>the fat of lambs</u>*.
    Ps. 114.4 The *mountains* skipped <u>like</u> *<u>rams</u>*, and the little *hills* <u>like</u>
        <u>lambs</u>. repeated at 114.6.
    Isaiah 53.7 he is brought <u>as</u> *<u>a lamb to the slaughter,</u>*
    Isaiah 65.25 The wolf and the lamb shall feed together
    Jerem. 11.19 But *<u>I was like a lamb or an ox that is brought to the slaughter</u>*
    Jerem. 51.40 I will bring *them* down <u>like</u> *<u>lambs</u>* to the slaughter
    Hosea 4.16 now the *<u>Lord will feed them as a lamb in a large place.</u>*
    New Testament:
    Luke 10.3 Go your ways: behold, I send *you* forth <u>as</u> *<u>lambs among wolves</u>*.

Acts 8.32 *He* was led <u>as</u> a *sheep* to the slaughter, and <u>like</u> *a lamb* dumb before his shearer

1 Peter 1.19 But with the *precious blood of Christ, <u>as of a lamb without blemish</u>*

Rev. 13.11 And I beheld another beast coming up out of the earth; and he had *two horns* <u>like</u> *a lamb*,

lion(s) 86 in Old Testament, 10 in New Testament:

Genesis 49.9 (3); Numbers 23.24 (2); 14.18; 2 Samuel 17.10;

Job 10.16; Psalm 7.2, 10.9; 17.12 (2), 22.13, 19.12, 20.2, 28.1,

Ps 28.15; Prov. 28.1, 28.15; Eccl. 9.4; Isaiah 5.28 (2), 31.4 (2), 38.13,

Isaiah 65.25; Jerem. 12.8, 25.38, 49.19, 50.44, 51.38 (2).

New Testament: 1 Peter 5.8, Rev. 9.8, 9.17, 10.3, 13.2.

oven

Ps. 21.9 Thou shalt make *them* [those that hate thee] <u>as</u> *a fiery oven* in the time of thine anger.

Lam/Jerem. 5.10 *Our skin* was <u>*black*</u> like *an oven* because of the terrible famine.

Hosea 7.4 They are all *adulterers,* <u>as</u> *an oven heated by the baker.*

Hosea 7.6 For they have made ready their *heart* like *an oven*,

Hosea 7.7 *They* are all *hot* <u>as</u> *an oven,* and have devoured their judges.

Malach. 4.1 For, behold, the *day cometh, that shall burn* <u>as</u> *an oven*,

[Odd the number of similes with 'oven' in Hosea.]

rock

Ezek. 26.14 And *I will make thee* <u>like</u> *the top of a rock*

Romans 9.33 *I* lay in Sion *a stumbling stone and rock of offense.*

II Samuel 22.2 And he said, The *Lord is <u>my rock</u>*, and *<u>my fortress</u>*,

Ps 18.2 The Lord is *<u>my rock</u>*, and my *<u>fortress</u>*, and my deliverer

Psalm 28.1 Unto thee will I cry, O Lord *<u>my rock.</u>*

Psalm 31.2 Be *thou* my *<u>strong rock</u>*,

Ps 31.3 thou art *<u>my rock and my fortress</u>*.

Ps 62.2 *He* only is *<u>my rock</u>* and my salvation; he is my defence.

Ps 78.35 Another 'God as a rock' translation.

Ps 71.3 again repeats the commonplace simile of calling God "my rock and my fortress." (not a simile in the Greek or Latin)

τοῦ σῶσαί με, ὅτι <u>στερέωμά μου καὶ καταφυγή μου</u> εἶ σύ.

Ps 92.15 Again 'the Lord is my rock' + 94.22; 95.1.

II Samuel 22.2 And he said, The *Lord is <u>my rock</u>*, and *<u>my fortress</u>*,

II Samuel 22.47 exalted be the <u>*rock*</u> of my *salvation*

NB – not in New Testament except in this context: a man who built his house on a rock.

sand

Gen. 22.17 I will multiply *thy seed* … <u>as</u> <u>*the sand which is upon the sea shore*</u>.

Joshua 11.4 And *they* went out … *much people, even* <u>as</u> <u>*the sand that is upon the sea shore*</u> in multitude.

Judges 7.12 and *their camels* were without number, <u>as</u> <u>*the sand by the sea side for multitude*</u>.

Job 6.3 For now it [*my grief*] would be <u>heavier than</u> *<u>the sand of the sea.</u>*

Job 29.18 Then I said, … I shall multiply *my days* <u>as</u> *<u>the sand</u>*.

Prov. 27.3 A <u>*stone is heavy, and the sand weighty*</u>;

Isaiah 10.22 For though *thy people Israel* be <u>as</u> *<u>the sand of the sea</u>*

Isaiah 48.19 *Thy seed* also had been <u>as</u> *<u>the sand,</u>*

Jerem. 33.22 <u>As</u> … *<u>neither the sand of the sea measured</u>*: **so** *will I multiply the seed of David*

Hosea 1.10 Yet *<u>the number of the children of Israel</u>* shall be <u>as</u> *<u>the sand of the sea,</u>*

Habak 1.9 and they shall gather the captivity <u>as</u> the *<u>sand</u>*.

New Testament:

Matt. 7.26 *Everyone that heareth these sayings of mine, and doeth them not*, <u>shall be likened unto</u> *<u>a foolish man, which built his house upon the sand</u>*.

Serpent cf. snake, adder

Ps. 58.4 Their [the wicked] *poison* is <u>like the</u> poison *<u>of a serpent; they</u> are* <u>like</u> *the <u>deaf adder</u>* that stoppeth her ear.

Ps. 140.3 T*hey have sharpened their tongues* <u>like</u> *<u>a serpen</u>*t; adders' poison is under their lips.

Prov. 23.32 At the last *it* [*red wine*] biteth <u>like</u> *<u>a serpent</u>*, and stingeth <u>like</u> *<u>an adder</u>*.

Jeremiah 46.22 The *voice thereof shall go* <u>like</u> *<u>a serpent</u>*;

New Testament:

Matt. 10.16 be ye therefore *wise* as *serpents* and *harmless* as *doves*.

John 3.14 And as Moses lifted up the serpent in the wilderness, even
so must *the Son of man* be lifted up.

2nd Cor. 11.3 But I fear, *as the serpent beguiled Eve* through his subtilty,
so *your minds should be corrupted.*

Rev. 9.19 for *their tails* were like unto *serpents*

sheep

Ps. 44.11 Thou hast given *us* like *sheep* appointed for meat.

Ps. 44.22 For thy sake *we* are counted as *sheep for the slaughter*.

Ps. 49.14 Like *sheep they* are laid in the grave.

Ps. 78.52 But [God] made *his own people to go forth* like *sheep*;

So-So. 4.2 *Thy teeth* are like a *flock of sheep that are shorn*

So-So 6.4 6 *Thy teeth* are as a *flock of sheep which go up from the washing*,

Isaiah 13.14 And *it shall be* … as *a sheep that no man taketh up*.

Isaiah 53.6 All *we* like *sheep* have gone astray; [+53.7]

Jerem. 12.3 Pull them out *like sheep for the slaughter.*

Micah 2.12 I will put *them* together as *the sheep of Bozra,* [+ 5.8]

New Testament:

Matt. 9.36 He [Jesus] was moved with compassion on them, because
they were scattered abroad, as *sheep having no shepherd.*

Matt. 10.16 Behold I send you forth as *sheep in the midst of wolves*;

Matt. 12.12 How much then is *a man* better than *a sheep*?

Matt. 25.32 And before him shall be gathered all nations: and he shall
separate them from one another, as a shepherd divideth his sheep
from the goats.

Mark 6.34 And Jesus, … was moved with compassion toward them,
because *they* were as *sheep not having a shepherd*,

Acts 8.32 *He* was led as a *sheep* to the slaughter, and like *a lamb* dumb
before his shearer.

snow

Exodus 4.6 And he put his hand into his bosom: and when he took
it out, behold, *his hand was leprous as snow.*

Ps. 51.7 wash me, and *I* shall be whiter than *snow*.

Ps. 68.14 When the Almighty scattered kings in it, *it* was *white as
snow* in Salmon.

Prov. 25.13 <u>As *the cold of snow in the time of harvest*</u>, **so** is *a faithful messenger* to them that send him.

Prov. 26.1 <u>As *snow in summer*</u>, and <u>as *rain in harvest*</u>, **so** *honour is not seemly for a fool.*

Isaiah 1.18 though *your sins* be <u>as *scarlet*</u>, they shall be as *white* <u>as *snow*</u>;

Isaiah 55.10 For <u>as *the rain cometh down, and the snow from heaven,*</u> ...
    11 **So** *shall my word be that goeth forth* out of my mouth.

Lam/Jerem. 4.7 Her *Nazarites* were <u>*purer*</u> than <u>*snow*</u>,

Daniel 7.9 and the Ancient of days did sit, *whose garment was white* <u>as *snow*</u>,

New Testament:

Matt. 28.3 His *countenance* was <u>like *lightning,*</u> and his *raiment* white <u>as *snow:*</u>

Mark 9.3 And his *raiment* became shining, *exceeding white* <u>as *snow;*</u>

Rev. 1.14 His head and his hairs were *white* <u>like *wool*</u>, as white as <u>*snow.*</u>

stars

Gen. 22.17 I will multiply *thy seed* <u>as *the stars of the heaven,*</u>

Gen. 26.4 And I will make thy seed to multiply <u>as *the stars of heaven.*</u>

Daniel 12.3 And *they that be wise shall shine* ... <u>as *the stars for ever*</u>

Obad. 1.4 <u>though</u> thou <u>*set thy nest among the stars,*</u>

a thief (in the night)

Job 24.14 The *murderer* rising with the light killeth the poor and needy, and in the night is <u>as *a thief.*</u>

Joel 2.9 They shall enter in at the windows <u>like *a thief.*</u>

New Testament:

1 Thes. 5.2 For yourselves know perfectly that *the day of the Lord* **so** *cometh* <u>*as a thief in the night*</u>.

2 Peter 3.10 But *the day of the Lord* will come <u>*as a thief in the night*</u>;

Rev. 3.3 If therefore thou shalt not watch, *I will come* on thee <u>as *a thief.*</u>

woman in travail

Isaiah 13.8 *they shall be in pain* <u>as a woman that travaileth</u>

Isaiah 21.3 *pangs have taken hold upon me* <u>as *the pangs of a woman that travaileth.*</u>

Isaiah 26.17 Like <u>as *a woman with child, that draweth near the time of her delivery*</u>, is in pain.

Isaiah 42.14 now I will cry <u>like *a travailing woman;*</u>

Jerem. 4.31 For I have heard *a voice as of a woman in travail,*

Jerem. 6.24 Anguish hath taken hold of us, and *pain,* as *of a woman in travail.*

Jerem. 30.6 Wherefore do I see *every man* with his hands on his loins, as *a woman in travail?*

Jerem. 49.22 *the heart of the mighty men of Edom* be as t*he heart of a woman in her pangs.*

Jerem. 50.43 Anguish took hold of him [the king of Babylon], and *pangs* as *of a woman in travail.*

Lam/Jerem. 1.17 *Jerusalem* is as *a menstruous woman* among them.

New Testament:

1 Thes. 5.3 For when they shall say, Peace and safety; then *sudden destruction* cometh upon them, *as travail upon a woman with child*;

Bibliography

Addison, Catherine. 1993. "From Literal to Figurative: An Introduction to the Study of Simile," *College English* 55.4 (April), 402–419 (Oxford University Press).

Baldwin, Robert and Ruth Paris. 1983. *The Book of Similes* (Futura Publications).

Bethlehem, Louise Shabat. 1996. "Simile and Figurative Language," *Poetics Today* 17.2 (Summer), 203–240.

Boys-Stones, G. R. (ed.) 2003. *Metaphor, Allegory, and the Classical Tradition* (Oxford University Press).

Brogan, Jacqueline Vaught. 1986. *Stevens and Simile: A Theory of Language* (Princeton University Press).

Bullinger, E. W. 2004. *Figures of Speech Used in the Bible (Explained and Illustrated) – 1898* (Baker Books, 1968).

Coffey, M. 1957. "The Function of the Homeric Simile," *American Journal of Philology* 78.2, 113–132.

Coffey, Michael and D. J. N. Lee. 1966. "The Similes of the Iliad and the Odyssey Compared," *Journal of Hellenic Studies* 86, 170–171.

Ehrman, Bart D. 2013. *The Bible: A Historical and Literary Introduction* (Oxford University Press).

Friedrich, Rainer. 1981. "On the Compositional Use of Similes in the Odyssey," *The American Journal of Philology* 102.2, 120–137.

Gibbs, Raymond, Jr (ed.) 2008. *The Cambridge Handbook of Metaphor and Thought* (New York: Cambridge University Press).

Hedges, James. 2011. "The Influence of the King James Bible on English Literature," posted online October 24, 2011 (Azusa Pacific University).

Hillers, Delbert R. 1983. "The Effective Simile in Biblical Literature." *Journal of the American Oriental Society* 103.1, 181–185.

The Holy Bible Authorized King James Version. 1901. (Cleveland and New York: The World Publishing Co.)

Innes, Doreen. 2003. "Metaphor, Simile, and Allegory as Ornaments of Style." In G. R. Boys-Stones (ed.), *Metaphor, Allegory, and the Classical Tradition*, pp. 7–27 (Oxford University Press).

Lee, D. J. N. 1964. *The Similes of the Iliad and the Odyssey Compared* (Melbourne University University Press). Reviewed by Frederick M. Combellack in *Classical Philology* 61.2 (April 1966), 125–127.

Lewis, C. S. 1950. *Literary Impact of the Authorised Version* (London: University of London, the Athlone Press). The Ethel M. Wood Lecture delivered before the University of London on March 20, 1950. In *Selected Literary Essays* by C. S. Lewis, edited by Walter Hooper, Cambridge University Press (1969).

McCall, Marsh H. Jr. 1969. *Ancient Rhetorical Theories of Simile and Comparison* (Harvard University Press).

Moulton, Carroll. 1977. "Similes in the Homeric Poems," *Hypomnemata, Untersuchungen zur Antike und zu ihrem Nachleben* 49 (Goettingen: Vandenhoeck und Ruprecht).

Nicolson, Adam. 2001. *God's Secretaries: The Making of the King James Bible* (New York: HarperCollins).

Scott, William C. 2009. *The Artistry of the Homeric Simile* (Dartmouth College Press).

Smith, Huston 1958. *The World's Religions* (revised 1991, HarperOne).

Sommer, Elyse (ed.) 1988. *Similes Dictionary* (Detroit Gale Research Co.).

Strong, James. 1890. *Strong's Exhaustive Concordance of the Bible* (Abingdon Press) (online).

Wiersbe, Warren W. 2000. *Index of Biblical Images: Similes, Metaphors, and Symbols in Scripture* (Better World Books).

Wilkins, Eliza G. 1920. "A Classification of the Similes of Homer," *The Classical Weekly* 13.19 (March 15) 147–150; 13.20 (March 22), 154–159.

Wilstach, Frank J. 1924 (1916). *A Dictionary of Similes* (New York: Grosset & Dunlap).

Ziolkowski, John E. 2014. *Plato's Similes: A Compendium of 500 Similes in 35 Dialogues.* <https://plato.chs.harvard.edu>

——. 2016. *Homer's Similes: A Compendium of Similes in the Iliad and Odyssey* (with Robert Farber and Denis Sullivan) GWU, ScholarSpace: <https://scholarspace.library.gwu.edu/files/rx913p90h>

* * *

Some Useful Online References

An Analysis of Figures of Speech in the Bible (including the Parable, the Allegory, the Simile, the Metaphor): <http://www.biblicalresearch.info/page545.html>

Douay-Rheims Catholic Bible + the Latin vulgate: <http://www.drbo.org/lvb/chapter/28014.htm>

The Fourfold Gospel: A Four Gospel Synoptic Parallel: By Alexander Campbell 145 events of Jesus' life in 8 parts: <http://www.bible.ca/b-four-gospel-synoptic. htm>

The Gospels in Parallel: <http://www.gospelsinparallel.com/gospels/g-4-55.html>

Greek Old and New Testament: <https://www.ellopos.net/elpenor/physis/ septuagint-genesis/default.asp>

Strong's Exhaustive Concordance of the Bible: <https://www.biblestudytools.com/ concordances/strongs-exhaustive-concordance/>

The Synoptic Gospel Parallels with John's Gospel: <http://www.gospelparallels. com>

Religions and Discourse

Edited by James M. M. Francis

Religions and Discourse explores religious language in the major world faiths from various viewpoints, including semiotics, pragmatics and cognitive linguistics, and reflects on how it is situated within wider intellectual and cultural contexts. In particular a key issue is the role of figurative speech. Many fascinating metaphors originate in religion e.g. revelation as a 'garment', apostasy as 'adultery', loving kindness as the 'circumcision of the heart'. Every religion rests its specific orientations upon symbols such as these, to name but a few. The series strives after the interdisciplinary approach that brings together such diverse disciplines as religious studies, theology, sociology, philosophy, linguistics and literature, guided by an international editorial board of scholars representative of the aforementioned disciplines. Though scholarly in its scope, the series also seeks to facilitate discussions pertaining to central religious issues in contemporary contexts.

The series will publish monographs and collected essays of a high scholarly standard.

Printed by
CPI books GmbH, Leck